LONDON
FIELDS

LONDON FIELDS

MARTIN AMIS

HARMONY BOOKS / NEW YORK

Published by Harmony Books,
a division of Crown Publishers, Inc.,
201 East 50th Street, New York, New York 10022.
Originally published in Great Britain
by Jonathan Cape Ltd. 1989.

HARMONY and colophon are trademarks of
Crown Publishers, Inc.
Manufactured in the United States of America
Library of Congress Cataloging-in-Publication Data

Amis, Martin.
London fields / Martin Amis.—1st ed.
p.   cm.
I. Title.
PR6051.M5L6   1989
823'.914—dc20
89-49558
CIP

ISBN 0-517-57718-6

10 9 8 7 6 5 4 3 2

First American Edition

to my father

Contents

Note

A word about the title. Several alternatives suggested themselves. For a while I toyed with *Time's Arrow*. Then I thought *Millennium* would be wonderfully bold (a common belief: *everything* is called *Millennium* just now). I even flirted, late at night, with *The Death of Love*. In the end the most serious contender was *The Murderee*, which seemed both sinister and deeply catchy. And I wavered and compromised with things like *London Fields, or The Murderee: Final Version*...

But as you see I kept ironic faith with my narrator, who would have been pleased, no doubt, to remind me that there are two kinds of title – two grades, two orders. The first kind of title decides on a name for something that is already there. The second kind of title is present all along: it lives and breathes, or it tries, on every page. My suggestions (and they cost me sleep) are all the first kind of title. *London Fields* is the second kind of title. So let's call it *London Fields*. This book is called *London Fields. London Fields*...

M. A.
London.

This is a true story but I can't believe it's really happening.

It's a murder story, too. I can't believe my luck.

And a love story (I think), of all strange things, so late in the century, so late in the goddamned day.

This is the story of a murder. It hasn't happened yet. But it will. (It had better.) I know the murderer, I know the murderee. I know the time, I know the place. I know the motive (*her* motive) and I know the means. I know who will be the foil, the fool, the poor foal, also utterly destroyed. And I couldn't stop them, I don't think, even if I wanted to. The girl will die. It's what she always wanted. You can't stop people, once they *start*. You can't stop people, once they *start creating*.

What a gift. This page is briefly stained by my tears of gratitude. Novelists don't usually have it so good, do they, when something real happens (something unified, dramatic and pretty saleable), and they just write it down?

I must remain calm. I'm on deadline too here, don't forget. Oh, the pregnant agitation. Someone is tickling my heart with delicate fingers. Death is much on people's minds.

Three days ago (is it?) I flew in on a red-eye from New York. I practically had the airplane to myself. I stretched out, calling piteously and frequently to the stewardesses for codeine and cold water. But the red-eye did what a red-eye does. Oh, my. Jesus, I look like the Hound of the Baskervilles . . . Shaken awake to a sticky bun at 1.30 in the morning, my time, I moved to a window seat and watched through the bright mists the fields forming their regiments, in full parade order, the sad shires, like an army the size of England. Then the city itself, London, as taut and meticulous as a cobweb. I had the airplane to myself because nobody in their right mind wants to come to Europe, not just now, not for the time being; everybody wants to go the other way, as Heathrow confirmed.

It reeked of sleep. Somnopolis. It reeked of it, and of insomniac worry and disquiet, and thwarted escape. Because we are all poets or babies in the middle of the night, struggling with being. There were hardly any Arrivals, apart from me. The business of the airport was all Departures. As I stood in some stalled passage and listened to the canned instructions I looked down on the lots and runways through the layered insult of dawn rain: all the sharks with their fins erect, thrashers, baskers, great whites – killers. Killers every one.

As for the apartment – well, it takes my breath away. I mean it. When I come in the door I go *tee-hee-hee*. The place kills me. All this for a personal ad in the *New York Review of Books*? I have certainly gotten the better of the deal. Yes, I have well and truly stiffed Mark Asprey. I tramp through the rooms and think with shame of my contorted little crib in Hell's Kitchen. He's a fellow writer, after all, and I would have felt happier, if not with exact equivalence, then with broad parity. Of course even I suspect that the décor is in regrettable taste. What does Mark Asprey write? Musicals? He writes charming notes. 'Dear Sam: Welcome!' his begins.

Not a thing in the place is content to be merely handy or convenient. The toilet brush is a mustachioed sceptre. The kitchen taps squirm with gargoyles. Clearly, here is someone who heats his morning coffee on the torched wind of Circassian dancing girls. Mr Asprey is a bachelor: no doubt about that. For instance there are a great many signed photographs on the walls – models, actresses. In this respect his bedroom is like some joint called Two Guys from Italy. But this guy's from London; and it isn't his pasta they're praising. The effortful inscription and looped signature: self-injury, done to the tender, the legendary throat.

On top of all this I get to use his car, his A-to-B device, which obediently awaits me on the ledge. In his note Mark Asprey apologizes on its behalf, letting me know that he has a better one, a

2

much better one, moored to his country cottage, or country house, or country estate. Yesterday I staggered out and took a look at it. Of the latest design, the car strives toward a state of stone-grey invisibility. Even my scrutiny it found inordinate and embarrassing. Features include fool-the-eye dent-marks, a removable toupée of rust on the hood, and adhesive key-scratches all over the paintwork. An English strategy: envy-preemption. Things have changed, things have remained the same, over the past ten years. London's pub aura, that's certainly intensified: the smoke and the builders' sand and dust, the toilet tang, the streets like a terrible carpet. No doubt there'll be surprises when I start to look around, but I always felt I knew where England was heading. America was the one you wanted to watch . . .

I climbed in and took a spin. I say *spin* to help account for the ten-minute dizzy spell that hit me when I came back into the apartment. I was impressed by its force. Giddiness and a new nausea, a moral nausea, coming from the gut, where all morality comes from (like waking up after a disgraceful dream and looking with dread for the blood on your hands). On the front passenger seat, under the elegant rag of a white silk scarf, lies a heavy car-tool. Mark Asprey must be afraid of something. He must be afraid of London's poor.

Three days in and I am ready – I am ready to write. Hear my knuckles crack. Real life is coming along so fast that I can no longer delay. It's unbelievable. Two decades of fastidious torment, two decades of non-starting, and suddenly I'm ready. Well, this was always destined to be the year of behaving strangely. Let me say with due modesty and caution that I have the makings of a really snappy little thriller. Original, too, in its way. Not a whodunit. More a whydoit. I feel sickly and enraptured. I feel bright green. I think I am less a novelist than a queasy cleric, taking down the minutes of real life. Technically speaking, I am also, I suppose, an accessory before the fact, but to hell with all that for now. I woke up today and thought: If London is a spider's web, then where do I fit in? Maybe I'm the fly. I'm the fly.

Hurry. I always assumed I'd start with the murderee, with her, with Nicola Six. But no, that wouldn't feel quite right. Let's start with the bad guy. Yeah. Keith. Let's start with *the murderer*.

Chapter 1 : The Murderer

KEITH TALENT WAS a bad guy. Keith Talent was a very bad guy. You might even say that he was the worst guy. But not *the* worst, not the very worst ever. There *were* worse guys. Where? There in the hot light of CostCheck for example, with car keys, beige singlet, and a six-pack of Peculiar Brews, the scuffle at the door, the foul threat and the elbow in the black neck of the wailing lady, then the car with its rust and its waiting blonde, and off to do the next thing, whatever, whatever necessary. The mouths on these worst guys – the eyes on them. Within those eyes a tiny unsmiling universe. No. Keith wasn't *that* bad. He had saving graces. He didn't hate people for ready-made reasons. He was at least *multiracial* in outlook – thoughtlessly, helplessly so. Intimate encounters with strange-hued women had sweetened him somewhat. His saving graces all had names. What with the Fetnabs and Fatimas he had known, the Nketchis and Iqbalas, the Michikos and Boguslawas, the Ramsarwatees and Rajashwaris – Keith was, in this sense, a man of the world. These were the chinks in his coal-black armour: God bless them all.

Although he liked nearly everything else about himself, Keith hated his redeeming features. In his view they constituted his only major shortcoming – his one tragic flaw. When the moment arrived, in the office by the loading bay at the plant off the M4 near Bristol, with his great face crammed into the prickling nylon, and the proud woman shaking her trembling head at him, and Chick Purchase and

4

Dean Pleat both screaming *Do it. Do it* (he still remembered their meshed mouths writhing), Keith had definitely failed to realize his full potential. He had proved incapable of clubbing the Asian woman to her knees, and of going on clubbing until the man in the uniform opened the safe. Why had he failed? Why, Keith, why? In truth he had felt far from well: half the night up some lane in a car full of the feet-heat of burping criminals; no breakfast, no bowel movement; and now, to top it all off, everywhere he looked he saw green grass, fresh trees, rolling hills. Chick Purchase, furthermore, had already crippled the second guard, and Dean Pleat soon vaulted back over the counter and self-righteously laid into the woman with his rifle butt. So Keith's qualms had changed nothing – except his career prospects in armed robbery. (It's tough at the top, and it's tough at the bottom, too; Keith's name was muck thereafter.) If he could have done it, he would have done it, joyfully. He just didn't have . . . he just didn't have the talent.

After that Keith turned his back on armed robbery once and for all. He took up racketeering. In London, broadly speaking, racketeering meant fighting about drugs; in the part of West London that Keith called home, racketeering meant fighting about drugs with black people – and black people are better at fighting than white people, because, among other reasons, they *all* do it (there aren't any civilians). Racketeering works through escalation, and escalation dominance: success goes to the men who can manage the exponential jump, to the men who can regularly *astonish* with their violence. It took Keith several crunchy beatings, and the first signs of a liking for hospital food, before he concluded that he wasn't cut out for racketeering. During one of his convalescences, when he spent a lot of time in the street cafés of Golborne Road, Keith grew preoccupied by a certain enigma. The enigma was this. How come you often saw black guys with white girls (always blondes, always, presumably for maximum contrast-gain), and never saw white guys with black girls? Did the black guys beat up the white guys who went out with black girls? No, or not much; you had to be discreet, though, and in his experience lasting relationships were seldom formed. Then how was it done? It came to him in a flash of inspiration. The black guys beat up the black *girls* who went out with white guys! Of course. So much simpler. He pondered the wisdom of this and drew a lesson from it, a lesson which, in his heart, he had long understood. If you're going to be violent, stick to women. Stick to the weak. Keith gave up

5

racketeering. He turned over a new leaf. Having renounced violent crime, Keith prospered, and rose steadily towards the very crest of his new profession: non-violent crime.

Keith worked as a *cheat*. There he stands on the street corner, with three or four colleagues, with three or four fellow *cheats*; they laugh and cough (they're always coughing) and flap their arms for warmth; they look like terrible birds . . . On good days he rose early and put in long hours, going out into the world, into society, with the intention of cheating it. Keith cheated people with his limousine service at airports and train stations; he cheated people with his fake scents and colognes at the pavement stalls of Oxford Street and Bishopsgate (his two main lines were Scandal and Outrage); he cheated people with non-pornographic pornography in the back rooms of short-lease stores; and he cheated people on the street everywhere with the upturned cardboard box or milk crate and the three warped playing cards: Find the Lady! Here, often, and occasionally elsewhere, the boundaries between violent crime and its non-violent little brother were hard to descry. Keith earned three times as much as the Prime Minister and never had any money, losing heavily every day at Mecca, the turf accountants on the Portobello Road. He never won. Sometimes he would ponder this, on alternate Thursday lunchtimes, in sheepskin overcoat, his head bent over the racing page, as he queued for his unemployment benefit, and then drove to the turf accountants on the Portobello Road. So Keith's life might have elapsed over the years. He never had what it took to be a murderer, not on his own. He needed his murderee. The foreigners, the checked and dog-toothed Americans, the leering lens-faced Japanese, standing stiff over the cardboard box or the milk crate – they never found the lady. But *Keith* did. Keith found her.

Of course, he already had a lady, little Kath, who had recently presented him with a child. By and large Keith had welcomed the pregnancy: it was, he liked to joke, quite a handy new way of putting his wife in hospital. He had decided that the baby, when it came, would be called Keith – Keith Jr. Kath, remarkably, had other ideas. Yet Keith was inflexible, wavering only once, when he briefly entertained the idea of calling the baby Clive, after his dog, a large, elderly and unpredictable Alsatian. He changed his mind once more; Keith it was to be, then . . . Swaddled in blue, the baby came home, with mother. Keith personally helped them from the ambulance. As Kath started on the dishes, Keith sat by the stolen fire and frowned at the new arrival. There was something wrong with the baby, something seriously wrong. The trouble with the baby was that it was a girl. Keith looked deep into himself, and rallied. 'Keithette,' Kath heard him murmur, as her knees settled on the cold lino. 'Keithene. Keitha. Keithinia.'

'No, Keith,' she said.

'Keithnab,' said Keith, with an air of slow discovery. 'Nkeithi.'

'No, Keith.'

'. . . Why's it so fucking yellow?'

After a few days, whenever Kath cautiously addressed the baby as 'Kim', Keith no longer swore at his wife or slammed her up against the wall with any conviction. 'Kim', after all, was the name of one of Keith's heroes, one of Keith's gods. And Keith was cheating hard that week, cheating on everyone, it seemed, and especially his wife. So Kim Talent it was – Kim Talent, little Kim.

The man had ambition. It was his dream to go all the way; he wasn't just messing. Keith had no intention, or no desire, to be a *cheat* for the rest of his life. Even he found the work demoralizing. And mere cheating would never get him the things he wanted, the goods and services he wanted, not while a series of decisive wins at the turf accountants continued to elude him. He sensed that Keith Talent had been put here for something a little bit special. To be fair, it must be said that murder was not in his mind, not yet, except perhaps in some ghostly *potentia* that precedes all thought and action . . . Character is destiny. Keith had often been told, by various magistrates, girlfriends and probation officers, that he had a 'poor character', and he had always fondly owned up to the fact. But did that mean he had a poor destiny? . . . Waking early, perhaps, as Kath clumsily dragged herself from the bed to attend to little Kim, or wedged in one of the traffic jams that routinely enchained his day, Keith would mentally pursue an alternative vision, one of wealth, fame and a kind of spangled superlegitimacy – the chrome spokes of a possible future in World Darts.

A casual darter or arrowman all his life, right back to the bald board on the kitchen door, Keith had recently got serious. He'd always thrown for his pub, of course, and followed the sport: you could almost hear angels singing when, on those special nights (three or four times a week), Keith laid out the cigarettes on the arm of the couch and prepared to watch darts on television. But now he had designs on the other side of the screen. To his own elaborately concealed astonishment, Keith found himself in the Last Sixteen of the Sparrow Masters, an annual interpub competition which he had nonchalantly entered some months ago, on the advice of various friends and admirers. At the end of that road there basked the contingency of a televised final, a £5,000 cheque, and a play-off, also televised, with his hero and darting model, the world number one, Kim Twemlow. After that, well, after that, the rest was television.

And television was all about everything he did not have and was full of all the people he did not know and could never be. Television was the great shopfront, lightly electrified, up against which Keith crushed his nose. And now among the squirming motes, the impossible prizes, he saw a doorway, or an arrow, or a beckoning hand (with a dart in it), and everything said – Darts. Pro-Darts. World Darts. He's down there in his garage, putting in the hours, his eyes still stinging from the ineffable, the heartbreaking beauty of a brand-new dartboard, stolen that very day.

Magnificent anachronism. The lights and mores of the modern criminal Keith held in disdain. He had no time for the gym, the fancy restaurant, the buxom bestseller, the foreign holiday. He had never taken any exercise (unless you counted burgling, running away, and getting beaten up); he had never knowingly drunk a glass of wine (or only when he was well past caring); he had never read a book (we here exclude *Darts: Master the Discipline*); and he had never been out of London. Except once. When he went to America . . .

He journeyed there with a friend, also a young *cheat*, also a darts-man, also called Keith: Keith Double. The plane was overbooked and the two Keiths were seated twenty rows apart. They stilled their terror with murderous drinking, courtesy of stewardess and duty-free bag, and by shouting out, every ten seconds or so, 'Cheers, Keith!' We can imagine the amusement of their fellow passengers, who logged over a thousand of these shouts during the seven-hour flight. After disembarking at New York, Keith Talent was admitted to the public hospital in Long Island City. Three days later, when he began to stagger out to the stairwell for his smokes, he encountered Keith Double. 'Cheers, Keith!' The mandatory health insurance turned out to cover alcohol poisoning, so everyone was happy, and became even happier when the two Keiths recovered in time to make their return flight. Keith Double was in advertising now, and had

8

frequently returned to America. Keith hadn't; he was still cheating on the streets of London.

And the world, and history, could not be reordered in a way that would make sense to him. Some distance up the beach in Plymouth, Massachusetts, there once lay a large boulder, reputedly the first chunk of America to be touched by the Pilgrims' feet. Identified in the eighteenth century, this opening sample of US real estate had to be moved closer to the shore, in order to satisfy expectations of how history ought to happen. To satisfy Keith, to get anywhere with Keith, you'd need to fix the entire planet – great sceneshiftings, colossal rearrangements at the back of his mind. And then the tabloid face would have to crease and pucker.

Keith didn't look like a murderer. He looked like a murderer's dog. (No disrespect to Keith's dog Clive, who had signed on well before the fact, and whom Keith didn't in the least resemble anyway.) Keith looked like a murderer's dog, eager familiar of ripper or bodysnatcher or gravestalker. His eyes held a strange radiance – for a moment it reminded you of health, health hidden or sleeping or otherwise mysteriously absent. Though frequently bloodshot, the eyes seemed to pierce. In fact the light sprang off them. And it wasn't at all pleasant or encouraging, this one-way splendour. His eyes were television. The face itself was leonine, puffy with hungers, and as dry as soft fur. Keith's crowning glory, his hair, was thick and full-bodied; but it always had the look of being recently washed, imperfectly rinsed, and then, still slick with cheap shampoo, slow-dried in a huddled pub – the thermals of the booze, the sallowing fagsmoke. Those eyes, and their urban severity . . . Like the desolating gaiety of a fundless paediatric hospital (Welcome to the Peter Pan Ward), or like a criminal's cream Rolls-Royce, parked at dusk between a tube station and a flower stall, the eyes of Keith Talent shone with tremendous accommodations made to money. And murder? The eyes – was there enough blood in them for *that*? Not now, not yet. He had the talent, somewhere, but he would need the murderee to bring it out. Soon, he would find the lady.

Or she would find him.

Chick Purchase. *Chick*. It's hugely unsuitable for such a celebrated bruiser and satyromaniac. A diminutive of Charles. In America it's Chuck. In England, apparently, it's *Chick*. Some name. Some country . . . Of course, I write these words in the awed hush that follows my completion of the first chapter. I don't dare go through it yet. I wonder if I ever will.

For reasons not yet altogether clear, I seem to have adopted a jovial and lordly tone. It seems antique, corrupt: like Keith. Remember, though: Keith is modern, modern, modern. Anyway, I expect to get better at this. And soon I must face the murderee.

It would be nice to expatiate on how good it feels, after all these years, to sit down and actually start writing fiction. But let's not get any big ideas. This is actually happening.

How do I know, for instance, that Keith works as a *cheat*? Because he tried to cheat *me*, on the way in from Heathrow. I'd been standing under the sign saying TAXIS for about a half-hour when the royal-blue Cavalier made its second circuit and pulled up at the bay. Out he climbed.

'Taxi, sir?' he said, and picked up my bag, matter-of-factly, in the line of professional routine.

'That's not a taxi.'

Then he said, 'No danger. You won't get a cab here, pal. No way.'

I asked for a price and he gave me one: an outlandish sum.

'Limo, innit,' he explained.

'That's not a limo either. It's just a car.'

'We'll go by what's on the clock, yeah?' he said; but I was already climbing into the back and was fast asleep before we pulled away.

I awoke some time later. We were approaching Slough, and the metre said £54.50.

'Slough!'

His eyes were burning at me warily in the rearview mirror. 'Wait a second, wait a second,' I began. One thing about my illness or condition. I've never been braver. It empowers me – I can feel it. Like looking for the right words and finding them, finding the powers. 'Listen. I know my way around. I'm not over here to see Harrods, and Buckingham Palace, and Stratford-on-Avon. I don't say twenty quids and Trafaljar Square and Bar*net*. Slough? Come *on*. If this is a kidnap or a murder then we'll discuss it. If not, take me to London for the amount we agreed.'

He pulled over unhurriedly. Oh, Christ, I thought: this really is a murder. He turned around and showed me a confiding sneer.

'What it is is,' he said, 'what it is is – okay. I seen you was asleep. I thought: "He's asleep. Looks as though he could use it. I know. I'll pop in on me mum." Disregard that,' he said, jerking his head, in brutal dismissal, toward the clock, which was of curious design and possibly home manufacture and now said £63.80. 'Don't mind, do you, pal?' He pointed to a line of pebbledash semis – we were, I now saw, in some kind of dormitory estate, green-patched, shopless. 'She's sick like. Won't be five minutes. Okay?'

'What's that?' I said. I referred to the sounds coming from the car stereo, solid thunks followed by shouted numbers against a savage background of taunts and screams.

'Darts,' he said, and switched it off. 'I'd ask you in but – me old mum. Here. Read this.'

So I sat in the back of the Cavalier while my driver went to see his mum. Actually he was doing nothing of the kind. What he was doing (as he would later proudly confide) was wheelbarrowing a lightly clad Analiese Furnish around the living-room while her current protector, who worked nights, slept with his legendary soundness in the room above.

I held in my hands a four-page brochure, pressed on me by the murderer (though of course he wasn't a murderer yet. He had a way to go). On the back was a colour photograph of the Queen and a crudely superimposed perfume bottle: '"Outrage" – by Ambrosio.'

11

On the front was a black-and-white photograph of my driver, smiling unreliably. 'KEITH TALENT,' it said:

* Chauffeur and courier services
* Own limousine
* Casino consultant
* Luxury goods and Celebrity purchases
* Darts lessons given
* London operative for Ambrosio of Milan, Perfumes and Furs

There followed some more information about the perfumes, 'Scandal', 'Outrage', and minor lines called Mirage, Disguise, Duplicity and Sting, and beneath, in double quotes, accompanied by an address and telephone number, with misplaced apostrophes: Keith's the Name, Scent's the Game. The two middle pages of the brochure were blank. I folded it into my middle pocket, quite idly; but it has since proved invaluable to me.

With sloping gait and two casual corrections of the belt, Keith came down the garden path.

There was £143.10 on the blatting clock when the car pulled up and I awoke again. Slowly I climbed from the car's slept-in, trailer smell, as if from a second aircraft, and unbent myself in front of the house – and the house massive, like an ancient terminal.

'The States? Love the place,' Keith was saying. 'New York? Love it. Madison Square. Park Central. Love the place.' He paused with a flinch as he lifted my bag from the trunk. 'It's a church . . .' he said wonderingly.

'It used to be a rectory or vicarage or something.' I pointed to an engraved panel high up in the masonry. Anno Domini. 1876.

'1876!' he said. 'So some *vicar* had all this.'

It was clear from his face that Keith was now pondering the tragic decline in the demand for vicars. Well, people still wanted the goods, the stuff for which vicars of various kinds were the middlemen. But they didn't want *vicars*.

Making no small display of the courtesy, Keith carried my bag in through the fenced front garden and stood there while I got my keys from the lady downstairs. Now, the speed of light doesn't come up very often in everyday life: only when lightning strikes. The speed of sound is more familiar: that man in the distance with a hammer. Anyway, a Mach-2 event is a sudden event, and that's what Keith

12

and I were suddenly cowering from: the massed frequencies of three jetplanes ripping past over the rooftops. 'Jesus,' said Keith. And I said it too. 'What's all *that* about?' I asked. Keith shrugged, with equanimity, with mild hauteur. 'Cloaked in secrecy innit. All veiled in secrecy as such.'

We entered through a second front door and climbed a broad flight of stairs. I think we were about equally impressed by the opulence and elaboration of the apartment. This is some joint, I have to admit. After a few weeks here even the great Presley would have started to pine for the elegance and simplicity of Graceland. Keith cast his bright glance around the place with a looter's cruel yet professional eye. For the second time that morning I nonchalantly reviewed the possibility that I was about to be murdered. Keith would be out of here ten minutes later, my flightbag over his shoulder, lumpy with appurtenances. Instead he asked me who owned the place and what he did.

I told him. Keith looked sceptical. This just wasn't right. 'Mostly for theatre and television,' I said. Now all was clear. 'TV?' he said coolly. For some reason I added, 'I'm in TV too.'

Keith nodded, much enlightened. Somewhat chastened also; and I have to say it touched me, this chastened look. Of course (he was thinking), TV people all know each other and fly to and from the great cities and borrow each other's flats. Common sense. Yes, behind all the surface activity of Keith's eyes there formed the vision of a heavenly elite, cross-hatching the troposphere like satellite TV – above it, above it all.

'Yeah well I'm due to appear on TV myself. Hopefully. In a month or two. Darts.'

'Darts?'

'Darts.'

And then it began. He stayed for three and a half hours. People are amazing, aren't they? They'll tell you everything if you give them time. And I have always been a good listener. I have always been a talented listener. I really do want to hear it – I don't know why. Of course at that stage I was perfectly disinterested; I had no idea what was happening, what was forming right in front of me. Within fifteen minutes I was being told, in shocking detail, about Analiese – and Iqbala, and Trish, and Debbee. Laconic but unabashed mentions of wife and daughter. And then all that stuff about violent crime and Chick Purchase. And New York. True, I gave him a fair amount to drink: beer, or lager, plentifully heaped like bombs on their racks in Mark Asprey's

13

refrigerator. In the end he charged me £25 for the ride (special TV rate, perhaps) and gave me a ballpoint pen shaped like a dart, with which I now write these words. He also told me that he could be found, every lunchtime and every evening, in a pub called the Black Cross on the Portobello Road.

I would find him there, right enough. And so would the lady.

When Keith left I sacked out immediately. Not that I had much say in the matter. Twenty-two hours later I opened my eyes again and was greeted by an unwelcome and distressing sight. Myself, on the ceiling mirror. There's a mirror on the headboard too, and one on the facing wall. It's a chamber of mirrors in there, a hell of mirrors . . . I looked—I looked not well. I seemed to be pleading, pleading with me, myself. Dr Slizard says I have about three months more of this to get through, and then everything will change.

I have been out and about a bit since then; yes, I have made several tremulous sorties. The first thing I noticed in the street (I almost stepped in it) struck me as quintessentially English: a soaked loaf of white bread, like the brains of an animal much stupider than any sheep. So far, though, it doesn't seem as bad as some people like to say. At least it's intelligible, more or less. Ten years I've been gone, and what's been happening? Ten years of Relative Decline.

If London's a pub and you want the whole story, then where do you go? You go to a London pub. And that single instant in the Black Cross set the whole story in motion. Keith's in the bag. Keith's cool. And I am now cultivating our third party, the foil, the foal, Guy Clinch, who, to my horror, seems to be a genuinely delightful human being. I find I have a vast talent for ingratiation. But none of this would ever have gotten started without the girl. It didn't have a hope in hell without the girl. Nicola Six was the miracle, the absolute donnée. She's *perfect* for me. And now she'll be taking things into her own hands.

The English, Lord love them, they talk about the weather. But so does everybody else on earth, these days. Right now, the weather is superatmospheric and therefore, in a sense, supermeteorological (can you really call it *weather*?). It will stay like this for the rest of the summer, they say. I approve, with one qualification. It's picked the wrong year to happen in: the year of behaving strangely. I look out at it. The weather, if we can still call it that, is frequently very beautiful, but it seems to bring me close to hysteria, as indeed does everything now.

14

Chapter 2: The Murderee

THE BLACK CAB will move away, unrecallably and for ever, its driver paid, and handsomely tipped, by the murderee. She will walk down the dead-end street. The heavy car will be waiting; its lights will come on as it lumbers towards her. It will stop, and idle, as the passenger door swings open.

His face will be barred in darkness, but she will see shattered glass on the passenger seat and the car-tool ready on his lap.

'Get in.'

She will lean forward. '*You*,' she will say, in intense recognition: 'Always you.'

'Get *in*.'

And in she'll climb . . .

What is this destiny or condition (and perhaps, like the look of the word's ending, it tends towards the feminine: a feminine ending), what *is* it, what does it mean, to be a murderee?

In the case of Nicola Six, tall, dark, and thirty-four, it was bound up with a delusion, lifelong, and not in itself unmanageable. Right from the start, from the moment that her thoughts began to be consecutive, Nicola knew two strange things. The second strange thing was that she must never tell anyone about the first strange thing. The first strange thing was this: she always knew what was going to happen next. Not all the time (the gift was not obsessively consulted), and not every little detail; but she always knew what was going to happen next. Right from the start she had a friend – Enola, Enola Gay. Enola wasn't real. Enola came from inside the head of Nicola Six. Nicola was an only child and knew she always would be.

You can imagine how things might work out. Nicola is seven years old, for instance, and her parents are taking her on a picnic, with another family: why, pretty Dominique will be there, a friend, perhaps, a living friend for the only child. But little Nicola, immersed in romantic thoughts and perfectly happy with Enola, doesn't want to come along (watch how she screams and grips!). She doesn't want to come along because she knows that the afternoon will end in disaster, in blood and iodine and tears. And so it proves. A hundred yards from the grown-ups (so impenetrably arrayed round the square sheet in the sunshine), Nicola stands on the crest of a slope with her new friend, pretty Dominique. And of course Nicola knows what is going to happen next: the girl will hesitate or stumble: reaching out to steady her, Nicola will accidentally propel her playmate downwards, down into the rocks and the briars. She will then have to run and shout, and drive in silence somewhere, and sit on the hospital bench swinging her feet and listlessly asking for ice-cream. And so it proves. On television at the age of four she saw the warnings, and the circles of concentric devastation, with London like a bull's-eye in the centre of the board. She knew that would happen, too. It was just a matter of time.

When Nicola was good she was very very good. But when she was bad . . . About her parents she had no feelings one way or the other: this was her silent, inner secret. They both died, anyway, together, as she had always known they would. So why hate them? So why love them? After she got the call she drove reflexively to the airport. The car itself was like a tunnel of cold wind. An airline official showed her into the VIP Lounge: it contained a bar, and forty or fifty people in varying degrees of distress. She drank the brandy pressed on her by the steward. 'Free,' he confirmed. A television was wheeled in. And then, incredibly (even Nicola was consternated), they showed live film of the scattered wreckage, and the bodybags lined up on fields of France. In the VIP Lounge there were scenes of protest and violent rejection. One old man kept distractedly offering money to a uniformed PR officer. Coldly Nicola drank more brandy, wondering how death could take people so unprepared. That night she had acrobatic sex with some unforgivable pilot. She was nineteen by this time, and had long left home. Potently, magically, uncontrollably attractive, Nicola was not yet beautiful. But already she was an ill wind, blowing no good.

Considered more generally – when you looked at the human wreckage she left in her slipstream, the nervous collapses, the shattered careers, the suicide bids, the blighted marriages (and rottener divorces) – Nicola's knack of reading the future left her with one or two firm assurances: that no one would ever love her enough, and those that did were not worth being loved enough by. The typical Nicola romance would end, near the doorway of her attic flat, with the man of the moment sprinting down the passage, his trousers round his knees, a ripped jacket thrown over his ripped shirt, and hotly followed by Nicola herself (now in a nightdress, now in underwear, now naked beneath a half-furled towel), either to speed him on his way with a blood libel and a skilfully hurled ashtray, or else to win back his love, by apologies, by caresses, or by main force. In any event the man of the moment invariably kept going. Often she would fly right out into the street. On several occasions she had taken a brick to the waiting car. On several more she had lain down in front of it. All this changed nothing, of course. The car would always leave at the highest speed of which it was mechanically capable, though sometimes, admittedly, in reverse. Nicola's men, and their escape velocities . . . Back in the flat, staunching her wrists, perhaps, or pressing an ice-cube to her lip (or a lump of meat to her eye), Nicola would look at herself in the mirror, would look at what remained and think how strange – how strange, that she had been right all along. She knew it would end like this. And so it proved. The diary she kept was therefore just the chronicle of a death foretold . . .

One of those people who should never drink anything at all, Nicola drank a very great deal. But it depended. A couple of mornings a month, stiff with pride, deafened with aspirin (and reckless with Bloody Marys), Nicola would adumbrate serious reform: for example, only two colossal cocktails before dinner, a broad maximum of half a bottle of wine with her meal, and then just the one whisky or *digestif* before bedtime. She would frequently stick to the new regime right up to and certainly including the whisky or *digestif* before bedtime the following day. By then, bedtime looked a long way off. There was always a lot of shouting and fistfighting to do before bedtime. And what about *after* bedtime, or after the *first* bedtime, with several bouts of one thing or the other still to go? So she always failed. She could see herself failing (there she was, clearly failing), and so she failed. Did Nicola Six drink alone? Yes, she drank alone. You bet. And why did she drink alone? Because she was *alone*. And she was alone, now, at night, more than formerly. What could never be endured, it turned out, was the last swathe of time before sleep came, the path from larger day to huger night, a little death when the mind was still alive and fluttering. Thus the glass banged down on the round table; the supposedly odourless ashtray gave its last weak swirl; and then the babywalk, the smudged trend to the loathed bedding. That was how it had to end.

The other ending, the real death, the last thing that already existed in the future was now growing in size as she moved forward to confront or greet it. Where would she see the murderer, where would she find him – in the park, the library, in the sad café, or walking past her in the street half-naked with a plank over his shoulder? The murder had a place, and a date, even a time: some minutes after midnight, on her thirty-fifth birthday. Nicola would click through the darkness of the dead-end street. Then the car, the grunt of its brakes, the door swinging open and the murderer (his face in shadow, the car-tool on his lap, one hand extended to seize her hair) saying, *Get in. Get* in . . . And in she climbed.

It was fixed. It was written. The murderer was not yet a murderer. But the murderee had always been a murderee.

Where would she find him, how would she dream him, when would she summon him? On the important morning she awoke wet with the usual nightmares. She went straight to her bath and lay there for a long time, round-eyed, with her hair pinned up. On important days she always felt herself to be the object of scrutiny, lewd and furious scrutiny. Her head now looked small or telescoped, set against the squirming refractions of the giantess beneath the water. She rose with dramatic suddenness from the bath and paused before reaching for the towel. Then she stood naked in the middle of the warm room. Her mouth was full, and unusually wide. Her mother had always said it was a whore's mouth. It seemed to have an extra half-inch at either wing, like the mouth of the clowngirl in pornography. But the cheeks of the pornographic clowngirl would be painted white, whiter than the teeth. Nicola's face was always dark, and her teeth had a shadowy lustre, slanting inwards, as if to balance the breadth of the lips, or just through the suction of the devouring soul. Her eyes

18

changed colour readily, eagerly, in different lights, but their firm state was a vehement green. She had this idea about the death of love . . .

The funeral, the cremation she was due to attend that day was not a significant one. Nicola Six, who hardly knew or remembered the dead woman, had been obliged to put in a tedious half an hour on the telephone before she managed to get herself asked along. The dead woman had briefly employed Nicola in her antique shop, years ago. For a month or two the murderee had sat smoking cigarettes in the zestless grotto off Fulham Broadway. Then she had stopped doing that. This was always the way with Nicola's more recent jobs, of which there had, for a while, been a fair number. She did the job, and then, after an escalating and finally overlapping series of late mornings, four-hour lunches, and early departures, she was considered to have *let everyone down* (she wasn't there ever), and stopped going in. Nicola always knew when this moment had come, and chose that day to stop going in. The fact that Nicola knew things would end that way lent great tension to each job she took, right from the first week, the first day, the first morning . . . In the more distant past she had worked as a publisher's reader, a cocktail waitress, a telephonist, a croupier, a tourist operative, a model, a librarian, a kissogram girl, an archivist, and an actress. An actress — she had gone quite far with that. In her early twenties she had done rep, Royal Shakespeare, panto, a few television plays. She still had a trunk full of outfits and some videotapes (poor little rich girl, spry newlywed, naked houri maddeningly glimpsed through fogsmoke and veils). Acting was therapeutic, though dramatic roles confused her further. She was happiest with comedy, farce, custard-pie. The steadiest time of her adult life had been the year in Brighton, taking the lead in *Jack and the Beanstalk*. Playing a man seemed to help. She did Jack in short blazer and black tights, and with her hair up. A million mothers wondered why their sons came home so green and feverish, and crept burdened to bed without their suppers. But then the acting bit of her lost its moorings and drifted out into real life.

With a towel round her belly she sat before the mirror, itself a theatrical memento, with its proscenium of brutal bulbs. Again she felt unfriendly eyes playing on her back. She went at her face like an artist, funeral colours, black, beige, blood red. Rising, she turned to the bed and reviewed her burial clothes and their unqualified sable. Even her elaborate underwear was black; even the clips on her garter belt were black, black. She opened her wardrobe, releasing the full-length mirror, and stood sideways with a hand flat on her stomach, feeling everything that a woman would hope to feel at such a moment. As she sat on the bed and tipped herself for the first black stocking, mind-body memories took her back to earlier ablutions, self-inspections, intimate preparations. A weekend out of town with some new man of the moment. Sitting in the car on the Friday afternoon, after the heavy lunch, as they dragged through Swiss Cottage to the motorway, or through the curling systems of Clapham and Brixton and beyond (where London seems unwilling ever to relinquish the land, wants to squat on those fields right up to the rocks and the cliffs and the water), Nicola would feel a pressure in those best panties of hers, as it were the opposite of sex, like the stirring of a new hymen being pinkly formed. By the time they reached Totteridge or Tooting, Nicola was a virgin again. With what perplexity would she turn to the voluble disappointment, the babbling mistake, at her side with his hands on the wheel. After a glimpse of the trees in the dusk, a church, a dumbfounded sheep, Nicola would drink little at the hotel or the borrowed cottage and would sleep inviolate with her hands crossed over her heart like a saint. Sulky in slumber, the man of the moment would nevertheless awake to find that practically half his entire torso was inside Nicola's mouth; and Saturday lunchtime was always a debauch on every front. She hardly ever made it to Sunday. The weekend would end that evening: a stunned and wordless return down the motorway, a single-passenger minicab drive of ghostly length and costliness, or Nicola Six standing alone on a sodden railway platform, erect and unblinking, with a suitcase full of shoes.

But let us be clear about this: she had great powers – great powers. All women whose faces and bodies more or less neatly fill the contemporary mould have some notion of these privileges and magics. During their pomp and optimum, however brief and relative, they occupy the erotic centre. Some feel lost, some surrounded or crowded, but there they are, in a China-sized woodland of teak-hard worship. And with Nicola Six the gender yearning was translated, was fantastically heightened: it came at her in the form of human love. She had the power of inspiring love, almost anywhere. Forget about making strong men weep. Seven-stone pacifists shouldered their way through street riots to be home in case she called. Family men abandoned sick children to wait in the rain outside her flat. Semi-literate builders and bankers sent her sonnet sequences. She pauperized gigolos, she spayed studs, she hospitalized heartbreakers. They were never the same again, they lost their heads. And the thing with her (what *was* it with her?), the thing with her was that she had to receive this love and send it back in opposite form, not just cancelled but murdered. Character is destiny; and Nicola knew where her destiny lay.

Fifteen minutes later, dressed for death, she called her black cab and drank two cups of black coffee and tasted with hunger the black tobacco of a French cigarette.

In Golders Green she dismissed the taxi, and it pulled away for ever. She knew she'd get a lift back: you always did, from funerals. The sky above the redbrick lodge she entered was certainly dull enough for a person to take leave of it with equanimity. As usual she was quite late, but the volley of pale glances did not pierce her. With no attempt at self-muffling she walked evenly to the back and slipped into an empty aisle, of which there was no shortage. The dead woman was not being populously farewelled. So this was all you got: the zooty sideburns and masturbator's pallor of an old Ted in a black suit, and the secular obsequies. Nicola longed equally for a cigarette and the lines you sometimes heard: a short time to live, full of misery. She was always especially stirred – this was why she came – by the spectacle of the bereaved elderly, particularly the women. The poor sheep, the dumbfounded sheep (even mere nature dumbfounds them), as reliable as professional mourners but too good at it really, too passionate, with hair like feather dusters, and frailly convulsed with brute grief, the selfish terrors . . . Nicola yawned. Everything around her said school, the busts and plaques, and all the panels with their use of wood to quell and dampen. She hardly noticed the discreet trundling of the coffin, knowing it was empty and the body already vaporized by fire.

Afterwards, in the Dispersal Area (a heavy blackbird was flying low and at an angle over the sopping grass), Nicola Six, looking and sounding very very good, explained to various interested parties who she was and what she was doing there. It solaced the old to see such piety in the relatively young. She reviewed the company with eyes of premonitory inquiry, and with small inner shrugs of disappointment. In the carpark she was offered several lifts; she accepted one more or less at random.

The driver, who was the dead woman's brother's brother-in-law, dropped her off on the Portobello Road, as instructed. Prettily Nicola said her goodbyes to him and his family, extending a gloved hand and receiving their thanks and praise for her attendance. She could hear them long after the car had pulled away, as she stood on the street readjusting her veil. Such a nice girl. So good of her to come. That skin! What hair! All the way back Nicola had been thinking how good a cigarette would look, white and round between her black fingers. But she was out of cigarettes, having almost gassed herself with tobacco on the way to Golders Green. She now progressed along the Portobello Road, and saw a pub whose name she took a liking to. 'TV AND DARTS' was the further recommendation of a painted sign on its door, to which a piece of cardboard had been affixed, saying, 'AND PIMBALL'. All the skies of London seemed to be gathering directly overhead, with thunder ready to drop its plunger . . .

She entered the Black Cross. She entered the pub and its murk. She felt the place skip a beat as the door closed behind her, but she had been expecting that. Indeed, it would be a bad day (and that day would never come) when she entered a men's room, a teeming toilet such as this and turned no heads, caused no groans or whispers. She walked straight to the bar, lifted her veil with both hands, like a bride, surveyed the main actors of the scene, and immediately she knew, with pain, with gravid arrest, with intense recognition, that she had found him, her murderer.

When at last she returned to the flat Nicola laid out her diaries on the round table. She made an entry, unusually crisp and detailed: the final entry. The notebooks she used were Italian, their covers embellished with Latin script . . . Now they had served their purpose and she wondered how to dispose of them. The story wasn't over, but the life was. She stacked the books and reached for a ribbon . . . 'I've found him. On the Portobello Road, in a place called the Black Cross, I found him.'

I think it was Montherlant who said that happiness writes white: it doesn't show up on the page. We all know this. The letter with the foreign postmark that tells of good weather, pleasant food and comfortable accommodation isn't nearly as much fun to read, or to write, as the letter that tells of rotting chalets, dysentery and drizzle. Who else but Tolstoy has made happiness really swing on the page? When I take on Chapter 3, when I take on Guy Clinch, I'll have to do, well, not happiness, but goodness, anyway. It's going to be rough.

The moment that Keith Talent saw Nicola Six — he dropped his third dart. And swore. The 32-gram tungsten trebler had pierced his big toe . . . I thought I might be able to make a nice play on words here. Cupid's dart, or something like that. Arrows of desire? But it wasn't desire that Nicola Six aroused in Keith Talent. Not primarily. I would say that greed and fear came first. Going for broke at the pinball table, Guy Clinch froze in mid-flail: you could hear the ball scuttling into the gutter. Then silence.

While the scene developed I melted, as they say, into the background. Of course I had no idea what was taking shape in front of me. No idea? Well, an inkling, maybe. This moment in the public house, this pub moment, I'm going to have to keep on coming back to it. Edging down the bar, I was intrigued only in the civilian sense — but powerfully intrigued. Every pub has its superstar, its hero, its pub athlete, and Keith was the Knight of the Black Cross: he *had* to step

23

forward to deal with the royal tourist. He had to do it for the guys: for Wayne, Dean, Duane, for Norvis, Shakespeare, Big Dread, for Godfrey the barman, for Fucker Burke, for Basim and Manjeet, for Bogdan, Maciek, Zbigniew.

Keith acted in the name of masculinity. He acted also, of course, in the name of *class*. Class! Yes, it's still here. Terrific staying power, and against all the historical odds. What *is* it with that old, *old* crap? The class system just doesn't know when to call it a day. Even a nuclear holocaust, I think, would fail to make that much of a dent in it. Crawling through the iodized shithouse that used to be England, people would still be brooding about accents and cocked pinkies, about maiden names and *settee* or *sofa*, about the proper way to eat a roach in society. Come on. Do you take the head off first, or start with the legs? Class never bothered Keith; he never thought about it 'as such'; part of a bygone era, whatever that was, class never worried him. It would surprise Keith a lot if you told him it was *class* that poisoned his every waking moment. At any rate, subliminally or otherwise, it was class that made Keith enlist a third actor in his dealings with Nicola Six. It was class that made Keith enlist Guy Clinch. Or maybe the murderee did it. Maybe she needed him. Maybe they both needed him, as a kind of fuel.

Do *I* need him? Yes. Evidently. Guy pressed himself on me, same as the other two.

I left the Black Cross around four. It was my third visit. I needed the company, hair-raising though much of it was, and I was doing all right there, under Keith's tutelage. He introduced me to the Polacks and the brothers, or paraded me in front of them. He gave me a game of pool. He showed me how to cheat the fruit machine. I bought a lot of drinks, and endured a lot of savage cajolery for my orange juices, my sodas, my cokes. Taking my life in my hands, I ate a pork pie. Only one real fight so far. An incredible flurry of fists and nuttings; it ended with Keith carefully kicking selected areas of a fallen figure wedged into the doorway to the Gents; Keith then returned to the bar, took a pull of beer, and returned to kick some more. It transpired that the culprit had been messing with Dean's darts. After the ambulance came and went Keith calmed down. 'Not with a man's darts,' Keith kept saying almost tearfully, shaking his head. People were bringing him brandies. 'You don't . . . not with his darts.'

I left the Black Cross around four. I went back to the apartment. I sat at the desk in Mark Asprey's bay-windowed office or study or library. Actually it's more like a trophy room. Actually the whole damned place is a trophy room. Walking from living-room to bedroom — and I'm thinking of the signed photographs, the erotic prints — you wonder why he didn't just nail a galaxy of G-strings to the walls. In here it's different. Here you're surrounded by cups and sashes, Tonis and Guggies, by framed presentations, commendations. Cherished and valued alike by the critical establishment, the media, and the world of academe, Mark Asprey has honorary degrees, pasteboard hats, three separate gowns from Oxford, Cambridge, Trinity College Dublin. I must look at his books, of which there are a great many, in a great many editions, in a great many languages. Hungarian. Japanese.

I left the Black Cross around four. I went back to the apartment. I sat there wondering why I just can't do it, why I just can't write, why I just can't *make anything up*. Then I saw her.

Across the way from Mark Asprey's bay-windowed library there is a lot-sized square of green, with two thin beds of flowers (low-ranking flowers, NUPE flowers) and a wooden bench where old-timers sometimes sit and seem to flicker in the wind. On this green patch, rather regrettably, rather disappointingly (how come Asprey stands for it?), there is also a garbage tip: nothing outrageous, no compost or bathtubs or abandoned pantechnicons, just selected refuse, magazines, old toys, a running shoe, a kettle. This is a London theme; the attempt at greenery would itself appear to attract the trash. The cylinders of wire-netting they put up to protect young trees sufficiently resemble a container of some kind, so people cram them with beercans, used tissues, yesterday's newspapers. In times of mass disorientation and anxiety . . . But we can get back to that. On with the story. The girl was there: Nicola, the murderee.

I was sitting at Mark Asprey's vast desk — I think I might even have been wringing my hands. Oh Lord, these chains! Something I have suffered for twenty years, the steady disappointment of *not writing* — perhaps exacerbated (I admit to the possibility) by Mark Asprey's graphic and plentiful successes in the sphere. It shocked my heart to see her: a soft blow to the heart, from within. Still wearing her funeral robes, the hat, the veil. In her black-gloved hands she held something solid, ribboned in red, the load settled on her hip and clutched close as if for comfort, like a child. Then she raised the veil

25

and showed her face. She looked so . . . dramatic. She looked like the vamp in the ad, just before the asshole in the helicopter or the submarine shows up with the bathcubes or the chocolates. Could she see me, with that low sun behind her? I couldn't tell, but I thought: Nicola would know. She would know all about how light works on windows. She would know what you could get away with in the curtainless room, what adulteries, what fantastic betrayals . . .

Nicola turned, wavered, and steadied herself. She dropped her burden into the trash and, embracing her shoulders with crossed hands, moved off in a hurrying walk.

For perhaps five minutes of stretched time I waited. Then down I went and picked up my gift. Not knowing what I had, I sat on the bench and pulled the ribbon's knot. An adorably fat and feminine hand, chaos, a menacing intelligence. It made me blush with porno-graphic guilt. When I looked up I saw half of Nicola Six, thirty feet away, split by a young tree-trunk, not hiding but staring. Her stare contained – only clarity, great clarity. I gestured, as if to return what I held in my hands. But after a pulse of time she was walking off fast under the wrung hands of the trees.

I wish to Christ I could do Keith's voice. The *t*'s are viciously stressed. A brief guttural pop, like the first nanosecond of a cough or a hawk, accompanies the hard *k*. When he says *chaotic*, and he says it frequently, it sounds like a death rattle. 'Month' comes out as *mumf*. He sometimes says, 'Im feory . . .' when he speaks theoretically. 'There' sounds like *dare* or *lair*. You could often run away with the impression that Keith Talent is eighteen months old.

In fact I've had to watch it with my characters' ages. I thought Guy Clinch was about twenty-seven. He is thirty-five. I thought Keith Talent was about forty-two. He is twenty-nine. I thought Nicola Six . . . No, I always knew what she was. Nicola Six is thirty-four. I fear for them, my youngers.

And meanwhile time goes about its immemorial work of making everyone look and feel like shit. You got that? And meanwhile time goes about its immemorial work of making everyone look, and feel, like shit.

Chapter 3: The Foil

GUY CLINCH WAS a good guy – or a nice one, anyway. He wanted for nothing and lacked everything. He had a tremendous amount of money, excellent health, handsomeness, height, a capriciously original mind; and he was lifeless. He was wide open. Guy possessed, in Hope Clinch, a wife who was intelligent, efficient (the house was a masterpiece), brightly American (and rich); and then there was the indubitable vigour of the child . . . But when he woke up in the morning there was – there was no life. There was only lifelessness.

The happiest time of Guy's fifteen-year marriage had come during Hope's pregnancy, a relatively recent interlude. She had taken her fifty per cent cut in IQ with good grace, and for a while Guy had found himself dealing with an intellectual equal. Suddenly the talk was of home improvement, of babies' names, nursery conversions, girlish pinks, boyish blues – the tender materialism, all with a point. Never entirely free of builders, the house now thronged with them, shouting, swearing, staggering. Guy and Hope lived to hormone time. The curtain hormone, the carpet hormone. Her nausea passed. She craved mashed potato. Then the nesting hormone: an abrupt passion for patching, for needle and thread. Seeing the size of her, the barrow boys of Portobello Road (and perhaps Keith Talent had been among them) would summon her to their stalls, saying sternly, masterfully, 'Over here, my love. I got the stuff you want.' And Hope would rootle to the base of damp cardboard boxes – rags of velvet, scraps of satin. In the eighth month, when the furniture had begun its dance round the house, and Hope sat with regal fullness in front of the television, darning and patching (and sometimes saying, 'What am I *doing?*'), Guy consulted his senses, scratched his head, and whispered to himself (and he didn't mean the baby), *It's coming . . . It's on its way.*

Oh, how he had longed for a little girl! In the sparse gloom of the private clinic, the most expensive they could find (Hope distrusted any medical care that failed to stretch searchingly into the four figures: she liked the scrolled invoices, with every paper tissue and soldier of toast unsmilingly itemized; she had no time for the bargain basements and the Crazy Eddies of the National Health), Guy did his share of pacing and napping and fretting, while titled specialists looked in from dinner parties or popped by on their way to rounds of golf. A girl, a girl, just an ordinary little girl – Mary, Anna, Jane. 'It's a girl,' he could hear himself saying on the telephone (to whom, he didn't know). 'Five pounds twelve ounces. Yes, a girl. A little under six pounds.' He wanted to be with his wife throughout, but Hope had banned him from labour and delivery wards alike – for reasons, soberly but unanswerably stated, of sexual pride.

The baby showed up thirty-six hours later, at four in the morning. He weighed nearly a stone. Guy was allowed a brief visit to Hope's suite. Looking back at it now, he had an image of mother and son mopping themselves down with gloating expressions on their faces, as if recovering from some enjoyably injudicious frolic: a pizza fight, by the look of it. Two extra specialists were present. One was peering between Hope's legs, saying, 'Yes, well it's rather hard to tell what goes where.' The other was incredulously measuring the baby's head. Oh, the little boy was perfect in every way. And he was a monster.

Guy Clinch had everything. In fact he had two of everything. Two cars, two houses, two uniformed nannies, two silk-and-cashmere dinner jackets, two graphite-cooled tennis rackets, and so on and so forth. But he had only one child and only one woman. After Marmaduke's birth, things changed. For fresh inspiration he reread *The Egoist*, and Wollheim on Ingres and the Melting Father. The baby books had prepared him for change; and so had literature, up to a point. But nothing had prepared him or anybody else for Marmaduke . . . World-famous paediatricians marvelled at his hyperactivity, and knelt like magi to his genius for colic. Every half an hour he noisily drained his mother's sore breasts; often he would take a brief nap around midnight; the rest of the time he spent screaming. Only parents and torturers and the janitors of holocausts are asked to stand the sound of so much human grief. When things improved, which they did, though only temporarily (for Marmaduke, already softly snarling with asthma, would soon be emblazoned with eczema), Hope still spent much of her time in bed, with or without Marmaduke, but never with Guy. All night he lay dressed for disaster in one of the two visitors' rooms, wondering why his life had suddenly turned into a very interesting and high-toned horror film (one with a Regency setting, perhaps). His habitual mode of locomotion around the house became the tiptoe. When Hope called his name – 'Guy?' –and he replied *Yes?* there was never any answer, because his name meant *Come here.* He appeared, and performed the necessary errand, and disappeared again. Now, with Hope's requests, the first time of asking sounded like the second time of asking, and the second time of asking sounded like the ninth. Less and less often Guy would try to hoist the baby into his arms (under the doubtful gaze of nanny or night-nurse, or some other of Marmaduke's highly-paid admirers), saying, rather self-consciously, 'Hello, man-cub.' Marmaduke would pause, reviewing his options; and Guy's bashfully inquiring face would somehow always invite a powerful eye-poke or a jet of vomit, a savage rake of the nails, or at the very least an explosive sneeze. Guy shocked himself by suspecting that Hope kept the infant's nails unclipped the better to repel him. Certainly his face was heavily scored; he sometimes looked like a resolute but talent-less rapist. He felt supererogatory. The meeting, the rendezvous, it just hadn't happened.

So two of everything, except lips, breasts, the walls of intimacy, enfolding arms, enfolding legs. But that wasn't really it. What had meant to come closer had simply moved further away. Life, there-fore, could loom up on him at any moment. He was wide open.

Guy and Hope had been away twice since the birth, on doctor's advice: their doctor's, not Marmaduke's. They left him in the care of five nannies, plus an even more costly platoon of medical commandos. It had been strange, leaving him behind; Guy fully participated in Hope's dread as the cab made its way to Heathrow. Fear was gradually eased by time, and by half-hourly telephone calls. The inner ear was tuned to infant grief. If you listened closely, everything sounded like a baby crying.

First, Venice, in February, the mist, the cold troubled water – and miraculously carless. Guy had never in his life felt closer to the sun; it was like living in a cloud, up in a cloudy sea. But many of the mornings were sombre in mood and sky (dank, failed), and seemed best expressed by the tortured and touristless air of the Jewish Quarter, or by the weak dappling on the underside of a bridge (where the pale flames pinged like static, briefly betrayed by a darker background) – or when you were lost among the Chinese boxes, the congestion of beauties, and you could have likened yourselves to Shakespearean lovers until there came the sound of a wretched sneeze from an office window near by, then the nose greedily voided into the hanky, and the resumption of the dull ticking of a typewriter or an adding machine.

On the fifth day the sun burst through again inexorably. They were walking arm in arm along the Zattere towards the café where they had taken to having their mid-morning snack. The light was getting to work on the water, with the sun torpedoing in on every pair of human eyes. Guy looked up: to him the sky spoke of Revelation, Venetian style. He said,

'I've just had a rather delightful thought. You'd have to set it as verse.' He cleared his throat. 'Like this:

> The sun, the sun, the . . . daubing sun:
> The clouds are *putti* in its hands!'

They walked on. Hope's oval face looked resolute. The juices in her jaw were already addressing the toasted cheese-and-ham sandwich she would presently enjoy; then the notebook, the little Amex guide, the creamy coffee. 'Dreadful pun, I suppose,' Guy murmured. 'Oh, God.' A press of sightseers confronted them. As they forged through, with Hope taking the lead, their arms were sundered. Guy hurried to catch up.

'The *tourists*,' he said.

'Don't complain. That's idiotic. What do you think *you* are?'

'Yes but –'

'Yes but nothing.'

Guy faltered. He had turned to face the water and was craning his neck in obscure distress. Hope closed her eyes longsufferingly, and waited.

'Wait, Hope,' he said. 'Please look. If I move my head, then the sun moves on the water. My eyes have as much say in it as the sun.'

'. . . *Capisco*.'

'But that means – for everyone here the sun is different on the water. No two people are seeing the same thing.'

'I want my sandwich.'

She moved on. Guy lingered, clutching his hands, and saying, 'But then it's hopeless. Don't you think? It's . . . quite hopeless.'

And he whispered the same words at night in the hotel, and went on whispering them, even after their return to London, lying in sleep's caboose, seconds before Marmaduke woke him with a clout. 'But then it's hopeless . . . Utterly hopeless.'

In excellent fettle, in the pink or the blue of boyish good health during their absence, Marmaduke sickened dramatically within a few hours of their return. Evenhandedly he dabbled with every virus, every hatching, afforded by that early spring. Recovering from mumps, he reacted catastrophically to his final whooping-cough shot. Superflu followed superflu in efficient relay. Doctors now visited him, unasked and unpaid, out of sheer professional curiosity. At this point, and for no clear reason (Sir Oliver asked if he might write a paper about it), Marmaduke's health radically improved. Indeed, he seemed to shed his sickly self as if it were a dead skin or a useless appendage: from the feverish grub of the old Marmaduke sprang a musclebound wunder-kind, clear-eyed, pink-tongued, and (it transpired) infallibly vicious. The change was all very sudden. Guy and Hope went out one day, leaving the usual gastroenteritic nightmare slobbering on the kitchen floor; they returned after lunch to find Marmaduke strolling round the drawing-room with his hands in his pockets, watched by several speechless nannies. He had never crawled. Instead, he appeared to have worked it out that he could cause much more trouble, and have much more fun, in a state of peak fitness. His first move was to dispense with that midnight nap. The Clinches hired more help, or they tried. An ailing baby was one thing; a strappingly malevolent toddler was quite another. Up until now, Guy and Hope's relationship, to the child and to each other, had been largely paramedical. After Marmaduke's renaissance, it became, well – you wouldn't say paramilitary. You'd say military. The only people they could get who stayed longer than an hour or two were male nurses sacked from lunatic asylums. Around the house, these days there was a kind of SWAT team of burly orderlies,

31

as well as a few scarred nannies and au pairs. Dazedly yet without bitterness, Guy calculated that Marmaduke, now in his ninth month, had already cost him a quarter of a million pounds. They went away again.

This time they flew first-class to Madrid, stayed at the Ritz for three nights, and then hired a car and headed south. The car seemed powerful and luxurious enough; it was, without question, resoundingly expensive. (Hope whaled on the insurance. Guy studied the gold-rimmed document: they would airlift you out on almost any pretext.) But as they cruised, as they cruised and glistened one evening through the thin forests near the southernmost shore of the peninsula, a great upheaval or trauma seemed almost to dismantle the engine at a stroke – the manifold, the big end? In any event the car was clearly history. Around midnight Guy could push it no longer. They saw some lights: not many, and not bright.

The Clinches found accommodation in a rude *venta*. What with the bare coil of the bulb, the lavatorial damp, the flummoxed bed, Hope had burst into tears before the señora was out of the room. All night Guy lay beside his drugged wife, listening. At about five, after an interval reminiscent of one of Marmaduke's naps, the weekend roistering in the bar, the counterpoints of jukebox and Impacto machine, exhaustedly gave way to the shrieking gossip of the yard – with a cluck-cluck here and a whoof-whoof there, here a cheep, there a moo, everywhere an oink-oink. Worst or nearest was a moronic bugler of a cock, playing tenor to the neighbours' alto, with his room-rattling reveille. 'Cock-a-doodle-do', Guy decided, was one of the world's great euphemisms. At seven, after an especially unbearable tenor solo (as if the cock were finally heralding the entrance of some imperial superrooster), Hope jerked upright, swore fluently and foully, applied valium and eyemask, and bunched herself down again with her face pressed to her knees. Guy smiled weakly. There was a time when he could read love in the shape of his sleeping wife; even in the contours of the blankets he used to be able to read it . . .

He went outside, into the yard. The cock, the grotesque *gallo*, stood in its coop – yes, inches from their pillows – and stared at him with unchallengeable pomp. Guy stared back, shaking his head slowly. Hens were in attendance, quietly and unquestioningly supportive, among all the dust and rubbish. As for the two pigs, they were yahoos even by the standards of the yard. A dark half-grown Alsatian dozed in the hollow of an old oildrum. Sensing a presence, the dog jerked upright, waking sudden and crumpled, with sand dried into the long trap of the jaw, and moved towards him with compulsive friendliness. It's a girl, he thought: tethered, too. As he went to pet the animal they became entangled, entangled, it seemed, by the very amiability of the dog, by its bouncing, twisting amiability.

In pastel daubings the new prosperity lay to east and west but this place was kept poor by wind. Wind bled and beggared it. Like the cock, the wind just did its wind thing, not caring wherefore. Hot air rises, cool air fills the space: hence, somehow, the tearing and tugging, the frenzied unzippings of this sandpaper shore. In his tennis shorts Guy stepped off the porch and walked past the car (the car avoided his gaze) on to the tattered croisette. A motorbike, an anguished donkey shackled to its cart — nothing else. The sky also was empty, blown clean, an unblinking Africa of blue. Down on the beach the wind went for his calves like an industrial cleanser; Guy gained the hardened rump of damp sand and contemplated the wrinkly sea. It opened inhospitably to him. Feeling neither vigour nor its opposite, feeling no closer to life than to death, feeling thirty-five, Guy pressed on, hardly blinking as he crossed the scrotum barrier; and it was the water that seemed to cringe and start back, repelled by this human touch, as he barged his way down the incline, breathed deep, and pitched himself forward in the swimmer's embrace of the sea . . . Twenty minutes later, as he strode back up the beach, the wind threw everything it had at him, and with fierce joy the sand sought his eyes and teeth, the hairless tray of his chest. A hundred yards from the road Guy paused, and imagined surrendering to it (I may be gone some time), dropping to his knees and folding sideways under the icy buckshot of the air.

He queued for coffee in the awakening *venta*. The daughters of the establishment were mopping up; two men boldly conversed across the length of the dark room. Guy stood straight, barefoot, his skin and hair minutely spangled by the sand. An interested woman, had she been monitoring him with half an eye, might have found Guy Clinch well made, classical, above all healthy; but there was something pointless or needless in his good looks; they seemed wasted on him. Guy knew this. Stocky mat-shouldered Antonio, leaning against the pillar by the door, one hand limp on his round belly — and thinking with complacence of his own blood-red loincloth, with the good shoelace-and-tassel effect down there on the crotch — registered Guy not at all, not at all. And the poling daughters had thoughts only for Antonio, careless, drunken, donkey-flogging Antonio and his crimson bullybag . . . Guy drank the excellent coffee, and ate bread

33

moistened with olive oil, out on the banging porch. He then took a tray into Hope, who ripped off her mask but lay there with her eyes closed.

'Have you achieved anything yet?'

'I've been swimming,' he said. 'It's my birthday.'

'. . . Many happy returns.'

'Young Antonio here is apparently pretty handy with a spanner.'

'Oh yes? The car's dead, Guy.'

Moments earlier, out on the banging porch, a ridiculous thing had happened. Hearing a rhythmical whimpering in the middle distance, Guy had raised his hands to his temples, as if to freeze-frame the thought that was winding through his head (and he wasn't given to them. He wasn't given to pornographic thoughts). The thought was this: Hope splayed and naked, being roughly used by an intent Antonio . . . Guy had then taken his last piece of bread into the yard and offered it to the tinned dog. (He also took another incredulous look at the cock, the stupid *gallo*.) The dog was whimpering rhythmically, but showed no appetite. Dirty and gentle-faced, the bitch just wanted to play, to romp, to fraternize, and just kept tripping on her tether. The length of filthy rope – six feet of it – saddened Guy in a way that Spanish cruelty or carelessness had never saddened him before. Down in the yard here, on a wind-frazzled stretch of empty shore, when the only thing that came free and plentiful was space and distance – the dog was given none of it. So poor, and then poor again, doubly, triply, exponentially poor. *I've found it*, thought Guy (though the word wouldn't come, not yet). *It is . . . I've found it and it's . . . It is –*

'So?'

'Why don't we stay here? For a few days? The sea's nice,' he said, 'once you're in. Until we get the car fixed. It's interesting.'

Hope's impressive bite-radius now readied itself over the first section of grilled bread. She paused. 'I can't bear it. You aren't going *dreamy* on me, are you Guy? Listen, we're out of here. We are *gone*.'

And so it became the kind of day where you call airlines and consulates and car-hire people in a dreary dream of bad connexions and bad Spanish: that evening, on the helipad at Algeciras, Hope favoured Guy with her first smile in twenty-four hours. Actually nearly all of this was achieved (between meals and drinks and swims) from the control tower of a six-star hotel further down the coast, a place full of rich old Germans, whose heavy playfulness and charmless appearance (Guy had to admit) powerfully reminded him of Marmaduke.

Thereafter it was all quite easy: not clear and not purposeful, but not difficult. Guy Clinch looked round his life for a dimension through which some new force might propagate. And his life, he found, was sewn-up, was wall-to-wall. It was closed. To the subtle and silent modulations of Hope's disgust, he started to open it. Guy had a job. He worked for the family business. This meant sitting about in a bijou flatlet in Cheapside, trying to keep tabs on the proliferating, the pullulating hydra of Clinch money. (It, too, was like Marmaduke: what *would* it get up to next?) Increasingly, Guy stopped going in and just walked the streets instead.

Fear was his guide. Like all the others on the crescent Guy's house stood aloof from the road, which was all very well, which was all very fine and large; but fear had him go where the shops and flats jostled fascinatedly over the street like a crowd round a bearpit, with slot-game parlours, disastrous beaneries, soup queues, army hostels, with life set out on barrows, on pingpong tables, on decapitated Portakabins – the voodoo and the hunger, the dreadlocks and dreadnoughts, the Keiths and Kaths of the Portobello Road. Naturally Guy had been here before, in search of a corn-fed chicken or a bag of Nicaraguan coffee. But now he was looking for the thing itself.

TV AND DARTS, said the sign. AND PIMBALL. The first time Guy entered the Black Cross he was a man pushing through the black door of his fear . . . He survived. He lived. The place was ruined and innocuous in its northern light: a clutch of dudes and Rastas playing pool over the damp swipe of the baize, the pewtery sickliness of the whites (they looked like war footage), the twittering fruit-machines, the fuming pie-warmer. Guy asked for a drink in the only voice he had: he didn't tousle his hair or his accent; he carried no tabloid under his arm, open on the racing page. With a glass of medium-sweet white wine he moved to the pinball table, an old Gottlieb, with Arabian-Nights artwork (temptress, devil, hero, maiden) – Eye of the Tiger. Eye of the Tiger . . . A decrepit Irish youth stood inches away whispering *who's the boss who's the boss* into Guy's ear for as long as he seemed to need to do that. Whenever Guy looked up a dreadful veteran of the pub, his face twanging in the canned rock, stared at him bitterly, like the old man you stop for at the zebra who crosses slowly, with undiminished suspicion: no forgiveness there, not ever. The in-

35

prehensible accusations of a sweat-soaked black girl were finally silenced by a five-pound note. Guy stayed for half an hour, and got out. He took so much fear away with him that there had to be less of it each time he returned. But going there at night was another entry.

Keith was the key: Keith, and his pub charisma. Keith was the pub champ. The loudest, the most booming in his shouts for more drink, the most violent in his abuse of the fruit machine, the best at darts – a darts force in the Black Cross . . . Now plainly Keith had to do something about Guy, who was far too anomalous to be let alone, with his pub anticharisma. Keith had to ban him, befriend him, beat him up. Kill him. So he pouched his darts one day and walked the length of the bar (regulars were wondering when it would happen), leaned over the pinball table with an eyebrow raised and his tongue between his teeth: and bought Guy a drink. The hip pocket, the furled tenners. Keith's house had many mansions. The whole pub shook with silent applause.

Cheers, Keith! After that, Guy belonged. He sailed in there almost with a swagger and summoned the barmen by name: God, or Pongo. After that, he stopped having to buy drinks for the black girls, and stopped having to buy drugs from the black boys. The heroin, the cut coke, the Temazepam, the dihydrocodeine he had always refused, fobbing them off with small purchases of dope. He used to take the hash and grass home and flush it down the waste-disposer; he didn't drop it in the gutter for fear that a child or a dog might get hold of it, a needless precaution, because the hash wasn't hash and the grass was just grass . . . Now Guy could sit in a damp pocket of pub warmth, and watch. Really the thing about life here was its incredible rapidity, with people growing up and getting old in the space of a single week. Like the planet in the twentieth century, with its fantastic *coup de vieux*. Here, in the Black Cross, time was a tube train with the driver slumped heavy over the lever, flashing through station after station. Guy always thought it was life he was looking for. But it must have been death – or death awareness. Death candour. I've found it, he thought. It is mean, it is serious, it is beautiful, it is poor; it fully earns every compliment, every adjective, you care to name.

So when Nicola Six came into the Black Cross on a day of thunder and stood at the bar and raised her veil–Guy was ready. He was wide open.

'*Bitch*,' said Keith, as he dropped his third dart.

Being a dart, a little missile of plastic and tungsten, it combined with gravity and efficiently plunged towards the centre of the earth. What halted its progress was Keith's left foot, which was protected only by the frayed webbing of a cheap running-shoe: you could see the little bullseye of blood. But there was another arrowman or darter in the Black Cross that day; perhaps this smiling *putto* lurked in the artwork of the pinball table, among its sinbads and sirens, its goblins and genies. Eye of the Tiger! When he saw her green eyes, and the breadth of her mouth, Guy gripped the flanks of the machine for comfort or support. The ball scuttled into the gutter. Then silence.

She cleared her throat and inquired of Godfrey the barman, who cocked his head doubtfully.

As she turned to go Keith stepped in, or he limped in, anyway, moving down the bar with his unreliable smile. Guy watched in wonder. Keith said,

'No danger. They don't sell French fags here, darling. No way. Here? No danger. Carlyle!'

A black boy appeared, panting, triumphant, as if his errand were already run. Keith gave the instructions, the mangled fiver, then turned assessingly. Death wasn't new in the Black Cross, it was everyday, it was ten-a-penny; but tailored mourning wear, hats, *veils*? Keith searched his mind, seemed to search his mouth, for something appropriate to say. In the end he said, 'Bereavement innit. God? Get her a brandy. She could use it. Nobody close I presume?'

'No. Nobody close.'

'What's your name, sweetheart?'

She told him. Keith couldn't believe his luck.

'Sex!'

'S-*i*-x. Actually it's *Six*.'

'Seeks! Relax, Nicky. We get all sorts in here. Hey, *cock. Guy* . . .'

Now Guy moved into her force field. Intensely he confirmed the line of dark down above her mouth. You saw women like this, sometimes, at the bars of theatres and concert halls, in certain restaurants, in aeroplanes. You didn't see them in the Black Cross. She too looked as though she might faint at any moment. 'How do you do?' he said (in his peripheral vision Keith was slowly nodding), extending a hand towards the black glove. 'Guy Clinch.' His fingers hoped for the amperes of recognition but all he felt was a slick softness, a sense of moisture that perhaps someone else had readied. Little Carlyle exploded through the pub doors.

'You must let me pay for these,' she said, removing a glove. The

37

hand that now attacked the cellophane was bitten at the five tips.

'My treat,' said Keith.

'I suppose,' Guy said, 'I suppose this is by way of being a wake.'

'Weren't family?' said Keith.

'Just a woman I used to work for.'

'Young?'

'No no.'

'Still. Does you credit,' Keith went on. 'Show respect. Even if it's just some old boiler. Comes to us all as such.'

They talked on. With a violent jerk of self-reproof, Guy bought more drinks. Keith leaned forward murmuring with cupped hands to light Nicola's second cigarette. But this was soon finished or aborted, and she was lowering her veil and saying,

'Thank you. You've been very kind. Goodbye.'

Guy watched her go, as did Keith: the delicate twist of the ankles, the strength and frankness of the hips; and that concavity of the tight black skirt, in the telling underspace.

'Extraordinary,' said Guy.

'Yeah, she'll do,' said Keith, wiping his mouth with the back of his hand (for he was leaving also).

'You're not –'

Keith turned, in warning. His gaze fell to the hand, Guy's hand (their first touch), which lightly held his forearm. The hand now slackened and dropped.

'Come on, Keith,' said Guy with a pale laugh. 'She's just been to a funeral.'

Keith looked him up and down. 'Life goes on innit,' he said, with most of his usual buoyancy. He straightened his windcheater and gave a manful sniff. 'Dreaming of it,' he said, as if to the street outside. 'Begging for it. Praying for it.'

Keith shoved his way through the black doors. Guy hesitated for a moment, a pub moment, and then followed him.

That night in Lansdowne Crescent, at 8.45, his twelve-hour tryst with Marmaduke now only minutes away, Guy sat on the second sofa in the second drawing-room with a rare second drink and thought: How will I ever know anything in the middle of all this warmth and space, all this supershelter? I want to feel like the trampolinist when he falls back to earth and to gravity. To touch the earth with heaviness – just to touch it. God expose us, take away our padding and our room.

I watched them go.

Keith followed Nicola out of the Black Cross. Guy followed Keith.

I wish to Christ I'd followed Guy, but those were early days, before I was really on the case.

A promising routine is forming around me. I can finish a chapter in two days, even with all the fieldwork I have to go out and do. Every third day, now, I do more fieldwork, and wince and gloat into my notebook. I write. I'm a writer . . . Perhaps to offset the looming bulk of Mark Asprey's corpus, I have laid out my two previous publications on the desk here. *Memoirs of a Listener*. *On the Grapevine*. By Samson Young. Me. Yes, you. A valued stylist, in my native America. My memoirs, my journalism, praised for their honesty, their truthfulness. I'm not one of those excitable types who get caught making things up. Who get caught improving on reality. I can embellish, I can take certain liberties. Yet to invent the bald facts of a life (for example) would be quite beyond my powers.

Why? I think it might have something to do with me being such a nice guy, originally. Anyway at the moment reality is behaving unimprovably, and nobody will know.

I'm so coiled up about the first three chapters, it's all I can do not to Fed-Ex – or even Thrufax – them off to Missy Harter, at Hornig Ultrason. There are others I could approach. Publishers regularly inquire about my first novel. Publishers dream nights about my first novel. So do I. I'm getting old, and at a peculiar rate. Missy Harter, of course, has always been the most persistent. Maybe I'll call her. I need the encouragement. I need the stimulation. I need the money.

Keith came over this morning. I suppose he *has* to be teeing me up for a burglary, because the place is full of portable baubles.

He wanted to use the VCR. Naturally he has a VCR of his own; he probably has several dozen, somewhere. But this, he said, was a little bit special. Then he produced a tape in its plastic wallet. The front cover showed a man's naked torso, its lower third obscured by two discrete cataracts of thick blonde hair. The sticker said £189.99.

It was called *When Scandinavian Bodies Go Mouth Crazy*. The title proved to be accurate — even felicitous. I sat with Keith for a while and watched five middle-aged men seated around a table talking in Danish or Swedish or Norwegian without subtitles. You could make out a word now and then. *Radiotherapy. Handikap-toilet.* 'Where's the remote?' Keith asked grimly. He had need of the Fast Forward, the Picture Search. We found the remote but it didn't seem to be working. Keith had to sit through the whole thing: an educational short, I assume, about hospital administration. I slipped into the study. When I came back the five old guys were still talking. The thing ended, after a few credits. Keith looked at the floor and said, '*Bast*ard.'

To cheer him up (among other motives) I applied to Keith for darts lessons. His rates are not low.

I too have need of the Fast Forward. But I must let things happen at the speed she picks. I can eke out Chapter 4 with Keith's sexual confessions (vicious, detailed and unstoppable), which, at this stage, are the purest gold.

Guy Clinch was no sweat to pull, to cultivate, to develop. It was a shame to take the money. Again, fatefully easy.

Knowing that Keith would be elsewhere (busy cheating: an elderly widow — also fine material), I staked out the Black Cross hoping Guy would show. For the first time I noticed a joke sign behind the bar: NO FUCKING SWEARING. And what's with this *carpet*? What do you want a *carpet* for in a place like this? I ordered an orange juice. One of the black guys — he called himself Shakespeare — was staring at me with either affection or contempt. Shakespeare is, by some distance, the least prosperous of the Black Cross brothers. The bum's overcoat, the plastic shoes, the never-washed dreadlocks. He's the local shaman: he has a religious mission. His hair looks like an onion bhaji. 'You trying to cut down, man?' he slowly asked me. Actually I had to make him say it about five times before I understood. His resined face showed no impatience. 'I don't drink,' I told him. He was nonplussed. Of course, non-drinking, while big in America, was never much more than a fad over here. 'Honest,' I said. 'I'm Jewish.' . . . Quite a kick, saying that to a barful of blacks. Imagine saying it in Chicago, or Pittsburgh. Imagine saying it in Detroit. 'We don't, much.' Gradually, as if controlled by a dial, pleasure filled Shakespeare's eyes – which, it seemed to me, were at least as malarial and sanguinary as my own. One of the embarrassments of my condition: although it encourages, or enforces, a quiet life and sensible habits, it makes me look like Caligula after a very heavy year. What with all the grape and the slavegirls and everything, and all those fancy punishments and neat tortures I've been doling out . . . 'It's all in the eyes, man,' said Shakespeare. 'All in the eyes.'

In he came – Guy – with a flourish of fair hair and long-rider raincoat. I watched him secure a drink and settle over the pinball table. Smugly I marvelled at his transparency, his flickering, flinching transparency. Then I sidled up, placed my coin on the glass (this is the pinball etiquette), and said, 'Let's play pairs.' In his face: a routine thrill of dread, then openness; then pleasure. I impressed him with my pinball lore: silent five, two-flip, shoulder-check, and so on. We were practically pals anyway, having both basked in the sun of Keith's patronage. And, besides, he was completely desperate, as many of us are these days. In a modern city, if you have nothing to do (and if you're not broke, and on the street), it's tough to find people to do nothing with. We wandered out together and did the Portobello Road for a while, and then – don't you love the English – he asked me home for tea.

Once inside his colossal house I saw further avenues of invasion. I saw beachheads and bridgeheads. His frightening wife Hope I soon neutralized; I may have looked like a piece of shit Guy'd brought back from the pub (on the sole of his shoe) but a little media talk and Manhattan networking soon schmoozed her into shape. I met her kid sister, Lizzyboo, and looked her over for possible promotion. But maybe the current *au pair* is more my speed: a ducklike creature, not young, with a promisingly vacuous expression. As for the maid,

Auxiliadora, I didn't mess around, instantly hiring her for the apartment . . .

I kind of hate to say it, but Mark Asprey was the key. Everyone was frankly electrified when I let slip my connexion to the great man. Hope and Lizzyboo had seen his latest West End hit, *The Goblet*, which Asprey is even now escorting to Broadway. Dully asked by me if she'd liked it, Lizzyboo said, 'I cried, actually. Actually I cried twice.' Guy didn't know Asprey's stuff but said, as if to himself, in amazement, 'To be a *writer* like that. Just to sit there and do what you do.' I fought down an urge to mention my own two books (neither of which found an English publisher. Run a damage-check on that. Yes, it still hurts. It still exquisitely burns).

So one dud writer can usually spot another. When we were alone together in the kitchen Guy asked me what I did and I told him, stressing my links with various literary magazines and completely inventing a fiction consultancy with Hornig Ultrason. I can invent: I can lie. So how come I can't *invent*? Guy said, 'Really? How interesting.' I sent a sort of pressure wave at him; in fact I was rubbing my thumb and forefinger together beneath the table when he said, 'I've written a couple of things . . .' 'No kidding.' 'A couple of stories. Expanded travel notes, really.' 'I'd certainly be happy to take a look at them, Guy.' 'They aren't any good or anything.' 'Let me be the judge.' 'They're rather autobiographical, I'm afraid.' 'Oh,' I said. 'That's okay. Don't worry about *that*.

'The other day,' I went on. 'Did Keith follow that girl?'

'Yes he did,' said Guy instantly. Instantly, because Nicola was already present in his thoughts. And because love travels at the speed of light. 'Nothing happened. He just talked to her.'

I said, 'That's not what Keith told me.'

'What did he say?'

'It doesn't matter what he said. Keith's a liar, Guy . . . What happened?'

Later, I got a look at the kid. Jesus.

I'm like a vampire. I can't enter unless I'm asked in over the threshold. Once there, though, I stick around.

And come back whenever I like.

Now here's a pleasing symmetry. All three characters have given me something they've written. Keith's brochure, Nicola's diaries, Guy's fiction. Things written for different reasons: self-aggrandize-

42

ment, self-communion, self-expression. One offered freely, one abandoned to chance, one coaxingly procured.

Documentary evidence. Is that what I'm writing? A documentary? As for artistic talent, as for the imaginative patterning of life, Nicola wins. She outwrites us all.

I must get into their houses. Keith will be tricky here, as in every other area. Probably, and probably rightly, he is ashamed of where he lives. He will have a rule about it – Keith, with his tenacities, his berk protocols, his criminal codes, his fierce and tearful brand-loyalties. Keith will naturally be tricky.

With the murderee I have a bold idea. It would be a truthful move, and I *must have* the truth. Guy is reasonably trustworthy; I can allow for his dreamy overvaluations, his selective blindnesses. But Keith is a liar, and I'll have to doublecheck, or triangulate, everything he tells me. I must have the truth. There just isn't time to settle for anything less than the truth.

I must get inside their houses. I must get inside their heads. I must go deeper – oh, deeper.

We have all known days of sun and storm that make us feel what it is to live on a planet. But the recent convulsions have taken this further. They make us feel what it is to live in a solar system, a galaxy. They make us feel – and I'm on the edge of nausea as I write these words – what it is to live in a universe.

Particularly the winds. They tear through the city, they tear through the island, as if softening it up for an exponentially greater violence. In the last week the winds have killed nineteen people, and thirty-three million trees.

And now, at dusk, outside my window, the trees shake their heads like disco dancers in the strobe lights of nightlife long ago.

Chapter 4: The Dead-End Street

'**D**REAMING OF IT. Begging for it. Praying for it.'
    Keith pushed his way out of the Black Cross and girded himself there on the stone step, beneath the sign. TV AND DARTS. He looked right, he looked left; he grunted. There she was. There was Nicola Six. She stood out clearly like a rivulet of black ink against the rummagings and barter pastels of the market street. Past the stalls she moved wanderingly, erring, erring. If it had occurred to Keith that Nicola was waiting for him or leading him on, that he was included in any design of hers, he would have dismissed the idea. But there was pressing invitation in the idleness with which she wandered, the slow shifts of weight in the tight black skirt. For a brief passage of time Keith had the odd idea that Nicola was watching him; and that couldn't be right, because Keith was watching Nicola, and Nicola hadn't turned. Something tugged him. She's leading me on, he thought, and started following her. *Beauty, extreme yet ambiguously available*: this, very roughly, was what Nicola's entrance into the Black Cross had said to Keith. But he didn't know the nature – he didn't know the brand – of the availability. Keith burped hotly. He was going to find out.
    Now Nicola paused in profile, and bent to inspect the cheap china of a covered barrow. Raising her face she had words with the barrow's owner, a *cheat* Keith knew well. She raised her veil . . . When she'd raised her veil in the pub Keith had looked at her with sharp interest, certainly, but not with desire. No, not exactly desire;

44

the point of the dart in his foot precluded desire, hurt too much for desire. Nicola was tall – taller than Keith in her heels – and, it would seem, delicately made, the curve of the ankle answering to the curve of the throat. She looked like a model, but not the kind of model Keith generally preferred. She looked like a fashion model, and Keith generally preferred the other kind, the glamour kind. The demeanour of the glamour model proclaimed that you could do what you liked with her. The demeanour of the fashion model proclaimed that she could do what she liked with you. Besides, and more basically, Keith generally preferred short girls with thick short legs and big breasts (no theoretical limit) and fat bums – girls in the mould of Trish Shirt and Peggy Obbs, of Debbee Kensit (who was special) and Analiese Furnish. The legs appeared to be particularly important. Keith couldn't help noticing that the legs he most often forced open, the legs he most often found dangling over his shoulders, tended to be exceptionally thick in the ankle, tended, in fact, to be ankleless, and exceptionally thick in the calf. He had concluded that fat legs were what he must generally prefer. The discovery pleased Keith at first, then perplexed and even worried him, because he had never thought of himself as being fussy. Nicola's ankles: you were surprised they could bear all that height and body. Perhaps she just wasn't his type. Oh, but she was. Something told him that she definitely, she deeply *was*.

Nicola moved on. Keith followed. Other possibilities aside, she interested Keith in the same way that Guy Clinch or old Lady Barnaby interested him. She was in the A.1. bracket. Keith wasn't the sort of bloke who disapproved of people who had a lot of money. He liked there to be people who had a lot of money, so that he could cheat them out of it. Keith was sorry, but he wouldn't want to live in the kind of society where nobody was worth burgling. No way. Thus, as he trailed Nicola through the trash of the barrowed street, thinking that her backside might well be fatter than it looked and anyway the thinner bird often made it up to you in the crib, several considerations obtained.

He waited until she approached the flower stall and stood there removing her gloves. Then he went in. Giving the nod and the pointed finger to old Nigel (who owed Keith and had good reason to be wary of him), and moving with his usual confident clumsiness, he wrenched a handful of brown paper from the nail and edged along the barrow picking the soaked bunches from their plastic tubs and saying,

45

'Discover the language of flowers. And let their soothing words . . .' He paused, trying to recapture the full jingle. 'Soothe away all your cares like.' No wedding ring, he thought. Could tell that, even under the glove in the Cross. 'Daffodils. Glads. Some of them. Some of them. The lot. A time like this.' He held forth the throttled posy. 'Why be retiring? On me.' Bites her nails but the hands are lazy. Dead lazy. 'You heading on down this way? Or I got the Cavalier round the corner.' Without quite touching her, his hands merely delineating the shape of her shoulders, Keith urged Nicola forward along the street. Expensive suit. Not cheap. 'I see a girl like you. Bit of a beauty. Head in the clouds as such. You said you got your own place.' She nodded and smiled. 'Now.' The mouth on her. That veil'd be useful too. 'Me? I'm Handy Andy. Mr Fixit innit. You know, the fuse's gone. The boiler's creating or the bell don't work. You need somebody with a few connexions.' The shoes: half a grand. Got to be. 'Because I know. I know it's hard, Nicky, to engage *any* real services these days. To be honest with you,' he said, and his eyes closed with stung pride, 'I don't know what the fucking country's coming to. I don't.' She slowed her pace; briskly she removed her hat and the black clip that secured her chignon. With a roll of her throat she shook out her hair, Jesus: high *priced*. They walked on. TV. 'All I'm saying is I'm a man can get things done. Any little prob like. Cry out for Keith. This it?'

They had approached the entrance to the dead-end street.

'I live down there,' she said. 'Thank you for these.'

As she slowed, and half turned, and walked on, and slowed again, Nicola fanned herself with the flap of a glove. Her colour was high. She even hooked a thumb into the V of her black jacket and tugged. She's hung, too, he thought. The bitch. Remarkably, this final bonus began to have a dispiriting effect on Keith Talent. Because perfection would be no good to him. Rather wistfully, he imagined she might have a big scar somewhere, or another blemish that he, for one, might willingly overlook. Failing that, in her mental instability he would repose his hopes. The condition of her nails was some comfort to him. Cold comfort only, though. By Keith's standards, they weren't that bad. They were bitten; but they weren't bitten off. That left her accent, which was definitely foreign (Europe, thought Keith: somewhere in the middle), and they might do things funny where she came from. Well, there was no harm in trying, he decided, although there'd been a lot of harm in trying as hard as *he* had, once or twice in the past.

46

She said, 'It's very muggy, don't you find?'

'Torrid,' said Keith.

'Goodness.'

'As close as can be.' His smile was playfully abject as he pitched his voice low and thick and added, 'Anything you want, darling. Anything at all.'

'Well as a matter of fact,' she said, in a tone so clear and ordinary that Keith found himself briefly standing to attention, 'there are one or two things that certainly need looking at. Like the vacuum cleaner. It's very good of you.'

'What's your phone number, Nick,' said Keith sternly.

She hesitated; then she seemed to give a sudden nod to herself. 'Have you got a pen?'

'No need,' said Keith, re-emboldened. 'Got this head for figures.' And with that he let his mouth drop open, and rested a large tongue on the lower teeth as his bright eyes travelled downwards over her body.

Her voice gave him the seven digits with a shiver.

'Sweet,' said Keith.

Thoughtfully Keith retraced his steps to the Black Cross. He had in mind a few drinks, to loosen the throwing arm; and then some serious darts. In the Portobello Road he encountered Guy Clinch, apparently browsing over a stall of stolen books. Keith never failed to be amazed that books fetched money. 'Yo,' he said, and paused for a few words. He considered. His circle of acquaintances was definitely expanding. It was through Guy, basically, that Keith had been introduced to Lady Barnaby. That's how it's done: the old-boy network . . . Keith had, of course, been friendly with people like Guy before: in prison. They were in for fraud, mostly, or drugs, or alimony default. White collar. They were okay (Guy was okay); they were human; they showed you respect, not wishing to get beaten up all day. But Guy wasn't in prison. He was in a huge house in Lansdowne Crescent. According to Keith, people like Guy admired and even envied the working man, such as himself. For some reason. Maybe because the working man lived that bit harder, in both work and play. When Guy now gamely asked him, 'Any luck?' – meaning Nicola – Keith waved him away, with a groan of hard-living laughter, saying he had too many birds on as it was.

They parted. Keith's plans changed. He looked in at Mecca, his turf accountants, for an expensive few minutes, then hurried off to do some work.

Keith used the heavy knocker. Slowly the door opened, and a pleading face blinked out at him. Filled, at first, with extreme caution, the pale blue eyes now seemed to rinse themselves in delight.

'Why, Harry! Good afternoon to you.'

'Afternoon, Lady B.,' said Keith, striding past her into the house.

Lady Barnaby was seventy-seven. She wasn't one of Keith's birds. No way.

In his bachelor days Keith had been a regular romeo. He had been a real ladykiller. In truth, he had been quite a one. Even Keith's dog Clive, in his dog heyday, had been no keener or less choosy or more incapable of letting a female scent go by without streaking after it with his nose on the ground and his tongue thrown over his shoulder like a scarf. Then came change, and responsibilities: Kath, his wife, and their baby girl, little Kim. And now it was all different. These days Keith kept a leash on his restless nature, restricting himself to the kind of evanescent romance that might come the way of any modern young businessman on his travels (the wife or sister or daughter or mother of some *cheat* in the East End, perhaps, where Keith went to get the perfume), plus the occasional indiscretion rather closer to home (Iqbala, the single parent in the next flat along), plus the odd chance encounter made possible when fortune smiles on young lovers (closing time, pub toilet), plus three regular and longstanding girlfriends, Trish Shirt, Debbee Kensit, who was special, and Analiese Furnish. And that was it.

Most interesting, in her way, most representative, most modern, was sinuous Analiese. Naughty, haughty, dreamy and unreliable, given to panic attacks, swoons, hysterical blindness, Analiese, in Keith's view, was mental. She read books and wrote poems. She sent letters to celebrities in all walks of life. She hung around outside TV studios, concert halls, the Institute of Contemporary Arts. In the letters she sent to people whose faces she had seen on the television and in the newspapers Analiese Furnish often enclosed a photograph; as a result, she often got replies. Not that these photographs were lewd or revealing or fleshy. Oh no. Snapped by one or other of her male protectors (abject, tongue-tied types, platonic attendants: she thought, absolutely wrongly and with characteristic lack of imagination, that they loved her for her mind), these photographs showed Analiese in pensive poses, gazing out of windows, or in sylvan settings, bending in her frock, perhaps, to relish the touch of a flower. Yet the replies came in, guarded, cajoling, exploratory. Why? What did the photographs say? The wideness of the eyes told of a heavy dream life; the brow was the brow of someone who could be lied to, and successfully; and the wide mouth and tropical henna of the hair suggested that when Analiese gave herself to you, she would give herself utterly, and probably wouldn't ring the house. In this last particular alone, appearances were deceptive. *Analiese* was deceptive, but not predictably. Also, she had a figure of full womanly power and beauty, except for her legs (which were fat and always hidden up to the last moment. These legs were the bane of her life). What you did with famous people just wasn't your fault. Different rules applied. You were swept away. And when it was over (and it was usually over quickly), well, you were wryly left with your albums and scrapbooks, your poems, your train-tickets, your memories, your dreams, your telephone calls to his wife and children, your letters to the editors of all the tabloids.

Keith had met Analiese on the street. She came up to him and asked, in her husky and theatrical voice, if he was television's Rick Purist – Rick Purist, of TV quiz-show fame. Keith hesitated. So might some medieval hermit have hesitated when the supplicant poor staggered through the dripping forest to his hovel, and asked if he was the Emperor Frederick or Baldwin IX, Count of Flanders, risen from the dead and come to redeem them, to give succour, to free from sorrow. Well now, the hermit must have wondered in his rags: am I or aren't I? It might be fun for a while. On the other hand . . . Keith peered at Analiese's heaving chest, and trusted to instinct. He admitted it to be so: he *was* television's Rick Purist. Thus the opening, tone-setting phoneme of their relationship – his slurred 'yeah' – was an outright lie. He accepted an invitation to join her for tea in her West Hampstead bedsitter. Keith drank the sherry while she showed him her memorabilia of the great and talked about the primacy of the human soul. Twenty-five minutes later, as Keith leadenly climbed into his trousers and headed for the door, he glanced back at the sofabed in the confident hope that he would see Analiese no more. But one night, a month or two later, he grew fond and wistful, and called her at three o'clock in the morning from the Black Cross. She read out a poem she'd written him. Keith went round there anyway. A month after that he opened his tabloid and saw a piece entitled STOLEN HOURS WITH TV'S RICK. There was a picture of Analiese, in her frock, savouring the scent of a municipal bloom. There was another picture of Analiese, without the flower, and without the frock (and cut off at the knee). There was also a picture of a puzzled Rick Purist: he did indeed look a bit like Keith. Here in cold print Keith learned that he was 'very romantic' and 'a fantastic lover' who was, moreover, 'built for love'. Rick Purist denied it all. Rick's wife Traci was standing by him. Words could not describe the elation Keith felt. He bought thirty copies of the newspaper and was about to shower the Black Cross with them. But just in time he realized that this would be an inappropriate response to a really singular slice of luck. Powerfully eroticized all the same, Keith called in on Analiese that very week. She knew by now, to her cost and embarrassment (or to the cost and embarrassment of the tabloid's editors), that Keith was not Rick Purist. But she forgot and forgave, and invented new fictions for him: Keith as fly-by-night, as man with no name, a crossword of aliases, a Proteus and Pimpernel. Keith didn't get it; but he certainly liked it. Never before had his unreliability and heartless neglect been seized on and celebrated as the core of his appeal.

Obviously there were little complications: obviously. Sometimes, when he stumbled into her bedsit in the small hours, Analiese was not alone. An adoring baldy or four-eyes – some wally, wimp, nerd or narna – might be sleeping on the chair, or on the floor, like a dog, in which case Keith would speed them into the night with a taunt and (whoops!) a kick in the arse, pick himself up off the floor and join Analiese in the sofabed with her warmth and her breasts and her laughter. On other occasions he surprised her in bed with famous people. This didn't happen very often (Keith didn't go round there very often), and the famous people were no longer very famous; but it did happen. A classical musician, some terrified poet: these were the kind of celebrities, and non-tabloid readers, to whom Analiese was now reduced. No hard feelings. Fair was fair. Keith would take a few swigs of whatever was available, crack a few jokes, and be on his way, usually to Trish Shirt's. Once he surprised her in bed with Rick Purist. Analiese was making amends (she later explained) for the disruption she had brought to Rick's marriage. On came the bedside lamp: Keith and Rick looked quite alike. Keith stared. He'd seen Rick on the telly! It was one of the strangest moments in Keith's strange life. He soon hopped it . . . That night seemed to sum it all up, really. She lived out in Slough now, did Analiese; and Keith was a busy man.

And Debbee? Little Debbee? Well, Debbee was *special*. Dark, rounded, pouting, everything circular, ovoid, Debbee was 'special'. Debbee was special because Keith had been sleeping with her since she was twelve years old. On the other hand, so had several other people. All completely kosher and Bristol-fashion because she'd had her tubes done and you just gave cash gifts of seventy-five quid to her mum, who wasn't bad either. Keith was very straight with Debbee Kensit. Respect. Consideration. Nothing dirty. Natural love. You got a ghostly feeling as you separated from her, on the small bed, in the small room, its walls fadedly rendering the lost sprites and dwarfs and maidens of childhood; and the white smell of very young flesh. Plump and prim (and fat-legged) on the man-made lower sheet lay little Debbee. And shockingly naked: untasselled, ungimmicked, unschool-uniformed. Such extras were to be found, plentifully enough, in her top drawer; but Debbee was always naked for her Keith, as nature intended. She wouldn't suggest wearing those things – no, not with Keith. And Keith was always too embarrassed to ask. Last autumn, Debbee had celebrated her fifteenth birthday. In the past Keith had gone round there as often as he could afford (or more often: he had sometimes knowingly bounced cheques on Mrs K.). Since November, though, he was less frequently to be seen there. But Debbee would always be special to Keith. She would always be special. At least until she was eighteen. Or sixteen.

And finally, invariably finally, there was Trish Shirt, blonde and pale and getting on a bit now, thinnish Trish (but sturdy-legged), who couldn't remember how old she was or what kind of blonde her hair had been when she started out, so many years ago. She lived under a supermarket on Ladbroke Grove, which was convenient, and even necessary, because she hated going out. Trish needed several tumblers of vodka before she could face the strip lighting and the caged goods. Keith brought Trish her dole, sparing her the fortnightly mortification, with money subtracted for her drink, thus sparing her a much more frequent ordeal. This figured strongly in the steady increase of his powers. Keith was like a god to Trish. 'I'd do anything for you, Keith. Anything,' she said. And Keith took her up on it. But every time he strode out of CostCheck clutching the keys to the heavy Cavalier, or silently got dressed (or rezipped himself) while staring at her pale body, Keith vowed that this visit would be his last.

Every time he pushed open the plywood door, every time Trish came to welcome him on her knees, Keith was that little bit angrier. For this he would give Trish payment. God save us, what was he *doing* to himself? Why was he here, with her, with that, when he had funloving little Debbee, and sinuous Analiese (and Peggy and Iqbala and Petronella and Fran)? Well, it was true that Trish had something to be said for her. Trish had a certain quality. She was nearest.

How to account for Keith's way with women, such as it was? How to account for Keith's talent? He had a knack. Keith could tell women what they were thinking. No doubt this has never been easy. But it's quite an accomplishment, with these women, in these days.

On the other hand, how much of a way with women did Keith really need? One was drunk, one was nuts, and one was fifteen. The ladykiller. These, then, were Keith's birds.

The nearest he had ever come to love, funnily enough, was with Chick Purchase. For years Chick had invaded and usurped his thoughts: Keith *hated* him, with a passion. And Keith could have loved the guy . . . It all went back to that business disagreement, at the plant off the M4 near Bristol. But there were also rumours, legends, about an incident at a party, an incident involving Keith and Chick's sister, Charlotte Purchase. Some spoke of improper suggestions; others, of attempted rape. Whatever the truth of the matter, Keith, fresh out of hospital after a daring raid on a rival's drugs pub, had been promptly rehospitalized by Chick. Looking back on it now, with mature hindsight, Keith said that it was all crap about the attempted rape (which, he claimed, had been an unqualified success), and that a darker tale lay behind the enmity, something of which a man might not easily speak. At the bar of the Black Cross it was generally agreed, in fearful whispers, that the two men had fallen out over a disputed darts score. Well, there was no coming back from that. And Keith could have loved the guy.

'And how are you, Harry?' asked good Lady Barnaby.

'Good,' said Keith. 'I'm good, Lady B. Everything shipshape?'

Keith made a perfunctory tour of the house, checking the refurbished boiler, the patched and sanded kitchen floorboards, the shifted furniture, the new window pane . . . The old window pane had been personally smashed by Keith Talent a few days ago, as a means of speeding his introduction to Lady Barnaby. It was Guy Clinch who had first drawn Keith's attention to the old woman, pointing out a stooped figure on Ladbroke Grove: 'Knew her husband . . . the house is far too big for her now.' Keith did what he usually did when he wanted to get to know a member of the opposite sex. He followed her home. Then the brick in the soiled handkerchief. 'Excuse me, missis,' Keith had panted when Lady Barnaby eventually came to the door (and peered through the letterbox), 'some black kids just put a brick through your downstairs window. I chased them but the little – but they got away.' It took a while before she let Keith inside. The old dear was all aflutter; she had been humming over a flower arrangement a few feet from the exploding glass. She wept on his shoulder. They drank half a bottle of cognac. Keith calmed her with tales of his unpleasant experiences with our coloured brethren . . . Ever since that day Keith was always looking in on Lady B., to do odd jobs, or rather to supervise them. He had no idea about any of that, merely leasing out the work to various cowboys he knew in White City. Lady Barnaby was fiercely grateful to Keith. She often said that it did her old heart good that people like him still existed.

'Well, Harry? What do you think?' asked Lady Barnaby uneasily.

Uneasily Keith slapped the boiler and pronounced it a fine piece of work. In fact even he could tell that something very serious indeed was about to go wrong with it. He felt nervous being in the same room – or on the same floor – as this labouring gravity-bomb in its padded vest.

'Real craftsmanship,' he said.

'Listen to it, though, Harry. That terrible clanging. And those *spitting* noises.'

'That's just the vents, adjusting to the new, to the increased flow, Lady B. The – the *cladding*. It's the cladding as such.'

'Wait for me!'

In the kitchen Keith said,

'You're going to have a smashing time in Yugoslavia, Lady B. What? Are you sure! *I* saw your mouth water when you took a look at that brochure. Your own suite, private pool, five-star dining. It's going to be heaven out there, love. Oh, heaven.' Briefly Keith thought of the holiday package he had concocted with his mate in the bucket-shop off Harrow Road: the hotel half-built and half-rotting; the shadow of the abandoned factory; the blighted shore. 'You never know,' he said, 'you might meet someone nice.'

'Harry!'

'No, come on. Because you're a pretty old lady, Lady B. You are. Not like my mum. Tell you what: I'll run you out to the airport on Friday morning. Shut up. Nothing simpler. I'll see you then then. And if you have any probs, Lady B., you know what to do. Any little thing, cry out for Keith. I mean Harry.'

Keith had a late lunch at the Amritsar and then returned to the Black Cross and played darts for eleven hours.

Expedient to a fault in most things, Keith was a confessed romantic when it came to his darts . . . The deal went something like this. A house in Twickenham or thereabouts: in the environs of Twickenham. An aviary. Park the wife and kid. Keep greyhounds. A household name. Figure in the England manager's plans: throw your heart out in an England shirt. An ambassador for the sport, a credit to the game. Give every barmaid in Britain one: no female pubgoer on earth can resist a celebrity darter, a personality. Tours of Scandinavia, Australia, Canada, the States. Build up a personal library of every victory on video. Be on television, a face known by millions. On TV innit. TV. TV . . .

Earlier in the summer, while completing (with infinite pain and difficulty) his entry form for the Duoshare Sparrow Masters, the knockout interpub darts competition in which he was doing so well now, Keith pondered and agonized for several days before filling in the section marked HOBBIES. He wanted to put *darts* and leave it at that. But darts was work. It would be like saying that his hobbies were *cheating*, *burgling* and *receiving*. Besides, he had in the past won two self-sufficiency awards from the British Darts Organization – darts bursaries, darts scholarships, as it were, to help him in his bid to go pro. He wasn't too clear on all this (and the cash grants had kept Keith self-sufficient for about fifteen minutes each in the turf accountants), but a struggler in the world of small businesses wouldn't tell you that his 'hobby' was *expanding a timber-yard* or *running a fag shop*, now would he? What, then, *were* Keith's hobbies? He couldn't put *birds*. It might get back to Kath. He couldn't put *horses* or *walking Clive* or *going to the pub*. *Pool* and *fruit machines* had, if little else, the stamp of authenticity . . . He toyed with certain fictions: *potholing*, *rallying*, *growing vegetables*. But his pride rebelled against the imposture. Growing vegetables? You must be . . . In the end he searched his soul for the last time, white-knuckled his grip on the biro, and put *TV*.

It was no less than the truth. He watched a very great deal of TV, always had done, years and years of it, aeons of TV. Boy, did Keith burn that tube. And that tube burnt him, nuked him, its cathodes crackling like cancer. 'TV,' he thought, or 'Modern reality' or 'The world'. It was the world of TV that told him what the world was. How does all the TV time work on a modern person, a person like Keith? The fact that he would have passed up a visit to the Louvre or the Prado in favour of ten minutes alone with a knicker catalogue – this, perhaps, was a personal quirk. But TV came at Keith like it came at everybody else; and he had nothing whatever to keep it out. He couldn't grade or filter it. So he thought TV was real . . . Of course, some of it *was* real. Riots in Kazakhstan were real, stuff about antiques was real (Keith watched these shows in a spirit of professional dedication), mass suicides in Sun City were real, darts was real. But so, to Keith, was *Syndicate* and *Edwin Drood: The Musical* and *Bow Bells* and *The Dorm That Dripped Blood*. Not an active reality, like, say, darts, on which the camera obligingly spied and eavesdropped. No, an exemplary reality, all beautifully and gracefully interconnected, where nothing hurt much and nobody got old. It was a high trapeze, the artists all sequin and tutu (look at that bird!), enacted far above the sawdust, the peanut shells and poodle droppings, up there, beyond a taut and twanging safety-net called *money*.

In the days after their first meeting, the image of Nicola Six began to work on Keith's mind. It worked like television. He thought of her often – while inspecting a shop window in Oxford Street, while haring after his scattered urges in the last moments before sleep, while finishing himself off with Trish Shirt. Although many of these thoughts were frankly pornographic (but class porn, you know? Not like the rubbish you get here), by no means all of them were. He saw himself in lace-up swimming-trunks, on a lounger, frowning over a balance-sheet by a personal plunge-pool, and Nicola walking past in bikini and high heels, bringing him a drink and tenderly tousling his hair. 'LA innit,' he whispered. Or Keith in a tuxedo, on a patio, outside Palermo: glass table and candles, and her in a flowing gown. An international entrepreneur with wide business interests. Redeemed, and freed from sorrow. On the other side. Where darts might yet take him. Where he belonged.

He left it for a bit, then called her.

His exit from the Black Cross that afternoon was marked for its air of studious and purposeful calm. Outside, the day was still; the flares of Keith's trousers billowed gracefully as he walked to the heavy Cavalier. With lips compressed and sternly pushed forward, he picked his way through the doubled traffic.

In fact, Keith was displeased. He hadn't much cared for the sound of her, on the phone. That small voice might be doing no more than wasting his valuable time. Or playing it cool. But that was okay. No woman could play it cooler than Keith – Keith, with his prodigies of thoughtlessness. Like being late. Keith was always late for his dates, especially for the first one. And if he had a standby he seldom showed up at all.

'I'll be right over,' Keith had said. He now doubleparked outside the Indian Mutiny on Cathcart Road. Seated at his usual table, Keith ate poppadams and bombay duck while the staff fondly prepared his mutton vindaloo. 'The napalm sauce, sir?' asked Rashid. Keith was resolved, in this as in all things. 'Yeah. The napalm sauce.' In the kitchen they were busy responding to Keith's imperial challenge: to make a curry so hot that he couldn't eat it. The meal arrived. Lively but silent faces stared through the serving-hatch. The first spoonful swiped a mustache of sweat on to Keith's upper lip, and drew excited murmurs from the kitchen. 'Bit mild,' said Keith when he could talk again. That day, the Indian Mutiny had no other customers. Keith chewed steadily. His lion's hair looked silver in the shadows. Tears inched their way over his dry cheeks. 'Bland, Rashid,' said Keith, later, as he paid and undertipped. 'What you looking at? It's five per cent. Bland. Dead bland.'

'Nicky? Keith,' said Keith, after the long push on the buzzer.

A second buzz, and the door succumbed to his touch. He turned and looked out at the dead-end street.

Keith contemplated the stairs. The mutton vindaloo ripped another stunning burp out of him. Lingering only to inspect a lock and to hold a brown envelope up to the light, and to lean against the wall for five minutes with his brow on his wrist, Keith began the heavy climb.

He came to the top, and found a door. He opened it. 'Jesus,' he said. More stairs.

Nicola stood on the brink of this final storey, wearing a soft woollen dress the colour of a Siamese cat, three of its nine buttons, its nine lives, already unfastened, and emerald earrings like tiger's eyes in the pockets of her black hair, and the silver collar, and every finger of her clenched hands barbed with rings.

'Come on up.'

'Champagne,' said Keith. 'Cheers,' he added. 'Jesus.'

He followed her down the passage and into the sitting-room, wiggling a finger some millimetres from her backside. Then, with a serious sniff, he confronted the room and its mental arithmetic. Nicola turned to face him, and Keith's calculations continued. The sum got bigger. Including jewellery. Outlay. TV, he thought. When she raised a hand to her throat Keith fumbled and crashed round his mind, looking for a pun on *choker*. He didn't find one.

He said, 'Prestigious.'

'. . . Do you want a drink or something?'

'Work before pleasure, my love,' said Keith, who was quite drunk already. On the whole he wished he wasn't, because hangovers played havoc with a man's darts. But he had seemed to need those seven pints of lager (you got to, with that stuff) and the chain of brandies with which he had rounded off his meal. Keith wondered why. It was out of character, so early in the day. Not that it mattered, because Keith could hold his drink. No one knew the difference. He thought with all modesty of the times he had burst through Trish Shirt's plywood door and walked straight into the wall, and she never said a word. Keith just carried it off.

'You're quite drunk already, aren't you, Keith,' said Nicola.

'Little celebration,' said Keith smoothly. But – you don't do that, he was thinking. You don't say it. No, you don't. That's what you *never do* . . . Keith looked at his feet, wrong-footed, and felt her eyes move strictly over his pub hair. Nicola's legs, he saw, were set combatively apart, and the last button of her dress was unfastened. Nicola's dress: Keith had been intending, at an early stage in their encounter, to ram his hand up it. But not now, he thought. No way.

She looked at her watch and said, 'I suppose we might as well get started.' And Keith was being led into the kitchen. Grimly and without profit he fingered the faulty vacuum cleaner, peered into the block-prone waste disposer, manhandled the hingeless ironing-board.

'This is hopeless,' said Nicola.

I'm a busy man, thought Keith. I can't just drop everything. I come up here . . . 'I come up here,' he said. 'I'm a busy man. I can't just drop everything.'

'There's the coffee-grinder.'

57

The coffee-grinder was produced. They both stared at it. It looked okay to Keith.

'Do you think it's the fuse?' she asked confidentially.

'Could be.' Grinder, he thought. Here we go. Grind her. A good –

She offered him a screwdriver and looked on with interest. 'I can't do it. The screw's too tight.'

Screw, thought Keith. Too tight. Yeah. He was surprised, again, to find no joke, no icebreaking salacity, on his slowly smiling lips. Hang about: it's coming. Too tight. Screw. If it's . . . you can't have a . . .

He applied the tool with will. The blade ground into the scratched head – and skidded off into the mons of Keith's thumb.

'*Fuck*,' he said, and dropped everything.

Now I had no choice but to end that chapter *right there*. I too had to drop everything. Maybe I can go back later and soften the transition, if there's time.

Keith's version just couldn't be trusted for a second longer. She loves him up in the bathroom? She makes him a cash offer? No. No. I had to make my move (no rest for the wicked). I had to get out there.

Up to that point the Talent narrative was of such mortifying squalor – it had to be no less than pedantic truth, in my opinion. It was relayed not to me alone but also to Dean, Thelonius, Fucker and Bogdan, in the Black Cross. Everyone tacitly agreed that Keith was emerging well from the tale.

How is this? Remember: modern, modern. Because it was all a tribute to Keith's indifference. To Keith not caring about anything. This would pave the way for still greater triumph in the sexual arena, where, of course (in Keith's version), an impenetrable mendacity took hold.

A real shock this morning. A cockroach – in Mark Asprey's apartment. It dashed the length of the kitchen, from beneath one labour-saving facility to another. It looked like a little coach-and-four, with a tiny driver, wielding a tinier whip.

Now I knew they'd reached here, these big fat black ones, and colonized the place. But in Mark Asprey's apartment! The Clinches evidently have them too. I expected and hoped that the first roach wave would respect the local traditions. I thought they'd all hang out at Keith's. But try explaining class to a cockroach. Cockroaches don't understand the English, like I do. I understand the English. I'm ashamed to say I pride myself on it.

I want to hang out at Keith's. I long to be asked over. Darts lessons, which turn out to be incredibly horrible, only get you into Keith's garage. The lone tower block at the end of Golborne Road: I can see it from my bedroom window. I'm working on it.

Auxiliadora will start coming in this week. I am beset by invitations from Lansdowne Crescent. I see myself standing outside the master bedroom, naked, with my clothes in a little bundle, knocking on the door.

So I tethered the diaries in their original ribbon and went around to Nicola's apartment. That's the thing: I just *did* it. Unlike Guy Clinch, I have Nicola's address and phone number. I have all her past addresses and phone numbers too. They're all there, on page one: her nomad progress through the city. Chelsea, Blackfriars, Regent's Park, Bloomsbury, Hampstead, and so on. And now the dead-end street. She's never been so far west before. Nicola Six has lived *care of* an awful lot of people. But they didn't take enough care, and she soon moved on.

'6: SIX,' said the tab. 'Yes, hello?' The voice was guilty and defiant. No one likes to be surprised, at home, on late afternoons. No one likes to be surprised. And I could have been Keith. I said, 'My name is Samson Young. Hello. We met in the pub, remember, the Black Cross? And later that day we saw each other on the street? I have something of yours I would like to return to you.' '. . . I don't want it.' 'Yes you do.' 'No I don't.' 'Okay. Then I'll try the police.'

'Christ,' she said. 'Another literalist. Look. Come back in an hour.'

I played a mild hunch. That's what writing is, a hundred hunches, a hundred affronts to your confidence, a hundred decisions, every page. I said, 'There's no need for you to dress up for me. I'm not a contender in all this. I'm – disinterested. I won't stay long and I don't care how you look. I won't dissuade you . . .' There was a silence. Then she hung up. There was another silence. Then the buzzer sounded and I pressed my way through.

It took me at least as long as it took Keith to get to the top. I passed the usual stuff: lurking bikes, the loathed mail of tan envelopes, mirrors, potted plants. On the last flight, past the inner door – you could feel it, well before she actually appeared on the stairs. Now I'm no chaser, and I failed in love, but I've felt these powerful feminine auras, these feminine shockwaves. Nothing like this, though, such intensity poised and cocked, and ready to go either way. Oh, entirely ready. And when she appeared at the top of the stairs – the white dressing-gown, the hair aslant over the unpainted face – I fielded the brutal thought that she'd just had fifteen lovers all at once, or fifteen periods. I followed her into the low room.

'It's characteristic,' I said. 'Pleasantly anarchical.' Meaning the room. I couldn't get her to look up at me. Her demeanour appeared to express great reluctance, or even physical fear. But it's hard to know what's really happening, on a first date.

'Do you want a drink or something?'

'You have one.' A half-empty bottle of red wine stood on the table by the window. On another table Keith's flowers stood dying in their bowl. Nicola left the room; I heard the surge of the faucet; then she returned with the rinsed glass. The cork came off silently. Set against the clear light of the panes, the glass bore two faint smears of red, wine at the base, lipstick at the rim. Today's wine, yesterday's lipstick. She wore no lipstick now. Nor had her dressing-gown been recently washed. There was a certain pride in this. Her body had after all been recklessly adored, every inch of it. Even her secretions, even her waste (she perhaps felt), even her dust was adorable. She smelled of tragic sleep and tobacco. Not cigarette smoke but tobacco – moistly dark.

Two wicker chairs faced each other, by the small table and its lamp. She sat in one chair and rested her feet on the other. The phone was at arm's length. So this was her telephone posture. I felt hope: she would communicate. I was looking at her but she wouldn't look at me. Everywhere else, but not at me.

'Siddown,' she said wearily, indicating the couch. I placed the diaries on the floor at my feet. 'So you read them.' 'It wasn't difficult,' I said. 'I couldn't put them down.' She smiled to herself, secretively, so I added, 'You have a way with language, and with much else. In fact I'm envious.' 'Everything? You read everything.' 'Yup.' She blushed – to her fierce annoyance. It was quite a light-show for a while, the olive skin thickening with violet. Yes, some tints of rose were present in her darkness. She arranged the hem of her dressing-gown and said,

'So you know all about my sexual . . .'

'Your sexual . . . weakness? Predilection? Bugbear?'

'Perversion.'

'Oh. It's quite common.'

'Is it?'

She looked at me now all right. Her lower lip hung in considered hostility. I'd better get this one right, I thought. Or it could be all over. And if I wanted the truth from her, then I had to give the truth too. And I *must have* the truth.

'Are you going "to go to the police" about it?' she asked.

'We are most of us', I said, 'in some kind of agony. I'm not here to judge you.'

'Thanks. What *are* you here for?'

I was close to full confession, but I said, 'I'm just an observer. Or a listener.'

'What's in it for me? For me you're just an unwelcome complication.'

'Maybe not. Maybe I'll help simplify. I'm intrigued by what you say about the death of love . . . Nicola, let me be your diary.'

At this point she must have made her decision. I found out why she made it, just before I left. We started with Keith's visit and talked for about forty-five minutes. She answered all my questions, even the most impudent, with considered clarity, and intense recall. I had to resist the temptation to take notes. And she threw in a tour of the apartment: through the inner passage, into the bedroom, and out again.

'I'm going to keep my promise and slip away,' I said. 'Can I call you tomorrow? Oh – you're a Scorpio, right? When *is* your birthday?' This was vicious. What's the matter with me? Who do I think I am? But she didn't seem to mind. 'Isn't that Guy Fawkes' Night?'

'Yes. Bonfire Night.'

'You know it's also the day of the full eclipse?'

'Yes I know. It's good, isn't it?'

We both stood up. Then we did something that people hardly ever do in real life. We looked at each other – for twenty seconds, thirty, forty. It was especially tough for me, with my eyes and everything. In the flinch that at one point she gave I noticed that her teeth, strongly slanted, wore the faintest signs of neglect. The discoloration (vertical, resinous) was itself fatalistic. Well, why bother? Those stains gave me my first and only erotic pang of the afternoon, not the warm outlines of the breasts, nor the conviction of nakedness beneath the cotton, sweetly soiled. No one had looked at me that way for quite a time; and I was moved. When she shaped herself for a question or statement, I could see what was coming, and I knew it was fully earned.

'You're —'

'Don't say it!' I said (I astonished myself), and clasped my hands over my ears. 'Please. Not yet. Please don't say it.'

And now she raised a hand, to stifle or cover a smile she knew to be wicked. 'My God,' she said. 'You really *are*.'

On the way back two swearing children offered me a handful of sweets: Jimmies, or Smarties. I considered, as I listened to the squeaked, the squandered obscenities of the seven-year-olds.

I really ought to think about what I'm doing, accepting candy from strange children.

Before I left, Nicola gave me back her diaries and told me to throw them on a skip somewhere. I tried to look casual about it. I couldn't tell her that I'd spent half the day Xeroxing them in their entirety. Mark Asprey has a Xerox, a beautiful little thing. It seems to work like a toaster, when it works, which it doesn't, not right now. I went to the Bangladeshi stationer's in Queensway. It was a real drag and cost just enough to tip me into a money panic. I cracked at once and rang Missy Harter at Hornig Ultrason. Naturally I didn't talk to her direct, but I had words with her assistant, Janit. Not quite true. I had words with Missy Harter's assistant's assistant, Barbro: Janit's assistant. Missy Harter will apparently return my call.

Of course it's far too early to start thinking about an advance. Or it was then, a couple of hours ago. But I don't see how I can be stopped, now I've found common cause with the murderee.

I'm ridiculously pleased, in Chapter 4, with that bit about the Emperor Frederick and Baldwin IX, Count of Flanders. When Analiese comes up to him in the street, and he wonders whether to go with the Rick Purist ticket, or stick to Keith. I stole it from *The Pursuit of the Millennium* by Norman Cohn. Like everybody else I'm finding it harder and harder to pick up a book, but I can still manage brief engagements with Cohn, with his fascinated, his fully gripped intelligence. Also I'm nearly halfway through Hugh Brogan's one-volume history of America. Soon I'll have to rely on Mark Asprey's shelves (or Mark Asprey's writings), which don't look promising.

These pseudo-Baldwins and pseudo-Fredericks, medieval hermits (medieval bums, often) deified by desperate populations, by the inspired hordes of the poor. They had a good run, some of them. They led uprisings; they marched on capitals and squatted in palaces. They screwed around, they partied like there was no tomorrow – for a time. But they all paid the price – on the stake. And when they did, pseudo-pseudo-Fredericks and pseudo-pseudo-Baldwins sprang up to replace them, quickly risen from the dead. Then they got torched too.

Even the Old Testament expected the Apocalypse 'shortly'. In times of mass disorientation and anxiety . . . But I am trying to ignore the world situation. I am hoping it will go away. Not the world. The situation. I want time to get on with this little piece of harmless escapism. I want time to go to London Fields.

Sometimes I wonder whether I can keep the world situation out of the novel: the crisis, now sometimes called the Crisis (they can't be *serious*). Maybe it's like the weather. Maybe you can't keep it out.

Will it reach the conclusion it appears to crave – will the Crisis reach the Conclusion? Is it just the nature of the beast? We'll see. I certainly hope not. I would lose many potential readers, and all my work would have been in vain. And that would be a *real* bitch.

Chapter 5: The Event Horizon

LIKE THE FLOWERS on a grave bearing the mother of a
sentimental hoodlum, Keith's bouquet leaned and loitered in
its bowl on the round table. Nicola always beheld these flowers
with disbelief. The colours spoke to her of custard, of blancmange
– a leaden meat tea served on pastel plates, the desiccation of a
proletarian wake for some tyrant grandad, or some pub parrot of
a granny, mad these thirty years.

She found that, far from brightening the place up, as Keith had
predicted they would, the flowers rendered her flat more or less
uninhabitable. In India (where Nicola had once been) certain colours
are associated with the colours of certain castes. These were low-
caste flowers, casteless flowers, untouchable flowers. But Nicola
didn't throw them away. She didn't touch them (you wouldn't want
to touch them). Keith Talent was expected, and the flowers would
remain. Nicola didn't yet know that Keith's blue eyes were
completely flower-blind or flower-proof. He wouldn't see the
flowers, and he wouldn't see their absence. Just as a vampire
(another class of creature that cannot cross your threshold unin-
vited) gives no reflection in glass or mirrors, so flowers, except in the
common-noun sense (he knew birds liked them, as did bees), sent no
message to Keith's blue eyes.

He telephoned on time, the day the flowers died. Even as she
picked up the receiver she felt – she felt how you feel when the
doorbell goes off like an alarm in the middle of the night. An

unpleasant mistake, or really bad news. She steadied herself. After the repeated pips, themselves punctuated by Keith's ragged obscenities, she could hear the squawkings and garrottings of the Black Cross at a quarter past three. Even though pubs were now open more or less round the clock (there was one near the entrance to the dead-end street), they still exploded at the old closing times: coded memories deep in the genes of pubs . . . Keith's tone was mawkishly pally, seeming to offer the commiserations due to a shared burden (faulty household appliances; shoddy workmanship; life, life), as if they had known each other for years – which, in a sense, she thought, they almost had.

'Tell you what then darling,' he said with that lugubrious lilt, 'yeah, I'll be right over.'

'Sweet,' he added when Nicola said yes.

She arranged herself for Keith's visit with considerable care.

When Nicola was just a little girl she had a little friend called Enola Gay. Enola shared in all Nicola's schemes and feints, her tantrums and hunger-strikes, in all her domestic terrorism. She too had the knack or gift of always knowing how things would unfold. Enola didn't exist. Nicola invented her. When adolescence came Enola went and did a terrible thing. Thereafter she kept a terrible secret. Enola had borne a terrible child, a little boy called Little Boy.

'Enola,' Nicola would whisper in the dark. 'What have you done, you wicked girl? Enola! *Enola Gay* . . .'

Terrible though the child was, Enola shone through Little Boy with the light of many suns. Nicola knew that she would never generate such light herself. She was vivid; she was divinely bright; when she walked the streets she seemed to be lit by her personal cinematographer. But it wasn't the light that burned in Enola Gay from Little Boy. That light came from the elemental feminine power: propagation. If Nicola had had that light her power might have approached the infinite. But she didn't have it, and never would have it.

With her, light went the other way . . . The black hole, so long predicted in theory, was now, to Nicola's glee, established astronomical fact: Cygnus X-1. It was a binary system; the black hole was orbiting a star thirty times the mass of our sun. The black hole weighed in at ten solar masses, but was no wider than London. It was nothing; it was just a hole; it had dropped out of space and time; it had collapsed into its own universe. Its very nature prevented anyone from knowing what it was: unapproachable, unilluminable. Nothing is fast enough to escape from it. For mother earth the escape velocity is seven miles per second, for Jupiter thirty-seven miles per second, for the sun 383 miles per second. For Sirius B, the first white dwarf they found, the escape velocity is 4,900 miles per second. But for Cygnus X-1, the black swan, there is no escape velocity. Even light, which propagates at 186,287 miles per second, cannot escape from it. *That's what I am*, she used to whisper to herself after sex. *A black hole. Nothing can escape from me.*

Sodomy pained Nicola, but not literally; it was its local prevalence, as it were, that pained her so greatly. It was the only thing about herself that she couldn't understand and wouldn't forgive. How *generally* prevalent was it (and an unwonted humiliation, this, to seek safety in numbers)? It wasn't like masturbation, which everyone secretly knew everyone secretly did, apart from the odd fanatic or ostrich or liar. Masturbation was an open secret until you were thirty. Then it was a closed secret. Even modern literature shut up about it at that point, pretty much. Nicola held this silence partly responsible for the industrial dimensions of contemporary pornography – pornography, a form in which masturbation was the *only* subject. Everybody masturbated all their lives. On the whole, literature declined the responsibility of this truth. So pornography had to cope with it. Not elegantly or reassuringly. As best it could.

When you came to sodomy . . . Instinct declared that nowhere near everybody did it, but one could harbour one's suspicions here too. Nicola remembered reading, with a blush of pleasure, that fully seventy-five per cent of female v. male divorce suits featured sodomy under one subhead or another, anything from *physical cruelty* to *unreasonable demands*. How unreasonable was it? How cruel? What did it mean when a woman wanted it? The tempting location, so close to its better sister . . . But wherever it was (in the armpit, behind the kneecap), it would have its attractions. Be literal, and look at the human mouth. The mouth was a good distance away. And the mouth got it too.

Literature *did* go on about sodomy, and increasingly. This hugely solaced Nicola Six. Now, if she could consider it as a twentieth-century theme . . . Just as Keith Talent would be proud to represent his country in an England shirt, so Nicola, in garter-belt and stockings and ankle-bracelet, would be perfectly prepared to represent her century. It started, she supposed, with Joyce, who was clearly interested in it: a murky *nostalgie*. Lawrence was interested in it: earth, blood, *will* (yes, and enforced degradation). Beckett was interested in it: a callowly uncomplicated yearning (Nicola decided) to cause distress and preferably damage, trauma, to the female parts. As for the Americans, they *all* seemed to be interested in it: with John Updike, it was mainly just another thing humans could do, and everything human interested Updike; of Norman Mailer one didn't need to inquire too deeply (a mere timekiller, before greater violence); Philip Roth, with what must be farcical irony, bedroom-farcical irony, refers to it as 'anal love'. V. S. Naipaul, on the other hand, who was very interested in it, speaks of 'a sexual black mass'. Well, *black*, anyway. And a black hole was mass, pure mass, infinite mass.

No, not everybody did it. But Nicola did it. At a certain point (and she always vowed she wouldn't, and always knew she would) Nicola tended to redirect her lover's thrusts, down there in the binary system . . . She had a thing of readying herself with the third finger of the left hand. The marriage finger. It was appalling, the crassness with which the symbolism suggested itself: the marriage finger, seeking a different ring, in the place whence no babies came. It was the only time she ever lost control. Not during (certainly not), but after, later, with silent tears of dismay. How much had she cried about it? How much tearfall? How many inches a year?

What saddened and incensed her was the abdication of power, so craven, the surrender so close to home. And power was what she was in it for. Nicola had lived deliciously; but she was promiscuous *on principle*, as a sign of emancipation, of spiritual freedom, freedom from men. She was, she believed, without appetite, and prided herself on her passionless brilliance in bed. But then, the subtle rearrangement, and the abject whisper . . . And it poisoned everything, somehow. Again, not literally. Although Nicola liked doing what nobody else did, although she liked danger, she didn't like *that* kind of danger, vandal danger, with no form to it. She was promiscuous, but her lovers weren't (they usually had wives instead); and her gynaecologist assured her, one night, when she still had time to care about such distant matters, that it was safe enough if you *did it last*. Well, when else would you do it – would you do the last thing? The thing itself was the last thing. It always seeded the end of the affair. And Nicola took some comfort from that fact: maybe it was just her strategy for sending love back the other way.

The only other compensation was an artistic one. At least it was congruous with her larger tribulation; at least sodomy added up. Most types have their opposite numbers. Groups have groupies. There are molls for all men, and vice versa. The professional has his perkie; scowlers get scowlies; so smuggies, loudies, cruellies. So the failed suicide must find a murderer. So the murderer must find a murderee.

After about fifteen minutes Nicola was sure that Keith was going to be late – significantly late. She changed her plan. She adopted Plan B. Her *life* had a Plan B, or it had had: to live on. But intimations of early middle age had settled that. With these intimations, other intimations: the second half of life; and natural death. These intimations were very informative, they were packed with news – and no thanks! You got old quick, like the planet. Like the planet, you could only prostrate yourself before the wonders of modern medicine, modern can-do. But can-do was nothing, when compared to already-done. You had to trust in cosmic luck. The heavenly operation, facelift, transplant. Divine rain.

She changed her immediate plans. Had Keith been prompt, he would have 'surprised' Nicola in tennis shorts, T-shirt and reversed baseball cap, the outfit she wore when, in an ecstasy of vexation, she did her weekly dusting. But he was late. So she took off her shorts and put her jeans back on and coolly went to the shops with the canvas bag.

When Nicola walked the streets she was lit by her personal cinematographer, nothing too arty either, a single spotlight trained from the gods. She had a blue nimbus, the blue of sex or sadness. Any eyes that were available on the dead-end street would find their way to her: builders in the gutted houses, a frazzled rep in a cheap car, a man alone at home pressing his face against the window pane with a snarl. There were three shops at the junction: tobacconist's (and sub-post-office); Asian grocery (and off-licence); and, incongruously, a travel agent's, a shop that sold travel. At the first Nicola bought fuses, and picked up her French cigarettes. The tiny old creature behind the counter (impossible to entertain the idea that she had ever been a woman) ordered the cigarettes especially; and Nicola felt the ghost of an obligation to give warning to stop: I can tell her I've quit, she thought. At the grocer's she bought lemons, tonic, tomato juice and what she confidently hoped would be her last-ever plastic bottle of toilet cleanser. The tobacconist overcharged her, the grocer gave short measure . . . Passing the travel agent's, with its great lists of destinations (and prices, hysterically reduced, in normal times, but now brutally upped: even Amsterdam cost the earth), Nicola abruptly realized that she would never go away again. Would she, ever? Not even a few days with Guy in Aix-en-Provence or a weekend with Keith in Ilfracombe or Jersey or some other paradise of duty free? No. There just wouldn't be time.

On the way back, near the entrance to the dead-end street, she was stared at by two builders who sat half-naked eating Scotch eggs and drinking beer on the porch steps of a corner house they were supposedly or at any rate cursorily renovating. Nicola had noticed them before, this exemplary pair. One was sixteen or seventeen, lean and suntanned and wholly delighted by the onset of his powers; the other, the senior man, puffy, thirty, with long hair and few teeth, and quite ruined, as if he got a year older every couple of months. The boy climbed to his feet as Nicola approached.

'Miss World!' he said in a quavering voice. He wore an expression of ironic entreaty. 'Give us a smile. *Please*. Ah, come on – light up. It might never happen!'

Nicola smiled. Nicola turned to him as she passed and smiled beautifully.

She arranged herself for Keith's visit with considerable care, despite the fact that she knew how things would go anyway, more or less. Of course, she was in a funny situation with reality (though this never occurred to her with any weight), coaxing it into a shape she knew it already had – somewhere, in phantom *potentia* . . . Simply doing the next thing that came naturally, Nicola had what she called a whore's bath, standing naked on a towel before the basin and the mirror. As she washed, she mentally developed an erotic design. It would be humiliating, and quite unnecessary, to think too specifically on the matter; but one had to be prepared. Taking an example at random, the pretty divots of her armpits, so aromatic and erogenous, so often praised and slobbered over, clearly such excellent value – these might have to go. He might want them shorn. Not yet. It would depend.

Her underwear she selected without a flicker of hesitation: suspender-belt, stockings, brassière – but all white this time, all white. She sat on the bed, tipping backwards, then stood up with her head bent sharply, making the right adjustments. Nicola was amazed

– Nicola was consternated – by how few women really *understood* about underwear. It *was* a scandal. If the effortless enslavement of men was the idea, or one of the ideas (and who had a better idea?), why halve your chances by something as trivial as a poor shopping decision? In her travels Nicola had often sat in shared bedrooms and cabins and boudoirs and powder parlours, and watched debutantes, predatory divorcees, young hostesses, even reasonably successful good-time girls shimmying out of their cocktail dresses and ballgowns to reveal some bunched nightmare of bloomers, tights, long johns, Y-fronts. A prosperous hooker whom she had hung out with for a while in Milan invariably wore panties that reminded Nicola, in both texture and hue, of a bunion pad. To ephemeral flatmates and sexual wallflowers at houseparties and to other under-equipped rivals Nicola had sometimes carelessly slipped the underwear knowledge. It took about ten seconds. Six months later the ones that got it right would be living in their own mews houses in Pimlico and looking fifteen years younger. But they mostly got it wrong. Over-elaboration or lack of self-love, or sheer lack of talent; plus minor vagaries, like the persistent and profitless fallacy of *black* underwear, which showed the right brothelly instinct, and beat boxer shorts and training-bra, but missed the point. Perhaps women couldn't believe how simple men really were – how it could all be decided in five minutes at the hosiery store. At this particular end of this particular century, they wanted tight bright white underwear, white underwear. They wanted the female form shaped and framed, packaged and gift-wrapped, stylized, cartoonified, and looking, for a moment at least, illusorily pure. They wanted the white lie of virginity. Men were so *simple*. But what did that do to the thoughts of women, to the thoughts of women like Nicola Six?

Never in her life, not ever, had Nicola decisively discarded any item of clothing. The flat's large second bedroom had become a supercloset – it was like a boutique in there, the suits, the party dresses, the theatrical costumes and disguises, the belts, the scarves, the hats. Imelda Marcos herself might have wondered at the acreage of Nicola's shoes . . . If Keith Talent were dressing her now, if Keith were designing her (she speculated), how would he want things to go? What did he want, at the top of the stairs? Nicola in thigh-high pink boots, rayon mini-skirt and bursting blouse. Yes, either that or Nicola in low-corsaged opal balldress and elbow-length ivory gloves, with a sable-trimmed brick-quilted dolman, a comb of brilliants and a panache of osprey in her hair. Queen of Diamonds, Queen of Hearts. But of course you couldn't do it quite like that.

'Come on up,' she said.

As Keith followed her heavily into the apartment, Nicola did something right out of character: she cursed her fate. Then she swivelled and inspected him, from arid crown to Cuban heels, as he cast his scavenging blue eyes around the room: Keith, stripped of all charisma from pub and street. It wasn't the posture, the scrawniness of the shanks and backside, the unpleasant body scent (he smelled as if he had just eaten a mustard-coated camel), the drunken scoop of his gaze – unappealing though these features certainly were. Just that Nicola saw at once with a shock (I knew it all along, she said to herself) that the capacity for love was extinct in him. It was never there. Keith wouldn't kill for love. He wouldn't cross the road, he wouldn't swerve the car for love. Nicola raised her eyes to heaven at the thought of what this would involve her in sexually. And in earnest truth she had always felt that love in some form would be present at her death.

'Well let's get started,' she said, directing Keith towards the kitchen and its dead machines. Once there, Nicola folded her arms and watched, increasingly astonished by how things evidently stood between Keith and the inanimate world. Such flexed and trembling helplessness, such temper-loss and equipment-abuse. She was inept in the kitchen herself; she had never, for instance, produced anything even remotely edible from the electric cooker, now long disused. But this frenzy of domestic quackery . . . Keith went at the ironing-board like the man in the deckchair joke. The tube of the hoover became a maddened python in his grasp. After his final misadventure with the coffee-grinder plug and the screwdriver Nicola handed him a paper tissue for his gouged thumb and said in a puzzled voice,

'But you're completely hopeless. Or is it just being drunk?'

'It's all right, it's all right,' said Keith rapidly. 'See, I don't normally do none of this myself. I got a team in White City. Real craftsmen. Here we go.'

With difficulty – there were blood and sweat and tears on the bakelite by now – Keith at last wrenched off the cap. Together they stared down at the pastel tricolour of the plug's innards. Their faces were close; Nicola could hear the soft baffled panting through Keith's open mouth.

72

'Looks okay,' he volunteered.

'It could be the fuse.'

'Yeah. Could be.'

'Change it,' she suggested, offering him a new fuse from the paper bag.

Chipping a yellow fingernail, swearing, dropping screws, confusing fuses, Keith accomplished this deed. He then slapped the plug into the wall, pressed the switch, and briskly actuated the coffee-grinder. Nothing happened.

'Well,' said Keith after a while. 'It's not the fuse.'

'Then could you take a look at the lavatory seat at least.'

The bathroom was unexpectedly spacious – carpeted, and full of unnecessary air; there seemed to be a great distance between the fat bathtub and the red chaise-longue. Here was a room, here was a set that had experienced a lot of nakedness, a lot of secretions and ablutions and reflections. Through the round window above the bath the sun cast its spotlight. Keith's face flickered or rippled as Nicola closed the door behind them.

'The toilet,' he announced with savage clarity. He approached the commode and raised the wooden lid. Nicola tingled suddenly – her armpits tingled. She knew what Keith was looking at: the small faecal stain on the cold white slope. On seeing it there earlier, Nicola had resolved to clean the bowl. She knew, however, that if she didn't do it at once, then she wouldn't do it. She hadn't done it at once. So she hadn't done it.

'The seat wobbles,' she said. 'And it slips.'

As Keith knelt and toyed doubtfully with the lid, Nicola sat herself down on the red sofa. She assumed a thinker's pose, chin on fist. Keith glanced her way and saw what was there to see: the light-grey cashmere, the white stockings, the brown underflesh of her crossed left leg.

'Wobbly toilet,' Keith said to her in a gurgling voice. 'Can't have that. Might do yourself an injury. Might ruin your married life.'

Nicola stared at him. There was perhaps an infinitesimal swelling in the orbits of her eyes. Several replies offered themselves to her with urgency, like schoolboys raising their hands to please the pretty teacher. One was 'Get out of here, you unbelievable lout'; another, remarkably (and this would be delivered in a dull monotone), was 'Do you like dirty sex, Keith?' But she stayed silent. Who cared? There wasn't going to *be* any married life. She stood up.

73

'You're dripping blood. Here.' She fetched a tin from the shelf. The light changed as she moved towards him.

Now she applied plaster to the meat of Keith's gently quivering thumb. Seen close up, flesh looks genital: minutely hair-lanced, minutely pocked. If his hands looked genital, what would his genitals look like, close up? The physiological effects of this thought told her all over again that he was the one. Their hands dropped. In different dizzinesses they saw, against the cold bowl, his bright blood meandering through the dark of her waste. This is disgusting, she thought. But it's too late now.

'Through here,' she said.

Five seconds later Keith was standing in the passage as Nicola zestfully loaded him up with ironing-board, iron, hoover, coffee-grinder. While she did this she talked to him as if he were subhuman, or merely representative. Would you very kindly. A great help. If you could also. Be most grateful . . . She loomed above him. Keith's Cuban heels began to edge backwards down the stairs. He peered up at her, so very hampered. He looked like a busker. He looked like a one-man band.

She said, 'I'd better give you a deposit,' and reached for something on the side table. She came closer. 'The man in the Black Cross. Guy.'

'Yeah. Guy,' said Keith.

'He's someone – he's someone of importance, isn't he, Keith.'

'Definitely.'

'Oh really?' Nicola had expected Keith to balk at any favourable mention of Guy Clinch. But his tone was respectful, even admiring. At this moment he seemed to need all the support and associational glamour he could get.

'Definitely. He works in the City. He's titled. I seen it on his chequebook. The Honourable, innit,' said Keith shrewdly.

Nicola stepped forward. With her fingers she was rolling two fifty-pound notes together. Keith twisted himself, in preparation. 'Wait,' she said. 'You'll drop everything.' He was wearing a black fishnet shirt with a patched chest pocket. But his darts were in that. So she rolled the money tight and placed it in his mouth. 'Is he rich?' she asked.

Keith worked the tubed notes sideways, as if his lips were used to having money between them. 'Definitely.'

'Good. There's a thing you and I might do together. A money thing. Have him call me. Will you do that? Soon?'

He twisted again, and nodded.

74

'There's just one other thing.' And what was it, this one other thing? She had a sudden, antic desire to lift her dress to the waist, to pivot, and bend – like a terrible little girl, with a terrible little daddy. She said erectly.

'My name is Nicola. Not Nicky or' – her lips closed in a flat smile – '"Nick".'

'Right.'

'Say it.'

He said it.

Her eyes returned to the black fishnet shirt. She placed a finger on one of its wide central squares. 'This sort of stuff', she said thought-fully, '– it should be on my legs. Not on your chest. Goodbye, Keith.'

'Yeah cheers.'

Nicola returned to the sitting-room and lit a cigarette. She heard him crash down the stairs – Keith, with the money in his mouth. For a minute or so she smoked intently, with dipped head, then moved to the tall window in the passage. She saw him, across the street, toppling in graphic difficulty over the open boot of his car. It was the right car: the murderer's car. With a boyish flinch Keith looked up into the evening sky, whose pale pink, as usual, managed to suggest the opposite of health, like the face of a pale drinker. Their eyes met slowly through the glass. Keith was about to essay some kind of acknowledgment, but instantly ducked into a fit of sneezing. The reports of these sneezes – quacked and splatty – travelled towards Nicola at the speed of sound: Keith's cur's sneezes. With his hand flat over his mouth he worked his way round the car and climbed in, and moved off softly down the dead-end street.

'Sneezes like a cur,' said Nicola to herself.

It was six o'clock. She yawned greedily, and went to the kitchen for champagne. Lying on the sofa, she sketched out the next few moves, or she turned up the dial, revealing the contours that were already there. Guy would call the day after next. She would arrange to meet him in the park. She would choose a cold day, so that she could wear her blond fur coat. Beneath that, at least, she would be able to keep some entertaining secrets. Her shoulders shook as she laughed, quietly. When she laughed, her whole body shook. Her whole body laughed.

In the popular books, when they tried to get you to imagine a black hole, they usually conjured a sample photon of light wandering near by, or (more popularly, and more phallically) an astronaut in a spaceship: a man in a rocket. Approaching the black hole, the traveller would encounter the *accretion disc*, circling matter bled from the neighbour star (and containing, perhaps, the wreckage of other men, other rockets); then, notionally, the *Schwarzschild radius*, marking the point at which the escape velocity equalled the velocity of light. This would be the *event horizon*, where spacetime collapsed, the turnstile to oblivion beyond which there was only one future, only one possible future. Now there can be no escape: during the instantaneous descent, all of eternity has passed on the outside. Caught in the imploding geometry, the man and his rocket enter the black hole.

Or look at it the other way. Nicola Six, considerably inconvenienced, is up there in her flying saucer, approaching the event horizon. She hasn't crossed it yet. But it's awfully close. She would need all her reverse thrust, every ounce, to throw her clear . . .

No, it doesn't work out. It doesn't work out because she's already there on the other side. All her life she's lived on the other side of the event horizon, treading gravity in slowing time. She's it. She's the naked singularity. She's beyond the black hole.

Every fifteen minutes the telephone rings. It's Ella from LA, it's Rhea from Rio, it's Merouka from Morocco. I have to break in over their hot cooings to tell them an unappetizing truth: I am not Mark Asprey. He's in New York. I give them my number. They hang up instantly, as if I'm some kind of breather.

Scented letters with lipstick imprints pile up on the mat. The girls, they come around the whole time: they practically picket the place. When I tell these pictures and visions, little duchesses, dazzlers and *poules de luxe* that Mark Asprey isn't around – they're devastated. I have to reach out to steady them. The other morning an adorably flustered-looking creature called Anastasia was there on the stoop, hoping for a few minutes with Mark. When I broke it to her, I thought I might have to call an ambulance. No, not so good for a guy not so lucky in love, or in art, as I stand in the passage scratching my hair in thought, and look up to see the framed dream-queens and the inscriptions scribbled wildly across their throats. *To my Apollo. Nobody does it quite like you. Oh I'm so completely yours . . .*

Anastasia couldn't have been sweeter (I gave her a good hug and she stumbled off mouthing apologies, her face a mask of tears). But some of the other ones, some of the snazzier ones, look at me with incredulous distaste. Can I blame them, especially when I'm in mid-chapter, exhausted, exalted, quilted in guilt, and unshaven to the whites of my eyes?

*

77

Yesterday evening there was an unusual telephone call. It was for me.

When I heard the sound, the subtle crepitation, that 3,000 miles makes, I thought it might be Missy Harter, or Janit, or at any rate Barbro. It was Slizard.

I like him personally and everything, but calls from Dr Slizard fail to set my pulse racing. He wants me to go and see some people in a research institute south of the river.

'How's America?'

'Crazy like an X-ray laser,' he said.

Slizard admits that the visit isn't really necessary, but he wants me to go along. 'Send me the pills,' I said. But I also said I'd think about it.

'Tell me, Auxiliadora,' I began, 'how long have you worked for the Clinches – for Hope and Guy?'

Auxiliadora was great. She gave me, while she worked, at least three chapters' worth of stuff in about fifteen minutes. A good cleaner Auxi may well have been, but she was certainly a sensational gossip: look how she smears and bespatters. She read their letters and eavesdropped on their telephone calls; she went through trashcan and laundry basket alike with the same forensic professionalism. Interesting sidelights on Lizzyboo. Fine material on Marmaduke. I listened, seated boldly at Mark Asprey's desk – not his working desk in the study but his writing desk in the living-room (where, I imagined, he tackled his lovemail). I was recuperating from Chapter 5. Heavy stuff, some of it. I can already hear Missy Harter telling me that America won't want to know all this (particularly if we're looking at a pub-date in say late spring, when the crisis, and the year of behaving strangely, will both be over, one way or another). But *Nicola* is heavy stuff. Nicola *is heavy*. I guess I could tone it down, if there's time. But tone it down to what? I guess I could 'make something up', as I believe the expression goes. Spanking or whatever. Her on top. Lovebites. But I can't make anything up. It just isn't in me. Man, am I a reliable narrator . . . I was sitting at the desk, as, with equal flair, Auxi cleaned the flat and dished the dirt, and making notes with a casual doodling action (and warmly looking forward to the domestic haven, the blameless hearth of Chapter 6), when there was a light rattle of keys, a slam of the door – and another woman strode furiously into the room.

78

She was Spanish too. Her name was Incarnacion. And she was Mark Asprey's cleaning-lady. She told me this in English, and said something of the same to Auxiliadora in a volley of oath-crammed Andalucian. I quickly located Mark's welcome note: sure enough there was a P.S. about his Spanish 'treasure', who was holidaying in her native Granada but would shortly return.

It was all very embarrassing. In fact it was all very frightening. I haven't been so scared for weeks. I took Auxi to the door, and apologized and paid her off. Then I went and hid in the study. When Incarnacion flushed me out I moved back into the sitting-room to find the large walnut table – previously bare but for a bowl of pot-pourri – infested with new gongs and cups and obelisks (dug up by Incarnacion from some bottomless trophy chest) and about a dozen photographs of Mark Asprey, making acceptance speeches, being fawned over by starlets, or in frowning conversation with deferential fellow bigbrains . . . He looks like Prince Andrew. Maybe he *is* Prince Andrew: the Prince as a bachelor, before he got so stout, on Fergie's cooking. The grinning eyes squeezed by the fleshiness of the cheeks. The inordinate avidity of the teeth.

Dinner tonight at Lansdowne Crescent. Lizzyboo will be there.

On the way over I'm due to stop in at the dead-end street: cocktails with Nicola Six.

As against that, I'm close to despair about getting into Keith's place. I have just this one idea, and it's a long shot: Kim, the kid. The little girl.

Keith's house is not a home. (And it's not a house either.) It's somewhere for the wife and child, and somewhere to flop, until Keith comes good on the ponies or the darts. Though often lost in praise of his dog Clive, he never mentions his girl Kim, except when he's especially drunk. Then it's *I think the world of that little girl* and *That little girl means the world to me*. But if prompted, or goaded, he will deign to denounce Kath's idleness and lack of stamina, when it comes to the kid.

'I mean,' he said to me in the Black Cross, or it may have been the Golgotha, his drinking club (the Golgotha is open twenty-four hours a day. But so is the Black Cross), 'what she expect? Moaning on. Baby this. Baby that. Can't sleep. Babies is what skirt *does*.'

'It can be very hard, Keith,' I cautioned. 'I've looked after children – babies. They worship their mothers but they torture them too. They torture them with the sleep weapon.'

He looked at me consideringly. You don't need much empathic talent to tell what Keith's thinking. He doesn't do that much thinking in the first place. The very difficulty, the disuse of the muscles, writes headlines on his forehead. Keith, and his tabloid face. Shock. Horror. You just read his flickers and frowns. Now it was something like *What would a* bloke *look after babies for?* He said, 'Yeah but it's not like real work as such. Half the time you just bung them in their –in that *pen* thing. Why was you looking after kids?'

'Two years ago I lost my brother.' This was true. Also unforgiveable. David. I'm sorry. I owe you one. It's this *writing* business. 'Oh yes. They had a two-year-old and another one just arrived. I was with them through all that.'

Keith's face said, Sad, that. Happens. Say no more.

But I did say more. I said, 'All Kath needs is a couple of hours a day with the baby off her hands. It would transform her. I'd be glad to do it. Guy employs male nurses,' I threw out. 'Take her to the park. I love kids.'

Well he didn't much like the idea, clearly. (He started talking about darts.) No, I thought – you've lost this one. Babies, infants, little human beings: they're a skirt thing. The only blokes who love babies are transvestites, hormone-cases, sex-maniacs. For Keith this was all very turbulent ground. The child-molester – the nonce, the short eyes – was the lowest of the low, and Keith had come across that sort before. In prison. He talked freely about prison. In prison Keith had gotten his chance to beat up child-molesters; and he had taken it. In prison as elsewhere, everyone needs someone to look down on, someone categorically *worse*. The serial grannyslayer got his go on the exercise bike, the copycat sniper had his extra sausage on Sunday mornings, but the short eyes . . . Suddenly Keith told me why: the hidden reason, beneath all the visible reasons. Keith didn't *say* it; yet it was written on his brow. The prisoner hated the child-molester, not just because he needed *somebody* to look down on, not only out of base sentimentality either, but because it was the one place left for his parental feelings. So when you striped the short eyes with your smuggled razor you were just showing the lads what a good father you were.

80

I was grateful to Keith for the insight. That's right, I remember now: we were in Hosni's, the Muslim café where Keith sometimes briefly recuperates from the Golgotha and the Black Cross. Just then, one of the pub semi-regulars passed our table. He leaned over and said to me:

'Here. I know what you are. A four-wheel Sherman.'

An explanation was effortfully supplied. Four-wheel = four-wheel skid = yid. Sherman = Sherman tank = yank.

'Jesus,' said Keith. 'Jesus,' he added, with an iconoclast's weariness. 'I hate that crap. "Your almonds don't half pen." Jesus. You ever going to stop with that stuff? You ever going to *stop*?'

Most of Mark Asprey's apartment quite likes me. But some of it hates me. The lightbulbs hate me. They pop out every fifteen minutes. I fetch and carry. The mirrors hate me.

The bits of Mark Asprey's apartment that hate me most are the pipes. They groan and scream at me. Sometimes at night. I've even considered the truly desperate recourse of having Keith come in and look at them. Or at least listen to them.

After its latest storm, after its latest fit or tantrum or mad-act, the sky is blameless and aloof, all sweetness and light, making the macadam dully shine. Sheets and pillows in the wide bed of the sky.

Still no word from Missy Harter.

Chapter 6: The Doors of Deception

IN HIS DREAM Guy Clinch edged closer to the bare body of a softly faceless woman. For a moment of dream time she turned into a thirteen-year-old baby, smiling, crooning, then once more became a woman without a face. Not even a baby face. This wasn't a sex dream. It was a love dream, a dream of love. He edged towards an oozing *yes* . . .

In actuality, in real life, Guy Clinch was edging towards a rather different proposition. Inches from his touch lay Hope in her dressing-gown, unblinkingly wakeful, and far from faceless: the healthy oval and its long brown eyes. Inches from his head, on the innumerable pillows, crouched Marmaduke, his hands joined and raised. As Guy entered the warmth-field of his wife's body, Marmaduke's twinned fists thumped down into his open face.

'Ow!' said Guy. The flesh fled in rivulets. He looked up in time to see the blurred arrival of Marmaduke's next punch. '*Ow!*' he said. Unplayfully he sat up and wrestled Marmaduke to the floor.

'Take him,' said Hope in a tranced voice.

'Was he very bad?'

'And quick with breakfast.'

'Come on, you little devil.' He picked up Marmaduke, who embraced the opportunity to sink his teeth gum-deep into Guy's neck. Guy gasped and began the business of trying to force open Marmaduke's jaws.

Hope said, 'He needs changing. He seems to have eaten most of his nappy again.'

'Loaded or unloaded?'

'Unloaded. Hold his nose. He'll give up in a couple of minutes.'

Guy pinched the sticky nostrils. Marmaduke's teeth tightened their grip. The seconds ticked by. Finally he released his mouthful, sideways, for greater tear, and sneezed twice into his father's face. Holding the screaming child out in front of him like a rugby ball or a bag of plutonium, Guy hurried towards the adjoining bathroom. This left Marmaduke with only one option for the time being – the reverse kick to the groin – which he now duly attempted. Guy put him face down on the far corner of the bathroom carpet. He managed to shut and bolt the door and crouch on the lavatory seat before Marmaduke was up and at him again . . . There were two reasons why Guy favoured the seated position: first, because it helped accommodate the unenlargeable erection he always woke up with; and secondly because Marmaduke, while feigning babyish absorption in the flush handle, had once smacked the seat down on him with incredible suddenness and force, dealing Guy a glancing blow that had none the less empurpled his helmet for a month and a half. As Guy used lavatory paper to staunch the flow of blood from his neck, Marmaduke paced yelling round the room looking for good things to smash.

'Milt,' said Marmaduke. 'Toce. Milt. Toce. Milt! Toce! Milt! Toce! Milt! Toce!'

'Coming!' sang Guy.

Milk toast, thought Guy. An American dish, served with honey or syrup. Hope likes that, and so does Lizzyboo. Hello, something missing: the strainer.

Marmaduke paused and spitefully watched his weaving father, the man with two pairs of hands. 'Toce,' he said, in an altogether more menacing tone. 'Toce *daddy*. Daddy. *Toce* daddy. Daddy *toce*.'

'Yes *yes*.' He stood there, skilfully buttering toast as Marmaduke clawed at his bare legs. Then the moment came and Marmaduke sprang for the knife. After a fierce struggle beneath the table Guy disarmed him and climbed to his feet, holding his nose where Marmaduke had bitten it. The knife again. He adored all knives. A calling, but for which occupation? Friends and relatives, on their rare and foreshortened visits, always said that Marmaduke, when he grew up, would join the army. Not even Guy's ancient father, a brigadier in World War II, had seemed to draw much comfort from this prospect.

Now he crouched smiling and offered up a piece of toast to Marmaduke's drooling mouth.

'Good Lord,' he murmured.

Guy had often suggested that they get specialist advice about Marmaduke's eating. After all, they were getting specialist advice about everything else he did. The child had of course been to several celebrated dieticians, and had been placed on regimes designed to quench him of vigour. The most recent one, said the doctor in his teak-panelled consulting rooms, would have reduced an Olympic sprinter to helpless enervation within a matter of days. It hadn't worked on Marmaduke, whose natural taste, incidentally, was for chips and hamburgers and monosodium glutamate and any kind of junk . . . Guy had seen greedy infants before – but nothing like this. The famished desperation, the neck-ricking bolts and snaps, the coruscating saliva. Halfway through his fifth brick of honey, butter and bronzed wholemeal Marmaduke released a dense mouthful and ground it into the tiles with a booteed foot: a sign of temporary satiation. Guy stuck a bottle in him and carried the child upstairs at arm's length. He locked him into the bedroom, then returned for the tray.

Hope lay back on her barge of pillows. This was more like how things were supposed to be: the tea tray, the telephone, the wallet of mail. The weekend skeleton staff had arrived and were amusing Marmaduke in the nursery above; only faintly could you hear his screams and theirs, and the occasional sickening impact. Guy lay on the sofa, reading the papers. Hope ran her glance cruelly over one gold-trimmed invitation after another. She said,

'I saw Melissa Barnaby yesterday. Out back.'

'Oh yes?' said Guy. Lady Barnaby: good, sad Lady Barnaby, with her milky eyes. She babysat for Marmaduke in the old days, once or twice. No. Once. The telephone call to the restaurant, just as the cocktails were arriving . . .

'She was looking rather well. She said she felt ten years younger. She's found this marvellous young man. He's fixed up the house. And now she's off to Yugoslavia for a week.'

'How nice.'

84

'We need one.'

'What? A holiday in Yugoslavia?'

'A marvellous young man.'

'It says here that tourists are advised not to visit COMECON countries. Idiots. They're deploying QuietWall. Darling,' he asked, 'how was it? Did you get any sleep at all?'

'Some, I think, between five and five-fifteen. Lizzyboo relieved me. He was terrible.'

Hope's sleep was a sacred subject in this house — more sacred, possibly, more hedged with wonder and concern, than the subject of Marmaduke himself. Guy had recently come across a scientific description of the amount of sleep Hope got, or claimed to get, during her nights with Marmaduke. It arose in speculation about the very early universe, nanoseconds after the Big Bang. *A trillionth of the time it takes the speed of light to cross a proton.* Now that really wasn't very long at all . . . On the alternate nights when Guy did Marmaduke, he usually got in a good three-quarters of an hour, and frequently dozed while the child wearily belaboured him or beat his own head against the padded walls.

'Poor you.'

'Poor me. Guy,' said Hope. She held a waxed document in her hand. 'What', she asked, 'is *this* shit?'

Guy went on reading, or at least his eyes remained fixed to the page. In the last month he had given £15,000 to charity, and he was feeling terribly guilty.

'Fifteen *grand?*' said Hope. 'Save the Children, huh?' She herself had given a similar amount to charity in the last month, but to galleries and opera houses and orchestras and other repositories of social power. 'What about *our* child? Who's going to save him?'

'Marmaduke', said Guy, 'will have plenty of money.'

'You've seen how he gets through it? Eighteen months old and already it burns a fucking hole in his jeans. In his Osh Kosh B'Gosh! You need therapy, Guy. When this whole thing started I *begged* you to have therapy.'

Guy shrugged. 'We're rich,' he said.

'Get out of here. You're giving me cancer.'

After a deft and speedy bowel movement Guy showered, then shaved: the French soap, the cut-throat razor. He dressed in an assortment of profoundly expensive and durable odds and ends, hand-me-downs some of them, clothes worn by his father, by

85

cousins, eccentric uncles. His closet was a City of business suits – but on most days now his clothes no longer needed to *say* anything. The outer man was losing his lineaments. Soon there would just be an inner one, palely smiling. A flowingly tailored tweed jacket, shapeless khaki trousers, a bright blue shirt, the thumping shoes (Guy's feet were enormous). As he came down the stairs he met with a rare sight: Marmaduke calmly ensconced in his mother's arms. Hope held him protectively while denouncing a nanny, a brawny Scandinavian whom Guy had not seen before. In his left fist he clutched his bays: a posy of long blonde hair.

'And where do you think you're going?' said Hope, turning from one defendant to another.

'Out. Out.'

'Where to? What for?'

'See some life.'

'Oh. Life! Oh I get it. *Life.*'

Reflexively, but with all due caution (and a shrewd glance at Marmaduke's free hand), Guy bent trimly to kiss his wife goodbye. Then everything went black.

He was in Ladbroke Grove by the time his vision returned. The sloped length of Lansdowne Crescent had reeled past him in the sun, popping and streaming in gorgeous haemorrhages; and only now at the main street, with its man-made noise and danger, did he feel a real need for clear sight. The eye-fork again: the first and second finger of Marmaduke's right hand, searchingly poked into Guy's candid orbits. Wonderfully skilful, you had to admit: such timing. He shook his head with the respectful admiration one knows before a phenomenon, and thought of the six-foot nurse he had seen the other week running down the front doorsteps, not even pausing to sue, with a bloody handkerchief pressed to her nose. Personal-injury suits were another way Marmaduke had found of costing Guy money. None had so far proved serious, but there were now quite a few pending. Marmaduke, and his permanent tantrum; the only thing that silenced him was a parental tantrum, one that left the adult actors still shaking and weeping and staggering, long after Marmaduke's original tantrum had resumed . . . Guy came to a halt on the street and blinked twice with his whole forehead. He raised a hand. With two soft pops he freed his lower eyelids, and waited for the sluicing tears. He had begun to enter the world of duplicity. He was

86

passing through the doors of deception, with their chains of lies. And all London swam.

What kind of man was this? How unusual? Guy gave money to charity. For every other man in his circle, charity began at home. And ended there too. Or not quite: charity continued for a mile or so, into the next postal district, and arrived at a small flat with a woman in it. These men winced at their wives' touch; they jerked up too soon to kiss them hello or goodbye. And Guy wasn't like that.

The thing was, the thing was . . . he was straight arrow. His desires described a perfect arc: they were not power-biased, they were not perverse. He may have had at least two of everything, but he had only one lady. Hope was it, his single woman. When they met at Oxford – this was sixteen years ago – there was something about Guy that Hope liked. She liked his curly-ended fair hair, his house in the country, his shyness about his height, his house in Lansdowne Crescent, his habit of hooding his eyes against a low sun, his title, his partiality to cherries (especially ripe ones), his large private income. They lived together during the last academic year, and studied together at facing desks in the double sitting-room ('Is *Samson Agonistes* epic or tragedy?' 'What were the long-term effects of Pearl Harbor, as opposed to those of Sarajevo and Munich?'), and slept together, vigorously, in the small double-bed. They had both been unhappy at home, had both felt underloved; now they became each other's family. So marriage, and London, and the City, and . . . Hope's social ambitions took Guy by surprise. The surprise wore off after a while (during the thousandth dinner party, perhaps), which was more than could be said for the social ambitions. They didn't wear off: they shone with a gathering brilliance. One of their effects was that Guy naturally came across many beautiful and accomplished and dissatisfied women, at least a dozen of whom propositioned him, in secluded corners, in crush bars, towards the end of masked balls. Nothing really happened. These advances were often sufficiently subtle to escape his notice altogether. True, every few years he secretly 'fell in love'. The redhaired wife of the Italian conductor. The seventeen-year-old daughter of the computer heiress. It was like an illness that passed after a couple of weeks; the love virus, efficiently repelled by a determined immune system. Most worrying and dramatic by far was the case of Lizzyboo, Hope's big little sister. Hope knew something was up the minute she found Guy in the visitor's room weeping over Lizzyboo's ballet pumps. Lizzyboo was sent away that time: seven years ago. All forgotten now, or not even forgotten: a scandalous family joke. Hope herself normally retained several menfriends (a partygoing philosopher, a dandy architect, a powerful journalist), but she was so strict and impeccable that it never seriously occurred to Guy – no no, nothing of that kind. For himself, the world of other women shaped itself into a great gallery, like the Hermitage, crammed with embarrassments of radiance and genius, but so airless, so often traversed, so public – a gallery where Guy sometimes sauntered for an hour, or where he sometimes hurried, looking straight ahead (squares of sublimity moving by like passing cars), or where he was sometimes to be found, though not often, standing before a blazing window and wringing his hands . . .

Marry young, and a melancholy comes over you at thirty, which has to do with thwarted possibilities. It was worse for Guy. Hope was a little older, and had had her fair share of guys at Oxford, earlier on, and at NYU, and for that matter in Norfolk, Virginia. So a new adventure: they overcame their ecopolitical anxieties and decided to go ahead and have a baby. Even then there were difficulties – Guy's difficulties. A process that began with him equably switching from jockey pants to boxer shorts ended up with him out cold and his legs in stirrups while a team of Japanese surgeons and a particle-beam laser rewired his nethers. Thus, after half a decade of 'trying': Marmaduke. For years they had worried about the kind of world they were bringing their child into. Now they worried about the kind of child they were bringing into their world. The gap or hollow that the baby had been meant to fill – well, Marmaduke filled it, and more; Marmaduke could fill the Grand Canyon with his screams. It appeared that from here on in a mixture of fatigue, depression and incredulity would be obliged to keep them faithful. Most of the psychiatrists and counsellors agreed that Hope's unreasonable fear of getting pregnant again might soon start to fade. Their last attempt at lovemaking had featured the pill, the coil, the cap, and three condoms, plus more or less immediate *coitus interruptus*. That was July. This was September.

But he wasn't about to stray. He was straight arrow. Divagation, errancy – to Guy this spelt humiliation. It would be disastrous, and inexpiable. No second chances. She'd kill him. The girl in the Black Cross with the extraordinary mouth – he would never see her again. Good, good. The flu, the malaria she had given him would be gone in a week. The thought of his life with an absence where Hope now stood (or wearily reclined) was enough to make him stop dead in the street and shake his hair with his hands raised and clawlike. He walked on, steadily. He would never stray.

'I mean – that's life,' said the young man. 'You can't argue with it. It's just one of them things.' He paused, and without fully straightening his body leaned forward and spat through the open door into the street. 'Okay,' he resumed. 'I got into a fight, I came out the wrong side of it, and that's life. No complaints. Fair enough. That's life.'

Guy sipped his tomato juice and stole the odd glance over his broadsheet. Good God: so *that's* life. The young man continued his tale. The two girls he told it to listened in postures of mild sympathy.

'I was out of order. Got taught a lesson.' He shrugged. 'That's it.'

Conversationally, philosophically, and often pausing to hawk blood into the street, the young man explained how this very recent altercation had cost him a broken nose and cheekbone and the loss of nearly all his top teeth. Guy folded his newspaper and stared at the ceiling. The rapidity of change. Anyone in Guy's circle who sustained equivalent damage would have to go to Switzerland for a year or two and get completely remade. And here was this wreck, back in the pub the very next morning, with his pint and his tabloid, his ruined face, and the occasional *phthook*! through the open doors. Already he had changed the subject and was talking about the weather, the price of beer. The two girls thought no less of him for it, particularly the scarred brunette; if he was lucky, and assuming he had one, he might get to take her home. Life goes on. And this *was* life, it really was, uncared for, and taking no care of itself.

Keith came in, causing the usual low pub murmur. He saw Guy and pointed a finger at him, then wagged his thumb backwards, indicating John Dark: John Dark, the corrupt policeman – the bent copper, the tarnished badge, the iffy filth. Dark was short and well-scrubbed, of that no-hair-but-good-teeth mould of man, and a horrid-jumper expert. He was the only regular in the Black Cross who looked at Guy with critical inquiry, as if he (Guy) really should know better. Dark's own position was ambiguous. He had a certain standing; but nearly everyone treated him with theatrical contempt.

Especially Keith . . . Guy inferred that Keith would be with him in a minute. And sure enough, after a few words with Fucker about the Cavalier (Fucker being the pub car-expert), Keith came over and leant forward seriously on Guy's table.

'You know that skirt who was in here? Nicola?'

'Yes, I know who you mean.'

'She wants you to . . .' Keith looked around unhappily. With impatience he acknowledged the salutes and greetings of Norvis, Dean, Thelonius, Curtly, Truth, Netharius, Shakespeare, Bogdan, Maciek, and the two Zbigs. 'We can't talk here,' he said, and suggested they repair to the Golgotha, his drinking club, and discuss things over a quiet glass of *porno*, the drink he always drank there (a Trinidadian liqueur). 'It's a matter of some delicacy.'

Guy hesitated. He had been to Keith's drinking club once before. The Golgotha, while no more private than the Black Cross, and no less noisy, was certainly darker. Then he found himself saying, 'Why not come back to my place?'

Keith hesitated. It occurred to Guy that the offer might seem offensive, since it was an invitation that Keith could never return. A one-way offer, unreturnable. But Keith glanced at the pub clock and said cannily, 'Good one.'

They moved together through the activity of the Portobello Road, Guy tall and questing in the sun, Keith stockier, squarer, his hands bunched in his jacket pockets, his flared trousers tapered and throttled by the low-flying wind, his rolled tabloid under his arm, like a telescope. Out on the street they couldn't talk about Nicola Six because that's what they were going back to Guy's place to talk about. As they turned into a quieter avenue their own silence grew louder. Guy chose a subject which had often helped him out in the past.

'Are you going to the match?'

Both men supported Queens Park Rangers, the local team, and for years had been shuffling off to Loftus Road on Saturday afternoons. In fact they might have come across each other earlier, but this had never been likely: Guy stood in the terraces, with his pie and Bovril, whereas Keith was always to be found with his flask in the stands.

'They're away today,' said Keith through his cigarette. 'United, innit. I was there *last* week.'

'West Ham. Any good?'

Some of the light went out in Keith's blue eyes as he said, 'During the first half the Hammers probed down the left flank. Revelling in the space, the speed of Sylvester Drayon was always going to pose problems for the home side's number two. With scant minutes remaining before the half-time whistle, the black winger cut in on the left back and delivered a searching cross, converted by Lee Fredge, the East London striker, with inch-perfect precision. After the interval Rangers' fortunes revived as they exploited their superiority in the air. Bobby Bondavich's men offered stout resistance and the question remained: could the Blues translate the pressure they were exerting into goals? In the seventy-fourth minute Keith Spare produced a pass that split the visitors' defence, and Dustin Housely rammed the equalizer home. A draw looked the most likely result until a disputed penalty decision broke the deadlock five minutes from the final whistle. Keith Spare made no mistake from the spot. Thus the Shepherd's Bush team ran out surprise 2–1 winners over the . . . over the outfit whose theme tune is "I'm Forever Blowing Bubbles".'

Keith's belated sigh of effort reminded Guy of the sound that Marmaduke would occasionally emit, after a rare success with some taxing formulation like *more chips* or *knife mine*. Guy said, 'The new boy in midfield, Neil . . . ? Did he do all right?'

'Noel Frizzle. He justified his selection,' said Keith coldly.

They walked on. Guy had of course been friendly with people like Keith before: in the City. But the people like Keith in the City wore £1,000 suits and platinum wrist-watches and sported uranium credit cards; at weekends they sailed yachts or donned red coats and mounted horses and went chasing after some rabbit or weasel; they collected wines (at lunch they crooned over their Pomerols and Gevrey-Chambertains) and modern first editions (you often heard them talking about what *New Year Letter* or *Stamboul Train* might nowadays fetch). They weren't poor, like Keith. Keith had his fistfuls of fivers, his furled tenners and folded fifties; but Keith was poor. His whole person said it. And this was why Guy honoured him and pitied him and admired him and envied him (and, he sometimes thought, even vaguely *fancied* him): because he was poor.

'Here we are,' said Guy.

He assumed his wife would be out or sleeping. She had been out, and would soon be sleeping, but Hope was right there in the hall when

91

Guy showed Keith Talent into the house. It went quite well, considering, Guy thought. When he introduced them, Hope put considerable energy into dissimulating her astonishment and contempt. And Keith confined himself to an honest nod (and a not-so-honest smile); he didn't look at all uneasy until Hope said that Lady Barnaby was downstairs, saying goodbye to Marmaduke before gallivanting off to Yugoslavia.

'If you got company . . .' said Keith, edging back towards the door.

From below came a harsh shout of childish triumph, followed by an unforced scream. Lady Barnaby sprinted up the stairs and appeared holding her forehead in one hand and her spectacles in the other. Urgently Guy moved forward, but Lady Barnaby seemed to recover very quickly.

'Perfectly all right. Perfectly all right,' she said.

'If you're sure? Oh, Melissa, I'd like you to meet Keith Talent. A friend of mine.'

Keith did now appear to be quite overwhelmed by the occasion. Perhaps, it's the title, thought Guy. It's a good thing he doesn't know about mine.

Lady Barnaby blinked up gratefully, raised her glasses to her eyes, and slowly nodded towards the hatstand.

'Oh my God,' said Guy. 'This is awful. Did Marmaduke do that? How? You simply must let us pay for them. Not with his fingers, surely.'

A nanny now stood at the top of the stairs. Resignedly she explained what had happened. Lady Barnaby had come ill-advisedly close to the highchair to feast her eyes on the boy. Marmaduke had cobwebbed both lenses with a skilful stab of the sugar-tongs.

'Have you got another pair?' asked Guy. 'Whoops! Darling, I think perhaps you ought to see Melissa home.'

In the drawing-room Keith asked for brandy, and was given one. He drank that, and asked for another. Guy, with whom alcohol did not always agree, poured himself a derisory Tio Pepe. They sat down facing each other on broad sofas. Guy felt that his instinct had been sound. Good to hear this in your own house: there could be little harm in it now.

'It's like this,' said Keith, and hunkered that little bit closer. 'I went round there, okay? See if I could help her out with anything. I do that. It's like a sideline. Nice place she got. And I thought, in addition . . .' Keith tailed off fondly. 'Well, you know what I'm like.'

But Guy did not know what Keith was like. He waited.

'You know,' said Keith, 'I thought she might want seeing to.'

'The flat?'

'No. Her.'

'How do you mean?'

'Christ.' Keith elucidated the point.

'And?' said Guy nauseously.

'Well it's hard to tell, you know, with some birds. She's funny. An enigma innit – you know the type. Half the time she's coming on dead tasty. And I mean *sorely* in need of it. And then, you know, suddenly it's Lady Muck.'

'So – nothing happened.'

Keith considered. At least one nice memory seemed to tickle his nose. But he said, 'Nah. Fuck all, really. And, I'm taking my leave and, as I say, she asks about you. Wants you to phone her like. Says she requires your help.'

'What about?'

'Don't ask me, mate.' He looked around the room and back again. 'Maybe she likes her own sort. I mean I'm nothing, am I. I'm *just a cunt.*'

It was hard to know how to react, because Keith was smiling. Throughout he had been smiling, when he wasn't coughing. 'Oh, come on, Keith!' said Guy palely.

The door opened. Hope stood there inexorably. 'I'm going to bed. Kenneth,' she said, 'would you put that cigarette out please? I took her back and she's calmer now. She's a little worried about going to Yugoslavia with only one set of glasses. Her boiler sounds terrible. It's lucky she's deaf. I was glad to get out of the house. If you use the kitchen I want everything cleared away. Without trace.'

'Birds,' said Keith when Hope had gone. He was taking a last few draws of his cigarette, one hand cupped under the long coal, as Guy searched for an ashtray. 'Can't live with them, can't live without them. Tell you what. Your wife's a cracker. And that kid of yours ain't bad neither. Either,' said Keith.

Duplicity consumed time. Even deciding to have nothing to do with duplicity was time-consuming. After Keith left, to run a local errand, Guy spent an hour deciding not to call Nicola Six. The urge to call her felt innocent, but how could it be? He wasn't about to run upstairs and share the experience with his wife. A pity in a way, he mused, as he paced the room, since all he wanted was the gratification, the indulgence of curiosity. Sheer curiosity. But curiosity was still the stuff that killed the cat.

At four o'clock, leaving Hope asleep and Marmaduke safely cordoned by nannies, Guy popped out to make a telephone call. He imagined it would take about ten minutes of his time, to find out whether there was anything he could reasonably do for this unfortunate girl – why, there was a telephone box at the very junction of Lansdowne Crescent and Ladbroke Grove . . . There was no one in the telephone box. But there was no telephone in it either. There was no trace of a telephone in it. And there was no hint or vestige of a telephone in the next half-dozen he tried. These little glass ruins seemed only to serve as urinals, as shelters from the rain, and as job-centre clearing-houses for freelance prostitutes and their clients. In widening circles Guy strayed, from one savaged *pissoir* to another. He hadn't used a telephone box in years, if indeed he had ever used one. He didn't know what had happened to them and to vandalism – though a serious glance at the streetpeople who glanced at him so mirthfully, as he rummaged behind the dark glass or stood there shaking his head with his hands on his hips, might have told Guy that vandalism had left telephone boxes far behind. Vandalism had moved on to the human form. People now treated *themselves* like telephone boxes, ripping out the innards and throwing them away, and plastering their surfaces with sex-signs and graffiti . . .

By now feeling thoroughly foolish, Guy queued for the use of a telephone in the General Post Office in Queensway. On a floor that smelled and felt to the foot like a wet railway platform, Guy queued with the bitter petitioners of the city, all of whom seemed to be clutching rentbooks, summonses, orders of distraint. It was time for Guy's turn. His hands were shaking. That number: easy to remember, impossible to forget. She answered, to his horror, and well knew who he was – 'Ah, yes'. She thanked him for calling, with some formality, and asked if they could meet. When, following Keith's course (and Nicola's silence), he suggested her apartment, she murmured demurringly about her 'reputation', which reassured Guy, as did her accent, whose faint foreignness now seemed not French so much as something more East European and intellectual . . . Another silence ensued, one that deducted twenty pence from Guy's original investment of fifty. The park, tomorrow?

Sunday, by the Serpentine. And she gave him instructions and thanks.

The telephone call had taken two and a half hours. Guy went out into the street and buttoned his jacket against the sudden cold. The clouds, which were behaving so strangely these days, had gathered themselves into a single cylinder, east to west, like a god's rolled towel, like the slipstream of a plane the size of America. He ran home ecstatically to relieve the nannies, get hollered at by Hope, and spend sixteen hours alone with Marmaduke.

At dawn on Monday morning Guy sat in the pale light of the kitchen. He had relieved Lizzyboo at about 3 a.m., and helped bandage her, after remarkable scenes in the nursery. But then, around five, something like a miracle happened. Marmaduke fell asleep. Guy's first impulse was to call an ambulance; but he was calmer now, content to monitor the child on the closed-circuit TV screen with the volume turned up full and look in on him every five minutes or so and feel his forehead and his pulse. For the time being Guy just sat there whispering words of thanks and pinching himself in the amazement of all this silence.

Quietly he approached the twin doors that led to the garden. The garden twinkled and simpered at him in its dew. Guy thought of Nicola Six and the continuous and inexplicable waves of suffering which the planet had somehow arranged for her – the lips, the eyes, averted in their pain. He blinked, and imagined he could see a dark-braided girl playing alone beneath the curtain of the willow tree. Perhaps it was Enola, perhaps it was Enola Gay. Enola, searching for Little Boy.

Guy unlocked the doors to the garden.

'*Guard, guard*,' Marmaduke would have said (it had previously been *garner, garner*), if he had been there to warn him. But Guy went out through the doors.

On Sunday he had walked with Nicola Six in London fields . . . Kneeling, the children launched their boats into the cold agitation of the water; the smaller craft wobbled all the more eagerly, as if activity could redress their want of size; among them, a black-sailed unfamiliar . . . Her story came at him now like a series of paintings, or *tableaux vivants* – no, more like memories of another life: the orphanage and charity school; her years as governess, nurse, novitiate; her current life of good works and scholarly seclusion.

95

Impeccable, innocent and tragic in her blond fur coat . . . Guy raised his fingertips to his eyelids, then lifted his head and stared. On days alone with Marmaduke, how he had tried to invest every minute with wonder and discovery. Daddy's getting dressed! Shirt, trousers, shoes, yes, *shoes*. Look: bathroom. Tap, sponge, toy boat! Now – ho ho ho – Daddy's making coffee. That's right: coffee. Not tea. Coffee! Oh, look out there. The garden, *and* flowers, *and* grass, *and* a little bird – singing! And such lovely clouds . . . The oohs and aahs of ordinary life had made little impression on Marmaduke, who just shouldered his course through the day with the usual grim ambition. But something had now made wonder work for Guy. He woke up and he thought, Air! Light! Matter! Serious, poor, beautiful: everything you care to name.

Marmaduke was stirring. Marmaduke was waking. Marmaduke was screaming. He's alive. Thank God, thought Guy. I'll not touch her. No, I'll not touch her. Ever.

I'd say she really did a number on Guy Clinch. No half-measures there. It beats me how she keeps a straight face.

She really did a number on him. What was that number? It was Six. Six. Six.

One thing about London: not so much dogshit everywhere. A lot still. Compared to New York, even old New York, it's the cloaca maxima. But nothing like it used to be, when the streets of London were *paved* with dogshit.

Explanation. The English still love their dogs, for some reason. But the dogs aren't living as long as they used to. Nothing is. It's weird. I mean, one expects snow-leopards and cockatoos and tsessebes to buy the farm eventually. But *dogs?* I have an image of fat Clive, sitting in a zoo.

How will we teach the children to speak when all the animals are gone? Because animals are what they want to talk about first. Yes, and buses and food and Mama and Dada. But animals are what they break their silence for.

Keith's account of the football match. I've heard many such summaries from him — of boxing matches, snooker matches, and of course darts matches. At first I thought he just memorized sections of the tabloid sports pages. Absolutely wrong.

Remember — he is modern, modern, despite the heels and the

97

flares. When Keith goes to a football match, that misery of stringer's clichés *is what he actually sees.*

A pleasant enough evening at the Clinches' last week. Publisher and his wife, architect and his wife, director of the National Portrait Gallery and his wife, sculptress and her husband. A lone tennis player called Heckler, the South African number seven. All the men were extremely attentive to Hope, and the thought occurred to me that she may be sleeping with one of them, or will be soon, which would liven things up even further.

Me, I am developing Lizzyboo. A fulsomely pretty girl. She is also voluble, indiscreet and, I think, not too bright. She's perfect for me.

So maybe I will have a little love-interest of my own. I need it. I sit here at Mark Asprey's vast desk. Incarnacion has adoringly divided his mail into two stacks: the love-letters and the royalty checks. Among the quills and antique inkwells there is an exquisite geometry set – nineteenth-century, Arabian. The clasp comes away with satisfying slickness. I'm going to try it.

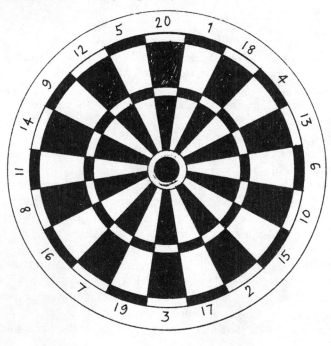

Look at that. It's beautiful. Admittedly it took me all morning, what with the dummy-runs and everything, the ridiculous errors, all that shading. It was great, though. I felt about eleven. Bespectacled, hunched sideways over the desk with my tongue out the corner of my mouth, alone in the universe.

I took as my model the illustration in a booklet of Keith's, *Darts: Master the Discipline*. I also used the pen he gave me, the one shaped like a dart.

Look at that. It's beautiful. Oh, Keith – take me home!

I must avail myself of Mark Asprey's car, that dinky A-to-B device of his, which seems to shimmer to attention every time I walk past it and lour at me reproachfully on my return. The cab fares are killing me. It's curious. You seldom see a black London taxi any more. You can call them, and arrange a rendezvous within a mile of Marble Arch; but apparently they stick to the West End and the City. Black cabs are like the buggies on Central Park, a tourist thing, a nostalgia thing. And a money thing: they're blindingly expensive. The drivers wear modified beefeater outfits.

You can see how it happened. Envy-preemption. Or the simplest prudence. Black cabs are socially insensitive. Traffic jams can get ugly, or uglier still; people get dragged out of these burnished hearses. So nowadays cabs aren't even minicabs. They're just any old heap with a removable sign up on the dash. You get in front. Then the driver removes the sign. Or sometimes he doesn't. He leaves it there. It's okay. It's cool. It looks sufficiently shitty inside; no one outside can be bothered to mind.

The place in Clapham is a research institute. I sit and wait. It feels like school. It feels like London Fields.

The truth is I am stalled. You wouldn't call it writer's block. You might call it snooper's block. Tower block.

I can see Keith's tower block from the bedroom window. I scan it with Mark Asprey's powerful binoculars. He's up there on the eleventh floor. I bet it's the one with all the ruined satellite equipment dangling from the little balcony.

Chapter 7 looms like Keith's tower block. A fortress. There's no way in.

When I entered the garage for my first darts lesson Keith turned suddenly and gripped my shoulders and stared me in the eye as he spoke. Some kind of darts huddle. 'I've forgotten more than you'll ever know about darts,' says this darting poet and dreamer. 'I'm giving to you some of my darts knowledge.' And I'm giving him fifty pounds an hour. 'Respect that, Sam. Respect it.'

Our noses were still almost touching as Keith talked of such things as the *address of the board* and *gracing the oché* and the *sincerity of the dart*. Oh yes, and *clinicism*. He then went on to tell me everything he knew about the game. It took fifteen seconds.

There's nothing to know. Ah, were I the kind of writer that went about improving on unkempt reality, I might have come up with something a little more complicated. But darts it is. Darts. Darts . . . Darts. In the modern game, or 'discipline', you start at 501 and score your way down. You must 'finish', exactly, on a double: the outer band. The bullseye scores fifty and counts as a double, too, for some reason. The outer bull scores twenty-five, for some other reason. And that's it.

In an atmosphere of tingling solemnity I approached the oché, or throwing line, 7ft 9¼ ins from the board, 'as decided', glossed Keith, 'by the World Darts Federation'. Weight on front foot; head still; nice follow through. 'You're looking at that treble 20,' whispered Keith direly. 'Nothing else exists. *Nothing*.'

My first dart hit the double 3. 'Insincere dart,' said Keith. My second missed the board altogether, smacking into the wall cabinet. 'No clinicism,' said Keith. My third I never threw: on the backswing the plastic flight jabbed me in the eye. After I'd recovered from that, my scores went 11, 2, 9; 4, 17, outer bullseye (25!); 7, 13, 5. Around now Keith stopped talking about the sincerity of the dart and started saying 'Throw it *right* for Christ's sake' and 'Get the fucking thing *in there*'. On and on it went. Keith grew silent, grieving, priestly. At one point, having thrown two darts into the bare wall, I dropped the third and reeled backward from the oché, saying – most recklessly – that darts was a dumb game and I didn't care anyway. Keith calmly pocketed his darts, stepped forward, and slammed me against a heap of packing cases. Our noses were almost touching again. 'You don't never show no disrespect for the darts, okay?' he said. 'You don't never show no disrespect for the darts . . . You don't never show no disrespect for the darts.'

The second lesson was a nightmare too. The third is tonight.

Warily I eye my pimpish darts pouch. £69.95, darts *compris*, courtesy of Keith.

Guy came over just now, for tea, and I returned his short stories with a few words of quiet discouragement. He was right: they weren't any good or anything. He's a sweetheart, and he has some nice perceptions; but he writes like Philboyd Studge. I told him, with an inner titter, that the stories ran too close to life.

He just gathered them up shyly, nodding his head. See, he didn't care any more. He didn't care. Just smiled and gazed out of the window at the speeding clouds. All in all, debriefing him was quite a sweat. I was reminded of the line in *More Die of Heartbreak*, and I checked in the dictionary: the second definition of *infatuation* is 'inspired with extravagant passion'; but the first definition is 'made foolish'. Guy asked my advice about Nicola. I gave my advice (it was bad advice), and with any luck he'll take it.

Then he left. I walked him downstairs and out into the street. The pigeons waddled by, in their criminal balaclavas. Pigeons have definitely seen better days. Not so long ago they were drawing Venus's chariot. Venus, goddess of beauty and sensual love.

Somewhere else in *More Die of Heartbreak* Bellow says that America is the only place to be, because it contains the 'real modern action'. Everywhere else is 'convulsed' in some earlier stage of development. That's true. But England feels like the forefront of something, the elegiac side of it, perhaps. It makes me think of Yeats's lines (and here my memory still holds):

> We have fallen in the dreams the ever-living
> Breathe on the tarnished mirror of the world,
> And then smooth out with ivory hands and sigh.

Now I must go to Keith's garage. How I suffer for my art.

Midnight. I return in a state of rapture. I have an hysterical urge to burst right into Chapter 7, to write all night and beyond! Oh, something is tickling my heart with delicate fingers . . .

Easy now. Courage. What happened?

Keith and I were packing up after my darts lesson. I sat there on a stolen case of *porno*. The atmosphere was better tonight, because toward the end I threw a treble 20. That's right. I got a dart to go in the treble 20, the flattened nose of the board's face – the treble 20, what darts is all about. Keith picked me up and whirled me around in the air.

Actually, it was bound to happen in the end. The darts went wherever they liked, so why not into the treble 20? Similarly, the immortal baboon, locked up with typewriter and amphetamines for a few Poincaré time-cycles, a number of aeons with more zeros than there are suns in the universe, might eventually type out the word *darts*.

I was sitting there going on about how tired Kath must be and how good I was with children. I also threw in some lies about the impossible squalor of my earlier years. So many times I've said all this – I'm almost toppling over with boredom myself.

'Oh, sure,' I said. 'When I was your age I was still dodging the shit in the South Bronx. The rats were this big. You'd come out of the walkup and see the body of a child, like a broken –'

'You got the – ?'

I gave him the £50. Intolerably he started talking about darts again – my darts, or rather my *mechanical security*. We began to leave. I grimly assumed that we would be looking in at the Black Cross for a nightcap and a few dozen games of darts. But as we went out through the little door Keith paused and looked at me unhappily.

'We going indoors,' he said. 'First.'

For the 300-yard journey we relied on the heavy Cavalier. We parked under the shadow of the craning block – which sparked and flickered like ten thousand TV sets stacked up into the night. Keith hurried. He summoned the elevator but to his silent agony the elevator was dead or elsewhere. We climbed the eleven floors, passing a litter of sick junkies sprawled out on the stairs in grumbling sleep. With referred rage Keith denounced them through his wheezes: a mixture of personal oaths and campaign slogans from the last election. We walked the walkway. Avoiding my eyes he leaned on the bell. And when the door opened I . . . I understand. I understand how Guy felt, as the veil went up (like a curtain or a skirt) to reveal the woman in the Black Cross. It comes in leaps and bounds. Sometimes it comes, not as thunder, but as lightning. Sometimes love comes at the speed of light. There's just no getting out of the way.

Faded, patient, Kath Talent stood in the kitchen colours, in the pale margin of the kitchen. She had Kim in her arms. And the child . . . the child was an *angel*.

Chapter 7: Cheating

'GOOD MORNING, LADY B.'

'Good morning to you, Harry.'

'So,' he said as he swept through the door. 'Today's the big one.'

'I – I've been watching the news.'

Keith strode into the sitting-room and switched off the television, pausing briefly to wonder how much it would fetch.

'The weather there,' said Lady Barnaby. 'And Yugoslavia is listed as one of the –'

'All stuff and nonsense, Lady B. All stuff and nonsense. This the lot? Then we're off. Oh yeah. Lady B., we got a little prob. The motor's on the blink. Never mind: we'll take yours. The holiday of a lifetime. What, are you sure!'

Listening to Lady Barnaby's decidedly hysterical laughter, and calmly aware of the set of housekeys and documents she always kept in the glove compartment, Keith barrelled up the motorway, giving her 'It's a Long Way to Tipperary' and a lightly bowdlerized version of 'Roll Me Over in the Clover'. They drove through veil upon veil of scalding heatmist. The sky pulsed blue, blue, blue. Whereas the cyclones and ball lightning in Yugoslavia and Northern Italy had even made it on to the pages of Keith's tabloid.

'It seems silly to be going away in this weather.'

'Greenhouse,' said Keith dismissively. '*El Niño* innit. Tomorrow just be pissing down.'

The remark carried little conviction. But Lady Barnaby seemed to take a surpising amount of comfort from it. Her bones knew the old English weather; whereas Keith was accustomed to a more versatile sky. Just piss down is what it just didn't do in England, not regularly, not any longer. It did that now in places like California and Morocco.

'Look at the *congestion*,' said Keith.

After a half-hour delay in the rotting exhaust-pipe of the access tunnel, and a rather longer wait at the short-stay carpark, Keith guided Lady Barnaby to the check-in stall at Terminal 2. Here the computer pronounced Lady Barnaby's ticket near-worthless. Keith took the news with cold resignation: the *cheat* at the bucket-shop had cheated him. What he didn't yet know was that the *cheat* who had cheated him had been cheated by the *cheat* who supplied the bucket-shop. As a result, Lady Barnaby was flying to a non-holiday, and flying one-way. Keith managed to panic her about missing her flight – and about losing her luggage, which they had luckily relinquished at the door. He stood there smoking and whistling and coughing and swearing as Lady Barnaby countersigned all but three of her traveller's cheques. She entered Departures in a ragged dash.

Vowing vengeance on her behalf, Keith picked up some bent duty frees from his contact at Freight, drove smartly to Slough for a breakneck get-together with Analiese Furnish, and then, back in London, rounded off a busy morning by selling Lady Barnaby's car.

'Enlah,' said the baby. 'Enlah,' said Kim. 'Enlah.'

Keith glanced up longsufferingly from his tabloid and his lunch. His lunch consisted of Chicken Pilaff and four Bramley Apple Pies. His tabloid consisted of kiss and tell, and then more kiss and tell, and then more kiss and more tell. Aliens Stole My Boobs. Marilyn Monroe And Jack Kennedy Still Share Nights of Passion: In Atlantis. My Love Muscles Tightened From Beyond The Grave. All his life Keith had been a reader of the most vulgar and sensational of the mass-market dailies. But two years ago he had made a decision, and gone down-market: to the smaller-circulation *Morning Lark*. He was still adjusting to the wrench. The *Morning Lark*, in Keith's view, made up for what it lacked in coverage with a more positive and funloving approach to life. There was no chance of tragedy or disaster driving Beverli or Frizzbi off page three, or page two, or page one. And although the girls in the *Morning Lark* weren't as pretty as the girls in the mass-market daily, they were certainly more numerous. Ah, the lovely smile on her – cheers you up for the rest of the day.

But now Keith was soberly rereading the filler about the death toll in Yugoslavia. He pointed at the pram with a finger. Kath slipped slowly forwards from her chair.

'Enlah,' said the baby.

The pram dominated the hallway. The pram *was* the hallway, and more. Its handles stuck into the kitchen, its fluted bonnet took up half the lounge. Again Keith glanced up longsufferingly as Kath returned, or pivoted, with the baby in her arms. The baby, who was neither tired nor wet nor hungry, established position on her mother's lap, demurely.

Kath gave a quick nod and said, 'I'm very worried, Keith.'

Keith drank tea with a mouthwash action. 'Yeah?' he said.

'War,' said the baby.

Kath said, 'It's the news.'

'Oh that,' he said with relief.

'The verification,' said Kath.

'Lie,' said the baby.

Keith said, 'Nothing in it. What *reason?*'

'I don't know. You look at the . . .'

'Oil,' said the baby.

Kath said, 'A flare-up. A flashpoint somewhere.'

'Eh?'

'Wall,' said the baby.

Keith said, 'Jesus. It'll blow over, okay?'

'Or,' said the baby.

'They've been cheating,' said Kath. 'Both sides. They've been cheating for fifteen years.'

'Who says?' said Keith. There was nothing about it in Keith's tabloid. 'TV?'

'I been down the library,' said Kath lightly. 'The proper papers.'

This touched a nerve in Keith (for he was very loyal to his tabloid, regarding its readers as one big family); but it also touched a chord. It was through the library that Kath had won Keith's heart. She had taught him how to read and write – easily the most intimate episode of his life. Oh, easily. The thought of it made tears gather behind his eyes, tears of shame and pride, tears of difficulty, of intimacy.

'Fuck off,' said Keith equably – his usual way of registering casual disagreement. 'So who's cheating who?'

'They both started cheating as a hedge against the other side doing so,' said Kath with the Irish fluidity that Keith had always silently admired, and now silently hated. 'They're accusing one another of non-compliance and inaccurate denial.'

Keith started on his first Bramley Apple Pie. He knew all about inaccurate denial. Keith used it a lot, this technique. He was forever inaccurately denying things. Quite recently he had had to do some very concerted inaccurate denial – with regard to his wife. Instead of inaccurately (and routinely) denying to someone or other that this or that was stolen or worthless or broken or ruined, Keith had been obliged inaccurately to deny that he had given Kath non-specific urethritis. It was the sternest test this tactic had ever faced . . . Keith had been cheating on Kath with a girl who had been cheating on Keith. Her name was Peggy Obbs. First, Keith went round to the clinic; next, he offered a cash gift to Petronella Jones and a bottle of pills to Trish Shirt; then he hastened across town and started beating up Peggy Obbs. While he was beating up Peggy, Peggy's brother Micky came home and started beating up Keith. When Keith explained why he was beating up Peggy, Micky stopped beating up Keith and started beating up Peggy, with Keith's help. After that was over, things got a little unpleasant: he came home to find Kath crying by the cooker, and saw the doctor's slip and the chemist's bag. But Keith was ready. He denied it. He denied it hotly, indignantly, and inaccurately. He seized her shoulders and told her to put her coat on *that minute*. They were going straight round to the doctor and have *him* do some denying. He was kneeing her out of the door by the time she shook free and went to comfort the weeping baby. As Keith started off to the Black Cross he told Kath not to *dare* blame him for her woman's troubles ever again. For a couple of weeks he gave her hell about it, then let the matter drop, exhausted (apart from everything else) by all this inaccurate denial, which was admittedly effective but, he found, uniquely tiring. And, by the way, this non-specific urethritis wasn't the old kind of non-specific urethritis, which everybody in Keith's circle already had. It was the new kind of non-specific urethritis, implying widespread inflammation of the lumbar regions, heavy and repeated doses of antibiotics, and (in an ideal world) at least a couple of months in bed. But who could manage these months in bed? Who had time for them? The planet needed a couple of months in bed. But it wouldn't get them – it wouldn't ever get them.

Keith finished his fourth Bramley Apple Pie and said, 'Shut it.'

A soft female cough came through the kitchen wall from the

neighbouring flat. Then they heard a contented swallow, and the sound a paper tissue makes when run across a smooth upper lip.

'Iqbala,' said Keith. 'She got a cold.'

'She got a new boyfriend too.'

'She *never*.'

'Yodelling her head off again she was this morning. Like a pig having an operation.'

'. . . The dirty little bitch.'

'Hark at him so indignant. You never said anything about the other boyfriend.'

Keith fell silent. This was true. He never said anything about the other boyfriend. He never said anything about the other boyfriend because *he* was the other boyfriend. Many times he had slipped next door, one finger raised to his lips. Being indignant about the other boyfriend had proved to be quite beyond his powers. He just told Kath (and Iqbala) to turn the telly up loud.

Kath said, 'Look at that now.'

Little Kim was asleep, seated more or less upright on her mother's lap. The baby's powerful face, fully formed but in miniature, with its collection of glassy roundnesses, its crescents and half-moons, lolled forward on the white trim of her jumpsuit. The cheeks broadened at the base, pushing out the lower lip, as brightly succulent as a slice of sushi, the likes of which neither Keith nor Kath had ever seen.

'Good as gold,' he said. 'Get her down, girl.'

To free the passage they backed the pram into the kitchen. To accommodate the pram, the table had to be shoved still tighter to the walls; Keith then faced the draining task of pushing Clive in under it with his feet. When two adults were active in the kitchen they performed closely, as in a dance, almost a smooch. But Keith wasn't feeling affectionate. His mode changed. He thought of Guy's house and found himself in the rare state of total cluelessness; he had no clue to that kind of space and what it might mean. Keith grew up in a low-rent basement flat in Chesterton Road (about six streets further down the Grove from Lansdowne Crescent), where, so far as he knew, his mother lived on speechlessly. Two rooms, kitchen and bathroom. All his youth he had sat in this flat and wondered how he was going to get out of it. Conversely, a great deal of his adulthood had been spent wondering how he was going to get back into it. A while ago he learned that on his mother's death the flat would revert to the council, and that, in Keith's estimation, was the end of that. It was certainly the end of his mother. He confronted the image, the bright astronomy, of what

107

Guy had and Keith's stream of consciousness simply stopped flowing. It dried up. TV, he thought. It was the best he could do.

Kath edged back into the room. Keith dogged her with his eyes, revising his catalogue of her physical deficiencies. Everything he cherished, everything he looked for in a woman, Kath didn't have. She was no Analiese Furnish or Debbee Kensit, no stocky little braburster with pumpkin bum and milkbottle legs. (Maybe short legs were shortcuts . . . Yeah. They didn't mess about. Short legs were shortcuts to the biz.) When he met her five years ago she looked like the girl in the advert for double cream: the eyebrows rurally pale, the hair and its innocent russet. Now she looked to Keith like a figure glimpsed at dawn through a rainy windscreen.

'Look at the state of you,' said Keith, and watched her shoulders tighten over the sink.

She paused in her work. 'I'm tired,' she said to the window. 'I'm so tired.'

You don't say, thought Keith. Oh really. He couldn't express let alone feel any sympathy for someone so proclaimedly in need of an ambulance. And when you considered the simple heroism with which Keith endured his bad chest, his curry-torn digestive system, the itchings and burnings of his sedimentary venereal complaints, his darts elbow, his wall-eyed hangovers . . .

He stood up, saying, 'I happen to be under considerable pressure at the minute. I work my guts out.' He made an expansive gesture. 'Who do you think's paying for all this?' In the kitchen, or indeed anywhere else in the flat, making an expansive gesture was not necessarily a good idea. One of Keith's outflung hands banged into the door, the other into the fridge. 'Get your head down now, for Christ's sake.'

'I think I will.'

'What. After you made my tea?'

'Yes,' said Kath. 'After.'

An hour later Keith sat catching up on his viewing, his knees inches from the screen (not that he had much say in where his knees went).

'Enlah,' said the baby. 'Enlah, Enlah, Enlah, Enlah. En*lah*. Enlah Enlah Enlah Enlah Enlah Enlah Enlah Enlah . . .'

With a sigh and some slow nodding Keith extinguished his most recent cigarette, switched off the shootout he was watching, and climbed to his feet. He looked down at Kim, whose moses-basket was wedged between the TV and the inactive two-bar fire. He stretched, barking his right elbow nastily against the wall, and flexed his back, yawning, until his head bumped into the door . . . Outside, the balcony was strewn with satellite receivers, all stolen, all broken. No space out there. No space where Clive could furiously swivel.

Keith shook Kath awake and then took the dog for his evening walk – Keith always did this, religiously, when he wasn't up to no good elsewhere. All you had to do was step into the street and you were surrounded by royalty. The Prince Albert, the Duke of Clarence, the Earl of Warwick. Maharajah Wines. In the yellow light of the shops, while Clive sniffed at some or other excrescence, Keith looked again at a certain brunette in the *Morning Lark*. She was pretty. Her name was Pritti, too – or Pritti, at any rate, was what she called herself, with grinning literalism. A bit like Nicola, thought Keith. Or Nikki. But Nicky wasn't pretty exactly, like Pritti. I blew that one. Or go round there and teach her a lesson . . . The arguable connexions between pin-ups and pornography and sex and violence: just to clear *them* up, while Keith is at hand. With people like Keith, a pin-up was enough to get him going, going in that general direction. But almost anything was enough to get people like Keith going. Five minutes in a populated region of Saudi Arabia would get Keith going. And you can't yashmak female reality, with its legs, its breasts, its hair, its eyes . . . A shame about Petronella getting married like that, even though she was tall and skinny, but still quite keen by the sound of her. Thus Keith would pay another farewell visit to Trish Shirt. Later. He walked the full 300 yards and let Clive precede him into the Black Cross, not wanting to miss Guy.

Keith wasn't disappointed. Six hours after his own arrival, Guy Clinch stepped over Clive's ash-strewn body and stood there swathed in the smoke and the spores. Eleven o'clock and the Black Cross was loud and crowded, and cocked tight, hairtrigger: one false move and it could all explode. The smoke was hot, the air was hot (hot Clive lay like a doorstop), even the wind outside was as hot as the late-night breath of Keith's TV . . .

Jesus. Keith shouted into a wall of sound. Earlier in the evening someone had gone and put a brick through the jukebox; but God the barman had started playing Irish folksongs over the PA system, at balding, teeth-loosening volume. Apart from making God cry, the main effect of these folksongs (which promised a fresh dawn for a proud and drunken nation) was to make everybody shout all the time: their third and unforeseeable effect was to make Keith even angrier with his wife, with Trish, with darts and debts, with all the pressures on the modern *cheat*. He shouted and shouldered his way through to

Guy, who lingered with his usual site-tenacity by the pinball machine, inoperative, because a girl was sleeping on it, or lying on it anyway. Also near by were Shakespeare, Dean, Thelonius, Bogdan and Zbig Two.

'Did you call her?' Keith shouted.

Guy flinched. 'Yes,' he shouted back.

'Did you see her?'

Guy nodded and mimed an affirmative.

Then Keith shouted, 'Did you fuck her?'

Guy staggered back from him. He shook his head and his hand in time. 'You don't understand,' he shouted. 'She doesn't . . . she's not –'

'Her?' shouted Keith. '*Her*?' he shouted even louder. Keith took Guy's arm and pulled him through the open doors into the street, suddenly pausing, on the way, to stroke Clive's back with his foot. Then he turned.

'What are you after then?'

'Nothing. She's not like that.'

'They're all the fucking same. Did you try her?'

Guy smiled palely and said, 'Of course not. You know me, Keith.'

But Keith did not know Guy. All he knew about Guy he got from TV. He said, 'Listen. I want something? I go for it. Me? I'm in there. Boof.'

'You're barking up the wrong tree, Keith.'

'I'm like a dog,' said Keith. 'You kick me? I don't run and hide. I'm back. I'm in there.'

Keith didn't look as pleased by this simile as he thought he was going to be. In fact his sweating face spoke of general disappointment and confusion.

'Keith, you're upset.'

'You're all the fucking same,' he said, and turned back through the doors, with an exemplary briskness. He knew Guy wouldn't be man enough to follow.

Two hours later, as Keith lurched with Clive down Lancaster Road, to pay his last call on Trish Shirt, he reviewed something Nicky had said to him that time ('Is he rich? . . . There's a thing you and I might do together. A money thing'), and furiously wondered if there was any way he could *sell* her to Guy Clinch.

'I've hit form just when I needed it,' said Keith. 'Come good at the right time. As long as I maintain my composure I don't fear no one, Tony, not throwing like I am. No way will I crap or bottle it on the night. I'd just like to thank you and the viewers for the superb support. The fans is what darts is all about.'

You're known for your big finishes, Keith, said the voice, which was – which was what? Which was TV, dream life, private culture, learning how to read and write, worldly goods. *I believe they call you Mr Checkout, or the Finisher.*

'That's right, William,' said Keith. 'But I've worked on my power. It's an improved Keith Talent you're looking at tonight. A more complete darter. Still, you know what they say. Trebles for show, doubles for dough. You can get all the maximums and ton-forties in the world but if you can't kill them off, if you can't stick it in at the death –'

Keith coughed for a few minutes. He wasn't on TV or anything. Far from it: the garage, the dusty morning light. He was sitting slumped on a cardboard box, in a posture of weary meditation. Just now on the phone Dean had given him some chastening news. Guess who was in the other half of the draw for the Sparrow Masters. Chick Purchase, whom Keith hated. Chick, whose very name tasted in Keith's mouth like hospital food. To tell the truth, Keith was looking and feeling distinctly seedy. In fact he had a wall-eyed hangover . . . Not that he'd tarried overlong at Trish Shirt's. Clive was still sniffing about the stockroom, looking for a good place to lie down, when Keith reeled back out of there. But then he had stopped by at the Golgotha for a pensive glass of *porno*. And later, around five, he had gone back to Trish Shirt's. On the other hand – as against that – you wouldn't catch him going *there* again. No way.

Seedily he peered round the garage, feeling its dust in his throat. He lit another cigarette. The bottles of drink on the workbench he now viewed with contempt. He generally found a vodka or two quite refreshing at this hour (it was ten in the morning), but he wouldn't be touching a drop, not now. No danger. It would be Lucozade until Friday. He had his darts match coming up – an away fixture at the Foaming Quart in Brixton, at Brixton's Foaming Quart – and he found, as he got older (and like the planet he was getting older at a peculiar rate), that darts was a stern mistress. Take this morning. Throw a dart? He couldn't even hold one. He couldn't even *lift* one. And Dean Pleat was expected with the van at ten-thirty.

As they peered seedily about, Keith's eyes registered certain items scattered among the debris and the contraband. They lay where he had first hurled them: vacuum-cleaner, coffee-grinder, ironing-board, iron. What were his plans for these appliances? When feeling at his most rancorous he thought that on a Wednesday or a Saturday, if he happened to be passing, he might dump them for ten quid on the tinker in Golborne Road. Now he reconsidered. Maybe that was just more short-end money, just more small thought. That time in her flat, when he gashed his thumb, with that screwdriver. She dressed his wound, while he stared into the brown sluice between her breasts. TV, Keith speculated. Brings them closer together innit. Like a bond. He remembered the taste of her money in his mouth and the way she put it there. A nauseous gust ruffled his head and seemed to clear it; he bent forward and whispered, with certainty, 'She . . . she has need of me.' Yes she did. In a way that went beyond his known parameters, she – she had need of him.

Keith stood up, and began to pace the floor, his hands clasped behind his back. In this matter of posh birds Keith was, after all, by no means inexperienced. There had been the odd housewife in his window-cleaning and petty-theft period (Keith with ladder, bucket, and unreliable smile), the odd daughter too when he was on stake-outs for the local firm, appearing at the front door with some choice plausibility or other. Keith knew that some of these rich ladies liked a bit of rough; but they didn't *all* like it, not by any means. A lot of people had difficulty with this point. Try drumming some sense into Norvis and Thelonius. They thought that *all* white women liked black men; they thought that the only ones who didn't, or pretended not to, were racist. Misguided, sadly misguided, thought Keith sadly. Some women didn't like otherness; they didn't like the other, when it came to the other. Hope Clinch, now: there was a perfect example of a rich lady who didn't like a bit of rough. They looked right through you and out the other side; for them you were nothing, not even animal – you were nothing. And Keith knew very well that he *was* a bit of rough, relatively speaking, at least for the time being.

On the whole he found posh skirt shockingly arrogant in bed, always wanting to get on top and other rubbish, and often drawing the line, if you please, at some of Keith's most favoured stunts. There was, for instance, that mad bitch in South Ken. Miranda. She was at least forty, and a wild one. Single in those days, Keith had spent many a night in her mews bedroom being oiled and teased and clawed. It went on all summer and Keith nursed high hopes of the relationship: a car, maybe, a cash gift or at least a loan. But he went off her, right off her, after she got the police round that time, when Keith paid a call on her one night, with some pals. All right, it was late (he remembered switching the car lights off on the way there), and – okay – things *were* taken (namely goods, drink and liberties) and it looked bad for a minute there when they formed that queue behind him. But to scream so loud the neighbours called the filth in: that was betrayal. Soon after that she changed her phone number and went away for a while. Keith was still in a state of high indignation when he showed up with the van and the boys (the same boys) and started bitterly stripping the house.

Keith sighed. Tomorrow he would take Nicola's stuff to GoodFicks in Cathcart Road. They would, of course, cheat Keith, and, having brought it all home, he would have to take it all back again. The original faults would perhaps be corrected, but new ones would also be introduced. You had to do everything, and pay for everything, at least twice; that was the way it was. Raising a yellow finger to his lower lip, Keith pondered the whole future of cheating. Cheating was his life. Cheating was all he knew. Few people had that much money any more but it was quite clear that they had never been stupider. The old desire for a bargain had survived into a world where there weren't any; there weren't any bargains. Unquestionably you could still earn a decent living at it, at cheating. Yet no one seemed to have thought through the implications of a world in which *everyone* cheated. The other morning Keith had bought five hundred vanity sachets of Outrage, his staple perfume. At lunchtime he discovered that they all contained water, a substance not much less expensive than Outrage, but harder to sell. Keith was relieved that he had already unloaded half the consignment on Damian Noble in the Portobello Road. Then he held Damian's tenners up to the light: they were crude forgeries. He passed on the notes without much trouble, in return for twenty-four bottles of vodka which, it turned out, contained a misty, faintly scented liquid. Outrage! The incident struck Keith as a sign of the times. Everyone was cheating. Everyone was cheating – because everyone was cheating. Poor Keith, and the tragedy of the commons . . . In such times the thoughtful man looked elsewhere: to his darts. Meanwhile, and always accepting that he might taste defeat on the oché (that was darts after all, making the game what it was), the cheating situation called for readjustment, for daring, for vision. Keith would have to cheat more, cheat sooner and cheat harder than the next guy, and generally expand *the whole concept of cheating*.

He picked up the darts and threw. Hah! a 20, a 5 and a 1: 26 – the joke throw. As he plucked the darts from the board Keith rehearsed his sneer of incredulous amusement and acknowledged the jeers of the crowd: even Keith was human. That was the only thing wrong with darts. That was the only thing wrong with cheating. You couldn't cheat at darts. No way.

There was the sound of a van outside. He recognized the faulty silencer.

'Keith!' yelled Dean.

'Dean!' yelled Keith. 'Okay. Let's go to *work*!'

The days passed. Though making himself no stranger to pub or club Keith drank nothing and worked hard because of the life that was in him. He sensed the pulse and body of the street-trade and heard the cars lowing in the furrows. Like new corn the young Swedes and Danes formed lines at his stall, and were reaped. He walked dog and burped baby and drew the keening of wife after his will. The hot macadam pulled on his shoes, like desire, and he had the surety a man knows when there is a sickly Saudi granny in the back of the Cavalier. He harkened to the chirrup of fruit-machine and the tolling of pinball table, humped the dodgy goods and defrayed life's pleasures with sweat of brow and groin and armpit, knew also the firm clasp of Analiese's ankles around his neck, the coarse reassurance of Trish Shirt's hair in his fist. And ever dazed from staring at the sun, the source of all generation. Heaven and earth was teeming around him. And how should this cease?

Keith drove up the dead-end street and braked with needless violence. He didn't park, although a space was available. He doubleparked. Then he emerged – in flared toreador pants, halfsmock shortsleeved darts shirt, oxblood cowboy boots.

The door buzzed open for him. Keith lugged the stuff up the stairs. Despite the heat, the journey seemed a lot shorter than it had the time before. Just goes to show: peak fitness. He climbed the final flight, dropped his cargo in the hall, and moved through . . . and moved through the intoxicating emptiness of the four large rooms. It reminded him of something. What? Oh yeah. Burgling. He called her name – the trisyllable this time. Then he returned to the hall and saw the stepladder, the tipped skylight. He ascended slowly into the brilliant photosphere. As the colours dripped from his vision, he saw a brown elbow, and a brown shoulder, and the rest of her, lying there in white underwear.

'Hello,' said Nicola Six.

Hello, thought Keith Talent.

114

Incarnacion is melting to me, but very slowly, on some glacial time scale. I am appreciably less frightened of her now. It's funny who has the power to frighten, and who has not.

Tall, broad, handsome, queenly, Incarnacion wears black at all times. Some of her outfits have been recently purchased; others are silvery-grey with use. There is probably enough steady death in the hills of her native Andalucia to keep Incarnacion in black for the rest of her life. How old are these Spanish ladies, when they make the big switch to black?

She is coming round to me. The hiring of Auxiliadora – that disgraceful solecism – we have started to put behind us. I am deferential. I spring-clean the apartment before she gets here. I give face. Christ, as if I need to spend more time kissing ass than I do already.

Incarnacion gives the odd smile now. She isn't exactly communicative yet; but on occasion she can be induced to discuss, or haughtily enumerate, the achievements of Mark Asprey.

Like Kath Talent, who is a worried woman, I have been consulting the *proper papers*. A great deal of comment (most of it stodgily pharisaical), some analysis (jovial stuff about the verification procedures) – and no news, not of a geopolitical nature anyway. The Gulf, Israel of course, Germany of course, Hungary, Cambodia and so on. But no *news*. I'll have to go to Queensway for a *Trib*.

The television is even worse. Those glamorous ladies read out the bulletins as if they're fronting *Blue Peter* or *Jackanory*. The bright smile of kindergarten kindnesses. Endless human-interest pieces about the weather. Soap and sitcom. Oh, and a quite incredible amount of darts. There's practically a whole channel of it, a whole network of darts.

The weather is certainly playing along and doing its bit. Yesterday I went for a walk with Guy in the park. Above, the clouds were moving with preternatural speed; you felt as if larger units of weather were passing overhead like meteorological discs on a chart – months, entire seasons sweeping by in less than thirty seconds. And great heat. The clouds sped, and not just laterally either. They seemed to bounce and romp and tumble. Yes, there was definitely something puppyish, something almost faggy, going on up there, when like plays with like.

At one point as I walked under a tree I felt the warm kiss of a voluptuous dewdrop on my crown. Gratefully I ran a hand through my hair – and what do I find? Birdshit. Pigeonshit. I'm feeling okay for once, I'm feeling medium cool, and a London pigeon goes and takes a dump on my head. It had this effect on me: despair. I swore and stumbled around, bedraggled, helpless, the diet of a London pigeon being something that really doesn't bear thinking about. I mean, what the digestive system of a London pigeon considers as *waste* . . . Guy laughed briefly, then fell silent and produced a skyblue handkerchief (used but clean: in bold contradistinction to a London pigeon, Guy's wastes would be clean). From his height he dabbed at the quick-drying matter. He did this unsqueamishly, and with delicacy. 'Hold still,' he told me. I tried. I put an arm around his waist to steady myself. But the top of my head doesn't really bear thinking about either, what with the writing I now find on my pillow at dawn, and the daddylonglegs that come and gather in my brush.

Later we sat at a sidewalk table and drank coffee. Around us young Arab husbands grumbled while their wives shopped. That mustache grumbled at this mustache. This mustache grumbled at that mustache.

'Written anything recently?' I asked him.

Guy paused and smiled and flinched. 'Yes, I have actually, Sam. Poetry,' he said.

'Sorry. I don't handle poetry,' I said daringly (and who does these days?). But I offered to take a look at it anyway. I know what his poetry will be about. What poetry is always about. The cruelty of the poet's mistress.

I myself attempt a call to Missy Harter at Hornig Ultrason. Barbro McCambridge's secretary Olivia eventually puts me through to Barbro. Next, Janit Slotnick's secretary Rosalind puts me through to Janit. At this point I am a mere secretary away from Missy herself; but that's as far as it goes.

I negotiate with Janit and her infuriating voice. She wants a sample. I offer to Fed-Ex – or even Thrufax – the first three chapters to her. Janit says okay, but she also wants a treatment. I try to conceal the difficulties this would involve me in. I suggest a 'projection'. We compromise on an *outline*.

I could stall, but for how long? Money anxieties are starting to smirk and gibber at me – and an artist shouldn't have to work under that kind of pressure. I want patronage. True, I get some free meals at the Clinches', and Lizzyboo, I hope, will insist on going Dutch when I take her to the movies. But Keith's darts lessons, rounds of drinks at the Black Cross, little presents for Kim – I have overheads.

I guess I could just wing it. But all I know for sure is the very last scene. The car, the car-tool, the murderer waiting in his car, the murderee, ticking towards him on her heels. I don't know how to get to the dead-end street. I close my eyes, trying to see a way – how do writers *dare* do what they do? – and there's just chaos. It seems to me that writing brings trouble with it, moral trouble, unexamined trouble. Even to the best.

I know. I'll ask Nicola. She already has an outline. *She* can damn well do it.

No news, but plenty of rumour. Where do they come from, all the rumours? A kind of inverse scepticism takes over, when there's no news.

An Apollo object, ripped loose from the asteroid belt, is heading toward us at ten miles per second. It's so big that when its leading edge hits, if it hits, its trailing edge will be up there where the aeroplanes fly.

A unique configuration of earth, moon and sun will cause hemispherical flooding. There will be sunquakes, and superbolt lightning.

A nearby supernova will presently drench the planet in cosmic rays, causing another Great Extinction.

Oh, and nuclear weapons: *those* dinosaurs.

The supernova stuff strikes me as a pure *definition* of rumour. How do we know about the supernova until we can see it? Nothing, no information, can reach us faster than cosmic light. There's a speed limit up there. The universe is full of signs, circled in red, saying 186,287.

And let's not forget the Second Coming, also awaited, in quiet confidence. Or not so quiet. On the street the poor rock and sway, like burying parties. All their eyes are ice.

'Call it off, Nicola,' I said (I felt I had to say it some time). 'So far, there's absolutely nothing inevitable about what you've entrained. Forget it. Do something else. Live.'

'It's funny, isn't it,' she said, 'that there's nothing more boring, in any kind of narrative, than someone vacillating over something you know they're going to do. I keep noticing it in the trash I watch and read. Will the spy come out of retirement for one last big mission. Will the gangster heed his wife's warnings or go for the clinching bank job. It's a nightmare sitting through that stuff. It's dead, dead.'

'Is it necessarily such a drag?' I said, sparing a protective thought for my paragraph about Guy and the telephone call. 'Sexual vacillation is okay, surely.'

'Oh yes. Will the priest succumb to the Jezebel? Will the gypsy seduce the virgin? These are questions that deserve question marks. They *are* the story. With the other stuff there's no story until they're out of the way.'

I said uneasily, 'But you're not in a story. This isn't some hired video, Nicola.'

She shrugged. 'It's always felt like a story,' she said.

Nicola was sitting opposite me, by the table and the telephone, in her white dressing-gown. The dressing-gown had been washed recently, and now it was the elderly wicker chair that looked used and intimate and Nicola-steeped. She folded her legs up beneath her. She had sat curled that way for many, many hours of her life here: introspections, piercing boredoms, incensed outwaitings. But with me she can let her hair down.

'Has Guy been here yet?'

'No. Soon. It's the next but one thing. I'm going to speed things up. Massive escalation.'

'Do you really need Guy? Couldn't you just edit him out?' I felt I had to say this too. For a moment I also felt real alarm that she might accede. If she did, I was looking at a very grim novella. Besides, I'd already Fed-Exed the first three chapters to Janit Slotnick.

'I agree it's a drag in a way but I do need him. Keith can't go it alone. There's not enough in him. Of course it could be managed. Easy. A bungled rape, strangulation. I could have managed that on the first date. The time he followed me home I could have managed that. But what do you think I'm after? A "senseless killing"? Anyway events are moving now. I just let the next thing happen.'

'Oh yeah. Nicola the determinist. "The next thing." Well how's it going to go? Could you – could you outline it for me?'

She exhaled, in weariness and irritation. I felt the same with Janit. She said, 'Clearly things will progress along two broad fronts. There'll be some intermeshing. I don't like . . . Why am I telling you all this?'

'I'll tell you why you're telling me all this. It's because,' I went on archly, 'it's because I'm a civilian. I'm immune. I salute your beauty and your originality and so on. And your power to shape reality. But for me it doesn't work. None of it. The bedroom voodoo, the Free Spirit nihilistic heroine bit, the sex-actress bit – it just doesn't get to me.'

She did a fish mouth, and her eyes lengthened. 'Get you. Aren't *you* the one.'

I raised a hand.

'That isn't why,' she said. 'I'll tell you why.' She looked around the room and back again. 'Are you ready? Can I say it now?'

I looked around the room and back again. I nodded.

'You're dying, aren't you.'

'We all are,' I said.

Well, yes, we all are, in a way. But in different lanes, at different speeds in different cars.

Nicola's streamlined A-to-Z device is travelling at a hundred miles an hour and will not swerve or brake when it hits the wall of death.

Keith's personal Cavalier needs decoking, and pinks on cheap fuel, and has far too many miles on the clock (no use fiddling the speedo on this highway), with bad trouble brewing in big end and manifold.

Guy might drive for ever at a prudent thirty-five, with tons of gas — but here comes the fog and the pile-up dead ahead.

Me I'm in a rattletrap lurching much too fast over bumpy ground. I have left the road. I am out of control. The hood flies up. There goes a wheel. Only one outcome.

Bury my bones in London Fields. Where I was raised. That's where I bought the farm. Yes I bought the farm out there in London Fields.

I must do something for the child.

Chapter 8: Going Out With God

ENOUGH OF HER childhood had been spent in church to give Nicola an interest in religion. She was interested in religion, in a way. (And it's a rare goodtime girl who waives all hope of Sugardaddy.) Nicola was certainly mighty keen on blasphemy. And so she often found herself imagining that she was going out with God.

Or not going out with Him – not any more. He had slept with her once, and once only: she did that to show Him what he would be missing for ever and ever. In bed Nicola had made Him do the act of doubledarkness: the doublebeast with only one back. Then never again. God cried in the street outside her apartment. He telephoned and telepathized. He followed her everywhere, His gaze imparting that fancy blue nimbus. God got Shakespeare and Dante working as a team to write her poems. He hired Parthenope, Ligeia and Leucosia to sing her lullabies and romantic ballads. Appearing in various forms, He tempted her with His charisma: he came as King David, Valentino, Byron, John Dillinger, Genghis Khan, Courbet, Muhammad Ali, Napoleon, Hemingway, the great Schwarzenegger, Burton Else. Preposterous flowers materialized on the stairs. Exhaustedly she flushed the innumerable diamonds down the toilet. God knew that she had always wanted her breasts to be very slightly larger and infinitesimally further apart: he offered to arrange it. He wanted to marry her and have her come and live at His place: in heaven. All this could be achieved at the speed of light. God said He would fix it so she lived for ever.

Nicola told Him to get lost.

Of course, there was another man in her life. His name was the Devil. Nicola didn't see nearly as much of the Devil as – in a perfect world – she would have liked. Sometimes, when the mood took him, he called her late and got her round to his soul club after hours, and abused her on stage while his friends looked on and laughed. Her thing for the Devil – it wasn't love. No, she could take or leave the Devil in the end. Nicola only did it because it was good fun and it made God mad.

Guy Clinch in the park had been quite an experience.

You know how it is when two souls meet in a burst of ecstatic volubility, with hearts tickling to hear and to tell, to know everything, to reveal everything, the shared reverence for the other's otherness, a feeling of solitude radiantly snapped by full *contact* – all that? Well, such interactions of energy are tiring enough when you're in love, or think you are. But let Nicola trumpet the assurance that they're much more tiring when you're not: when you're just pretending.

Guy Clinch in the park had been murder.

'Let's talk about you. That's enough about me . . .'

'I'm sorry, am I rambling on terribly . . . ?'

'It's funny, but I don't think I've ever talked about this before . . .'

'That's enough about me. Let's talk about you . . .'

While, with an expression of dreamy self-pity, she frailly hugged her fur coat to her body (the day was helpfully cold) and spoke about her spiritual struggles at the convent, it was only the thought of the spangled garter-belt and cathouse panties, the riot of underwear she wore beneath, that prevented Nicola from flopping back on the bench with her feet apart and saying, 'Oh, I can't bear this stuff. I'm lying. Never *mind*.' She had to maintain an actress's discipline: it was like the fifteenth rehearsal with some dud leading man who kept on flubbing his lines. Time and again Nicola nearly corpsed. Yes: it'll be all right on the night. She played for time (taking little rests) by staring in saintly silence at the water: the toy galleon with black sails, in whose wake . . . And when Guy was in full voice – on the Third World, on his writing, on the material inequities he found he just couldn't accept – Nicola stayed conscious by wondering how she would have processed Guy Clinch a few years ago, or a few months ago. She would have seduced him that afternoon and sent him back to his wife with a graphic lovebite on either buttock. Suddenly he was talking about the subsidizing of thermal underwear for the elderly in winter; and Nicola suddenly felt she had done enough. As they parted on the Bayswater Road it took all she had to make that second fake-impulsive swivel and give that second vague wave goodbye.

When she got home she slipped out of her coat and twirled into bed still wearing her high heels. When she awoke around midnight she bathed and then compulsively cooked herself a bushel of pasta and sat eating it and watching television and drinking nearly two bottles of Barolo.

He called the day after the day after, which was just as well. As it was, Nicola listened patiently enough to the furtive, the terrified, the pantwetting pips of the public telephone.

'I've been thinking where it might be nice to meet tomorrow lunchtime,' he said, 'if you still can and want to? . . . The Wallace Collection – do you know it? Off Baker Street. It's always soothing, I find. Or the Soane Museum in Lincoln's Inn Fields. Extraordinary little place, rather melancholy, but in a pleasant kind of way. Or we could meet in the V & A.'

'Yes,' said Nicola. 'Or in a restaurant.'

'. . . Yes. What kind of restaurants do you like?'

'Expensive ones' was the answer. But Nicola didn't say that. She simply named a restaurant of world-historical costliness in St James's and said she would see him there at one.

Guy was early. He came rearing up out of the banquette when she walked through the door. The boyish brightness of his rough silk tie spoke to Nicola of an insufficiently examined self, or an insufficiently critical one.

'This was a mistake,' she said timidly as she removed her gloves and lay them on the tablecloth. 'I mean the restaurant. I didn't know it would be so pretentious. I've hardly ever been to restaurants. The name just popped out.' Speaking sideways Nicola ordered a Tanqueray gin martini straight up with three olives. 'I'm sorry.'

'Nothing for me, thank you. Oh don't worry.'

She lit a cigarette and regarded him with respectful amusement. 'Are you shocked by my dependencies?' she asked. '*I* am. As you've gathered I'm rather a nervous person – rather a ridiculous person, I'm afraid. It's not very often I go out into the world.'

'Actually I find it touching.'

123

'You're very generous. Well this is – good fun. And I did so enjoy our talk in the park.'

'I think I went on a bit.'

'No. No. In the modern world it's not often . . . But today I must be sensible. I do have something I want to ask of you.'

She was dressed for business. This was the story.

During her early years in the orphanage (that peeling warren of municipal mortification) Nicola had befriended a little Cambodian girl – beautiful, abandoned, with hurt four-lidded eyes. Like partners in a concentration camp where the enemy wasn't cold or hunger or outright torture but lovelessness, lovelessness, they kept each other going – indeed, the tiny pals exalted themselves with the intensity of their secret and their bond. When she was twelve Nicola went on to the charity school (cum blacking factory) while her soulmate was 'adopted' or farmed out to a pitiless Iraqi. The man abused her. There was violence. She – she fell. Did Guy understand?

Guy nodded grimly.

Little Nicola, turning away from her rotting textbook or the headmaster's switch, would weep over her friend's long letters. She had the child: a son. She was then repatriated, never to return.

'Cambodia? She's still there? My God.'

'The Proxy War,' said Nicola coldly.

Occasionally a blood-smudged dispatch written on toilet paper or Elastoplast found its way through to her. Mother and child were variously sighted in a refugee camp in Thailand, a resettlement facility in Burma, a prison in Laos.

'It's hopeless there,' said Guy. 'The whole area.'

'You know, in a way it's ruined my life as well as hers. I feel so desperately incomplete without her. I think that's why I never . . . but that's another story. I must bring them back. I'll never feel whole until I bring them back. You have connexions, don't you, Guy? Is there perhaps something you could do? Inquire?'

'Yes. I could certainly try.'

'Could you? Their names are here. I'd be eternally in your debt.' She smiled fondly. 'Little Boy was always known simply as Little Boy, though he's almost a man now. *Her* name is En Lah Gai. I called her Enola. Enola Gay.'

She checked Guy's face. Nothing. And a little knowledge might have helped him here. A little knowledge might even have saved him . . . With a crisp fingertip Nicola directed the waiter to replenish her glass with the Chardonnay she had picked. She watched Guy's uplifted face as it filled with purpose. Then she squeezed lemon on to her eleventh oyster, and waited before adding the Tabasco. It flinched reassuringly. After all, you eat them alive.

'I take it you're married,' she said abruptly.

'Yes. Yes. And I too have a little boy.'

Nicola inclined her head and smiled without opening her mouth.

'My wife Hope and I have been married for fifteen years.'

'Nuclear,' said Nicola. 'That's not so common any more. How romantic. Well done.'

'I wonder if there's any more black pepper,' said Guy.

Later, on the street, they were getting ready to part. Feeling the need of contrast, badly feeling the need to mix things up, Nicola walked away from him, stretching her arms as if they were wings for flight. Her dark-grey business suit was, she knew, none the less flatteringly cut, making much of her hips, making little of her waist. The city heat, re-established, and used and trapped for some days now, prompted her to unbutton and remove her jacket. She slung it over her white-shirted shoulder and turned to him with a shake of the hair and a hand on her hip, giving herself a thought instruction that went like this: You're something very negligent on a catwalk somewhere with a lot of old men watching and wondering how hard and how expensive you'd be to fuck.

'Are you all right? I must say . . . I must say you're looking terribly well.'

'Am I?' She shrugged. 'Perhaps I am. But what for?'

Additional wine, and two glasses of Calvados, had got her through a deadly hour during which Guy, in innocent and meandering style, had sought to convey certain information about his heart: that it was a good one; that it was in the right place; that it would seem to belong to another; and that it was true. The alcohol and the conversation combined to assist Nicola in her next project, which was to start crying. Years ago, when she studied the Method, her instructor told her that sadness – misery, tragedy – wasn't always the way. You had to think about the things that made you cry in real life. Whereas her classmates all got by with images of lost puppies, vanished fathers, *Romeo and Juliet*, starving Namibians, and so on, Nicola found that her one sure path to tears lay through memories of irritation and above all boredom. So as she picked out the orange beak of a black cab in the cyclotron of one-way West End traffic and then turned to

Guy distractedly, her head was full of missing buttons, passport queues, utility bills, wrong numbers, picking up broken glass.

'You're crying,' he said joyfully.

'Help me. I'm so terribly alone. Please help me.'

As her taxi edged up St James's to Piccadilly, Nicola turned in her seat. Through the dark glass she watched Guy swaying – swimming, drowning – in the heavy air. And he was quite nice in a way, the fool, the poor foal. Guy: the fall guy. On paper, at least, he certainly didn't deserve the humiliation and havoc she planned to visit on him. But this was how it was, when (among other considerations) you had really *got to the end* of men.

Paradoxically, or at any rate surprisingly, Nicola Six disapproved of bikinis. She execrated bikinis. For twenty years and all over the world she had been ricking necks on fashionable beaches: the double doubletake. A modern beuty in a racing one-piece? The men stared, and so did the women. The girl's belly, though enviably contoured, for some reason had no interest in being seen. Ditto the breasts (for toplessness, too, she held in contempt). Women sometimes thoughtfully covered themselves for a while after Nicola strode by. Here was a person who didn't want her body familiarized. Looking down at their own torsos, bared alike to sun and eyes, the women resentfully sensed this prideful gamble. And the men: they knew that if they ever magicked themselves into the hotel room, the quiet villa, the cabin, the changing-hut, they would see something that the beach had not seen, that the sun and the waves and the eyes had not seen.

Nicola loathed bikinis; the bikini she regarded as the acme of vulgarity (and how the lines demarcated the godlike thorax, making polyps of the breasts); nevertheless, a bikini was what she was wearing when Keith Talent jacked himself out on to the roof that day, and stood there blinking in the blaze . . . She had bought it that morning; and it was exceptionally vulgar, Nicola's bikini, cutely skimpy with cutaway thighs, and bright white against her Persian flesh. At first, Keith clearly thought – as he was meant to – that she was sunbathing in her underwear: he looked away for a moment, alarmed at having surprised her in this disquieting improvisation. But then he made out the silk-aping waterproof of the curved white.

'Hello,' she said.

Keith coughed a few times. 'She wore an itsy-witsy teeny-weeny,' he then volunteered. 'Yeah cheers.'

'Do you know the etymology of *bikini*, Keith?'

'Who?'

'Yes, you're right. Origin is more like it. *From* is more like it. *From* Bikini Atoll in the Marshall Islands, Keith, the site of the US weapons tests in 1946 and 1954. First, atomic bombs. Then, in the Fifties, the Super: the hydrogen bomb.' She laughed ruefully, and continued: 'I still don't see how this inevitably leads to a "scanty two-piece beach garment worn by women". I looked it up in Brewer before you came, Keith. He chummily suggests a comparison between the devastating effects of the explosion and the devastating effects of the costume.'

As she spoke Nicola was looking, not at Keith, but at her bikini and what it framed. She rightly imagined that he was doing likewise. The interproximate breasts, concavities of throat and belly, white pyramid, the racing legs. Keith did not know, could not have guessed, would never have believed, that half an hour ago this body had stood naked before the bathroom mirror while its mistress wept – drenching the feet of the god of gravity. Beauty is in the eye of the beholder. Which is fun for the beholder; but what about the owner, the tenant? Nicola wondered whether she'd ever had a minute's pleasure from it. Even at sixteen, when you're excitedly realizing what you've got (and imagining it will last for ever), you're still noticing what you haven't got, and will never get. Beauty's hand is ever at its lips, bidding adieu. Yes, but bidding adieu *in the mirror*.

'Bang!' said Keith.

'What American men did there – one of the greatest crimes in human history. If you got the world's most talented shits and cruelty experts together, they couldn't come up with anything worse than Bikini. And how do we commemorate the crime, Keith?' She indicated the two small pieces of her two-piece. 'Certain women go about wearing this trash. It's very twentieth-century, don't you think?'

'Yeah. Diabolical.'

'You know those coral lagoons will be contaminated for hundreds of years?'

Keith shrugged. 'Chronic, innit.'

'. . . You're looking very pleased with yourself, Keith,' said Nicola – affectionately, as it might be. 'And that's quite an outfit.'

'Yeah well I'm on a roll,' he said. 'I'm playing tonight.' His head dropped in a bashful reflex, and then he looked up again, smiling. 'Onna darts.'

'Darts, Keith?'

He nodded. 'Darts. Yeah. My confidence is high. I'm oozing confidence.'

Keith went on to rehearse some of his darting hopes and dreams, and told how he planned, shortly, to burst into the arena of World Darts itself. Nicola questioned him keenly; and Keith responded with a certain rough eloquence.

'I know the knockers take the piss, but there's considerable prestige in the sport these days. Considerable. The final's televised. If I taste victory there I go on to play Kim Twemlow, the world number one, before the cameras. Kim Twemlow – the man's like a god to me.'

'I see. Well I'm sure you'll prosper, Keith. And I wish you luck.'

'I – I got all your stuff fixed, uh, Nicola. It come out a bit dear in the end.' He took the invoice – or the piece of paper with figures written on it – from within his darts pouch. 'But forget it. This one's on me.'

'Oh nonsense.'

And she stood up. Keith turned away. She approached. With their shoulders almost touching they looked out over the steamy roof-scape, life's top floor, its attic or maid's room, with washing, flower boxes, skylights and groundsheets, huts and tents and sleeping-bags, and then the lone steeple of the tower block, like the severed leg of a titanic robot.

'Look!' said Keith, and pointed babyishly, with bent forefinger. Immediately beneath them, in a half-shadowed roof-ridge, water had been able to gather and remain. Birds played in the pool. 'Like . . .' Keith grinned fondly. 'It's like birds playing in a pool.'

'*Like* birds playing in a pool, Keith?'

'You know. Girls. Playing in a swimming-pool.'

'Ah yes.' Nicola thought of the kind of video Keith might occasionally get his hands on. The white villa, the baby blue of a Marbellan swimming-pool, the handful of topless English slags, 'playing': my, how they frolicked on diving-board and lilo! Then, as the music modulated, one or two or three of them would slip away, with or without Manolo the gardener, for the lucratively backbreaking siesta. 'Let's go down,' she said.

They entered a world of blackness, and moved heavily through the heat from room to room. One by one they activated coffee-grinder, vacuum-cleaner, flat-iron. All worked – all were renewed. All would break down again, of course, as they both knew, within a few hours. For the backroom boys at GoodFicks were destiny artists, were reality tinkerers, also, in a way, bending the future to serve their own ends.

Nicola asked Keith what she owed him, and Keith spread his hands, Hindu-style. Leaving him in the passage (and feeling the force of his blue eyes on her rump), she went to the bedroom, and closed the door behind her. She took a thick roll of fifty-pound notes from beneath the mattress. Then she slipped her feet into her tallest white high heels, which were there by the bed, waiting. Standing in front of the mirror she felt, in succession, like a chorus girl, like a horse, like a cartoon. Suddenly she was obliged to muffle a sneeze of laughter – wincing, horrified, but definitely laughter, laughter that showed signs of slipping off its ratchet and out of control. Was she just mad? Was that what it was? The same body, the same mirror, the same pair of eyes: tears and laughter within the space of forty-five minutes, all very dangerous, dangerous. Across the street was a dead house whose windows were corrugated metal. On its door was a white sign bearing red letters: DANGEROUS STRUCTURE. This was her body. This was her plan.

Lightly Keith accepted the money and folded it into the pocket of his toreador pants. He took one step backwards down the stairs and then halted and looked her up and down with maximum insolence. 'Well,' he said slowly. 'Now I'm at it. Got you fixed up. Is there – is there anything else you like me to do for you?'

'You mean sex?' said Nicola, glancing at her watch. 'We'll see, Keith. All in good time. First some questions. You're married.'

'Not really. Put it like this. My wife thinks she is. But me I'm not so sure.'

'Children?'

'No. Well, yeah, I got a little girl. She's not even one yet.'

At this point the intercom buzzer sounded, with timid brevity, like a snatch of Morse. Nicola ignored it and said, 'I expect you could use some money, couldn't you, Keith, particularly now?'

'Yeah. Absolutely.'

'Can you keep your mouth shut, Keith? Do you have to run and tell the boys about all your good times?'

He coughed and said, 'No way. Never do that.'

'All right,' she said sternly. 'Unimaginable treats await you, Keith. Forget about everything you've had before. This will be a different *class.* Sweetheart, don't look so worried! I'll expect certain things in return. You know what I mean. The qualities of patience and coolness, Keith, that I imagine you apply to your darts. Are you going to trust me? We're going to do this at my speed. All right? '

'You're on.'

'Take these.' She handed him a shower attachment and a book, a paperback. 'You don't have to do anything with them. They're props. They're just props.'

'Who's that?' said Keith warily, for the buzzer had sounded again: the merest blip.

'The first test of your discretion is on his way up the stairs,' she said, pressing her thumb down on the release. 'Remember: why should *he* have all the money? Watch.' With terrible intentness she placed the roll of money into the prow of her bikini bottoms, and patted it. 'Keith! It looks like – it looks like a . . .'

'Yeah.'

'It looks like a . . .' Five minutes ago she had been close to hysteria. But now the hysterical lilt in her voice, although hideous to her own ears, was entirely willed. 'It looks like a gun-barrel in a holster, doesn't it, Keith!'

'Uh . . . yeah.'

'Here.'

In a slow glaze he reached out with the back of his hand. The trembling knuckles.

'Don't touch,' she said, and stood her ground.

And he didn't touch. He just touched the material, and the money.

When she arranged this meeting with Guy, over the telephone, Nicola stressed the need for commando or bank-caper synchrony ('Unpunctuality throws me utterly. It's tiresome, I know. The orphanage, perhaps . . .'); but this didn't stop her keeping him waiting for a good fifteen minutes ('Please sit down!' she called from the bedroom. 'I do apologize'). She needed fifteen minutes. One to envelope her bikini in a plain white cotton dress. Another to give the bedclothes a fantastic worrying. What was the delightful phrase in *Lolita*: the guilty disarray of hotel linen suggesting an ex-convict's saturnalia with a couple of fat old whores? The rest of the time Nicola needed for makeup. Out came the actress palette; on went the actress bulbs. A profound and turbulent postcoital flush was the effect she was after. She even cobbled together the imprint of a punch or a hefty slap on her right cheekbone. (This was surely going too far; but then that was the idea, wasn't it, to go too far?) Her hair she vigorously tousled. It was ironic, sweetly ironic: because in fifteen minutes she could have straightened hair and bedding, had they needed straightening, and powderpuffed away the very plumes and blotches with which she now lewdly and firily daubed her face. But that's art. Always the simulacrum, never the real thing. That's art.

Nicola emerged from the bedroom in a subtle hobble, patting her hair with one hand and limply fanning herself with the other . . . Guy stood sideways-on at the bookcase. He was holding a slim volume up to his face, arms half-folded, in a posture of clerical perusal. He turned, and looked at her reproachfully.

'I see you have a weakness', he said, 'for D. H. Lawrence. Well I have too. Of course he can be a complete embarrassment. But the *expressiveness* is the thing. In fact,' he went on, looking around brightly, 'I can see many, many shared enthusiasms here. Your fiction shelves are the mirror image of mine. Apart from the Americans. And the astronomy, the popular physics. And you're interested in chess!'

'Fairly interested,' said Nicola.

He turned to her again. She edged forward, extending a lower lip to blow the hair from her brow. Behind her the bedroom door was open and a large movable mirror had been specially positioned, reflecting the bed and its satyr's heaven of throttled sheets and twisted pillows.

'Do you play? Or is it just theory?'

'What?' With bandy-legged gait she came on into the room. Negotiating the round table, she winced twice – deeply private twinges, as if a ghost had gently goosed her. Guy's gaze of polite inquiry did not falter. With low indignation she said, 'Did you meet Keith on the stairs?'

He seemed to need to concentrate for a second before agreeing that he had.

'Keith was just picking up some stuff for me,' she said, and gave her hair a defiant tremor.

Guy's face now showed concern. 'He had a book with him,' he murmured to himself. He heard her exhale, and added, 'I'm sorry. You're tired. And my news isn't terribly encouraging. Would you rather I came back another time?'

Waving a hand at him she flopped on to the sofa. She didn't listen at all as Guy, taking a seat opposite, began chronicling his efforts to locate her friends. It was no surprise to her that the trail had proved cold . . . In truth (though it didn't strike her like this – the truth never struck her like this), she was thoroughly galled. What would she have to *do* to arouse suspicion in this man? If he'd come in and found her lying naked on the sofa with one leg hooked over the back of it, satedly mumbling to herself and relishing a languorous cigarette – he would have assumed she was suffering from the heat. Even if she got *pregnant* she could spin him the line about immaculate conception. God did it. It was God's: the oldest trick in the book . . . Nicola had been looking forward to the series of good expressions with which she would have greeted his jealous bafflement: dawning comprehension, incredulous disgust, definitive dismissal. The time had come, she reckoned, in the interests of variety and elbow-room (and in the interests of interest), to show him something of her temper. But here he was, in his blissful blandness. Perhaps the earlier act had worked too well. Sex with Keith: such morbid perversity was beyond his experience, and was now beyond his imagination. Mind you, it was beyond her experience too: men of the people, men of the British people anyway, had never been her cup of tea. But nothing was beyond Nicola's imagination. Nothing.

So then: Plan B. Quite a significant fraction of her life was now tending to feel like Plan B, and not like Plan A. Guy looked well-aired, and annoyingly sweatless, in his plain blue shirt; whereas the wanton pancake seemed to be thickening in Nicola's pores, and between her legs she could sense the inadmissible cheapness of the white bikini. Well, the B-road would take her – more dully – to the same destination. Perhaps, too, a useful doubt had been subliminally established. Nicola folded her arms. With vengeful frumpishness she watched as Guy talked, the way his expression childishly mimicked his speech, with its soft frowns and hopeful glimmers. And suddenly she thought: maybe it isn't in him. Christ. She had always been sure (it was one of her predicates) that Guy contained a strong potentiality of love, which she needed, because the equation she was working on unquestionably needed love in it somewhere. And if it wasn't the real thing, if it was just a contemporary dilution or simulacrum – friendliness, helpfulness, goody two-shoes love . . . Perhaps love *was* dying, was already dead. One more catastrophe. The death of God was possibly survivable in the end. But if love was going the same way, if love was going out with God . . .

'I don't want to be a total wet blanket,' he was saying. 'The man I know at Index is trying to make contact with a clearing-house in Khorat. There are several avenues still untried.'

The air grew still and silent. Tears had formed on her painted cheeks.

'I'm sorry,' he whispered. 'I'm so sorry.'

'I have a confession to make. Hear me out, and then go away for ever. Oh what a strange, strange life. I never thought it would change – my life. I thought it would just go on, like this. Or I would end it. I never thought I'd meet anyone good enough. And I don't mean beautiful enough or grand enough. I just mean *good*. Good enough. And now it's happened and . . . oh, Guy, I'm so completely thrown.'

She waited (quite a time) until he said, 'Say it.' Then she made her eyes burn with all their green, and said,

'I'm in love. With you. There's just one other thing. I warned you I was a ridiculous person.'

He waited. He inclined his head. He asked, 'What is it?'

She sighed and said with the exasperation of despair, 'I'm a virgin.'

When God got mad he was a jealous God. He said that if she didn't come across at least one more time He'd wash his hands of the whole planet. He had other planets, thanks, and in better parts of the universe. He promised plague, famine, mile-high tides, sound-speed winds, and terror, ubiquitous and incessant terror, with blood flowing bridle deep. He threatened to make her old and keep her that way for ever.

She told Him to fuck off.

To my everything, He is *nothing*. What I am I wish to be, and what I wish to be I am. I am beyond God. I am the motionless Cause.

Cross that firebreak, and then cross that one. Go too far in all directions. Extremity upon extremity, and then more extremity, and then more.

The moment I set eyes on him I thought Keith Talent was an anachronistic kind of character. I thought that time and inflation and the new demographics would have mopped him up by now or sent him somewhere else: to the North, or at least to the suburbs. Not so. The streets are full of jokers, dodgers, jack-the-lads and willie-the-dips – whole crews of Keiths . . . Of course, hardly any of them will make it, will win through to the Cavalier, the printed brochure, the dreams of darts. They will stay out there on the street until whenever, in dumb hats and seam-busted zootsuits, looking fantastically greedy and devious, and fooling no one.

Fagin himself would have nothing to do with them. He'd be horrified. And these are the best and the brightest (and Keith is the best and the brightest of the best and the brightest). The others are yokels and village idiots, turnip-swaggers, ditch people – but this is London; and there are no fields. Only fields of operation and observation, only fields of electromagnetic attraction and repulsion, only fields of hatred and coercion.

Only force fields.

Keith is anachronistic, too, in this matter of his libido. He's not in the satyromaniac league (and the satyromaniacs, I guess, will always be with us). He's an obsessional tailchaser of the type that was meant to have died out years ago. He drools and slurps at everything remotely bim-like on the street; he regales the entire pub with the things he does to Analiese Furnish and Trish Shirt; he'll even give you fifteen minutes (no berk protocols here) on how it went with Kath the other night. On top of all this he makes no secret of his heroics in the handjob realm. And on his diet I'm amazed he even gets around.

Is it just me, or does Keith's hormonal tumult have something to do with reduced life-expectancy? Never very extensive when looked at against an historical mean, Keith's life is now doubly compressed, condensed – and therefore speeded up. His life is on fast-forward, or picture-search. It's not just the animals who aren't living so long.

Now they're briefer still, but animals have always lived brief lives. What we take from animals, what we take from our pets (without trying, and without asking), is a lesson about death: an overview of the shorter span. After two cats and nine hamsters, the adolescent is a bit better equipped for the awful call to his grandmother's bedroom.

We're all keeping step, just about. At eight years of age, Clive is already an old, old dog.

To the movies with Lizzyboo Broadener. Lizzyboo: Hope's big little sister, taller, blonder, rounder faced, fuller figured. Lizzyboo's breasts are a family joke. Ah, those family jokes. Ah, those secondary sexual characteristics – those SSCs! This is the big question about Lizzyboo's breasts: where did they come from? No other Broadener, past or present, has got Lizzyboo's breasts. Hope hasn't got Lizzyboo's breasts. She makes do with Hope's instead, which are a whole lot smaller. It was felt (the family joke continues) that Marmaduke might give Hope Lizzyboo's breasts, or at least make Hope's bigger. But there's Marmaduke for you – disobliging to the last. When Marmaduke was done with Hope's breasts, they were mauled and drained and chewed and tugged all right, but no bigger. A lot sorer – but no bigger. And there's childless Lizzyboo (thirty-one, and just starting to worry) with her beautiful twins. It's very hot still, and she wears just a sleeveless T-shirt on the way to the flick. The clear lineaments of her embarrassing perfection spread agony on the street. The guys can't take it. She makes Keiths of us all – or everyone except me, everyone except the man at her side, who doesn't dare look. The SSCs on her. Will you look at those SSCs.

It was an old horror film, from the Seventies, a piece of shit called *The Dorm That Dripped Blood*. Various coeds got sliced up in their underwear. Chainsaw, hunting-knife, straight razor. The slicer was some species of ghoul, demon or zombie – definitely a dead guy at any rate – with a grudge against the Dean. He looked like a normal fat janitor most of the time, until he neared naked or lightly-clad female flesh: then the inner mutant burst out, rippling with worms and maggots and the usual appurtenances of the grave. I identified. Especially when, during a supposedly scary bit, Lizzyboo took my hand in hers. Hers is a warm hand, a light hand. I would have been more grateful for it, if I hadn't been dying. Her hand stayed where it was, well after *The Dorm That Dripped Blood* had stopped being scary, well after the ghoul had been torched and staked. The lights came up and she turned to me with her whole body and took her hand back with slow care. Her mouth was open. God, the wonder of female teeth.

'What did you think?' she asked, really wanting to know.

She likes me. She digs me. Why? I have one or two ideas on this. Mainly she likes me because Hope does too. I detect considerable sexual influence, or sexual plagiarism, between these sisters. Lizzyboo may be the kind of girl who isn't quite sure who she likes until prompted by a larger approval. I felt this approval, even as we walked to the movie, the image of Guy and Hope looming in the air behind us (smiling encouragingly, her hand resting on his shoulder), like parents. Secondly, of course, I am generally retiring with the ladies, and this has a lulling effect, especially on very pretty blondes with big SSCs, accustomed as they are to living in a garrison of hard-on and hairtrigger. I have never screwed around (why *not*, God damn it?) and I have never minded not screwing around (until now), and I think it shows. I'm certainly unlikely to have any of those unpleasant diseases. Thirdly – or maybe this is just point 2(b) – I'm not interested. Which is always a come-on. Genuine lack of interest is bound to work in your favour. And when you're dying (I find), you really have no problem playing it cool.

After our kiddie movie we enjoyed milkshakes in a café on Kensington Park Road. It's all very difficult. She likes me. She puts a hand on my forearm for emphasis. She practically wets herself at all my jokes. She brandishes those SSCs. Lizzyboo digs me, which is just as well, because if she wants to find the way to my heart she's going to need a fucking shovel. She's going to need to dig up London Fields. Lizzyboo is so pretty and keen and affectionate and straightforward that I'll have to come up with a really world-class excuse.

Got some good stuff about Guy's crush on her. Then I said I had to go home and work on my novel.

*

No word yet from Missy Harter, or from Janit Slotnick, or indeed from Barbro McCambridge. The minute after I Fed-Exed the first three chapters off to Hornig Ultrason (at trouncing expense) I sat there by the phone waiting for it to ring – to ring, to bounce about on its cradle, like in a cartoon. But three days now and nothing.

A terrifying night in Brixton, watching Keith's darts match at the Foaming Quart. I lay down my life or what's left of it for this lousy novel and do I get any thanks?

Pretty well every day now, at noon, I walk or drive to the tower block of Keith Talent, to take Kim off Kath's hands for an hour or two, to look after Kim – to protect and to cherish little Kim. Talent himself is rarely at home when I call. He is out cheating. He is at the Black Cross. He is in his garage, in his cave of darts. When I do run into him on these occasions he wears a hostile leer. Kath blinks up at me when I enter. She is sitting at the table with her head in her hands. I hope she will feel some benefit soon. But misery seems to have a way of making you forget what the other stuff is like, which is probably just as well, from misery's point of view, or you wouldn't put up with it. Sometimes you're down, and sometimes you're down. The rough with the rough. For worse and for worse.

'Hi,' I said as I squeezed into the kitchen (Keith having passed me wordlessly at the door).

'Oh, Sam.' She stood up – she paused. The aftermath of Keith's heavy breakfast still crowded the small table (which in turn filled the small kitchen): fat mug of cold tea, grease-furrowed plate, V-sign of cigarette butts in the dollop of brown sauce. Crazily Kath surveyed all this.

'Why don't I take Kim out.'

'Yes. That's best.'

The child raises her arms to me as I lean to take her. She got used to me very quickly. I smoothtalked her into it. She came across. I have this way with chicks. Of course I don't want anything from her. Though the tales she could tell . . .

I carry her to the Memorial Park – to the park, with its punks and drunks. I'm not really worried. The adult-and-infant combination is a relatively safe one; you don't get bothered, or not much anyway. Baby-related muggings have fallen off. The guy bending over the pram whispering threats with a broken beer bottle in his fist – now this is not a popular kind of guy. In slum-and-plutocrat Great

Britain, so close to the millennium, he isn't popular, he is doubly unpopular; no one's behind him. Sentences reflect this. It's not worth it, for what the average mum has in her purse. So it doesn't happen. Or not much anyway.

What impresses and stays with me is the power of the baby's face – *the power*. It is knit tight, like a tautly prominent navel, chockful of possibilities, tumescent with potentiae, as if the million things that could happen to her, the essences of the million Kims there might one day be out there, are concentrated in this powerful face . . . But I wonder. Nicola's face is powerful too. The very thinness of the skin that coats her closed eyes is powerful. Perhaps with her the effect is reversed or diametrical. Because Nicola's face, Nicola's life, contains only one future, fully shaped, fully designed, toward which she now moves at steadily climbing speed.

So the municipal gardens, the *harijan* flowers, the pastel totems of the playground (how do we interpret them?), the untouchable youths in their spikes, the meteorology of the sky, the casteless old wedged into benches, and the baby with her sweet breath and faceted roundnesses, as tender as an eyeball. You wouldn't want to touch her. You wouldn't want anything to touch her.

Chapter 9: Doing Real Good

WEARING HOUSECOAT AND slippers, and carrying her mail in her armpit, Hope Clinch strode out on to the terrace, mechanically pausing to chuck a potted plant under the chin. The plant was an amaryllis, and had cost considerably more than the average weekly wage; but it wasn't thriving. It wasn't working. Soon it would have to be returned – by Melba or Phoenix, or by Lizzyboo, perhaps – to the dishonest florist for replacement or repair.

She sat at the table and opened her first letter. Looking down, she said, 'I just talked with Melba. About Lady Barnaby. Disaster.'

Guy had looked up from his crossword. He was still wearing his white cotton nightie. Guy often slept in a nightie. Hope had found this endearing for a while, fifteen years ago. 'Oh yes? Tell,' he said.

Beyond their garden lay the communal green, moistly overgrassed in every season – but not in this season. Guy knew what female dogpee did to lawns; and it seemed to him that a bitch the size of a behemoth might have caused those swathes of brown. But dogs were not allowed in the communal garden. It was just the September sun that was doing it. The sun! Guy shut his eyes and wondered how something ninety million miles away could turn his lids into a Hockney swimming-pool awash with fresh blood . . . Out on the lawn, like milkmaids at work, small children played among the fat guards and fatter nannies, who lowed about them, urging caution. Marmaduke was not to be seen there. He was in his nursery, trying out a new au pair. They listened to his hearty ululations – Tarzan, as it might be, showing Jane how it went on the lianas – flinching every few seconds to the sound of some egregious collision. Guy smiled promptingly at his wife's bowed head. The marriage was there (breakfast being its chief sacrament), like the crockery on the awkward table, waiting to be invaded.

'The Yugoslavia trip,' said Hope, opening another letter and reading it. 'She arrived in the middle of the night. For some reason the plane went via Oslo. The next morning she was cleaned out by the cabbie who drove her to the hotel. Only it wasn't a hotel. You expect a toilet but this was ridiculous: some kind of barracks full of mad thugs.' Hope opened another letter and started reading it. 'At this point she completely flipped. No one knows quite what happened next but she was found a couple of days later wandering around Zagreb airport without any bags and without her *glasses*, which I feel kind of badly about.'

'Marmaduke.'

'Marmaduke. Someone at the consulate shipped her back. She got home and the house had been stripped bare. Melba says there's nothing there except floorboards and paint. Then she apparently passed out. But luckily she came to on the stairs just before the boiler exploded. It's still under a ton of water over there.'

'How frightful. Is there anything we can do? Where is she now?'

'In hospital.'

'Insurance?' asked Guy doubtfully.

Hope shook her head. 'She's wiped out.'

'My God. So her marvellous young man –'

'Wasn't so marvellous.'

'. . . You can't trust anyone these days,' said Guy.

'You never could,' said Hope.

Now here came Marmaduke. Defeatedly watched by the stunned au pair (her presence diluted to a mere reflection in the glass), the little boy erupted through the double doors. Although Guy and Hope responded with grooved swiftness, Marmaduke was not to be denied. Surmounting Guy's challenge he harpooned himself face first into the table leg before Hope had a chance to lift the tray. Then the world rocked: broken glasses, chipped china, childblood, spilt milk, spilt milk.

Saddened as he was by Lady Barnaby's recent reverses, Guy easily succeeded in keeping a sense of proportion. After all, when it came to tales of extremity in strange lands – disorientation, shelterlessness, blinded decampment – he couldn't help but feel he was playing in a higher league. Well, not playing, just watching: a pale spectator among tens of thousands, high up in the bleachers.

All week he had been driving into Cheapside, quite early, and closeting himself in his office with his coffee and his four telephones. He dialled. His voice knew the circularizing tones of charity, the quiet cajolery of good works. Bad works are all about money. So are good works. But of bad works he was ignorant: and he knew it. Of course, you said the word Indochina and at once you caught the sound of breath escaping through telephone teeth – right through the receiver's helix and into your own inner ear. 'Forget about everywhere else,' said his contact at Index, with a brio to which Guy was not yet attuned. 'Forget about West Africa and Turkmenistan. This is the shitstorm.' He'd had no idea. Nobody had any idea. It seemed that there was no *idea*. Faced with this, and confusedly feeling the need of some bold and reckless act, Guy went out and bought some cigarettes, and sat there awkwardly smoking as he dialled.

Why was he doing this? Like everybody else, Guy had little appetite for the big bad news. Like everybody else, he had supped full of horrors, over breakfast, day after day, until he was numb with it, stupid with it, and his daily paper went unread. The expansion of mind, the communications revolution: well, there had been a contraction, and a counter-revolution. And nobody wanted to know . . . Why am I doing this? he wondered. Because it's good? Thought – consecutive thought – ended there. In his head Guy had rescreened his lunch with Nicola so many times that the film was worn thin, and pocked with the crud and curds and queries that tarnish tired eyes. He could see her throat, her moving lips. On the soundtrack her voice remained virginally clear, with its foreignness, its meticulous difficulty. She said she had Jewish blood in her. When Guy tried to pinpoint the attraction he thought not of her breasts, not of her heart, but of her blood, and her blood's rhythmic tug on him. What could you do with someone's blood? Smell, it, taste it, bathe in it? Make love to it. *Share it.* Perhaps you could put this down to protectiveness, which always contains something fierce, something animal. Was that what he was after? Was he after her blood?

Though planetary and twentieth-century, and entirely typical of both, the events in Indochina demanded to be thought of astronomically. To begin with, they were obscure, distant, they were deepest black. The Proxy War had put a curve on things when both sides agreed, or when 'both sides agreed', to play their game in the dark. This condition they quickly brought about by a declared policy, much publicized in the press and on television, of killing all journalists. No longer could the foreign correspondents hop from foxhole to foxhole with their MEDIA tags in their hatbands and then telex their stories over cocktails from the garden rooftops of scorched Hiltons. In response, rogue camera crews chartered jeeps and choppers; malarial war-freaks climbed out of opium bunks and firmed up their stringerships; one-legged photographers with lumps of Ho's shrapnel still lodged in their brainpans stood on border roads with their thumbs in the air. They went in, but they didn't come out. Guy smoked and flinched and rubbed his eyes, and wondered whether anyone could really bear to watch.

What came out came out slowly or wrongly or weakly, like tired light. On the one hand the monosyllabic affirmatives or distracted giggling of survivors thrown clear by the crash or the blast; on the other, the unsleeping testimony of the satellites, triumphantly affectless, seeming to exclude everything human from their diagrams of the dead – corpse fields, skull honeycombs. This was a new kind of conflict; *spasm war* and *unfettered war* and, unavoidably, *superwar* were among the buzzwords; *proxy war* because the world powers seeded it and tested weapons systems in it and kept each other busy with it; but the money was coming from Germany and Japan (and China?), and other brokers of the balance of power. 'If you want to get an idea of what's happening there,' said his informant at the Red Cross, 'read an account of what the Khmer Rouge did in the Seventies and multiply everything by ten. Body count. Area involved. No. Square it. Cube it.' Guy did just that. And here was the astronomical. Because if millions were circling in the vortex of war, then other millions needed to know whether they were living or dead, and if there were millions who cared for the millions who cared, then pretty soon . . . pretty soon . . .

He had never felt more alive.

He had never felt happier – this was the ugly truth. Or not for many, many years. He came home in the evening to his wife's surprised approval (he suddenly had value after his day at the office – novelty value, as well as the usual kind) and to Marmaduke's derisory atrocities. He fixed Hope's drink and took it to her at the dressing-table and kissed her neck, his mind on other things, other necks. It was drunk-making stuff all right, an excitation that sparkled the way her tonic did when it hit the ice. She patted his office cheek and smoothed his calculator brow, confident that he was out there making money. And what was he really doing? Guy had need of the great chaos he had tuned into. Feel the tug of mass misery and you want more – more misery, more mass. You have to get addicted. No wonder everybody on the sidelines had the urge to paint it black.

'Tough day?'

'Not really.'

'Poor you.'

Poor them. But good, good! His motives didn't bear inspection, not for an instant. He thought (when he thought) that he was learning something about life, which always meant death. He thought he had a chance to do real good. His motives didn't bear inspection. Nor did they get any. Love, of all things, saw to that – modern love, in some wild new outfit. I've got enough now, surely to God. Call her tomorrow then, he thought, as he zipped Hope up.

Guy was coming along nicely. He was doing real good.

Lost, then, in his new mood of exalted melancholy, Guy climbed the stairs to Nicola Six's door – past the prams and bikes, the brown envelopes, the pasted dos-and-don'ts of parenthood, citizenship, community. He paused halfway up, not for rest but for thought. You know of course that it's a myth or half-truth about the inexorable prosperity of the Asian subculture in the United States. The first wave of mostly middle-class Vietnamese – they did well, right enough. But the next lot, the Cambodians: just imagine. The last time you saw your house it was a hundred feet off the ground and in flames, with your mother and your father and your six children inside it. You'd need time to recover from that. After that, you'd want a rest before taking on America. And presumably the next batch, if it ever comes, the next batch will be even more . . . As Guy went on up he heard somebody coming down: a sniffling, shuffling figure, with heavy boots. Guy stood to one side on what he assumed to be the penultimate landing, his chin abstractedly upraised. And all this was on top of the crisis, or rather *beneath* the crisis, under its wing. This idea of the delegation of cruelty . . .

'Hello, mate.'

'– Keith . . . Sorry, I'm half-asleep.'

'I know the feeling.'

But Keith did look different. And it wasn't just the liontamer getup and the freshly blowdried hair. Actually these extras seemed to go against the new slant of his presence, which was one of furtiveness or humility. He stood on restless legs with his head bowed, clutching some sort of bathroom attachment to his chest – and a book, a paperback. Neither was Guy empty-handed. He couldn't deliver two grateful refugees, but he had a present with him, a present for Nicola Six. He had thought long and fervently about this present. What could he buy her? A Titian, a yacht, a diamond as big as the Ritz. Guy had wanted to buy her the earth, but he had bought her a globe. Not the old kind: the new kind. A literal globe, the planet as seen from space, heavy, mysterious, baby-blue in its shawls. He held it, like Hamlet.

Suddenly Keith shrugged and wagged his chin sideways and said, 'I just been – helping out.'

'Yes of course. That's what I'm here for too.'

'Same difference.'

'I'm trying to help her trace someone. Without much luck, as it happens.'

'Still. You do what you can.'

'Exactly.' Guy looked at Keith now with pitying fondness. Poor Keith . . .

'Oh yeah. You coming tonight?'

'I'm sorry?' said Guy.

Keith stared at him with full hostility. 'To the darts.'

'The darts, yes. Of course. Absolutely.'

'BMW. Mercedes 190E. 2.5–16. Uh, it's up there, mate.'

And Keith shuffled and sniffed and hurried off down the stairs – with that *book* under his arm . . .

Guy called her name in the passage, and advanced with respectful evenness of tread. The sitting-room was empty. It was also much as he had imagined: interesting disarray beneath a lowish ceiling (tall Guy warily sensed a certain pressure on his crown), a teacup here, a foreign magazine there, past-their-best tulips collapsing over the sides of a glass bowl (as if seasick), a certain indolence in the furnishings, the usual pistol-grips and worn webbing of too much video equipment (his own house was a Pinewood of these inexpensive toys), the tobacco tang of thoughtful bohemianism. On the table beneath the window, by the wicker chair, an unfinished letter . . . 'Nicola?' he said again, with a light shake of the head. Her voice, somewhat muffled, responded from the neighbour room with a patent untruth: she said she wouldn't be a second. He glanced uncensoriously at his watch, and stood to attention with his hands behind his back. After a while he moved to the window and looked backwards over his shoulder and then sideways at the writing pad. 'Dear Professor Barnes,' he read. 'Thank you for sending me Professor Noble's paper, which I'm obliged to say I found misleading and shoddily argued. I take his word for it that artists often have sexual relations with their subjects. One is amply persuaded that such things happen. But his anecdotes can have no useful bearing on the representational argument. I was on pins, wondering when he was going to say that Rembrandt's portraits of Saskia – or, perhaps, Bonnard's of Marte – were "suffused" with sexual knowledge, or reflect on the painter's yearning to "get inside" his sitter, or recliner. Such coarse speculation is where this line always leads. To lend a personal note,' read Guy, completing the page. His hand reached out to turn it. But then he desisted with a soft shudder. She knows about art, he thought bracingly. And a beautiful hand: not as strictly elegant as Hope's, rounder, more expressive, with something of Lizzyboo's feminine corpulence. It abruptly occurred to Guy that he had never done anything like this before. He had never been alone with a woman of his own age in the place where she lived, and in secret, without Hope knowing. Nicola's sitting-room was 'much as he had imagined'. What, exactly, *had* he imagined? He could claim, perhaps, that his reveries were chaste. But his dreams went their own way. Well, he thought, we can't help dreaming what we dream. Guy swept his gaze round to the bookcase and approached it with brisk relief. He took out *The Rainbow* and looked at its opening page. What was it Keith had with him? Ridiculous. Slipped my mind. *Villette? The Professor? Shirley?* No, much more obvious but not *Jane Eyre . . .*

I see. She's obviously been crying, Guy said to himself as Nicola stepped out of the bedroom. Her colourful face addressed him declaratively – saying what, he didn't know. It didn't strike Guy that her erectness at such a moment was unusual, because Hope was like that too: she always addressed you with her tears, or their aftermath; she would never cringe or hide. Looking past Nicola for an instant Guy saw in the mirror the sorry anarchy of neglected linen. Yes: the habitat of deep, deep depression. My God, look! – the poor creature can hardly walk. Such disorientation in the tread. And the suffering face, seeming to flex from inner pain. Mm. Nasty welt or spot on the cheekbone there. Of course these days even the most radiant complexions . . . She'll bump into that table if she's not careful. Whoops. It's the same thing I always have with her, the urge, the need to reach out and steady her, if I dared.

'It's so *hot*,' she said, as if in accusation.

'Yes I know,' he said apologetically.

For a while Guy attempted some praise of her bookshelves, and there were other marginalia (chess, Keith, the heat again); but it seemed heartless to tug on these tenterhooks. As gently as he could, he began. And her presence, her force field, went quite dead as it withstood the first volley of the disappointments he had brought her. With her hands clasped on her lap she sat bent forward on the sofa, the bare knees together, the ankles apart but the toes almost touching, like a child in the headmaster's study. Nicola's full face never flickered – except once, maybe, when he mentioned the man at Greenpeace, in whom the name Enola Gay had briefly rung a bell, another lead that led nowhere. It was almost a deliverance when grief came and those slow tears, astonishingly bright, began to map her cheeks.

'I'm sorry,' he said. 'I'm so sorry.'

A minute passed and then she said, 'I have a confession to make.'

As she made it, as he heard it, a series of soft explosions, of intimate rearrangements, seemed to take place in the back of his skull. Delicious and multiform, a great heaviness exerted itself on him – the force of gravity, reminding you of all the power you need just to lug this blood around.

'One other thing. I warned you I was a ridiculous person . . .'

It was thrown out, with baffled impatience. Guy smiled to himself. Palely, inwardly, Guy smiled, and said, 'I guessed as much.'

'You *what*? I'm sorry I . . . I didn't know people could tell.'

'Oh yes,' he said calmly. 'In fact it's quite obvious.'

'Obvious?'

He had long guessed it, he now felt, the pinkness and purity of Nicola Six. And after all it wasn't such a rare strategy, not in these cautious times, these times of self-solicitude. It made sense, he thought – it rang true. Because if you took Hope away then Nicola and I are the same. Virgin territory. Guy was now feeling the novel luxury of sexual experience. He had never knowingly met anyone less experienced than himself; even Lizzyboo, with her four or five unhappy affairs, struck him as an amatory exotic (love-weathered), like Anais Nin. And this might even mean that I will be able to love safely . . . But where did the contrary impulse come from? What alternate message from what alternate world was telling him to wrench open that chaste white dress, to take that brown body and turn it inside out?

'Only that you have this dark glow to you. Something contained. Untouchable.'

In pathetic confusion she stood with her hands still clasped and moved towards the window. Guy groaned, and got to his feet, and crept up behind her.

'Is this for me?' she asked. The globe stood there on her desk. She turned to him and raised both hands to her cheeks. 'It's still quite pretty, isn't it?'

'My dear, you're —'

'No, not me. The earth,' she said. 'Please go now.'

'. . . May I call you tomorrow?'

'Call me?' she said through her tears. 'This is love. You don't understand. Call me? You can do what you like to me. You can kill me if you like.'

He raised a hand towards her face.

'Don't. That might just do it. I might just die if you touch me.'

Over breakfast the next morning Hope informed Guy that the car had been done again and he'd have to take it in. Guy nodded and went on with his cereal (the car got done about once a week). He watched his wife as she flowed up and down the kitchen in her dressing-gown. Previously, if she had known *everything*, she might have called a psychiatrist. But now, after yesterday, she might feel justified in calling a lawyer, a policeman . . . As he got up to go Guy felt the need to say something to her.

'What are those pills you're taking? Oh. Yeast.'

'What?'

'Yeast.'

'What about it?'

'Nothing.'

'What are you talking about?'

'Sorry.'

'Christ.'

The car got done about once a week. In the street Guy opened the door of the VW (it was never locked) and covered the broken glass on the driver's seat with the sign that said STEREO ALREADY GONE. He drove to the garage in St John's Wood. Before he climbed out he removed the service book from the frazzled wound in the dash where the stereo used to be (years ago). The usual shrugs and nods. As Guy waited for the usual unreliable promise he might have reflected on how easy the Other Woman had it: she didn't make you take the car in ever, and she swallowed her yeast in private.

Guy walked down Maida Vale. Having lost their leaves too early, the trees sunbathed, wrinkled and topless and ashamed. London birds croaked in pity or defiance. The sun was doing what it did and always had done, day and night, for fifteen billion years, which is burn. Why didn't more people worship the sun? The sun had so much going for it. It created life; it was profoundly mysterious; it was so powerful that no one on earth dared to look its way. Yet humans worshipped the human, the anthropomorphic. They worshipped promiscuously: anybody. An Indian keep-fit fanatic, an Ethiopian mass-murderer, a nineteenth-century American angel called *Moroni* – Guy's own Catholic God or Nobodaddy. Almost humorous in some lights, the down on her upper lip. The sun was a unit away: an astronomical unit. But today you felt that the sun was no higher than Everest. Not good to be out in it, really. Giver of all life, the sun was now taking life away, the lifetaker, the carcinogenic sun. A trick of perception, or is there a certain spacing in the join of her hips and legs, a curved triangle of free air between the thighs, just at the top? Guy walked on, down Elgin Avenue. He felt happy – in obedience, perhaps, to the weather (and if this sun were rendered in a children's book it would surely be smiling); happy anticipations, happy memories, an embarrassment of happiness. He remembered one morning over a year ago. Yes, he had just burped Marmaduke; in fact the child had been sick on his shoulder (the drycleaning man comes and scratches the corduroy with a doubtful fingernail and you say 'Baby sick', and everyone smiles, forgivingly, everyone understands). I was sitting on the bed with the baby, while she changed or bathed next door. I felt cold suddenly – his sick was cooling on my shoulder – and there was the baby's head, the hair slicked flat with womb-gloss, biospherical, like a world. Or a heavenly body. I felt its heat, the warmth of the baby's head, and I thought (oh these puns and their shameful mediocrity – but I meant it, I really meant it): I've got, I now have . . . I now have a little sun.

148

And God – look out! – the Portobello Road, the whole trench scuffed and frayed, falling apart, and full of rats. Guy could feel the street frisking him – to see what he had and what he might give up. A queue of tramps had formed at the gates of the Salvation Army Hostel, waiting for soup or whatever was offered, the troops of the poor, conscripts, pressed men, hard pressed. Tall, and with clean hair, clean teeth, Guy moved past them painfully, the tramps and their tickling eyes. All he saw was a montage of preposterous footwear, open at the toes like the mouths of horses, showing horse's teeth . . . Once upon a time, the entrance to the Black Cross was the entrance to a world of fear. Nowadays things had changed places, and fear was behind him, at his back, and the black door was more like an exit.

Eleven-thirty, and the moment they'd all been waiting for: heralded by his dog, a plume of cigarette smoke and a volley of coughing, Keith Talent was so good as to step into the Black Cross. Keith's status, his pub twang, always robust, was now, of course, immeasurably enhanced, after the events of the previous night. An interested general murmur slowly coalesced into light applause and then slowly dissipated in fierce, scattered cries of goading triumph. Relief barman Pongo was the most eloquent, perhaps, when, having readied Keith's pint, he extended a plump white hand and simply said: 'Darts.'

'Yeah well cheers, lads,' said Keith, who had a wall-eyed hangover.

'You did it, man,' said Thelonius. 'You did it.'

Keith rinsed his mouth with lager and said thickly, 'Yeah well he crapped it, didn't he. No disrespect, mate, but there's always going to be a question mark over the temperament of the black thrower. First leg of the second set I was way back and he goes ton-forty and has three darts at double 16? When he shitted that I knew then that victory was there for the taking. In the third leg of the vital second set I punished his sixties and then – the 153 kill. Treble 20, treble 19, double 18. Champagne darts. Exhibition. That was probably the highlight of the evening. You can't argue with finishing of that quality. No way.'

'It was a stern test,' said Thelonius deliberately, 'of your darting character.'

Bogdan said, 'You responded to the – to the big-match atmosphere.'

'The choice of venue could have posed problems to a lesser player,' said Dean. 'You fended off the . . .'

'You disposed of the . . .'

'Challenge of the . . .'

'Brixton left-hander,' said Thelonius with a sigh.

Keith turned to Guy Clinch, who was leaning on the pintable and watching them with a diffident smile. 'And *you*,' said Keith, coming towards him. 'And *you*,' he said, with prodding finger. 'You handled yourself superb. Handled himself excellent last night. Handled himself excellent.'

Guy gazed gratefully enough into Keith's eyes – which did indeed (he thought) look most peculiar this morning. Keith's eyes contained a bright array of impurities and implosions, together with a vertical meniscus of unshed tears; but the strangest thing about them was their location. The mortified pupils seemed to be trying to put distance between either socket – they were practically in his temples. My God, thought Guy: he looks like a whale. A killer whale? No. Some benignly wheezing old basker. A blue whale. A sperm whale. Yes and with the incredible pallor . . . Guy sipped his drink and listened to Keith's praise, and to the praise of Bogdan, of Norvis, of Dean and Pat and Lance. He inspected their faces for evidence of irony. But all he found was approval, and welcome.

'I never knew,' said Keith, 'I never knew you was so tasty.'

Had there, after all, been that much to it? After his meeting with Nicola, Guy returned home and spent teatime with Marmaduke. Hope was playing tennis with Dink Heckler. He then had a long shower (can be difficult, sometimes, getting all that custard and treacle out of one's hair), changed, and, at about seven, made his entry into the Black Cross. And into a delirium of darts. Banners and hats bearing the legend KEITH, and shouts of 'Darts, Keith!' and 'Keith!', and Keith himself, highly charged, hoarsely yelling '*Darts*!' Outside, two vans revved tormentedly. In they all piled, with the natural exception of Keith, who was relying on alternative transport. 'I'm taking him,' Fucker had said, 'in *that* fucker,' and pointed through the doors at a gunmetal Jaguar. Then Guy got forty minutes in the back of the van, where the whites and the Asians smoked and laughed and coughed all the way, and the blacks silent with unreadable hungers, and half-bottles of Scotch grimly and unquestioningly passed from hand to hand.

'On the way in they was obviously going to start something,' said Dean.

'Really?' said Guy, who hadn't noticed anything untoward, except for the jostling and the raillery, and a great presence, a great heat of bare black muscle. 'How could you tell?'

'They stabbed Zbig One,' said Zbig Two.

'Nothing serious,' said Keith. 'Zbig One? He's all right. Out next week some time.'

The darts contest took place, not in the Foaming Quart proper (with its stained glass and heavy drapes and crepuscular funk), but in an adjoining hall, such was the intensity of the local interest. As Keith said, the fixture had captured the imagination of all Brixton. Standing ankle-deep in sawdust, Guy guessed that the hall had been used recently, and no doubt regularly, as a discotheque and also as a church; less recently, it had served as a school. He just sensed this. There were no especially pointed reminders of the establishments he had attended (their thousand-acre parklands, olympic swimming-pools, computer studios, and so on); but the low stage, the damaged skylights, the Roman numerals of the clock, the quelling wood – all told Guy *school*. A boys' school, too. He looked around (this *did* worry him) and there were no women anywhere . . . Benches had been set out as in an assembly room, many of them tipped over in outbreaks of horseplay, and eventually everyone sat down. But when the match began, with no ceremony, everyone stood up. If everyone had sat down you could have watched from your seat. But everyone stood up. So everyone stood up.

Not that there was a great deal to see, in the way of darts. Keith's opponent was very young and very black, and strikingly combined the qualities of violence and solemnity, the face perfect and polished, and the shaved head holding a tint of violet, like an impeccable penis, impeccably erect. With many hesitations and corrections, two old black men refereed and kept score with chalk and mike. Loping and sidling in electromagnetic shirt and toreador flares, Keith was easily the most coarse and slovenly figure on the stage; but he looked by far the best adapted.

'You wound them up beautiful,' said Dean.

'The hostility of the crowd', Keith agreed, 'put me under pressure. What they didn't know is – Keith Talent *thrives* on pressure.'

'You wound them up beautiful,' said Dean.

'Showmanship innit,' said Keith. 'Sheer showmanship.'

151

The hostility of the crowd, Guy had noticed, was certainly marked. Early on it assumed the form of screaming and coin-throwing and foot-stomping, together with at least three quite serious attempts on Keith's life. Later, though, as Keith's darts told, as the crowd's dream was pricked into nightmare . . . there was much weeping and keening and beseeching (had the women got in here at last?), and Guy watched a man holding a slice of beerbottle to his own neck, muttering fast with his lids half-shut and flickering. On stage, Keith responded – with showmanship. This showmanship consisted of a wide variety of obscene gestures, a series of feinted kicks aimed at the heads of the groundlings, and a habit (especially incensing) of appearing to free, or of actually freeing, his underpants from between his buttocks just as he turned and prepared to throw.

Anyway, after half an hour in the howling bodyheat, with Guy contributing to both the heat and the howl, shouting 'Darts!' and 'Keith!' and 'Darts, Keith!' with more and more licence, it seemed to be generally agreed that the match was over and that Keith had won it. In a flourish of forgiveness Keith turned to his opponent, who advanced on him suddenly with one dart raised like a knife.

'Stabbed himself. In the hand. With his own dart.'

'Passions were running high,' said Norvis.

'Yeah,' said Keith. 'Beyond a doubt he was rueing that costly miss in the second set.'

'Had to be,' said Dean. 'Had to be.'

It was in the carpark that Guy was unanimously held to have distinguished himself. He thought back: the ground's scooped and rutted surface exposed by the line of headlights under the familiar blackness of a London night, and the blackness of the human line in front of the two vans and Fucker's Jag, torches, eyes and teeth, the jink of chains, the smell of petrol or kerosene. At this point Keith himself had fallen silent and hung back, a part of the company enfolding him, their champion or thoroughbred.

'I'd have gone in there myself,' said Keith.

'Nah.'

'Didn't want to give them the satisfaction.'

'True, Dean, true,' said Keith. 'Conserving my energies. Already pondering the quarter finals as such.'

But Guy had gone in there. He made his way forward, with rectilinearity, with giraffe straightness of posture; and the lack of hesitation, the unanswerably clear ring of his voice as he simply said

'Excuse me', and, when the black boy ran at him, 'Don't be a tit', and went on through; and then, once the line had been broken to let him in, how everything just fell away . . . Guy sipped on drink and praise, and wondered. His father had been brave. In the war he had risen to brigadier, but he made his name as a teenage lieutenant in the guerrilla action in Crete, coming down from those hills coated in blood and medals. The night before, Guy had sensed no personal danger. He felt the black crew had something else in mind, something inscrutable. And anyway the carpark and its actors had seemed to occupy no more than ten per cent of his reality. At any moment, with mighty bounds, he could be free. Free, on the mighty bounds, the quantum leaps of love.

'No,' said Keith, peering at him earnestly with his soaking eyes. 'No. You did real good.'

If I'm brave, thought Guy, or brave for now, then what do I feel in the street (the way the air just shakes you down, that *Guernica* of hoboes toes!), and still feel? Not fear, then. Shame and pity. But no fear.

A little later, at Keith's suggestion, they repaired to the Golgotha for a discreet glass of *porno*. The bar was three drinkers deep, and as they waited Keith cocked a tenner and turned sideways to Guy, saying, 'You uh, see that Nicky then?'

Guy considered. He often had trouble with Keith's tenses. 'Yes, I saw her – that time . . .'

'Helping her out.'

'That's right.'

'That's right.'

It couldn't be said that a *silence* fell between them, for there were no silences in the Golgotha. But by the time they reached the bar (where they would remain as long as possible, like everybody else, out of brute territoriality), a hiatus had arrived and now made itself comfortable, getting fatter and fatter and shoving out its elbows.

Guy said, 'I was . . . Sorry?'

'No. You was saying?'

'No. Go ahead. Please.'

'No I was just saying – I can't be doing with all these birds. Saps a man's darts.' Keith coughed for a while and then said tearfully: 'I respect my body. I got to take care of myself. Now. Onna darts. It's tough, with all this spare minge around but you got to draw the line somewhere. You got to.'

153

Edged out from the bar, they stood by a pillar with their drinks, right in the teeth of the snapping steel band.

'You wouldn't believe,' Keith shouted, 'you wouldn't believe what I'm turning down. Take yesterday.'

And as Keith launched into a squalid decameron of recent gallops and tumbles, instant liaisons, valiant cuckoldries, eagerly requited grabbings and gropings, quickies and workouts and hip-twangers and knee-tremblers, Guy reflected – and reflected wryly – on the utter artlessness of the standard male strategies. Class strategies too, he allowed. It would take a stretch of cosmic time before Keith would acknowledge the cosmic distance that separated himself from a woman like Nicola Six. You had to be quite near to see and to feel. After all, if you looked out from the virusless morgue of Pluto (Guy was thinking of the latest *Journeyer* photographs), the sun was no more than an exceptionally bright star, admonitory and cruciform, a bright star – a cold, bright star, like the brandished sword of God, long before you felt its heat.

When he telephoned her early that afternoon (from a Mexican snackbar in Westbourne Park Road), Nicola's voice was everything he had hoped it would be: direct, uncomplicatedly friendly, low with charged warmth – and sane. Yes, he had hoped for the firm clasp of her sanity, because he often feared for that delicate equilibrium. If not too good for this world, she was, in his view, far too good for this time; it was the way he saw her, as an anachronism: a museum piece, time-orphaned . . . She was just dashing off to a lecture (and here Guy screened an image of dedicated hurry, of books crushed to the breast and a length of scarf held up by the breeze), but she did so terribly want to talk to him. Could he very sweetly ring her later this evening, at six o'clock, at six o'clock precisely?

'Of course. What's your lecture?'

'Mm? Um – "Milton and Sex".'

'Well that won't last long,' said Guy, whose humour always came from the overflow of happiness, never from the undertow of irony. In any case, he mildly regretted the remark.

'Actually I think they mean gender.'

'Oh yes. He for God. She for God in him. That kind of thing.'

'Yes. That kind of thing. Must run.'

Guy had the Mexican lady make him up a kind of omelette hero (he hoped to use her telephone many more times) which she put in a

bag and which he guiltily secreted in an empty rubbish basket on
Ladbroke Grove.

'Well what did you think?' said Hope.

'Thank you,' said Guy. He said it, not to Hope, but to the man
whose job it was to monitor – or stand fairly near to – the automatic
checkout of the underground garage beneath Cavendish Square. He
had seen Guy many times now and knew his face. Not that he
appeared to be much bucked by this familiarity, or by anything else
that happened to him down there.

Guy retrieved his credit card and steered them up into the light.
'The *traffic*,' he said.

'Jesus, how many times? Listen: You Are The Traffic.'

'. . . I thought he made a lot of sense.'

'Three hundred *guineas* of sense?'

'On the fresh-air question.'

'I knew you'd say that.'

'If not on the hostility-to-me question.'

'I knew you'd say that.'

The Harley Street doctor they had just consulted was an expert on
infant hypermania. He had seen Marmaduke at his surgery and had
also paid a stunned visit to the house, where, as promised,
Marmaduke was able to relax and be his normal self. Absolutely
impossible at the surgery, Marmaduke had been absolutely unbelievable at home. Even today, nearly three weeks later, the doctor was
still wearing a patch of gauze over his right eye. All parties agreed
that the legal matter need not affect their professional relationship.
Recently, Guy had taken out insurance on Marmaduke-related
personal-injury suits, on what seemed to be highly advantageous
terms. More recently, he had taken out insurance on the insurance.

'On the hostility-to you question,' said Hope, 'I thought he made a
change from Freud.'

'So did I. But I prefer Freud. I'd rather Marmaduke didn't like me
for Freudian reasons. I don't like him not liking me because he just
doesn't *like* me. Why shouldn't he like me? I'm incredibly nice to him
all the time.'

Guy turned his head. Hope was staring out expressionlessly at the
car-crammed street. With some caution he patted her twice on the
knee. Their last real embrace had, in fact, been staged for that very
doctor's benefit – a paramedical embrace, as part of a demonstra-

tion. At home, in the kitchen, Guy had embraced his wife while the doctor looked on. As predicted, Marmaduke dashed the length of the room and sank his teeth into Guy's calf. Requested to tolerate it, Guy tolerated it, and maintained the embrace up to the point where Marmaduke started head-butting the cooker.

'To return to the fresh-air question,' said Guy. 'Or to the half-hour question.' This referred to one of Hope's most controversial rulings: Marmaduke was not allowed outside for more than half an hour a day. 'He seemed to think that an hour was safe.'

'No he didn't. He said it could be regarded as tolerable.'

'It's the confinement. Children like to whirl around. How about forty-five minutes? He needs some fresh air.'

'We all do. But there isn't any.'

There wasn't any. And hard to explain that one away, hard to justify it – to the young (Guy meant), to those who would come after. How would you begin? Well, we suspected that sacrifices might have to be made, later, for all the wonderful times we had with our spray cans and junk-food packaging. We knew there'd be a price. Admittedly, to you, the destruction of the ozone layer looks a bit steep. But don't forget how good it was for us: our tangy armpits, our piping hamburgers. Though maybe we *could* have got by with just roll-ons and styrofoam . . .

'*Look!*' they both cried, in childish unison. They were driving down the Bayswater Road and a sick squirrel stood trembling by the park railings.

Guy and Hope laughed – at each other, at themselves. 'Look!' they had cried – to please Marmaduke. There was the squirrel, leaning on a tree stump, and retching apologetically. But Marmaduke was not in the car. And Marmaduke wouldn't have been pleased anyway, since he showed no interest in animals except as new things to injure or get injured by.

On the stroke of seven Guy called Nicola from a booth in the lobby of a hotel for the homeless in Ilchester Gardens. The Mexican snackbar was closed; but spotting usable telephones had become something of a hobby for Guy Clinch. In this way Nicola kept showing him more life. He stood there poised with his coins. Behind his back filed whole families bearing plates with little suppers on them. Clearly the kitchen was in the basement and everyone ate in their rooms. Guy exhaled in exquisite pity. One and a *half* fishfingers? For a growing boy? And then probably the mothers have to –

He fumbled. 'Hello?' he said. 'Hello? . . . Nicola?'

'Guy? Wait,' said the voice. 'This isn't me.'

'Hello?'

'It's a tape. I apologize, but I didn't trust myself to talk to you unmediated. I didn't trust my resolve. You see . . . Dear Guy, thank you for all the sentiments you have awoken in me. It was wonderful to learn that I *could have* these feelings. My reading, in future, will be much vivified. I shall look at Lawrence with new eyes. My love, if you . . . But I suspect there is something deeply frivolous about pursuing a course that holds so little prospect of good. And that's what we want, isn't it? The good? I'll never forget you. I shall just have to – but no matter. Never make any attempt to contact me ever again. If you had any tenderness for me – and I think you did – then you'll know how absolutely and unconditionally I mean that. If you get news of my friends, well, perhaps a note. I'll never forget you.

'Think of me sometimes.

'Goodbye.'

'Goodbye,' he whispered, after a while.

Nine hours later, at four in the morning, Guy turned the page and said:

'The north wind doth blow, And we shall have snow, And what will poor Robin do then, poor thing?'

Marmaduke looked up from a modern edition of *Goodnight, Moon*, which he was patiently, almost studiously, tearing to pieces. You could read to Marmaduke – it soothed him, or kept him happy or at least busy. But he had to be allowed to tear up the book directly afterwards. Soon he would be tearing up *Mother Goose's Treasury of Children's Rhymes and Fables*. And yet for the moment the child hesitated and his father read on:

'He'll sit in a barn, And keep himself warm, And hide his head under his wing, poor thing!'

Marmaduke watched with his mouth open. The scragged copy of *Goodnight, Moon* fell from his grasp. He got to his feet with a sigh and approached the low chair where Guy sat. He grinned suddenly and reached out a round hand that trembled with approving interest to touch the tears on his father's cheek.

157

Of course, I keep trying to tone Marmaduke *down*. I thought he was funny at first – but really that kid is no joke. He devastates his parents twenty times a day. I censor him. I bowdlerize him too. There's some stuff you just can't put in books.

Turn your back for ten seconds and he's in the fire or out the window or over in the corner, fucking a light socket (he's the right height for that, with a little bend of the knees). His chaos is strongly sexual, no question. If you enter his nursery you'll usually find him with both hands down the front of his diaper, or behind the reinforced bars of his playpen leering over a swimsuit ad in one of the magazines that some nanny has thrown in to him. He goes at that bottle like a top-dollar Vegas call-girl, like a grand-an-hour sex diva. Yeah, that's it. Marmaduke looks as though he is already contemplating a career in child pornography: he knows it's out there, and he can tell that there's a quick buck in it. Naturally he's hell with the help and any other woman who strays within range. He's always got a hand up the nurse's smock or a seigneurial tongue in the au pair's ear.

I wouldn't have thought Lizzyboo was his type but he goes for her in a big way.

Incarnacion and I are the best of friends. There's absolutely no problem, any more, about her talking to me.

'Living alone, you know,' she said today, 'it's all right – it's good.' Queenly Incarnacion lives alone. Her husband is dead. Her two children are grown up. They live in Canada. She came here. They went there. 'You have advantages. When you living alone, you do things when you want. Not when they want. When you want.'

'True, Incarnacion.'

'You want a bath. You have a bath. You want to eat. You eat. You don't need them to say so. It suit you. You sleepy, you want to go to bed. You go to bed. Don't ask. You want watch the TV. Okay! You watch the TV. Up to you. You want a cup of coffee. – Coffee. You want clean the kitchen. You clean the kitchen. You want maybe listen to the radio. You listen the radio.'

Yes, and the same goes for any solitary activity you care to name. But after twenty minutes on the upside of living alone, we get twenty minutes on the downside of living alone, like there never being anyone else around and things like that.

A letter from Mark Asprey.

He mentions a restless desire to pop back to London for a few days, next month sometime. He adduces the wonderful convenience of the Concorde. He allows that it would also be convenient, and pleasingly symmetrical, if I could be prevailed upon to return to New York for those same few days and reoccupy my apartment –which, he adds, he doesn't use much anyway. He drops hints about a certain rather celebrated lady whom it is imprudent to entertain in his suite at the Plaza.

By now an habituated snooper, I have gone through all Mark Asprey's desk drawers. More trophies, but not for public viewing. Under-the-counter stuff. Pornographic love letters, locks of hair (head and nether), arty photographs. The deep central drawer is firmly locked. Maybe it's got a whole girl in it.

I have even looked at some of his plays. They are terrible. Frictionless romances, down through the ages. *The Goblet* has an Arthurian setting. It's all pretty-pretty; but not very pretty. I don't understand. He's one of these guys who hits an awful note and then is uncontrollably rewarded, like Barry Manilow.

Now here's an intolerable thought. I was looking again at Nicola's diaries. She uses initials for her menfriends. The docile GR, the well-fleeced CH. NV, with his suicide bids. HB, who cracked up after his divorce. TD and AP both hit the bottle. IJ, who fled to New Zealand. BK, who apparently went and joined the Foreign Legion. Poor PS, who bought the farm.

159

The only one she kept going back to, the only one who was half a match for her, 'the only one I've ever been *stupid* for', the handsomest, the cruellest, the best in bed (by far): he's called MA. A resident of West London. Connected to the theatre.

I burn no torch for Nicola Six. So why does this thought *kill* me?

It's happened. A call from Missy Harter, or, to be more accurate, a call from Janit Slotnick.

'This is Janit Slotnick? Miss Harter's assistint?' 'Yes yes.' 'Well, sir, there's certainly a lot of excitemint here today at Hornig Ultrason.' 'There is?' 'We know we're paying megamoney for it.' 'You are?' 'Mm-hm. The new book on the death of John Lennin!'

I won't transcribe all the crap she talked about the death of John Lennon. How the KGB did it, and so on.

'Miss Harter wanted to have me call you – about your treatmint.' 'Well it's hardly a treatment, Miss Slotnick. More of an outline. What's the feeling on it?' 'Disappointmint, sir.'

At this point the receiver shot out of my hand like a bar of wet soap.

'. . . agrees that the opening is strong. So is the denouemint.' 'What? The ending?' 'It's the middle we're disturbed about. What happins?' 'How should I know? I mean, I can't tell until I've written it. A novel is a journey, Miss Slotnick. What was the feeling on the first three chapters?' 'We feel they're a considerable achievemint. But we're disturbed, sir. It's a little literary.' '*Literary*? Jesus, you must . . . I'm sorry. I beg your pardon.' 'Sir.' 'I need an advance, Miss Slotnick.' 'I'm not sure we're ready yet to make that kind of commitmint. On this point Miss Harter and myself are in total agreemint.'

I abased myself with promises of cuts, rewrites, tone-downs and spruce-ups until Janit very coolly consented to take a look at chapters four to six.

'And we're unhappy about the names, sir.'

'No problem,' I said. 'I was going to change them anyway.'

Usually it's late at night, now, when I get the call from Nicola Six. One, two. Even three. It's then that she wants to proceed with our debate or battle-plan or script conference. She summons me. I always show.

160

I'm up to it, apparently. Not so long ago I was sleeping like a newborn: I couldn't keep my eyes open for more than five minutes running. Then for a while I slept like a baby: I woke twice an hour in floods of tears. But now I'm really getting on top of my game. Soon I'll be like some coppery old ascetic in the caves of Ladakh, or like Marmaduke: sleep will be something that I can take or I can leave. So, not without difficulty, with night fear, with the heaviness of fatigue indefinitely postponed, I get out there. It's my job.

Three nights ago, or three dawns ago, as I was girding myself for Chapter 9, I got the call around two-thirty and went straight over in the car. She took my coat and hat with a humorous expression on her face. She was dressed up – black velvet – and drinking champagne. One of her private parties. I sat down and ran a hand over my face. She asked me how I was and I told her I was good.

'What are you dying of anyway?'

'A synergism.' See our interdependence? We don't, we can't talk to anybody else like we can to each other. I can look into her eyes and say it.

'Communicable? No. Direct or indirect? Indirect.'

'Non-communicable,' I said. 'But possibly direct. Radiogenic, naturally. They don't know. It's quite an unusual case. You want to hear the story? Takes about ten minutes.'

'Oh yes please. I'm interested.'

'London Fields,' I began.

She knew about the clusters – though of course she didn't know that I was in the centre of the bunch. And she is interested. She is *familiar* with it all. At one point she said, 'Hang on. So your father was working for *her*.' 'Her? Pardon me?' 'HER. High Explosives Research. That's what they called it.' 'Right.' Or again she'd come out with something like 'And plutonium metallurgy. That was another area the British were behind on.' She smoked intently, narrowing her eyes each time she exhaled. One thing about that face: it is always beautifully lit.

'You've really gone up in my estimation,' she said when I was through. 'So in a way you're at the heart of all this. In a way, you are the Crisis.'

'Oh no,' I said modestly. 'I don't think so. I'm not the Crisis. I'm more like the Situation.'

'So you know about Enola Gay.'

'Oh yes. And Little Boy.'

Later, she showed me the 'letter' she'd placed on the table for Guy to read. 'Professors Barnes and Noble,' I said. 'That's a cheap shot, Nicola.'

'It gets cheaper,' she said. 'Read on.'

'". . . Rembrandt's portraits of Saskia – or, perhaps, Bonnard's of Marte – were 'suffused' with sexual knowledge, or reflect on the painter's yearning to 'get inside' his sitter, or recliner. Such coarse speculation is where this line always leads. To lend a personal note . . ."'

'Turn the page.'

'". . . I've sat for perhaps a dozen painters in my life, and slept with most of them, and it never made any difference to anything, not to me, not to them, and not to that thing on the canvas."'

I looked up. She shrugged one shoulder. I said,

'I wish you wouldn't take these unnecessary risks. Very imprudent, what with you being a virgin and all. Still, I take my hat off to your confidence. You just *knew* Guy wouldn't turn the page?'

'Come on. You know, with him, *passive* prying is all right. You don't avoid what's there to see, but it's an indignity to move any closer, to listen any harder. Actually I'm surprised he dared to read a word.'

'Hubris, Nicola. Hubris. Guy is quite capable of surprises, especially where you're concerned. You should have seen him at the darts. Like a lion. I was half-dead with fear. Though I didn't read it right, I now think. There wasn't any real danger, not for us. Those guys, they weren't going to hurt us. They were going to hurt themselves. You're yawning. It's late. But don't you be snooty about the darts. They matter in all this.'

She yawned again, more greedily, showing me her plump back teeth. 'That's why I iced Guy. To concentrate on Keith. God help me.'

I held up the letter. 'Do you mind if I take this?' She shook her head. 'Nicola, what do you think *I'm* up to?'

'I don't know, I suppose you're writing something.'

'And you don't mind?'

'At this stage? No. In fact I approve. Let me tell you something. Let me tell you what women want. They all want to be *in it*. Whatever it is. Among themselves they all want to be bigger-breasted, browner, better in bed – all that. But they want a piece of everything. They want *in*. They all want to be in it. They all want to be the bitch in the book.'

Boy, am I a reliable narrator.

I finally limped to Queensway for a *Trib*.

Two main stories. The first is all about Faith, the First Lady: a remarkably full account, in fact, of her recent activities. I was baffled; but then I remembered the speculation earlier in the summer about Faith's health. Presumably all this stuff about hospice work, White House redecorations and anti-pornography crusading is offered in courteous rebuttal. And as reassurance. Everybody knows how totally the President loves his wife. He campaigned on the issue.

The second main story is puzzling also. Something about the Soviet economy. Lots of human-interest snippets: how it's going down with Yuri in Kiev; what Viktor thinks in Minsk. I had to read the thing twice before I realized what the story was. The Soviet Union is working a seven-day week.

Op-ed pieces about solar disturbances, university prayer, Israel, Mustique and summer-home winterization. Leaders about grain tariffs and Medicare.

In Queensway I encounter the same bag-lady I used to see there ten years ago. Still around! Christ, her *strength*. Still arguing with herself (the same argument). Still arguing with her own breast. She takes her breast out and argues with it.

That lady has an unreliable narrator. Many people in the streets have unreliable narrators.

Watching the children in the park when I go there with Kim – it occurs to me, as I try to account for childish gaiety, that they find their own littleness essentially comic. They love to be chased, hilariously aware that the bigger thing cannot but capture them in time.

I know how they feel, though of course with me it isn't funny, the bigger thing loping along in my wake, and easily gaining.

163

Chapter 10: The Books in Keith Talent's Apartment

K EITH PRESSED THE Pause button and removed from his jacket pocket the book that Nicola had given him. He weighed it in his hand and assessed it from several angles. He read in a deep whisper: 'HE was born a gypsy – and lived and loved like a lord. SHE was the daughter of fashion – and he drove her to her grave.' Keith coughed, and continued: 'The story of Heathcliff's un . . . guvnor . . . ungovernable passion for the sister he never had.' He read on for a while, with much flexing of mouth and brow. Then he looked up and thought: Keithcliff! . . . Of humble origin, success was soon his. Wed to Kathleen, all the birds were on his case. Enjoying plenty on the side, there was one that stood out. Rich and well-born, Keithcliff she craved. And then the day came to pass when she took him to her bed. With ungovernable passion . . . He looked at the front cover; he stood up, and placed Nicola's gift in among his other library books: *Darts*; *The World of Antiques*; *Darts Yearbook*; *Dogs Yearbook*; *On the Double: The Kim Twemlow Story* by Kim Twemlow (with Dirk Smoker); and a brief history – wrapped in polythene and never opened – of the regiment that Keith's father had cooked for, and later deserted from, during World War II. Costume drama, thought Keith. Awful old load of old balls. The class system innit.

TV, thought Keith. VCR. Dynacord. Memorex. JVC. Keith pressed the Pause button and went on watching TV, or 'watching' TV – watching TV in his own way. It was a habit. Every evening he taped six hours of TV and then screened them on his return from the Black Cross, the Golgotha, Trish Shirt's or wherever. At 3 a.m. there would still be live transmissions, some old film, say (in fact Keith was missing a quite salacious and sanguinary *policier*); but he could no longer bear to watch television at the normal speed, unmediated by the remote and by the tyranny of his own fag-browned thumb. Pause. SloMo. Picture Search. What he was after were images of sex, violence and sometimes money. Keith watched his six hours' worth at high speed. Often it was all over in twenty minutes. Had to keep your wits about you. He could spot a pinup on a garage wall in Superfastforward. Then Rewind, SloMo, Freeze Frame. A young dancer slowly disrobing before a mirror; an old cop getting it in the chest with both barrels; an American house. Best were the scenes that combined all three motifs. An oil baron roughing up a callgirl in a prestige hotel, for instance, or the repeated coshing of a pretty bank teller. He also watched major adaptations of works by Lawrence, Dreiser, Dostoevsky, Conrad – and anything else that sparked controversy in the pull-out TV section of his tabloid. For skirt, you often did better with something like *The Plumed Serpent* than you did with something like *Vegas Hooker*. He didn't like all those petticoats, though. No way. Keith's screenings were usually over quickly, but some items, he found, repaid days or even weeks of study. Anything about lady wrestlers. Or women's prisons. The female body got chopped up by Keith twenty times a night: what astronomies of breast and belly, of shank and haunch . . . Now the great thumb moved from Fast Forward to Rewind to Play, and Keith sat back to savour the pre- credits sequence of a serial-murder movie. Bird running through park at night. Psycho hot on her heels.

'Enlah . . . Enlah . . . En*lah.*'

Keith sighed heavily (his lips flapped) as the baby came to life; her assertions, her throaty provisos could be made out in the interstices of shirtrip and headbang. The spooky exiguity of the flat, the startling slenderness of its partitions, often gave grounds for depression. But there was an upside. Keith shouted for Kath and thumped on the wall with his free fist until he heard Kath fall out of bed. These shouts and thumps entrained a relay of counterthumps and countershouts from their nearest neighbours. Keith shouted and thumped some more, reserving a special vehemence, perhaps, for Iqbala's new boyfriend. Kath appeared. She was tired, but Keith was tireder, or so he reckoned. He'd been out until three doing car stereos. Dispiriting work: when you stove in the window bearing the inevitable sticker STEREO ALREADY GONE – on a windy night, with glass everywhere – to find the stereo already gone. Fifteen of them running and you wanted a nice meal when you got in: Sweet and Sour Pork and Six Milford Flapjacks.

'Jesus,' he said.

Five minutes later and Keith was seven or eight murders into his serial-murder movie. He came to a good bit: a very good bit. He rewound and went to SloMo. The redhead climbed from the bath and reached for the – Oi! Hint of pube there. Amazing what gets through, even these days. All you need's a bit of patience. Bit of application. Though when they're just naked though, it's not enough. You want something to – to frame it with. A garter-belt'll do. Anything. Keith's thoughts turned to Analiese Furnish, who, in his judgment, tended to err in the other direction. A bra with two holes in it: looks stupid. Not to mention them pants. All them frills and fringes. Zlike going to bed with a sack of dusters. Now the redhead slipped into a light gown while behind her a shadow straightened. Even that's better than nothing. She still wet so you can see the outline. Here comes the nutter with the mallet. Watch out darling! Boof.

'Keith?'

' . . . *Yeah*?'

'Would you burp her for me? Just for a second?'

'Can't. Watching TV innit.'

'She's got the hiccups and I've come over dizzy.'

It had to be admitted that Kath never bothered Keith with the baby except in the most drastic emergencies. He turned slightly in his chair and reached over his shoulder to open the lounge door. To give Kath her due, she did seem to be on the verge of authentic collapse: down on one knee and leaning backwards against the wall with the baby awkwardly crooked in her grasp.

Keith thought about it. 'Give her here then,' he said. 'Jesus, what's the *matter* with you?'

He sat there watching TV with Kim on his lap. Then he even got to his feet and jogged about a bit, the better to soothe the pulsing child. After at least three minutes of that he started shouting Kath's name as loud as he could until she reappeared with a warmed bottle – and finally Keith got a bit of peace. He rescreened the redhead's murder half a dozen times, and had a proper look at her, with the Freeze Frame. It being Friday, the night when Keith did his chores and generally helped out in the home, he then switched off the TV, put his coffee mug in the sink, aired the dog (or, to be more specific, stood there impatiently while Clive shat all over the walkway), had a quick wash, took off his clothes (leaving them in a neat stack, or at any rate a single pile, on the floor of the lounge), and woke up the wife and gave her one. It took quite a while to wake her up but it didn't take long to give her one, the wet-gowned redhead, Trish Shirt on her knees, Nicola Six and the fat moneygun in her clean white pants.

Keith turned over and lay there furiously wanting services and goods.

When Nicola asked Keith about his romantic discretion, about his ability to keep his mouth shut on the subject of women and sex, Keith coughed and answered in the following terms: 'Never do that. No way.' This was untrue. It was by no means the case. He *always* did that. When it came to kissing and telling, Keith was a one-man oral tradition.

He knew it to be a fault. Ah, he knew! He could tell it was a fault because it kept getting him into trouble. And here was another complicating factor: being the sort of bloke who couldn't get by without a regular bird, even before marriage: someone indoors, taking care of things, and being cheated on. Keith had tried getting by without a regular bird, and his subsequent disintegrations were invariably dramatic. All the more reason to keep your mouth shut, if you could, silence being golden, as they said.

Many times, fresh from a session, and out of sheer habit, he would find himself boasting to the boyfriend or the husband of the woman he was cheating with; alternatively, he would find himself boasting to the father or the brother of the woman he was cheating *on*. Dear oh dear. In the early days of their marriage, he had come to the brink of regaling Kath with hot news of an uncovenanted encounter. Also, and far more seriously (how he suffered for it: the recriminations, the self-hatred), he kept hurrying and botching and underdoing his conquests, such was his eagerness to get back to the pub and give all the details to his mates. He wanted to stop people in the street and tell them about it. He wanted to take out announcements in the tabloids. He wanted it on *The Ten O'Clock News*. Boing. Unemployment: encouraging figures. Boing. Keith Talent fucks another woman: more later. Boing. He wanted to tell everyone everything about women and sex.

Keith loved to kiss and tell. But what could he tell about Nicola?

Not even a kiss. In normal circumstances, lies would have done, and Keith had a paragraph ready in his head (beginning, 'Posh foreign birds are the worst'). But these were not normal circumstances. The conversation Keith wanted and needed would be with God the barman or with Shakespeare, both of whom, like Keith, had a peculiar difficulty with girls. Shakespeare for preference, Shakespeare being more passive and sympathetic a listener, and Shakespeare being more discreet (Shakespeare being, in fact, routinely speechless on drugs or drink). The conversation would go like this – and this is how it went in Keith's head:

'Shakespeare? Listen. I nearly did it. I nearly did it, mate.' 'Bad?' 'Yeah. That close.' 'She aggravate?' 'Yeah. In a bikini innit.' 'You *using* on that, man.' 'Yeah. But you should have seen her. Praying for it.' 'That the single worse thing you can think.' 'Yeah yeah.' 'But you control you aggression.' 'Yeah.' 'You show Restraint and Respect.' 'Yeah. And Regard. Talked myself down.' 'You did good, man.' 'Yeah cheers.'

The peculiar difficulty with girls experienced by God, Shakespeare and Keith was this difficulty: they raped them. Or they used to. They had all been on the same rehab courses and buddy programmes; they had mastered some jargon and tinkertoy psychology; and they didn't do it any longer. They could control their aggression. But the main reason they didn't do it any longer was that rape, in judicial terms (and in Keith's words), was no fucking joke: you just couldn't ever come out a winner, not with this DNA nonsense. The great days were gone. Shakespeare and God had both spent a long time in prison for it, and Keith nearly had. Of his two court appearances on rape charges, the first had been more or less okay ('Why, Jacqui, why?' Keith had hollered woundedly from the dock). But the second case was *very frightening*. In the end the girl dropped charges, thank heaven, after Keith sold his motor and gave three and a half thousand quid to her dad. Of course, Keith's rapes were to be viewed quite distinctly from those numerous occasions when, in his youth, he had been obliged to slap into line various cockteasers and icebergs (and lesbians and godbotherers). Rape was different. Rape was much more like all the other occasions (not so numerous, if you kept Kath out of it) when he had candidly used main force to achieve intercourse and the woman, for one reason or another, hadn't reported him.

Rape was different. And rape capability was what he felt when she

168

loomed above him on the stairs, her legs planted apart and laughing like a madwoman, and he reached out his knuckles and touched. His whole body felt like a human throat, his own, full of hot caffeine, full of tannic, pleading and sobbing for its first cigarette. 'We'll do this at my speed,' she said. No. No, *not* your speed. *My* speed. With the Fast Forward and the Freeze Frame and a bit of the old SloMo near the end. At a man's speed, with none of the brakes women use if you let them. *Rape*, he thought, with abstract terror. Rape is different. It is maximum, like fighting, massively preemptive, with all time gambled or cashed, and nothing mattering. One two three four five six seven eight nine ten. Regard, Respect, Restraint. Lucky there was someone coming up the stairs (who was it? Guy. Guy!). Lucky Trish Shirt lived so near. Lucky for Keith. Unlucky for Trish.

Keith was glad he hadn't. Keith was glad he hadn't raped Nicola. Definitely. He was thrilled about the whole thing. The doublefight of rape, with all it asked of you, the colossal investment of politico-sexual prestige, and the painful regrets (and minor injuries) it often left you feeling, was no kind of preparation for a long game of darts – especially a stern test of your character, such as Keith had faced at the Foaming Quart. Besides, raping Nicola would have been quite unnecessary, as his next visit, the next day, had made – in Keith's view – abundantly clear. Rape, when it happened, was always deeply necessary; and then deeply unnecessary, half a second later.

Finally, there was no money in rape. Show Keith a rich rapist. Go on: just point one out. There was no money in rape. But there was money, it seemed, in Nicola Six.

Financially, this was not a good time for Keith. Few times were, financially. Even during his best periods, his purple patches of epiphanic swiping and stiffing, of fiddling and gypping and duping and diddling, when money was coming in hard from all directions, Keith never had a good time, financially. Always, at some point in the day, a bitter destiny lay in wait for him: pennilessness, at Mecca. Always he lost everything, without fail. Well, sometimes he won; but he always persevered until he had lost everything. Kath, who didn't know the tenth of it, used to ask where all the money went: where did they actually *go*, those tenner-crammed brown envelopes, those toilet-rolls of twenties? For the day usually began and ended with Keith upending her handbag over the kitchen table or banging at the electricity meter with his fists. Where did it all go? Kath had asked this question gently, patiently, and not recently. For it made Keith mad. How could he get anywhere, how could he progress, tied down to a wife with such limited horizons – who thought so small? 'Christ. Investments like,' he told her. 'Currency speculation. Futures.' In fact, Keith did not understand that money could be accumulated, except, perhaps, on an Accumulator, at the betting-shop. On the other hand, to give him credit, Keith didn't *like it* in the betting-shop. It was not a human option to *like it* in the betting-shop. Keith didn't mind the banked TV screens, the earache voiceover, the food scraps and dog-ends: it was more the atmosphere of longshot desperation, as guys in dead shoes and fifty-pence suits stood around trying to predict the future, with nothing to help them but the *Evening News*.

Now Keith stood at the bar of the Black Cross, having words with Thelonius. You couldn't hear them in the noonday surf. Keith wore bomber jacket, flared white slacks, white chisels; he drank lager thirstily. Thelonius was immersed in a bristling full-length fur coat, and only rarely consulted his glass of orange juice. Both their faces were lit by amusement as Thelonius enumerated something on raised ringed fingers. Thelonius laughed with his salmon-coloured tongue. Two blondes stood just outside their force field: Juniper and Pepsi. Lightly bronzed, and with a silvery Scandinavian sheen to her, Juniper was younger, and was Thelonius's. Pepsi was older, and was anybody's, and had been anybody's for an awful long time. If the stray listener moved closer, he would soon discover that Keith and Thelonius were discussing semi-violent crime.

'*Calm*, man. That's the whole thing: *calm*,' concluded Thelonius. 'A golden opportunity. Think about it, man. Give it your considera-tion. All I ask.'

'Nah,' said Keith. He shook his head. 'Nah. I appreciate it, pal. Don't think I don't. I wish you all the luck in the world. In all sincerity. I'm not like some. I like seeing my mates making decent bread. It's, it's just –'

'It's your darts. Say no more, man. It's your darts.'

'Yeah.' Keith nodded. He was greatly moved. He sniffed and said, 'I can't do it, mate. No way can I imperil my darts, not now. No way. As I move into the public eye.'

'I hear you,' said Thelonius, also moved.

'Yeah cheers, Thelonius.'

Thelonius gripped Keith's shoulder. 'But if you reconsider . . . ?'

'Yeah.'

'Yeah.'

'Yeah.'

Thelonius studied the heavy ingot of his watch and wiggled a finger for his blonde. Juniper came forward. Pepsi remained, and looked meaningly at Keith, who stared hard at her as he headed for the door.

Keith and Clive made their way down the Portobello Road. As they passed Mecca, Keith slowed to a halt. Then he straightened his shoulders, and walked on. He wasn't going in there. No way. He wasn't going in there because he didn't have any money – because he had *already* been in there. A honk sounded: Thelonius flashing past, the girl's blonde hair scrabbling at the half-open side window. Keith waved, feeling the asceticism of him who strives along a quieter road, to a far greater prize. The spade lifestyle, though, he thought, as he turned down Elgin Crescent – it made a lot of good sense. Especially the way they dealt with their birds. When they took out their wallets and showed you their photos: after the blondes, after all the Pointer Sisters and Marvellettes and Supremes, there'd be one black bird with buck teeth and young eyes. And you'd say, 'That your cousin or something then, Wes?' And they'd shake their heads (they took your point) and say: 'Babymamma.' You see, that was the bird they had babies with, or at least gave babies to. Thelonius has four or five kids in a basement in Leamington Road Villas. Only go round there once a fortnight, on Giro day. Then you're back in the pub with the blonde and the child benefit. Now even the flashest white bloke didn't seem to be able to swing that. If Keith had been inclined to think in Darwinian terms, he might have said to himself that the additional blondes were pure gravy for the brothers, because they kept the black bird-pool high. Nevertheless, he understood, and nodded slowly. Ideal arrangement. Brilliant, really. And that way you got the enjoyment of having children (that lovely warm glow of pride) without them ever being around. Stay well clear, until they're older: football. No more nappies. When *was* that? At two? At nine? The spades had their own traditions. Others, others of us chose to accept and duly shoulder our responsibilities. White man's burden. Civilization as such. His mood steeply worsening, Keith shoved himself through the CostCheck doors, gave the nod to Basim, leaned through the cage and borrowed a half of vodka from Harun, tethered Clive to the stockroom doorknob, and furiously trudged down the stairs to pay his last call on Trish Shirt.

*

And it was definitely going to happen with Nicola Six – financially, too. Of this Keith was now supremely confident. The only worry was *when*. With the rape moment successfully endured and mastered, he could probably wait for the sex. But could he wait for the money?

It was all about *time*. Time was everywhere present, was massively operational, in the life Keith moved through. He saw how it strafed people (look at Pepsi!), how it blew them away, how it wasted them. He saw the darts players on TV: every year there was always a fresh new face – and after half a season it looked like an old one. In common with Leo Tolstoy, Keith Talent thought of time as moving past him while he just stayed the same. In the mirror every morning: same old Keith. None the wiser. But in his soul he could tell what time was doing. Keith, who had gone through his midlife crisis at the age of nineteen, didn't expect time to leave him alone, no, not for a moment.

Look at Pepsi. It used to do Keith's heart good watching little Pepsi Hoolihan as she flitted like a butterfly from pub to pub along the Portobello Road. And this, it seemed, was only the other day! Popular girl – a breath of fresh air. Everybody loved little Pepsi. Some nights, when she'd had more Peculiar Brews than were strictly speaking good for her, why, Keith himself would take her round the back and they'd have a bit of fun. All it cost you was a Peculiar Brew. Riding high, was Pepsi: had the world – in the form of a few pubs along the Portobello Road – at her feet innit. It was hard to credit this now. Keith hated to see her these days. And so did everybody else. Alas. It was fair enough and a sound career move for a bird to change tack when she was getting on in years. You go where you're appreciated, and black blokes did love blondes. For a while, anyway. And then they got old even faster. A shocking sight, today, Pepsi Hoolihan in the Black Cross, whining for drinks from the dudes round the pool table with whiskers coming out of her ears. I mean, at twenty-four . . . Of course, Trish Shirt was much older: twenty-seven. If Keith dumped her, which he intended to do, and do soon, like today at the latest, Trish wouldn't have many options, even supposing she was mobile. He couldn't see her enjoying a long second wind, a year, six months, poncing vodkas off the brothers in return for God knows what. They've their own way of doing things and you got to respect that, but they didn't half treat birds horrible. Then, looking at it realistically (I'm a realist, thought Keith – always have been), if she had a bit of sense and looked after herself, she might make babymamma for some old Rasta. Like Shakespeare. Shakespeare's babymamma. Jesus. Keith exhaled through tubed lips.

Time waits . . . Time don't wait. It just don't wait. Just marches on. At the double. *Take me*, thought Keith (and it was like a line of poetry twanging in his head, like a cord, drawing him in), *take me — take me where rich women want to fuck me.*

'Poor you. You're hungover. All that celebrating, I should think, from your darts. Well you deserve it. Now take off your coat and sit down at the table and read your paper. I'll make you a nice spicy Bullshot. Believe me, it's the best thing.'

Keith did what he was told, pausing, as he sat, to wipe a tear from his eye, a tear of gratitude perhaps. On the other hand, the weather had turned again, and everyone's eyes were smarting in the dry mineral wind, a wind speckled with dust and spore, with invisible lamentation. A log fire, Keith noted, burned confidently in the hearth. Coming up the stairs Keith had been uneasily aware that he had nothing in his hands, no prop, no marker; his fingers missed the feel of the shower attachment, the coffee-grinder, the heavy iron. He had no burden. Only the folded tabloid, which was with him all day, under the armpit like Nelson's telescope . . . This he now carefully unfurled and flattened out on the table among the books and fashion magazines. *Elle. Women in Love.* He looked up coolly every now and then, in the gaps between jokes, horoscope, cartomancy column, agony aunt, kiss and tell. He could see her in the kitchen, efficiently, elegantly and as it were fondly preparing his drink. Nicola was wearing a shirt and tie, and a pinstripe suit of playfully generous cut. She might have been the illustration to an article about the woman who had everything. Everything except children. Nicola Six: nobody's babymamma.

'Seychelles,' said Keith half-absently as she placed the interesting drink near his bunched right hand. Then he raised his head. But she had moved past his back and was now standing in quarter-profile by the desk, calmly going through a diary, and humming to herself. 'Bali,' Keith added.

'Them that's got shall get,' sang Nicola, 'them that's not shall lose. So the *Bible* said . . .'

Lovely moment really, he thought. I ought to savour it. She has a way of slowing everything down. She doesn't just plonk herself on a chair, like some. Yack yack yack. She lets you get your bearings. Why don't more birds do that? So fucking important to a man. Look at her hair. Beautiful cut. Christ, they must do it strand by strand. None of this ten minutes under the blaster at Madame Pom-Pom's. I bet she goes to Bond Street or somewhere . . . and Keith's mind slid off down a gleaming arcade of rich mirrors, black velvet, ticking heels, stockinged ankles. The funny thing is, the really funny thing is: soon, one of these days (okay: her own speed), the woman over there is going to be sitting on the couch over *there*, by the TV, sitting on my lap, well fucked, and watching the darts.

'I've been watching the darts', she said, '– on television. Tell me something, Keith. Why do all the players drink lager? Only lager?'

'Intelligent question. Good talking point. It's like this. Your top darter is travelling the land, from pub to pub. Now beers vary. Some of them local brews, couple pints and you're well pissed. But lager . . .'

'Yes?'

'But lager's *kegged*. It's *kegged*. Standard. You know what you're getting. Now the darter has to drink. Has to. To loosen the throwing arm. Part of his job. But within reason. You know like you set yourself a limit. Like ten pints. Pacing it out over an evening.'

'I see.'

'Kegged. You know what you're getting.'

As a talking point, the part played by lager in the working life of a top darter seemed to be close to exhaustion. But then the telephone rang. Nicola looked at her watch and said,

'Excuse me for a moment, Keith. I'll need silence . . . Guy? Wait. This isn't me. It's a tape. I apologize, but I didn't trust myself to talk to you unmediated. I didn't trust my resolve. You see – dear Guy, thank you for all the sentiments you have awoken in me. It was wonderful to . . .'

Tape? thought Keith. Keith wasn't altogether comfortable. Among other things, he was trying to suppress a cough, and his watery gaze strained over the clamp of his hand. Goes on a bit. And I don't like the sound of this Lawrence she'll be looking at with new eyes. Brush-off innit, he thought, with sadness, with puzzlement, even with anger. Jesus, might as well be off out of here and get to work. Hark at her.

'. . . how absolutely and unconditionally I mean that. I'll never forget you. Think of me sometimes. Goodbye.'

Nicola turned to Keith and slowly kissed the vertical forefinger she had raised to her lips.

He held silence until the receiver went down. Then he coughed long and heavingly. When Keith's vision cleared Nicola was standing there with her open and expectant face.

Lost for words, Keith said, 'Shame. So it didn't work out.' He coughed again, rather less searchingly, and added, 'All over, is it?'

'To tell you the truth, Keith, it hasn't really begun. For him the idea is the thing. Guy's a romantic, Keith.'

'Yeah? Yeah, he does dress funny. He said, he told me he was "tracing" someone.'

'Oh that,' she said boredly. 'That was just some crap I made up to get money out of him. It'll come.'

This bird, thought Keith, now hang on a minute: this bird is really seriously good news. She's a fucking miracle. Where she been all my life?

'Money for you, Keith. Why should he have it all?'

'Caviare. Uh, when?'

'I think you can afford to be patient. I must do this at my own speed. Not very long at all. And really quite a lot of money.'

'Beluga,' said Keith. He nodded sideways at the telephone and went on admiringly, 'You're quite a little actress, aren't you Nick?'

'Nicola. Oh, literally so, Keith. Come and sit here. There's something I want to show you.'

It was all electrifying, every second of it. Every frame of it. Keith watched the screen in a seizure of fascination. In fact he was almost sickened by this collision or swirl of vying realities: the woman on the couch whose hair he could smell, and the girl inside the television, the girl on the tape. It might have overloaded him entirely if the electric image hadn't clearly belonged to the past. So he could still say to himself that TV was somewhere else: in the past. Not that Nicola had aged, or aged in the sense he knew, become gruesomely witchified, like Pepsi, or just faded, nearly faded from sight, like Kath. The woman on the couch was more vivid (time-strengthened), richer in every sense than the girl on the screen, who none the less . . . Brooding, tousled, lip-biting Nicola, poor little rich girl, in a play; tanned, keen, wide-mouthed Nicola, in a series of adverts, for sunglasses; white-saronged, ringleted, pouting Nicola, not actually Cleopatra but one of her handmaidens, in Shakespeare. Then the

175

finale: the pre-credits sequence of a feature film (her debut, her swansong), a striptease in the back room of a gentleman's club full of sweating young stockbrokers, and Nicola up on a table wearing a metal showercap and, at first, the usual seven veils, dancing with minimal movements but with fierce address of eyes and mouth until, just before she vanished in the smoke and the shadow, you saw all her young body.

'That it?' said Keith with a jolt.

'I get killed later on. You don't see it. You just hear about it. Later.'

'Jesus, beautiful. You know,' he said, not because it was true but because he thought she would want to hear it, 'you haven't changed a bit.'

'Oh I'm *much* better now. Listen. You run into Guy pretty often, don't you?'

'Consistently,' said Keith, suddenly very pitiless.

'Good. Next time, but leave it a day or two – tell him this.'

Soon afterwards, as she was showing him out, Nicola added,

'Have you got all that? Are you sure? And for God's sake don't overdo it. Lay it on, but don't overdo it. And mention the globe.'

'Jack Daniels.'

'Well then. Be good. And come and see me again very soon.'

Keith turned. She was right. She *was* better. When you see photos and that of them young, you think they're going to be as good as they are now, only newer. But it wasn't like that, not with Nick. Only the eyes, only the pupils, looked as though they'd been around. What was it? Class skirt – and some foreign skirt too – they needed time for the flesh to get interesting. They pour oil on themselves. Massage. TV. Idle rich innit . . . Class skirt, he thought: but she wasn't wearing a skirt. Them baggy trousers (not cheap), so puffy there you had no notion of the shape that was hiding within.

'Old Grandad,' said Keith, and coughed lightly. 'Come on, Nick. Your speed – okay. I respect that. I'll exercise restraint. But give me something. To keep me warm at night. Show me you care.'

'Nicola. Of course,' she said, and leant forward, and showed him she cared.

'. . . Yeah cheers.'

'Look! I've got one more thing to show you.'

She opened a closet, and there, pinned to the back of the door, was a poster from the long run at Brighton, Nicola full length in tunic and black tights with her hair up, hands on hips and looking over her shoulder, the wild smile graphically enhanced: *Jack and the Bean-stalk*.

She laughed and said, 'What do you think?'

'Jim Beam,' said Keith. 'Benedictine. *Porno.*'

'. . . *What?*' said Nicola.

The books in Keith Talent's apartment. There weren't many books in Keith Talent's apartment. There weren't many books in his garage, either. But there were some.

There were six: the *A – D*, the *E – K*, the *L – R*, the *S – Z* (the modern *cheat* being heavily and exasperatedly reliant on the telephone), *Darts: Master the Discipline*, and a red pad which had no title apart from *Students Note Book – Ref. 138 – Punched for filing* and which, perhaps, could be notionally christened *A Darter's Diary* or, more simply, *The Keith Talent Story*. Here it was that Keith logged his intimate thoughts, most (but not all) of them darts-related. For example:

> You cuold have a house so big you could have sevral dart board areas in it, not just won. With a little light on top.

Or:

> Got to practice the finishing, got to. Go round the baord religiously. You can have all the power in the world but its no good if you can not finish.

Or:

> ~~Tedn Tendnen~~ Keep drifting to the left on the third dart, all them fuckign treble fives.

Rereading this last gobbet, Keith made the *tsuh* sound. He reached for his dart-shaped biro and crossed out *fuckign*. Letting out a brief grunt of satisfaction, and dotting the *i* with a flourish, he wrote in *fucking*. Keith wiped a tear from his eye: he was in a strange mood.

The conversation with Guy Clinch, completed earlier that day in the Black Cross, had developed naturally enough. Keith could at least say this for himself: he had been good, and done as he was told.

'Whew, mate,' he'd remarked as Guy joined him at the bar. 'You don't look too clever.'

'Yes I know.'

Keith peered closer with a wary sneer. 'No. You definitely do *not* look overly brill.'

'I think I must have a bug or something.'

Not that Guy ever looked as radiant as Keith believed he ought to. Personally, and having seen Guy's house, Keith wondered why Guy wasn't rubbing his hands together and grinning his head off all the hours there were. But oh no: not him. Keith was habitually impatient with Guy's habitual expression, one of temporary and precarious serenity, the face raised and slightly tilted, and the eyes wanly blinking. Today, though, his head was down and he seemed to have lost his colour and his money glow. Like every other male Caucasian in the pub, Guy was being shot in black and white. He was war footage, like everybody else.

'It must be going round,' said Keith. 'I tell you who else ain't in the best of health: that Nicola.'

Guy's head dropped another inch.

'Yeah. I went round there. You know I got all that stuff mended for her? Well they all went wrong again, you know, like they do.' This was true enough; but when Keith quietly offered to go another mile with GoodFicks, Nicola just shrugged and said it wasn't worth it. 'Anyway she's definitely under the weather. Know what it looked like to me? Apaphy. Apaphy. Staring out of the window. Playing with that globe thing. Sad little smile on its face.'

Guy's head dropped another inch.

'Like –' Keith coughed and went on, 'like she was pining. Pining. Pining its little heart out . . . Jesus Christ, look at the state of that Pepsi Hoolihan. I can't get over it. I haven't seen her for a few weeks, that's what it is. She looked bad enough in the summer but look at her now. She looks like fucking Nosferatu. Cheer up, pal. Here. I got one for you.'

And then, after Guy had crept off and Keith was standing there thinking how nice and simple life could be sometimes, God and Pongo took him aside and told him, in accents of grim apology, about the visit to the Black Cross of Kirk Stockist, Lee Crook and Ashley Royle . . .

This news shouldn't have surprised Keith, and it didn't surprise him. It merely frightened him a very great deal. Ah, money, always the money. As noted earlier, Keith was not in the healthiest shape, financially. His position as regards rent, rates, utilities, police fines and Compensations, hire purchase, and so on and so forth, was an inch from disaster. But it was always an inch from disaster . . . In the garage there Keith's dusty face hardened as he spat on to the floor and reached for the bottle of stolen vodka. This was the thing: he had been borrowing money on the street, more particularly on Paradine Street, in the East End. He had been borrowing money from a loanshark called Kirk Stockist. Unable to repay Kirk Stockist, he needed money for the heavy interest – the vig, the vig, the vertiginous vigesimal. To pay the vig, he had been borrowing money from another loanshark called Lee Crook. It seemed like a neat arrangement at the time, but Keith knew it to be fraught with danger, especially when he started borrowing money from Ashley Royle to pay the vig on the loan from Lee Crook. Through it all Keith had hoped and expected everything to come good at Mecca. And it hadn't. And nothing else had either. His own business interests had recently unravelled in a chaos of no-shows on the part of other *cheats* – catastrophic welshings and skankings that caused low whistles even among Keith's acquaintance, among poolroom hoodlums, touchy car thieves, embittered granny-jumpers. Now Keith thought venomously of his betrayal at the hands of that fucking old fraud Lady Barnaby, and gave a shudder as he recalled the price that her jewellery had fetched. Driving down Blenheim Crescent the other day, Keith had clenched his fist and said '*Yesss*' when he saw that Lady B's psychopathic boiler had eventually blown its top; the roof of the house looked like Reactor No. 4 at Chernobyl – or Reactor No. 6, at Thierry. Oh, how Keith longed to forget his cares and throw himself into his darts! Darts it was that had caused him to neglect his cheating: the hours of practice, and also the days of celebration, when that practice bore fruit at the oché. And there was Nicola: time-consuming too in her way, and promising uncertain rewards. Old Nick: does it at her own speed like. Keith's jaw dropped open affectionately as he thought of their session in front of the TV, how he had begged for the Freeze Frame and the normal Play, and how she had whisked them on brutally with the Fast Forward from highlight to highlight . . .

The telephone rang and Keith did something he hadn't done in a while: he answered it. 'Ashley!' he said. Keith didn't say much after that. He just periodically said 'Yeah' – perhaps half a dozen times. Then he said, 'Right. Right. Yeah cheers, lads.'

Solemnly Keith picked up *Darts: Master The Discipline* and turned to one of its most stirring passages. He read:

Whilst darts is basically a twentieth-century sport, darts go way back into the English folk Heritage. Those famed English archers are said to have played a form of darts prior to defeating the French at the proverbial Battle of Agincourt in 1415.

Keith looked up. 1415! he thought. 'Heritage,' he murmured richly.

How many times, how many, many times had he chalked for his father, at the chalkboards of the dartboards of the pubs of London, where he was raised. Dad would be playing, usually, with Jonathan Friend, or with Mr Purchase: Chick's dad. And if little Keith made a mistake with the sums . . . Standing in the garage, Keith raised a palm to his cheek and felt it burning, still burning, always burning . . .

But we mustn't go too far back, must we, we mustn't go too far back in anybody's life. Particularly when they're poor. Because if we do, if we go too far back – and this would be a journey made in a terrible bus, with terrible smells and terrible noises, with terrible waits and terrible jolts, a journey made in terrible weather for terrible reasons and for terrible purposes, in terrible cold or terrible heat, with terrible stops for terrible snacks, down terrible roads to a terrible room – then nobody is to blame for anything, and nothing matters, and everything is allowed.

Ashley Royle, Lee Crook and Kirk Stockist had told Keith that if he didn't give them all the money they wanted by Friday, then they would, among other things, break the middle finger of his right hand. This, of course, was Keith's courting finger: even more centrally, it was his darting finger. He finished his vodka, straightened his flares, put on his windcheater (even the wind Keith cheated) and went off to try to find Thelonius, to talk to him about semi-violent crime.

Keith has started asking me for money. I knew this would happen.

Late last night we had a stand-up snack at Conchita's. Keith had words with Conchita's daughter. He wanted the *chili rilienos*. In due course a plate of devilled plutonium was set before him. It bubbled audibly, and gave off thick plumes of ebony and silver. I was reminded of the splattings and belchings of Sulphur Springs, in St Lucia (land of Thelonius's fathers). Keith took a matter-of-fact first mouthful and stood there with smoke coming out of his nose and asked me to give him money.

I want to give him money. I really don't need this Thelonius business. Thelonius is a joke criminal anyway, riding a farcical lucky streak. What if it all goes wrong, which it will? Keith canned: Keith out of the action. I can't bear to see them hunkered down together in the Black Cross, saying things like 'Payday' and 'Bingo'. They've even got a crappy little map. On the other hand I don't want Keith's darting finger broken either, that precious, multi-functioned digit, on which he further depends for his Americanized obscene gestures.

No, I want to give Keith money. (I want to give Thelonius money too.) But the trouble is I don't have any. And Keith needs so much, so soon, and will presently need more. Why no call, no deal, no rapturous jackpot from Missy Harter? Why? Why?

Mindful of Heisenberg's principle that an observed system inevitably interacts with its observer – and aware too that the decent anthropologist never meddles with his tribe – I decided not to tell

181

Nicola about Keith and semi-violent crime. Then I told Nicola about Keith and semi-violent crime. I told her to get moving and give Keith money. It's okay, she says. She just 'knows' that the crime of semi-violence will take place, and it'll be okay. How I wish I could share in her hope – the awakened, lips parted, the new ships . . .

Well, I told Keith no. He stared my way in what I took to be anti-Semitic silence for about fifteen seconds, and then went taciturn on me. At least I think he went taciturn on me. I don't know what that *chili rilienos* was doing to his insides (it even *means* 'red-ass'), but his tongue looked like a reefer knot. 'That's more like it, Conchita,' he eventually croaked.

I felt bad. I do owe him something. After all, where would I be without Keith?

The snack was cheap and I handled it.

Death seems to have solved my posture problem – and improved my muscle tone. What jogging and swimming and careful eating never quite managed, death is pulling off with no trouble at all. I recline with burger and fries, while death completes its own stay-fit programme. And with none of that sweating and grunting which some of us consider so unattractive.

Yes, for the present I flatter myself that death is having a good effect on my appearance. I definitely look more intelligent. Is this why Lizzyboo digs me? I look almost messianic. The skin is tightening under my jaw and over my temples, and gaining in glow. In death I shine. In death I am – I am beautiful. As cosmeticist and shape-up coach, my condition is doing a fine job. It's a little painful, true – but all good things hurt. Apart from what it does to the eyes (red-tendrilled, and swelling, or growing), the death-effect really isn't too bad. Apart from the eyes and the death.

I accompany Lizzyboo and Hope and Guy and Dink Heckler to the tennis club in Castellain Road. I sit on an umpire's chair and watch. Mixed doubles: Guy paired with Lizzyboo, facing Hope and Dink, the South African number seven . . . I don't think Guy sees what's brewing between Dink and Hope. Poor Guy. He's like me, myself. We're here. But we're not here. When we look up our eyes find the same cloud, heavy and queasy and low-flying, the colour of an avocado, yes, and with a query of vinaigrette in its core.

Unsmiling, in supercasual sportswear, and as hairy as a tarantula, Dink is the one they all want to see, here at the club; the pale secretaries and treasurers, the ageing pros, the brilliant black kids come by to admire and envy Dink's power and touch, his rollover backhand, his snorting smashes. Wearing grey socks, grey shoes, khaki shorts and half a kaftan, Guy is easily the most rhythmless of the four, the least determined, and the worst adapted (his generous confirmations and disavowals, his compulsive apologies, almost as regular as the sound of bat on ball) . . . But it was the ladies I had come to see.

Equally tall and brown and resplendent they are also both equipped with bravura backhands and the special looping second serve. Optimum use has been made of the available material, with investment here and outlay there, at the tennis ranch and the tennis clinic. They swoop and swoon in their whites. Of course, Lizzyboo boasts even more sap and down than Hope, her older sister. *Yuck*, they both say, when the shot goes awry.

Hope plays with severity (she is as firm and strict as the pleats on her skirt), Lizzyboo with laughter and friendly ambition. Hope assumes a vexed expression when she plays her shots (fending off that big fuzzy bug). Get lost! her strokes seem to say. Lizzyboo 'persuades' or 'caresses' the ball. *Come here*, says her racket. *Come back*. But if the girls were playing singles, there would be nothing in it – they would be perfectly matched. Their throats shine as they grin and shriek. They must have a hundred teeth between them. When the balance and the skill and the timing were being handed out, the sisters were given the same amount of tennis talent. But Lizzyboo definitely got the tits.

The set went to six-six, to the tie-break. Withdrawn and indolent until now, Dink exploded with a horrible competence, lunging from tramline to tramline to poach his volleys, beetling backwards on tiptoe for the whorfing overheads. He came on all masterful with Hope: hand on shoulder for the jock-intimate huddles between each point, and the approving, the legitimizing pat of his rackethead on her rump. Also, to my fascination, he started thinking it would be good if he gunned for Guy at the net. Lizzyboo's short second serve would kick up in girlish invitation, and there would be Dink, wriggling into his ravenous wind-up, cocking every muscle to drill that yellow bullet into Guy's waiting mouth. And Guy never flinched. He fell over two or three times, and one ball scorched his hairline; but he didn't back off. He just got to his feet and apologized. At six-zero Dink aced Lizzyboo with shameless savagery, and then half-turned, his mouth white and tight and starkly crenellated, as he cuffed the spare ball toward my chair. Nobody takes a set off the South African number seven. Nobody. Unless of course he's the South African number six. That asshole. It didn't occur to him that Lizzyboo and Hope and Guy would be pretty good at tennis too, if they did *nothing else the whole time.*

Lizzyboo came and stood beside me and laid a hot head on my shoulder. I commiserated. Hope sat with Dink. Guy sat alone. He sat alone staring straight ahead with a towel across his knees . . . Of course, Lizzyboo had a thing with Dink, some time ago. And there is this sexual plagiarism which operates between the two sisters. Lizzyboo had a thing with Dink. And it didn't work out.

And it won't work out with me either. Pretty soon she will start wondering what is wrong with her. She will become ashamed. Aren't people amazing? I guess I ought to come clean. But I can't. I don't want it to get around. I'll just have to tell her that I love another.

This feels terrible. She rests her head on my shoulder. I should be taking powerful drags of her toasty sweat, her life vapours. Instead, I avert my jaw. This feels terrible, like a mean parody of love. On the tennis court, I notice, Dink says *nothing* instead of *love*. Fifteen-nothing. Nothing-thirty. Even on the tennis court love has gone; even on the tennis court love has been replaced by nothing.

I've started reading books to little Kim. They're about the only books I can manage these days. She's interested, and seems to concentrate, particularly when she's lulled by her bottle.

When she drinks from her bottle she sounds like someone winding a watch. She's winding a watch, against her future time.

'How I wish – how I wish, Nicola, that I could share your confidence, your belief that all will yet be well.' 'Yes, it's nice to have such a rosy view of things.' 'I've got to run. Or go, anyway. Listen. This is somewhat embarrassing.' 'For you or for me?' 'There are two things I need from you – from the horse's mouth. First off, could you get Keith to unbutton a little. I need his P.O.V.' 'His what?' 'His point of view. I'm not sure he knows what "discretion" really means. He still sings, but it cramps his style. Lift the D-notice a little. Just tell him to shut up around Guy.' 'Okay. Consider it fixed.' 'Great.' 'That's not embarrassing. What's the other thing?'

I dropped my head. Then I raised it and said, 'Your kisses. It would help if I knew how you kissed.'

She laughed recklessly. Then she gathered herself up from the chair and came forward.

I held up a finger. 'This isn't a pitch or anything.'

'No no. My stuff doesn't work on you. Isn't that right?'

'That's right. Come on. You kissed Keith.'

'After a fashion.'

'And I figure you'll kiss Guy next time.'

'Absolutely. But wouldn't this be a dangerous precedent? I mean, where's it going to end?'

'So you'll be going further. With both of them. Of course. How far? All the way. Where else. Relax,' I said. 'Sexually I'm dead already. Sexually I'm Postman Pat. I just need a couple of pointers for the next chapter.'

'Can't you make *anything* up? All this literalism. You know, it's the death of love.'

'You needn't worry. You won't catch my fatal disease.'

'Why would *I* care?'

We were standing there with our force fields touching. I felt nothing in the heart but my face had begun to tremble. 'Go on,' I said. 'Give me a kiss.'

She placed her wrists on my shoulders. She shrugged and said, 'Which one?'

I get back late and the goddamned pipes are at full throttle. Such moronic bugling – I think of Guy's cock or rooster, Guy's *gallo*, so far away, so long ago. I walk at speed around the apartment with my hands pressed over my ears. Christ, is the whole *house* dying?

Oh, the pipes, and their brute pain. I hear you. I hear you, brother. Brother, I *hear* you.

Chapter 11: The Concordance of Nicola Six's Kisses

IN THE CONCORDANCE of Nicola Six's kisses there were many subheads and subsections, many genres and phyla – chapter and verse, cross-references, multiple citations. The lips were broad and malleably tremulous, the tongue was long and powerful and as sharp-pronged as a sting. That mouth was a deep source, a deep source of lies and kisses. Some of the kisses the mouth dispensed were evanescent, unrecallable, the waft or echo of a passing butterfly (or its ghost, hovering in the wrong dimension). Others were as searching and detailed as a periodontal review: you came out from under them entirely plaque-free. The Rosebud, the Dry Application, Anybody's, Clash of the Incisors, Repulsion, the Turning Diesel, Mouthwash, the Tonsillectomy, Lady Macbeth, the Readied Pussy, Youth, the Needer, the Gobbler, the Deliquescent Virgin. Named like a new line of cocktails or the transient brands of Keith's perfumes: Scandal, Outrage . . . Named like the dolls and toys – the rumour and voodoo – of an only child.

One kiss was especially tricky (it resisted description – it resisted everything), featuring as it did two apparent opposites: passionate demurral and outright inexorability. You had to fix things so that your partner, or opponent, felt your desperate reluctance even as your lips homed in on his. Halfway between the Needer and the Deliquescent Virgin, it was particularly handy after fights, or when you wanted to turn a man around again within the space of a few seconds (out of decrepit satiation it snatched shocking renewal). This was the kiss she would bestow on Guy Clinch. Looming forward, he would enfold her with his height. She would blink up at him in adorable distress – a distress not altogether feigned, because she did pity him the torments that were destined to come his way. With this kiss, you didn't move your feet but it felt like tiptoe. A straining aspiration in the breast, while the mouth, if it could, seemed to want to turn and hide. But it couldn't. Now overseen by an invisible interaction, their lips would inch closer. The kiss was called the Wounded Bird.

Physically, it was among her mildest. At the other end of the escalation ladder – intense, athletic, hard core – was a kiss she seldom used: unforgivably, it was called the Jewish Princess. Nicola learned it from a pornographic film she had seen long ago in Barcelona, but its associations all lay elsewhere. Rich, vulgar, young, plump, effortlessly multiorgasmic and impossibly avid: a squanderer's kiss, the kiss of an impossible self-squanderer. Whereas, in the Wounded Bird, the tongue was conspicuous only by its shimmering absence (that butterfly again, caught in a screened chamber), the Jewish Princess was *all* tongue – and not its tip but its trunk, its meat: brute tongue. Here, the tongue did duty for every organ, male and female, the heart included. Such a kiss was more a weapon than a wand; a weapon of the exponential kind (one that called upon the speed of light), because it was almost unusably powerful. The Jewish Princess was *inordinate*. Applied at the right moment, it made a man kneel on the floor with his chequebook in his hands. Applied at the wrong moment (and Nicola could certainly pick these wrong moments), it could finish a love affair in half a minute: the man would be backing towards the door, and staring, one hand raised, and the sleeve pressed to his lips. 'I'm sorry – don't go,' she once said. 'I didn't mean it: it was an accident.' No use. To achieve the Jewish Princess you brought your tongue out to its full extent and let it rest on the lower lip *before the kiss began*. Thus the kiss, when it came, was from the second mouth.

The kiss was called the Jewish Princess – unforgivably. But then the kiss itself was unforgivable. The Jewish Princess was unforgivable.

And what about a kiss for Keith? What about a smacker for the kisser of Keith Talent?

When he came in that time – tabloid wedged under armpit, winded jeans, wall-eyed hangover – Nicola couldn't help it. She made herself huge and bristled above him saying,

'You know the iron and the coffee-grinder and the vacuum-cleaner you had fixed?'

'. . . Yeah?'

'Well they've *all* gone wrong again.'

Keith stared back at her, the dry tongue waiting on the lower teeth.

Nicola waited, too, until the itch, the heat-flash, the eczema of detestation had passed through her and moved on somewhere else. Then she changed: she made herself small. She could be big and she could be small but mostly she was big and when things went wrong they went wrong on a big scale. Bath overflows, heavy tumbles, broken beds.

'Yeah well it's the way of the fucking world innit. Jesus. I come up here . . .'

She made herself small. She compressed her body into the gamesome folds of her pinstriped suit. She clasped her hands. She dropped her head – so that she could peer up at him as she gently said,

'Poor you. You're hungover. All that celebrating, I should think, from your darts. Well, you deserve it.' She reached out to help him off with his electric-blue windcheater, promising him a nice spicy Bullshot. 'Believe me,' she said, 'it's the best thing.'

Nicola halved the lemon, opened the can of consommé, ground the pepper, poured the vodka. Every now and then she looked at him as she worked, shaking her head and whispering to herself. Her project had been to get through men – to get to the end of men. And what did that leave her with? There he sat at the table, fiercely frowning over his paper, as if it were a route-map, guiding him to buried treasure. The round and hairless forearms lay flat on either margin. You could end the thing now: by going over and whisking it out from under his gaze. Keith would kill for his tabloid. Any day.

'Seychelles,' he said, impermissibly, as she placed the glass six inches from his fat right hand. Unable to do more for the moment, Nicola effaced herself, standing at the corner table and looking down blindly at her diary. Heat scattered through her. 'Bali,' he added . . .

She had a question ready: to do with darts. In a silent trauma of contempt, broken only by the occasional incredulous cackle, Nicola had been watching the darts on television. A twenty-stone man threw a twenty-gram nail at a lump of cork, while the crowd screamed for blood. Tiddlywinks in a bearpit. This was some destiny.

Anyway she asked the question, and he answered it; then she moved up behind him and looked over his shoulder. The centre pages of

Keith's tabloid were devoted to tabloid-sized photographs of the movie-star Burton Else and his bride Liana. Big Liana wore a small bikini. Burton Else wore some kind of thong or opaque condom. His head, no larger than an avocado, blazed out above an inverted pyramid of organ meat. The accompanying text concerned itself with the Elses' marriage agreement: damage-limitation for Burton, in the event of a divorce.

'Burton Else, innit,' said Keith, with what seemed to be a touch of pride. 'And Liana.'

'They come and they go,' said Nicola. 'Every few years the world feels the need for another male literalist.'

'Pardon?'

'I wonder how many million she gets a year,' Nicola continued, 'for going along with the notion that he isn't a faggot.'

Could anything surprise Nicola? Was she surprisable? One wonders. Keith now half-turned to her slowly, all patience lost, gone, as if she'd been bugging him for hours and *this was it*.

'Him?' he said loudly. 'Burton Else? Fuck off.'

She took a step backwards, away from this. Then she folded her arms and said, 'An obvious and well-known faggot. A celebrated faggot.'

Keith's eyes closed longsufferingly (give him strength).

She said, 'Come on. I mean, who cares, but look at his face. On top of that body? She deserves the money. It must be a full-time job looking the other way.'

'Not Burton Else. Not Burton.'

Nicola wondered how far she ought to go with this. It was, in fact, common knowledge about Burton Else. Anyone who followed the movies knew about Burton Else (and Nicola followed them closely). It was even clear from the trades: constant static between certain pressure groups and the studio lawyers. Yes, it was common knowledge about Burton: but not as common as the *other* knowledge about him, the big-screen and video knowledge, which said how much he loved his country and his women and his machine-guns. Burton had a new wife in every film (before she got slain by samurai or Red Indians or Guatemalans, or some other band of intellectuals): how these blondes adored their Burton, how they oiled and ogled him, and encouraged him with his bodybuilding! Christ, thought Nicola, hasn't everyone caught on by now? (She was intrigued by the homosexual world, but finally disapproved of it, because she was excluded from it.) The workout king, the erection lookalike: however fearless and patriotic you made him, however many wives and Bibles and three-foot Bowie knives you gave him, he still belonged to locker rooms, cuboid buttocks, testosterone hotels.

'Burton Else's a happily married man,' said Keith. 'He loves his wife. Loves the woman. Do anything for her.'

Nicola waited, thinking about love, and watching the dull invitation to violence subside in Keith's eyes.

'Camera don't lie like. That last film he was always giving her one. She wasn't complaining, no way. She said nobody did it quite like Burton.'

'Yeah,' said Nicola, and leant forward with her hands on the table like a teacher, 'and he probably had to stagger into his trailer or his bungalow to throw up between takes. He's a fruit, Keith. And as I said, who cares? Don't worry. It does your masculinity credit that you can't see it. It takes one to know one. And you aren't one, are you Keith.'

'No danger,' he said automatically. Then for a few seconds he blinked steadily on a heartbeat rhythm. And his face creased in childish unhappiness. 'But if . . . but then . . . but he . . .'

Film, Keith, she could have said. *Film. All that not real. Not real.*

It was six o'clock precisely, though, and the telephone rang, right on the button, and Nicola smiled ('This is a tape'), and did her thing with Guy.

Later, after her own film show, as she escorted a hugely, an almost speechlessly gratified Keith to the stairs, as she prepared to usher him out into the wind and the rain, Nicola said reflectively, strollingly (her hands in the trouser pockets of the pluming suit),

'He's a romantic, remember. So work on that. Tell him I'm pale and drawn. Tell him I sit by the window, sighing. Tell him I finger the beautiful globe, and ruefully smile, and turn away. You know the sort of stuff. In your own style, Keith, of course.'

'Jack Daniels.'

It seemed now that she would finally have to kiss him. Well, he asked for it. Nicola felt a noise, a soft rearrangement, go off inside her, something like a moan – one of those tragic little whimpers, perhaps, that thwarted lovers are said to emit. She breathed deep and leaned down and offered Keith the Rosebud: fish mouth, the eyes thankfully closed. 'Mah,' she said when it was over (and it lasted half a second). 'Patience, Keith. You'll find with me,' she said, 'that when it rains, it pours. Look!'

Jack and the Beanstalk. How the young legs sped up into the purple tunic. And the impetuous, the life-loving smile!

'Jim Beam. Benedictine. *Porno*.'

'*What?*'

'*Porno*. It's this drink. You get it down the Golgotha. Or by the case from the bloke at BestSave. Dead cheap, cause it's been nicked *twice*.'

'. . . Run along, Keith.'

'Yeah cheers.'

She came back into the sitting-room and, seeing a patch of brief and sudden sunlight on the sofa, flopped herself down in it, her limbs outstretched, like a dark star. Nicola's round tummy pushed upwards three or four times as she laughed – in helpless exasperation. Yes, all right. Porno: porno. Yes of course. If you must. Surprisingly, Nicola disliked pornography, or she disliked its incursion into her own lovelife. Because it was so limited, because there was no emotion in it (it spoke straight to the mental quirk), and because it stank of money. But she could do pornography. It was easy.

A performing artist, a bullshit artist, something of a piss artist, and a considerable sack artist, she was also an *artist*; and although she knew exactly where she wanted to go, she didn't always know exactly how she was going to get there. You could never admit this, however, even to yourself. You had to make the mind shoot like a puck over all that creaky ice. You trusted your instinct, or you were dead. She laughed again, with a brisk snort that had her stretching for the paper tissues (now who planned that – who planned that burst bubble of humorous mucus?), as she remembered the killer line she had laid on Guy Clinch. 'There's just one other thing: I'm a virgin.' A *virgin*. Oh, *yeah*. Nicola had never said those words before, even when she had the chance: twenty years ago, in that little gap between finding out what it meant and ceasing to be one. She had never said it when it was true (especially not then. And would it have made much odds to the drunken Corsican in his mag-strewn boiler room, beneath the hotel at Aix-en-Provence?). 'I'm a virgin.' But there was a first time for everything.

The joke was, the real joke was . . . she had come close – she had come *that* close – to muffing her big line. She almost said something that would have wrecked the whole performance. Really, the actress training was a liability in real life: if you're the dramatic type anyway, then *don't* go to Drama School. Because the associations of the moment, the tears, the indignation, the extremity, had prompted another line, another lie, one she had delivered pretty well routinely

191

throughout her teens and twenties, in ultimatum form, on the crest of various rages, various dissolutions. She almost said: 'There's just one other thing: I'm pregnant.' Whoops! Now that would have been quite bad. No coming back from there. 'I'm pregnant.' *Those* words, at least, had fairly often consorted with the truth. She didn't go on about it or anything, internally or otherwise, but she acknowledged the scar tissue of her seven abortions.

Nicola blew her nose noisily and lay there clutching the rolled tissue. Two broad fronts: the cloudy trophies of Guy's archaic heart; Keith Talent, and his reptile modernity. She was an artist, in reasonable control, and knew everything that was going to happen, more or less. But she never knew this. She never knew this about her final project. She never knew it was going to be such hard *work*.

The black cab pulled away, thanked and tipped by the, by the . . . Disgustingly attired (how *could* she?), and making her way into the pregnant blackout of the dead-end street. The car waited; now it nosed forward, with sidelights burning. The door opened. *Get in*, he said. And she had been so very very bad . . . *You*. Always you, she said. And in she climbed.

Nicola awoke, and heard the rain, and went back to sleep again, or she tried. The rain sounded like industrial gas escaping from the rooftops – tons of gas, enough to fill the storage vat that overlooked the Park (corseted and flat-topped, the snare in God's drum set). Mauling and worrying the pillows, she squirmed and bounced around the bed. She persevered for perhaps an hour while ten thousand sensations ran through her like a metropolitan marathon. She sat up suddenly and drank most of the pint of water that had colourlessly monitored her sleep. There came the sound of thunder, the premonitory basses and kettles of God's new drum solo. She hung her head. This morning, at any rate, Nicola Six could look forward to a whole day off.

She micturated angrily, as if trying to drill a hole through the hard marble. Having wiped herself she stepped on to the scales in her heavy white nightdress – her decidedly non-vamp nightdress, what she wore in bed when all she wanted was comfort, frump-warmth and comfort. The dial shivered and settled. Eh! But the nightdress was heavy, the sleepy in her eyes was heavy, her hair (she made a mustache of one of its locks) was heavy and smelled of cigarettes: the tobacco, not the smoke. With a silent snarl she cleaned her teeth for the taste of the toothpaste, and spat.

Back in the bedroom she drew the curtains and released the blind. She opened the window to the wet air: three inches, a distance that corresponded in her mind to a single raised notch on the passage thermostat. Normally, on a working day, she would have aired the bed – but she planned to return there very soon. Ten o'clock, and it was dark outside. Against such darkness the rain might be expected to take on the glow of silver or mercury. Not today. Even the rain was dark. She listened to it again. What was the point? What could the rain say but rain, rain, rain?

In ritual vexation she ran a tap for her morning tea. The tapwater, she knew, had passed at least twice through every granny in London. Previously she had relied on bottled water from France, more costly than petrol, until it was revealed that Eau des Deux Monts had passed at least twice through every granny in Lyon. You had to run the tap for at least ten minutes before it stopped tasting like tepid soy sauce. Just how much of people's lives was spent waiting for hot water to run hot, for cold water to run cold, standing there with a finger, pointing, in the falling column. She went and switched on the television: the soundless, telex-like news channel. Sternly she reviewed the international weather reports. MADRID 12 RAIN. MAGNITOGORSK 9 RAIN. MAHABAD 14 RAIN. MANAGUA 12 RAIN. The RAIN in the right-hand column formed a pillar of drizzle. That's right: it was raining all over the world. The biosphere was *raining*.

With the tap still poling into the sink Nicola put on her dressing-gown and flew barefoot down the stairs for her mail. The men who lived beneath her . . . The men who lived beneath her got less and less keen on Nicola the nearer to the top they got. Speechlessly revered by the man in the basement, openly acclaimed and fancied at street level, she was heartily endorsed by the man on the first floor, who tended to pooh-pooh the suspicion of the man on the second, who none the less associated himself with the settled hostility of the man on the third. The man on the fourth floor didn't like her one bit. In fact, on almost any reckoning, she was ruining his life. She kept him up at night with her banging and pacing; his days she poisoned with her music, her frantic scene shifting, her vampire and vigilante videos; odds and ends tossed from her windows littered his balcony; three of his inner walls reeked of wet-rot from her leaking pipes, her overflowing baths . . .

In bed again, leaning on a rampart of pillows, with her teatray and

193

her mail . . . And there was a time, five years ago, three years ago, when her mail weighed in at half a stone, and smelled of toilet water and pot-pourri: well-turned tributes, grovellings, poems, invitations, and a lot of free airline tickets. Now? Cathode script from computerized mailing lists. 'Richard Pinkley has completed the preparation of his Autumn Exhibition and is pleased to invite you to the Preview.' '*I* don't *care*,' said Nicola. 'Lucky you! Your name has been selected for a chance to win the holiday of a lifetime with Vista International!' '*I* don't *care*,' said Nicola. 'We understand that the lease on your property will shortly expire and we would be delighted to help you with your relocation in any way we can.' '*I* don't *care*,' said Nicola. Her lease was due to expire at the end of December. Short lease. None of this millennial stuff: nine hundred and ninety-nine years. Just thirty months was all she had wanted. The lease was running out; and so was her money.

Now the real toilet – beginning with the toilet. The toilet: rightly so called. Interesting word, toilet. 'Toilet.' *Toilet*. 'Arranging the hair . . . (*make* one's *toilet*) . . . *an elaborate toilet; a toilet of white satin* . . . (room containing lavatory) . . . (Med.) cleansing of part after an operation or at time of childbirth . . . The reception of visitors by a lady during the concluding stages of her toilet; very fashionable in the 18th C . . . Preparation for execution (in Fr. form *toilette*).' Toilet was right. She had known girls who went to the toilet in fleeting thoughtlessness: it was something that got done between doing other things. Nicola wasn't like that. Nicola was heavy weather. She realized, with regret (but what can you do?), that she was mannish when it came to the toilet. Not ridiculously mannish: she didn't need a pack of cigarettes and *War and Peace* and a section of horse-brass to chew on; she didn't need to hold up traffic beforehand, and clear the street with a bullhorn. Yet the whiteness of the bowl was tinged with difficulty, with onerousness. She flipped up her non-vamp nightdress and sat there making unreadable faces. It shouldn't really happen to a heroine – or only behind closed doors. But the reception of visitors by a lady during the opening stages of her toilet was very fashionable in the twentieth century. And now the twentieth century was coming to an end.

Naked, she weighed herself a second time, while the bath thundered – while it slobbered and rumoured. Then, in an abrupt about-turn, the full-length mirror . . . Yes! Good, still good, all very very good. But time was getting ready to finger it, to make its grab; time was drying that belly with the heat of its breath. She looked at the pots and tubs on the bath's rim; cleansers, conditioners, moisturizers. She looked at the nail varnish, the hair dryer, the fairground lights of the dressing table – the mirror hours, the looking-glass war! No one could seriously stand there and expect anybody to be forever having to do with all *this* shit.

Something about the indomitability of the human spirit (and felt death in its full creative force): back into battle she came the next day, pressing forward under the spiked dome of her black umbrella. Fresh air – or fairly fresh anyway, relatively free-range and corn-fed: outer air, not inner air, not just personal gas. In bygone times of average lassitude she had been capable of spending a week and a half wondering whether to post a letter or return a library book or paint her toenails. But these days (the last days) her need for activity was clearly desperate. She swayed in the rain as she re-experienced the killing etiolation of the previous day, all its pale delinquency. Sitting there beside the bookcase, trying to read, in a growing panic of self-consciousness. Why? Because reading presupposed a future. It had to do with fortification. Because reading went the other way. She sent the book flying through the air with its petticoats flapping. *Women in Love*! She wanted a drink, a pill, a drug (she wanted a Greenland of heroin), but she didn't want it. She wanted the concentrated, the consuming, the undivided male attention known as sexual intercourse (imagine the atomic cloud as an inverted phallus, and Nicola's loins as ground zero), but she didn't want it. Formerly the telephone would have led her off into altered states. And now the telephone's tendrils led nowhere. All you could do was heavily move from room to room to room . . . So it was good to get out and busy oneself with something really useful.

The rain made toadstools of the people on the street. They had a toadstool smell, too (a sodden softness), she noticed, as the wet souls converged at the entrance to the underground, faceless stalks, in mackintoshes, beneath the black flowers of their umbrellas. But Nicola's personal cinematographer (the cause, perhaps, of all her trouble) was still hard at work, and lit her like a chasuble. It was hot, and the rain was hot, but Nicola would be cool. She wore a plain dress of silvery linen. The rain would ruin it, the scuff and the shuffle and the tyre squirt would certainly ruin it (her shoes were already ruined). That didn't matter. Because she was killing off her clothes, one by one. In the damp-dog airlessness of the train (a taxi would have taken all morning), Nicola suffered a sense of deafness from the sleeping pills she had eventually taken the night before. And she also feared an incriminating pallor. Yesterday had devolved into an epic of largely pleasureless – and entirely solitary – excitation: the terrible teenager's clogged *cafard*. And yet the adolescent (she now formulated it to herself), no matter how terrible, no matter how torpid and graceless and hormone-slowed, always had the prospect of love. Nicola did not have the prospect of love – love, which distinguishes this place from all others in the universe. Or it tries. Indeed, her flexings and squeezings, her compulsive caresses of the self, were further haunted by the thought that nothing significantly better was taking place anywhere on earth: no act of love that was undesperate, unmediated, unsneeringly observed. She was wrong about that, wrong also about the way she looked, though in the Spanish burnish of her face there was maybe half a dab of hoar, the hoar of smoke or cloud or milk. Now Nicola stared at a schoolboy until he vacated his seat for her, like a somnambulist. Proudly she sat, and looked straight ahead.

An hour and a half among the warm dust and the microphotography of the Public Records Office in Marylebone High Street gave her everything she needed to know about Walker Clinch. She knew the evidence would be there and of course it was, superabundantly. Thence to the nearby Wallace Collection, where she made a twenty-pence purchase: a single postcard. On the front was a suit of sombre armour, the tin soul of a robowarrior slain long ago. On the back, this:

> Dear Guy – Why do I come here? This is just to say that I am well. It doesn't matter, because by now one has grown so used to this devastating solitude. I am not without employment. And I can always sit and watch the rain – and watch the poor birds getting iller and iller. No tears!
>
> Nicola
>
> *Please* don't reply.

She had written these words in a state of simulated self-pity and indignation, but as she read them now, why, Nicola fairly beamed. Oh the very land where they grew the trees that yielded the paper for writing love-letters on – its soil was dying, neutered with chemicals, overworked, worked to dust. She had this idea about the death of love . . .

Which began with the planet and its fantastic *coup de vieux*. Imagine the terrestrial timespan as an outstretched arm: a single swipe of an emery-board, across the nail of the third finger, erases human history. We haven't been around for very long. And we've turned the earth's hair white. She seemed to have eternal youth but now she's ageing awful fast, like an addict, like a waxless candle. *Jesus, have you seen her recently?* We used to live and die without any sense of the planet getting older, of mother earth getting older, living and dying. We used to live outside history. But now we're all coterminous. We're inside history now all right, on its leading edge, with the wind ripping past our ears. Hard to love, when you're bracing yourself for impact. And maybe love can't bear it either, and flees all planets when they reach this condition, when they get to the end of their twentieth centuries.

Nicola found a chair and placed the card in the thick envelope she had brought along for it. She addressed it to Guy's office (and imagined his face reflected in a visual display unit, and branded by the green figures). In her manly wallet Nicola's fingers finally found one last creased stamp. As she licked, a queue formed ahead of her in her mind, edging towards the turbaned shadow in its caged stall at the subsidiary post-office. But then she nodded, realizing that this letter was the last she would ever send, this stamp the last she would ever lick. Good, good. Stamp queues (in fact queues of any kind) put Nicola into a daylong fury. You bought thousands and then the following week the price of mail went up again. No more of that. Good: one more of life's duties, one more of life's pieces of shit, discharged for the very last time.

With the promise of a little danger money Nicola secured a black cab and sailed up, high on Westway to keep her date for lunch.

'I once slept', she said experimentally, 'with the Shah of Iran.'

Nicola paused. Keith blinked and nodded. She gave him time to work out the dates: Nicola would have been fourteen at the time of the Shah's death. But of course he didn't work it out.

'I was twenty-one at the time. The Shah of Iran, Keith.'

'The towelhead,' Keith said firmly.

She looked at him with her head at an angle.

'But they're religious,' he went on.

'No *no*. This was before the revolution. The Shah . . . the Shah was the king, Keith. An extremely profligate one, too. Have you never heard tell, Keith, of the Peacock Throne? Anyway he scoured the planet for the very best and hottest young women, and paid them lots of money to go to bed with him. It was quite an experience.'

The dark-suited waiter approached, rubbing his hands together and saying, 'Is everything all right, sir?'

'Uh,' said Keith, 'give us some fucking privacy here, Akhbar, okay?'

Keith was waiting for her when she arrived, stolidly established in the very hearth of the dark restaurant. Offered a treat lunch anywhere he liked, Keith had unhesitatingly opted for the Retreat from Kabul, describing it, after some encouragement, as providing a whiff of the Orient at a competitive price. 'Afghani innit,' he had added. 'And you can't beat a good hot curry. No way.'

The murderer remained seated as she approached his table. Nicola wondered whether it was the light, or the food he was already eating, or some routine proletarian ailment he had come down with – but Keith's face was quite yellow. The kind of yellow you saw in a healing black eye. 'Don't be shy, darling,' he said, and tensely opened a hand at the opposite chair. He had the pint of lager and the cigarette and the tabloid and the half-finished sandwich of poppadam and pickle. 'Akhbar! A menu for my uh, for my uh – give her a menu, and don't gimme no meat. What, in here? Three hard-boiled eggs and bung my special sauce on it. Not a germ on earth'll live through that. No danger.' Nicola returned the menu unopened and ordered her first gin and tonic, pleading a diet. For ten minutes or so Keith poured scorn on diets, arguing that you had to keep your strength up and that men preferred fat women. Then his meal arrived. Three additional waiters and two smocked cooks stood and watched, murmuring eagerly among themselves. The murmuring ceased, on the instant, as the first spoonful of sauce entered Keith's mouth, and then you could hear through the hatch an explosion of adolescent laughter – from the boys in hell's kitchen . . . He chewed, then stopped chewing, then chewed again, exploratively, like a puppy testing a hard chocolate. He closed his eyes and fanned his hand placatingly. When, at last, he started to speak, there was so much smoke coming out of his mouth Nicola thought for a moment that he must have quietly lit another cigarette. Keith asked Akhbar to correct him if he was wrong but didn't he ask for the hot one?

'I was having breakfast alone at the Pierre in New York,' Nicola later resumed, 'as was my habit in those days. Two men approached me. Swarthy, and mean of forehead, but perfectly polite and very expensively dressed. Compliments were paid, and an envelope was produced. A promissory note for $50,000 and undated first-class air ticket, return, to Teheran. One night with the Peacock. I later learned that the Shah had many teams of such people at work in all the great capitals, recruiting hefty starlets from Los Angeles, the palest blondes from Stockholm and Copenhagen, fantasy sex-scholars from the geisha houses of Tokyo and Osaka, hysterical goers from Copacabana Beach in Rio de Janeiro, Keith. Quite a thought! The wide world was his brothel. Now that's imperialism. I mean, you have to think: how did he *dare?*'

At this point Keith extended a dissenting forefinger. His sympathies, clearly, were as yet very much with the Shah. He sat hunched forward over his meal, the spoon limply dangling as he finished a long mouthful. Smoke was coming out of his nose now, too, as he said, 'Ah. But for him—no way would that be out of order for a towelhead Royal. Ancient privilege as such. A right exercised from way back. Time immemorial.'

'Time immemorial? Time immemorial? *No, Keith,*' she said, with soothing urgency. 'The Shah's father was just some corporal in the army before he made his *coup.* The purest scum, Keith. The Peacock was born a pauper. You see what I'm saying? It's all will and accident. Anyone can burst out. You can burst out.'

Slowly Keith looked down and to the right, frowning. Nicola lipread his thoughts. TV. Robes. Hot out there. Yul Brynner. Keith in equivalent finery. The Shah of Acton. Keith of Iran. He savoured a fresh spoonful. Smoke was now coming out of his ears.

'Well I said yes, of course. $50,000 was quite a lot of money in those days, and I was intrigued. And unattached. You remember those TV ads for sunglasses I showed you?'

'How could I ever –?'

'That's what I looked like. The CD pimps gave me a couple of fancy presents – jewellery, Keith – and said I would be hearing from them. Nothing happened for a while. Then the telephone call, the limousine, more presents, Kennedy Airport.'

'New York? Love the place. Love it.' He chewed on. Was it Nicola's fancy, or was smoke now coming out of his *eyes?*

'At the other end they took me off to some resort in the south. First, a searching medical. Then I sunbathed for a week: if you were brown already, the Shah liked you browner. The Scandinavian blondes and the pale colleens, I imagine, were kept in a cupboard under the stairs. Plus several hours a day of massage, and workouts with the Shah's dirty-minded physios. Exercises designed to enhance one's twang and twist and give. People do want value for money, don't they, Keith.'

'Definitely,' said Keith seriously. He had stopped eating. An obscure agitation began to play over his lumpy brow.

'I was told it was going to happen in the Summer Palace at Qom. But there was a hitch. I was driven to Teheran. The Sharina was abroad somewhere, frenziedly shopping. You can imagine the scene, Keith, I'm sure: the salutations, the gifts, the pre-war champagne, the flaming dinner on the dusky terrace. There was some kind of demonstration in the square outside which soon developed into a riot. But there we were, with the smalltalk and the servants . . . I was led off. Humming maidens prepared me. Then a middle-aged French madame with big tits and rockinghorse eyes came in, practically armoured in bracelets and necklets and armlets, and spent about forty-five minutes listing all the treats that the Shah would be expecting of me. Final ablutions, perfumes, oils, unguents, Keith. Two lines of the choicest cocaine. And the most miraculous underwear. The panties, I would guess, were worth about a thousand times their weight in gold.'

Keith lit a cigarette. His fingers flickered like the flame. He stared at her with ponderous illegibility. Most of the time Keith's lips were easy to read – his forehead was easy to read. But not now.

'The thing was they didn't weigh *anything*. I'm very interested indeed in underwear, Keith, as you will soon cheerfully discover, but I've never in my life come across anything like those panties. Elite silkworms, no doubt, specially bred and trained. Cool-pants silkworms. It was quite a sensation, pulling them up tight, as instructed. Quite insubstantial but palpably there, like wetness.'

A pulse passed, and he nodded at her to proceed.

'When the Shah eventually removed this shrunken wisp he threw it with gusto high towards the domed ceiling. The panties hovered, Keith, in the warm thermals of the air, and began to fall, like an autumn leaf. When he was finished, they were still falling. And His Excellency took his time. I couldn't sleep because of the gunfire. At noon the next day another pimp appeared and drove me to the airport.'

'Djyou.' Keith cleared his throat and said, 'Did you see him again?'

'The CD pimp?'

'Yeah. No, the . . . His Excellency.'

'The Shah never slept with the same whore twice. And I think I must have been one of his last flings. Six weeks later there was the revolution. And the Shah was dead within a year. But he did look in the next morning and used me rather brutally on the way to a meeting with his American advisers and his Chiefs of Staff. I begged him for those panties – I *begged* him, Keith – but they were already being microtweezered and blowdried for the next slice of . . . Are you all right?'

'Nicola?'

She felt a light shock at the sound of the three syllables. This was Keith's high style.

'Nick, I'm desperate.' He clenched a crackling fist just under his nose. 'I'm fucking desperate. I got to have it *now*. Now. Not soon. Not next week.' At this point, even more surprisingly, he straightened a sallow middle finger. 'Or I just kiss goodbye to this. See? I got to have it like *now*.'

'What?'

'The money!'

'Oh for Christ's sake.'

Keith leaned back and imposingly drew in breath through his nose. She saw that the yellow in his face wasn't the colour of need or fever; it was the colour of fear, open pored, like a grapefruit.

'You don't know the kind of pus I'm dealing with here. Okay, call me a cunt, I took double money on the street. Plans of mine did not reach fruition. Now I made the list and come Friday I get a kicking and they break my fucking darting finger and all.' Again the sallow digit was held up for admiration or review. 'That's how low they'll stoop. See, it brooks no delay. This happens, I'm *out of it*. I'm history. I'm a fucking dinosaur.'

'All right. See Guy tomorrow. Tell him this. Call me when it's done.'

With a genuine performance ahead of her – albeit a matinee or a dress rehearsal – Nicola the love actress felt better, felt much better: she felt twice the price. You see how thin, how poor it would all be, without Guy? The next morning, stern-faced and motionless in the scarcely bearable heat of her bath, with one steaming shank hooked over the side, she gave herself up to the disciplined play of thought. The tale of Ali Baba and the Magic Panties had not gone down as well, or as enlighteningly, as she had hoped. It hadn't been much fun to tell, either (Plan A: have fun telling the story; Plan B: don't have much fun telling it), under the glare of Keith's rancid inscrutability, his wide eyes tipped at an angle, as if he was trying to identify something – the number of a bus slowly surging through the rain, a racing result on the back page of an evening paper. Was he unmoved? Could it be that Keith was cold to the notions of enthusiastic whoredom, foot-deep luxury, tyrant sex, and gravity-defying underwear? A Shakespearean lament would be in order (the world was out of joint) if Keith didn't like underwear, invaluable underwear, underwear worth all his tribe. Perhaps, however (and here her fringe fluttered, as she gasped upwards to cool her brow), Keith just liked *cheap* underwear. One thing, anyway: he believed her story. He fully credited her Arabian Night. A reliable taxonomy of Keith's mind, his soul, his retractile heart—it couldn't be done. None of it parsed, none of it scanned. His libido would be all tabloid and factoid. Such a contemporary condition was pretty well recognized, if imperfectly understood. It had to be said that Nicola liked the idea of trying to get to the bottom of it. Synthetic modernity (man-made), qualified by something ancient and ignoble and reptilian. Like darts: a brontosaurus in nurene loons. All the more reason, then, to wipe the money fear off his face, to see what was in him (his dreams and dreads, the graphs and spools of his nocturnal erections) and find out what would move him to murder.

Wearing a T-shirt only and sitting on a towel, in the kitchen, with the spread newspaper, the pot and the wooden spoon, Nicola depilated her legs for the last but one time; she unpeeled the sections of simmering beeswax, like industrial elastoplasts, from her smarting calves; she sang while she worked . . . Nicola didn't know this (and knowing it wouldn't have made any difference), but she was emerging from the kind of mid-project doldrums that all artists experience, in the windless solitude halfway between outset and completion. The thing is there now, and you know you can get to the end of it. It is more or less what you wanted (or what you felt you'd finish up with); but you start to wish that the powers that be, the talent powers, had thrown you a little further or higher. How to keep that spring in the stride, that jounce in the rump, as black-stockinged Jack mounts the beanstalk for the hundredth time? The tricks she was going to play on Keith and Guy were *good* tricks; but they were low and cruel and almost unrelievedly dirty. If she could do it all sitting upright, fully clothed (indeed, beautifully turned-out), pressing buttons with impeccable fingertips, and not a hair out of place! But it wasn't going to be like that. She would have to get all hot and sweaty, and roll up her sleeves and her skirts, and put in a lot of time down there on the kitchen floor.

Nicola Six was a performing artist, nothing more, a guest star directed by the patterning of spacetime, and there it was. It was written.

Keith called at three.

She said, 'Hello? . . . Good . . . What exactly did you say? . . . And how did it go down? . . . – No no. That's what I expected. That's by the book, Keith. With luck we'll sort it all out in time.'

Nicola listened, or at least stood there with the telephone pressed to her ear, while Keith discoursed with husky briskness on his upcoming darts clash – the quarter-finals of the Duoshare Sparrow Masters. Keith had done as he was told, and told Guy what Nicola had told him to tell. That meant that Guy would come very soon, within fifteen minutes, twenty at the outside. Already in her mind she could hear the terrified *peep* of the buzzer, his pale hello?, his colossal bounds up the stairs. But now she obeyed a long-incubated impulse and said to Keith,

'Tell me something . . . What happens if you win this game? . . . All right – this "match". . . And what, and what if you win the semi too?'

Keith talked boldly of the final: the venue, the format, the purse, the TV coverage, the chance to face world number one Kim Twemlow (also before the cameras), the lively promise of a career in professional darts with its highflying lifestyle, the very real possibility of some day representing his country in an England shirt.

Yes, she thought, or in an England tent.

'Wait,' she said. 'The final. Is there a date set for it? . . . When would this be?'

As he told her, she gave a soft shout, and dropped her head, and felt within herself a warm flood of vindication, a movement and a pang, something like peeing in a cold sea. For a moment she feared the untimely onset of her penultimate period. But that was five days away; and in this area, if in no other, she was as regular as time itself. Women are clocks, after all. They are timekeepers – keepers of the time.

'Listen,' she said. 'I have to go. Whatever happens, you're going to reach the final, Keith, don't worry. I know it. I feel it. With me behind you. You're going to get to the final. You're going all the way. Call me tonight. I must get ready.'

Actually she was pretty well ready as it was. In her multipurpose black cashmere dress, with its dozen black buttons down the middle, she was dressed for anything, she was ready for anything. Nicola had need of only one last prop. Seating herself before the bulb-ridged mirror, she reached for the bottle of glycerine and its little plunger.

Glycerine: a quintessentially modern substance – a viscous liquid formed by the chemical conversion of fats and used as an ointment, a drug component, a sexual lubricant, an element in high explosives. Used also for false tears, by actors and actresses. That's where Nicola found this bottle of tears: in her box of tricks, the box of tricks of the actress.

As the first crocodile tear began to smear her vision, Nicola gazed into the fingerprint contours and saw – and saw crocodiles. She saw the reptile house in Keith Talent's brain. What iguanas and anacondas, what snoozing geckos languished there, presided over, perhaps, by a heraldic basilisk, a rampant cockatrice! All the reptiles were waiting, waiting. And when reptiles wait when there is food around, they are waiting for the food to get weaker, deader, rottener. Not a jungle, not a swamp (for this was a modern brain): a smalltown zoo, an underfunded game reserve, a half-abandoned theme park. Deeply, unimprovably stupid, the creatures are none the less aware that they are being watched. Keith's face appeared before her: the bashful salacity of his alligator smile. It wouldn't be her who romped and basked with Keith and rolled with him in the mud. It would be Enola, Enola Gay. In the theme park, in cold blood, the blindworms and salamanders gave a sudden twitch – a shrug of ooze. Then silence. Reptile vigil . . .

Nicola's head snapped back to the frightened *peep* of the buzzer. She went to listen to Guy's pale hello? Of course she had adored dinosaurs as a little girl. She knew all their names by heart, and loved to toll them through her mind. Dinosaur: terrible reptile. Brontosaurus: thunderlizard. (Now she could hear him scale the stairs with mighty bounds.) A planetary society, built from bones. Would the same thing happen when the human beings were gone? Would we be exhumed (the *cheat*, the foil, the murderee), would we be reconstructed and remembered by the rat, the roach, the triumphal virus?

She took up position at the top of the stairs.

Ankylosaurus. Coelophysis. Compsognatus.

Crookedlizard. Hollowform. Pretty jaw.

Ornitholestes. Maiasaura. Oviraptor.

Birdrobber. Childguarder. Eggstealer.

I've been poring over her diaries again – the stuff about 'MA'. My, how those two went at it. Hammer and tongs. Like Kilkenny cats.

Nicola and MA? Nicola and Mark Asprey? I have to know.

So I in my turn have laid a trap for Nicola Six. Very simple: I just asked her over.

'What's the address?' she said on the phone.

I told her: no audible response. 'You know. Near where you dumped your diaries.'

She'll come clean. Or I'll tell by the look on her face.

'It's terrible,' said Incarnacion in the kitchen this morning, as she removed her mack and the zippered groundsheet she wears on her head, and as she slurped out of her galoshes and gestured toward the window and the terrible rain: 'the terrible rain!' She's right, of course. The rain is terrible. It wouldn't look so bad in a jungle or somewhere, coming down like this, but in a northern city, suspended from soiled clouds. It's all so desperate when you try to wash something unclean in unclean water.

'Is terrible, you know?' proceeded Incarnacion, as she set about the vague preparations for her first pot of tea. 'It brings you so low. When the sun shines? You happy. Feel good. Cheerful, you know? Full of the get up and go. But when is raining like this. Rain, rain, rain. When is raining? You sad. Is miserable, you know? You get depress. You wake up? Rain. Go out? Rain. Inna nights? Rain. Rain,

rain, rain. How you going to cheer up and feel good and happy and cheerful when is all this rain? How? Rain! Just rain, rain, rain.'

Ten minutes of that and I picked up my hat and coat and went out and stood in it. Standing in the rain isn't a whole lot better than being talked to about it by Incarnacion, but it's got the edge. The street corners are swagbellied with rain. They all have these spare tyres of rain. These guts of rain.

At last. Oh happy day.

The call from Missy Harter. In mid-afternoon, under another ton of rain.

First, though, I am screened, not by Missy's assistant Janit, nor yet by Janit's assistant, Barbro, but by a male interrogator with an armpit-igniting way with him, whose name, if he has one, is not revealed. Even when they call you, it takes for ever to get to the top. I suspect they might even run your voice through the computer, in case you're trying to give someone senior a disease over the telephone.

'At last. Missy. How are you?' 'Good. Here's the deal.' 'The deal?' 'The deal. I have my doubts but it's been with Marketing and they project it'll go.' 'Marketing!' I said. (Marketing: I was very moved.) 'Marketing,' she said: 'Here it is: we tight-option volume rights at twenty per cent.' 'Explain, Missy.'

Missy explained. Or she went on talking. So far as I could follow, I got some money now against a renegotiable advance; the latter sum would dramatically decrease if I attempted to place the book elsewhere, but they reserved the right to match any offer from a rival publisher, whom they would immediately sue; if they didn't like the finished book and someone else did, I repaid their money and they returned the typescript, or else they sat on the typescript and I sued Hornig Ultrason; and if I accepted a better offer elsewhere, then Hornig Ultrason sued me.

'Well I suppose it sounds okay.'

'It's standard,' she said. 'You'll hear from the lawyers. I'm time-urgent. The reason: I have a meeting. Goodbye there.'

'Oh Missy? Before you run. Is there anything you can tell me about the – the international situation? Over here it's –'

'Next question.'

I had an image of Missy Harter, scandalized in a skyscraper, looking as prim as her name. But of course the conversation would be taped at her end. And then she added relentingly, 'It's serious. But we feel we're in good hands. Much depends on Faith's health. Forty-five seconds. Next question.'

Faith's health. They talk about Faith as if the First Lady were the only lady. Or the Last Lady. 'You said you had your doubts about my – about the work. Would you care to elaborate on that?'

'It ran counter to expectation. It's so unlike you. Where did it come from?'

'I really need the money, Missy. I'm time-urgent too, you know.'

'I know you are. And I'll try.'

But the money will not come through in time.

The coincidence of Keith's darts final and her own birthday (or appointed deathnight) has filled Nicola with fresh hope. She is rejuvenated. Oh, it's encouraging, I agree. Yes. I guess the future looks bright.

Except Keith has to reach that final. And he won't reach the darts final without his darting finger. In such cases, they don't just bend the darting finger until it breaks. No. The darting finger is placed in the crack of a doorway, and the door is then kicked shut. End of darting finger. Farewell, O darting finger. Nor will Keith reach the darts final if he is locked up in prison at the time. And prison is where Keith will surely languish (picking his nose, perhaps, with a speculative darting finger) if he does this heist with Thelonius. Another thing stands in his path, as he heads toward the darts final. It has at last dawned on me that Keith isn't very good at darts.

I am fond of Thelonius, of course.

He has many excellent qualities: gaiety, warmth, considerable beauty. In him the human essences are rich: life flows from his face and body in a silent roar. He takes care of himself, Thelonius, fanatically, adoringly, inside and out. Boxing at the air, he runs backwards to the gym to work out with the weights. He does yoga, and spends entire weekends standing on his head. As part of his quest for physical perfection Thelonius eats nothing but fruit: even a string-bean, even a radish, would gross him out. His teeth are as flawless as any dolphin's. The secondary smoking and drinking, the tertiary snacks – the drooling meat pies – of the Black Cross reach out for him but their spores can't make it through his purple haze. He always looked after himself. And now that he's in the money, well, no imperial infant ever had it so good. Of course, it has to be conceded that Thelonius is not without faults. One is his habit of breaking the law the entire time. Another is bad taste.

Explosive, exponential bad taste, a kind of antitaste: there is nothing semi-violent about Thelonius's bad taste. I recently asked him if in his younger days he had ever visited America (and perhaps spent a few years on Forty-Second Street or Hollywood Boulevard). When Thelonius was poor, he looked like an athlete; now that he's rich (and the transformation is a very recent one), he looks like a pimp. The animal kingdom may be untroubled by Thelonius's diet, but it has a lot to fear from his dress sense. His pimpsuits, pimphats and pimpshoes are made out of bison and turtles, zebras and reindeer. Among the stolen goods in the pimpboot of his pimpcar are more pimpclothes, swathed in pimppolythene. Every other day, as the pimpwhim takes him, his pimphair is either superfrizzed or expensively relaxed. His pimpfingers are dustered with pimprings. Boy, does Thelonius look like a pimp.

He has a further blemish: an exaggerated view of his own skills and merits. For instance, he is not a good criminal. He is a very lucky criminal, so far. He is heading towards prison at a hundred miles an hour, and taking Keith with him.

True to the logic of the moral fix I'm in, I find myself wishing that Thelonius had much more criminal talent than reality has in fact blessed him with. If I were running things, he would inviolably prosper — he could do what the hell he liked. He could hurt the weak, he could steal and punch and lie and club as much as he wanted, and I would sleep all the sounder.

I don't know why I say Keith isn't good at darts. Keith *is* good at darts. Very often, the darts go where he throws them. His darts genius shines, and brightly. But he is no better at darts than practically everyone else in England. This is a darts culture here: darts is what the Brits do best, in the afterglow of empire. And Keith certainly isn't as good at darts as the darters on TV. The darts *always* go where *they* throw them.

Keith, I think, is not unaware of his possible shortcomings at the oché of today. 'In today's darts,' he will concede, 'standards are outstanding.' He is becoming more and more internally reliant on what he calls his 'gift for rising to the big occasion'. He gets himself going with fiery oratory about the address of the board, gracing the oché, and the sincerity of the dart.

And what about the other Big Occasion? The other Final?

Yeah well cheers, Keith. I know he'll go out there and give me two hundred per cent. Keith a quitter? Keith Talent? You must be – Do you want your – ? No danger will Keith bottle it when the cosh comes down. Pressure? He fucking *phrives* on it. He'll do the necessary. Keith'll do the biz. No way is he going to go out there and not go all the way.

Is moral 'fix' really the word I want? Does fix really cover it? Keith and Guy will both survive, after a fashion. But I mean my position with the murderee.

She just came over. She's been and gone.

On her way up the stairs and into the apartment Nicola did a first-rate imitation of somebody who had never been here before. In retrospect, I salute the actress talent. At the time, I was fooled. (And I was happy.) The way she looked around with caustic glances at the framed photographs – but only parenthetically, just giving the place the edge of her attention, while we talked.

I was fooled. But then I left her in the sitting-room for a minute, and silently returned, framing a question in my head about Keith and the money. And there she was: bent over Mark Asprey's desk, trying the one locked drawer. With a hard look on her face.

Silently I retreated. I don't want her to know I know. Not yet.

All most painful. All most *painful, painful.* My only consolation is that according to her diaries Nicola did something sensationally wicked to that MA of hers. Oh, she was very very bad . . . I can't understand my own feelings. This nausea. I am implicated. I can't understand the implication.

This is no *fix*. This is moral horror, no two ways about it.

The Black Cross. A good name, I always thought, sent my way by reality. The cross, darkly cruciform, the meeting place of Nicola and Keith and Guy.

A cross has three points. Depending on how you look at it, though, it might be said to have four.

And my love thing for Kim immediately involves me in new anxiety. There was no honeymoon period.

While Kath sleeps, with morbid abandon, in the bed-sized bedroom, I play with Kim on the sitting-room floor. Kim bears small bruises about her small person. You can see how it happens. Almost any movement in Keith's flat involves the movement of something else. You get these little chain reactions. Always you're beetling over the child. Turn around and your nose bangs into the door. Shift in your seat and something else shifts. I worry.

Jewellery, precious minerals, intricate glasswork, and so on, dead beauty: none of it does anything for me. But Kim's eyes make me understand. Jewellery, precious minerals, intricate glassware, dead beauty, it's all fine: an attempt to summon the living galaxy of a baby's eyes. The baby's sparklers, the Milky Way of babies . . . Babies don't mind if you stare at them closely. Everyone else does. The dying do.

At some point in the afternoon Kim likes to take a nap. Often she is woken by bad dreams. It is strangely pleasurable to pick her up and comfort her. All you do is just stand there and be the great shoulders, the godlike thorax.

Chapter 12: The Script
Followed by Guy Clinch

GUY SAT AT the kitchen table and gazed, with steady incomprehension, at his veal: its pallor, its puddled beach of juice. He had cooked the dinner himself, as usual, expressionlessly busying himself with meat-pounder, pasta-shredder, vegetable-slicer. The kitchen was a spotless laboratory of time-saving devices. Time was constantly being saved. But for what? Guy used to enjoy cooking, in the relatively old days, when you did some of it yourself. He liked to cook in an apron, not in a lab-coat. Really, Guy could have made the grade as a proletarian female. He was obedient, industrious and uncomplaining. He had what it took. Now he gazed at his veal and briefly felt the allure of vegetarianism (that friendly black boy in the Black Cross) until his eye fell on the smug pellets of the broad beans, the endlessness of the pasta. The wine, a powerful Burgundy, seemed, at least, non-alien, definitely terrestrial: forgetfulness, the warm south, it said to the juices of his jaw. These schooled juices searched also for another presentiment. For the flavour of reconciliation, perhaps? No. Of forgiveness. Guy looked up carefully at his wife, who sat across the table consuming her meal in vigorous silence.

A little while later he said,

'I'm sorry?'

'I didn't say anything,' said Hope.

'I'm sorry.'

'Why don't you go to the doctor?'

'No need. Really. I'll be all right.'

'I didn't just mean for your sake . . . So how much more of this do we get?'

'More of what?'

'Of the famished mute. You don't eat anything. And you look like death.'

It was certainly the case that he wasn't eating anything. A literalist (and a rather literary literalist), Guy had eaten awfully little since his last conversation with Nicola Six; in fact his appetite had begun to decline the very day they met, and since their parting (yes: for good – for the best) it had disappeared altogether, just as the woman had disappeared. When he did eat – and the activity wasn't distasteful so much as madly irrelevant – he had to hurry off after a minute with his hand held high. You could then hear him vomiting efficiently in the basement lavatory. What kept him going were his breakfasts – his hearty bowls of MegaBran. He could digest his MegaBran because (or so he often thought) the thick, dark, all-fibre cereal was precisely one stage away from human shit in the first place. MegaBran was on a chemical knife-edge between cereal and human shit. Guy wondered whether MegaBran shouldn't rename itself HumanShit: the lettering could be done wavily and mistily, to suggest an imminently dawning reality. One drop of saliva was all MegaBran needed. Marmaduke, who adored spitting on people's food, had once successfully spat into a full packet of MegaBran. The results had been spectacular – though it ought to be said that Marmaduke's saliva had often shown itself to possess surprising and maleficent properties . . . Not so long ago Guy would have thoughtlessly chopped a banana into his morning bowl of MegaBran; but now he was overwhelmed by the reek of the potassium enhancement. Everyone hated MegaBran. Everyone ate it. Hope couldn't bear cooking or even being in the kitchen but she was intensely strict and vigilant about everything everyone ate.

Guy poured more wine and said in a puzzled voice, 'Can't bear that noise.'

'I know. How does he do it?'

'Can't we turn him down a bit?'

'No. I'm listening for the phlegm.'

They were alone tonight. But they were not alone. Marmaduke was present, in electronic form: the twin screens of the closed-circuit TV system shook and fizzed to his rage. There were twin screens in most rooms, on every floor. Sometimes the house felt like an aquarium of Marmadukes. Guy thought of all the video equipment in Nicola's apartment (what use did she have for it?) and then thought of his own, of how he and his wife had gamely wrestled with the webbing and the pistol-grips in the months after Marmaduke was born, gathering footage of Marmaduke screaming his head off in the playpen, Marmaduke screaming his head off in the park, Marmaduke screaming his head off in the swimming-pool. They soon stopped bothering. After all, there was so little difference between the home movie and the closed-circuit monitor, which gave them Marmaduke screaming his head off twenty-three hours a day as it was. And when the twin screens weren't giving it to them (two different angles of Marmaduke screaming his head off), Marmaduke was giving it to them: live.

Now, against the background of the child's obscure agonies, a tremendously long silence gathered. This silence was shaped like a tunnel. It seemed to Guy that there was no way out of it, none at all – except full confession. Or this:

'We could have another child,' he said, staring seriously at his wife.

'. . . Are you out of your mind?'

Guy's eyebrows lifted and he resettled himself like a moody pupil. It was true that they had been most gravely advised – on many different occasions, in many different clinics and consulting rooms, in Geneva, in Los Angeles, in Tokyo – to renounce the possibility of a second child, or to delay it indefinitely, or at any rate until Marmaduke was at least fourteen (by which time Hope, besides, would be fifty-one). The billionaire specialists and Nobel Laureate child-psychiatrists had always warned of the disturbing effect on Marmaduke if a little newcomer should succeed him. None had been heartless enough to suggest that the second child might be just like the first.

'What if it's just like Marmaduke?' said Hope.

'Don't *say* that. My God. What's he doing now?'

'He's trying to make himself sick.'

'But he's got his whole fist down there.'

'He won't manage it.'

Guy looked at Hope – surprised, heartened.

'He threw up his tea long ago. And his milk and cookies. His only hope now is with the phlegm.'

'He wasn't sick after lunch. Can't bear that noise. Or was he?'

'Yeah – he slimed Melba. Then he bit Phoenix on the tongue. Quite far back. I hope she wasn't letting him French-kiss her again.'

Guy uneasily reviewed Hope's policy about Marmaduke and

213

kissing. Members of the staff were allowed to kiss Marmaduke. But only Hope was allowed to French-kiss him.

'I had to call Terry.'

'Terry!'

Even more uneasily Guy thought of Terry – his platform shoes, his brutal singlet. 'I hate Terry.'

'So do *I*. He's strictly last-resort. And even he looked pretty shaken.'

Guy looked down and gave a smile – not of affection but of wonder. He loved Marmaduke. He would joyfully die for Marmaduke. He would die for Marmaduke, not next week, not tomorrow, but now, right now. He loved Marmaduke despite the clear sense, constantly refreshed, that Marmaduke had no lovable qualities. Marmaduke gave no pleasure to anyone except when he was asleep. When he was asleep, you could gaze down at him and thank the Lord that he wasn't awake.

'Oh yes,' said Hope. 'Lady Barnaby. She's been struck dumb.'

'Literally?'

'Yup. Since she got back. Shock.'

'That's terrible.'

'You know what you look like?' said Hope. 'A hermit.'

Guy shrugged and looked away. He didn't seem to mind the comparison. But then he looked back again: Hope was staring at him with concentration. He feared this stare. He readied himself.

'Not a hermit who lives in a cottage,' she went on slowly. 'In the Orkneys or wherever. I mean the kind of hermit who lives in a hotel in Las Vegas. A sordid maniac with lots of money who never goes out. The kind of person who has a "shrine" in his bedroom for some fat dead moviequeen.'

He had kept up with the Cambodia thing – with the remote and groping search for Little Boy and En Lah Gai: the displaced persons. Making his calls each morning at the office (it was his only reason for going in), Guy was by now on first-name terms with various contacts – various telephonic entities – at the American Refugee Committee, the British Refugee Council and the UN Border Relief Operation. His limp fingers regularly sought his brow as he sat there and listened to the war stories. Guy had grown up in the age of mediated atrocity; like everyone else, he was exhaustively accustomed to the sad arrangements, the pathetic postures of the dead. But you couldn't see Cambodia, the torturee nation, whose redoubling sufferings took place behind a black curtain or a slammed door. This darkness seemed to have a pornographic effect on the concerned imagination. You just couldn't escape the excitement in the voices that told tales of Cambodia. Guy himself had been sent copies of the satellite photographs and seen the death silhouette: the diagrammatic honeycomb was evidently a landscape, a wide horizon of human skulls. He too felt the excitement, the rush of boyish manliness, which in his case soon subsided into a distant nausea. The satellite massacres: human death as a god might see it. Guy's faith, a feebly gleaming heirloom (a locket, perhaps, that once belonged to his dead mother), was much tarnished for a while by the clear impossibility of anything surviving such a thorough subtraction of the human body. Take life away, and all you have is the anatomical torment of a single skull. 'I was there all through the Eighties,' one of the telephone ghosts roared at him (he was an American from UNBRO), bringing him messages from the other side. 'I have an image for you. You all set?' The voice was eager, greedy. 'A child's prosthetic foot, in a flipflop, marching to war. That's Cambodia, pal.' Guy nodded quickly, in placation. 'And there's no way out.'

Though of course, as always, there was a way out, it transpired – there *was* one way out . . . Guy had persuaded himself that he wasn't making a hobby of Cambodia. But this research of his remained in some sense a labour of love, a romantic duty, a means of thinking about Nicola in relative and arguable guiltlessness. No denying that a fantasy was being quietly and queasily unspooled. Guy would mount the stairs of her house (against a background of flags and bunting), coolly shepherding the two shy figures; Nicola would be ready on the top landing, her hands tightly clasped, with beautifully viscous tears on her cheeks. How the laughter of En Lah Gai would nervously sound as warming broth was prepared in the small kitchen! How the eyes of Little Boy would burn – would burn with unforgettable fire! And down there at hip height Nicola's fingers would entwine his own in fond conspiracy . . .

Even Guy could tell that there was something wrong with this motion picture, something awful, something aesthetically disastrous. The scene would have a livid colour, the music would roll along in its corrupt or sinister gaiety, the dialogue would feel dubbed, and the actors would simper like charmless children on the brink of being found out. Again the word pornography came to mind: to Guy's mind, where there wasn't any – where there wasn't any pornography.

215

None at all? No, not really. There had been those occasions (increasingly frequent, until his operation) when a nurse holding a test-tube like a glass condom had disgustedly ushered him into a curtained room equipped with 'books' – torn heaps of men's magazines. Guy had turned the strange pages (in the end he relied on his wallet photograph of Hope). And there was the sprinkling of stag films he had been obliged to watch half of during business trips to Hong Kong and other eastern Mammons. Always there came a terrible moment, in between the carnal sections, when the cast stood around pretending to be interesting with all their clothes on, just like proper actors and actresses, obeying a properly inventive director, in a proper film. The imposture seemed to be doubly shaming for everyone, including the viewer. Even Guy could tell that his interest in Nicola Six and his interest in Indochina did not sit well together (with a wag of the head he thought of a plump pinup he had once seen, fondling a piece of hardware in a weapons brochure). Love and war – love and historical forces – did not sit well together.

Besides, his musings were on the whole dreadfully tender and tentative. His dreams, which appeared to emanate from the pool of warm pressure in his chest, all followed adolescent storylines of surveillance, custodianship, brilliant rescue (rowing boats, a car's flat tyre magically repaired and replaced). He thought of her always, even at moments of sudden stress in the office or the nursery; her face was like a curlicue floating in his peripheral vision. Daily, cosynchronously, he dogged her through her day, her waking, her light breakfast, her idealized toilet – and so on. He thought of his thoughts as explorers, in virgin territory. Of course, he didn't know how much male thought had already gone into Nicola Six, those millions of man hours; he didn't know that every square inch of her had been *ransacked* by men's thoughts . . . Sometimes, to buy his weekly packet of cigarettes (or an extra daily paper), he went to the shop near where she lived. As if round a doorway he bent and peered up the dead-end street. Seen through eyes of love, how fiercely she would have illumined the ordinary prospect: the trees already leafless in September, two builders eating Scotch eggs on a stoop, a dead cloud collapsing into the fog of dark rain. This day Guy straightened his dirty mack with a smile of pain, and walked back and round to the Black Cross.

Keith was standing by the fruit machine, contentedly picking his teeth with a dart – or with the *point* of a dart, as Guy had learned to distinguish (*flight, shaft, barrel, point*), after a few of his early darting solecisms had been menacingly corrected, here in the Black Cross. Guy found that he was glad to see Keith, and took comfort also from the damp lineaments of the ruined pub. Conspicuous elsewhere, his own colourlessness easily merged with the circumambient grey. The white people in here were black-and-white people, monochrome, like World War II footage. Like World War I footage. Guy thought further of the stills that form the countdown to an elderly movie: 6, +, 5, *, blank, clapperboard; and the white areas of the screen grained with dust and nostril hairs, like the whites of soiled eyes. Keith always made Guy think of eyes.

'Fucking sickening. It disgusts me. No, it does.'

'Absolutely vile.'

'Wicked.'

'It's filthy.'

'Persistent low atmospheric pressure innit.'

By moving his head a centimetre to the left, Keith indicated that Guy might join him. As Guy came forward he accidentally stepped on the surprising solidity of Clive's tail. Clive lifted his chin from the carpet and snarled or swore at Guy wearily.

'Sorry. Well,' said Guy. 'Haven't seen you for a while.'

Keith nodded. This was true. And what of it? Keith took the trouble to point out that he was the sort of bloke who had places to go and people to see. He wasn't the sort of bloke who just sat around getting pissed all day in the Black Cross on Portobello Road. No. Keith's restless nature demanded variety. This week, for instance (it laboriously emerged), he had been sitting around getting pissed all day in the Skiddaw on Elgin Avenue. But in fact Keith did look pleasantly surprised to be in the Black Cross. Why, Guy didn't know.

'Few drinks. Relax.' Keith suddenly refocused and said, 'Whew, mate, you don't look too clever. No. You definitely do *not* look overly brill. It must be going round. I tell you who else ain't in the best of elph either. Neither.'

At the sound of her name (a duosyllable in this case: for a moment it sounded like a further grammatical adjustment) Guy felt something soft exploding in the transept of his chest. His head dropped and he reached out a hand for the bar. Nicola was suffering. This was heavenly news.

'Sad little smile on its face. Like – like she was pining. Pining. Pining its little heart out.'

Guy looked up. Keith seemed to be inspecting the saloon-bar ceiling – wondering, perhaps, how many Londons of cigarette smoke had gone into its golden brown. With evident relief he now talked of other matters, and Guy thought, with a mild seizure of affection: he knows. Keith knows. He has divined it. Nicola and I – in a sense we're way above his head. But he can see what binds us (the ropes of love); and with due respect.

'Here. I got one for you.'

Guy tried to concentrate. Keith was about to tell a joke – he was already chuckling ruminatively to himself. In the past Guy had struggled rather with some of Keith's jokes. They were often reasonably mild, turning on a childish whimsicality, a lugubrious pun. Only rarely, or relatively rarely, did Keith lean forward bearing his incisors and impart some tale about a rotten haddock and the knickers of an unfortunate lady. But that could happen to you anywhere. In the billiards room at the club. In a starred restaurant in the City. And as he had just shown, despite his superficial roughness Keith had a lot more natural delicacy than many of the –

'How can you tell when your sister's having her period?'

'Um,' said Guy. He didn't have a sister. He shrugged. He said, 'I don't know.'

'Dad's cock tastes funny!'

Guy stood and stared into the tempest of Keith's laughter. This tempest, this *tormenta*, kept on coming for a very long time, until, after a series of lulls and false calms, orderly waters returned once more. Guy was smiling palely.

'Gah!' said Keith, lifting a fist to his streaming eyes. 'Dear oh dear. Well. It puts a smile on your face. And you got to keep laughing. You got to. In this life . . . Dear oh dear oh dear.'

Now Guy hung back as Keith took his new joke on a tour of the pub. Its punchline was soon ricocheting from group to group. In the damp light there was many a spray of Scotch-egg crumbs, many a dull flash of Soviet dentistry. The joke went down well in all quarters, though one or two of the older women (were they really old or only old-young?) confined themselves to a long glance of affectionate reproach. Drinking brandy, seated by the back door, and scratching his neck, Guy watched all this in his numb fever. Compliments that come second-hand are said to be the sweetest; and never in his life had Guy Clinch been so flattered. He sat there pulsing with the flattery of love. Today's rushes, in the screening-room of his mind's eye, showed nothing more than repeated scenes of reunion, breathless and unfettered reunion. Just a hug. Not even a kiss . . . Not even a hug. These rushes were like the last frames of *Incident at Owl Creek*, with the dead hero racing through the dark dreamfields, and under false skymaps, racing towards her, and racing, and racing, and getting no nearer with each heartbursting surge . . . God and Pongo took Keith aside and then he left hurriedly. He tried to shovel Clive up with his foot and then leaned backwards forty-five degrees on the lead, like the last man in a tug-of-war team. Twenty minutes later, as Guy was leaving, three men filed into the saloon bar and asked for Keith; they asked the pub for Keith – as if (Guy mused fleetingly) the black cross were daubed on the door and not on the sign above, and they were telling the pub to give Keith up or to bring him out. If Keith had been trying to avoid this trio (the white-haired one sported half a dozen earrings per ear, and had the blue lips of a cold child), then Guy didn't blame him: they did look extremely tiresome.

The ceiling of Marmaduke's nursery swarmed with strange shadows, Medusa heads, beckoning goblins . . . Children love their toys, don't they. It's so obvious. But why? Why do they?

'*Please* don't do that, darling,' he said.

Guy was sitting on a low chair, surrounded, like Joan of Arc, by kindling – in his case the scattered planks of a wooden train-set, together with a few torn picture-books and eviscerated teddybears. Turning from the wrecked mobile, Marmaduke was now 'playing' with his toy castle. It was 5.45 in the morning.

Children love to touch their toys because their toys are the only things they *can* touch: the only things they can touch freely. Manmade objects, blunted, detoxified, with pleasure possible and pain counterindicated. Or that was the idea. Marmaduke could find mortification almost anywhere. A fluffy birdling was cute enough until a child engulfed his own larynx with it.

'Milt,' said Marmaduke, without turning round. 'Big it.'

Guy looked at his watch. He went and unlocked the crammed refrigerator on the landing. He returned with a full bottle – and four wholewheat biscuits, which the child now repulsively dispatched.

'My God,' said Guy.

'More big it,' said Marmaduke out of the corner of his mouth (its centre being occupied by the bottle). 'More big it.'

'No!'

'More big it.'

'Absolutely not!'

The teat slid from Marmaduke's lips. 'Big it. More big it . . .' Instead of raising his voice, Marmaduke lowered it: he sometimes got a far more chilling effect that way. 'Big it, Daddy. More big it . . . More big it, Daddy . . .'

'Oh all right. Say please. Say please. Say please. Say please.'

'Police,' said Marmaduke grudgingly.

Toys were symbols – of real things. That toy monkey stood for a real monkey, that toy train for a real train, and so on: in miniature. But there seemed to be a disturbing literalism abroad in Marmaduke's nursery. That toy baby elephant, for instance, pink and gauzy and five feet high, with its imperial tassels and convincing little howdah (the launchpad of many sickening falls): the baby elephant was about the size of a baby elephant. And the same sort of thing could be said for Marmaduke's howitzers and grenade-launchers and cartridge belts, not to mention all the plastic broadswords and cutlasses and scimitars – *and* his cudgels and knobsticks and battleaxes. Marmaduke's latest deployment (part of a permanent modernization programme), a DID, or Deep Interdiction Device, a pucklike boobytrap which could take out three or four toy tanks at a time, was certainly far larger than the actual contrivance now fielded by Nato. Nato. Assault Breaker. How old it all was. Though Marmaduke himself would unquestionably favour First Use. Marmaduke was a definite First-Use artist. Fight like hell for three days and then blow up the world.

The door opened. Hope stood there, in her small-hour glow. A sentinel in a white nightdress. One arm was raised, as if to hold a candle. He became aware of the sound of rain on the streets and rooftops.

'It's six.'

'He's being very good actually,' Guy whispered. The lines of his brow invited and encouraged Hope to contemplate her son, who was playing with his toy castle, methodically weakening each ridge of the outer rampart before snapping it off. Doing this caused him to grunt and gasp a good deal. Only the very old grunt and gasp so much as babies. In between (Guy thought), we strain all right yet keep holding silence.

'Upstairs.'

Upstairs on the third floor there was a room known locally as the Padded Cell. It was furnitureless and covered in three thicknesses of duvet, wall to wall, floor to ceiling. Its only irregularity was a chest-high ledge with an extra duvet and some pillows for attending adults to climb up to and throw themselves down on. Thither they carried the screaming child . . .

Outside, day was forming in terms of rain-deadened light; Guy now joined his wife between the sheets. Rolling his neck, he took one last look at the monitor: a ceiling-to-floor shot of Marmaduke silently screaming his head off in the Padded Cell. As he screamed, Marmaduke bounced skilfully on his slippered feet, trying to generate enough height for a damaging dive. Guy sank back. His wife searched him for the reliable body warmth he knew she still needed him for.

'It's our cross to bear,' she said vaguely.

Guy bent his throbbing neck and kissed her mouth, which was half-open and half-awake and tasted of dreams and fever. He lay there vigilantly, hoping and not hoping. The weak delirium of dawn, when the body is childishly tired and tender, with surprising tangs and hurts and tastes: it had happened, during shared insomnias, after summer balls, and, much longer ago, at the end of nights of soldierly study. Is *Troilus and Cressida* an anti-comedy? Explore the formation of the Special Relationship . . . He was in fact grotesquely erect: the skin down there was tugged tight as a drum. His auxiliary heart, refusing to become disused, or taken lightly. Just by pressing into the linen here one could perhaps quite easily . . .

'I'll do it,' murmured Hope, sliding from the bed in quiet animal obedience – for Marmaduke's great cries were by now of the volume and timbre that no mother could sleep through. It was morning. Today was another day.

He turned on to his back. He had this toy of Nicola in his head, oval, blue-backed, like a Victorian miniature. Symbol of the real thing. The real thing. Three brutal jolts would certainly finish it. But all kinds of considerations – including squeamishness, another kind of *amour propre*, and the thought of all the mess it would leave – combined, as always, to stay his hand.

You wouldn't want to play with it like that.

Two days later Guy did something ordinary. And then something strange happened.

He helped a blind man cross the street. And then something strange happened.

On Rifle Lane a very old blind man was standing at the zebra crossing. Rangy, propulsive, briskly strolling, Guy paused when he saw him. It was perhaps not such a common sight, not any more. One doesn't often see the blind in the streets now. One doesn't often see the very old. They stay inside. They don't come out much, not any more. Not this year.

Tall, thin, the blind man stood with blind erectness, backward-tending, as road and pavement users crisscrossed past. Something wavery in his stance suggested that he had been there for some time, though he showed no distress. In fact he was smiling. Guy strode forward. He took the blind man's blind arm. 'Would you like a hand, sir?' he asked. 'Here we are,' he said, guiding, urging. On the far kerb Guy cheerfully offered to take the blind man further – home, anywhere. Sightless eyes stared at his voice in astonishment. Guy shrugged: offer the simplest courtesy these days and people looked at you as if you were out of your mind. And then astonishment became general, for the blind man tapped his way to the nearest wall, and dipped his head, and used his eyes for something they were still good at. Tears came from them readily enough.

Guy reapproached the blind man with embarrassment and some panic.

'Leave him,' said an onlooker.

'Leave him alone, for fuck's sake,' advised another.

Guy wandered off into the rain. Hours later, at home, when his confusion and his heartbeat had started to steady, he thought of something he had read somewhere . . . about the traveller and the starving tribe. How did it go? The sun-helmeted anthropologist revisits a tribe which he had once celebrated for its gentleness. But now the tribe was starving; such food as there was went to the strong; and the strong laughed at the weak, the flailing, fading weak; and the weak laughed too. The weak laughed too, sharing in the hilarity of vanished feeling. One time, an old woman stumbled on the edge of a drop. A passing strongman – a food expert, a swaggering food champ – helped her over the edge with a kick in the rump. As she lay there, laughing, the traveller hurried forward to give comfort. And the comfort was intolerable to her. Two strokes of the hair, soft words, a helping hand: *this* was what made the woman cry. The present seemed perfectly bearable – indeed, hilarious – until you felt again what it was like when people were kind. Then the present was bearable no longer. So the old woman wept. So the blind man wept. They can take it, so long as *no one* is kind.

222

Guy was kind, or kind that day. It was all right for him. He had Nicola's postcard in his pocket. The suit of armour: the brave words. Any other time he might have walked right past. Love is blind; but it makes you see the blind man, teetering on the roadside; it makes you seek him out with eyes of love.

'Darling? Come and sit on my lap.'

'. . . Go way.'

'Come on. And read a book. Come and sit on Daddy's lap. There's a good boy.'

'Zap.'

'Lap. Very good! *Good* boy. Look. Food. You like food. What's that?'

'Bam.'

'Bam? . . . Spam. Sssspam. Very good. What's that?'

'Agh.'

'Egg, yes. Egg. What's that? . . . What's that? . . . We're in the garden now. What's that? What's that, darling?'

'Dick.'

'Stick. Very good. Sssstick. Now here's a flower. Say "flower" . . . Those are the petals. And this bit down here is –'

'Dork.'

'Very *good*, darling. Excellent. Now what do you call this? Where the tree used to be. Like in our garden. Where they've chopped it down.'

'Dump.'

'Marmaduke, you're a genius. What's that? . . . A tree. What's that? . . . Grass. Don't do that, darling. *Ow*. Wait, look! Animals. Animals. What's that?'

'Jeep.'

'Yes, sheep. Very good. What's that?'

'Zion.'

'Lion. Lllion. Lllion. Very good. And what's this squidgy thing here?'

'Nail.'

'Snail. Excellent! Aha. Here's your favourite. Here's the best animal of them all. No wait, darling. Hey! One more. You like this one. What is it? What is it?'

'. . . Gunk!'

'Yes! And what does it do? What does it do that no other animal can? What does it do?'

'. . . Dink!'

'*Very good.* You know, sometimes you can be the most adorable man-cub.'

As Guy bent forward to give a farewell kiss to the increasingly restless child – Marmaduke caught him with the reverse headbutt. It was probably at least semi-accidental, though Marmaduke did do a lot of laughing and pointing. In any event the combined movement resulted in a fairly serious impact. Anyone who has ever marched into a lamp-post, or into a fellow pedestrian, knows that 3 m.p.h. is quite dangerous enough for human beings, never mind 186,000 miles per second. He was still spitting doubtfully into a paper tissue when, about fifteen minutes later, there was a knock and the door opened.

'Doris,' said Guy.

'Guy,' said Doris.

Guy flinched a little at the familiarity – or one of his genes did. A recent recruit, Doris was a portly blonde of thirty or forty, with mutinous legs. She was already a martyr to the Clinches' stairs.

'There's someone at the door for you.'

'Oh? Who is it?'

'Don't know. Says it's urgent. It's a *man.*'

Guy wondered what to do. Hope was playing at the Vanderbilt with Dink Heckler and wouldn't be back till just after seven. There was something of a nanny famine at present; even Terry had succumbed to the pressure, gratefully accepting some post at a prison gymnasium. And he couldn't ask Doris, who would in any case certainly refuse. Alone with Doris, within range of Doris, Marmaduke spent every moment trying to kick her swollen shins or jeeringly punching her breasts.

'Bring him up. Sorry, Doris. Show him up. Thank you.'

In due course Keith sailed into the room – in his sailor trousers with their spinnaker flares. His hair was flattened by the rain, and the soaked tabloid hung from his armpit, like an extra limb of little utility. He gave a confidential nod and said,

'Audi.'

Guy thought for a moment and said, 'Howdy.'

'Saab Turbo,' Keith went on. 'Fuel injection. Listen, mate . . .' Keith glanced over his shoulder and then at Marmaduke, who peered up with interest from the remains of his toy castle. 'Listen. I popped round there with some stuff and – Nicola. Between you and me, pal, it don't look too shrewd.'

Guy stared at him with earnest incomprehension.

'I mean, you seen them marks on her wrist.'

'No?'

'The left wrist. Little white scars. You know. Tried it once. Might try it again.'

'Christ.'

'Says to me: "Don't fix that. Don't fix this. No point. What's the point. Why bother. What's the point. No point." All this. Face like a – she's really down. Emotionally withdrawn. Showing suicidal tendencies innit. I'm just worried she's gone do itself an injury.'

'You really think?'

With a craven expression on his face Keith said, 'Go round and see her, mate. She's been very good to me, she has. You know: a really nice lady. And if she . . . I'd never . . .'

'Yes of *course*.' Guy's pupils moved around in thought and then he said, 'Keith, I couldn't possibly ask you to watch the child for twenty minutes, could I?'

'Course you can. Glad to. Oh uh . . .' And again he peered up at Guy heedfully. 'Use your phone?'

'Yes of course. Down one floor and the second door on your left.'

'Kath might be preparing my evening meal.'

When Keith returned – after a long and taxing interval – Guy himself went and burst into the master bedroom to pick up his keys and his money. Driving a hand through his hair, he noticed the heavy indentation of Keith's buttocks on his wife's side of the bed. He felt something had to be done about that. Hurriedly he pummelled the duvet with his fists.

One more visit to the nursery: Keith was down on his haunches, his hands raised, snorting and sniffing – softly sparring with Marmaduke, who looked well pleased with his new friend.

'You *are* good, Keith,' said Guy.

'Yeah cheers,' said Keith.

Intense but more or less disinterested concern prevailed until he rang her doorbell: after he heard the sound of her voice (its soft moan of assent or surrender or defeat), he felt nothing more than the simple tug of beauty. '6: SIX', said the oblong sticker next to her button. Such prodigal symmetry. Even her telephone number was somehow minutely glamorous, with the curves of its eights and zeros, like an erotic cipher. With mighty bounds he scaled the stairs.

Guy expected – or wouldn't have been surprised – to find her on a creaking stool with a noose round her neck, or lying on the sofa with a mother-of-pearl derringer in her ear . . . In reality he found her standing over her desk, and leaning on it capably with her small fists, and for some reason staying that way for a couple of beats after he had chased his chariot heart into the low sitting-room. (The sitting-room meant nothing to him: it was just the place where certain things could happen.) Then she turned.

'You shouldn't have come,' she said warmly. 'But I must admit I'm terribly pleased to see you.'

Guy knew that he would never forget the varieties of light in her face, the prismy clarity of the eyes, the smile with all its revelatory whiteness of tooth – and those teartracks, their solid shine, like solder, on her cheekbones. When women cry (what was that line in *Pygmalion*?), the hayfever russet is part of the pathos and the whole snotty helplessness, but with her, with her –

'Just an hour ago,' she said, and smiled down at her desk, 'I got the most wonderful news.'

'That's wonderful,' he said, quite unable to keep the disappointment out of his voice. Don't tell me she's crying for *joy*. How woodenly, now, those wonderfuls echoed in the low room.

An envelope was held up towards him. Airmail: the striped red-and-blue trim.

Nicola said, 'They're alive. Enola is alive. And – and Little Boy. They're still in transit somewhere between Sisophon and Chantha-buri. But everything is clear now. Completely clear.'

Guy shrugged one shoulder and said, 'Fantastic.'

She came forward and bent over the table for her cigarette lighter. With mournful disquiet Guy saw her breasts through the open neck of black bodice. He looked away, and felt relief when she straightened up and the material tautened. So brown! So close together!

'I fly to Seoul tonight.'

It was fatherly, the whole thing was fatherly – even the way he took her wrist like that was fatherly, fatherly. She was unwilling but after a while consented to sit beside him and hear what he had to say. He said that in his view she wasn't allowing herself to face the truth of what was really happening – in Cambodia. He was gentle, yet firm. There was, he felt confident, nothing lingering in the way he smoothed and patted her hand: a reflex of protective suasion. Guy took stern pleasure in the doubts he saw gathering in her open face. Nicola was nodding, and biting her lip, and leaning forwards at a penitent angle. The neck of her bodice was so disposed that he might have availed himself of her inattention; but he became absorbed, rather, in the solicitous caresses with which he now favoured her hair, her neck, her throat. So brown. So close together. After a silence she said,

'Then I'll have to do the other thing.'

He said quickly, 'The underground railway?'

She looked up at him with no expression on her face. ' . . . Yes.'

'It's unreliable. A real gamble.'

'Oh. I know.'

'And a lot of money.'

'How much, do you think?' He named a sum and then Nicola added grimly, 'Yes, that's more or less the figure I've heard mentioned. By my contact in . . . Tunisia.' She opened her eyes to their full extent, saying, 'Well it's perfectly simple. I'll sell my flat. The lease isn't all that long but it will probably realize almost that amount. I'll find a room somewhere. And then there's one's jewellery and clothes and so on. That fridge is nearly brand-new.'

'Surely there's no need for all that. Surely.'

'You're right. It won't be enough. Still. There are things a woman . . .' She paused, and said with slow intentness, 'A woman can do certain things.'

'*Surely.* I won't hear of it.'

Nicola smiled at him wisely. 'Oh no. I see your scheme. Guy, that would be completely out of the question.' She placed a consoling hand on his thigh and turned to look towards the window. 'I'm sorry, my dear one. No no. I couldn't possibly let you lend me so much money.'

It was seven o'clock when Guy got back to the house of cards, where love sent him bounding up the stairs again.

Unbelievably, Marmaduke was sitting motionless on Keith's lap, his stocky form partly obscured by the upraised tabloid – and by a hip-high shelf of cigarette smoke. Guy hoped it didn't seem too pointed or censorious, the way he strode in there and hurled both windows open to the rain. Claiming that Marmaduke had been as good as gold, Keith left promptly, and with a willing anonymity, a few minutes before Hope returned with Dink. This gave Guy time to air the room (he waved a towel about while Marmaduke gnawed at his calves) and to rootle out the six or seven dog-ends which Keith had crushed into an aperture of some mangled toy. Then the house of cards reshuffled.

Hope came up and Guy went down, taking Marmaduke, at Hope's impatient request. Lizzyboo was in the kitchen. And so was Dink Heckler. The South African number seven sat at the table in his fuming tenniswear; as usual, he was passing the time in calm inspection of various portions of his arms and legs; perhaps (Guy speculated) it was their incredible hairiness that held his attention. As he warmed the yelling Marmaduke's half-hourly bottle Guy could hear more yelling upstairs, a reckless exchange of voices that rose to the abrupt climax of the slammed front door. Then Hope skipped down the stairs, resplendent from her tennis, and from her latest domestic achievement: sacking Doris.

'She stole my earrings. They were right there on the dresser,' said Hope.

'Gumbag,' said Marmaduke.

'Can I get a shower?' said Dink.

'Which ones?' said Guy.

'They're worthless. Or I'd have strip-searched her,' said Hope.

'Gumbag,' said Marmaduke.

'You hear that? That's Doris. She's been teaching him new swearwords,' said Hope.

'Auntie wants a hug. *Ow*,' said Lizzyboo.

'Could I get that shower?' said Dink.

'Isn't it amazing, the way he always gets you bang on the nipple? I mean, what's the point of anyone if they're so fat they can't even *walk*,' said Hope.

'Guzzball,' said Marmaduke.

'Listen to him. I mean his chest! I knew it: Doris has been smoking in the nursery. He'll have to be nebulized,' said Hope.

'Intal or Ventolin?' said Guy.

'I'll help hold him down,' said Lizzyboo.

'No way,' said Marmaduke.

'Can I get that shower?' said Dink.

There was a big mirror in the kitchen, and a big kitchen in the mirror, and Guy kept glancing secretively at himself, a singular figure in this busy world of glass. Figures swept to and fro on its surface; Dink Heckler, with his one hopelessly repeated question, was the room's only pocket of rest. Guy explored his lips with a slow tongue: he now barely noticed the swelling where Marmaduke had butted him. That night, he decided, he would forbear to clean his teeth. The meeting of mouths (I'm in it now), the way their faces seemed to stall and then

228

lock into the same force field. Some people think that just because one works in the City there are these huge chunks of money lying around. He had felt no reading on his personal tiltmeter and yet their mouths were definitely homing. Of course, she's completely innocent, completely green, about money, as about everything else. Her eyes were closing with the slightest of tremors. Bonds would be best: might take a day or three. And there was a flicker too in the lips somewhere. Talk to Richard in the morning. When it happened he could sense the tongue behind the teeth, stirring or cowering like a wounded bird.

Hope said suddenly, 'Look at the anorexic.'

Guy laughed. He found he was piling food into his mouth: a lump of cheese, a slice of ham, a halved tomato. 'I know. I've only just realized,' he said, and laughed again, bending his knees to lick the gob of mayo dangling from his little finger, 'that I'm absolutely starving.'

'Could I get that shower?' said Dink.

'It's blood,' said Lizzyboo.

'There's blood on his hair. Guy! There's blood on his hair!' said Hope.

'Don't worry,' said Guy. 'It's only minc.'

Outside, the rain stopped falling. Over the gardens and the mansion-block rooftops, over the window boxes and TV aerials, over Nicola's skylight and Keith's dark tower (looming like a calipered leg dropped from heaven), the air gave an exhausted and chastened sigh. For a few seconds every protuberance of sill and eave steadily shed water like drooling teeth. There followed a chemical murmur from both street and soil as the ground added up the final millimetres of what it was being asked to absorb. Then a sodden hum of silence.

Two days ago I changed Marmaduke's diaper. It was right up there with my very Worst Experiences. I'm still not over it.

I guess it had to happen. There are nanny-lulls, still centres in the hurricane of nannies. I am always hanging around over there. I am always hanging around where people are hanging around, or going where they're going, eager to waste time at *their speed*. In the end Lizzyboo helped me get him under the shower. Then we mopped the nursery wall. And the ceiling. I'm still not over it.

Marmaduke possesses his mother with a biblical totality, and he is always goosing Melba and frenching Phoenix (and watch him splash his way through the au pairs); but Lizzyboo is his sexual obsession. He shimmies up against her shins and drools into her cleavage. He won't have a bath unless she's there to watch. He is forever ramming his hand – or his head – up her skirt.

Of course, and embarrassingly, Lizzyboo is becoming more and more certain that she needn't fear any such nonsense from me. No, in my condition I'm not about to get fresh. She sometimes gives me a puzzled but interrogatory look – the eyes seem to cringe – while Marmaduke is scouring her ear with his tongue. Or trying to force her hand down the front of his diaper. Being human, she is starting to wonder what is wrong with her. I could tell her I'm gay or religious, or just frightened of catching some fatal disease. I suppose I really shouldn't continue to trifle with her affections. Especially now that I don't need to.

I have Thrufaxed all twelve chapters off to Hornig Ultrason, where, it seems, my stock is already rising high. You can tell by the way everyone speaks to you. Unless I am mistaken, even the computerized voice of the reception bank betrays a secret liking for me. 'One momint. I have Missy Harter for you,' said Janit Slotnick, in the tone of somebody preparing a three-year-old for a particularly winsome treat. 'Oh, and have you heard the news that's causing such excitemint here?' I was already romping and tumbling in the zeros of a paperback or book-club deal when Janit said: 'She's pregnint!' But I never did get through to Missy Harter. The computer screwed up and twenty minutes later Janit called and said that Missy would soon get back to me, which she hasn't.

On impulse I said, 'Janit? Say spearmint.' 'Spearmint.' 'Now say peppermint.' 'Peppermint.' 'Thank you, Janit.' 'Sir.'

Incarnacion wraps up or abandons a long anecdote about her adventures in the supermarket (a story from which she emerges with obscure credit) to inform me that Mark Asprey has phoned while I've been out – while I've been out avoiding Incarnacion.

Mr Asprey, relates Incarnacion, is endearingly keen to pay a flying visit to London. Of course, at a single snap of his fingers, he can put up at a top hotel, or find a bed with any number of heartsick glamour queens – but Mr Asprey would find it far more agreeable to stay right here, in the place he calls home, and where, in addition, Incarnacion can bring all her powers to bear on the promotion of his comfort. She is altogether sympathetic to this sentimental yearning of Mark Asprey's. In fact I get thirty-five minutes on the primacy of home, with its familiar surroundings and other pluses.

Incarnacion herself suggests that I could conveniently return to New York. For her, the symmetry of such an arrangement is not without its appeal.

I don't say anything. I don't even say anything about the difficulties of non-supersonic East–West transatlantic air travel, in case I get an hour on, say, the inadvisability of central thermonuclear war. I just nod and shrug, confident that in the very nature of things she must eventually shut up or go away.

Last night I attended a dinner party at Lansdowne Crescent. Also present were Lizzyboo and Dink. The main guests were not distinguished; they were just born rich. Three brothers, Jasper,

Harry and Scargill, three joke representatives of the English gentry (down from Yorkshire, near Guy's dad's place, for an agribusiness conference), together with their speechless wives. The boys from Bingley – and they *were* boys: time-fattened, time-coarsened, but boys, just boys – did a lot of shouting at first and then fell silent over their plates: devout and sweaty eaters. Dink kept looking at Hope with a bored scowl in which some other message was impatiently enciphered; Guy hardly said a word. There wasn't any competition or, for that matter, any choice: I was the life of the party. And I have so little to spare.

It broke up just after eleven, when Marmaduke's hollerings and thunderings could no longer be ignored or even talked through. I saw the pummelled au pair trying to free his hands from the banisters. Guy and Hope looked as though they would be gone some time.

Exhaustedly I stood with Lizzyboo on the stoop and watched the four cars steal off into the hot night. She turned to me with her arms folded. I was afraid. She did that thing with the lowered head and the childishly questioning fingers on my shirtbuttons, giving her somewhere to look while she asked me why I didn't like her. I was afraid. I was afraid of something like this. What was the nature of this fear of mine? Like the weight of a million adulteries, complications, untruths, chances for betrayal. Also the inexplicable sense that I had already loved her or liked her or felt male pride in her, long ago, and kissed her breasts and held the pressure of her legs on my back already, many times, until what love there was all ran out, and I didn't want to do it, ever again. I wished I had a little certificate or badge I could produce, saying that I didn't have to do it, ever again. I was afraid of her body and its vigour, of her flesh, of her life. I was afraid it might hurt me. I was afraid it might break me.

'I like you very much.' All I saw was the perfect evenness of her parting as she said,

'Do you? Do you want to come to my room for a little while?'

'I uh, believe not.'

'Why? Is there something wrong with me?'

Actually the nails on her big toes are beginning to lose symmetry, she has a steep-sided mole on the back of her neck, and generally her skin (when compared to someone like Kim Talent) is definitely showing signs of wear, of time, of death. But I said, 'You're beautiful, Lizzyboo. Give yourself the benefit of the doubt. The thing is, I'm in love with someone else.'

Then I went over to Nicola's for an update. I'm not in love with Nicola. Something intertwines us, but it isn't love. With Nicola it's more like the other thing.

Missy Harter comes through on the line to say that she has a check on her desk – enough to front me for another few months: enough. I said. 'Thank God. You must have cut some corners. I take it this call is not being monitored?' 'Right. It's a virgin.' 'Good. Any other news?' 'On what you call the world situation? Why yes. Next week: breakout.' 'Surely you mean breakdown.' 'Breakout. Frank renegation.' 'But that's terrible.' 'Not so. The reason: if we don't, they will. Goodbye now.' 'Wait! . . Any other news?' 'Yes. I have news for you. I'm expecting a baby.'

'And I have news for you. It's mine.'

'Bullshit,' she said.

'I knew it. It is!'

'Bullshit.'

'That last time. On the Cape.'

'Please let's not do this. I was drunk.'

'Yeah, and I bet you were drunk in the morning too. That's when it happened. In the morning. I felt a pop. I even heard it. A distinct pop.'

'Bullshit. I'll end this now. I'm ending this.'

'Don't hang up! I'm coming back. Now.'

'Back? To America?' She laughed sadly. 'Haven't you heard? There's no way in.'

It is with great, with ineffable – it is with the heaviest ambivalence that I –

I don't want to go. I don't want to go. I'm not in good enough shape to take on America. I'm not up to America. I want to stay here, and see how it all turns out, and write it down. I don't want to go. But I'm going. Not even I could live with myself if I stayed. Besides, there is a sky up there that looks like a beach and I mean with white sand and blue ocean and helixed volleyballs and cumulus *putti* exploding out of the surf. Good for flying. Maybe good for love.

So I'm sitting here now with my bag packed and waiting for a car that doesn't show. I just called the minicab people again (their proud slogan: YOU DRINK, WE DRIVE). A taped message, followed by three Engelbert Humperdinck numbers, followed by the slurred evasions of a guy who speaks no English. Hard to believe that in this hovel of stop-gap there yet abides a smouldering genius who knows the way to Heathrow Airport. Still, no doubt someone or other will make some kind of attempt to get here in the end.

The sky is telling me that I might just get away with it. Oh hey nonny nonny, or however it goes. Having failed in art and love, having lost, I may win through with both, even now, so late in the goddamned day. My affairs are in order. My actors are on hold. But where's my cab?

I called Guy and told him not to do anything rash while I'm gone. I don't want him to do anything rash until after I get back. With luck, he'll have a quiet time of it. Or a noisy time of it. I foresee a recurrence of Marmaduke's bronchial troubles. Left in sole charge of the child for over an hour, Keith Talent, I happen to know, did more than fulfil his normal quota of one cigarette every seven minutes. On top of teaching Marmaduke how to box and swear and gurgle over the pinups in the tabloid, Keith taught Marmaduke how to smoke.

Keith himself of course I couldn't do anything about. All his life people have been trying to do stuff about Keith, and they never got anywhere. They've tried locking him up. I'd lock him up too, if I could, just for a couple of weeks. Like me, like Clive, like the planet, Keith's debt is getting old; and Keith will do whatever Keith needs to do . . . Anyway I went over. I trudged up the concrete stairway, through the pinged obscenities. Christ, even ten years ago, in London, it was quite an achievement to get past two men talking in the street without hearing the word *fuck* or one of its cognates; but now they're all doing it – nippers, vicars, grannies. I let myself in, Kath having wordlessly presented me, some days ago, with a single gnarled key. Mother and child were at home: no dog, no *cheat*. Kim was pleased to see me – so pleased, in fact, that if I didn't have this love-mission to blind and dizzy me, I might have to admit that something serious is seriously wrong at Windsor House. An hour of Keith's parenting is enough to hospitalize Marmaduke Clinch: and so Kim Talent – and so Kim Talent . . . On the nature short the adult crocodile reaches for the baby with its jaws. You fear the worst: but that ridged croc mouth is delicate enough to handle new-born flesh, cat-and-kitty style. On the other hand reptiles don't normally tend their young. And when daddy gets mad, big jaws will stretch for other reasons, for other hungers . . . Kim cried when I said goodbye. She cried when I left the room. I think she must love me very much.

234

I've been loved before, but no one ever cried when I left the room. Incredibly, Missy used to cry when I left the apartment. And so did I. Before I went I wrote a note for Keith (plus £50 for the skipped darts lesson) and left it on the kitchen table, unmissably close to the October *Darts Monthly*.

Jesus, I could drive to the airport myself. The bigger question is: could I drive back? And Mark Asprey will want the use of his car. 'I couldn't ask you, could I, Nicola,' I said on the phone, 'to be prudent, and keep activity to the minimum while I'm gone?' She was eating something. She said, 'What takes you there?' 'Love.' 'Ooh. What a shame. I'm planning some hot moves. You're going to miss all the sexy bits.' 'Nicola, don't do this.'

She swallowed. I could hear her inhaling masterfully. Then she said, 'You're in luck. In fact I just told Guy I'm going away for a few days. To my *retreat*.'

'Your what?'

'Don't you love it? A place with a couple of nuns and monks in it. Where I can think things over in a sylvan setting.'

'It's good. And I'm grateful. Why are you stalling?'

'No choice. So don't worry. You've got a few days' grace.'

'What is it?'

'Guess . . . Oh come *on*. The thing I can't control.'

'I give up.'

She sighed and said, 'It's the fucking *curse*.'

A lordly Indian has just chewed me out for even expecting a cab to show up anywhere definite in the calculable future. He seemed to feel I was living in the past. Things, he told me, just aren't *like* that any more. But he'll see what he can do. I'll take the notebook, of course. And leave the novel. Neatly stacked. Many pages. Do I want Mark Asprey to read it? I guess I do. I'll take the notebook: with all the waiting around and everything – I envisage having a lot to say. Will America have changed? No. America won't have come up with any new ideas, any new doubts, about herself. Not her. But maybe I can take a new reading: a think piece, maybe, based on my own experiences, a substantial (and publishable?) meditation, extending to some eight or ten thousand words, on the way America has started to fulfil –

Oh, this is rich. Outside – what a pal – Keith has just pulled up in the royal-blue Cavalier. I get to my feet. I sit down again: again, the heavy reluctance, in the haunches, in the loins, whence love should spring . . . Now how will the etiquette go on this? He's climbed out of the car and glanced warily down the street. I've waved. He has raised his longbow thumb – his bent, his semicircular thumb. Keith sports a fishnet shirt and pastel hipsters but his chauffeur's cap nestles ominously on the hood. He is polishing the chrome with a J Cloth. If he opens the back door first then I'm out another fifty quid.

Enough. I'm ready. Let's go to America.

Well I'm back.

I'm back.
Six days I've been gone. I didn't write a word. The way I feel now I might never write another. But there's another. And another.
I lost. I failed. I lost everything.
Unlucky thirteen.
Jesus Christ if I could make it into bed and get my eyes shut without seeing a mirror.
Please don't anyone look at me. I really took a tumble – I really took a tumble out there. Oh, man, I'm in bits.

Apart from the fact that on account of the political situation they and their loved ones might all disappear at any moment (this sentence needs recasting but it's too late now), my protagonists are in good shape and reasonable spirits. They still form their black cross.
They look a bit different. But not as different as I look, catapulted into my seventies and still recovering from the fall.
I go into the Black Cross and nobody recognizes me. I'm a stranger. And it all has to begin again.

Perhaps because of their addiction to form, writers always lag behind the contemporary formlessness. They write about an old reality, in a language that's even older. It's not the words: it's the rhythms of thought. In this sense all novels are historical novels. Not really a writer, maybe I see it clearer. But I do it too. An example: I still go on as if people felt well.

I look to the kids, who change quick too. Marmaduke, so far as I can tell, is exactly the same except in one particular. He has stopped saying 'milt'. He now says – and he says it often and loudly – 'mewk' or 'mowk' or 'mulk' or, more simply, 'mlk'.

All right, if we are going to go on with this thing there'll have to be some changes around here. Apart from anything else I think I'm going blind: so let the colours run. Actually Nicola herself, with her recent outrages, has already forced this on me. Who says these people need so much air and space? We're all in it together now.

Kim has stopped saying 'Enlah'! She cries normally, humanly, complicatedly. No longer does she pay homage to the sudden, the savage god of babies: Enlah!

We're all in it together now. As is the case with the world situation, something will have to give, and give soon. It will all get a lot woollier, messier. Everything is winding down, me, this, mother earth. More: the universe, though apparently roomy enough, is heading for heat death. I hope there are parallel universes. I hope alternatives exist. Who stitched us up with all these design flaws? Entropy, time's arrow – ravenous disorder. The designer universe: but it was meant to give out all along, like something you pick up at GoodFicks. So maybe the universe is a dog, a pup, a dud, slipped our way by the *Cheat*.

'Milt' I reckon I can live without. But 'Enlah'? Already I miss it. And I'll never hear it again. Nobody will, not from her lips. How did it sound? How well can I remember it? Where has it gone? Oh, Christ, no, the hell of time. I never guessed that you lost things coming this way too. Time *takes* from you, with both hands. Things just disappear into it.

Keith is under the impression that he has come through a stern examination of his character and emerged with flying colours. There he stands, with one hand under his nose, with courting finger resting in the cusp between barrel and shaft, with pinkie raised – Keith's integers! And Guy's okay, considering. The fall guy: fool, foal, foil. I went to see him in hospital. There he lies, in white nightie, palely smiling. He really had us worried for a time. But they're both on course.

I'm not getting something and what I'm not getting has to do with the truth and it so happens that I'm well placed to take a crack at it – the truth, I mean – because this story is *true*.

The form itself is my enemy. All this damned romance. In fiction (rightly so called), people become coherent and intelligible – and they aren't like that. We all know they aren't. We all know it from personal experience. We've been there.

People? People are chaotic quiddities living in one cave each. They pass the hours in amorous grudge and playback and thought-experiment. At the camp fire they put the usual fraction on exhibit, and listen to their own silent gibber about how they're feeling and how they're going down. We've been there.

Death helps. Death gives us something to do. Because it's a full-time job looking the other way.

A highly civilized note from Mark Asprey, rounded, well turned, like the man himself, and left in the study, propped against my stacked typescript:

My dear Sam: Two things are missing. (Have you been keeping low company?) I don't expect you to have used or even noticed these items, because you're a blameless non-smoker – whereas I adore the harsh cut of Turkish tobacco with my morning coffee no less than I relish at the other end of the day the rough solidity of a colossal Havana between my lips. Item 1: onyx cigarette-lighter. Item 2: ormolu ashtray. Yours ever, MA

No mention (except between those brackets?) of my novel, which I'm sure he has looked at – though the pages, it's true, aren't even infinitesimally misaligned.

I wonder if MA met with the murderee while he was here. I wonder if MA slept with the murderee while he was here. Just now, none of that seems to matter. Wait, though: I can feel something gathering around me once again. Ambition, obsession. It had better be obsession. Nothing else is likely to keep me out of bed. All about, the study shelves are ranked with Asprey's piss . . .

In-depth updatings and debriefings have been necessary, and she has been awfully sweet and patient with me. This much is certain: I'm going to miss her.

The weather has a new number, or better say a new *angle*. And I don't mean dead clouds. Apparently it will stay like this for quite a while: for the duration, in any event. It's not a good one. It will just make everything worse. It's not a wise one. The weather really shouldn't be doing this.

He frowned. She laughed. He brightened. She pouted. He grinned. She flinched. Come on: we don't *do* that. Except when we're pretending. Only babies frown and flinch. The rest of us just fake with our fake faces.

He grinned. No he didn't. If a guy grins at you for real these days, you'd better chop his head off before he chops off yours. Soon the sneeze and the yawn will be mostly for show. Even the twitch.

She laughed. No she didn't. We laugh about twice a year. Most of us have lost our laughs and now make do with false ones.

He smiled.

Not quite true.

All that no good to think, no good to say, no good to write. All that no good to write.

Chapter 13: Little Did
They Know

SHAPED LIKE A topheavy and lopsided stingray, elderly, oil-streaked, semi-transparent, and trailing its coil of feathery brown vapour, a dead cloud dropped out of the haze and made its way, with every appearance of effort, into the dark stadium of the west. Guy Clinch had looked up. Now he looked down. To him, clouds had always been the summary of everything that could reasonably be hoped for from the planet; they moved him more than paintings, more than exciting seas. So dead clouds, when he saw them, brought a strong response also (it was much worse since fatherhood). Dead clouds made you hate your father. Dead clouds made love hard. They made you want and need it, though: love. They made you have to have it.

This was how things stood with Guy. Or this was how they swayed and wavered. On the night of the Wounded Bird – the kiss, when his lips had strained to meet or shun the lips of Nicola Six – Guy had checked into hospital a little after ten.

He felt fine himself. If anyone had asked him how he felt, he would have said that he 'felt fine'. Apart from an itchy left eye, a sore throat, his mild mono and controllable colic (all of which fell within the ever-roomier parameters of *feeling fine*), plus his more or less permanent height-related lower back pain and the numerous rumours of whatever else was in store for him mortally, Guy felt fine. Marmaduke's asthma attack, on the other hand (it developed suddenly that evening), had every appearance of severity. The doctor came, and admired from a distance the desperate inflations of Marmaduke's belly. It's not that they can't get air in; they can't get air out. Many telephone calls were made – lights sent probing into the nooks and crannies of the health system. Now of course Guy and Hope had a system too. If the best care available was private, then Hope went in with the child; if non-private, then Guy did. Such an arrangement, said Hope, answered to his egalitarian convictions, his interest in 'life', as she called it, with all due contempt. By eleven o'clock, at any rate, Guy had his pyjamas and toothbrush ready in a briefcase and was soon backing the car out into the street.

Guy went in the next night too, straight after he finished at the office, relieving Hope, who pulled aside the surgeon's mask she was wearing long enough to inform him that inch-high eczema had broken out across Marmaduke's chest and was heading, at a speed almost visible to the human eye, for his neck and face. With a gesture of quiet challenge she lifted the sheet. Guy stared down in wonder at the jewelled child.

Even more strangely and frighteningly, Marmaduke lay perfectly still, and was quite silent. During past hospitalizations, when Guy had arrived with his flowers, his bananas, his toys and cuddly animals, his overnight bag, Marmaduke had reliably climbed out of even the deepest troughs of weakness and disorientation to give his father a weary swipe. But today – not the smallest gob of spit. Not so much as a snarl! Marmaduke's red-smudged eyes stared up in bafflement and appeal. When the child suffered like this, it was as if Guy himself, or Guy's little ghost, were hawking and writhing, somewhere lost, in an alternate world. Looking down on him now, Guy felt the familiar equidistance between tears and nausea. The latter impulse he managed to resist. But then Hope wept. And then Guy wept. They embraced each other. And together, and very carefully, they embraced the child.

That night Guy thought about Nicola a good deal, but unwillingly, and without pleasure. And he cleaned his teeth with some violence, abolishing from his mouth the last memory of her lips. As he lay on the campbed in the sweltering cubicle, and jerked to his feet every few minutes to review the red rubies which fantasticated the surface of Marmaduke's drugged sleep, her image flapped in on him in little coronaries of self-hatred and dismay. That stolen hour: Keith and his cigarettes: if Hope knew – her anger, rightful and limitless. The connexion between the illicit kiss and the child's sufferings was

243

perhaps as tenuous as the smoke that issued from the crafty burn of Keith's brief vigil; but he felt it as a certainty. This is the girl that kissed the man that asked the friend that smoked the fag to mind the kid that lived in the house that Hope built . . . Better just to wash my hands of the whole thing. It will be bearable. It won't *kill* me. I'll give her the money and that'll be the end of it. This vow, repeatedly uttered, felt calming, ascetic and renunciatory. At four he smoothed Marmaduke's forehead for the last time and collapsed into sleep moments before the first nurse strode into the room.

In the morning, Marmaduke looked unbelievable, and sounded as if . . . Well, if you'd shut your eyes, you would have quickly imagined two lumberjacks stooped over the handles of their doublesaw, and patiently felling some titan of the woodlands. And yet the child was widely pronounced to be stabilizing. The cutaneous vesicles, for instance, had already started to weep. Guy stared at the face on the bloodstained pillow and was unable to imagine that this was anything even a child could really recover from. But Marmaduke would recover from it. And Guy would recover from it. Actually he knew, to his shame, that recovery was near, because Nicola's face was back, and no longer half-averted; it was candid and aroused and voluptuously innocent. Being in a hospital anyway, Guy felt the urge to ask around, to find somebody who could get this face (this image, like the sun's imprint, but never fading) surgically removed. Of course, doctoring hadn't worked for the Macbeths; and it wouldn't work for him. When Hope arrived at half past ten with Phoenix and Melba and the odd au pair, Guy slipped away and called the office, and got Richard, who said he could go for the money at noon. He returned just as the doctor, the in-house asthma expert, was taking his leave.

Guy asked, 'What did he say?'

'Him?' said Hope. 'I don't know. Part allergenic, part reactive.'

'When he's better,' said Guy, who was thinking, Not too far: anyway she could meet me at the station, 'we'll move out of London.'

'Oh yeah? Where to, Guy? The moon? Haven't you heard? Everywhere's a toilet.'

'Well we'll see.'

'You can go now.'

But he stayed for a while, the good father, and watched the child. My God (Guy thought), he looks like Io. He looks like Io, Jupiter's molten moon, covered in frosty lava, from cold volcanoes. Io's volcanoes, caused by sulphur dioxide boiling at many degrees below zero in contact with sulphur . . . Just then, Hope unbuttoned her shirt and bared a breast, and offered it to the boy, for comfort. Of course, Io is connected to the mother planet by a kind of navel string. A 'flux tube' of electrical energy. Ten million ampères.

Later, as he bent to kiss Marmaduke's lips (the only part of his face unaffected by the popping swamp of the inflammation), the child flinched and gave a definite sneer. Pretty feeble by his standards; but Guy was heartened, and emboldened, to find his son capable of even such a spiritless grimace. He was wearing plastic handcuffs, to stop him scratching.

A mile to the west, Keith Talent lit a cigarette with the remains of its predecessor and then pressed the butt into an empty beer can. In this way did he scorn the ormolu ashtray and the onyx cigarette lighter, two recent acquisitions, which lay near by. He reached for a full beer can, tussling with the six-pack's elastic yoke. He swore. He coughed. He straightened up in bed. He burped astonishingly.

The noise that burp made was doubly disproportionate, disproportionate to his bulk, disproportionate to the podlike restriction of the room he lay in. Even Keith was slightly taken aback by it. A horror-film burp, a burp that cried out for at least two exorcists. Perhaps one of hell's top burp people was plying his trade in Keith's body. But Keith didn't care. He burped again, voluntarily, defiantly. From the kitchen the dog barked back. 'Keith,' called Kath. And even little Kim filed the possibility of protest. Keith gave them another.

Lying there among the knouts and nooses of cheap sheets and damp blankets, in his pink-tinged Y-fronts, with the beercan on his gut and the fizzing snout in his fingers, Keith had a fairly accurate idea of who and what he was. He could taste his own essence. The sourness of locker rooms, municipal duckboards, dormitories, prisons.

Things were bad. On the phone: 'Keith? It's Ashley. I'm going to have to hurt you, mate. All right? I'm going to *hurt* you.' Keith Talent, who had done a lot of hurting in his time, who knew about hurting from both points of view, Keith Talent understood. 'I understand.' It wasn't TV, hurting. It was real. It didn't come much realer: finger-cracking reality. Yeah, and kicked senseless and left upside down in a fucking dustbin somewhere.

Have the fucking bailiffs round here anyway in a minute. Characteristically you were sent two fat guys, with ginger beards, murmuring — money's janitors (they didn't want any trouble). Everything you owned got priced. Then you really found out how little you were worth. At this moment Keith himself felt like a coin (he could taste it in his mouth), nicked and grimy, and of low denomination. In three nights' time he was meant to be throwing in the Duoshare. Quarterfinals. 'Nationwide sponsorship,' said Keith. He stared with his mouth open at the middle finger of his right hand. Prestigious endorsements. No help from that lying cow either. Was the darts dream about to end? Was the whole darts bubble about to burst?

Keith? What's the matter? The truth was that in addition to his usual woes Keith happened to be suffering from the after-effects of violent crime. You can almost hear him saying it, in moody explanation: 'I happen to be suffering from the after-effects of violent crime.' There *are* after-effects of violent crime, and they are onerous. We can be sure of that. Look: even Keith was capable of feeling the worse for them. The after-effects of violent crime *have* to be considerable, to get through to people like Keith who are always feeling lousy anyway. Now he burped again and the dog barked back and he burped back again — 'Keith,' called Kath — and it all felt as ragged as that, trying to outburp an old dog under a blanket of fagsmoke in the low sun.

By his participation in violent crime, Keith had worked a little gamble. In at least three or four senses, Keith had worked a little gamble with *time*. He had ploughed many days' worth of the stuff into the intensity of a scant forty-five minutes; and now those gambled hours were being subtracted from the present. A gambling man, Keith had gambled those hours; and he had lost them. He had lost. Not everything, because he reckoned he'd got away with it okay and wouldn't be doing the kind of time you measure in years. But he hadn't won. Those gambled hours, where had they gone?

The whole thing was a farce from the start. Never work with our coloured brethren, Keith said to himself. It should be pointed out that the injunction had little bigotry in it. It was like saying: Never drive down the Golborne Road on Friday or Saturday afternoons. Rubbish trucks innit. Occasioning pronounced congestion. You nip up Lancaster Road instead. Common sense. Keith wasn't prejudiced. No danger. Keith had lots of foreign mates, believing that it took all sorts to make a world. Look at horse-toothed Yaroslav, of Polish extraction. Look at Fucker Burke, pure bog-and-spud Irish. And Pongo was a Cornishman. No, Keith liked all sorts, all sorts of men, just as he liked all sorts of women, all colours, all creeds. Look at Balkish and Mango and Leeza and Iqbala. Look at Thelonius. In the end, though, he felt the wisdom of the traditional view: that when it came to *work*, your average bongo'll be as much use as an ashtray on a motorbike. Same difference with the black darter. All the sincerity in the world. But no clinicism.

Their plan was deceptively simple. Thelonius's babymamma Lilette worked as a cleaning-lady – but never for very long. As soon as any household felt the time was right to entrust her with a doorkey, Lilette felt the time was right to entrust it to Thelonius (who had it copied) and then quit the following day. The following night Thelonius would be stopping by in the small hours . . . Thelonius seemed offended by Keith's mild hint that the filth would soon put two and two together.

'Filth don't know shit,' he said. 'This is the big one. It have long bread, man.'

'Bingo,' said Keith.

As planned, Keith showed up at the Golgotha shortly after nine. Thelonius was there, as planned. Quite untypically, and not very encouragingly, Thelonius was drunk. 'Sdoveo,' said Thelonius. 'Svodeo.' He was trying to say 'Videos'. Another stretch of time passed while Thelonius tried to say 'Digital'. Well, in for a penny, thought Keith (prophetically enough). Outside, Thelonius opened a trembling palm in presentation of his new car – a souped-up, low-slung maroon Mini, with rallying lights, customized chrome fenders and celebrity windows. Not discreet, thought Keith, as he bent to climb into it.

'We won't be getting too many digital videos in here, mate,' said Keith, pleased, at least, to be sparing the Cavalier from such a mission. 'What happened to the BMW?'

'Had to let it go, man. Had to let it go.'

Keith nodded. That's how it went. Thelonius had committed every last fiver of his most recent windfall to the purchase of the BMW. He had bought the BMW off a *cheat*. A couple of days later he was without the means to buy the car a litre of petrol, let alone the repairs and spare parts (item: new engine) that the BMW cried out for. So he had sold it back to the *cheat* – at a heavy loss. And what does he do with such funds as remain? Gets this eyecatching minge-wagon, plus a new fur coat. The new fur coat would already be gathering oil in the Mini's boot, and Thelonius would be without the means to get it cleaned. That's how it went.

'Fifteen minutes,' Thelonius was saying sleepily, 'and we be back inna Black Cross, rich men. Sonofabitch!'

'What?'

The car contained no petrol.

And neither of them had any money.

So it was upon the Cavalier that they relied to take them to the dark corner off Tavistock Road. On the way Thelonius rehearsed his dreams of early retirement: the tickertaped, blonde-flanked return to St Lucia, land of his fathers; the ranch-style villa, the private beach, the burnished helipad. No moon, no streetlamps, and a low ceiling of cloud. The lock gave slickly to Thelonius's key.

'Bingo,' said Keith.

Little did they know that the place they were about to burgle – the shop, and the flat above it – had already been burgled the week before: yes, and the week before that. And the week before that. It was all burgled out. Indeed, burgling, when viewed in Darwinian terms, was clearly approaching a crisis. Burglars were finding that almost everywhere had been burgled. Burglars were forever bumping into one another, stepping on the toes of other burglars. There were burglar jams on rooftops and stairways, on groaning fire-escapes. Burglars were being burgled by fellow burglars, and were doing the same thing back. Burgled goods jigged from flat to flat. Returning from burgling, burglars would discover that they had been burgled, sometimes by the very burglar that they themselves had just burgled! How would this crisis in burgling be resolved? It would be resolved when enough burglars found burgling a waste of time, and stopped doing it. Then, for a while, burgling would become worth doing again. But burglars had plenty of time to waste – it was all they had plenty of, and there was nothing else to do with it – so they just went on burgling.

'Sonofabitch!' said Thelonius.

'What?'

'Torch onna blink!'

They thrashed around for a while by the light of Keith's Ronson. Thelonius found the till, smashed it open and triumphantly wrenched out a fistful of luncheon vouchers.

'LVs, man. Sonofabitch LVs.'

'Wait a minute,' said Keith, with a sweep of his dark-adapted eyes. 'I know this place. It's just a fucking corner shop. There's no *videos*. All they got here's a load of fuckim porp pies!'

Thelonius had hoped or predicted or at any rate affirmed that the owners would not be there when they called – would, in fact, be enjoying a late holiday on the west coast of England. How was it, then, that they could hear footsteps on the floor above, and the sounds of exasperated protest? The owners, of course, had gone nowhere: much impoverished by recent burglaries, they were stopping home. Thelonius looked up. 'Joolery, man,' he said, with the sudden calm of deep inspiration. 'She dripping with joolery.' He ducked into the back room and climbed the stairs with long silent bounds. Acting on pure instinct, Keith slowly filled his pockets with cigarettes. He went to the front door and opened it, wondering what he was feeling. Down All Saints, outside the Apollo, great numbers streamed against the light. Keith stuck his head out and had a look at the shop sign. Yeah, that's right. N. Poluck, the sign said grimly. Cornish Dairy. Confectioner & Newsagent. Yeah: tabloids, packet cakes, and milk cartons. Old Polish couple ran it, with an air of great depression and disobligingness. Typical *corner* shop: never had anything that anybody might ever want. Long live CostCheck and BestSave. Keith shut the door. Then, having checked the Eat-By date on the cellophane, he ruminatively consumed a pork pie.

In the upstairs bedroom Thelonius was rattling through the oddments on the dressing-table with truly unbearable agitation. Keith had never watched Thelonius at work before. A grave disappointment, with none of that relaxed concentration you're always hoping to see. He looked around for Mr and Mrs Poluck and soon picked them out, under a heap of clothes and upended drawers, and not stirring overmuch. Thus he also ascertained that there was nothing semi-violent about this particular crime. With a clear conscience, then, Keith strode up to the trembling figure of Thelonius and did two things. He tousled Thelonius's hair; he put a cigarette in Thelonius's mouth and lit it. Thelonius took one distracted drag before jerking his head back: enough. Keith left the butt on the dressing-table, among the specks of hair-dust. Bingo, thought Keith: DNA innit. Now Mr Poluck groaned; Thelonius shouted '*Where?*' and thumped a gleaming gym-shoe down into his cheek. 'You don't do it like that, mate,' said Keith, peering about

249

for something you could carry water in. 'You get them both sitting up and hurt one till the other . . . You know.'

Keith had been hopeful at first. Nobody trusted banks any longer, thank God; and you could stroll out of the most improbable places with some quite decent lifesavings under your arm. But the bright dream was fading. Mr and Mrs Poluck were as tough as old boots – and as cheap. Thelonius did everything with tears of imploring rage in his eyes. What a life, eh? The exertion, the inconvenience, the unpopularity you incurred, and nothing going right any of the time. Keith had to do a bit of judicious slapping and shaking and hair-tugging. He disliked the touch of old bodies and wondered if it would be any better working with the very young. Looking round the room he felt something like bafflement or even sadness at the whole idea of human belongings: we get them in shops, then call them our own; we all had to have this precious stuff, like our own hairbrush each, our own dressing-gown each, and how soon it all looked like junk – how soon it got trampled into trash. For their part, to be fair, the Polucks did well, with no excessive complaint, seeming to regard the episode as largely routine. Keith met with, and longsufferingly endured, their stares of deep recognition, which wasn't a matter of putting a name to a face but of looking into you and seeing exactly what you were. No fun. No jewellery either. In the end they came wheezing down the stairs with a fake fur coat, a damaged TV set, a broken alarm clock and a faulty electric kettle. Then the stony light of Keith's garage and the bottle of *porno* passed through the dust to settle the crime buzz and crime flop that played on their flesh like fever.

Those on the receiving end of violent crime feel *violated*: injury has been dealt out to them from the hidden chaos, which has shown itself briefly, and then returned to where it lives. Meanwhile, in chaos's hiding place, what happens? Rocks and shells catch and grate in neither sea nor shore, and nothing is clean or means anything, and nothing *works*.

'I'm a piece of shit,' Keith whispered into his beercan. He thought of everybody else who never had to do this. Guy, Guy's wife, in endless mini-series. Shah of Iran. Tits. A rich bird: and then you're *out* of here.

The money came in four buff envelopes. They contained used fifties. Much-used fifties. Sitting in his office (with its Japanese furniture and single Visual Display Unit and clean desk), Guy offered up his delicate and increasingly emotional nostrils to a familiar experience: the scurfy smell of old money. It always struck him, the fact that money stank, like the reminder of an insidious weakness in himself. Of course, the poets and the novelists had always patiently insisted as much. Look at Chaucer's cock. Look at Dickens (Dickens was the perfect panning-bowl for myth): the old man up to his armpits in Thames sewage, searching for treasure; the symbolic names of Murdstone and of Merdle, the financier. But all that was myth and symbol, a way of saying that money could somehow be thought of as being smelly, of being scatological. It was frightfully literal-minded of money, he thought, to be actually stinking up the place like this. *Pecunia non olet* was dead wrong. *Pecunia olet.* Christ, heaven stops the nose at it . . . Guy sealed and stacked the packets. He couldn't wait to get rid of them – all this hard evidence of deception. So far, no outright lies. He fancied he had been rather clever with Richard, adopting the smug yet faintly rueful uncommunicativeness of someone settling a gambling debt. It had come naturally. But it seemed quite likely that men were just easier to deceive. Guy put the money into his briefcase and smoked half a cigarette as he contemplated – in its physical aspects only – the drive across town.

Everything was going perfectly normally or acceptably but he was finding it impossible to meet her eye. He could point his face in the right direction, and try to will himself into her looming gaze. At one juncture he made it as far as her bare shoulder before his vision went veering off to some arbitrary point on the bookcase, the carpet, his own huge shoes. Otherwise, Guy clung to the belief that he was behaving with conviction and control. The tremendous snaps of his briefcase locks seemed to underscore his worldliness, the briskness of all his dealings. This was certainly one way of doing it: you gave the money, as it were disinterestedly; and then the adult verdict. Guy laid out the envelopes on the low table, and mentioned one or two of the slight difficulties he had encountered. Directing a rictus smile towards the ceiling, he spoke, for instance, of the tenuous connexion between the endlessly malleable symbols on the display screen and the hard cash in one's hand, with all its bulk and pungency.

'Will you do me the kindness', said Nicola Six, 'of looking at me when we're talking?'

'Yes of course,' said Guy, and steered his stare into the sun of her face. 'I do apologize. I – I'm not myself.'

'Aren't you?'

With a limp hand half-hooding his eyes (it was all right so long as he concentrated on the cleft between her chin and her lower lip), and with his legs crossing and uncrossing and recrossing, Guy ventured to speak of the recent struggles of his son Marmaduke, of the successive nights in hospital, the sleeplessness, the serious thinking . . . By now Guy was staring at the bookcase again. As he began to outline the chief theme of all this serious thinking, Nicola said,

'I'm sorry to hear that your little boy's been ill. But I must say I think it's rather tactless of you to bring that up now. If not downright cruel. Under the circumstances.'

This promised something inordinate, and Guy was duly alarmed. He couldn't help feeling the pathos of her formulations (how theatrically we speak when we're moved); at the same time, he couldn't help feeling that her choice of outfit was perhaps a trifle unfortunate. Well, not 'choice': arriving several minutes early, he had caught her, she said, between her exercises and her shower. Hence the little tennis skirt or tutu or whatever it was, at the brim of her bare legs; hence the workout top, which was sleeveless. Also backless. The effect was altogether inappropriate, what with those girlish white socks she must have quickly slipped on. He looked her in the eye and said, 'Under the circumstances?'

Now it was her turn to look away. 'I see,' she said, with deliberation, 'I see that once again I am a victim of my own inexperience. It's an awful handicap. You never know what other people might reasonably have in mind.' She hugged herself, and gasped softly, and said, 'You want to go. Of course. You want to be safe again. Away from complication. I understand. May I . . . ? Before you go, may I say something?'

She stood up with her eyes closed. She came towards him, loose of body, with her eyes closed. She knelt, and folded her arms to make a pillow for her cheek on his knees, with her eyes closed. The room darkened. Guy felt that intimacy could actually kill you – that you really could die from all this pressure on the heart.

'It's sad, and ridiculous, but I make no apologies, I suppose. We can't help wanting what we want. Can we. It may have sometimes seemed that I singled you out for a purpose. You were to take me out of my life. Take me to the other side. Through love. Through sexual love. But really my plan went deeper than that. I'm thirty-four. I'll be thirty-five next month. The body ticks. I . . . I wanted to bear your child.'

'But this is too much,' said Guy, sliding his knees out from under her and trying to clamber himself upright. 'I'm speechless. I can't breathe either! I think it —'

'No. Go. Go at once. And take your money with you.'

'It's yours. And good luck.'

'No. It's yours.'

'Please. Don't be silly.'

'Silly? Silly? I can't accept it.'

'Why?'

'Because it's *tainted*.'

How incredibly lucky that everyone was at the hospital. Let's hear it for hospitals. And for asthma, and for eczema, and for infant distress. By the time he got home, Guy was in no condition to dissimulate, to act normal, whatever that was. He was in hospital shape himself, cottony, lint-like, as if his torso were just the bandage on an injured heart. In the second drawing-room he threw off his jacket and watched himself in the mirror as he raised the brandy bottle to his lips. Then a cold shower, and the welcome coldness of the sheets . . . How, exactly, had the fight started? It started when she threw something at him, something so small that he barely saw its passage or felt its impact on his chest. Then she was on her feet and thrusting the envelopes at him, and he held her slender wrists, and then the staggered collapse backwards on to the sofa — and there they were, in clothed coition with their faces half an inch apart. For a moment Guy could feel the hard bobble at the centre of everything.

'What did you throw at me?' he said.

'A Valium.'

He snorted quietly. 'A *Valium*?'

'A Valium,' she said.

With relief, almost with amusement, Guy readjusted his shocked body; and even his peripheral vision managed to renounce all but the quickest glint of her leggy disarray. Soon he found himself lying on his back with Nicola's head resting on his chest, his nostrils tickled by her hair as she wandered weepily on. Here she was giving him the detailed confession: how she had hoped to step with him into a world of physical love; how they might, if he, the perfect man, agreed, and after 'a lot of practice', try to make a baby; how thereafter she would be content if he looked in once a week, or perhaps twice, to play with his little daughter and (the suggestion was) to play with his little daughter's mother. This dream, of course, she now cancelled and cursed . . . 'A lot of practice': there was something pitiably callow about the phrase. There was plainly something else about it too; callow or not so callow, the words entrained a physical reaction, one that tended to undermine his murmured demurrals and tender mewings. Guy hoped she hadn't noticed the ignoble billyclub which had now established itself athwart his lap. And when she accidentally rested her elbow on its base (turning to ask if this was all just sentimental tosh), Guy was glad he couldn't see his own archly agonized smile as he slid out from under her.

They parted. Yes, Guy and Nicola were to part. She stood. She stood there, corrected. She was mistress of herself once more. As Guy moved heavily towards the door he looked down at the velvet chair and saw the Valium she had thrown at him: not much of a missile, not much of a weapon, a yellow tranquillizer the size of a shirtbutton, and partly eroded by the sweat of her fist.

'I thought I might need it', she said, following his eyes (which were misting over at this comic poem of female violence), 'for after you left. But then I lost my temper. I'm sorry. I'm absolutely all right now. Go to your son. Don't worry. Goodbye, my love. No. No. Oh, be *gone*.'

Well he was gone now, and wouldn't be back. Guy was in his own bed, where he ought to be. He wouldn't be back – except perhaps in circumstances of great extremity. He found that the current situation, or the Crisis, had a way of prompting the most shameful fantasies – discrepant, egregious, almost laughably unforgivable. What if you survived into a world where nothing mattered, where everything was permitted? Guy lifted the single linen sheet. He had never thought of himself as being impressively endowed (and neither, he knew, had Hope). Who, then, was this little bodybuilder who had set up a gym in his loins? . . . So in his own way Guy Clinch confronted the central question of his time, a question you saw being asked and answered everywhere you looked, in every headline and haircut: if, at any moment, nothing might matter, then who said that nothing didn't matter already?

Just when you thought she was a complete innocent or 'natural' or maybe even not quite right in the head (manic depression? in mild, interesting and glamorous form?), she came out with something really devastating. How had it gone? Tainted. The money was *tainted*.

Certainly those fuming fifties had quite a genealogy: privatized prisons under Pitt, human cargo from the Ivory Coast, sugar plantations in the Caribbean, the East India company, South African uranium mines. This was all true: sweatshops, sanctions-busting, slain rainforests, toxic dumping, and munitions, munitions, munitions. But none of it was news to Guy. As Nicola talked he had sat there listening to a kind of commentary on the last ten years of his life: the horrified discoveries, the holding actions, the long war with his father. For ten years he had been dealing with cruel greeds and dead clouds. Nowadays the company was a good deal cleaner. And a whole lot poorer. Hope's money stank too: everywhere, vast bites out of the planet. Go back far enough and all money stinks, is dirty, roils the juices of the jaw. Was there any clean money on earth? Had there ever been any? No. Categorically. Even the money paid to the most passionate nurses, the dreamiest artists, freshly printed, very dry, and shallowly embossed to the fingertips, had its origins in some bastardy on the sweatshop floor. She'd taken it. Nicola had taken it. That put paid to another thought, also uncontrollable (and here the linen sheet gave another jolt): her on a street corner and a man walking past in white flares (hello sailor), and the woman on her knees in the alley, and the money dropped on to the wet concrete.

Guy thought he heard Marmaduke screaming and looked with terror at his watch. No panic: time to get up. Time to return to the sinister cheer of the Peter Pan Ward. He heard the sound again, from the street; but he was accustomed, by now, to the auditory trickvalve that turned a fizzing pipe or a tortured gearbox – or even birdsong or Bach – into a brilliant imitation of his absent son's screams. As he climbed from the bed Guy heard the thump, and felt the internal shockwave, of the slammed front door. Five seconds later he had hopped into his trousers and was veering round the doorway with a whiplash of shirt-tails.

The child was home! The child was home, borne aloft, it seemed, on the shoulders of the crowd, the little hero returned from the war, and screaming himself black in the face. Guy skimpleskambled down the stairs and ran high-kneed through the hall with his arms outstretched. And as the child joyously launched himself into his embrace, and, with the familiar, the inimitable avidity, plunged all his teeth into his father's throat, Guy thought that he might have been precipitate, or inflexible, or at any rate none too kind.

*

255

A mile to the north, Keith Talent lit a cigarette with the remains of its predecessor and then pressed the butt into an empty beer can. Two new televised conversations joined the surrounding symposium. Several types of whining were going on: the giant's dentistry in the street below, Mr Frost above who was mad and dying, Keith's fridge, various strains of music, and Iqbala next door going on at her boyfriend about the clothes money he'd borrowed off her last week and promised to refund on Wednesday. Keith listened closer: someone somewhere was actually shouting, 'Whine! . . . Whine! . . . *Whine!*' Ah yes. Keith managed an indulgent leer. That would be little Sue down below and to the left, calling to her son Wayne. There came another repeated shout: 'Sow! . . . Sow! . . . *Sow!*' That would be Kev, calling to Sue. Keith leered again. He and Sue had once been close. Or was it twice? His place. Kath in hospital. Now Keith called to his wife, who duly appeared in the doorway with Kim in her arms.

'Idea,' said the baby.

'Lager,' said Keith.

'Here,' said Kath.

'Adore,' said the baby.

'What's that?' said Keith, meaning the TV.

'Ordure,' said the baby.

'News. Nothing on the Crisis,' said Kath.

'I'll give *you* a crisis in a minute,' said Keith.

'Adieu,' said the baby.

'Lager,' said Keith.

'Adieu, adore, ordure, idea.'

The doorbell rang, or rattled faultily.

'*Check it Kath,*' he said in warning as she turned.

Keith sat up straight with long eyes and open mouth. If that was Kirk and/or Ashley and/or Lee, if that was the boys, then Keith had miscalculated, and seriously. Over the past week, with all this talk about the breaking of his darting finger, Keith had had time to ponder, with many an elegiac sigh, the steady erosion of criminal protocol. In the old days you kicked off by threatening someone's family. None of this nonsense about starting in on a man's darting finger. How about Kath and Kim? Weren't they worth threatening? But maybe that was what Kirk and Ashley and Lee had decided to do: threaten his family. (They couldn't have come here for Keith, after all, or not directly: home was the last place they'd reckon on finding him.) In principle he might have approved. Still, threatening

256

his family wasn't any good if he happened to be *with* his family at the time. He could hardly hide under the bed. Hide under the bed? Keith? No way: there was ten years of darts magazines down there.

'It's all right. Just a woman,' said Kath.

Two beats later he heard the front door croak open, Kath's cautious *Yes?* and a foreign female voice saying, *Good afternoon. I'm your new worker.* Keith sank back.

Chronic innit, he thought (he was gorgeously relieved). Diabolical as such. They come in here . . . *Where's Mrs Ovens? Ah, well, I'm working in conjunction with her. We'll liaise.* Liaise. I'll liaise you in a minute. Keith thought of his probation officer, the absolute lustrelessness of her hair and skin and eyes and teeth, the vertical lines that busily lanced her upper lip. Runs me ragged. All this about the *Compensations.* He had skipped their last five appointments: she'd have him reporting on Saturday afternoons, minimum, or swabbing out the Porchester Baths. *And how is the little one?* Yeah, that's it. Call it the little one because she can't remember its name. How's diddums? How's toddles? They come in here . . . *And is your husband in employment at present?* Power like. Stick their fucking oar in. Got no kids or one family's not enough. Keith craned forward and saw one flat black shoe suspended in the air beneath the kitchen table and slowly rocking.

'And is your husband at home at the moment', he heard the voice ask, 'or is it you who's smoking all these cigarettes?'

At that Keith let out a savage and protracted belch, a belch that said to all that he would never yield.

Clive barked. Kath said, 'He is, yes. He's not been well.'

'So it would appear. The child . . . You're aware, no doubt, of the harm caused by passive smoking?'

'I smoked passively every day of my life and it never did me any harm.'

'Didn't it?'

Keith was now burping in varied and horrid volleys.

'I'm afraid I might have to see about a hygiene order.'

'Hygiene? Listen. I mean we haven't got what some have. We're just *trying*, you know?'

'You tell her, Kath,' shouted Keith.

'I mean you come in here . . .'

'Speak your mind, girl,' shouted Keith.

Kath said, 'I'm starting to wonder about what *you're* doing and

257

how *you're* feeling. There's nothing I wouldn't do for my baby. Nothing.'

'Except you haven't got any *money*, have you. You just haven't got enough *money*. My God, the smoke. And I can't say I like the look of that dog. Do you abuse your daughter, Mrs Talent?'

'Oi!'

Keith could stand for this no longer. His protective instincts were stirred. Loyalty: it was a question of loyalty. Nobody talked that way about Keith's dog – or about his cigarettes, which were superking-sized and had international standing. He was out of that bed by now and struggling with the mangled length of his ginger dressing-gown. Heavily he appeared in the doorway – browngowned Keith, fag in mouth, one arm working at the flapping sleeve, in variegated whiteness of pants and vest and flesh – and looked into the eyes of Nicola Six.

What was she doing?

What was she doing?

If the intelligent eye could lift off and climb past eaves and skylights, and speed over rooftops, and settle as it liked where people thought they were alone – what on earth would it see?

Nicola backing towards her bed with a glass of champagne in one hand and the other raised and beckoning, in black elbow-length gloves and a cocktail dress the colour of jealousy, and on her face an unrecognizable smile. Now she sat, and placed the glass on the bedside table, with a languid stretch of her wings, and remained for a moment in perfect profile, facing the window: pensively. Then her black gloves began to take rapt interest in the presumably exquisite texture of her dress – that bit that housed her breasts. Oh, the look of young wonder! She shook back her hair and started to unclasp.

Who was watching? Who saw her stand and lower the dress to her feet and step out of the lillybed in her high heels? And turn, and look up sleepily, and blow a little kiss, and wiggle a black finger. Nobody. Or nobody now. Just the single eye of the pistol-grip camera, placed on the chest by the door.

This would undoubtedly be for Keith.

'Jesus,' I asked her, 'what are you doing?'

'Oh, it's nice to get out and about. Look who's talking. What about you and your crazed excursion?'

I held up an open palm at her.

'Your love-quest . . . I'm sorry. Are you very sad?'

'I'll live,' I said. Not the happiest choice of words. 'It wasn't meant to be.'

Nicola nodded and smiled. She was sitting opposite me, the lower half of her body strongly curled into the lap of the wicker chair. It was about two a.m. When she spoke you could see deep darkness in her mouth. 'Your nerve went,' she said.

'Listen. We're not all puppetmasters like you. And even you need the run of the play. You need accidents, coincidences. I happen to know there's a nice little accident that'll help speed things up with Guy.'

'I do need real life. It's true. For instance, I need the class system. I need nuclear weapons. I need the eclipse.'

'You need the Crisis.'

Blinking steadily, she sipped red wine and lit another black cigarette. A strand of tobacco stuck to her upper lip until her tongue removed it. With gusto she scratched her hair, and then frowned at her fingernails, each of which seemed to contain about a quid deal of hashish. Yes, she certainly looked off-duty to-night. I'm the only one who ever sees her like this. She lets me. She likes me. I'm a hit with all the wrong chicks: Lizzyboo, Kim, Incarnacion.

'Nicola, I'm worried about you, as usual. And in a peculiar way, as usual. I'm worried they're going to say you're a male fantasy figure.'

'I *am* a male fantasy figure. I've been one for fifteen years. It really takes it out of a girl.'

'But they don't know that.'

'I'm sorry, I just *am*. You should see me in bed. I do all the gimmicks men read up on in the magazines and the hot books.'

'Nico*la*.'

'So they'll think you're just a sick dreamer. Who cares? You won't be around for that.'

'You neither. I was thinking. You're hard to categorize, even in the male fantasy area. Maybe you're a mixture of genres. A mutant,' I went on (I love these typologies). 'You're not a Sexpot. Not dizzy enough. You're not a Hot Lay either, not quite. Too calculating. You're definitely something of a Sack Artist. And a Mata Hari too. And a Vamp. And a Ballbreaker. In the end, though, I'm fingering you for a Femme Fatale. I like it. Nice play on words. Semi-exotic. No, I like it. It's cute.'

'A Femme Fatale? I'm not a Femme Fatale. Listen, mister: Femmes Fatales are ten a penny compared to what I am.'

'What are you then?'

'Christ, you still don't get it, do you.'

I waited.

'I'm a Murderee.'

We went out walking. We can do this. *Oh* — what you see in London streets at three o'clock in the morning, with it trickling out to the eaves and flues, tousled water, ragged waste. Violence is near and inexhaustible. Even death is near. But none of it can touch Nicola and me. It knows better, and stays right out of our way. It can't touch us. It knows this. We're the dead.

My love-quest did something to me. *Heathrow* did something to me. I can still feel the burning vinyl on my cheek. What happens, when love-thoughts go out — and just meet vinyl?

Now I've had some bad airport experiences. I've been everywhere and long ago stopped getting much pleasure from the planet. In fact I am that lousy thing: a citizen of the world. I've faced utter impossibilities, outright no-can-dos, at Delhi, São Paulo, Beijing. But you wait, and the globe turns, and suddenly there is a crevice that fits your shape. Heathrow provided no such fuel for optimism, or even for stoicism. Zeno himself would have despaired instantly. The queues, the queues, cross hatched by the extra-frantic, the extra-needing. Too many belongings. Too many people all wanting to do the same thing . . .

And now the dreams have come. Something happened to me. I fell, down, down, tumbling end over end.

The dreams have come, right on schedule, as Dr Slizard warned. And if the dreams have come, then can the pain be far behind?

I always thought I was up to anything that dreams could throw at me: I'd just sleep right through them, and get some much-needed rest. But these dreams are different, as Slizard said they would be. After Incarnacion has been here the bed is plump and impeccably uniformed, and I repose trust in its square-shouldered pride, its bursting chest! On most nights, though, it looks about ready for me, intricately coiled, waiting for the stripped creature on his hands and knees.

As Slizard foretold, the dreams are not recuperable by memory, or not yet anyway, and this suits me right down to the ground. I have the impression that they deal with the very large and the very small — the unbearably large, the unbearably small. But I can't remember them, and I'm glad. Bad news for me, these dreams turn out to be bad news for Lizzyboo, too. I always used to think how heavenly it would be — at least in the abstract — to wake up to her, to wake up to all that honeytone and health (the sun lights this scene gently: her back bears warm creases from the press of her fanned hair; and then she turns). No longer. I'm not going to wake up to anybody ever again. I couldn't let Lizzyboo wake up to me, a gaunt zero, zilched by death. I can feel the unslept hours and the unremembered dreams queuing in waves above my head.

Quaintly, Slizard advises me not to eat cheese. This from his office in the Pan Am building in New York, the envy of the universe. I heed his words. Cheese? No thank you. I stay right off that shit. Don't grate no cheese on my pasta. Not a single Dairylea split with Kim. At the Black Cross, I take a pass on the cheese-and-onion crisps. Offered cocktails at the Clinches', I don't touch so much as a cheese football. And yet when I sleep what reeking stiltons, what slobbering camemberts and farting gorgonzolas come and ooze across my sleep.

Lizzyboo says she eats too much when she is unhappy. She tells me this, between mouthfuls, in the Clinch kitchen. She tells me more over her shoulder from the icebox or the cooker. It's a terrible thing with her. Always the kiddie stuff: fish fingers, milkshakes, baked beans, sticky buns. Her weight shoots up. Lizzyboo and her weight! I didn't know? Yes, the slightest sidestep from her starvation diet — and grotesque obesity is at the door with its bags. I wonder if it can be the force of suggestion, but over the past few days a quarter-moon seems to have formed beneath her chin, and an extra belt of flesh around her midriff. She takes her head out of the bread-bin to tell me that she doesn't know what she's going to do about it.

Although I could point a finger at the world situation, I'm clearly meant to take the blame for this. For this disaster also I am obliged to pocket the tab. 'Come on, honey,' I say to her. 'There are plenty of fish in the sea.' Again, a poor choice of words, perhaps. Because there aren't plenty of fish in the sea, not any more. Lizzyboo shakes her head. She looks at the floor. She gets up and heads for the grill and sadly makes herself a cheese dream.

When entering America these days it is advisable to look your best. Wear a tuxedo, for instance, or a vicar outfit. Penguin suit, dog collar: take your pick. Me? I looked like a bum, in bum suit, under bum hair, on bum shoes, when I crept into a cab, twenty miles from Missy Harter. My eyes felt as red as cayenne pepper — as red as the digital dollars on the cabby's moneyclock. It was night. But I could see the cabby's signs as clear as day. Passengers were asked to stow their own bags (DRIVER HANDICAPPED) and, of course, to refrain from smoking (DRIVER ALLERGIC). PLEASE TALK LOUD was a third notification of the cabby's many disabilities and cares. Even with three of the four lanes down we made good speed into the city. Just enough moon to see the clouds by, clouds shaped like the tread of a gumboot, or a tyre, or a tank. Over the sky's sandflats the gibbous moon seemed tipped slightly sideways and smiling like a tragic mask. Beneath, half-cleared rustbelt. SHERATO. TEXAC. Even the big concerns losing their letters. Then the city: life literalized, made concrete, concretized, massively concretized. Here it comes. And as we passed the

Pentagon, the biggest building on earth, visible from space, I saw that every last window was burning bright.

That was my American dream. America? All I did was dream her. I woke up and I was still in Heathrow Airport, with my cheek on the hot vinyl. For fifteen minutes I watched a middle-aged man chewing gum, the activity all between the teeth and the upper lip, like a rabbit. And then I just thought: Enough.

It was hard getting back into London: I nearly flunked even that. Even getting back into London took my very best shot (No danger. You won't get a cab here, pal. No way). Before, I never thought I'd be able to live with myself if I failed to get to Missy and America. But maybe I can. After all, it won't be for terribly long.

That *dream* . . . So dogged, so detailed – so literal. One of those dreams where things happen at the same speed as they do in real life. It included a convincing four-hour wait in Reimmigration. Missy Harter used to dream like that, always; she used to lie by my side, and spend half the night in the Library of Congress or shopping at Valducci's. Something tells me that I won't dream like that ever again. From now on, each night, it'll be special relativity – Einsteinian excruciation. So maybe the American dream was a farewell to dreams. And to much else.

What was I doing? The whole thing, the whole love-quest, the whole idea: it was from another world. Forget it. Turn back. Back to try the art and dice with death and hate, and not fight for love in some unreal war . . .

Chapter 14: The Pinching Game

IF WE COULD pass through her force field (and we can't quite do this, force fields being strongest round the beautiful and the mad), we would know that her stomach wall hurt and weighed heavily, that she felt occasional drags and brakings of nausea, that all sorts of salmon were bouncing upwards against the stream. But here she comes, the character, Nicola Six on the street, on the Golborne Road, bringing a packet of light through all the random hesitation. Not that the street was without colour and definition on this day: it looked shorn in the low sun, plucked and smarting, with a bristle of golden dust. But Nicola brought light through it, human light, even dressed as she was, for simple authority: black cord skirt and tight black cashmere cardigan, white shirt with blue ribbon serving as bowtie, hair back (before the mirror, earlier, a daunting emphasis of eyebrow). She was getting all the right kinds of look. Women straightened their necks at her; men glanced, and dipped their heads. Only one discordant cry, from the back of a truck, and fading: 'Miss World! Miss World!' Everyone else seemed to be shifting sideways or diagonally but Nicola was travelling dead ahead.

The entrance to Windsor House immediately extinguished all her light. Nicola slowed for an instant, then kept going; she used a mental trick she had of pretending not to be there. The steeped concrete shone in the low sun, and even fumed slightly with the fierce tang of urine. It would have been a humiliation to approach them, so clearly were the lifts defunct – slaughtered, gone, dead these twenty years. She peered up the vortex of the stone stairwell and felt she was underneath a toilet weighing ten thousand tons.

'Want I mind your car?' said a passing four-year-old.

'I haven't got a car.'

'Die, bitch.'

She climbed up past scattered toilet-dwellers, non-schoolgoing schoolboys and schoolgirls, non-working men and women, past the numb stares of the youthful and the aged. She faced them all strongly; she knew she looked enough like the government. She felt no fear. Walking naked up these steps (she told herself), with her bare feet on the wet stone, Nicola would have felt no fear. That was part of it: no more fear. She paused on the tenth floor and smoked half a cigarette, watching an old toiletman tearfully trying to uncap a damaged can of Peculiar Brew.

Like everybody else, Nicola knew that council flats were small — controversially small. In a bold response to an earlier crisis, it was decided to double the number of council flats. They didn't build any new council flats. They just halved all the old council flats. As she walked along the ramp of the fifteenth storey, open to the search of the low sun, Nicola could hardly fail to notice that the front doors alternated in colour, elderly green interspliced by a more recent but even flakier dark orange. The front doors were also hilariously close together.

She halted. Faultily the bell sounded.

It was Nicola's view that she was performing very creditably, especially during the first two or three minutes, in that storm or panic of sense-impressions. To begin with there was the kaleidoscopic wheeling that her entry forced upon the kitchen, the chain of rearrangements made necessary by the admission of *one more person* into the room. Then vertigo relaxed into claustrophobia – armpit-torching, heat-death claustrophobia. Distractedly her parched eyes searched for a living thing. There was a plastic pot on the minifridge. In it, some kind of maimed gherkin was apparently prospering; it rose from the soil at an unforgivable angle. Then she had to confront the pallor and distress of the mother, and the surprising child on the floor (the intelligent valves of its watchful face), and the flummoxed dog. Christ, even the dog looked declassed. Even the dog was meant for better things. Next door to the left a man and a woman were quarrelling with infinite weariness. The room was split-levelled with cigarette smoke. Nicola pressed her thighs together to feel the good silk between her legs. She hadn't been anywhere this small since she was five years old.

Still hidden from sight, Keith hardly went unnoticed. As the olfactory nerve-centre of this particular stall or cubicle, Keith hardly went unnoticed. Although he remained at the far end of the flat, he was none the less only a few feet away. Keith was very close. Nicola could hear a beercan pop, a lighter worked and sworn at, the severe intakes of air and smoke. Then the inhuman hostility of his eructations . . . Time to flush him out. Time, because the place could not be borne – was astonishingly unbearable, even for an expert, like her. Feeling you were in Nigeria was one thing. In Nigeria, and trapped in Nigeria, and not at the scene of a drought or a famine but of an industrial catastrophe caused by greed. And there for your own advancement, to make what you could of the suffering. The talk was two-way torture. She said,

'Except you haven't got any *money*, have you. You just haven't got enough *money*. Do you abuse your daughter, Mrs Talent?'

'Oi!'

They waited.

And Keith loomed, loomed large in the Keith-sized kitchen. He wasn't that big; but he was gigantic in here. When their eyes met he paused heavily. Up from the depths of the brown dressing-gown came a sallow blush of shame or rage or both.

'I'm sorry,' said Nicola, with some haughtiness, 'but it seems to me that self-hatred is more or less forced on one in conditions like these. There'd be no way round it. Without self-hatred you wouldn't last five minutes.'

'Hey,' said Keith. '*Hey*. You. *Fuck* off out of it.'

Kath turned slowly to her husband, as if he were a wonderful doctor, as if he were a wonderful priest. She turned back to Nicola and said, 'Yes. Care? What kind of care do you get from an office? And from someone like you, doing your hobby or whatever it is you're doing. Get out.'

'Tell her, Kath,' said Keith calmly.

'Get out, you old witch. Get out. You vicious thing.'

'Well as I said before,' said Nicola, gathering herself and looking up into Keith's considering sneer, inches from her eyes, 'it's nothing more nor less than a question of money.'

She swayed out on to the ramp. Violently yanked from inside, the door gave an agonized creak and then closed almost noiselessly.

Nicola found that she was short of breath and taking great bites out of the air. Now to get back and prepare for Keith's coming. As she turned she heard the voices from the toy house.

'Vicious. Purely vicious.'

'They can't touch you, girl. You are who you are. Don't ever forget it. You are who you are, girl. You are who you are.'

So when he rang *her* bell, when he buzzed and blurted and came jinking up the last flight of stairs, Nicola was ready for this summit meeting, ready to turn all the new energies her way. She had done Keith violence, but she wanted no violence done to her, not yet. She wanted that violence violently stoppered. It was all right: she had the money. And any innocent or idiot could tell that a considerable sex-deflection would also be called for. Thinking this, Nicola had breathed in sharply and embraced herself, bristling – even her breasts had bristled. Love wouldn't do it. (Keith wasn't the type.) Sex wouldn't do it either, all by itself. Not even Nicola's sex, whose power had so often astonished even Nicola Six: the threats, the reckless bribes (money, marriage), the whimperings, the unmannings and unravellings, the bared teeth, the tendons of the neck so savagely stretched . . .

Keith entered. Nicola stood at the table in the darkened room, counting money under an angle lamp. She wore a black nightgown of candid vulgarity. With her hair freed and a third of each breast showing and no smile on her business face, she hoped to resemble a Monaco madame after a hard week in her first tax year of semiretirement, or something like that, as seen on TV. She removed her dark glasses and looked into the shadows for him. He looked back into the light. Silently, their force fields touched. And said:

Home was his secret. Nobody had ever been there before. Oh, there *had* been ingress: rentmen and census people, the police, and cheating electricians and would-be plumbers and so on as well as real social workers and probation officers – but nobody he knew. Not ever. Only the dog, and the woman, and the child: the insiders. They, too, were secrets. Home was his terrible secret. Home was his dirty little secret. And now the secret was out.

'Once upon a time,' said Nicola carefully, 'your wife must have been very lovely.'

'You shouldn't've fucking done it, Nick.'

'And the little girl is divine. What did you say your dog was called?'

267

'You shouldn't've fucking done it, Nick.'

'Such a noble beast. Keith, I *understand*. You didn't want me to know, did you, that you lived like a pig.'

'That's so . . . That's so out of *order*.'

She had a bottle of whiskey and two long glasses ready. One of the glasses she filled with perhaps a quarter of a pint of neat spirit. She took two swallows, and came round the table towards him.

'Have some of this.'

And he took two swallows.

Nicola could be taller than Keith when she wanted to be. She was certainly taller than him now, in her four-inch high heels. Keeping her legs straight she leant back on the table and dropped her head, murmuring, 'I took some of your money and spent it on new stockings and things. I hope you don't mind.' She looked up and said, 'You do know why I'm doing this, don't you, Keith? You do know what this whole thing is really all about?' Nicola didn't feel like laughing. But she did think it was wonderfully funny.

'What?'

'It's your darts: listen.'

The speech went on for five or six minutes. She then took him by the hand and guided his leaden body towards the sofa, saying, 'I've made a little tape for you, Keith, which in its curious way will help show you what I mean.'

. . . The black elbow-length gloves, the look of young wonder, the jealous dress, the blown kiss, the wiggling black finger, beckoning.

'Slow it,' moaned Keith, as the fade began. With a soft snarl he snatched at the remote. Then Nicola's quarter-clad brown body dashed backwards, and became a clockwork mannequin, then a living statue, as Keith froze the frame of choice.

'That,' said Keith, and sighed, not with yearning so much as with professional sincerity, 'that is the real thing.'

She gave him the money now, negligently tossing handful after handful into a tradenamed shopping-bag, and then led him into the passage. Every now and again Keith tried to look shrewd and deserving, but his lips kept scrolling into an adolescent leer. Standing above him at the top of the stairs, she folded her arms and appeared to gaze downwards at herself. 'The eternal appeal of the cleavage, Keith. What is it, I wonder. The symmetry. The proximal tension.'

'Prestigious,' said Keith. 'Looks nice.'

'In the books, they say, rather wistfully, that men want to put their faces there. Return to mother, Keith. But I don't agree. I don't think men want to put their faces there.'

Keith nodded his head, and then shook it.

'*I* think they want to put their cocks there, Keith. *I* think they want to fuck the tits. Ooh, I bet they do.'

'Yeah cheers,' said Keith.

This wasn't the real thing. Just a mannequin, on the remote. 'Remember. Next time you see him: mention poetry. I don't care how. And meanwhile, masturbate about me, Keith. Beat off about me. As a form of training. A lot. All those things you wanted to do to girls and were too shy to. Or they wouldn't let you. Do them to me. In your head.'

Keith's eyes seemed to be seeping upwards beneath his lids. 'Give me a taste. Come on, doll. Give me a taste.'

She must touch him. With three long fingers she felt his hair: as dry as fire-hazard gorse. One spark and it would all go up. She took a grip near the snagged parting line and pulled back slowly. Then, leaning into his opened face – and already hearing the swill of mouthwash, the twanging floss (it isn't me doing this: it's Enola, Enola Gay) – she gave him the Jewish Princess.

The telephone was ringing. Nicola drank whiskey. She lifted the receiver, heard the panicking pips, paused, and dialled six. 'I'm afraid I'm not here,' she said. And she even meant it, in a way. 'If you'd like to leave a message, please speak after the tone.'

Of course, there was no tone, and they both waited. Christ, how many seconds?

'Hello? Hello, Nicola? . . . God, I'm completely soaked. It's so awkward, talking to a machine. Listen. I've been –'

She pressed down with a finger.

Carefully Guy ducked his head out of the telephone cubicle and turned to face the street-wide wall of rain. Music was playing – it came and went beneath the thunder-racetrack of the sky. The right music, too. Guy turned: an old black man in the corner with a sax and the fierce melancholy of Coleman Hawkins. What was it? Yes. 'Yesterdays'. Guy would certainly be giving him money.

He stood in the steeped emptiness of the underground station on Ladbroke Grove, barely half a mile from the house, where he had recently discovered a live telephone box – in a long rank of dead ones. Quite a find. Like seeing a pterodactyl, complacently perched on a telegraph wire among the sparrows and worn old crows. Forever intensifying, the rain was now coming down so hard that even the cars seemed to be wading off home. Just buses, like lit fortifications, stalled in the wet night. That song: such complication, such grievous entanglement. First you go through this, it was saying. Then you go through *this*. Then you go through *this*. Life, thought Guy. When at last the man was finished Guy went over and pressed a ten-pound note into his styrofoam cup. 'That was beautiful,' he said. No answer. Guy turned and walked. And then the man called out: 'Hey buddy. I *love* you.'

Five long strides got him under the bus-stop shelter. Already he was farcically drenched. Rather than go straight home, where Marmaduke was in any case well-attended despite the nanny shortage (two night nurses until he was better again), Guy dreamed up reasons for breaking the journey with a visit to the Black Cross: two hundred yards along Lancaster Road. He kept on waiting for the rain to slacken. But it didn't. It kept on doing the other thing. It was lashing down, just like they said, whipstroke after whipstroke, in climbing anger. Extremity upon extremity, and then more extremity, and then more.

As Guy dodged and jumped towards the Portobello Road and its low-strung lights he saw a figure splashing about like a stage-drunk in the swollen gutter beneath the lamp. *Keith*. And he wasn't staggering. He was dancing, and laughing. And coughing.

'Keith?'

'. . . Yo!'

'My God, what are you doing?'

Keith sank backwards against the lamp-post, his head up, his gut softly shaking with laughter or exasperation – with laughter or defeat. He had a green carrier-bag, crushed to him beneath his crossed arms. 'Oh, mate,' he said. '*You* tell me. What's it all about, eh? Because I don't fucking get it.'

'Come on in. Look at us.'

'Because I don't fucking get it.'

'What?'

'Life.'

Now a tomato-red Jaguar jerked round the corner and came to an urgent halt beneath the lamp.

'Here comes summer.'

The back door opened and a voice said from the contained darkness, 'Get in the car, Keith.'

'Cheers, lads.'

'Get in the fucking car, Keith.'

Guy straightened, showing all his height. Keith held up a dripping hand. 'It's okay,' he said. 'No, it's okay. Only messing.' Keith stepped forward, and stooped. Then he said casually over his shoulder, 'We'll have a drink. Not in there. Inna Golgotha. I'll –' A hand came out of the shadow and Keith flopped suddenly into the back seat. 'Ten mim*ff*. Oof!'

He shouted something else and sustained another blow but Guy couldn't hear in all the rain's swish and gloss.

Re-entering the Golgotha meant rejoining it, at heavy expense, because Guy hadn't brought his stencilled nametag and could do nothing with the doorman's wordless stare. With some reluctance he ordered a *porno* (in the context of the Golgotha, Keith frowned on all other drinks) and secured a table by the fruit-machines, some distance from the band. As he did so he marvelled at this new thing he had: guts. Guy didn't even look around for another white face. For some reason the physical world was feeling more and more nugatory. He thought that perhaps this was a consequence or side-effect of the time he was living through: the sudden eschatology of the streets; the tubed saplings and their caged trash, marking the place where each human being might be terribly interred; her leggy disarray and the bubble at the centre of everything . . . Keith came in; he held up a bent thumb, and then vanished, soon to reappear with a glass and an unopened bottle of *porno* – a litre bottle, too, or possibly even a magnum.

'Are you all right?'

Keith's grinning face looked hot and swollen, and one of his ears was a startling crimson, with the beginnings of a rip showing beneath the lobe. A patch of blood on his hair had had time to dry and then to deliquesce again in the rain. He kept looking at the middle finger of his right hand as if it had a ring on it, which it didn't.

'Nah, load of nonsense. They're good as gold really. All forgotten now as such.'

His clothes were smoking. But so were Guy's. Everyone was smoking in the Golgotha, and everyone's clothes were smoking too. This was what happened when water met with warmth; and the rain that fell on London now gave off smoke for reasons of its own.

After a few quick glasses Keith said, 'I'm going to treat meself tonight. Debbee Kensit. Debbee – she's special to me. You know what I mean? Not yet fully mature. And pure. Natural love. Not like some. Nothing dirty. No way.'

'Dirty?' said Guy.

'Yeah. You know. Like gobbling and that. Seen uh . . ?'

At once Guy raised a forefinger to his eyebrow. 'Not in a while.'

'I don't understand you, Guy Clinch. I don't. Know what she said to me the other day? She said, "Keith?" I said, "Yeah?" She said, "Keith?" I said, "Don't start." She said, "Keith? You know, there's nothing – I wouldn't do – when I go a bundle on a bloke like that." There. That's what she said.'

Guy was staring at him in addled incredulity. 'Wait a minute. She . . . told *you* –'

'Or words to that effect,' said Keith quickly. 'Now hang on. Hang on. You're getting off on the wrong foot here, pal. She didn't *say* it. Obviously. Not in so many words.'

'So she said what?'

'It was like from this *poem* or something,' said Keith, with what certainly seemed to be sincere disgust. 'Christ! How'm I supposed to know. Eh? I'm just scum. Go on. Say it. I'm just scum.'

'You don't –'

'Je*sus*. Oh, excuse me, mate. No no. I'm not sitting through this. I come in here. Relax. A few drinks. You try to bring two people together in this world.'

'Keith.'

'I expected better of you, Guy. I'm disappointed, mate. Very disappointed.'

'Keith. It's not like that. Look. I really apologize.'

'Well then. And listen: I didn't mean no disrespect to her either. Neither.'

'Keith, of course you didn't.'

'Well then. Okay. Yeah cheers. I'm glad we . . . Because you and me, we . . .'

Guy suddenly felt that Keith might be on the verge of tears. He had certainly been punishing the *porno*. Something else told Guy that the word *love* was not too far away.

'Because you and me, we – we ought to look out for each other. Because we're in this together.'

'In what?' said Guy lightly.

Keith said, 'Life. In this life.'

They both sat up straight and cleared their throats at the same time.

'I didn't see you there Saturday.'

'You were there, were you?'

'You didn't –'

'No, I couldn't. What was it like?'

Keith dropped his head and peered up at Guy with an expression of rich indulgence. He said, 'Obviously the visitors were keen to blood their new signing from north of the border, Jon Trexell. How would the twenty-three-year-old make the transition from Ibrox Park to Loftus Road? At just under a million one of Rangers' more costly acquisitions in the modern era, no way was the young Scot about to disappoint . . .'

Twelve hours later Guy came down the stairs of his house in Lansdowne Crescent, carrying the breakfast tray and humming *non più andrai*. He paused and fell silent outside the door of the main drawing-room. He put two and two together. Hope was interviewing, or importuning, a new nanny. Guy listened for a while to the conjuring of large sums of money. Nanny auditions were a constant feature of Hope's daily life. There had been a standing ad in *The Lady* ever since the week of Marmaduke's birth . . . He went on down to the kitchen, bidding good morning to a cleaning-lady, a maid, a nurse, two elderly decorators (the cornices?), and an outgoing nanny (Caroline?), who was openly drinking cooking-sherry and taking deep breaths as she stared in wonder at the garden. Blindingly lit by the low sun, the near end of the room was still a slum of toys. Both the closed-circuit TV screens were dead but Guy's attention was drawn by a portable intercom on the table. Its business end must have been in the room above, because you could hear Marmaduke in stereo. He was evidently being quite good, as was often the case when a new nanny was in prospect. To hear him now, a stranger might have thought that the child had suffered nothing worse in the past few minutes than a savage and skilful beating. Abruptly everyone in the kitchen yelped with fright at an atrocious crash from the room above.

'No no, Melba,' Guy sang, heading off the maid as she went for the industrial vacuum-cleaner beneath the stairs. 'I'll do it.' Present myself to the new nanny: present the normal smile. One behaves as if that's all nannies could possibly want: normality.

'*Melba!*' yelled Hope as Guy came swerving into the room, grappling with nozzle and base. Marmaduke had somehow toppled the full-length eighteenth-century wall mirror, and was now gamely struggling to go and throw himself in its shards. Hope held him. Between the child's legs the cord of a lamp dangerously tautened. Guy stared into the Kristallnacht of fizzing glass.

'Mel*ba*!' yelled Guy.

After a few minutes Guy helped Melba fold the crackling binliner. He got up from his knees, brushed himself down – ouch! – and turned as Hope was saying,

'. . . quite as hectic as this. Darling, don't. Please don't. This is my husband, Mr Clinch, and I'm sorry, what did you say your name was?'

'Enola. Enola Gay.'

You look for the loved one everywhere, of course, in passing cars, in high windows – even in that aeroplane overhead, that crucifix of the heavens. You always want the loved one to *be there*, wherever. She is the object of the self's most urgent quest, and you search for her sleeplessly, every night, in your dreams . . . Guy felt panic, and pleasure: she was here, she was closer, and how gentle she looked in pink. Obeying a lucky instinct, Guy came forward and kissed his wife good morning. Whatever other effects this had it predictably caused Marmaduke to attack him. Left free for a moment to wander down the room, the child saw the caress and ran back over to break it up. Thus Guy was busy pinning Marmaduke to the floor as he heard Hope say,

'The money I think you'll agree is extremely generous. I've never heard of anyone paying anything even approaching that. You can wear what you like. You'll have backup most of the day from Melba and Phoenix and whoever. You'll have the use of a car. You get a double rate for any Saturdays you might like to do, and triple for Sundays. You can have all your meals here. You can move in. In fact –'

Melba knocked and re-entered. Three builders or gardeners stood ominously in her wake.

'Do excuse me for a moment,' said Hope.

So then. Leeringly chaperoned by Marmaduke, Guy and Nicola sat ten feet apart, on facing sofas. Guy couldn't talk to her; he found, once again, that he couldn't even look at her.

But Marmaduke felt differently. He slid from his father's grip. He put his hands in his pockets and sidled across the carpet. Checking out a new nanny – checking out her tits and weakspots: this was meat and drink to Marmaduke.

'Hello then,' he heard her say. 'You're a cool customer, aren't you? Guy, I'm so sorry. I hoped you wouldn't be here. I had to do this – I had to see. Ow! I say, that's quite a pinch. I got your message and I felt so – I see. Well, two can play at that, young man. Come to me today. You must. It's called the Pinching Game.'

The door opened. Guy looked up: Hope was summoning him with

her strictest face. He trudged from the room in his enormous shoes. Hope knew: it was so *obvious*. Guy felt as though a new force had been introduced into nature, like gravity but diagonal and outwards-acting: it might take the lid off everything, the room, the house.

'Well?' said Hope in the hall with her hands high on her hips.

'I . . .'

'We take her, right? We grab her. We gobble her up.'

He hesitated. 'Has she any qualifications?'

'I didn't ask.'

'Has she any references?'

'Who cares?'

'Wait,' said Guy. At his back he felt the glare of what he assumed to be dramatic irony. 'Isn't she a bit goodlooking?'

'What? It's incredibly quiet in there.'

'You always said that the goodlooking ones weren't any use.'

'Who are we to be picky?'

Guy laughed briefly and quietly.

'I mean,' continued Hope in a loud whisper, 'he's worked his way through all the ugly ones.'

They heard a harsh moan from within. It was quite unlike any sound they had heard Marmaduke make before. The parents hurried in, expecting the usual scene. Nanny hunched in a corner or diagnosing some facial injury in the mirror. Marmaduke brandishing a lock of hair or a torn bra strap. But it wasn't like that. Enola Gay was looking up at them with unalloyed composure while Marmaduke Clinch backed away, nursing his wrist, and with a new expression on his face, as if he had just learnt something (one of life's lessons), as if he had never known such outrage, such scandal.

The house was a masterpiece. How it scintillated, how it *thrummed*. So much canvas, and so much oil. How confidently it put forward its noble themes of continuity and repose, with everything beautifully interlinked. And Nicola's presence was like a fuse. Because she could make the whole thing go up.

Of course, the house wasn't art. It was life. And there were costs. Naturally, money was one of them. The house didn't eat money. It scattered money. Money flew off it, like tenners fed to an open propeller. From miles around people came to scour and primp it, to doctor it for more use, more work. Scrubbers and swabbers on their knees, the quivering plimsolls of an electrician upended beneath the

275

joists, a plumber flat on his back, a mangled sweep slithering up the chimney, labourers, repairmen, staggering installers, guarantee checkers, meter readers; and, of course, Marmaduke's many myrmidons. Sometimes Guy imagined it was all laid on for the child. The dinky boy-drama of skip-removal. The spillikins of scaffolding. All the ruin and wreckage.

The other thing the house used up was *order*. Each day the doublefronted dishwasher, the water softener, the carrot peeler, the pasta patterner got closer and closer to machine death, hurtling towards chaos. Each day the cleaning-lady went home tireder, older, iller. A citadel of order, the house hurried along much entropy elsewhere. With so much needed to keep it together, the house must deep down be dying to collapse or fly apart . . . Feeling hunger, and the desire to do something suddenly serious, Guy went downstairs again, stepping over a carpet-layer and pausing on his way to exchange a few words with Melba, whose strength for years he had bought and sapped . . .

His hands were steady as he poured milk and buttered bread. Now here was another conjugal secret: he pulled out the morning paper from beneath a stack of Marmaduke's toy brochures, where he had earlier hidden it from Hope, and turned again to the op-ed page. There was the article or extract, unsigned, offered without comment. Of course, in these days of gigawatt thunderstorms, multimegaton hurricanes and billion-acre bush fires, it was easy to forget that there were man-made devices – pushbutton, fingertip – which could cause equivalent havoc. But then all this stuff was man-made, not acts of God but acts of man . . . So the first event would be light-speed. A world become white like a pale sun. I didn't know that. Didn't know the heat travelled at the speed of light. (Of course: like solar rays.) Everything that faced the window would turn to fire: the checked curtains, this newspaper, Marmaduke's tailored dungarees. The next event would come rather faster than the speed of sound, faster than the noise, the strident thunder, the heavensplitting vociferation of fission. This would be blast overpressure. Coming through the streets at the speed of Concorde, not in a wave exactly but surrounding the house and causing it to burst *outwards*. The house, in effect, would become a bomb, and all its plaster and order, its glass and steel would be shrapnel, buckshot. No difference, in that outcome, between this house and any other. His house, the thrumming edifice of negative entropy, would be ordinary chaos in an instant, would be just like wherever Keith lived, or Dean, or Shakespeare. Then everything would be allowed. Guy shut his eyes and helplessly watched himself running north through low flames and winds of soot; then her room, torn open to a sick sky, and an act of love performed among the splinters – forgivable, but with her beauty quite gone, and everything spoiled and sullen and dead.

'I've got to stop,' he said with a sudden nod.

'Pardon?' came Melba's voice sweetly.

'Oh, I'm sorry, Melba. It's nothing.'

'The Effects of Thermonuclear Detonations', taken from something they referred to as 'Glasstone & Dolan (1977, 3rd edn)', among the editorials on deforestation and nurses' pay, next to a report about Concorde moving into overall profit by the end of the year, and above the astronomy column, which said that the Apollo object torn loose from the asteroid belt would miss the earth by a quarter of a million miles. Which sounded good. But that was where the moon was. Farewells were sounding on the intercom when Guy crushed the newspaper into the bottom of the rubbish bin. He swallowed as he felt her force field leaving the house.

And the house was still there.

Guy peered into the hall. By the sound of it, Marmaduke had dispersed – upstairs with Phoenix and Hjordis, no doubt. Now Guy abruptly cringed to the greeting of Dink Heckler.

'Hey,' said Dink, and pointed with an index finger.

'Dink. How are you?'

'Good.'

The South African number seven was of course in tenniswear. His pressed shorts were candy-white against the scribbled slabs of his thighs. Encased in practically cuboid gyms, Dink's feet were planted stupidly far apart.

'You're playing', said Guy, 'in this weather?'

'For sure.' Dink stared through the half-glass front door at the bright October morning, and then stared back at Guy with an expression of fastidious disquiet. 'What's the matter? You see something I don't?'

'It's just the – the low sun. Rather blinding.'

Hope now came skipping down the stairs saying, 'That's good. She's starting today. At one.'

'*Is* she,' said Guy.

277

Hope looked at Guy, at Dink, at Guy again. 'Are you *okay?* . . . Actually I'm encouraged. I thought she was amazing. Marmaduke was quite silent with her. He looked completely stunned. She must have this terrific authority. You know he's having a *nap* up there?'

'Amazing,' said Guy.

Then Hope said with finality, 'I'm playing with Dink.'

Under the buxom duvet, in the vestiges of his wife's sleepy body-scent, behind half-drawn curtains, Guy lay staring at the ceiling, itself significantly charged with the milky illicit light of a bedroom still in use during the hour before noon. The trouble with love, he thought, or the trouble with this love anyway (it would seem), is that it's so *totalitarian*. In the realm of the intellect, how idle to look for the Answer to Everything; idler still to find it. Yet with the emotions . . . what's the big idea? Love. Love is the Big Idea. With its dialectical imperatives, its rewrites, its thought police, its knock on the door at three a.m. Love makes you use the blind man, makes you hope for death in Cambodia, makes you pleased that your own son writhes – deep in the Peter Pan Ward. Bring on the holocaust for a piece of ass. Because the loved one, this loved one, really could turn the house into a bomb.

He awoke around two. His mind was clear. He thought: it's over. It's passed on. And he tensed himself, listening for the first whisper of recurrence . . . Perfectly simple, then. He would tell Hope everything (though not about the money. Are you *serious?*) and submit to his atonement. How marvellous, how beautiful the truth was. Ever-present, and always waiting. Love must be an enemy of the truth. It must be. And it kept on making you like what was bad and hate what was good.

Footsteps passed his room and climbed the stairs.

And now life lent a hand.

Through the throttled wire of a stray intercom he heard noises, voices, laughter. Hope and Dink, upstairs, changing. Having played, they were now changing, changing. A yelp, *I'm all sweaty*, a comical interdiction, *Check it out*, a trickle of zip then a hot silence broken by a gasp for air and her serious *Quit it!* . . .

And Guy thought: My wife doesn't love me. My wife has betrayed me. How absolutely wonderful.

Soon she entered, wearing a dressing-gown, the hair released from its grips, and with burning throat. 'Get up,' she said. 'He's sleeping now but you're on duty when Phoenix leaves. We're nannyless for the rest of the day. That bitch didn't show.'

In the next room along, Marmaduke, who had been up all night, lay sprawled in a shattered nap. Toys were scattered about the cot like munitions in a stalled war. The little prisoner, with his brutal Scandinavian face, was shackled in his woollen blankets, in his tumbling baby rope. Flattened with sweat was his duck-white hair . . . Even in sleep the child was not unmonitored, unmediated. Drinking a cup of instant coffee, Phoenix watched over him from the kitchen, closing her long eyes for several seconds at each indication that he might be about to stir.

Before losing consciousness Marmaduke had gazed at and prodded the twin bruises on the back of his dimply fist. He regarded them with fear and admiration. Already he was forgetting the pain that had accompanied them, but something about the way they came to be there would live on gloriously in his mind. He wanted to do to someone else the thing that had been done to him. 'Nice,' he had whispered (as one might say 'nice' of a pretty girl in the street or of the straight drive on the cricket field: saluting skill, talent), before rolling over to twist himself into sleep, hoping to dream of the Pinching Game.

The Pinching Game was good. It was *nice*.

'Ow! I say, that's quite a pinch. Well, two can play at that, young man. It's called the Pinching Game.'

Marmaduke waited.

'Do you want to play?'

Marmaduke waited.

'Now first – you pinch me as hard as you like.'

Marmaduke pinched her as hard as he liked – which was as hard as he could.

'Good. And now I pinch *you*.'

Marmaduke watched, with stoned interest. Then his vision seeped through tears of pain.

'Now it's your turn again. You pinch me as hard as you like.'

Marmaduke reached out quickly. But then he hesitated. First looking up for a moment with an uncertain smile, he carefully gave the tenderest tweak to the back of her hand.

'Good. And now I pinch *you*.'

279

Although I don't eat much now I think I still have a good appetite for love. But it doesn't work out.

In all I spent six nights sleeping rough at Heathrow. Not much sleeping. But plenty of rough. And I despaired. The other people there were better at it than I was, stronger and quicker in the standby queue, with heftier bribes more heftily offered. I could see myself becoming, as the weeks unfolded, a kind of joke figure in the Departure Lounge. Then a tragic figure. Then a ghoulish one, staggering from news hatch to cafeteria with bits falling off me.

I think I still have a good appetite for love. But there's nothing I can eat.

Incarnacion relates that Mark Asprey was hardly to be seen here at the apartment. Her own eyes retreat and soften with a lover's indulgence as she talks of the kind of demand in which her employer constantly finds himself. This leads her on to explore one of life's enigmas: how some people are luckier than others, and richer, and handsomer, and so on.

Of course I'm wondering whether he took a stroll down the dead-end street.

In my new dreams I think I keep glimpsing Kim, and Missy, Missy, Kim. They're trying to be nice. But in my new dreams it just doesn't work out.

*

I love Lizzyboo in my own way yet when I consider her socio-sexual training or grounding I have the impression that there are only about four or five things that could ever really happen between her and men.

He Refuses To Make A Commitment. She Has A Problem Giving Him The Space He Needs. He Is Too Focused On His Career At This Time. They Think They Love Each Other But Given Their Temperamental Differences How Will They Ever Connect?

She's much more importunate these days, or she is when she's not eating. The restraints are gone. It's as if she's falling. She's falling, and at the usual rate of acceleration, which is plenty fast: thirty-two feet per second per second. Luckily, at least, with this falling business, it doesn't make any difference how heavy you are . . . I guess I could tell her I'm plain old fashioned. 'I guess I'm just a child of my time, Lizzyboo,' I can hear myself saying as I daintily remove her hand from my knee. Alternatively, there are any number of debilitating but non-fatal diseases I could bashfully adduce. Last night she took my hand on the stairs and said, 'You want to fool around?' Me? Fool around? Hasn't she heard that fooling around is on the decrease – though maybe it hasn't been, much, in her case, or not until recently. Dink Heckler, for example, has the look of a stern taskmaster in the sack. But she won't be getting any of that nonsense from me. I'm a child of my time.

In the wild days of my hot youth no one wanted to risk it and neither did I. Remember how it used to go . . . Are you free any night this week? I thought we might step out together – to the hospital. That nice place on Seventh Avenue. If it makes you feel more relaxed about it, bring your personal physician along. I'm bringing mine. I'll be around to get you about half past eight. In an ambulance. Aw honey, don't be late.

It's not quite like that any more. Let's consider. The vaulting viruses, all those wowsers and doozies and lulus, are of course increasingly numerous but they seem to have simmered down a good deal. Purely out of self-interest, naturally. They're only parasites, after all, and the career guest and freebie-artist doesn't really want to tear the whole place apart (except when unusually drunk). So the wisdom of evolution prevailed; they adopted a *stable strategy*, with their own long-term interests held sensibly in view; and now they're just part of the dance. Besides, we all know we're not going to live for ever. We do know that. We forgot it for a while. For a while, the live-forever option looked to be worth trying. No longer. Even in California the workout parlours and singlet clinics are paint-parched and gathering dust. Three score and ten is a tall order, even for the very rich, even for someone like Sheridan Sick. We subliminally accept that life has been revised downward, and once again we start sleeping with strangers. Or some of us do. The act of love takes place in a community of death. But not very often. Just as you won't find much corridor-creeping in the modern hospice, despite all the superb facilities.

I met her eleven years ago. We felt safe. More than that. We felt solved. We were *solved*.

Now she won't talk to me. My name is muck at Hornig Ultrason. I'm not feeling very well, and I *haven't got any money*.

I find myself indulging in vulgar reveries of a movie sale.

There must be a dozen hot actresses who would kill for the part of Nicola Six. I can think of several bankable stalwarts who could handle Guy (the ones who do the Evelyn Waugh heroes: meek, puzzled, pointlessly handsome). As for Keith, you'd need a total-immersion expert, a dynamic literalist who'd live like a trog for two or three years as part of his preparation for the role.

The only difficulty is Marmaduke. Typical Marmaduke. Maximum difficulty. Always.

Maybe you could dispense with an infant star and go with a little robot or even some kind of high-tech cartoon. It's amazing what they can do.

Or, because age and time have gone so wrong now, why not a youthful dwarf, wearing diaper and baby mask?

It's all gone wrong. The old are trying to be young, as they always have, as we all do, youth being the model. But the young are now trying to be old, and what is this saying? Grey-locked, resolutely pallid, halt in step and gesture, with panto-hag makeup, crutches, neck-braces, orthopaedic supports.

Then the next thing. You start fucking around with the way your babies look. First, you fuck around with the way *you* look (turn yourself into a bomb site or a protest poster), then, with that accomplished, you start to fuck around with the way your *babies* look. Dumb hairstyles – lacquered spikes, a kind of walnut-whisk effect. Magentas and maroons, wheat-and-swede combinations. I saw a toddler in the park wearing an earring (pierced), and another with a tattoo (bruised songbird). There are babies tricked out with wigs and eyeglasses and toy dentures. Wheeled in bathchairs.

Now I know the British Empire isn't in the shape it once was. But you wonder: what will the *babies'* babies look like?

Lizzyboo and I go to the new milkbar on Kensington Park Road. Her treat. She insists. The place is called Fatty's, which strikes me as unfortunate, and bad for business. On the way Lizzyboo will eat an ice-cream or a hot pretzel or a foot-long hotdog. Once there, once actually in Fatty's, she will start on the milkshakes, with perhaps a banana split or a fudge sundae. Over these dishes she will sketch in the prospect of lifelong spinsterhood.

This afternoon, a blob of chocolate somehow attached itself to her nose. I kept assuming she would eventually notice it – would feel it, would see it. But she didn't. And I let too much time pass, too much nose time, too much chocolate time. It was a big relief when she excused herself and went to the bathroom. As she lifted herself from the chair I observed that the zipper on her skirt was warped with strain. At least five minutes later she returned, and the blob of chocolate was still in place.

'Sweetheart,' I said, 'you have a blob of chocolate on your nose.'

She was mortified. 'How long has it been there?' she said tightly into her compact.

'Since way back. Since you had the éclair.'

'Why didn't you *tell* me?'

'I don't know. I'm sorry.'

Because to have done so earlier would have involved an admission of intimacy. Because it suits me if she looks ridiculous. Because I didn't know she had stopped looking in mirrors.

They both turn heads, these girls I squire. Lizzyboo by day. Nicola by night. They both embody whatever it is that means men *have* to look.

And what is it? One of the many messages that pulses off Lizzyboo has something to do with babies. It says: Big me. I'm big already but make me bigger. Let the SSCs get to work. Give these breasts a job. I lay it all before you, if you're the one. If you're the one, then I lay it all before you.

283

Interestingly, Nicola's appearance makes no mention of babies. All she has to say on that subject is Watertight Contraception. I'm not going to lose my figure and get up in the middle of the night. I won't be time-processed, medianized – not by *you*. It would have to be something special, something unique, something immaculate.

Like the Virgin Mary: Nobodaddy's Babymamma.

It doesn't particularly matter that I'm going blind because I can't read anyway. Five minutes with *Macbeth* on my lap and I'm in a senile panic of self-consciousness. Mark Asprey's many bookshelves are shelved with books but there's nothing much to read. It's all stuff like Good Bad Taste or Bad Good Taste or Things You Love to Hate or Hate to Love or why it's Frivolous To Be Important or The Other Way Around.

I get stuff from Nicola but who am I kidding. There are things I'm not seeing, or not understanding. The only writer who gives me any unfeigned pleasure is P. G. Wodehouse. And even him I find a bit heavy. He takes a lot out of me. Scratching my hair, with soft whistles, with lips aquiver, I frown over *Sunset at Blandings*.

Pretty soon I'll be obliged to ask Nicola to show me what she looks like in the nude. I find I'm looking forward to it. I can't imagine she will deny me this simple request. She knows how seriously I take my work.

Chapter 15: Pure Instinct

'ALL RIGHT THEN,' said Nicola. 'Shall we start?'
  'Yes,' said Guy. 'Let's.'

She gazed at him with an expression of sensitive expectancy.

He shifted position in his chair and said with a quavering voice, 'I really do find it quite extraordinary.'

'What?'

'Someone as beautiful as you. And never been kissed with passion.'

'I suppose it is in a way. But I know you'll be terribly patient and gentle with me.'

'I'll do my best. Oh by the way. Before we start. What did you do to Marmaduke? He was absolutely angelic until tea-time.'

'A silly thing. The Pinching Game.' She explained, with the briskness of impatience or even vexation (children: a delicate subject hereabouts). 'A little lesson in adult injustice. Or arbitrariness. They give you a soft pinch and expect a soft pinch back. Not a hard pinch.'

Literalmindedly, Nicola was wearing white. A full white party frock with many a flounce and purfle. The dress was certainly not meant to be provocative. Far from it: there was something forbiddingly juvenile in the way her arms emerged plumply from the puffed sleevelets and a special awkwardness conferred by the waist-thickening sash. She had also applied her makeup with excitable prodigality, as a twelve-year-old might prepare for her first big ball.

Nevertheless, Guy gazed at her dress, with its fringe of petticoat, and imagined the history of underwear being enacted within.

He said hoarsely, 'No attempts? Not even at parties or anything? Quite extraordinary.'

'Yes, my sexual life . . . just never happened. Perhaps it had to do with my parents dying when they did. An only child. Thirteen. My nature turning on its hinges. And I had seen what happened to Enola.'

'Oh yes.'

'I was curious, of course. I had longings.'

'You must have felt their interest. Men must have been intensely interested.'

'Do you know what I felt?'

'No?'

'I felt that my emotional – or sexual – being was like a little sister. A very spirited little sister. An inner sister. Whom I must always protect. I had to keep her in. Even though she yearned to come out and play.'

'It's almost tragic.'

'Though I've always suspected that my nature is in fact highly sensual. The way I respond to art tells me this. To poetry. To paintings.'

Guy had long been aware of a faint pulsing action in the middle of his lap. Now he noticed that with each passing second his teacup and saucer had begun to click. He recrossed his legs and said uneasily. 'I wonder what happens to all that – all that sap.'

Nicola straightened. She turned her face to one side. 'Does it curdle, do you mean?'

'I'm sorry.'

'No no. It's quite all right. Does the moisture . . . does the juice . . . ? It never felt like that. Perhaps it just wastes its sweetness on the desert air.'

'Yes, born to blush unseen. Yes I've always thought', Guy enthused (and she smiled so bravely!), 'that Empson was quite right about that. The situation is stated as pathetic but it doesn't exactly encourage you to change it. A jewel doesn't mind being in a cave, and a flower prefers not to be picked. If anything. You could –'

'There was a boy', said Nicola, 'with oil-black hair and the muscles of a panther. Pinto, the Corsican gardener's son. This was in Aix-en-Provence. Every night we would meet in the warm garden behind the abandoned villa. He caressed me so thoroughly with his tongue and his rough fingertips that I kept thinking I would unravel completely or fold myself inside out.'

'. . . When was this?'

'I was twelve.'

'Twelve?'

Nicola gave Guy time to complete the following train of thought – that of driving out to the airport with his foot on the floor, taking the first plane to Marseille and running the wily Pinto to ground in some flyblown shadowland . . .

And give the blacktoothed brute the thrashing of his life. Guy tried to imagine Nicola at twelve and saw a brown belly, a collection of clefts and flexed sinews, and the same face he faced now. She was smiling, and patting the cushion at her side.

'Come on then,' she said. 'We're not going to do much with you sitting all the way over there . . . Are you comfy? You're walking in a funny way. Okay then. Shall we start?'

'Yes. Let's.'

'What with?'

'With kissing, I suppose.'

'Right. Go on then.'

Twenty minutes later Guy whispered, 'This is heavenly. But do you think you could open your mouth a little bit?'

'I'm terribly sorry.'

'No it's all right. Or at least,' he said, 'at least don't shut it quite so tightly.'

Down in the street below Keith sat slumped in the Cavalier listening to a darts tape on the stolen Blankpunkt. They're taking their fucking time about it, he thought. He looked longsufferingly across the road at Guy's VW: on a meter. Still, he imagined there would be no great breach of decorum (he reviewed his instructions) if the Cavalier were to occupy the slot when Guy went on his way. Leave it here'll the car get a ticket. Or clamped. Fucking bastards . . .

What a difference a day makes. It was hard, in some ways, to credit the change that had come over Keith in a scant twenty-four hours. He sat back. The low sun warmed him. Blinking through the windscreen, whose fuzz and splat now subtly harmonized with the pond-mantle and the bobbing tadpoles of his tarnished vision, Keith recalled that recent self, that self of rage and terror, coming up her stairs with murder in its soul – or at least with murder in its brow. I might have taught her a lesson. Straight: I'd have swung for her yesterday. Happily hungover, Keith snorted (and coughed), and shook his head with a thickskinned smile. He comes into her lounge and it was all dark. Like a Danish sex club. No, not Danish. Er, Arab. With candles, and screens. She was wearing a black gown that was so – beautiful. No way here'll that not be an exquisite garment. Not cheap neither. Either. As for the woman it encased: you had to be giving her all kinds of credit for the nick she'd kept herself in. And all the money on the table like, like TV as such.

'You shouldn't have fucking done it Nick!'

'Keith, I *understand*. You didn't want me to know, did you, that you lived like a –'

His eyes opened, and flickered. He rubbed them, with his knuckles, like a child. And then, after that, after something so – after saying something so *well* out of order, she goes and changes my life, just like that. Magic. Because she understands me. She understands me. She's the only one that really understands me. About my darts . . . Keith sniffed and stirred, and wiped the tears from his eyes with a mahogany thumbnail. Not ashamed to admit it . . . A whole new life now. Keith's mind slid sideways: the last dart flying home (had to be a bull finish: had to be), and Keith turning to embrace the sporting shrug of his adversary; and then a pastel arcade of goods and services. And pastel women. The night before, after the quart of *porno* with Guy, a visit to Debbee Kensit, and a final call paid on Trish Shirt, Keith had gone home and caught up with some of his viewing: American football, and the frame-by-frame analysis of the cheerleaders in their flickety white skirts. You had to hand it to the Yanks: they got the sport groupies all there, and *in uniform.*

How did it go again? Your home life, Keith, is stifling your darting talents, and throwing a pall over your darting future. It's a question of darting attitude – getting your darting head right for the big one. I see you, Keith, as a young boy in the street with your face crushed up against the glass. But it's not a shop window. It's a TV screen. We're talking TV stardom here, Keith. Behind the screen is where you've got to get to. That's where all the other stuff is – all the stuff you want. Let me take you there, Keith. Let me take you to the other side.

'Yeaeaeah,' said Keith as the darts tape achieved its climax. He punched the buttons. Meteorologist Dennis Car: Hurricane Juanita. Phone-in: money matters. Geopolitics: another scan for the President's wife. Local news: police had made an arrest in the case of the murdered five-year-old in South London's Camberwell. Keith looked indignant. You *never* heard anything like that on the news any more. Said it just encouraged it. Don't ask Keith why. Kill a kid, he thought. Get your name on the radio. Or TV.

And then that video. Jesus. Keith had been – and still was – profoundly moved. The lighting, the production values, the sheer professionalism. Not overly explicit, but top-quality work within its own terms. In the past, Keith had done loads of videos with birds, and had taken it very seriously indeed. And to this day he felt puzzled by the monotonous squalor of his results. For with a video camera on his shoulder and a ladyfriend on the carpet or the couch – Keith was all aesthete. He tried to make it beautiful, and it came out ugly; and the birds looked mad. And mad in the wrong way. So when Nicola Six, alluringly reduced to two dimensions, had climbed out of the deep green dress and had gazed, in bra-and-panty set, so pensively out of the window, Keith had felt a tingle up his spine and a prickle of the hairs on the back of his neck. Had felt, in fact, that sense of pregnant arrest which accompanies the firm handclasp of art.

Actress like. Real pro: knows what she's doing. The others: amateurs. Nor was this favourable impression in any way dispelled when she talked dirty to him on the stairs. The poetry of the cleavage. *Nicola* seemed mad too, then, for a minute. But mad in the right way. And you expected a bit of that – indeed you looked for it – in the sex-genius sphere. To follow Keith's thoughts where they wouldn't quite go (and anyway he was thinking with his blood): only *imbalance* would lead a woman to invest such a lot of herself in such an unreliable area. Take Analiese. 'Masturbate about me, Keith,' Nicola had said. And Keith had honoured her plea. 'All those things you wanted to do to girls . . . Do them to me. In your head.' Keith considered. There wasn't anything, by now, that he had wanted to do to girls and hadn't gone ahead and done – as Trish Shirt, among others, could defeatedly attest. And he'd never raped Trish Shirt: he'd never seen the need. No, Keith did everything he wanted to do – except, occasionally, sexual intercourse, which had a habit of slipping his mind (fifteen minutes later, in the street, he would stop dead and snap his fingers), so busy was he with all his other stunts . . . Oh yeah. There *was* one thing he had wanted to do to girls and had never gone ahead and done. He had wanted to do it quite badly and often, too (when they nagged and cried and that, or

289

wouldn't let you do everything you wanted). He had never murdered any of them. He had never done that. And her kiss (Jesus), like falling into a swamp or quicksand . . .

Keith put a fresh darts tape into the Blankpunkt and resettled himself in the hot Cavalier. That classic encounter at the Embassy between Kim Twemlow and Nigel House. Such darts immersion was, in Keith's view, the ideal preparation for his upcoming quarter-final at the George Washington on England Lane. He bent his head and looked up wincing at Nicola's high window. He thought: they're taking their fucking time about it.

Guy felt a fiery crack on the side of his head. His neck jerked backwards into thin air, and gravity tugged him urgently to the floor.

After a moment of white flurry Nicola was kneeling by his side.

'On *no*,' she said. 'Oh my darling, I'm so sorry.'

Guy raised three fingertips to his temple. He closed his eyes, and then blinked mechanically.

'Let's see. Ooh. That looks quite nasty. I'd better get you some meat for it. I must have caught you with my ring. Oh God. You should have warned me about your *tongue*.'

Guy half sat up. He called after her, unable, for the moment, to keep the querulousness out of his voice, 'You said Pancho or whatever his name was used his tongue.'

With swollen eyes, and one hand clamped over her mouth, Nicola dropped to her haunches in front of the open refrigerator. Then her face cleared and straightened. 'In my ear,' she called back. 'Not in my *mouth*. He was just a dirty little gypsy or something.'

'Well how was I supposed to know?'

She returned. Guy noted her blush of contrition.

'Christ! What's that?'

'Pork liver. Anyway it's all I've got.'

The purple organ was dangling hideously close to Guy's eyeball. 'I don't even know', he said, '– I don't even know what this whole business with meat *is*. Do you?'

'I imagine it's meant to limit the swelling or something. I'm quite shocked at myself. It was pure instinct.'

'Oh I'm all right.'

'Mm. It certainly isn't working, this meat. It's coming up rather alarmingly. You've got such delicate skin. Like a child's. Oh dear. Whatever will you tell your wife?'

'What, it's a proper black eye, is it?'

'I fear so.'

He held her gaze for a moment. 'Isn't there something in *Jude* like this? She throws a pig bladder at him or something? I mean, it's not thought to be terribly friendly.'

'It hasn't been a great success, has it. Our first session.'

'No, but . . .' Guy placed a fist on his heart. '*In here.*'

This surprised her, and softened her, and made her partly relent. Nicola's eyes moved meaningly across his face. After all, it would do Keith good to wait. 'I'll tell you what,' she said. 'Let me lead. I'll just use my imagination. Close your eyes and I won't be so shy . . . Let me kiss it better. I'll just get rid of this disgusting meat.'

Without will, he sat back against the base of the sofa. As she moved round him on the floor, all he felt were her lips, her fingertips, her breath on his face. He heard sighs and rustlings, and the sound of his own blood. At one point he felt a soft weight on his groin – the pressure, perhaps, of the gathered material of her dress or petticoat. Anyway, it wasn't serious, because her next kiss had the shape of a smile.

She gave him the Rosebud, the Pouter, Youth, Cousins Touching Tongues, the Deliquescent Virgin, the Needer.

'Don't stop,' he whispered.

She gave him Anybody's, the Toothcount, Lady Macbeth, the Grand-A-Night Hooker, the Readied Pussy, the . . .

'Please,' he said, his eyes still closed but starting to struggle. 'Please. No.'

Here we go: he's coming . . . *now*. Keith struggled into position. To make things 'look good', Keith had obtained, at Nicola's suggestion, a workmanlike prop: a stolen leather bag full of stolen tools – spirit-level, light hammer, chisel, tyre-iron. Doesn't see me. They can do that: look right through you.

Guy was coming back down the garden path, and moving awkwardly, half doubled-up, and listing. He looked round in fear with the ghost's eyes of the deceiver. Always this problem of re-entry. How the strands of duplicity tightened, like the veins on the surface of a sclerotic soul. *Why did you come to the house?* he had asked her. *To establish something. Your wife doesn't love you. Poor Guy* . . . Guy couldn't bear to believe this, Dink or no Dink. But in any case the duplicity was now all doubleknotted: one would have to go at it with fingernails, with tweezers. He paused (winded, battered); he felt as if he had been flying for twenty-two hours in economy class, and that the dead-end street, with its unstirring trees dust-feathered in the low sun, might just as well be Australia. Guy scanned the scene, not for faces, not yet, but for figures with their inimitable weight and outline, as Giacometti might: Phoenix, Richard, Terry, Lizzyboo – Hope!

'Yo!'

Guy gave a stark yelp.

'Prestigious,' said Keith, shuffling stockily across the road with his bag. 'Eurobank. Motorway contraflow. Intercool.'

'Keith.'

'Oi!'

'What?'

'Whew. That's a bit tasty.' Keith's scowl of concern now widened into a friendly sneer. 'You come on a bit rough, did you? Forced to defend her honour, was she?'

'No, I tripped on my way up the stairs.'

'Course you did. Listen.'

Keith reached up and put an arm round Guy's shoulder. Guy flinched but then quickly fell in with Keith's confidential amble. Was it okay, asked Keith, if he *took his place*. He'd nip in where Guy'd just been.

'I wait for you to go and then slot in after you. I'll ease in there. No sweat.'

Guy looked down at the upturned rhomboid of Keith's nose, its scored bridge, its tunnel-of-love nostrils.

'Because they fucking clamp you round here.'

'Do they? Yes of course, Keith.'

'Bollinger. Veuve Clicquot. Oh uh. Tomorrow night.'

Tomorrow night? What fresh hell was this? Guy opened his eyes as wide as they would go.

Keith's cigarette-bearing hand suddenly froze on its way to his lips. 'You forgotten,' he said with full menace.

'No no. I'll be there.' Where? Judging by the energy that Keith continued to trap in his stunned visage, Guy felt that the date must be of high significance, like a visit to the dogs or to the shrine of some sainted bookie.

'Onna darts,' said Keith at last.

The VW Estate was wedged tight into its bay, with perhaps three inches spare at front and rear; it took Guy a long time to work the car out into the street, and Keith was always there, directing matters like a policeman, beckoning, fending off, beckoning again, and finally raising the great bent thumb.

Be no good at fighting, decided Keith as he climbed the stairs. A total banana. When a man was called on to look to his fists – and his feet, and his knees, and his teeth, and his chisel and his tyre-iron and his beer bottle – Guy'd crap it. Hopeless! Keith saw the likes of Guy all the time (on TV): jeered from the bedroom, snivelling in their tweed suits. Aboard the *Titanic* he'd be one of the blokes that dressed up as birds, whereas Keith would meet his fate like a man. What though the cocktail bar be at forty-five degrees, Keith would be down there propping it up, and murdering the Scotch. On the second-floor landing he paused to catch his breath. He lit a cigarette and slumped back against the window sill. By the time he had stopped coughing the cigarette was down to its filter. So he lit another one. He had nothing to blow his nose on but found an old tit magazine in his stolen bag and did what he could with that. Plus there was the curtain. Then he staggered on up the third flight, wondering what Lady Muck had in store.

'We all have a dirty little secret, don't we, Keith?'

'Yeah?' said Keith, with slow hauteur, as if he didn't have a dirty little secret. In fact, of course, Keith had lots of dirty little secrets. He had dirty little secrets galore. To make no more than a brisk selection, to name but a few: Trish Shirt and his father and his darting doubts and the crate of ripped knicker brochures in the garage and his failure in the eyes of Chick Purchase and Debbee Kensit's birth certificate framed on her bedroom wall and an unshakable conviction of worthlessness and Kath-and-the-flat.

'It has always been a disappointment to me, a bitter disappointment, Keith, that literature – that art – has failed to own up to it. To the dirty little secret. Which is, of course . . .'

'*That* ain't no secret. I'm at it all the –'

'Oh, there's Larkin's "Love again: wanking at ten past three" and a few bursts of confessionalism from the Americans. But surely this is the responsibility of the novelist, who works with the quotidian, who must become the whole of boredom, among the just be just, among the filthy filthy too, Keith.'

'Yeah,' said Keith absently. 'Same difference.'

'You'd think that the twentieth century, unfastidious enough in every other respect, would go ahead and grasp the nettle, wouldn't you, Keith? But no.'

'I seen a film', said Keith, 'where a girl did it. The other day.'

'Which film was this?'

Keith cleared his throat. '*Miss Adventures in Megaboob Manor*,' he said carefully.

'We'll get round to that in a minute, Keith.'

'Two hundred and seventy-five quid.'

'I suppose one of the great things about masturbation is that nobody wants to be seen doing it. Generally, they don't want the news to get around. Why should people be staring at the ceiling with *that* kind of expression on their faces? Let me freshen that for you, Keith.'

'Er, thanks, Nick. Ola.'

Keith watched her pass: the soft shake of her dress. Employing the darting finger, he made an up-and-under feint at her white-flounced rump. The friction of underthings: quite *noisy*, that dress. Like the bird inside it. Keith sucked hard on a section of his upper lip. He considered himself to be thoroughly at ease, and nicely holding up his end of the sexual lecture or exchange or foretalk. He thought of the ecstasy aunts in the magazines, and of their certain approval. Breaking new grounds in frankness. An adult exchange of views innit. Mutual pleasure. We all have our needs. But both his legs were dead they were that tightly crossed. And his palms felt siltily viscid. Jesus, hang around here all night. This rate the Cavalier'll get a ticket. Or clamped. Fucking bastards . . .

'Like so much else, Keith, it's all to do with time. How old are you?'

'Twenty-nine.' Said boldly, as if his age were one of his less arguable virtues or qualifications.

'A child. A baby. You're reaching the age when, according to literature, you'll soon be putting all that behind you. You won't of course. Ever. They won't stop you stropping it, will they, Keith. Oh no. I look at you, and I see a man', she said, her face flooding with roguish admiration, 'who'd be *proud* to die with his Johnson in his hand.'

'Yeah cheers.'

'Cheers! But don't worry. We won't be watching. It's okay until you're about the same age as Christ was at Calvary. Thereafter, no one wants to know. Because it just gets sadder. Sadder and sadder all the time.'

Keith shrugged. He could feel himself sinking into the privacy of his hangover – into the deep and settled privacy of how he felt. Here all the difficulties were undivulged. Oops. Oi. Hello. Oof. Jesus. Dear oh dear. But in silence. Whole'll . . . whole thing'll go up anyway. And Thelonius with his mangos and his weights. And Guy.

Now Nicola came and joined him on the sofa. The great layered spread of frock and petticoat. The legs folded seethingly underneath. Her face dipped but her eyes still sought his. 'You're clearly something of a connoisseur', she said softly, 'of pornography. What's your special taste? Be frank. I understand. As you know I – I'm quite "non-judgmental".'

Keith liked this word. To him it evoked a new dawn, a better world, one finally free of all juries and magistrates and QCs. He flexed his eyebrows and said, 'Same as the next man.' He knew – he even hoped – this was probably false (and felt the formation, across his upper lip, of a Zapata mustache of sweat). On average Keith spent between two and three hours a day in a largely fruitless quest for the sort of pornography he liked (i.e., pornography, whore-art, and not the sex-free sex films slipped his way by other *cheats* or the rubbish you get in the shops). But there was a time when pornography had played an altogether more central role in his life. When he was a bachelor, Keith had done pornography the way some people did heroin. Pornography pauperized Keith and made him fear for his sanity and his eyesight. Pornography was the main reason he had sought Kath's hand in marriage. Videos. From a towelhead – Abdelrazak – in Brixton. (Abdelrazak was nonjudgmental too. You could say that for him: 100 per cent nonjudgmental, was Abdelrazak.) Keith knew that he had no resistance to pornography. He had it on all the time, and even that wasn't enough for him. He wanted it on *when he was asleep*. He wanted it on *when he wasn't there* . . . 'Just nude birds,' said Keith. 'Basically. Obviously.'

'It's funny, isn't it. The dirty little secret may be neglected elsewhere. But here's a genre, starting as *samizdat* and ending up as a global industry, which is about *nothing else*. Women don't usually approve of pornography, do they, Keith. I shouldn't think, for instance, that your *wife* approves of it.'

Oi, thought Keith. What was the matter with all this? In his head, ideas wanted to be named, but remained nameless. Something to do with sinning singly, invisibly. You locked the door behind you. Only the porcelain saw, and the old towel. He felt the desire to speak and opened his mouth but there was nothing there.

'Women talk about the violence it does to them. But I don't know. Look at the most innocuous entertainment imaginable: a magic show. The assistant minces around in a bikini, and then lies down grinning her head off to get sawn in half. I think women don't like pornography because it excludes them. Women are there when pornography is made. Ruined sisters. But they're not there when pornography is used. That's men's work. They don't share their little secret with women. They share it with pornography.'

She stood up. Look: she had the remote in her hand. The TV gave its electric crackle. She laughed musically (crazily) and said, 'Really, the Englishman's taste! Nurses and schoolmarms and traffic wardens. It's so *sweet*. I suppose it all comes from nannies and public schools and things. Though not in your case.'

'No danger,' said Keith (he was busy watching).

'Still, there *are* lots of randy plumbers and winking window-cleaners and so on.'

'Yeah cheers.'

'I'm going to have a bath. Would you unzip me, Keith? Thank you. I'll be in the tub, oh, for at least fifteen minutes. It's the little catch at the top. That's it. Thank you. There are some paper tissues on the table there. Let me know when you're done . . . It's all right, Keith. I understand.'

She welcomed and applauded the death of just about anything. It was company. It meant you weren't quite alone. A dead flower, the disobliging turbidity of dead water, slow to leave the jug. A dead car half-stripped at the side of the street, shot, busted, annulled, abashed. A dead cloud. The Death of the Novel. The Death of Animism, the Death of Naive Reality, the Death of the Argument from Design, and (especially) the Death of the Principle of Least jAstonishment. The Death of the Planet. The Death of God. The death of love. It was company.

The death of physics, for example. Physics had died only the other day. Poor physics. Perhaps fifty people on earth understood it fully, but physics was over, just in time for the millennium. The rest was mopping up. The rest was funeral direction. They had found proton decay, at 10^{32} years, uniting the strong and the weak atomic forces, giving the strongelectroweak. Then all they needed, for the Grand Unified Theory, for the Theory of Everything, was gravity. And then they got it. They got gravity.

She had read the cautious popularizations in the news magazines; and everyone agreed that the Theory made beautiful sense. The maths were beautiful. The whole death was beautiful. As she understood it – well, it was very simple (it courted intuition) – the key to Everything was this: time was a force as well as a dimension. Time was a force; but then of *course* it was. Elementary. Six forces. And time was the sixth force, not just a measure but a motivator too. Time 'softened up' quanta for all the other interactions, saving a special intimacy for its workings with gravity; the tug didn't tug without the massage of time. Uranium felt time as a force easing its journey into lead. Yes. And human beings felt time that way too (how anthropomorphic the Theory was, how sentimental!), not just as a temporal arena, but as a *power*. Don't we feel time as a power, and doesn't it feel like gravity? When we rise from the bed to face another year. When we reach and bend, when we try to strain upwards. What is it that is always pulling us back down?

As for the death of love . . . Was it really coming? Was it already here? Naturally she had wondered, as all artists do, whether she was just arguing out from her own peculiarity. But now the news was abroad and everybody was talking about it. And how to explain her red-throated anger and bitterness (she felt violated, plagiarized) when she first saw the phrase in print? The diagnosis was in on love, the diagnosis was coming in; and love was as weak as a kitten, and pitifully confused, and not nearly strong enough to be brave or even understand. Dying, the human being can formulate a strategy for death, gentle or defiant; but then death moves in completely and decides to run the show, at some point, near the end. Near the death. (She wasn't having any of that. *She* would be running things right up to the very last second.) And now the twentieth century had come along and after several try-outs and test-drives it put together an astonishing new offer: death for everybody. Death for everybody, by hemlock or hardware. If you imagined *love* as a force, not established and not immutable, patched together by all best intentions, kindness, forgiveness – what does love do about death for everybody? It throws up its hands, and gets weaker, and sickens. It is crowded out by its opposite. Love has at least two opposites. One is hate. One is death.

297

All her conscious life she had loved the dinosaurs (to this day she often imagined herself as a kind of moll tyrannosaurus, greedy, savage, faithless, yet still fought-over often and atrociously, and living for eighty million years). What killed *them*? She had the theories cold. An exploding star that drenched the globe in cosmic rays. A meteorite shower that kicked up a coating of dust. A new breed of baby stealers, oviraptors, velociraptors. Or, more bathetically, and more hauntingly, the notion that evolutionary success, a billennium of good living, rendered them incapable of propagation. In other words (she put it), they got too fat to fuck. She played with the idea, trying to combine it with the death of love, and imagined the heavy richness of a distempered paradise, where something was not quite right; and here the ancient creatures slowly sensed that their world had begun to fall away. They smelled the death-ubiquity. It wasn't just that they were all too fat and generally out of shape. They weren't *in the mood*. And so beyond the fuming purple of the mire and beneath the blood-boltered sky, in a forest full of snoozing teeth and spikes, still shattered and reeking from another day of chase and snatch and chomp, on a low branch one lovebird turns to the other and says (she translated from the pterodactylese): 'Leave me alone. The scales have fallen from my eyes. You're a monster. Leave me alone. I'm not *in the mood*.'

Their story was over. More than that, their reality was concluded. You can feel it coming. Women would of course be expected to soldier on a little longer, with their biological imperative and so on, and the gentle feeling for children would naturally be the last thing to disappear, but women would never get very far with lovelessness and they too would weaken in the end. Nicola used to think (not often, and long ago) that even she might have been saved by love. Love was Plan B. But it never happened. She could attract it, she could bring love in, modern love anyway: she could make a man feel he was at last really living, she could give his world high colour – for a couple of months. But she couldn't generate it, she couldn't send love out. Not even kitten love, curled and purring, with kitty smile. And if love was dead or gone then the self was just self, and had nothing to do all day but work on sex. Oh, and hate. And death.

Keith coughed outside the bathroom door. This cough of Keith's started out as a butler's discreet reminder but quickly developed into a ragged diphtheria of barks and snarls. While it raged, while it wrecked itself on the other side of the wall, Nicola had plenty of time to take up the shower attachment and rinse her breasts, her belly, her deep backside, to pat herself down with a wide volume of towel, to take up position by the door in her pink bathrobe, and wait. He wouldn't want to face her. Sad animal, having sinned singly. Now he was wishing that he hadn't done it. In ten minutes he would be wanting to do it again.

'Are you all right?'

Keith gave a cough like a full stop.

'Off you run then. There's a present for you. On the table there.'

'. . . This?'

'It's a briefcase.'

'Looks . . . It's more like kind of a *satchel*.'

'Never mind. It's full of money.'

She opened the door a single notch, no greater distance than its own thickness. Just the lightest touch of force fields, the white steam and pink towelling and rosy flesh escaping like draught into the gloom of the passage: not much solider, in fact, than their congress of moments before, with her electronic presence meeting whatever issued from Keith's eyes. But still he looked up now in temporary terror from his nosebag of notes. His downturned face seemed adolescent, even childish. If she had yanked the door open and stepped out to confront him, he might have cringed, collapsed – he might have unravelled completely.

'Appreciate it,' he said. 'Genuinely appreciate it.'

'My pleasure.'

'And uh, loyal tape, Nicola. Quality. They ought to give you an Oscar.'

She paused and said, 'What should we call it, Keith?'

'Uh. Hang about. "Bobby . . ." Uh. Wait. "Bobby . . ." It's coming. "Bobby . . . on the Beat." There you are. "Bobby on the Beat."'

'Very good, Keith.'

'Or just "Tithead".'

'"Tithead", Keith?'

'It's what you call them. The hat.'

'I see.' The plastic hat had cost £3.50 from the toyshop in Kensington Park Road. Everything else had come out of her actress trunk. How many other outfits could she find in there? Smouldering barrister. Lewd prison wardress. Had there ever been any lady executioners? A steaming Amazon, maybe, with lifted *panga*. She said, 'Always bring the satchel with you when you come to see me. Spend the money. There's lots more: it's all Guy's. Express yourself with it. Remember what *kind* of money it is, Keith. Get some new clothes. Accessories for your car. Relax with a few drinks. Clear your mind completely and concentrate on one thing. Which is?'

Keith nodded grimly. 'My darts.'

'Your darts.'

'Ton-forty,' said Keith. 'Maximum. Bull check-out. Sincerity finishing.'

With satchel and toolbag Keith came carefully down the front steps. He halted. He adjusted his belt. He peered downwards at his zipper. He laughed loosely. Keith was in fact sustaining a mild attack of *esprit de l'escalier*. 'Filth', he thought. Yeah. Would have been best. Just call it 'Filth'. Blimey. He looked up, back over his shoulder: the high windows burning in the low sun. Keith made a face. The face of a man recalling pain. But soon his violently buckled features resolved themselves into a forgiving sneer. Whistling, whistling piercingly (some sentimental ballad), Keith started forward, opened the garden gate, and headed for the heavy Cavalier.

Behind and to the right, flanked by flaking pillars in a doorway further up the dead-end street, Guy watched him go.

I receive a quite fantastically offensive letter from Mark Asprey. I've read it eight or nine times now and I still can't believe what he's trying to do to me. On Plaza notepaper:

My dear Sam:

I can't refrain from this hurried missive. Yesterday, after a rather good lunch, I was musing and browsing at Barnes & Noble, down in the Village. How clean and airy the Village is now! Imagine, if you will, my elation on seeing a goodly stack of *Memoirs of a Listener* – by Samson Young. Well, naturally, I snapped one up. And seldom have I gained such pleasure from the outlay of a mere 98 cents.

I paced the room. I paced the room on my new *shtetl* legs – my twanging pool-cue legs. I tore at my hair. *What* hair? I phoned the Handicraft Press. Oh, the fearsome blast I would give Steve Stultifer. No answer. It was three a.m. over there. 'A poignant charm', Asprey goes on,

is afforded by the helpless contortions of your prose. But why do you think anyone wants to hear about a lot of decrepit old Jews? Still, I admire your nerve. An autobiography is, by definition, a success story. But when some pipsqueak takes up his pen as the evenings lengthen – well, full marks for gall! And the remainder shops do deserve our full support.

Of course, I knew that sales of my book were modest. But this is a savage blow. And the reviews were good. Both of them. And they printed so few – I mean, they can't have sold *any at all*.

You should turn to fiction and the joys of the unfettered fancy. I had rather a hectic time in London, seeing friends old and new and clinching that book deal you might have read about. I gather you spent the entire week at Heathrow. Why didn't we link up? You could have treated me to 'a wad and char'. Or I could have smuggled you into the Concorde Lounge!

Yours ever,
Mark

P.S. Oh, yes. Always thinking of ways to amuse you, I have left a favourite of mine on the bedside table – Marius Appleby's *Crossbone Waters*. Now *that's* non-fiction.

There goes my confidence. I could feel it leaving. I could even *hear* it: it rushed out the door and whistled through the street. Until this morning I was, as they say, up and down about this project of mine. Half the time I mentally polished my Pulitzer acceptance speech. The other half I planned incendiary suicide with *The Murderee* in my arms.

Let me soberly state that I don't think my book is really prizewinning material. Though the panel might feel differently about it if they knew it was true.

Christ, it's only just occurred to me: people are going to imagine that I actually sat down and made all this stuff up.

For now I devote myself to the small concerns. I go where even I feel huge and godlike.

My new project: teaching Kim Talent to crawl. I am her crawling coach. Kim and I are really working on her crawling. Crawl, crawl, crawl. And it isn't easy, in Keith's joke pad. I wait until Kath is asleep or out pacing the walkways with the alcoholic housewives, the tranqued mums, the bingoid single parents. I shove at the squat armchair until most of it is wedged into the hallway. Then I lay out a towel on the floor and plonk Kim down in the middle of it. I scatter rattles and squeaky toys at an inviting distance from her nose. In training shoes, in tracksuit bottoms (with my stopwatch and my steroids), I cheer her on from the touchline. Come on, Kim. You can do it, baby. Get out there and *crawl*.

With tiny grunts and pants, with sublime patience and resolve, she squirms and edges and inches. The expression she wears is one of demure audacity. Do you really want to see something? Well watch this! Watch that! *I'll* show you . . . On she shoves and shoulders. She licks her lips. On she inches and edges. And what happens? She just goes backward. And not very far. How like life. How like writing. All that effort, and the result is just a small minus. She starts to frown and wince. She starts to see that it's a poor deal (and no one gave her fair warning). She starts to cry.

After some comfort, some juice, some deep breaths, she is ready to go again. She nods her head: she is ready. I cheer her on from the margin of the towel, as her frowning face recedes from the rattles, the squeaky toys. As her face recedes from me. Next door, the mother rests. Teaching Kim to crawl.

Kath doesn't let me change her any more. I wonder why. Some Irish imperative, as the child's first birthday approaches? I keep thinking I see bruises, welts, in the shadowy cracks of her Babygro.

Yesterday I arrived on the walkway, and stood there fidgeting with the key, wondering if I'd need it. I peered in through the window. Keith at the table, humped over his tabloid. Kath at the sink. And Kim on the floor, in her bouncer chair. But she wasn't bouncing. And she wasn't sleeping. Her shiny head was bowed; the shape of the shoulders . . . I thought of that terrible phrase. And I thought: Kim has what Kath has, what Keith has. It is called failure to thrive.

I hope I'm just imagining this. I'm waiting for the pain and it hasn't come. Slizard is amazed it hasn't come.

I'm wired for pain. My eyes are wired for pain.

Vladimir Nabokov, encouragingly, was a champion insomniac. He believed that this was the best way to divide people: those who slept; those who didn't. The great line in *Transparent Things*, one of the saddest novels in English: 'Night is always a giant but this one was especially terrible.'

Fee fie fo fum, goes the giant. How did VN ever slay the thing? I wander. I write. I wring my hands. Insomnia has something to be said for it, in my case. It beats dreaming.

God knows why but I've started *Crossbone Waters*. Travel. Borneo. Handsome Marius Appleby and the glamorous photo-

303

grapher who's been assigned to him, Cornelia Constantine. It's an awful little piece of shit. But there's the adventure, and the love interest, and I have to admit I'm hooked.

Now wait a minute. How did Asprey know about me holing up at Heathrow? I don't think I said anything to Incarnacion (with whom he is in constant and sinister touch). I don't think I've ever said anything to Incarnacion, except 'Really?' and 'You don't say?'

So who does that leave? Perhaps, in a sense, I'm being wise after the event – though 'wise' might be putting it a bit high. Just now I was sitting at his desk next door. I noticed, on the expanse of green leather, some new displays of trinketry, the altered disposition of the mailstacks. I imagined Asprey pottering here, with his plumed pen and his calculator. Idly I reached out and tried the locked drawer. It opened smoothly to my jerk.

Notes, letters, cards. Photographs.

Well, there's no longer any very pressing need for me to ask Nicola to show me what she looks like in the nude. But I think I'll ask her anyway.

'It's too adorable,' said Nicola. 'And did you both have little animal nicknames?'

'You have to realize', I said, 'that I was a tremendous sweetie before all this started.'

'Let me guess. You were Daddy Bear, and she was your little cublet.' 'I'm not saying.' 'Little meals on trays. Warmed slippers.' 'Me correcting proofs. Her reading manuscripts. Happiness.' 'And she always did what Daddy Bear said?' 'Not at all. In fact she was on the bossy side. I used to call them the Hitler Sisters. Her and Page. Another tomboy. They were always pouring with blood from some fight they'd just had. Like you and MA.' 'I'm getting the picture. You were Goody Two-Shoes. And she was little Miss Bossy Boots. What did she look like? It's too adorable.'

I got to my feet and went and stood over her. I produced the wallet photograph, Missy eight years ago, brightly lit: the tidal drifts of down from temple to jawbone.

'Mmm,' she said. 'Still. You must have hardly dared to pinch each other, in case you woke up. To the twentieth century.'

I couldn't resist it. I produced the second photograph and held it

304

up to my face. 'What kind of camera did Mark Asprey use? One with a time delay? Or did you employ some sniggering third party?'

Nicola took a time delay before she said, 'Time delay.' And she said it softly.

I said, 'No dreaming here. Plenty of pinches. Fully awake.'

She flinched as I tossed it on to her lap. She straightened, and said, 'I suppose you and Missy never went in for any of that.'

'Actually we did try spanking once. It hurt. My hand, I mean. I even said, "Ow."'

'I can see it does look rather ugly,' she said, and her long fingers began to tear. 'It was what he liked. And one will do things for . . .'

'Yes. Well you did say you were "stupid" for him.'

'For a genuine artist.'

'Come on. It's shit. Oh come *on*.'

'I absolutely don't agree. There's a purity in his work that reminds one of Tolstoy.'

'*Tol*stoy?' I just couldn't take this. It was like the world. It was like fundamentalism. The planet was insane. The truth didn't matter. As I picked up my coat I said, 'Did you see him? When he was here.'

She made no reply.

'It's over between you two. Isn't it?'

'Some things are never over.'

There is a woman who stands in the middle of the Tavistock Road, for an hour every evening, just after dusk, with her head up and her arms outstretched: cruciform.

Not old, not shabby, not stupid-looking, she stands right there in the middle of the street. She smiles fixedly at the oncoming cars, which slow down as they pass, and the drivers stare – but few shout out. Actually, it is terrible, this smile of hers: martyred, trusting, admonitory. Why doesn't somebody come and drag her off somewhere? One drunk is all it would take. When you drive by, and especially if you approach her from the rear, you always think of car metal meeting female flesh and blood, the forced and instant rearrangements of collision, with flesh and blood going where it suddenly has to go. She's perfect for the book, but I can't think of any good way of getting her in.

She's out there now. I can see her from the window. Why don't they come and take her away? Oh, why don't they *come*?

Chapter 16: The Third Party

THE NEXT TIME Guy saw Keith he looked utterly transformed. The Black Cross, at noon; down the length of Lancaster Road and in through the pub doors the low sun burned unpreventably . . .

'Cink paint,' said Keith. 'Rear final drive.'

First, and most obviously and graphically, the clothes. Keith wore a brown shirt of moiré silk with raised stripes (its texture reminded Guy of pork crackling), hipster cream flares, and a new pair of coarse-furred ferret-like loafers (with a hint of the scaramouch or the harem-creeper in their curled tips).

'Intake manifold,' said Keith. 'Central differential.'

The cream flares had a striking arrangement at the fly. Bootstrap or bodice effects Guy was familiar with (Antonio, the rude *venta*, so long ago), but he had never seen anything quite like Keith's crotch.

'Underbody sealant,' said Keith. 'Wheel housing liners. Flange design.'

Individual loops, each tied in a bow, and tasselled with fringe and pom-pom; and the trousers were so dramatically, so disconcertingly low on the hip that there was only room for two or three of them. The trousers held Keith's substantial rump as reverently as a Grecian urn holds its essence. Guy, who found the outfit ridiculous and even alarming, none the less envied Keith that pert rear-end, having often thought that his own life had been quite poisoned by his want of real buttock. Their occupant seemed well pleased with the new trousers, and especially the fly, whose bows and bobbles he would occasionally run a hand over.

'Joint trapezium arm rear axle,' said Keith. 'Cataphoretic dip priming. Galvannealed zincrometal.'

Keith was, today, in particularly baronial mood, his manner suggesting an unpierceable detachment from the froward concerns of pub life. The reason for this was not hard to fathom, was indeed well known and still being talked about: at the oché of the George Washington, in England Lane, on Thursday night, Keith had tasted victory. He thus took his place in the semi-finals of the Duoshare Sparrow Masters.

'A shame you uh . . . let us down Thursday,' said Keith. He was now cleaning his fingernails with a dart. Guy looked again: Keith had been manicured! Gone were the frayed cuticles, the scabs of kippered nicotine. 'There was . . . it caused considerable disappointment.'

'No I feel very bad about that,' said Guy. 'But the boy was sick again. And at the moment we haven't got any – any choice. I was up all night with him.'

Keith looked puzzled. 'Your wife okay is she?'

'Sorry?' -

'Still walking is she?'

'I'm sorry?'

Keith no longer looked puzzled. He just looked mildly surprised, and mildly displeased. Turning an inch or two, he jerked his eyebrows at Pongo, who smartly refilled his tankard. Then Keith pointed his darting finger at Guy until Guy said,

'Oh I'll have the same.'

Now Keith looked away. He seemed to be unhurriedly probing his teeth with his tongue. He began to whistle – just three casual notes on a rising scale. He ran a hand through his hair, which had been recently cut, and moussed, and extravagantly blow-dried.

'I'm sorry I missed it,' said Guy. 'Anyway well *done*, Keith.' He reached out a hand towards Keith's shoulder, towards his streaming brown shirt, but then thought better of it. 'I hear you really –'

'Keith? Carphone!'

'Er, excuse me for a minute, would you, Guy?'

Guy stood there tensely with his drink, every now and then reaching to scratch the back of his neck. Time passed. He turned and looked (the angle of his head feeling vaguely craven) as Keith stepped back in from the radiance of the street and paused by the door to have words with Fucker and Zbig One. 'Jesus,' Keith was saying in his deepest voice. 'These birds. No peace. Relax. Few drinks.' Guy looked away again.

Now with full gravity and silent promise of discretion Keith drew Guy to the fruit-machine, into which he began to insert a series of one-pound coins, and along with whose repertoire of electronic ditties and jingles he would confidently sing.

'I'm glad you're seeing Nicky again,' said Keith. 'Derdle erdle oom pom. Unrecognizable.'

'Sorry?'

'No comparison innit. Derdle erdle oom pom. Meemawmeemawmeemaw. None of this moping around, what's the point, no point. What's the point. She's transformed.'

'Ah yes, you went round there to . . .'

'The boiler.'

'Ah yes.'

'To look at the boiler. Puckapucka*pucka*pucka. Bah bar dee birdle dee bom: ploomp! A, an exceptional woman, that. Not overly versed, though, in the, in the ways of the world. You agree?'

'– Yeah,' said Guy.

Keith shook his head and smiled with affectionate self-reproach. 'First time I went round there I thought she was one of them – Derdle erdle ooom pom. One of them birds that's really, well, you know.'

Guy nodded suddenly.

'Meemawmeemawmeemaw. Oozing for it. You know. Dripping for it. Sliding all over the floor. You're in there five minutes, minding your own business, and suddenly – Bah bar dee birdle dee bom: ploomp!'

'I know the sort.'

'Not been in there five minutes and she's smacking your cods all over the park. Puckapucka*pucka*pucka. You come through the door, you take off your coat, you look down. She's got your gun in her gob. Derdleerdle oom pom. Bah bar dee birdle dee bom: ploomp! . . . Derdle erdle oom pom. Derdle erdle oom pom. Derdle –'

'Yes,' said Guy.

'Yeah well. Not a bit of it. Her? No way. Keeps herself *to* herself. The real article: a lady. *Look* at this fucking thing.'

308

After several shoves and slaps Keith left the fruit-machine rocking steadily on its base and led Guy back to their drinks. Keith positioned himself comfortably, inclining backwards with his elbows on the bar.

'Yes,' said Guy, who seemed somewhat calmer, 'she's quite naive in some ways.'

'Doesn't surprise me.'

'Almost otherworldly.'

'Same difference.'

'That's right.' Guy's face cleared further. He even began on a smile.

'She's not . . .' The angle at which Keith was leaning afforded him a rare glimpse of his waist. He appeared to become absorbed by the tasselled loopings of his groin, weighing each bobble in turn with his clean fingers. For a moment a look of amusement or fond memory crossed his face. But then his solemnity returned. He raised his hand to his hair, and looked upwards at the ceiling. He said, 'She's not just some fucking old slag like some.'

Out on the street Guy groped his way into a lamp-post and stood for a moment with his forehead pressed to the damp rust. He kept casting his mind back . . . No, his mind kept going there under its own power, with great sudden backward vaults through time. Guy kept thinking of his very first visit to her flat. Keith coming down the stairs – Hello, mate – and Nicola lingering (or recovering) in her bedroom; and then emerging (he glimpsed the tousled linen in the mirror), walking awkwardly, bowlegged and bent in the middle, with her lewd and feverish face – It's so *hot* – and a welt or graze on her temple, as if, perhaps, in their rough passion . . . 'Oh my dear,' Guy found himself whispering (to whom?), with an incomprehensible smile on his lips. 'Such repulsive thought. Cannot be. Simply cannot be.' He moved off, but soon paused again, and paused again, and always with fingertips poised near his eyes.

And so Guy headed home, into the low sun. Quite uncanny, the sun's new trajectory, and getting lower all the time. Seen from the rear, I must look exactly like I feel: a silhouette, staggering blind into the photosphere of an amber star . . . And just as the sun burns off mist from the warming land, so the cumulus and thunderheads gave way, as Guy walked, to cores of silver, and even spots of blue, in the sky of his mind. The only evidence: Keith's face. The face of Keith

Talent, on the steps (with his toted toolbags). That unmistakable contortion of gross lechery, and of lechery *in some way* gratified. But look at it from another angle; and bear in mind that, for all his better points, and through no real fault of his own, Keith remained an unbelievable berk. He might have a spyhole somewhere and peep on her in the bedroom or the bathroom. Window-cleaner wiles, keyhole cunning. Perhaps he steals or at least inspects her underwear: quite easy to imagine Keith with his whole head in the laundry basket. Possibly he has contrived a way to exploit her innocence – some little procedure, insignificant to her, significant to him. Builders and plumbers are always manoeuvring women into close contact. Remember Hope complaining about it. Get you into the airing cupboard. He might ask her to bend down so that she can – she can look at a pipe or something. Even I couldn't avoid seeing her breasts when she leaned over that afternoon. So brown. So close together. Or he gets her to go up a ladder. As she strained to reach the skylight or whatever it was, her buttocks, in their white panties, would be locked together, and muscularly tensed, and sweetly unaware . . .

By the time Guy approached his front garden the adolescent chaos of his thoughts had in fact disqualified him from returning home. He was unpresentable. And he didn't even notice until he reached for his key and found that he could hardly get his hand into his trouser pocket. Guy swivelled, and dropped his head, and walked away fastening all three buttons of his long tweed jacket. A brisk jog up the steep bit of Ladbroke Grove, and a five-minute reverie about Pepsi Hoolihan, proved to be of little help. In the end Guy fashioned a kind of splint with his belt and ducked fast through the front door straight into the lavatory beneath the stairs. He could hear women's voices downstairs until they were drowned by the rush of the cold tap.

'So how's Room Service?' asked Lizzyboo, who had just been crying, and was now eating.

'*What* Room Service?' said Hope. 'He's willing enough, some-times, but the orders come out wrong. He brings me tea with sugar. He brings me coffee with milk. I hate milk.'

'What do you think's up?'

'With Room Service? I have two theories. Either he's flipped. You know, that was always possible.'

'Or?'

'Or he's dying.'

'. . . I don't think he's dying,' said Lizzyboo.

'I don't either,' said Hope. 'Of course there's a third possibility. He's in love.'

'Room Service?'

'Like he was with you.'

'He was never *in love* with me.'

'Sure he was. I found him snivelling over your dress, remember?'

'What dress?'

'The ballet dress. Flo-Flo's ballet dress. The blue one.'

'It wasn't blue.'

'Yes it was.'

'It was white.'

'No it wasn't.'

With his big feet Guy now started coming down the stairs. Hope stood up and started clearing away. Lizzyboo went on eating Shreddies.

'Hi,' he said.

'Hi,' said Lizzyboo.

'You get in any good fights today?' said Hope. 'Have you shown Lizzyboo your black eye?'

'Wow,' said Lizzyboo.

'It's clearing up now,' said Guy.

'Yeah,' said Hope. 'It only looks like someone just spat a bad oyster in your face.'

'Hope!' said Lizzyboo.

'Where's Marmaduke?'

'Out with Terry somewhere.'

Terry was back. Terry was back, and at rock-star wages. But not for long. The Clinches were passing through the nanny choke-point of autumn: several new ones would be starting over the next couple of weeks. Terry found it easier, or at any rate practicable, if he took Marmaduke off somewhere. Hope permitted it, so long as Marmaduke was in the open air for no longer than thirty minutes, or at most forty-five. They had stopped asking where Terry took him. The Toy Museum. Some snooker hall. Marmaduke would be back, soon enough.

'Have you eaten?' asked Lizzyboo with her mouth full.

'Yes. No. Anyway I'm not hungry. Feeling rather weird, actually. I think I'll just go and lie down for a bit.'

And up the stairs he went on his big feet.

The sisters stayed silent for quite a time.

311

'Flipped,' said Lizzyboo.

'Dying,' said Hope.

These, then, were the terms in which Keith encapsulated his Thursday-night victory at the George Washington on England Lane: 'In the final analysis' – and Keith had said this often by now, leaning backwards on the bar of the Black Cross, the shrewd sweep of his eyes including Dean, Norvis, Bogdan, Fucker, Curtly, Netharius, Shakespeare, Zbig One – 'the senior player could find no answer to the fluency of my release.'

In truth there were other things that the senior player could find no answer to the fluency of: namely, the whispered taunts and threats with which Keith had regaled him immediately before the match, during the announcements, and in between every leg and set (while the two darters stood solemnly side by side, marshalling their thoughts). This was a questionable ploy, and Keith was always loth to resort to it: I mean, you tell your opponent you're going to rip his ear off and flob in the hole, then you step up there, breathing hellfire, lose your concentration – and throw 26! Rebounds on you. Defeating its own purpose. But when Keith laid eyes on Martin Permane, the fifty-five-year-old ex-county thrower, with his exophthalmic stare, his wary smile and his village-idiot physique (not to mention the darting medals on his breast: had some phenomenal averages in his classic seasons), well, he decided to give it a try. Although Martin Permane showed no response to the white-lipped cataract – hormone pills, prostate operations, walking frames, hearing aids and coffin prices were some of the themes Keith played on – his darts definitely suffered. Let himself down, did the senior slinger. Failed to throw to his full potential. And when, after the match, Keith ordered octuple Southern Comforts for himself, Dean and Fucker, and proceeded there and elsewhere to get unfathomably drunk, the older man merely frowned into his consolation shandy, observing that darting styles had progressed a bit since he was a lad, and falling silent altogether as Keith lurched over to pound him on the back.

No matter. All that was in the past: you take each match as it comes. Keith now girded himself for the future, getting his darting head right for the big one.

He threw himself into his darts. Darts was in his blood (his only patrimony, except for the darts pouch itself and the Ronson cigarette-lighter). The darts in his blood coursed through him, feeding his darts brain. A darts brain, that's what he had: darts nerve, darts sinew. A darts heart. A darts soul. Darts. 158? Two treble 20s, double 19. Or two treble 18s, bull. Darts. 149? Treble 20, treble 19, double 16 (the best double on the fucking board). Darts. 120? You just shanghai the 20: treble 20, big 20, double 20. Tops. Darts. Darts, darts, darts. Darts. *Darts.* Keith Talent: Mr Checkout. Keith Talent – the man they call the Finisher.

When not actually practising his darts (brief breaks for a *porno* or two, and a ruminative smoke, as opposed to all the non-ruminative smokes he had while actually practising), Keith pored over his darting bible: *MTD: Master the Discipline: Darts:*

> If your opponent does a bad shot, like 26, punish him, capitalize, kick him when he is down with a maximum or a ton plus. If you do that no way will he get back in.

Yeah, thought Keith. You capitalize.

> Never ask about an opponent. You play the darts not the man.

Never ask about an opponent, thought Keith. You play the darts not the man.

> Those Pilgrim Fathers are said to have thrown darts while sailing to America in 1620 on the so-called Mayflower.

1620! thought Keith.

> Christ knows how they managed it as they only had a small boat as they were tossed about on the 'Atlantic' Ocean. King Arthur was also said to have played a form of darts.

'Heritage,' Keith murmured. Following an unwonted but enticing train of thought, Keith saw himself as a key figure at the court of King Arthur, hailed initially for his darting skills, but going on to win more general acclamation for his dirty jokes, his ability to hold his ale, his frenzied wenching. Not King Keith, granted (no way), but Sir Keith, possibly. Tall-backed chairs, and a great pile of Clives by the fire. Had enough, sleep there if you like. Once a simple country lad. Of humble extraction. Sings for his supper as such. And then until the wonderful lady, with her hanky, and her fan, and her heaving bosom, takes his hand and leads him up, up, to the great tower . . . All this the girl in the dead-end street was making possible. Keith realized, as he stood there in the dusty garage, his right toe on the chalk line, exactly 7ft 9¼ ins (2.37 metres) from the board, with his darts in his hand – Keith realized that his entire face was covered in tears. Gratefully, exaltedly, he raised the cigarette to his lips: a falling teardrop – here was more marksmanship – landed on its smoking coal. But by puffing hard Keith succeeded in keeping the fire alive.

Tears at the dartboard, lachrymae at the oché: this was Keith's personal vision of male heroism and transcendence, of male grace under pressure. He remembered Kim Twemlow in the semi of last year's World Championship. The guy was in agony up there (and now Keith flinched as he saw again the teartracks on that trex-white face), trailing four sets to nil and two legs down in the fifth. No one, not even Keith, had given him a fucking prayer. A burst gastric ulcer, they said later, brought on by a few curries and a late night out. But what does the guy do? Calls a ten-minute medical delay, sinks a few Scotches, wipes away his tears, picks up his darts – and he throws. And he throws . . . Five-four it was in the end. And the next night he only goes out there and butchers Johnny Kentish in the big one. Seven-fucking-nil. INNIT.

Kim and Keith: they were men. Men, mate. Men. All right? Men. They wept when they wept, and knew the softnesses of women, and relished their beer with laughter in their eyes, and went out there when it mattered to do what had to be done with the darts. Take them for all in all. That was what the Guy Clinches of this world would never understand. Keith had often wondered why Nicola Six was doing him all these favours. And the thing or area known as his *character* was the last place he had looked for an answer. But now (the tears, the darts, the sawdust) it all seemed possible. We're talking success. And I can handle it. A guy like Keith – and she must have sensed this – there was nothing he couldn't do, there was nothing beyond him. A guy like Keith could go all the way.

The baby saw the father in his usual chair. She made towards him. After a while she was no nearer. After a while she was no nearer. Keith stepped over her from the living-room to the bedroom. The baby wheeled around, or she tried. Keith just got further off-centre. He stepped over her from the bedroom to the bathroom. The baby wheeled again. She pressed down on her hands and looked up and inquired of him. Keith bent and picked up the heavy life (and they *are* heavy, even the slightest of them, the possibilities, the potentiae, all densely packed) and took a single stride into the middle of the kitchen.

314

His wife stood there in her tired light. Wordlessly Keith offered her the smiling child. Without moving his feet he leaned back on the doorjamb and watched critically as Kath prepared the bottle, fumbling and staggering every now and then, little Kim hooked awkwardly over her thin shoulder. Keith sighed. Kath turned to him with a pale flicker in her face: a request for leniency, perhaps even a smile. Well, dream husband innit, thought Keith. Loads of money suddenly. Cheerful round the house. And all this was true, except for the bit about being cheerful round the house. Keith was in a constant and unprecedented fury round the house. Everything round the house prodded and goaded him.

He sat down and began on his Boeuf Stroganoff and Four Individual Milford Flapjacks. Keith's mouth was full, and he had been drinking all afternoon, and all morning, at the Black Cross, so he seemed to say,

'You got your *boeuf* statificate on you?'

'Got my what?' asked Kath cautiously. Could it be that Keith was now complaining about her cooking, something he had never done before? She gave him what he wanted. Her hotpots and fondly spiced Irish stews had ceased unremarked about three days into their marriage.

'The bit of paper that says how old you are.'

'Not on me, no, Keith.'

He straightened a fork at her. 'When was you born then?'

'. . . Born?' said Kath, and named the year.

He stopped chewing. 'But that means you ain't even twenty-two yet! Got to be some mistake, love. Got to be . . . You know what it's like? It's like an horror film. You know, where the bird's okay until the last five minutes. Then she's just this boiler. Suddenly she's just ash and smoke. Ash and smoke.'

Keith completed his meal in silence, with a couple of breaks for cigarettes. Then he said, 'Come on, Clive. Up you get, mate.'

The great dog climbed stiffly to its feet, one back leg raised and shivering.

'Come on, my son. Don't sit around here in this fuckin old folks' home, do we.'

Grimly, his long head resting on an invisible block, like an executionee, Clive stood facing the front door.

'No way. We're off.' He looked at his wife and said, 'Where? Work. In the correct environment.' He extended an indulgent knuckle to the baby's cheek, and then added, with perhaps inordinate bitterness,

'You just don't comprehend about my darts, do you. What my darts means to me. No conception.' His eyebrows rose. His gaze fell. He shook his head slowly as he turned. 'No . . . con*cep*tion.'

'Keith?'

Keith froze as he opened the door.

'Would you give her a bottle when you come in?'

The shoulders of Keith's silver leather jacket flexed once, flexed twice. 'Ask me no questions,' he said, 'and I'll tell you no lies.'

Down on the street Clive lent his lumpy cooperation as Keith hauled him into the front passenger seat of the heavy Cavalier. So they weren't walking, not tonight. The dog could already taste the moist carpet of the loved pub, his aromatic lair in the corner beneath the table, the place that smelled of many things but mostly his own archaeological deposits, his drooling growls, his whimpering sleep, his maturity, his manhood, the distant fluxes of his distant dog days. Clive had spent about two years of his life in this agreeable spot: dog years, too, seven times longer, or quicker, than the human reckoning. Now, before they got there, Clive had reconciled himself to a chilly wait of ten or fifteen minutes, alone, on the front seat. But he could handle it.

Like a dog itself the car lumbered through the lampless streets, on snuffling treads, with yellow eyes, heading for Trish Shirt's.

While Keith drove, Guy showered. With costly inerrancy the bubbled pillar of water exploded on his crown; below, supplementary waist-high jets also sluiced his thighs, his insubstantial backside; and his great feet slapped about in the twirling wash. It's the Coriolis force that makes water spin like that; in the southern hemisphere it spins the other way, clockwise; and on the equator it doesn't spin at all. Guy looked down through the tempest, through the privatized prisms: yes, the bodybuilder was back. Like Terry. It had returned, recurred, craning into being, dumb and hopeful. The sheep look up. He had had this tumescence now, it seemed to him, for almost a month. And it was the *same* tumescence, not a series of new ones. In this respect it resembled Marmaduke's tantrums or screaming fits, which could be seen as essentially the *same* tantrum or screaming fit: twenty months old and beginning on the day he was born. Tumescence and tantrum alike spoke eloquently of mysterious pain. It hurt now, for example. Just as Marmaduke hurt now (hear him holler). It hurt a lot all the time. For the past few days Guy's groin had entertained an ache of steady severity; it seemed to drift or cruise about in his lower systems, variously snagging itself in his spine, his scrotum, his guts. Chainmailed in money, in health (he felt fine), in caution, Guy had never had much to do with *pain*. Except that shiner: pure instinct – the dear fist. How could pain ever find him? So in a way he welcomed and honoured it, the pain. It was like the pain in his heart, in his throat; it was love, it was life. He didn't want to touch it, the pain, didn't want to disturb or molest it. No. You wouldn't want to touch it.

And now it juddered before him like a vacated diving-board as he strode from the shower to the billowcloud of the Turkish towel, and he tented it tenderly in white cotton shorts, and dressed the pain quickly, and looked for a way out of the house on his taut leash, past the quiet wall of his wife's contempt – a contempt not doubled but squared or cubed by the presence of the sister, silently eating.

'Is the milk on?' said Hope.

By averting her eyes a quarter of a degree, Hope might have seen for herself that the child's bottle was indeed warming, like a missile in the silo of its Milton. But this was an expression of her higher responsibility (she was measuring medicines): so might the brain surgeon tell the lab char to give her mop a good squeeze.

'Yes,' said Guy. 'The milk's on.'

On the steps, the doublefronted house looked down on him, proudly – the masterpiece, the swelling arsenal of neg-entropy. All around the pressure was gathering, in pounds per square inch.

Nicola Six had just got Enola Gay out of Phu Quoc and was in the process of ferrying her to Kampot when Guy said suddenly,

'So really you see quite a lot of Keith.'

'. . . Yes. He's in and out a good deal.'

'The boiler and so on.'

'The boiler. And the pipes,' said Nicola (who in truth knew even less about this kind of thing than did Keith Talent).

'Do you ever – does he ever have you go up ladders or anything like that?'

Guy crossed his legs and realigned his buttocks. He was, he realized, succumbing to a reckless agitation. Not that the evening had – on paper anyway – provided much excitement so far: a two-hour one-man play, translated from the Norwegian and performed in a Totteridge coffee-bar, about the demise of the reindeers; then a simple though no doubt perfectly nutritious meal in a vegetarian Bangladeshi restaurant in Kilburn. There had certainly been no anxiety about running into anyone he knew. But Nicola at night was a novelty, and a revelation (and in the City money was moving in strange ways and Guy felt again that the time was short. Short, short was the time) . . . The sun does many things but it's far too busy to flatter the human being with its light. Human beings do that, with *their* light. Guy didn't quite say it to himself, but human light made Nicola look experienced: the thinness or fineness of the skin round the hollows of jaw and cheekbone; the dark breadth of the mouth. And how incontrovertibly illicit were the shadows of the apartment, the folds of her silver-grey cashmere dress, the glaze of her legs. At eleven o'clock at night – at her place – love was no allegory.

'Let me think. Does he have me go up ladders. No. *He* goes up ladders.'

'He doesn't get you in corners. By the sink or something.'

'In corners . . . No I don't think so.'

'How does Keith strike you? Generally, I mean.'

She shrugged minutely and said, 'I suppose he's rather an attractive character.'

'Of course you know', Guy heard himself saying, 'that in some ways he's little better than a common criminal. Or worse.'

'Or worse? Guy, I'm shocked. I think it's so unkind to judge people by hearsay. Or by their backgrounds.'

'Just so long as you know. I mean, you haven't found anything missing. Cash. Jewellery. Clothes.'

'Clothes?'

'Scarves. Belts. He might give them to his girlfriends. He's got lots of girlfriends, you know. Underwear.'

'Whatever would Keith want with my underwear?'

'These questions will seem quite pointless to you. But has he ever got you in the airing-cupboard.'

Nicola did a slow frown and said, 'It's funny you should mention the airing-cupboard.'

Guy sat back. He stretched his neck and looked along his nose at her.

'The other day there was some sort of problem to do with the airing-cupboard. Some . . . pipe thing. Well it's awfully cramped and stuffy in there. And I was wearing my short blue thing I do my exercises in.'

'Go on,' said Guy regally.

'Well he told me to read the nipple gadget on the stopcock. Are you sure you want to – it's all rather shaming. I had to strain upwards to see the dial. I had one foot on the chair. And one on the towel rack. Rather an undignified sight. And very uncomfortable, with my legs stretched apart like that. And then . . .' She gave a secretive smile.

'What?'

'You'll never guess.'

'I think I can. Keith did something. Didn't he.'

'No no. Keith was in there, in the bathroom, testing the temperature level in the bidet. No. The towel rack slipped and I tumbled to the floor with all the sheets and everything coming down on top of me!'

Guy smiled palely.

'Fortunately I was able to collect myself completely by the time he hurried along to help. No, the real reason I need him here so much – and you're not to be cross or tease me. The real reason . . . is the little one.'

'I'm sorry?'

'*Oh*. If at the other end of a great chain of ifs and buts, and far in the future and everything, if there is a future, and only when you want to, we do decide to have a baby daughter, then there are all sorts of things I might as well get done now. And if we're going to make any progress this evening then do please come and sit over here. I'm dying to do some kissing.'

Guy left about an hour later, soon after midnight. And something happened, just before he left, something dramatic, something painful – though Guy would later derive much complicated comfort from the incident. First he had paid a stooped visit to the bathroom, where, gasping and wincing, he had rearranged himself with the aid of his belt and the vibrant elastic of his boxer shorts. In the hall he joined Nicola, who stood in profile with her arms folded. 'This', she said, 'is the famous airing-cupboard.' In they peered. 'Come on,' she said, and stepped inside. Sober Guy suddenly felt rather drunk: the pine racks of bedding, the polythene puff of the heater, the narrow space where a man and a woman might very well contend with certain harassing proximities. 'You can just imagine me up there,' she said, as she turned to him, 'with one leg here and one leg there. Careful.' . . . As had been the case before, their farewell kisses, being emblems of their own termination, were by far the most liquid and

319

distended of the evening; and the heat in there was so furtive, so feminine . . . Not that their bodies were actually touching or anything like that; but Guy could feel the ghosts of various contours, of promising pendencies, or perhaps just the electric field, the cashmere nimbus, of her dress. To further this delicious calibration he slightly bent and parted his legs, urging himself forward half a famished millimetre. At one point, as she breathed thickly into his ear, his hand moved from her shoulderblade to the surprising bounty of her armpit, and then hovered and fell (he thought he heard a moan of assent) on her waiting breast.

Later, Guy could never finally decide whether he had in fact lost consciousness, though Nicola would always regretfully assert that he had. When the world's lineaments returned, in any event, he was lying in the foetal position with his head on the passage carpet and with both hands cupped and trembling over his groin. The colour of his face (Nicola would remark) had some interesting affinities with the colour of his healing black eye: grey on a background of pale green. She was calling his name as if through rain and from a considerable distance.

'Guy? Guy? Guy! Guy . . . I can't bear it. I did it again. Just pure instinct. Terrifying how dramatic it was. You went down like a ton of bricks. Have you been ill? Ooh. Does it hurt dreadfully? Come on . . . oof. I suppose we can look on the encouraging side. My breasts were *bursting* and when you touched me there was this great convulsion right through my body. Can you drive? Can you walk? Can you *speak*? Say something. Guy? Guy? Ah I can't *bear* this. Why is it that I always seem to be causing you pain?'

After Guy left, Keith called. Nicola stared at the seething booze in her glass as she heard the pips of the payphone, the bearpit clamour of sawdust and bloodlust . . .

Now this was a little bit naughty of Keith to call so late like this. But he wanted to see another one of those videos, being incorrigible as he was. And, quite frankly, after the kind of evening she'd had (that play! that meal!), well, where was the harm in a little bit of fun?

Nicola poured more brandy. She giggled uglily: ugly giggling. She knew the giggling was ugly but that only made her giggle all the uglier. She went to her dressing-room, taking the glass, and the bottle.

D'you know something? She was really in the mood. She was. Keith, he did love her to wear her frillies. Said it made him feel dead fruity. Now *this* . . . is a lovely garment. Dirty great brute like him but they're

320

all just little boys really when they see you in your scanties. (And they *do* like a spiky shoe.) All the pound notes Guy gave her she would spend on wondrous frillies and costliest scanties. For him! For Keith!

She unbuttoned her dress and slipped out of it. She let her hair down. Ugly giggling.

Guy parked the car in Lansdowne Crescent and sat waiting for the pain to go away. Seventy-five minutes later Guy was still there. But then so was the pain. With his lips as far apart as they had ever been asked to stretch he slid across the seat and out into the night.

The great house swam towards him, darkly streaming. He searched its face: no dreaded yellows of emergency or vigil. Was it possible that his return might coincide with Marmaduke's tortured small-hour drowse? The front door admitted him. His bones creaked and split and popped into the hall. With reckless swiftness he tiptoed towards the kitchen stairs.

Under surgical lights, surrounded by washers and driers and stacks of nappies, Guy inspected himself, unkindly, like an army doctor. His animal parts looked hard-done-by, traduced, but no more unprepossessing than usual. It was his face that seemed altered, shrunken, livid – his fool-for-love face, terrified by the bright mirror. Among Marmaduke's innumerable talcs and salves there was nothing for what ailed him.

As he came out of the washroom adjusting his trousers, a bolt of fear traversed the kitchen: a spectral nightdress in a mouth of white light. Not Hope – Lizzyboo. Raiding the icebox.

'Marmaduke quiet?' he asked.

'Mm-hm. As of ten minutes.'

He thought of their one embrace, the embrace Hope never knew about, in the bathroom, in Italy, the not-so-little little sister, flattered, foregrounded, breathlessly promoted. How big she was now. And how other. Poor Lizzyboo.

'Goodnight.'

She chewed and swallowed. 'Goodnight,' she said.

Guy stole upstairs, falling quieter on every step, and undressed in the dark of the visitor's room. Naked, he stole across the passage on the balls of his feet. The furious physics of the door fought him every inch of the way: its croaks and twinges, its rasp against the carpet's nap. When you're trying to be quiet, you see that everything is dying to be noisy. And Guy twanging there with the physics of everyday life. Hope lay in the darkness, curved like an ess or a zed, or a query.

Wehn Kieth got back that . . . When Kieth . . . Wehn Keith got back that nite, okay. Eezy does it. Where's the lite? Okay. No way was them last *pornos* too clever. Ditto going again to Shirt Trish again. But Nik siad OK to drink waht felt okay. Dim matter. Siad it dim matter. Man is the hunter . . .

He slammed the front door behind him. He stood at the sink and drank a lot of warm water. Then he felt better. Then he fell over. Suddenly, and in no particular order, Keith burped the wife, took the baby outside for a pee, and fucked the dog.

Kim Twemlow's lifestyle! Still strolling about in his white shoes. Even up here on the ceiling there were lights of cars. The house, the circular drive, and selected guests for luncheon. Why, Cymphia. Amphea! Generally find a glass of chapmange quite refreshing at this hour. Smampha. Corimphia! My dear Aramimpha! . . . Keith? You could have the lot, mate. Yeah, you cuold. You colud do it son. You culod. Yeah you fucking cloud . . .

What was it? Driving back like that – what was it? In the car, and Clive sleeping. The moon. And London like it used to be. Many moons of the street-lamps, many moons ago. TV. Jesus. Coming up on me now. Felt yung innit. Uh-oh. What goes down must – oop. Whoop. Yeah that was the phing. Yooph, mate, yooph!

I must go to London Fields, before it's too late.

If I shut my eyes or even if I keep them open I can see the parkland and the sloped bank of the railway line. The foliage is tropical and innocuous, the sky is crystalline and innocuous. In fact the entire vista has a kiddie-book feel. There in his van putts Postman Pat: Postman Pat and his black-and-white cat. It is all outside history. Vicars, spinsters, parkies, gardeners, widows so old, so long-widowed, that they have reverted to a state of virginity. The only hard evidence of sex is the children – and, in the distance (and not so hard), soft hills in the shape of breasts.

There was a stream, fordable, jumpable, not dangerous, perfectly scaled for five-year-olds, for boys, for my brother and me. David! Sam! Oh boys, you are heartbreaking and mysterious. The way you cock your weak bodies – to essay something, to dare something. Your love of war. Look! Watch! Oh, boys, why do you have to do this?

But boys have to do this.

I must go back. I mustn't leave it too late.

One can only assume that Missy has a thing for men and weapons – for arms and the man.

Look at me: pre-nuked and dead-already.

Look at Sheridan Sick. That time I met him. High up over Du Pont Circle, a party in the boardroom of Hornig Ultrason (Hornig

Ultrason: a beacon for everything bad). I asked him to explain the new phenomenon of superbolt lightning. Missy stood at his side, at my side. I knew nothing.

'Solar supergranulation,' said Sick. 'Sam? Imagine soup boiling in a pan 20,000 miles across. Even when it gets here the flare wind is still travelling at 400 miles per second. Then it hits a ghost basin in the magnetosphere. Bingo. Superbolt.'

Quite unenlightened, I said, 'You give the impression that you know a lot about these things.'

'I'm learning, Sam. We're working more and more with the QuietWall community.'

'Well, stop. And don't do it again.'

'That's funny,' he said. With a really disgraceful smile. On his really disgraceful face.

Sheridan Sick: a smart cookie. Yeah, a biscuit, with a haircut on top, powered by a certain je-ne-sais-quoi. It takes all kinds to make a world. It takes only one kind to unmake it. My father was of the latter school, though in an unrecognizably younger world, caught up in fresher historical forces. And not doing it for the money.

Of all the forces, love is the strangest.

Keith looks like love (though I'm sure he doesn't feel it. And given he's Keith). The spring in the step, like Johnny Head-in-Air.

And Guy looks like death.

Love can make a woman pick up a bus, or it can crush a man under the weight of a feather. Or it just lets everything go on as it was yesterday and will be tomorrow. That's the kind of force love is.

God knows why I persist with *Crossbone Waters*. I guess it emboldens me: that stuff like this gets published. It's an awful little piece of shit.

In his skiff or whatever, with his sweaty fatigues and his trusty guide Kwango, Marius Appleby retraces the old pirate routes of festering Borneo. Many long descriptions of celebrated pillagings and rapes. Especially rapes. Marius often seems to wish he were back there in the old days, and that the pirates were taking on new hands.

But the good bits are all about the photographer assigned to him by the colour magazine, Cornelia Constantine: five feet twelve, twenty-seven, octaroon complexion. Her eyes are *as black as ebony* and she has *flaming* waist-length red hair. He meets her at the airport. She's one of those natural blue-bloods, disdainful, self-sufficient, dedicated to the art of taking photographs. But Marius is posh too (he lets it be known), and handsome, and no stranger to the love of women. Cornelia's previous boyfriends include a world-famous sculptor, an EEC Prime Minister and a dead racing-driver. When she alights from the jeep, even the *bustling* streets of Samarinda go into freeze frame, like on Keith's TV.

They hire old Kwango and set off in the skiff, which is called *Aphrodite*. Invoking the deity, Marius vows to possess Cornelia. His chances don't look good, but you find yourself rooting for him somehow. As he awakes on the first morning he sees her standing naked in the cerise lagoon, her flaming hair perched on the crux of her muscular buttocks. On her way out, after her swim, she faces the travel writer boldly, without shame, as noble beauties will. And he raptly notes that her breasts are *proud* and her hair-colour *natural*.

Oh yeah. A story of natural love. The whole thing is like this: a thesaurus of miserable clichés. It's an *awful* little piece of shit. But I guess I'll keep going. The thing is, I really want to know how Marius makes out with Cornelia.

Like my heroine or villainness, like my murderee, Lizzyboo, too, has a strategy for getting to the end of men. Her strategy is this: Weigh Two Hundred Pounds.

There is a major obstacle in her journey towards two hundred pounds: food poisoning. Common sense: if you eat more food, then you eat more poison. I think this works in my favour, all in all. She's in bed now, sick, too sick to eat much or to feel like getting fresh.

Imagine the miraculous expansion of Missy Harter's girth. I keep getting the wild idea that if we could buy babies in stores or go look at them in zoos and theme parks, and they never grew up but stayed at fifteen months for say six or seven years, yes, we'd still be interested, some of us, we'd go look at them and maybe buy a couple and keep them under the ping-pong table in the basement and bring them out to show our friends.

Every day the sun is getting lower in the sky.

The pain hasn't come yet. Slizard is amazed. But I still have this strontium sting or plute ache in my ankles. I find the roads are getting longer, the hills steeper. I use the car.

Now – the streets, the traffic. We know that traffic reflects the temperaments of the great capitals (and here in a farewell flourish I invoke my world citizenship): the unsmiling triumphalism of Paris, the fury and despair of old New York, the cat-and-mouse audacity of Rome, the ragged murder of Cairo, the showboat longevity of Los Angeles, the industrial durance of Bombay or Delhi, where, four times a day, the cars lash the city in immovable chains. But here, in London – I just don't get it.

They adore doubleparking. They do. This is true love – a love whose month is ever May. They park in the middle of the goddamned street. I turned into the All Saints Road – and it wasn't a road any longer. It was a lot, a doubleparking lot. The traffic lights are barely more than decoration, like Christmas lights. You hit a red at the crossroads but you inch forward anyway, into the lock, into the headlock. You may even decide the time is ripe to get out and run an errand. Why? Why not? Everybody else does it. It seems clear to me, after five seconds' thought, that if everybody does it then nobody gets around, nobody gets anywhere. But everybody does it because everybody does it. And here's the other thing: hardly anyone seems to mind. At the crossroads the drunken youth drops out of his van and waddles into GoodFicks or Potato Love or the Butchers Arms, and the cars don't mind. They just nudge and shove each other, the old heaps, and not angrily, in this intimacy of metal and rust and not getting anywhere.

That was more or less how it was ten years ago. That was more or less how it was ten days ago. Now, in the last little packet of time, it's all changed. We have moved from purgatory to full inferno. And suddenly everybody minds. Even the gentler sex. And if plump mums scream over the grizzle of their strapped kids, if old ladies in old Morrises parturate with venom and smack freckled fists on the horn, then how are the *men* taking it? Four times in the last few days I have sat tight in the car, gridlocked under the low sun, with no way out, while jagged figures discover what the hard machine can do to the soft: what the hood of the car can do to the human nose and mouth, what the tyre-iron can do to the back of the human head. Traffic is a contest of human desire, a waiting gaɪ.ɪe of human desire. You want to go there. I want to go here. And, just recently, something has gone wrong with traffic. Something has gone wrong with human desire.

I don't get it. No – I do! Suddenly I do, though there's no real reason (is there?) why anybody else should. In traffic, now, we are using up each other's time, each other's lives. We are using up each other's lives.

Cornelia's morning swims have become a ritual. Marius will now stand on the deck with bronzed arms akimbo and openly admire her as she wades toward the shore. Her breasts, apparently, are —

A package, delivered by uniformed courier. I was expecting, with very little enthusiasm, the medication promised by Slizard. This was from Hornig Ultrason, however.

It contains the first chapters of my typescript. And the outline. And a check. Option-money. I don't know how she worked it. But this . . .

I'm aware that art can be sweet, and love sweeter, the recognition and forgiveness in the eyes, the hand and its needed touch, the mind-body problem so sweetly solved. But this, this (the money quivers in my fingers), *this* is true felicity.

The turbulence of my joy was such that I didn't notice, for a moment, that the pain had come.

And now the pipes are starting up again. The pain — the inorganic agony.

Jesus, the whole apartment is writhing and twisting with it.

Is it ever going to stop? Is it ever going to stop with that stuff?

Not *now*. But when? When's a good time for it — for pipes, for pain? It never is, it just never is, it just *never is the time.*

Chapter 17: Cupid's College

'LOVE JUICE. UNGOVERNABLE PASSION. The earth moved innit.'

'Hello, Keith. How are you?'

'Give herself utterly. The consummation of their bliss. One up the Khyber.'

'How are things?'

'Mutual body pleasure. The importance of sufficient foreplay. A full but firm figure. Consenting adults.'

When he was with her, Guy's trust was absolute and entire. Although Nicola's kisses sometimes shocked him – with their liquidity, their penetration, their hunger – her inhibition was unassailable, without blindspots, and impressively intransigent. How her whole body seemed to lock or jam whenever his hand entered the force field surrounding her breasts, her thighs, her heartbreaking belly. Elaborately conditioned by her sensitivity (and by the two powerful blows he had recently sustained), Guy was almost as tentative, as virginally hairtriggered, as Nicola herself. It was a relief for them both to be elsewhere, in all the places where nothing could happen. Sometimes, in the afternoons, they visited obscure museums or earnest cinemas. They went for walks, making the most of the clear weather: Guy relished a good tramp, and Nicola said she liked it too. The further out the better, Guy in his big wet shoes, Nicola in her dark-green wellies, her patched blue jeans: they held hands, and walked with their joined arms swinging. Just north of Barnet they found a wood they both adored. The muffled rustling, the way the trees husbanded moisture. Of course, there were little tricks and japes. She would knock his hat off into a puddle, then run and hide. Guy would scamper after her. She once wrote I Love You with a stick in the phlegmy mud of a dried stream. There were many delicious kisses under the branches of the tinkling trees. Birds stirred and damply flapped but they saw no animals, no small woodland creatures, not even a squirrel or a rabbit: only the animal fawns of the light cast by the low sun. Nicola said that these moments were especially precious, away from the city and its sense of approaching catastrophe.

When they got back to her flat Nicola would serve tea, on a tray, usually with biscuits. And for a while they would carefully neck on the sitting-room sofa. Yet when the time came for him to leave, and the kisses at the top of the stairs became kisses of farewell they also became wanton, and she would now squirm with vivid appetite in his arms. Smaller than him, and shoeless by this stage, Nicola would seem to be climbing up his body with the aid of various points of suction. Now, as he went on his way, his chest bore the fudgy imprints of her breasts, his belly was embossed by her culverts and contours. Further down, all was muscle memory: the tilt and camber of her excruciating pith. And she would soon be braver, she said. 'Soon I'll be braver,' she whispered hotly into his humming ear.

Still, Guy counted himself pretty lucky if he managed to get in and out of there without bumping into Keith. As Guy staggered down the stairs, bent, breathless, coated with electricity, Keith would be staggering up them. Alternatively, when Guy rang the buzzer on the porch, it would be Keith who personally yanked open the front door, looking glazed, lordly, propitiated. Something like this happened slightly more often than not. And once it happened twice: on the way in *and* on the way out – as if Keith was just politely and briefly vacating the eminence that was rightfully his. There were also other visits, Guy knew. Sometimes, when he was passing by or at any rate in the general neighbourhood, or when he had nothing better to do (a surprisingly capacious timeframe), Guy would haunt her dead-end street. On one occasion he saw Keith pull up and stolidly hoist satchel and toolbag from the boot of the heavy Cavalier. On another – and this was more or less pure accident – Guy's Volkswagen was involved in a minor delay, close to the significant junction; the delay was caused by Keith, who at some risk to himself and others was backing out into the main road; a few minutes later Keith drove past, sneering volubly into his new carphone.

In the early mornings Guy would lie in bed next to the shape of his sleeping wife (so distorted, now, in all his feelings about her, by the weight of what she didn't know) and stare at disgusting tableaux vivants, coarse grey travesties of potting shed and parkie hut, of elderly nurseries, with Keith saying, 'The doctor told me I have to do it once a day. Just lie down there,' or, more coaxingly, 'You just put it in your mouth until – it's just a funny game really.' Stealthily Guy drained himself from the bed. Next door he sat on the edge of the bath and moaned and shouted into the towel's cumulus. Then he looked down at his own loins with amazement and humiliation: there was the farcical animal, the winking elf. Godlike and archaic, he rose and began to cover the wound. In the mirror a pale warrior, vizor-boned, bodkin-browed – the starved lips! The two corners of his jawline had grown sharp rivets. His hipbones stuck out like the handles of a cooking urn. An urn that contained? The stew of all his stewed love.

And the century so close to its ending. The thing was, the trouble was, what it came down to was . . . No. Guy never dared think it. Set free, the thought would have gone like this. You could imagine Nicola, someone like Nicola, someone in her position, someone so placed, so cloistered, at the end of the nineteenth century or at the end of the eighteenth century or any other century that had a number. But not the twentieth century, which must leave its mark on everyone. Not the twentieth century. Not looking like she looked.

Keith said, 'What do you do with Guy then?'

'What do you think I do?' said Nicola. 'I tease his fucking cock off.'

Keith nodded slowly at her, with genuine affection. Then he stretched. 'Yeah. You know . . . he went to the university. Okay. But he done know fucking nothing.'

'It's a paradox, isn't it, Keith.'

'Nothing.'

'Whereas yourself, Keith, a student at the university of life . . . ?'

'Up the hard way. Street-smart as such. No, okay: he was born into a life of wealth and privilege like.' Keith lifted a finger. 'But he never lifted a finger for it. For me – for me, that's like unbelievable. Half the time he must think he's fucking *dreaming*.'

'Keith? May I demur? Happiness isn't relative, any more than suffering is. No one's going to feel grateful that his life isn't any worse. There's always enough pain, Keith. And the rich baby cries as lustily as the poor.'

'Yeah cheers.'

Keith was lying on Nicola's pretty bed, in his trousers and vest: thoroughly relaxed. His plump feet seemed to quiver lightly in their brown socks. Beside him rested the silver tray, the dregs of the devilish espresso, the saucer frilled with cigarette ends. Talentedly, Nicola was wearing a charcoal business suit and a white silk shirt fastened at the throat with an antique brooch of high formality. Her nails were varnished ovals; her linked bracelet stirred and settled with delicate distinctness. She sat on a straightbacked chair, in simple and streamlined authority. She corporate, he corporeal: the power breakfast.

'I'll leave you alone for a little while,' she said, standing and smoothing herself down. 'It's a rather glossy little piece I've prepared for you this morning.' She handed him the remote control, and reached for the tray. 'You'd never guess what these lady executives get up to in their offices. On a warm day, perhaps. After seeing some handsome window-cleaner going about his rough work. Oh, Keith: how discreet are you being these days?'

'Cross my heart and hope to die.'

'Yes yes. But how discreet are you being? It doesn't really matter. Of course, you don't say a word to Guy. But otherwise just do what comes naturally. He'll just think you're lying, anyway. Let me know when you're done.'

She drifted into the body of the flat, the sitting-room, the kitchen. She placed the silver tray on the wooden draining-board. She made another cup of coffee and smoked another cigarette and read *Time* magazine . . . This week's cover story was about the weather. As usual. It was hard to believe that *the weather* had until quite recently been a synonym for small talk. Because nowadays the weather was big talk. The weather made headlines all over the world. Every day. On TV a full reversal had taken place: the handsomest newscasters and the brainiest pundits were all weathermen now; and the whimsical tweed-suited eunuchs, who used to point rulers at charts and apologize about the rain, came on at the end to give the other news, or what was left of it. Meteorologists were the new war-correspondents: after John on hurricanes, and Don on glaciers, you got Ron on tropospherics. Rhythmically flicking the nails of her thumb and forefinger, Nicola read about the low sun, and the latest explanations. The change of angle was apparently caused by an unprecedented combination of three familiar effects: *perihelion* (when the earth is at its shortest distance from the sun), *perigee* (when the moon is at its shortest distance from the earth) and *syzygy* (when the earth, sun, and moon are anyway most closely aligned). The confluence made gravity put on weight, slowing the planet's spin and also *slowing time*, so that earth days and nights were now fractionally but measurably longer. 'Yeah cheers,' murmured Nicola, who had only twenty days and nights on earth to go. She tossed *Time* over her shoulder and arrived at her own explanation. Love made the world go round. And the world was slowing up. The world wasn't going round.

Still, the earth's new tilt meant that London would get the full eclipse. London would witness 'totality' on November 5. And already there were boys on the street with their guys, begging. 'Penny for the guy?' The guys themselves were insultingly perfunctory: so little thought had gone into them, so little care, so little love. They weren't *worth* a penny. And a penny was worth nothing.

After a long limbo (neglect, oblivion), she knocked on the bedroom door. Normally he alerted her with a confidential cough. But Keith's urbane throat-clearings, once begun, could rage on for over an hour. 'Yeah?' he said thickly. The moment she entered she was angrily aware that Keith had not availed himself of his solitary treat. Quickly she followed his gaze to the television screen: herself, freeze-framed, at her desk next door (and with one leg up on it), the charcoal suit in fascinating disarray. Nicola looked at him again, and shut her eyes as part of the effort of not laughing. For Keith was in tears. Warmly they had flowed; their tracks were yellowish on his porous cheeks. How she had underestimated her Keith! Pornography awakened all his finer responses. It wasn't just the sex. He really did think it was beautiful.

'I expect,' said Nicola, with relief, with amusement, with generosity (though not all the anger had been purged from her voice), 'I expect that after you visit me, you go off and see some girl, don't you Keith. Some little cracker. You do, don't you, Keith.'

Keith kept his counsel.

332

'That's good. I approve. Then you do to her all the things you want to do to me. All the things you *will* do to me, very soon. Ooh, I bet you do. You do, don't you, Keith.'

Keith kept his counsel.

'I just want you to do what feels right for *you*,' said Nicola. After the yob art, she thought she might as well throw in some yob love, on the off chance that it might make any difference to anything. 'Oh, I don't expect to hold you, Keith, not now or later, a man such as yourself. That's why I'm spinning things out like this. Especially not later. The girls will all be after you, and who can blame them? But I'll always be pushing for you, Keith, even when I'm just one of your memories. You won't have to let me know when the big one comes along: I'll *be* there for you, Keith. When you're throwing your darts for the Embassy, for the number-one spot, I'll be somewhere in the crowd, Keith, cheering you on.'

Keith sat up straight and put his feet on the floor. As he looked about for his shoes he said, 'Not *for* the Embassy. *At* the Embassy. Not *for*. *At*.'

She ducked into the bathroom, to change into her jeans and wellies for the next act. But first she threw on all the taps, pulled the lavatory flush, buried her face in a towel and almost killed herself laughing. It was a warm and timid little face that peeped through the crack in the door as Keith moodily took his leave.

'Guy,' said Keith, with his head down. 'What you tell him I come here for? Tell him I what? Fix the toilet? Lie on the kitchen floor with me tongue up a funnel?'

'. . . Something like that,' said Nicola.

Success has not changed me, thought Keith as he came down the stairs. Success, and recognition. Obviously it's nice to enjoy the fruits of stardom. Obviously. The money and the – the adulation like. The goods and services. I worked like a – like a dog for my crown. No danger I'll relinquish it in a hurry. But obviously basically I'll hopefully be the same Keith Talent I always was.'

Keith wiped the additional tears from his eyes and opened the front door. That sticklebrick of pallor, money, invented pain and good teeth – known as Guy Clinch – was feeding coins into a parking meter. His smile flickered up at Keith, who stood on the steps with his legs apart, shrugging into position the strap of his stolen toolbag.

'Good morning,' said Guy defeatedly.

But Keith moved past him with just a glazed wipe of the eyes and crossed the road for the heavy Cavalier.

Nicola was right. After he visited her, Keith went to see a ladyfriend. Moreover, Keith visited a ladyfriend *before* he visited her. Only certain unrepealable physical laws stopped him going to see a ladyfriend *while* he visited her. Nicola was right again. The girls were all after him, or at least they weren't getting out of his way. And Keith was really putting himself about, with an urgency, a cartwheeling canine frenzy he had never known before. Was someone putting something in his lager? It couldn't be healthy (even Keith was sure of this), and he genuinely feared for his darts, not to mention his sanity. Compulsive behaviour innit. But the birds were as bad. Indeed, over the great city, or in those flues and runnels where Keith scampered and paused, his whiskers working, a sewery fever seemed to be abroad, all wastepipes and floodgates and gargoyles, rat-borne. For Keith it was sharp and brackish, like the ever-present smell of urine in the streets. Of course, you had to be persistent, and having nothing to do all day unquestionably helped. After he'd fetched her milk for the ninth morning running, Iqbala consented, once again, to turn the telly up loud. Popping in on Petronella Jones with a series of high-octane gifts to celebrate her recent marriage to the oilrigger, Keith had found that one thing led to another. Since Thelonius's arrest, Keith had been doing the right thing, making regular and glad-handed visits to Lilette and the kids, and he could all too easily see himself developing an obligation there (Lilette okay for a baby-mamma, and not pregnant, or not very pregnant, just now: give the kids a tenner get lost for twenty minutes). It was getting so bad he hardly had time to hang around for hours on end relaxing over a few drinks with his colleagues in the Black Cross. While he performed – in bed, on the couch or the carpet, up against the radiator – while he jerked and stabbed and fought for breath, his thoughts, his desperate presentiments, were all of money, transformation, Nicola and, for the first time in his life, his own death. And here was one final proof that all was not well. He'd stumble in at Christ knows when, after doing Christ knows what to Christ knows who all day, followed by nine hours of darts and rounding it all off at Trish Shirt's – and find himself elbowing Kath awake at four in the morning! Now why would he go and do a thing like that? Kath. *Kath*, in whose body he had long lost all but a reflexive, Friday-night interest. It was like that time in the middle of the pregnancy, when Keith had been briefly stirred to find himself alongside this cool new *fat* chick with the big tits and the beer gut. I don't know what's got into me, he now thought, as he pressed her shaking shoulders down the bed. Really and truly I don't.

Keith pulled off in the heavy Cavalier. Being a professional, he drove with some sedateness, keeping his concentration, and his temper, as you had to do. The thick fingers depressed the indicator, and flashed the lights, in warning, in sufferance. The meat of the hand came down on the horn in brute denial, or tapped it tw ce, to say *hi* to a *cheat* or make a woman swivel and show her face . . . Mind you, Keith wasn't complaining. Complain? Keith? Not the type. Got on with it. Just as he imagined the world being held together by blind and hidden forces, so everything generally rested easy in his reptile mind. And guess what: Analiese Furnish had moved back into town. Keith accelerated, then braked, then traumatized a Learner with shout of horn and glare of lights. What they *doing* on the roads. Analiese, with her poems, her crushed flowers, her newspaper clippings (OUR SECRET LOVE), her Caramac hair, her bountiful summer dresses. Tired of Slough, tired of mildly scandalizing the blighted dormitory estate, Analiese had dropped her Heathrow baggage-handler, packed her many suitcases, and dramatically appeared on the White City doorstep of the unemployed violinist in whose love she knew she could always trust. 'After you, darling,' said Keith. 'Come on. Come on. Come on. Come *on*. Jesus. *COME ON*.' Yeah. Picked up sticks and moved back into town. I don't know how he wears it. Ah, but Analiese unquestionably had a knack or a power when it came to love – to love of a certain kind. With her scrapbooks, her costume jewellery, and her fat legs, Analiese had always been able to find a certain kind of man (fuddled, failed in art and love, patient, tender, older), who would house her, listen to her, worship her, and vow to keep his hands off her. 'What's this? Jesus, look at that stupid *bastard*.' Move it. '*Move it*.' Yeah. You heard: never lets him lay a finger on her. Before long Analiese was to be found in all her old haunts – the stage doors of the National Theatre, the carpark of the BBC, the van outside Ronnie Scott's – while Basil stopped home, scratching his beard, rereading her diary, and genuflecting in front of the laundry hamper. Basil's little flat in White City was dead convenient for Keith.

Now he wound down the window and stuck his head out of it. 'Don't fuckin say phankyou, whoah ya!' Christ, the manners of the road. Not that he was entirely happy with the situation. The postman

335

always rings twice as such. For instance, Keith liked to show up on impulse, going at things freestyle like, in his own way. And every time he sauntered whistling down the basement, with a sixpack of Peculiar Brews in one hand and his belt buckle in the other – there he'd be, mister misery. Get back. 'Get back, you little bitch.' It cramped a man's style. Where was the spontaneity. *Cheers, Baz*, Keith would say menacingly, and plonk himself down for a wait. Analiese just stared at Basil through the silence. As often as not she'd have to tell him. Honour my privacy, Basil. Respect my space, Basil. All this. And then with a shudder he'd rear up, fling on a mack and, Keith assumed, slope off down the drinker. Not ideal. But what could Keith do? That's it: block the whole fucking road. He couldn't entertain her at the garage – his lair of darts: even Trish Shirt used to balk at that, the way the grit got worked into the back of her dress. And Dean's flat was a tip. And so was Dean's van. Maybe if he put it the right way to Lilette, or Petronella, or Iqbala. Or Kath. Take your time, pal. I'm only here for my health. 'Cunt!' In theory, now that he had a couple of bob he could always take her to a nice little hotel. But there weren't any nice little hotels. There were only nasty little hotels. And the big ones frightened him. Anyway you don't want to lie around all day hearing her banging on about safe sex or religion. Got to be quick. Cavalier'll get a ticket. Or clamped. Fucking bastards. *Is* the Vodafone better than the Celmate, with improved specifications? Fucker'll know. 'll ask Fucker.

The traffic thinned, and Keith gratefully dropped into second gear. He had travelled perhaps five hundred yards. 'Freedom.' Besides, he needed his spare cash. For Debbee Kensit. Her mum had only upped the rates again. What with the petrol going all the way out there and a couple of quid for the gift he religiously took along, Debbee being special, you were talking almost a ton a visit. Keith maintained a considered silence about it but with Debs turning sixteen this month for sheer nerve it took your breath away. Hello. Give her a little beep. Now what have we –

A Krakatoa of truck horn atomized Keith's thoughts. For a sudden instant his windscreen was all chrome ribcage and scorching lights. Then the massed frequencies all fled past him in a deep scoop of air. Keith had straightened rigid in his seat: now he sank back, and decelerated, and pulled over – or at any rate he quenched the car of motion. For several minutes he sat there, doubleparked, rubbing his face with his hands. He lit a cigarette and exhaled vehemently. See what I mean? he thought, and felt brief love for the truckdriver and his skills. Another couple of feet. Another couple of feet and they'd be hosing me off the bonnet. See what I mean? It can't be healthy. And a calculated risk, that one: saw the truck coming and knew it was going to be tight. But I had to look, didn't I. Rarity value. Couldn't let that one walk on by, no way. Because you don't often see that. You don't. Had to look. An old woman not fat with really big tits.

Keith pulled out again, and proceeded to Ladbroke Grove and Trish Shirt's.

'I don't know how he does be doing it,' said Norvis, with honest bafflement as well as envious admiration. 'He here, he there. He everywhere.'

'Yes,' said Guy.

'No one approach he for energy. No one have he staying power. Soon as he finish, he off, looking for more.'

'So they say.'

'It have no one like Keith when it come to the chicks.'

Guy looked furtively along the bar. Keith was down at the darker and more fashionable end of it, with Dean and Curtly, near the microwave, the poppadam-warmer, the pie-nuker. Now Keith was delighting his friends with an anecdote, vigorously delivered: he was making a horn-squeezing gesture with his right hand, which then dropped only to rise again suddenly, darting finger first. The froth on Dean's beer exploded in mirth . . . Guy looked about himself, through the spore-filled air. Just when it seemed that Keith's pub prestige could rise no higher, it had yet jumped a palpable notch. But Guy himself, no less clearly, had been intolerably demoted. Here he stood, gratefully conversing with Norvis – comfortably the least celebrated of the Black Cross brothers (being unathletic, ill-favoured and hard-working) – fine-sprayed with spittle and obscenities and pork-pie crumblets, and transfixed by the hairless coccyx of an albino builder. Guy scratched himself with all ten fingernails. There appeared to have been a complementary revision of his status at Lansdowne Crescent. Guy's laundry, once discarded, no longer tangily rematerialized in his walnut chest of drawers. This morning he had wedged his shirt into the laundry basket and then, a minute or so later, tugged it out again.

'As I say, it beat me how he does be doing it.'

'Excuse me for a moment, Norvis, would you?'

With his head up, impelled by nothing more than inevitability, Guy squeezed and sidled his way forward, deeper into the pub's horn and hide and boiling fangs. Finally he gained the little clearing which always formed near where Keith relaxed with his favourites of the hour. Keith now stood in conference with Dean and Curtly: the tabloid was stretched open in his grip as he proudly showed the lads what Hurricane Keith had just done to Philadelphia. Sea surge and devil wind: one of the worst in history – even in *recent* history. That morning Guy had himself read up on Hurricane Keith's depredations. Seven feet of water dumped from the sky in twenty-four hours: a day when all the weather gods rush for the bathroom . . . Dean and Curtly straightened slightly on Guy's approach. Keith offered them both a last glance of silent facetiousness and then assembled his most solemn stare, like a sergeant turning from his corporals to face the gawky lieutenant.

'Morning, Keith. How have you been?'

Keith stared on. He made no answer. Dean and Curtly looked elsewhere – outwards, downwards.

'All set then', said Guy, with an archness that he had already begun to regret and revile, 'for the big push?'

Keith's expression slowly changed, or filmed over, the lids hooding Guy off. What was it? The eyes were in their pre-fight glaze, their search for animal severity. No. They looked like they looked after some stunning feat at the oché. Airless concentration, self-love, a darts trance. Keith's trance of darts!

'Bidding fair for the semi-finals,' said Guy, half-raising a pale thumb and turning jerkily to the bar. Here he faced Pongo. Guy indicated his empty tankard, which Pongo registered without interest, finding other instructions to attend to while Guy continued with his musical *excuse me*s.

'Ride comfort,' said Keith in a low voice. 'Anti-knock rating.'

Guy couldn't tell where the words were going, so quickly did he abort his turn of head and stricken smile. Maybe Keith was talking to the pub itself, its smoke, its dust.

'Aeroback. Her sobs of pleasure. Higher take-up. A veritable wildcat. Anti-perforation warranty. Lovejuice . . .'

There was some delay getting out, caused by an altercation near the front door. Things seemed to settle down; but then a blood-striped figure lurched up again off the floor, and it all began again. At this point Guy re-encountered Norvis, who shouted,

'He got another one now!'

'Sorry?'

'He got another one now!'

'Really?'

'Yeh. Oh yeh. She rich. Just round the corner. He go round there every morning and does be doing she arse off. And she make she videos. For he. Dark bitch. They the worse.'

Zbig Two, who was standing near by, abandoned or otherwise brought to an end a joke he was telling Manjeet (one that featured, as did all Zbig Two's jokes, a prostitute, a policeman and a purulent mackerel), and turned round and enthused, 'The first time he gone round there she came on like Lady Muck. But Keith's smart.'

'He patient.'

'Next time – bingo.'

'Yeh. Oh yeh. Frankly it get me how he does be doing it.'

'And this one *pays* him for it.'

'He she toyboy.'

'*Pays* him for it.'

They sounded ready to go on like this indefinitely, the information being so fresh in their minds. It seemed that Keith had just held a press conference on the subject, here in the Black Cross. Guy could imagine him: the tabloid rolled and raised . . . Another question from the back there . . . I'm glad you asked that. *Yes*. She . . . Grinning at the floor Guy listened on: her own penthouse, tall, well turned out, legs on the skinny side but good bum, tits so close together you could –

'What's her name?' said Guy hilariously.

Norvis and Zbig Two looked at each other, two experts, teetering quiz-contestants, stumped by the obvious. It's. Hang on. She call. Wait a bit. It have so many. Nita. Nelly. Nancy. With his mouth open Guy blinked and waited. The depth of their frowns, the temple-banging, the ecstasy of thwarted recall. He wondered if he could decently ask them to exert themselves so.

'Nicky! That's it.'

'Nicky. Yeh. Oh yeh.'

'Nicky. That's it: Nicky.'

'Nicky. That's it. Nicky. *Nicky*.'

The compact opened and Nicola's enlarged face filled the round mirror. It stared back at its mistress. It bared its teeth and licked its lips. With a sweep of wall and dimity and velvet the mirror closed again.

She looked up. 'There you are,' she said softly, and got to her feet. 'Are you all right? You sounded rather miffed on the telephone. Let's take off your mack.'

'No, I'd rather not, actually.'

Nicola backed into the sitting-room. As Guy followed her she looked up at him with humility and concern. 'Darling, what is it?' she whispered. 'Sit down. Can I get you anything?'

Guy shook his head; but he did avail himself of the low armchair. He raised his hand in a gesture of placation, a request for silence, for time. Then gently he rested the palm against his right ear, and closed his eyes . . . That morning, as he lay in bed, and as Marmaduke pried at his clenched lids, Guy felt an odd sensation, inappropriate, balmy, sensual: in fact, a trail of Marmaduke's hot drool was gathering in his ear. It hadn't bothered him at first, but now half his head was blocked and pulsing. Some glutinous – or possibly sulphurous – property of the child's spittle had done its maleficent work, deep in the coiled drum. The room tilted, then swayed. Maybe everything is so mad now, he thought.

'There's something I must ask you.'

She looked at him with unbounded willingness.

'I'm probably a complete idiot,' he went on, for her house, her windows, her curtains, had seemed so blameless from the outside. 'But there's something you ought to know too. Now you must promise in advance to forgive me if I – '

Guy hesitated. Quite clearly he could hear the sound of a toilet flushing nearby. Too near to be anywhere else. Then Keith came out of the bathroom. He had a silver leather jacket held over his shoulder and was saying, 'That was my favourite, that was. I like them when you – '

'Ah, Keith,' said Nicola lightly. 'I'd almost forgotten you were still here.'

Freeze-framed, italicized, caught absolutely redhanded, Keith's figure began to inch back into life, to move and breathe again – and to shrink, to shrink to nothing, as Guy rose reflexively to his feet.

'Hello, mate –'

The leather jacket, held a moment ago insouciantly shoulder-high, Keith now gathered into his hands where he could crease and crumple it. A strong interaction was taking place between the men:

the power of class, at its strongest over short distances. Guy looked at Keith with contempt. And this was the Knight of the Black Cross.

'I expect you'll want to be on your way,' said Nicola, 'here's your – case. I put something in it for you.'

A coughing fit seemed about to free Keith indefinitely from the obligation of speech; but then he gulped suddenly with a thickening of the neck and said, 'Appreciate it.'

'Oh and Keith? You couldn't bear to have another go with the grinder, could you? It's there. It packed up again, I'm afraid.'

'Willco,' said Keith, gathering his things.

'Same time tomorrow?'

Keith looked at Nicola, at Guy, at Nicola. 'Er, yeah!' He nodded, and tubed his lips, and shuffled sideways towards the door.

'Goodbye, Keith,' she called, and turned to Guy. 'I'm sorry. What were you saying?'

He waited. Keith's strained whistle started up and retreated down the stairs. 'Is he,' asked Guy, sitting, and looking around, 'is he here *all the time?*'

'I'm sorry?'

Guy said reedily, 'I mean, if he's not actually in here it's quite a rarity if I don't see him on the stairs.'

'Keith?'

'I mean, what does he *do* here day in and day out?'

'Does he say anything to you?'

'What? On the stairs? No, he just says "Cheers" or "Innit" or something,' said Guy, as his hand sought his brow.

'I mean generally. He hasn't told you our little secret?'

'Whose little secret?'

'Keith's and my little secret,' Nicola smiled at Guy with rueful mischief. 'Oh well. I suppose it's got to come out. I'm afraid I've deceived you rather.'

'I see,' said Guy, and raised his chin.

'He'd be horrified if you knew,' she said, and looked closely into Guy's crippled face. Its weakness she identified for the hundredth time as something predetermined, already etched, something made for a specific purpose, but too long ago. 'And of course he's very worried that his wife will find out about it.'

'I think,' said Guy, 'I think you'd really better tell me.'

Well, in a minute, she thought. A few more choice ambiguities, perhaps. No – all right. Okay: *one* more. 'I mean, what does it matter

341

if he's only a common working lad?' she asked. Then she widened her mouth and tented the lines on her brow and said with martyred calm: 'I *teach* him.'

'Keith? I don't understand.'

'Of course he's only just literate and a complete dunce in all sorts of ways but the desire is there, as it so often is. You'd be surprised. I learned that with my work in remedial reading.'

'When did all this start?'

'Oh, ages ago.' She frowned, seeming to remember. 'I gave him a copy of *Wuthering Heights*. I didn't know how serious he was but he persisted. And now we're doing it properly. We've just started on the Romantics. Look.' And she held up her Longman's *Keats*. 'I'm wondering if it's wise to start him off on the Odes. Today we had a quick look at "Lamia". The story helps. I was thinking perhaps "La Belle Dame Sans Merci". Or "Bright Star". It's a favourite of mine. Do you know it? "Bright Star! Would I were steadfast as thou art"?'

'Nicola. Has he done anything to you?'

Even she had her doubts about the look of radiant puzzlement she now gave him – doubts about its supportability, in any scheme of things. 'I'm sorry?'

'Has he ever tried to make love to you?'

Slowly it formed, the pure incredulity. After a moment she put a hand over her mouth to catch a silent hiccup; then the hand moved upwards to her eyes.

Guy got to his feet and came forward. In no uncertain terms, and with his mind half-remembering some analogous recital, some previous exercise in illusion-shattering (when? how long ago? what about?), he told her what Keith and his kind were really like, how they thought of women as chunks of meat, their dreams of violence and defilement. Why, only today in a rough tavern Keith had been blustering about the uses he had put her to – yes, her name shared and smeared in gross fantasies of enslavement, humiliation, appetite, murder.

Nicola looked up. He was standing over her with his feet apart.

She said, 'Oh – does it mean that much? They believe in each other's lies just like they believe in television . . . What's that?'

'. . . What?'

She drained her face of all experience and raised it towards him. Then her head levelled again and she pointed with a finger. '*That*.'

'Oh, that.'

'Yes. What is it?'

'What *is* it?'

'Yes.'

'You must know, you must have read . . .'

'Yes, but why is it so – so protuberant?'

'I don't know. Desire . . .'

'May I? It's like rock. No. Like that stuff that some dead stars are made of. Where every thimbleful weighs a trillion tons.'

'Neutronium.'

'That's right. Neutronium. Would I bleed?'

'I don't know. You've gone on horses and things.'

'And this bit under here is important too, is it? Oops! Sorry. This is fascinating. And in some circumstances a woman will take this in her mouth?'

'Yes.'

'And suck?'

'Yes.'

'I suppose the idea would be to suck absolutely as hard as one could. What a strange thing to want to do.'

'Yes.'

'So regressive,' she said, and briskly stroked and patted him, as one might dismiss a friendly but unfamiliar animal. 'Though I can see it might be fun for you.' She was smiling up at him, her mouth like a split fruit. 'What's the line in "Lamia"? "As though in Cupid's college she had spent sweet days"? That really is the worst thing in all Keats. *So* vulgar. But Cupid's college is where you'd better send me for a while, until I know all the tricks.'

He left about an hour and a half later.

His ear was worse. At least three-quarters of his face was unrecallably numb, and heavy, too, to the muscles of the cheek. That was Marmaduke's work. But his good ear had also received a lot of attention, from Nicola's lips and tongue; as he came down the stairs, stepping from carpet to bare board, Guy realized that he was in fact clinically deaf. Outside made his lips feel raw and chapped from kissing – and these kisses so wolvish all of a sudden, especially when he felt her breasts which he was now permitted to do (from without only), and the breasts themselves so responsive and distended and seeming to link up with all the complications of his own low wound.

343

Across the street he rode, on his rogue boner. Pale rider. Under the fantastic clarity of the evening sky. He looked up. The moon certainly did look closer than usual, but beautifully close, and not yet shining, like the crown of a skull or a Goth helmet; and not just a mask or a shell but a body, with mass and depth, a heavenly body. And the only one we ever really see, the planets too small, the stars too distant, and the sun too vast and near for human eyes.

Dead cloud. Just then – awful sight. Just then he saw that a dead cloud was lurking above the near rooftops. Awful sight. What did it think it was doing there, so out of kilter? They were always lost, dead clouds, lost in the lower sky, trembling drunkenly down through the thermals, always looking in the wrong place for their brothers and their sisters.

Guy pogoed on. The world had never looked so good . . . Bright star! And with so much doubt gone he could reproach himself in full measure.

Well might Guy curse himself for a brute and a swine. His thoughts were all crosspurposed, while hers were all of truth and beauty, beauty, truth.

I saw a dead cloud not long ago. I mean right up close. This was New York, mid-town, mid-August, the Pan Am building (you could feel its monstrous efforts to stay cool), the best piece of real estate in the known universe. How could some dump of a white dwarf or innocently hurtling quasar stand up to this golden edifice on heliographic Park Avenue? I was in Dr Slizard's office, just below the restaurant, the revolving carvery or whatever they have up there now. The dead cloud came and oozed and slurped itself against the window. God's foul window rag. Its heart looked multicellular. I thought of fishing-nets under incomprehensible volumes of water, or the motes of a dead TV.

'Science', said Slizard, in his epigrammatic style (his good colour, his busy eyes, his accountant's beard), 'is getting very good at explaining how it killed you. How it killed things. But we still don't understand dead clouds.'

Luckily I've known Slizard all my life. How else could I afford him? I always enjoyed his company, until I got sick. My father taught Slizard at NYU before he switched subjects. He used to come to the house one or two nights a week. He had long hair then. Now he has no hair at all. Only the talking beard.

Marius Appleby lives for the ritual of those morning swims, and so do I. Cornelia's breasts, apparently, are *magnificent, splendid, awesome, majestic* – and all the other words that mean 'big'. And

345

we're only on page fifty-nine.

Cornelia has Afghani blood. She rides a horse like a crazed ghazi. She shaves her legs with a Bowie knife. Marius has yet to win a smile from her, a civil word. Old Kwango (bent, pocked, muttering), himself deeply roused by her, for all his years, suggests the time-honoured and locally popular strategy of *rape*, where a man must roughly take what he claims to be his. Marius demurs. He's watched her with her bullwhip. But he also sees the need for something butch – some act of manly valour. Oh, it's tough, with Cornelia striding about so proudly and nobly the entire time. And she seldom has a stitch on.

The weight of her head and the plumpness of her cheeks cause Kim to pout while she sleeps. Her arms are arranged in one of her Spanish-dancer positions. If you could take twenty snaps of the sleeping child and flick them in a booklet, she would perform the movements of the castanet artist, one hand aloft and curved, one hand lowered and curved also, and always symmetrical.

She stirred. Every time, now, I'm frightened she won't recognize me. People don't. People I haven't seen for three days look right through me. I myself keep going to the mirror for an update . . . Her breath was deeply charged with sleep; and she looked momentarily disgraceful, as babies can look, her face puffed, and latticed with the ephemeral scars of sleep. She focused on me, and pounded her legs – but almost at once her face formed an appeal, as if straining to tell me something, something like *you wouldn't guess what's been done while you've been gone*. Of course, as babies inch toward speech, and their expressions so intelligently silent, you expect the first words to penetrate, to tell you something you never knew. And what you get is stuff like *floor* or *cat* or *bus*. But then with a bent finger Kim pointed at a lesion on my arm and said, with clarity and conviction:

'Ouch.'

I was astounded. 'Ouch? Kim. My God. So you can talk now, can you?'

The baby had no more to add. Not for the time being. I carried her into the kitchen. Kath was elsewhere (in the bedroom). I made the formula and put a slow teat on the bottle. She cried when she saw it. She cried because she wanted it and crying was all she had. I fed her with frequent burp-stops and burp-outs. She wiggled a leg as she drank. For of course if a leg is dangling attractively, then a baby must wiggle it, must never miss the chance to wiggle it. Toward the end of the bottle I felt the warm seep-swell of her diaper. So I put the mat on the table and got ready to change her.

Then Kath intervened, appearing suddenly. 'Ah there,' she said. She took the child from my arms and the Huggy from my hand. Some mick rule here – a chill of priestcraft?

She went with the child into the living-room. I watched the baby's rolling face as it bobbed on Kath's shoulder. The astonished eyes.

'Ouch,' the baby said to me, before Kath shut the door. '*Ouch*.'

' "For Galen knew that from that day forth he would always dream of she who had come to him that night in Toledo, and tousled him awake with a lover's impatience." There.' Nicola said nothing. 'Come *on*. It's so obviously terrible. It's not even literate. "Of *she* who." Of *her* who, for Christ's sake.' Nicola said nothing. 'The sentiment is repulsive enough. But I guess he didn't bother *you* with sentiment. Too busy climbing into his Beelzebub outfit.' Nicola said nothing. 'It's funny he's so bad at women. All powder-puffed and air-brushed. Without physical functions. He places them in that golden age, now alas long past. You know the one: before women went to the toilet.'

Nicola spoke. She looked at me mistily and said, 'You're wrong. His work speaks very directly to women because he idealized them so passionately. Isn't this a great theme – the struggle of the man, the warlike creature, to accommodate gentleness? Asprey is surely Lawrentian here.'

'. . . This shatters me, Nicola.' This shatters me. Because it discredits, it explodes her artistic sense. And her artistic sense is all I have to go on. 'Oh well. You must be a theatre-lover. More perversity. There's nothing there, in English anyway. Just Shakespeare, and that's that. Which is some kind of cosmic joke. As if Titian was a scene painter, or Mozart wrote movie scores. As if God just directed rep.'

I was now being a little too glib – or a little too something – for the enigmatic Miss Six. (These last sentences were in fact direct quotes from a long letter I was writing to Mark Asprey.) She left her chair and went to the table. She poured out and drank eight swallows of brandy. She looked at the black window. 'I go out walking,' she sang, 'after midnight, in the moonlight, just like we used to do. I'm always walking, after midnight. Searching for you.'

'. . . Your voice is pretty nice. I guess you sang when you did pantomime. But it's kind of a cold voice. Holds something back.'

When she sank down on the sofa beside me her legs went up about three feet in the air. Her gaze also had the caloricity of liquor. I felt I was fending it off.

'To work,' I said, and took out my notepad. 'Let me have some more on these nature rambles you take Guy on. These little love parodies – they're among the worst things you do.'

'You only have to write them up. I have to go on them. I hate walking. I mean, *where to?* It's like being in an ad. An ad for menthol cigarettes – remember? In the days of threepenny bits?' She thought for a moment and said, 'No, it's like being in an ad for love. An ad for love.'

'I still don't get it. The Guy-torture. But I'm expecting some cool twist. Oh yeah. It's about time I saw one of these videos. One of these ads for sex.'

'There aren't any. I don't keep them. I hate them.'

'How very disappointing. I take it Asprey's snaps are a little out of date. How disappointing. How am I meant to describe the delights of your body?'

She reached for her top button and said, 'I'll take all my clothes off.' She paused. She leaned closer. 'Don't you feel we could be like terrible little cousins and show each other everything. All the sticky smelly bits. Look at you. You don't fancy it, do you, in flesh and blood. Listen. I have a confession to make. I have this shameful habit. Every day I go to a bad place and do a bad thing. Well, some days I manage not to – but then the next day I might do it twice. I go to the toilet. Come on, Sam. Help me beat this thing. You be my bathroom buddy. Every day, just after breakfast, when I feel the temptation – I can call you up and you can talk me down.'

'Nico*la*,' I said. I got to my feet. 'At least tell me this terrible thing you did. To Asprey. It might cheer me up.'

'I put a brick through his windscreen. A big un, too.'

'Oh, sure. Come on. That would be no more than routine.'

'I'm not saying.'

'Why?'

'Why? Why? Why do you think? Because it's too *painful*.'

She's right in a way. There is no language for pain. Except bad

348

language. Except swearing. There's no language for it. Ouch, ow, oof, gah. Jesus. Pain is its own language.

The pain-kit arrived in good time. It came by courier, mid-afternoon, so I was able to call Slizard immediately. 'It's beautiful,' I croaked. 'Like a box of liqueurs. Or a chemistry set.' He knew I'd like all the labels: when it comes to pain-classification, he said, we're back in the middle ages, or the nursery. Suddenly I asked him, 'Hugo, what's happening? Worldwide I mean. I called some contacts in Washington. It's all leak and spin. Where's the *information*? How are you seeing it?'

'. . . It's serious.'

'How so?'

'It's like this. The pressure is coming from two directions. Do you go in now, and take the chance, or let the system degrade further. The Pentagon is for going in; State would prefer to ride it out; the NSC is torn. There is hypertension, also dyspnoea. There may be embolisms. Me, I'm for ride-out. They must get past the millennium. They can't risk it now.'

'Hugo, what are we talking about here?'

He sounded surprised. 'Faith,' he said.

'Excuse me?'

'The President's wife.'

Our world of pain, as here arrayed and classified: how like life it is, how like childhood and love and war and art. Shooting, Stabbing, Burning, Splitting. Tugging, Throbbing, Flashing, Jumping. Dull, Heavy, Tiring, Sickening. Cruel, Vicious, Punishing, Killing.

'The single pill in the black bottle,' I said. 'With the modern skull-and-crossbones . . .'

'That's for when the living will envy the dead. That's for the most painful condition of all. Life, my friend.'

On *Aphrodite*, Cornelia continues to disdain all congeniality. And all clothing. It's driving Marius and Kwango crazy.

It occurs to me that certain themes – the ubiquitization of violence, for example, and the delegation of cruelty – are united in the person of Incarnacion. There is, I believe, something sadistic in her discourses, impeccably hackneyed though they remain. I wonder if Mark Asprey pays her extra to torment me.

She has been giving me a particularly terrible time about the stolen ashtray and lighter. And I'm often too beat to get out of her way.

Endlessly, deracinatingly reiterated, her drift is this. Some objects have *face value*. Other objects have *sentimental value*. Sometimes the *face value* is relatively small, but the *sentimental value* is high. In the case of the missing ashtray and lighter, the *face value* is relatively small (for one of Mark Asprey's means), but the *sentimental value* is high (the gifts of an obscure but definitely first-echelon playmate). Being of high *sentimental value*, these objects are irreplaceable, despite their relatively low *face value*. Because it's not just the money.

Do you hear her? Do you get the picture? It takes me half a day to recover from one of these drubbings. I am reminded of the bit in *Don Quixote* when Sancho has spent about fifteen pages saying nothing but look before you leap and waste not want not and a stitch in time saves nine, and Quixote bursts out (I paraphrase freely, but I really understand): Enough of thine adages! For an hour thou hast been coining them, and each one hath been like a dagger through my very soul . . .

Chapter 18: This Is Only a Test

KEITH FROWNED, AND sipped on his cigarette, and read these words:

It is a definite historical fact that Boadicea played a form of darts. Quite a warrior for a woman, she was thought to have honed her skills, by playing darts. Little good it did the Queen of the Ancient Britons in the end, for she was defeated by the Romans and perished by her own hand in the year 'AD' 61.

'AD' 61! thought Keith.

Early dartboards have definitely been recovered from ancient locations. It is not known for definite what form of darts Boadicea played. Probably not 501, which shapes the modern game but some other form of darts.

Pensively Keith removed his darts from their purple pouch. Then, with the aid of this same pouch, he dabbed away his tears. A cigarette later, he sat with his pad, his darting diary, on his lap and a biro in his hand. The biroholding hand waved in the air for a while like a sketcher's. Then he wrote:

Eazy on the drink.

A cigarette later, he added:

The trouble with darts they are no good when you are pist.

He resumed his practice session, his darting workout at the oché. The darts thunked into the board. He retrieved them. He threw again. He retrieved them. He threw again. He retrieved them. He threw again . . . Eight cigarettes later, he sat down and wrote:

Get the basics right. Lean on front foot, nice eazy follow thrugh. In doors you just get moaned-at. Sap's a mans ability to concentrate completely on his darts.

The darts were thrown, retrieved, thrown again (they thunked into the board), retrieved, and thrown again, and again. The six cigarettes were torched, consumed, ground out on the crackling floor. He threw 26 four times running. A wave of self-pity went through him. No one outside the sport realized just how tragically *hard* it was to throw a dart 5ft 9¼ ins, with clinicism. He paused, and sat, and wrote:

Keep throwing fucking '26'. Better Tomorrow. Don't reckon Nicks skeem sceem skeem.

'Good morning to you, Keith.'

Scheme, thought Keith. TV had not prepared him for anything like this. Or scam. 'Good morning ah . . . Miss Six,' said Keith. Load of nonsense.

'Nicola, please! Now just sit in your normal place and I'll be with you in a minute. Coffee?'

Basically, Michael, I'm just the sort of guy who just likes to meet up with his mates down the pisser. Down the drinker. Down the pub. Basically I just drink to relax. To relax? To *relax*? thought Keith, and saw himself (last night, 3 a.m.) on his knees in the garage with a bottle of *porno* in either hand. Gracelessly Keith sat himself down on the sofa (he was thoroughly out of sorts). Earlier instructed by Nicola not to look at the camera, he looked at it anyway, through his low lids: on the little bookcase there, its twin red lights unkindly glowing. Keith rocked with the pulse of a contained cough or burp or retch, then lit a cigarette. Here she comes. Nicola wore a checked grey suit, squarely cut, and flat black shoes; her hair was swept up from her lightly painted face, the bun rich and grained and gordian. Looks the part all right, you could say (there was even an apple on the table). Schoolmarm outfit innit.

'Why don't we begin', she said, 'with Keats's "Bright Star"?'

'Yeah cheers.'

'Page eighty-six. It is five lumps, isn't it, Keith.'

86, thought Keith. Treble 18, double 16. Or you could go bull, double 18. Darts.

'Now.' Nicola settled herself erectly at his side. Humming somewhere just beneath their hearing threshhold, the video camera was positioned to Nicola's rear, over her shoulder, catching Keith in profile as he turned towards her grimly. She didn't really look like a schoolmarm. At that moment Nicola crossed her legs with a lift of the skirt and briefly shivered her rump into the cushion. On TV more like a Mother Superior who gets up to things. Or the dog in the office in the touching romantic comedy: take her glasses off and she's a goer. The skirt had a slit in it, or a fold, like a kilt.

'Keith? Why don't you take us through it.'

'You what?'

'Read it out loud. Use mine. Come a little closer.'

'Bright,' said Keith, 'bright – star!' He jolted, apparently rather taken aback by the exclamation mark. 'Would . . . I would I were –'

'Would I were steadfast,' whispered Nicola.

'As . . .'

'Thou.'

'Art.' Keith wiped his toiling brow. 'Not in lone, not in lone splendour.' He coughed: a single bark from the dog within. 'Pardon. Splendour hung aloft the night – and watching, with, with *eternal* lids, apart, like –'

'You seem to be reading one word at a time. As if you're lassoing it with your tongue. When was it you learned to read?'

Keith's open mouth went square. 'Yonks,' he said.

'Go on.'

'Er, like nature's . . . patient, sleepless . . .'

'Eremite. Hermit. Recluse. And 'patient' has the sense of de*vout*, Keith.'

'The moving. Jesus. At their . . .'

'At their priestlike task of pure ablution round earth's human shores,' said Nicola; and as she read on she opened up her skirt to the waist (and Keith could see the sheer of the stockings, the interesting brown flesh, the white silken prow):

> 'Or gazing on the new soft-fallen mask
> Of snow upon the mountains and the moors;
> No – yet still steadfast, still unchangeable,
> Pillowed upon my fair love's ripening breast,

To feel for ever its soft fall and swell,
Awake for ever in a sweet unrest,
Still, still to hear her tender-taken breath,
And so live ever – or else swoon to death.

. . . Well, Keith?'

'Yeah?'

'So what does it mean? Take your time.'

Keith read the poem again. Two vertical worms of concentration formed in the centre of his forehead. The letters on the page seemed as unanswerable, as crammed with silent quiddity, as the impurities in his own eyes. Keith moved through an awful dream of missed connexions, sudden disappearances, horrendous voids. He wondered if he had ever suffered so. Three or four minutes later, when he thought he might actually be about to lose consciousness, Keith felt words fighting their way to the surface and the air.

'There's this star,' Keith began.

'Yes?'

'And', Keith concluded, 'he's with this bird.'

'Well that's more or less the size of it. But what is the poet trying to say?'

And Keith might have put an end to everything, right then and there. But now Nicola turned the page: Keith's eyes were presented with an index card with writing on it – her corpulent, generous, feminine hand.

'Now I may not be an educated man,' read Keith, with only a little difficulty. It sounded halting, honest. It sounded good. 'But it seems to me to go against common sense to ask what the poet is "trying to say". The poem isn't a code for something easily understood. The *poem* is what he is trying to say.'

'Bravo, Keith.'

'The lover looks to the star as an image of, of constancy. What Keith – what Keats is expressing here is a yearning to be outside time. Suspended with his fair love. But I think the uh, movement of the poem gives a little twist to that reading. The star is identified with purity. The clean waters. The newly fallen snow. Yet the lover must be bold. He must come down from the heavens, and enter time.'

'Exactly, Keith. The lover knows he cannot escape the human sphere, with all its ecstasy and risk. "Swoon to death": for the Romantics, Keith, death and orgasm are equivalent.'

354

'Yeah, well, same difference.'

'The first eight lines really are quite beautiful, but I can't help feeling that the sestet is terrible tosh. What now? The Odes? I think not. Let's look at "Lamia" again. It's one of your favourites, isn't it, Keith.' She placed the book on her lap; she talked and read; she turned the pages with long fingers which then trailed across her bare thighs in negligent indication or caress. 'Some demon's mistress, or the demon's self . . . Real are the dreams of Gods . . . Cupid's college . . . Subtle fluid . . . Weird syrups . . . Dear me: all this melting and blushing and fainting and swooning. That purple-linèd palace of sweet sin.' Here they encountered another index card, and she smiled at him encouragingly.

'It would seem that Keats,' said Keith, more confidently, 'for all his celebrations of the physical, is not a little coy and uh, evasive, even in the safety of his enchanted forest.'

'A little fearful too. His maiden is a snake in disguise.'

'Exactly,' Keith improvised.

For a while Nicola talked of the life, the *Letters*, the neglect, the early death. Keith started to enjoy his weighty contributions, his voice becoming deeper, richer, with the imagined power of suddenly talking like this, feeling like this, thinking like this. He even began folding his arms in an authoritative way, and scratching his temple with what remained of the fingernail on his right pinkie.

'The story ends in Rome, in 1820.'

1820! thought Keith.

'He was twenty-six.'

Double 13, thought Keith. Not nice. You got three darts better go 10, double 8.

'The son of a rude stablehand, he died in a bitterer obscurity. "Here lies one whose name was writ in water" were the words he wanted engraved on his tomb.'

'It's tragic to reflect,' read Keith huskily, 'that Keats will never know how he lived on in the hearts of his many admirers. Admirers from such different walks of life. Now someone like Guy', Keith went on with a thick and sudden frown, 'clearly has something of the, of the poetic spirit in him. And I honour it. But I myself, in my, in my unschooled way, have also found my life enriched . . .' The index card here said, simply, 'by John Keats'. But Keith felt at this stage that he could do a little better than that. 'Enriched', he said, 'by the plucky little . . . by the . . . talented Romantic whose . . . whose untimely —'

355

'By John Keats,' said Nicola. The skirt was straightened, the book snapped shut — and, with it, Keith's wordhoard. 'I think that's enough for today, don't you? One final quote, Keith:

> Who alive can say,
> "Thou art no poet; may'st not tell thy dreams"?
> Since every man whose soul is not a clod
> Hath visions, and would speak, if he had loved
> And been well nurtured in his mother tongue.

And I think you've shown again today, Keith, the truth of those lines.'

Keith took a breath, and longed to soar and sing. But all was silence in his huddled mind. He nodded soberly, and said, 'Yeah cheers.'

She saw him out. On her return she walked through the sitting-room, across the narrow passage and into the bedroom. Guy was sitting primly on the bed, the broad hands palm upwards on his lap. Nicola kissed him on the mouth and held him at arm's length.

'*Now* are you satisfied?'

Guy smiled wanly at the television screen, which showed the sofa's back, the empty room. 'Revelation,' he said. 'I'm sorry. Feeling rather ridiculous and ashamed. I did say it wasn't really necessary. Quite amazing, though. I could hardly believe it. The judgment. The natural critical sense.'

'I told you he was keen.'

'You are good, Nicola.'

Yeah cheers, she almost said, as she took off her coat. 'One has to do what one can.' Tipping her head, she started to unbutton her blouse. 'A funny reason to enter a lady's bedroom for the first time. I don't think I'm quite ready, yet, to swoon to death. But as for your fair love's ripening breast . . . Ripening, indeed. Feel for ever its soft fall and swell. Ooh. I hope your hands are nice and warm.'

'These warm scribes, my hands. Just one thing. I thought you were terribly cruel', he said in a clogged voice, and smiling, 'to poor old Keats.'

John Keith, thought Keith, as he drove away. Top wordsmith, and big in pharmaceuticals. Books: one way to make a fast quid. Breakfast by the pool. Wife in good nick. 'Really, dahling, I got to stop writing them Hollywood scripts and get down to serious writing.' Fucking great study full of leather. Snooker! Jesus. Lady Muck with the schoolmarm skirt round her waist. Wasn't bad. No. In the end I thoroughly enjoyed it. Showed Guy. But an awful old load of old balls. Keith wondered, parenthetically, if Keats had ever played a form of darts.

He moved out into the main road. As he did so he felt a withered agitation in his gut, like the last wing-flickers of a damaged bird. Oi. He felt it in his throat and lungs too – waste, consumption. During one of several long delays Keith picked up the Vodafone and called Petronella. Line disconnected? Hard to tell: he couldn't even hear himself swear for the mind-ripping clamour of a nearby skip-remover. He felt again the coppery friction in his abdomen. It occurred to Keith that he ought to be under the doctor. This wasn't the welcome satyromania of old. It was like a panic attack. And although the spirit was willing – was ravenous, was desperate – the flesh was inexplicably weak. It was taking him ages, every time. He felt sore and ticklish: he thought with a wince of the snails he had killed with salt as a child.

This doubleparking! Keith queued and edged and weaved his way to Ladbroke Grove, and doubleparked in Oxford Gardens. He strolled into CostCheck, nodding to Manjeet. Past dairy products, past toiletries, past videos he whistled his way: an affecting ballad, Spanish, called 'Los Sentimentados'. He stepped aside as a fight got going between an attendant and some kid by the Alkool display, hopping backwards in a practised veronica when a bottle broke, fearful for his flares. Down in the storeroom Keith looked through the split in the hardwood door. Trish Shirt was lying on the ground with one leg hooked up on the cot: the exact-same position in which Keith had left her ten hours ago. Keith's teeth contrived a censorious squeak as saliva moved from lips to tongue. It would take half an hour to slap any sense into her, easy. Another consideration obtained: much earlier that day, as he wrenched off her crammed panties, Keith had been influentially reminded of his dartboard down in the garage, the bit near the treble 20 where there was a big fringed lump due to darting overuse. The modern dartboard, however, whilst known as the bristle board, is not made from animal hair but from vegetable matter; sisal, prepared from the spiny leaves of the agave plant, is imported from Africa, compressed into the requisite shape, backed by chipboard, and finished by screen-colouring and wiring. Innit. The resemblance had excited Keith at

357

the time, but not for long enough; soon, thoughts of power scoring –
the ton-forties, the unanswerable maximums – had wrecked his
concentration. Now Keith looked at his watch. He went back
upstairs, bought a six-pack of Peculiar Brews, and climbed into the
Cavalier for the ninety-minute mile to White City and Analiese
Furnish, in no mood for any nonsense from Basil.

Keith returned to Windsor House just after six. He stood in the
kitchen, as frazzled as London traffic. Invaluable hours of priceless
practice had been lost – so many thunks, so many precious retrievals.
You couldn't blame Basil: he had absented himself smartly enough,
after Keith had taken him aside, man to man, and given him a clip
round the ear. It wasn't Analiese's fault either: she had given of her
best, and hadn't complained, and Keith had seen for himself the
tortured tendons of her jaw. Nah: murder getting home, with the
streets full of personnel and Shepherds Bush cordoned off again . . .
Kath appeared, holding the baby like a magic shield against him.
Keith looked at her expressionlessly, at her tired light. Tomorrow:
the Semis. And a considerable dilemma. The match itself Keith
regarded, or thought he regarded, with titanic equanimity. What
worried him was his choice of guest. In the normal course of things,
no problem: Debbee Kensit or Analiese Furnish, showing a cleavage
you could park your bike in. But this was a high-profile fixture,
prestigious as such. Trish Shirt had got wind of it. And Nicky said she
wanted to be there. And even Kath had mumbled something about it
if you please.

'Where's my meal.'

'Would you come and look at this, Keith?'

'Jesus. What?'

'It's the TV.'

Keith pushed past her and stopped dead on the brink of the lounge.

'It's the same on every channel.'

Keith peered forwards with his lips moving. The screen said:

> This is only a test of the Emergency Broadcast
> System. If this had been a Real Emergency,
> this would show you which channel to turn to
> for the Latest Information.
>
> But this is only a Test.

'You know something?' said Keith to Kath. 'You scared the

fucking life out of me then. Thought the TV was down.' He wagged his head at the screen. 'That's all right. Look. Look! It's back on again now. Where's my meal?'

As Keith contemplated, with relish, his Mexican Chilli and Four Apricot Madeleines, Kath said,

'I went to the library. There's no newspapers.'

He took the tabloid from his armpit. 'What's this then. You gone blind or summing.'

'But they —'

Keith was now staring at his empty teacup. Kath stood, childishly erect, and went next door to put the baby down. She came back and reached across him for the shrouded pot.

'That's not a newspaper.'

His eyes swelled at her warningly.

'There's nothing in it. About the Crisis.'

'Fuck off,' said Keith conversationally. 'They, there's always something about it.' Over the past month Keith had kept himself abreast of the Crisis by sometimes reading the filler that his tabloid sometimes ran at the foot of page fourteen. The little headline varied. YANKS: &@ɸ*! or RED NYET or GRRSKI! Or, once, in unusually small type: TOWELHEAD DEADLOCK. Keith now turned to page fourteen with a flourish. There was an article by the Slimming Editor on the health of the President's wife. But no filler.

'Nah well. Can't be anything happening then.'

'You think not.'

Keith fell silent. He was immersed in an item about the movie star Burton Else. Burton's aides utterly refuted the rumour that Burton was bisexual. Since the mysterious death of his young wife, Burton had been entirely occupied in his attempts to make contact with Liana beyond the grave. By way of illustration there were two photographs, one of Burton, one of Liana, both topless.

'They say they'll —'

Keith dashed his knife and fork on to the tabletop and got to his feet. 'Look mind your own fuckin business okay? Jesus, you call yourself a wife I got a fuckin semi-final tomorrow night and you're giving me this crap? Sticking your fuckin oar in. Come on Clive, no point staying in here. Get to work. Come on Clive. Come on me old mate. *Jesus.*'

The baby was awake. But she wasn't crying. Her eyes glittered.

*

359

At nine o'clock in the Black Cross, Keith downed his darts and downed his drink and went out the back to the phone. It took ages for Manjeet to get Trish to come to the stockroom.

'Been cancelled,' said Keith perfunctorily.

'Why?'

'Question-mark over me fitness innit.'

'What?'

'Sidelined with a finger injury innit.'

'What happened? She cross her legs?'

'Shut it.'

'I'm coming anyway.'

'Free country innit,' said Keith, more or less truthfully for once.

'You coming round later?'

Keith hung up without saying maybe. Back in the bar he saw Guy.

'Cheers, Keith.'

'Hello, mate.'

Keith felt something he didn't feel often: embarrassment. Or rather he would have felt it – embarrassment – if he'd had the leisure. In truth Keith was seldom bothered by embarrassment: a book called *Keith and Embarrassment* would be a short book, trailing off after two or three pages . . . He looked up. Guy was gazing at him with an expression of pitying fondness.

'Demands,' said Keith. 'You got commitments. All these demands. On your time . . .'

Guy was nodding.

'The big occasion,' said Keith, flexing his darting finger. 'You dig deep.'

Guy kept on nodding. He seemed ready to accede to any proposition Keith might put forward.

'The big occasion. *That's* what I respond to. You coming tomorrow night? Course you are. Yeah well could you do me a favour, mate?'

'Sure.'

'See: I can't. Bring Nicky.'

'Sure.'

'Nicola. See: I can't.'

They leaned back for a moment with their elbows on the bar, like equals. Then Keith said absently, 'I'm up to here in minge.'

The bent copper, John Dark, came over. John Dark – the iffy filth. Keith bought the drinks: he owed Dark some money for settling the Thelonius business. More nonsense. Thelonius's name had popped out of the DNA computer smartly enough. But then, so had Keith's. Careless work: saliva on the pork pie crumbs. Keith would do a lot for pork pies, Keith would do a lot in the name of pork pies; but going to prison for them, he reckoned, was well beyond the call . . . The three men spent half an hour talking about the difficulties Rangers were having in asserting themselves up front and translating their aerial superiority into goals. Then the conversation moved on to the depressing attendance figures for the early months of the season. Dark said, with his permanent cheerfulness,

'It breaks your heart. And it could get worse. This morning, what comes up on the screens? Contingency plans. Partial evacuation of Central London.'

Keith looked sideways. Guy looked downwards.

'Where would Rangers be then, eh?' Dark laughed. 'This lot? Shift this little lot? They must be fucking *dreaming*.'

Shakespeare put his head through the door and gestured. Keith made his excuses. Outside, Big Dread was standing under the lamp-post, with Truth. They all huddled round as he unfolded a section of newspaper and bore its contents to the light.

'That them?' said Keith.

'That them all right,' said Truth.

'They the right kind?'

'From the gym,' said Big Dread. 'Anabolic innit.'

'It won't give me tits or nothing?'

'Never,' said Truth. 'Enhance your darts innit.'

'How much each?'

It was, of course, his darts he had in mind. But Keith took one steroid there and then (saving the other two for the following morning, on Truth's non-committal instructions), and went off to try it out on Trish Shirt.

Just before noon the next day Guy left Lizzyboo in the kitchen, where she was wordlessly eating corn on the cob, and wandered up the stairs and into the hall, nodding, now and then to a half-familiar nanny or au-pair. In the second drawing-room he went and stared without avidity at the whisky and brandy in their crystal tantalus. Next door, in the first drawing-room, so broad, so under-used, he tried music, something unstrenuous, something he knew well (the Concerti Grossi), and decided, after a few minutes, and to his amazement, that the piece no longer interested him. On his way up the stairs he saw another new nanny, dark-skinned, exotic, serenely slovenly. There had been a tacit relaxation of the rule about pretty nannies. Indeed, when the heat was up and the low sun filled the windows, the place had an air of luxurious ill fame: languid, ante-bellum. These nannies had come on the market suddenly over the last two or three weeks, and Hope had snapped them all up. At a time like this, Guy thought (but there had never been a time like this), young girls might feel an atavistic urge to get inside a big house. Inside a big cave.

Hope was in the bedroom, at the dressing-table, brushing her hair. Every time he encountered her now he saw their past life together flash by, as if their marriage were a person fatally drowning. He managed to take a little low comfort in the spectacle of her tennis gear. Dink had not been as much around as one might have liked.

'You're playing?' he said. 'With Dink?'

'No courts until six. What's the matter with everyone? Why aren't they working?'

'No one's working. Have you noticed? Building sites and every-thing . . . Is Lizzyboo pregnant?'

She turned to him: an intelligent oval in which indignation and coldness were equally represented.

'I only wondered. Not just her size but the way she eats. Cravings. She's eating corn on the cob down there. She had about nine in three minutes. I was put in mind of an electric typewriter.'

'It's just her way of dealing with it. Eating's okay, you know. You should try it.'

Guy was leaning against the doorpost with his hands in his pockets. He looked down the corridor. 'Did he have a nap last night? Anyway. He's stirring,' said Guy, unnecessarily, because you could hear Marmaduke's unfaltering roar and the ever-surprising violence of his rocking cot. 'Has he been out today? I thought I might stroll him.'

'The girls will take him out back.'

'I'd like to. What? No, I would.' This was of course a grotesque untruth. But Guy had need of a telephone. Not to call Nicola, whom he was seeing that night (he would squire her to the darts). No: to call Richard at the office. He had spoken to Richard at length and with urgency three times already that day and didn't want to alarm the household further. That was another thing about deception: your black lies made your white lies darker. Your stars were all dimming in heaven.

362

'Do you think it's really safe out there?'

'Oh, it's all right.'

He was now faced with the task of equipping Marmaduke for the outside world – of dressing him entirely, from soup to nuts, with the child throwing all he had at him every inch of the way. In the nursery Guy took off Marmaduke's nappy and despairingly wedged him into the potty. 'Are you going to make a present for daddy?' he asked, again quite hopelessly. Twenty minutes later, following Marmaduke's reliable failure to make a present for daddy, Guy wrestled him into nappy-liner, nappy, nappy pants, vest, shirt, trousers, socks, shoes, jumper and, downstairs, anorak, gloves, face mask, bobble hat, scarf. As he was dragging him towards the front door and reaching out to free the doublelock, Marmaduke 'went supervoid', in the local phrase (the phenomenon usually marked the end of Marmaduke's experiments in week-long, white-lipped constipation). The child, in other words, had swamped himself in ordure. When Guy unravelled Marmaduke's scarf he saw that some of it was even peeping over the collar of his shirt. In the nursery again Guy wrestled him out of bobble hat, face mask, gloves, anorak, jumper, shoes, socks, trousers, shirt, vest, nappy pants, nappy and nappy-liner, waved away the game but gagging nannies, hosed Marmaduke down in the master bathroom, and wrestled him back into nappy-liner, nappy, nappy pants, vest, shirt, trousers, socks, shoes, jumper, anorak, gloves, face mask, bobble hat and scarf. During these struggles, Marmaduke's lifelong enthusiasm for hurting his father – and, within that, his specialization in hurting his father's genitals – was given play only twice. A flying headbutt to the testicles, and an unrestrained blow with a blunt instrument (a toy grenade-launcher) to the sensitive tip. The new pains joined and reinforced and starred in all the ensemble pains that were there already. This time, he actually got the front door open before Marmaduke was noisily and copiously sick.

Well, Guy hardly bothered with that. A roll and a half of toilet paper later, and he was out on the street with the steaming child. Marmaduke was now lying face down on the pavement, entirely flaccid to the touch. Guy crouched, and coaxed, and flinched into the low sun.

'There's a good boy.'

'Nnno! . . . Ant mummy.'

'Come on, darling.'

'Ant cad jew.'

'Oh all right.'

During their walks, Marmaduke always insisted on being carried, because it made the business of hitting his father much easier. They started off towards Ladbroke Grove. The lofted child's fingers played playdough with Guy's face.

Royal prisoners, Guy thought: *that's* their status. Babies are royal prisoners, imperial internees, little Napoleons, tiny Hirohitos. Ouch! Must clip his nails. Passive resistance – well, within certain conventions of acceptable struggle. They consume the gaoler's man-hours. They sap the enemy's war-effort. 'Not in the eyes,' he said. When they're falling down the stairs, you can see it in their faces: they're saying – this is *your* problem. And just as you think the old boy is coming along quietly for once – 'Not in the eyes' – there'll be some frazzled lurch for the door, some fumbled sabotage. Or a last, heroic self-fouling. Ow. Ouch. Right up the nose with that one. Whose war is it? Aren't we their friends, their enemies' enemies? Of course, you can never treat the royal prisoners cruelly or harshly, because they're royal and must be seen to be perfect when hostilities end . . . Before he was a father Guy didn't realize just how many babies and children there always were about the place. But now – he was entering Ladbroke Grove with its shops and pubs and bus-stops – Guy saw that the royal prisoners were naturally everywhere, as they always have been, all sizes (the woeful ones, the terrible twos, the threatening threes, the fearsome fours), and all doing what royal prisoners always do.

The superior violence everywhere suggested by the flesh and mortar of the street had an emollient effect on Marmaduke, who was perhaps hoping to pick up some tips for use elsewhere. Presiding over the car horns and engine surges, and the turning wheels of ordinary commerce, small concerns, and the permanent smash and scuffle at the pubs' lantern jaws, came the dead notes of six or seven burglar alarms exasperatedly sounding. The post-office, whose floor stayed wet in any weather, was a skating rink of drunks and supplicants and long-lost temper – and self-injury, Guy thought, noticing how nobody noticed the woman in the corner rhythmically beating her head against the join in the wall. He queued for a callbox, or milled for a callbox, the queuing idea, like the zebra-crossing idea, like the women-and-children-first idea, like the leave-the-bathroom-as-you-would-expect-to-find-it idea, having relinquished its hold in good time for the millennium. Even Marmaduke seemed somewhat daunted by the swirl. Guy was thinking of trying his luck at Conchita's

364

or Hosni's or possibly the Black Cross when a booth became clear and no one serious interposed. He called Richard, who forthrightly confirmed what they had both suspected: all American money was leaving the City.

After the conversation was over Guy went on standing there, the telephone to one ear while Marmaduke patiently mangled the other. He never panicked; and he didn't panic now; he cleaved, as always, to what he felt was inevitable. The American retreat was in any case far less significant than the rollover it might entrain. And his own holding position was probably sound. But he suddenly felt a universal steepening. Guy held the child, but wants and needs now flailed out from him, basic, cheap, ordinary, the stuff we have to have. It occurred to him that he was perfectly free to call Nicola, and this he did. Sleepily she revealed that she was lying on her bed, after a bath, and that he was much in her thoughts. For some reason Guy laughed, and with childish gratitude or relief. He felt a new pain somewhere but didn't notice how his trousers rose a couple of inches from his shoes.

He went outside with the child and the sun was right there at the end of the street like a nuclear detonation. And Guy knew that the sun shouldn't be doing this. No, the sun really shouldn't be doing this. The sun shouldn't be coming in low at us like this, filling windows and windscreens with rosy wreaths of dust, setting the horizon on fire like this, burning so aslant like this, at this terrible angle, making everything worse. You want it out of your sight. Look round a corner— and there's nothing, the street is gone, it's just fire and blood. Then the eyes themselves burn through and you can see the wet asphalt sizzling in its pan. The sun turns slums into crystal battlements. But the sun shouldn't be doing this, it really shouldn't be doing this, branding our minds with this idea, this secret (special burning, special fire), arrowing in low at us all the time like this.

As they turned into Lansdowne Crescent a free dog bounded past, as if escaping from the scene of a crime. Guy sat Marmaduke down on a garden wall and tried to embrace him. Into the eager flurry of small fists he bent his face, his searching lips. He had just seen himself in the future: he was with Marmaduke, at the zoo in Regent's Park – the zooworld of annulment, dissolution, visiting rights, half-orphanhood. The cafés, the concourses were sparsely scattered with other divorced fathers, other sundered children. But the cages were empty, except for trails of smoke and the ghosts of animals. There weren't any animals. No animals any more. Not even a dog.

For some time now I have thought it possible to believe that America was going insane. In her own way. And why not?

Countries go insane like people go insane; and all over the world countries reclined on couches or sat in darkened rooms chewing dihydrocodeine and Temazepam or lay in boiling baths or twisted in straitjackets or stood there banging their heads against the padded walls. Some had been insane all their lives, and some had gone insane and then gotten better again and then gone insane again. America: America had had her neuroses before, like when she tried giving up drink, like when she started finding enemies within, like when she thought she could rule the world; but she had always gotten better again. But now she was going insane, and that was the necessary condition.

In a way she was never like anywhere else. Most places just are something, but America had to mean something too, hence her vulnerability – to make-believe, to false memory, false destiny. And finally it looked as though the riveting struggle with illusion was over, and America had lost.

I sit by the side of Lizzyboo's hammock-like bed, patting her hand and talking about all the rewards of the cloistered life. How very different from the sleeping arrangements and general atmosphere aboard *Aphrodite*, where Marius swelters in the port cabin, listening to Cornelia's insomnias of stopped longing in her starboard bunk . . .

There was a time when I thought I could read the streets of London. I thought I could peer into the ramps and passages, into the smoky dispositions, and make some sense of things. But now I don't think I can. Either I'm losing it, or the streets are getting harder to read. Or both. I can't read books, which are meant to be easy, easy to read. No wonder, then, that I can't read streets, which we all know to be hard – metal-lined, reinforced, massively concrete. And getting harder, tougher. Illiterate themselves, the streets are illegible. You just cannot read them any more.

'So you loved him,' I said.

'So you loved her,' said Nicola.

I didn't answer either. What happens? We endlessly circle everyone else, everyone else we can get in range, looking for the other, who is circling and waiting and, we hope, looking for us. Then, if you dare to, if you possibly can, you just think: *not a doubt*.

For some time now it seemed that the dreamlife of America might become too strong and troubled. What's that line in *early* Updike – in innocent, amorous Rabbitland? America is beyond power: she acts as in a dream, as a face of God. America thought she was awake, brightly awake, but in reality she was sleeping, and deep-dreaming; and she was all by herself. She wanted to be good, to be better – *special*. We all do. When you go insane, what happens? Wanting to be good and right: can this do it? Can love do it? Too much love, and all of the wrong kind. Love unreturned, tantrum love, collapsing into hurt feelings. Feelings ripped and torn. Inconsolable America, cruelly stung, breathing deeply, and not coming out to play. Marriageably she slept, and dreamt, and thought she was awake.

It makes it so no one can say how frightened they're feeling. Four months ago Missy Harter was whispering in my ear. Now she talks like *Time* magazine.

I call her everywhere and nothing happens.

Keith asked me if he could bring Analiese Furnish to the apartment. As he filed this request, and sensed some of my unease, he gave me the look of the star-crossed lover. In Keith's version of it, in Keith's spin-off of it, the star-crossed lover looks like an old chancer whose steed has fallen ten yards from the post. Just this once, I said.

Notes:

Of course, I'd admired the topless tabloid photo of her that Keith carries around with him, and physically she measured up. All in all she seemed (i) a little less pretty (ii) quite a lot more crazy (iii) about five years older and (iv) about nine inches shorter than the image formed by my typewriter.

I made ready to leave but they insisted I stuck around. Long silence from the bedroom. Then the sound of what I can only describe as intense mutual difficulty. Then a dozen furious cowboys finally hit Santa Fe.

Later, during the aftermath, I was alone with her in the sitting-room. 'Tell me something,' I said. 'Out of interest. When Keith comes over, where does Basil go?' 'He goes', she said haughtily, 'to the *park*.'

Air of flusteredness and falsity. Dumb hat. She reviewed the photographs on the walls like an art historian in a gallery. Hair and shoulders seemed to hum in minute response to my gaze. Even her club-like ankles, cringing under the floral print of her dress, seemed to know when I was looking at them. Christ: the expansion of mind, the communications revolution. All survivable, presumably; but Analiese just didn't make it. The mind doesn't expand. It stays the same. Other things fill it.

In the book, she stood for something. In the flesh, she was pointless: a complete waste of time. Or not quite. In the flesh, she broke your heart, as all human beings do. I watched her, an older man, failed in art and love. Fat ankles. Dear flesh.

And now in the same park but in different weather I stand with Basil side by side. Nothing divides us – just a screen of rain. You'd call us stuffed men but even the stuffing has been knocked out of us. We hug ourselves to hold what warmth remains and because no one we love will. Basil, the weeping violinist. And no good at that either. You and me, pal.

One fails to see how Marius is going to make any progress on the macho front. Cornelia doesn't need it. He keeps trying to protect her and rescue her and so on – but she's never in any trouble. For instance, they encounter a wild dog near a trading shack on some windswept shore. Marius does the butch thing and steps forward to confront it. The dog stares up, yawning and drooling with rabies. Clad, as usual, in only a cartridge belt, Cornelia pushes him aside (her magnificent breasts are *heaving*) and blows its head off. She reminds me of someone. I know: Burton Else.

And, like Burton Else, like *everyone* else, Cornelia has her softer side. Marius is definitely doing better on the campfire end of things, after old Kwango has retired. Here, under the tamarinds, under the throbbing stars, she tells him of her love for Bernardo, the doomed racing-driver – his flashing smile, his lustrous quiff. Here is a woman who will not give herself lightly to any man. But when she does, Marius figures, she gives herself *utterly*.

Nevertheless the sands of time are running out: he only has about fifty pages. Go for it, Marius. The suspense is killing me. Death is killing me. Everything hurts, and I think I'm going blind.

My eyes have become such pitiful instruments. In the vampire movie, when the cowgirl or barmaid comes too close with her white throat, and the Count thinks what the hell and really leans in there, and his eyes . . . that's what my eyes are like. Partly it's all this crying I do. I cry so much – I feel what femininity is. Crying is part of my repertoire, part of my day, my life. I wail and keen. I have sniffles. Oh, Lizzyboohoohoo. Sometimes, when I'm at a loose end, I have a refreshing little sob and feel much the better for it. I grizzle and blub. I weep it out. And still I must blow my nose and pipe my eyes and go out into the teargas of the unreadable streets. The chicanes, and the terrible cars.

For some time now it's all been bad timing. Bad timing, and then more bad timing, and then more. The millennium, coming so soon, so hard upon, is bad timing. In the year 999, in the year 1499, in the year 1899 (and in all the years between: the millennium is a permanent millennium) – it didn't really matter what people felt or what they felt like saying. The end of the world just wasn't coming. Nobody had the hardware. The end of the world was staying right where it was. Unless . . . We've all had that funny experience, after taking a leak: pull the handle, and watch the bowl froth with sewage. It went out. And now it's coming in again. The human being is standing on tiptoe, head cracked back on his neck, with only nostrils, pouting lips and a lump of straining forehead visible above the rising tide. They did good to put the weather reports on late at night, after the children have supposedly gone to bed. X-rated weather reports, and the weathermen like jumpy undertakers. Imagine the planet as a human face -- a *man's* face, because men did it. Can you see him through the smoke and heat-wobble? His scalp churns with boils and baldspots and surgeon's scars. What hair is left is worried white. The face beneath is saying: I know I shouldn't have tried that stuff. I know I shouldn't have messed with all that stuff. I really want to change and straighten out but I think I went and left it a little too late. I get an awful feeling that this is stuff you can't recover from. Look what it's done to me. Look what it's *done* to me . . .

In a sinister reversal I am now established as Keith's darts coach. He doesn't coach me any more. I coach him. It's easy.

I can't help him with the technique side of it (there isn't any), and I can't help him with the tactical side of it (there isn't any), but I can help him with the psychological side of it, and there's apparently plenty of that. Everything depends on the savagery of your desire to get that dart to go where you throw it. Afterward, eerily, the money still changes hands in the same direction. Keith looks elsewhere as he receives the notes.

So I was standing there last night saying things like 'Be accurate, Keith' and 'Keep it tight' and occasionally, of course (the supreme accolade), 'Darts, Keith'. Every now and then we get into recondite stuff about muscle memory and the destiny of the shaft and so on, but mostly I just stand there saying things like 'Be accurate, Keith'. 'Be accurate, Keith': what kind of advice is that? What does it cost me to say it? I make an effort and say it through the pain. The pain I'm at home with by now; but not the effort. It is the effort that is so new, unprecedented – and so tiring, like all efforts. Effort is full of effort and all that tiring stuff. There is a tab. Light bleeds out of the other things.

Last night, around eleven, something happened to Keith that should never happen to a *cheat*: he ran out of cigarettes. Flabbergasted, he searched the garage for his spare few dozen cartons – and couldn't find a single pack. That shows you just how long he has been neglecting his cheating.

When he went to get some, at the Offie (where they have everything a modern family needs: drink, videos, nuked pizza), I settled down for a leisurely look at his notebook, his darting diary. And among the little homilies about the wayward third arrow, the illiterate fantasies of sudden wealth, the grimly transcribed gobbets about how Hannibal probably played a form of darts, I came across the following:

Got to stop hurting K. No good just takeing it out on the Baby.

Get him gone. Christ, how much longer before we come to the end? Get him gone.

Enough. Finish. *Over.*

Chapter 19: The Ladies and the Gents

S EMI NIGHT!

The five-set semi-final of the Duoshare Sparrow Masters was, for Keith Talent, a home fixture. No way, on the other hand, was such a quality contest being staged at the Black Cross. On this night Keith looked to a far more prestigious venue: Acton's the Marquis of Edenderry. *That* was the drinker Keith had always represented – the foaming tankard, the purple arrowpouch, the clinical finishing. No way would you catch Keith throwing for the Black Cross, whose drunken troupe of cosmopolitan stylists had never come close to Superleague, had never, in fact, been known to win a darts match. Your more cultured arrowman was always going to be turning elsewhere for his sport. Basically it was to a more dart-orientated boozer that Keith was obliged to gravitate, where you found the darting dedication. The Marquis of Edenderry: its terraces of brothelly red velvet and tinkling chandeliers, the barman in braces, striped shirts and porkchop side burns, the barmaids with their milkmaid outfits, wenchy cleavages and sound knowledge of darts averages and lore. Magnificent facilities, with eight boards all in a line, and then, for the big occasions, the raised oché complete with mimic target and digitalized scoring. Kath helped dress him: the burnished Cubans, the toreador flares, the black shirt short-sleeved for flowing throwing with its silver-scripted admonition: KEITH TALENT – THE FINISHER. Then the bat-winged darting cape . . . In the damp shadows of the Black Cross the figure Keith cut could occasionally seem taciturn and remote; but put him in a class pisser like the Marquis of Edenderry and, well, the guy just came alive. Keith loved the Marquis of Edenderry. He sometimes came over all funny about the Marquis of Edenderry, and would tearfully beat up anyone who spoke slightingly of the place.

'Yes. This is it,' said Guy. He gave a sideways smile of encouragement and asked, 'Are you all right?'

Nicola smiled back at him without opening her mouth. 'I think so.' She took his hand. 'It's just that I'm not a great one for pubs,' said Nicola, who in truth had always preferred expensive cocktail bars and violent speakeasies.

'We met in a pub.'

'Well then. They can't be all bad.'

He got out and moved round quickly to her door. A hand appeared. He raised her up into the night.

'You look splendid,' he said, and added in a louder voice: 'I'm just wondering whether we oughtn't to leave your coat in the car.'

Nicola looked like a million dollars. Or a million pounds, anyway. Over the V-neck jacket and rear-split skirt of a black velvet suit was flung a blond mink coat ('It's fake,' she had lied); court shoes, sheer stockings, diamonds on her ears and on her throat at the end of a fine gold chain, and a gold watch, and a gold clasp on the black leather bag.

'I mean,' said Guy, 'they won't know it's not real.' When, earlier, as planned, she had come straight down the stairs in response to his buzz, Guy had been seriously alarmed (and, of course, seriously touched) by the guileless opulence of her dress. How hard, and with what intelligent success, she had tried to look sophisticated. And they were only going to the pub to watch the darts and root for Keith, who perhaps had told her that the place was rather grand.

'Who won't?'

'The people in the pub.'

'They'll try and steal it, do you mean? But you'll protect me. Anyway they wouldn't dare.'

Guy smiled palely. All he had meant was that the coat might cause ill feeling, in the Marquis of Edenderry. But of course he kept this to himself.

They entered the pub and its loud world of primitive desires, desires owned up to and hotly pursued and regularly gratified. Daily fears having been put aside for the night: that was the idea. The desiderata included goods and services, sex and fights, money and more TV, and, above all, in fateful synergy, drink and darts. A shifting tabletop caught Guy an early and awkward blow, flooding his vision with a familiar distress; so he just squeezed his way through after her, after Nicola, for whom the heavy press seemed to part as far as the tips of her coat's bristles. Hell will be noisy and crowded, he thought. Hell will be *busy*. Now they reached the body of the Marquis of Edenderry, and here was air, and space – and tables, and chairs. The pub was simply too big to be slaked by mere human beings. They sat, and were immediately attended by a uniformed waiter whose erectness and impatience declared that tonight would be high efficiency, high turnover, the managerial team having no doubt set their sights on an epic profit. There were also alert sweepers with longhandled brushes and dustpans, to tackle the upended ashtrays and the shattered glass. And when a fight broke out near by – surprisingly vigorous and sanguinary for so early in the evening – two ageing bouncers cruised along and floored the likely victor with crisp punches to the nose; they then administered some exemplary stomping with cross looks cast about. Guy hummed and hawed and twice apologized to the waiter before deciding on a beer, Nicola having asked, with an air of considerable timidity, for a cognac, which is what she had been drinking all afternoon. The waiter stiffened, wiring himself still tighter, and moved off. Guy was pleased, or at any rate looked pleased, to see some of the same old faces from the Black Cross. They now regarded Nicola with an admiration that expressed itself in frowns of pain, of grave disappointment. The sexual slanders, the lies told in the Black Cross, Guy felt, were somehow active here in the Marquis of Edenderry; but they could never really touch her. He gazed at Nicola, serious and inviolate, in her glad rags. He didn't know that her mind was working like silicon with incredible calculations as it might be the trajectory of the last dart bisecting the angle of his erection: arcs, tangents, targets.

'I hope Keith wins,' he said.

'Oh he'll win,' she said. Guy smiled at her with his head tipped, as if questioning her certainty. She could have told him what she believed to be true, that she felt it in her tits; I feel it in my tits. But of course she kept this to herself.

At 7.45 precisely North Kensington's Keith Talent pushed open the double doors of the Marquis of Edenderry and stood there removing his car gloves while all the heads turned. Stay cool but don't tighten up.

He lifted his chin, surveying his immediate responsibilities. There were some shouts from further back. Heavy support. Don't ask about an opponent. You play the board, not the man. Mike Frame, the landlord. And Terry Linex and Keith Carburton from Rare Perfumes: a nice gesture. Appreciate it. Now Mike Frame stepped forward and placed a serious hand on Keith's shoulder, urging him on to the cleared stretch of barspace. Two men in suits, sponsors from Duoshare. And Tony de Taunton from DTV. DTV. TV. With intense formality Keith was offered a selection of select wines, a choice of choice spirits. No way. Lager. Lager's kegged. It's *kegged*.

'I understand you usually throw number three for the pub, Keith.'

'Third gun. That's correct, Tony.' Keith explained that the pub's two top darters, Duane Kensal and Alex O'Boye, had both been unavailable when the Duoshare came round this year. Absently he added that such things were always unpredictable, where matters of parole and remand were concerned. 'No, I'm the underdog tonight,' said Keith. Lower expectations. 'Suits me down to the ground.'

'Well good luck.'

'Thanks, Tony. Yeah cheers.'

7.50 and the double doors swung open again, meaningly: the clatter faltered, and there was a schoolyard sound from within, whoops, harsh laughter. Keith turned. Not too quick. And faced the entrance with his ready sneer. Four Japanese. *That* one! Paul Go! Seen him down the Artesian! Fucking maniac on the treble twenties! Did two ten-darters in half an hour! Came out of his trap with a maximum! Never smiles! Did the 170 finish! . . . Don't ask about an opponent. Keith sipped his lager. So Paul Go beat Teddy Zipper. The fast-throwing oriental had what it took to put one over on the South London drayman. Keith parked his sneer at the bar while the exclusive huddle opened out to include his adversary. Then he turned, looked for a moment into the unknowable ferocity of Paul Go's lidless stare, nodded his farewells, circled his tongue round his right cheek, and slowly unmoored himself into the smoke and the noise – and the pub's waves of love.

'He's coming over,' said Guy. 'I think he's coming over. He certainly looks . . . ready for anything.'

'Doesn't he,' said Nicola. 'I love the stingray outfit.'

'I think we might need more chairs. If he joins us we might need more chairs.'

374

Still some distance off, Keith was now walking the gauntlet of his friends and fans. Handclasps and handsmacks, savage and farcical winking, the great dry head jerking in recognition and acknowledgment. Playfully he slapped the drinks from offering hands, and tossed spare cigarettes over his shoulder, like Henry VIII with his chicken legs. Laughing faces filled Keith's wake.

'He looks like the Pied Piper,' said Nicola.

'He looks . . .' said Guy, with doubt, but so raptly that it came out anyway. He couldn't imagine ever feeling superior to Keith again: the male principle, so positively charged. 'He looks', said Guy, 'like Marmaduke.'

Finally he was nearing their table, back first, and windmilling his arms — at Curtly, Dean, Fucker, Zbigs One and Two, Bogdan, Piotr, Norvis, Shakespeare.

'Best of luck, Keith,' called Guy, his glass raised, but much too early, for Keith was still craning to heed some chant or goad.

'Best of luck, Keith.'

'Yes, good luck, Keith,' said Nicola.

He was now looking beyond them and flapping his hands in authoritative summons.

'I think we might need more chairs,' said Guy.

'Right then,' said Keith, and gave a courtly sniff. 'Guy, Nick: Debbee. This is Debbee. Debbee? This is Analiese. Analiese? Petronella. Petronella? Say hello to Iqbala. Iqbala? Meet . . . meet . . . meet . . .'

'Keith!'

'Sorry, darling . . .'

'Sutra!' said Sutra.

'Sutra,' said Keith, who had not known Sutra long.

'I think we might need more chairs.'

'Right then. What's it going to be? Glass of milk for you is it Debs?'

'Keith!'

'Jesus,' said Keith, closing his eyes in the greatest disgust. 'Here comes summer. Look what the fuckin cat's dragged in. Look what's just crawled out from under its fuckin stone.'

Guy and Nicola both turned and looked up: behind them stood a faded blonde, or a blonde's ghost. She stared at Keith with what appeared to be numb yearning.

'I'll get another chair.'

375

'Guy? Don't move a muscle. She's pissed, innit,' said Keith, going over Guy's head. 'You. Fuck off out of it.'

'No. Uh, I think I *shall* get another chair.'

Guy was travelling ever further afield for his chairs; when he returned, having tugged and wiggled another one loose from the surrounding stockades of noise and need, he found Keith in mellower mood, hospitably waving a hand in the air.

'Trish like,' said Keith as Trish slowly sat. 'Pint of vodka, is it? Bucket of mephs?' And he started to order drinks, at no point and in no wise neglecting the flurry of ogreish winks and pouts and thumb-upping and triple-ringing with which he primed the hopes and assuaged the fears of the innumerable followers and disciples and other Keith Talent-addicts who had filled the place as thoroughly, it seemed, as they would have filled his own apartment. A home fixture: Keith was playing at home.

'Blimey. We'll have *Kath* in here in a minute. I'm like You fucky Nefner that's who I'm like. I have, I have never made no secret of my, my admiration of the, the female charms. Look at this,' said Keith, turning on Debbee with the hot wind of his stare. 'Miss Debbee Kensit. Sixteen today. On your feet, girl.'

Debbee rose. The black net T-shirt with its lively catch of breasts; the loose white knickers worn, fashionably, outside the tight black shorts; then the two bands of stark flesh before the thick pink tubing of her legwarmers. Debbee's round face was pleasant, more than pleasant, until it fully smiled. The smile did a lot for Debbee: it did things like halving her IQ. And it took you, if you would follow, into a world of gum and bone, of dismay, and childish deals to do with love and pain (though only Keith knew the touch of the terrible tenners left trembling on sideboard and mantelpiece). Guy, who found himself taking comfort from the vivid sprawl of Keith's commitments, had always believed that you had to be thirty-five or forty before you got the face that you deserved. Debbee showed that you could get that face on your sixteenth birthday. But *deserved* didn't come into it; no, not at all.

'Sixteen as such,' Keith was going on. 'Pure as soft-fallen snow. A virgin innit, saving herself for the man of her dreams. Me I never laid a finger on her. No danger. Because she's special. Special. Special to me.'

'How is your finger, Keith?' said Trish. 'How's your poor *finger*?'

'Not thy expect any you old slags to appreciate something like

376

that. Hey! Now now, girls,' he said with a priestly look. 'Now now, ladies.' Around the Marquis of Edenderry loudspeakers were clearing their throats. 'Best behaviour, all right? Don't do it for me. I'm not asking you to do it for me. Do it for darts. Okay? Do it for darts.'

Apart from feeling that she might, at any second, black out from neglect, or even die of it and save everyone the trouble, Nicola considered herself to be usefully placed for the time being, and well prepared, like an athlete or an artist, for a necessary audacity in the play. She sat sunk down into the shape of her chair and her coat with her shoulders combatively flexed, her legs crossed, and one shoe bobbing patiently. Looking from face to face – Debbee, Analiese, Sutra, Petronella, Iqbala, Trish – she felt no jealousy; but rivalry had always roused her. Only Petronella, she had incidentally concluded, would give her any trouble in a fight. Petronella was tall and thin but powerfully well-balanced in the thighs and, most crucially, would be hugely and astonishingly dirty, would go nuclear, in the very first instant. Nicola had always been both gratified and alarmed by how good she was at fighting with women, on the rare occasions when it had come up. She liked women, and women liked her, despite everything. In the past she had had many close girl friends, and one close girlfriend. But in the end there was nothing you could *do* to women (and there was nothing they could do to you). Except you *could* scratch and bite them, you could mark and twist their softness, if the need arose, and Nicola was good at fighting women. She had learned how in a much heavier league, fighting with men . . . It was Keith who worried her. Keith, she decided, was not at his best. She didn't at all mind his talk, his gruesome presence, his antigallantry. The trouble with Keith, tonight, in the Marquis of Edenderry, as elsewhere and at other times, was that he was formless – he had no form. He had gathered women round him or up against him to make an island of non or neg terror, for terrornight. And it hadn't worked out. He was terrified. She could see that he was terrified, pitiably brittle, with a disgraceful bad-stomach recalcitrance in the constant flicker of his face. So Nicola was now looking for a hook (knowing that a hook would be there), to get them through it, something to give him courage and lend form to his chaos. She wasn't going to let him be the louser-up of her reality. However, she didn't feel like talking yet, and was glad when Guy showed he had his uses by asking, with a frown of interest,

'Keith, who are you up against tonight?'

377

'Never ask about an opponent. You play the board, not the man. It's a thing between you and the darts . . . Paul Go.'

'Is he Japanese?'

'I got respect for every man I play.'

'A very determined people.'

'Fucking loansharks,' said Keith, assaying, for once, a racial slur. He could think of nothing worse to say about them, having, for example, barely heard of World War II. Keith's father, who had certainly heard of World War II, and had successfully deserted from it, might have asked if everyone knew the terrible things they did to some of our boys back then; but Keith was reduced to a few half-remembered grumbles from the fillers in his tabloid.

'They got a big yen for big yen. Tokyo Joe, he'll be stuffing his pockets.'

'Yes well they do have their critics.'

'So do I, mate! Oh yeah. I've heard them. They doubt my power. Question mark over my temperament – all this. I'm just a jammy bastard, according to some.' There came the spit and crackle of another announcement, and again Keith's face flickered huntedly. 'Well the shoe'll be on the other foot. I'm going out there to silence the knockers once and for all.'

But Keith stayed where he was, as time kept passing, and despite the general lurch the pub gave towards the streetward side of the arena. The women looked at him from their accustomed state when out on the town with their men: that of more or less frowzy silence. Trish had already gone off and faded away somewhere.

'Better be going to the dressing-room,' said Keith irresolutely. 'Compose my thoughts.' He smashed a palm into his chest and quickly staggered to his feet. A heart attack? No: Keith was feeling for his darts pouch. Brutally he yanked it out. 'It's not a dressing-room, not as such,' he went on, with a shy smile. 'The Gents. They clear the lot of them out. To allow the two contestants to – to compose their thoughts. Okay ladies! Wish me luck!'

The ladies wished him luck, all except Nicola, who excused herself and disappeared in search of the Ladies.

Where does a lady go, in a pullulating pub, if she wants to meet a gent, and enjoy a bit of privacy? Nicola knew the answer. Not the Ladies: you can't have a gent in there. The ladies wouldn't like it. Not the Ladies. The Gents, the Gents – the gents being so much more tolerant and fun-loving in this regard. Ladies aren't supposed to go in the Gents. Only gents are. But this was no lady. Unless she be – unless she be Lady Muckbeth . . .

At first Nicola lingered near the entrance, by the machines. What would they be dispensing these days? Not just cigarettes and condoms, not in here: also hairpieces and prostate-kits and pacemakers. After one last hopeless shout through the doorway the man in the frilly shirt moved off – and Nicola walked in, into the world of white testosterone.

She did so proprietorially. The big youth who came fast out of the stall looked at her and hesitated on his way out, thinking better of washing his hands. She lit a cigarette with detailed calm, and raised her chin for the first inhalation. There were three men in the men's room: Keith, who looked up from dabbing his face at the basin and frowned softly as he caught her eye in the mirror; a haggard milkman bent over the white pouch of a urinal, his forehead pressed to the tiles, weeping and faintly whinnying with pain as he micturated; and Paul Go. It was over to him in his corner she sauntered, to Paul Go, expressionlessly tending his darts, aligning flights, barrels, shafts, points. She stood so close to him that in the end he had to look up.

'Do you speak English?'

He gave a sudden nod.

'And where are you from? Japan, yes – but Honshu, Kyushu, Shikoku?'

'Honshu.'

'Tokyo, Kyoto, Nagoya, Yokohama, Nagasaki?'

'Utsonomiya.'

'What?'

'Utsonomiya.'

'Been with us long, have you Paul? Tell me. Do you know what I mean by Enola Gay?'

He gave a sudden nod.

She stared for a while at the black fluff on his upper lip and then turned her blond fur on him, and said to Keith, 'It's funny, isn't it, darling?'

Keith seemed ready to agree.

'People are always saying that the Japanese are different from us. From you and me. More different. More different than the black. More different than the Jew. More different, even, than that little creature over there.' She indicated the micturating milkman, who wasn't at all offended. Still entirely caught up in his lone drama of self-injury, he had lifted a hand to his tear-stained face, and altered his stance to that of one about to seat himself on a high stool. 'We should surely be able to address the matter in a liberal and inquiring frame of mind. I mean, when all is said and done, just how different from us, spiritually, humanly,' she said, and turned again, '*are* these fucking monkeys?'

Paul Go waited. Then he smiled.

'And now you're showing those teeth that nobody understands.'

The last words were said into a surprising silence, as some fresh disposition established itself in the hall beyond. The man with the frilly shirt had reappeared; and there were other onlookers. Losing no time now, Nicola clicked back across the floor, opening her handbag. She gave Keith a kiss, the Wounded Bird, and carefully wiped his mouth with a paper tissue. Standing back, she considered the whole man, with eyes of love.

'Keith, your shirt! It must have got a little creased in the car!'

She bent to straighten the ridged rayon. She bent lower.

'. . . On your knees, girl,' said Keith calmly.

So that was the necessary: the diaphanous stockings, meeting the other shine on the toilet floor. Nicola knelt. She tugged downwards on the shirt's hem, and wetted a finger to collect some fluff from the vertical stripe of the trousers. She said,

'Win, Keith. Dispose of the challenge of the – the *hibakusha*. Come to me tomorrow. I'll have more money for you . . . You're my god.'

'On your feet, girl.'

Paul Go moved past them. Even the old milkman levered himself free of the urinal and set his course for the door. Keith stayed for a while and looked at her, nodding his head. But she was the last to leave.

Guy patrolled the Marquis of Edenderry, his questing nose out front, the indeterminate mouth with its wince-smile and flinch-grin. The pub, the entire cavern of leather and glass, had been tipped sideways, its contents toppling towards the street, towards the raised dart-board, the trampled oché. All you could see up there was a man in a purple dinner jacket, above the crowd; his voice might not have been the worst voice of all time, but it was certainly the worst voice yet (a nightmare of fruity pomp); with this voice he was saying, 'So I'd like to thank you for kindly thanking us for bringing you this contest here tonight . . .' Guy could see Debbee and – was it? – Petronella standing together on a table, a few feet from the swaying rampart of heads and shoulders. He was afraid he had been rather a dub with Keith's harem; most awkward; they had seemed to look right through him, to look right through his well-enunciated questions about where they lived and what they did; though he did manage to exchange some words with Analiese about the theatre. He craned and flinched and felt the need for Nicola: a childish need, like being lost on some market street, and desperate for one of the bustling mannequins to slow and soften into the kind shape of the loved one. She must be still in the Ladies, Guy thought, as he went to use the Gents.

He couldn't imagine that Nicola would want to watch the whole thing, or even any part of it, so he returned to their table to wait for her there. Others, too, were sitting it out, busy drinking or petting or fighting. He emptied his glass and blinked at the crowd. Then he felt a light touch on his shoulder, and with a forgiving smile he turned to face the authentic ruin of Trish Shirt.

'Whoops! Are you all right?'

She stared into nothing, as he helped her sit; she stared into nothing – or she stared, perhaps, at her own thoughts, at her own insides. Here was a blonde to whom everything that could happen to a blonde had gone ahead and happened. As the darts crowd, the arrowshower, steadily grew in its growling, Trish Shirt said, with infinite difficulty,

'I don't know . . . I don't know what the world's . . . *going* to.'

This remark seemed to Guy about as shocking as any he had ever heard. He watched her carefully. To attempt so little in the way of speech, of response, of expression: and then to fuck *that* up.

'In the *toilet*,' she said.

Guy waited.

'He comes round my owce. Eel bring me . . . booze and that. To my owce. And use me like a toilet.'

'Oh I'm sure not,' said Guy, reflecting that even the word *owce* was an exalted epithet for where Trish lived, if of course Keith's unsympathetic descriptions of the place were to be trusted.

'Keep meself got up like a titmag. In my owce. Case he wants to come round and lam the yell out of me. In me oh *nous*. Where's the respect? Where's the appreciation. Does he . . . does he *talk* about me?'

'Keith?'

'Keith.'

381

She had asked the question with such total abjectness that Guy was at a loss for the right reply. He thought of straw: was this the kind you clutched at, or the kind that broke your back? Keith did in fact talk about Trish frequently, even routinely, as a way of advertizing his movements around town; and he backed up these mentions with as much violent detail as he had inclination or time to transmit. Guy said,

'He talks about you often, and fondly.'

'Keith?'

'Keith.'

'Oh I love him dearly with all my heart,' she said. 'Truly I do.' Her face softened further: a mother watching over a sleeping child. A mother who had been away some time, in an institution. A cracked mother. A mother – alas! – that you wouldn't want *your* child near, with her wrong type of love. 'Go on. What's he say?'

'He says,' said Guy, helplessly but rightly concluding that Trish would believe anything, 'he says that his feeling for you is based on deep affection. And trust.'

'Why then? Why, Keith, why? Why's he rub my nose in it? With her. In the *toilet*.'

'What, *here*? . . . Yes, well, he does behave impulsively at times.'

'On her knees.'

Guy looked up. What he saw made his shins shiver, like the anticipation and recoil he felt at the instant of Marmaduke's half-hourly injuries. Nicola was standing alone on the bar, her arms folded, her shoes held in her right hand, her blond fur coat like a low sun, and supervizing the contest with an expression of inexplicable coldness.

Trish was crying now and Guy took her hand.

'Everything,' she said through her tears, and again with infinite difficulty, 'everything's coming . . . to the dogs.'

And while Trish stared – stared, as it now seemed, into her own eyes – Guy held her hand and watched the crowd: how it bled colour from the enormous room and drew all energy towards itself, forming one triumphal being; how it trembled, then burst or came or died, releasing individuality; and how the champion was borne along on its subsidence, his back slapped, his hair tousled, mimed by female hands and laughing, like the god of mobs.

'So: the fairytale continues,' said Royal Oak's Keith Talent, draining his glass and wiping his mouth with his sleeve. 'Basically the complexion of the match changed in the second leg of the third set.

Recovering from his wayward start, when nothing would go right for the fast-throwing oriental, the little guy from the east was permitted three clear darts at the double 16, the board's prime double. The bigger man could only stand and watch. But his fears proved fleeting, for the young Jap crapped it. Relishing the home fixture, the North Kensington chucker went from strength to strength, stepping in to punish the smaller man, who never recovered from the blow. Yes, the slip cost him dear. After that, no way could he stave off defeat.'

So saying, Keith closed his eyes and yawned. Secretly he was amazed by his voice. Instead of not working at all, which would have been fair enough, his voice was working phenomenally well (though even he was shocked by how deep it had become since the last few drinks). But what authority, what rolling fluency! Keith yawned again: the inhalation, the ragged wail. It was so late now that the Marquis of Edenderry had in fact been shut for almost half an hour; but the party lingered on behind bolted doors, their glasses proudly rebrimmed by the manager, Mike Frame. Keith yawned again. Perhaps he was catching these yawns from his companions (who had had nearly five hours of his post-match analysis). They moaned suddenly and unanimously as Keith said,

'Going for a considerable finish in the nailbiting fourth set, the . . .'

Keith stopped, or paused. He noticed that Trish was asleep, or at any rate not conscious. The women all had their heads bowed, in fatigue, or in the piety of love. Keith felt so happy and proud that his mouth dropped open and these words emerged, as his right hand (with erect darting finger) counted from girl to girl: Debbee, Analiese, Trish, Nicky, Sutra, Petronella, Iqbala . . .

'Eeny meeny miney —'

Nicola sat upright. And Guy stirred. And in the general flurry of missed clues, ungot jokes, Trish Shirt came to with a shout. She left her chair but she didn't straighten: she stood there cocked in a haggard crouch and pointing with her whole arm at Nicola Six.

'You! It's you! Ooh, I saw you. In the Gents. She was down on her fuckin knees in the Gents! For Keith. She was down on her knees in the Gents *sucking his* —'

Keith stepped masterfully forward and hit Trish once on the cheekbone with his closed fist. He stood above her, panting, but the body didn't move. In the near background Mike Frame waited indulgently, jinking his keys.

*

383

'A chapter', said Nicola in the car, 'of epic squalor.'

'Yes. Surprisingly dreadful.'

'When I get home I shall have a scalding shower.'

'Hideous business. I'm sorry. We should have left straight after the match and let them get on with it.'

'You know, when Keith hit the madwoman, that was his idea of being gallant. To me. Like laying his jacket over a puddle.'

'You think?'

'Curious how madness and obscenity go together. Like madness and anti-Semitism. Shakespeare was right. Ophelia . . .'

'Oh yes. A rather sorry Ophelia, I'm afraid.' Guy was still awash with adrenalin and anger, and with confusion about his own response to the Talent enormity. He had felt no fear, only paralysis, as if everything he believed in had been wiped out of existence. Now Guy added to himself, 'Hard to see what to do . . .'

A little later she said, 'I love your tongue. All this kissing.'

'You're frightfully good at it.'

'Beginner's luck.'

They were parked in her dead-end street. She now gave him a series of literary kisses, Maud, and Geraldine, and Eve in the Garden, and (a happy creation) Ophelia Before and After the Death of Polonius. Then she threw in the Grand-a-Night Hooker. She did enough, in any case, she confidently imagined, to rebrim his sobbing boner. Then she reached for her handbag with the last of many sighs.

He said abruptly, 'Your stockings. The knees are both torn.'

'I know. I can't see the point of stockings when they're this sheer. Of course, a pair of good hardy tights is what one really wants. Watch me to the door. Don't get out.'

She climbed from the car and walked to the garden gate. But then she turned and walked back – walking as she would on another night, very soon, to another man in another car. She approached and bent before the driver's window, which Guy smartly lowered. Nicola put her head into the car and gave him the Jewish Princess.

When it was over, Guy involuntarily raised a hand to his mouth. 'That – that was . . .'

'Unforgivable?' said Nicola mysteriously. 'By the way. I'm going to stop teaching Keith.'

'Really?' said Guy lovingly.

'One tries to do what one can. But I've finally put my finger on what I can't bear about him.'

384

Which is?' said Guy, even more lovingly.

'He's so working-class.'

Working-class or not, Ken-Chel's Keith Talent was still abroad. The night was young. Though of humble extraction – the son of a simple criminal – Keith Talent was still very much at large.

He had made, in the heavy Cavalier, a magisterial tour of Greater London: Plaistow for Petronella, Arnos Grove for Sutra, Slough for Analiese (Basil was behaving strangely), then to Ickenham, to get little Debbee home safe and sound. And for a while he sat in her semi, drinking instant coffee and passing the time with her perfectly fanciable mother, who had heard of Keith's victory on the TV (it came in the form of a newsflash, in the middle of a darts match she was already watching) and had stayed up to congratulate him and, of course, to ensure that her little Debbee didn't give Keith one on the house. In no way had Keith neglected his responsibilities to Trish Shirt, personally helping Mike Frame to shove her into the minicab and himself standing there with the cocked twenty, giving the driver full instructions. Nor had he forgotten Iqbala, whom he had left until last, her being a neighbour, and who was now fast asleep (he'd checked) in the boot of the car.

The instant coffee was drunk, the cigarettes smoked, the time passed. A new Keith Talent. The taste of victory is sweet. In the old days Keith and Debs would have slipped away at some point for their little cuddle, Keith later settling with Mrs K. Or he might have waited in the Cavalier, smoking more cigarettes and listening to darts tapes, until Debbee threw a key down from her window, and he'd pop back in for a freebie. But tonight? Well, it was a new Keith Talent they were looking at. And Debbee was special. She cost £85. And he found that he wasn't really bothered one way or the other, now that she was sixteen, a good deal of the magic having gone out of it. No. He gave Mrs Kensit a kiss and a squeeze, and Debbee an even chaster goodnight on the doorstep, and was on his way. In the car he smacked a darts tape into the stereo (the Obbs-Twemlow final: evergreen) and drove to Trish Shirt's.

Twenty minutes later he sat in his garage and smoked twenty cigarettes and drank a bottle of *porno*. Tsk, tsk: bloodstains on his collar. In long but regular intervals, tears of pride dropped on to his lap. Another bockle? Already bit tiggly. That bull finish: right in the miggle. No diggling, but give Debs a lickle cuggle. Quick piggle.

385

From time to time he would stare up at the swimming beauty of the dartboard: the kaleidoscope of every hope and dream. She did it. Nicky did it. Old Nick. Then home, to the chores of love. He walked the wife, burped the dog, and . . . Semiconscious, then, also semi-literate and not even semiskilled, Double-U Eleven's Keith Talent rested his head against the semipermanent cork wall, and thought of semiprecious Nicola, beneath the cold black sky of seminight.

And now under the low sun I go to Kim Talent with a lover's impatience, with a lover's tearing impatience, fearful that the world will die before I meet the searching blaze of her eyes. On the way in the quiet riot of Golborne Road I see three young women walking along together, licking and sucking their fingers. Why? What profane novelty . . . But yes of course. They've been eating french fries, eating chips from the open bag covered in vinegar and salt. And now licking their fingers. Long may they do so. Long may they have the freedom, the fingers, and the lips. With a lover's impatience I shall unbutton her Babygro. With a lover's impatience I shall tear at the sticky tabs of her diaper.

Kim was sleeping. So was Keith, at three in the afternoon. He'd tried getting up; he'd tried the bracing stroll to the Black Cross. And he'd come right back again. His tortured snoring filled the flat. And Kim's sleep too was restless, pain-jabbed, caught up in the baby's passionate, eternal and largely obscure struggle not just to get through being a baby, an infant, a child, a young one, but to deal rawly with the knots and tricks of being. Even a baby knows that death isn't one idea: it is the complex symbol. Baby, what is your problem? Daddy, it's this: the mind-body problem. I asked Kath why she didn't take the chance to go to the shops. I said it forcefully or frantically. The resolute colourlessness of her face told me no, no; but then her eyes closed, and something was decided, something important was decided. And she left us.

387

Got to stop hurting K. With a lover's impatience I woke her. *No good just takeing it out on the Baby.* She cried in confusion and sadness as I unbuttoned her on the living-room floor. With a single wrench I pulled off her diaper . . . What kind of planet is it where you feel relief, where you feel surprise, that a nought-year-old girl is still a virgin? Then I turned her over.

On the right buttock, a bruise, perfectly round and shockingly dark, and grainy, like an X-ray, shining black light on the internal world of cells. On the left buttock, three cigarette burns, in a triangle.

I got up so suddenly that I banged into the standard lamp and if the room had been any bigger I would have fallen over backward right on to the deck. The wall held me up with a blow to the cranium. Showing effort and eagerness, Kim turned herself over, a new skill of hers, and looked up at me from the floor.

'He's been hurting you, hasn't he?'

'. . . Mm. Urs,' she said.

'It's daddy, isn't it.'

'. . . Earse.'

I went down on my knees and said through the sound of his window-rattling snore, 'I'll – I don't know what I'll do. But I'll protect you. Please don't worry. Please. My darling.'

'Please,' I said. 'Do this one big last thing for me. Please.'

Nicola pushed her face forward. 'Christ, I said *okay.*'

'But what good is your guarantee? You're alone. On what can you swear? You don't love anything or anybody.'

'Well you'll just have to take my word for it, won't you. I was going to do something like this anyway. What's the big deal?'

'Just bear with me,' I said. I had toothache in my knee and legache in my mouth and earache in my ass. I nodded. 'Good. So. You'll have Keith move in. Or spend a lot of time here. And make him happy. Until the big night.'

'I won't wake up with him. That's out of the question and is never going to happen. And you realize it'll mean sending Guy away for a while.'

'There go my unities.'

'I rather thought America.'

'America?' I sighed heavily. But we all have to make sacrifices. I took a breath and said, 'Outstanding work, by the way, at the Marquis of Edenderry. You got us out of a tricky situation.' I was there, of course,

388

at the Marquis of Edenderry. I was there. But am I anywhere? I look at my outstretched hand and expect it to disappear, to begin its slow wipe from the screen. I move in and out of things. I am an onlooker in my own dream. I am my own ghost, kissing its fingertips.

Indulgently she said, 'Have you finished your letter to Mark?'

'No. And it's about eight thousand words long.'

'Don't finish it. Or don't post it. Here's a better idea. Post it to yourself. Do you know the Borges story, "The Aleph"? It's very funny about literary envy.' She finished her drink and dashed the empty glass into the fireplace. Typical.

'Is it now?'

Here they come again, the pains. Gather about me, my little ones.

Exquisite *tristesse* on finishing *Crossbone Waters*. I can't think why. It's an awful little piece of shit.

Marius returns from a crepuscular soul-ramble to find Kwango packing his meagre possessions. Ridiculous conversation. Kwango says he will be gone for three moons. Why, O Kwango? The woman is ready. She waits. How, O Kwango, do you know this? How do you know this, O great Kwango? The birds whisper it. I smell it in the waters.

Nor does Kwango speak with forked tongue. Marius hastens to Cornelia's cabin, and gets the lot . . .

Or you infer that he does. Marius goes all posh and manly at this juncture ('Towards morning, I took her again'), with much Kwangoan rambling about water, femininity, ebbings, fluxes. I expected *her* to be manly. I expected her to really strap Marius on. But no: she's a simpering sonnet in the sack.

At any rate the seventy-two-hour debauch concludes with Kwango's return and a brisk voyage back to Samarinda, where Cornelia's seaplane is already bobbing in the harbour. No promises. No regrets. Just one last kiss . . .

I'm devastated. I really *am* falling apart. Why the sighs, why the tears, why the rich and wistful frowns? It's an *awful* little piece of shit.

My last act of love took place ninety days ago.

I ambushed and ravished her. I was frictionless and inexorable. How could she possibly resist me? Burton Else couldn't have handled it better. Kwango himself would have wept with pride.

It was a precision raid. Everything was sweet. On the appointed day I unsmilingly flew from La Guardia to Logan. Then the six-seater to the Cape: how aerodynamically carefree it was, how the baby plane was whisked up on the thermals, out over the boatless water. I looked back with a shrewd glance: Boston at dusk with the sun behind it – heaven's red-light district. We landed with extreme delicacy, as did the old open-prop stratocruiser that was coming down alongside, like a corpulent but thin-shanked lady, skirts raised to toe the moist tarmac. Onward.

Sand spills had closed the thruway. In my hired jeep I ruggedly drove through battened Provincetown, then on past the sign that says Cape Cod Light, and into the woods. Many times I climbed out to untangle the drag of queer growths, the grasp of nameless vines made bitter by their own ugliness, taloned briars, sharp-knuckled twigs, all under a storm of blackfly. Then at last the camp, the unlocked screen door, and Missy Harter on the piano stool, clasping her coffee cup in both hands.

She had come for remembrance, as she did every year: her father, whom she loved, whom I loved, Dan Harter, with his old-guy jeans, his Jim Beam and his Tom Paine. She was perfect for me.

I cried. I laced her coffee with bourbon. I told her I was dying too. I went down on my knees.

How could she possibly resist me?

Last night, as I entered, Nicola gave me her most exalted and veridical smile and said,

'I've reached a decision. God, it's all so clear now. I'm calling the whole thing off.'

'You're what?'

'I'll go away somewhere. Perhaps with Mark. It's simple. Plan B. I'll live.'

'You'll what?'

She laughed musically. 'The look on your face. Oh don't worry. I'm all talk. I'm just a big tease. It's still Plan A. Don't worry. I was just kidding. I was just playing nervous.'

Last night was our last night, in a sense. We both felt it. The world was coming into everything. The room where we now talked, Nicola's habitat, would soon be altered, compromised, as would Keith's, as would Guy's. These places would never be the same again. I said,

'I'm going to miss our talks.'

'There's another thing I've been teasing you about. Of all my recent deceptions, this was the hardest. Technically. I mean keeping a straight face. Pretending to be a virgin is a breeze in comparison. Mark Asprey.'

'Oh yes?'

'His work. His writing.'

'It's . . ?'

'It's *shit*,' she said.

'. . . My heart soars like a hawk.'

What was she wearing? I can't remember. No outfit or disguise of innocence or depravity. Just *clothes*. And she wasn't made-up either; and she wasn't drunk, and she wasn't mad. Very much herself, whatever that was, herself, fraying but shiny like worn velvet, extreme, aromatic, nervous, subtle.

She said, 'How do you feel about me? The truth.'

'The truth?' I got to my feet saying, 'You're a bad dream, baby. I keep thinking I'm going to wake up' – here I snapped my fingers weakly – 'and you'll disappear. You're a nightmare.'

She stood and came toward me. The way her head was inclined made me say at once:

'I can't.'

'You must know that it has to happen.'

'You've come across this. When men can't.'

'Only by design. It's easy: you make yourself leaden. Don't worry. I'll fix it. I'll do it all. Don't even try and think about love. Think about – think about the other thing.'

Later, she said, 'I'm sorry if you're angry with me. Or with yourself.' 'I'm not angry.' 'I suppose you've never done that before.' 'Yes, I did think I might get through life without it.' 'You may surprise yourself further. As Keith says, it's never over until –' 'Until the last dart strikes home.' 'Anyway,' she said, 'this will only happen once.' 'Anyway,' I said, 'I'm mostly grateful. It's made me ready to die.' 'That was my hope.' 'With Mark, what was the –?' 'Hush now . . .'

We put our clothes back on and went out walking, in the dripping alleys, the dark chambers of the elaborately suffering city. We're the dead. Amazing that we can do this. More amazing that we want to. Hand in hand and arm in arm we totter, through communal fantasy and sorrow, through London fields. We're the dead. Above, the sky has a pink tinge to it, the cunning opposite of health, like something bad, something high. As if through a screen of stage smoke you can just make out God's morse or shorthand, the stars arranged in triangles, and saying therefore and because, therefore and because. We're the dead.

Chapter 20: Playing Nervous

ALTHOUGH FOR HIM personally the future looked bright, Keith
was in chronic trouble, as *cheats* and suchlike always were, with
his Compensations.

His caseworker, a Mrs Ovens, was coming down on Keith hard.
Increasingly riskily, he had skipped their last seven appointments;
and the eighth, scheduled for the day after his historic victory at the
Marquis of Edenderry, he had noisily slept through. Now, if he
wasn't careful, he'd be looking at a court appearance and at least the
threat of a mandatory prison term. Keith rang Mrs O. the next day
on his carfone and ate shit in his poshest voice. For a consideration,
John Dark, the iffy filth, would also vouch for Keith's good
character. She gave him one last chance: on the morning of the Final
of the Duoshare Sparrow Masters, if you please. And Keith hated
this like a deformity because it was part of the failure he would soon
be gone from: turbid queues, and the office breath of afternoons, and
a press of difficulty, made of signs and symbols, that never began to
go away.

Keith's Compensations. They really were a torment. Oh, the
things he went through, the suffering he endured. For some people, it
seemed, a fiver a week (split sixteen or seventeen ways) just wasn't
good enough . . . Keith's Compensations represented the money he
paid, or owed, for the injuries he'd meted out during a career that
spanned almost two decades. You'd think that being a child prodigy
in the violence sphere would have its upside Compensationswise,

392

since some of the people you damaged and hurt (and naturally you were always going to be concentrating on the elderly) would be dying off anyway. But oh no: now you had to pay their relatives, or even their mates, so only the lonely forgave their debts, some of them going back twenty years, a crushed nosebridge here, a mangled earhole there, every one of them linked to double-digit inflation and continued-distress upgrade and spiralling medical costs and no end of a fucking pain all round.

'Is it your Compensations, Keith?' said Kath, as Keith replaced the carfone.

'I'll give you a Compensation in a minute.'

Thoroughly out of sorts, Keith was taking Kath to the hospital for her tube trouble, the ambulance service having been discontinued in their area for the foreseeable future. It was the first time since their marriage that Kath had been in Keith's car.

'What's that noise?' Kath asked, and looked more closely at the sleeping baby on her lap. 'Whimpering.'

Keith wrenched his head round to check on Clive; but the great dog was silent.

'And banging.'

Now Keith remembered – and scolded himself for not remembering sooner. Quickly he thumped a darts tape into the stereo and turned it up loud. 'It's the next *car*,' he said. They were in a traffic jam, and there were certainly plenty of other cars near by, and no shortage of banging and whimpering. 'All this *congestion*,' said Keith.

He dropped Kath and the baby at the gates of St Mary's. Then he drove round the first corner, pulled up, and got out. Preparing himself for yet more reproaches from the female end of things (even Trish would be having a go at him later), Keith longsufferingly let Iqbala out of the boot of the car.

'Lady Barnaby,' said Hope. 'Oh that's awful.'

'What?'

'She's dead.'

'How did you –?' said Guy, lengthening his neck towards her.

'There's an invite here to her funeral or whatever.'

'How frightful,' said Guy.

They were having a late breakfast in the kitchen. Also present were Melba, Phoenix, Maria, Hjordis, Auxiliadora, Dominique and Marie-Claire. Also Lizzyboo, bent over her muffins. Also Marmaduke: having spent a lot of time noisily daubing his breakfast all over the table, he was now quietly eating his paint set.

'Oh I suppose we can get out of it,' said Hope.

'I think we ought to go.'

'What for? We don't care about her friends and relatives, supposing she has any. We never cared about her, much, and now she's dead.'

'Show respect.' Guy finished his bowl of Human Shit and said, 'I thought I might go in.' He meant the office, the City. Or that's what he would have meant if he hadn't been lying.

'Trading has resumed?'

'Not yet,' he said. 'But Richard says it looks hopeful.' This was also untrue. On the contrary, Richard had said that it didn't look hopeful at all . . . Guy felt that he had just about reached the end of his capacity to inquire into contemporary history, into What Was Going On. He kept postponing that call to his contact at Index, somehow, to ask what the chances were that this time next week he would be folding his only child into a binliner. People were avoiding, avoiding. He cast an eye over Hope's mail: the goodbye to Lady Barnaby was all that was being offered in the way of social life, on which there seemed to be a merciful moratorium. But Richard, unmarried, childless – he loved nobody – was a mine of unspeakable information. That at the moment of full eclipse on November 5, as the Chancellor made his speech in Bonn, two very big and very dirty nuclear weapons would be detonated, one over the Palace of Culture in Warsaw, one over Marble Arch. That until the cease of the flow of fissionable materials from Baghdad, the Israelis would be targeting Kiev. That the President's wife was already dead. That the confluence of perihelion and syzygy would levitate the oceans. That the sky was falling –

Guy got up to go. As he drained his coffee cup he allowed himself a disbelieving stare at Lizzyboo, who was now addressing herself to the remains of Marmaduke's porridge. The bent head, and the motionless bulk of the shoulders beneath the dark blue smock, sent out a contradictory message: the self within was shrinking, even as the body billowed. And not long ago, only the other day, in her tennis wear . . .

Hope said, 'Before you go would you do the garbage and bring the wood in, and do the water-softener, and check the tank. And bring the wine down. And call the glazier. And the garage.'

The telephone rang. Guy crossed the room and picked it up. A brutish silence, followed by a brutish phoneme – some exotic greeting or Christian name, perhaps. Then the dialling tone.

'Wrong number.'

'All these wrong numbers,' said Hope. 'I've never *known* there be so many wrong numbers. From all over the world. We live in a time', she said, 'of wrong numbers.'

Nicola, who loved nobody, who was always alone, stared at the washing-up that lay there formlessly, awaiting resuscitation, awaiting form; dead and dirty now, the cups and saucers and glasses needed clean water, green liquid, brush, rag, and her gloved fingers, and then their pretty redeployment on the dresser's shelves. Excitingly, it was getting to the point where a teacup, say, could be used and put aside, unwashed (or thrown away, or shattered) – used for the very last time. Items of clothing could be similarly discarded. No more shampoo need be purchased now, no more soap, no more tampons. Of course she had plenty of money for luxuries and non-essentials; she had plenty of disposable income. And, in these last days, she would certainly give her credit cards a fearful ratcheting. The week before, her dentist and gynaecologist, or their secretaries, had coincidentally called, to confirm routine appointments, for scaling, smearing. She had fixed the dates but made no move for her diary . . . Now Nicola rolled up her sleeves and did the dishes for the last time.

Soon afterwards, as she was changing, the telephone rang. Nicola had had several such calls: a loan company, wanting to help her with her lease, which had just expired. She didn't care because she had a month's grace; and a month's grace was more grace than she would ever need. She heard the man out. Her lease could be renewed, with their help, he said, for up to a thousand years.

A thousand years. The loan company was ready, was eager, to underwrite a millennium. Hitlerian hubris. From what she knew about events in the Middle East, from what she gathered from what remained of the independent press (contorted comment, speculation), it seemed possible to argue that Hitler was still running the century – Hitler, the great bereaver. Although they were entering November now, there was still time for him to reap exponential murder. Because what he had done you could do a thousandfold in the space of half an afternoon.

Was she nervous? Without question it would be disagreeable, at this late date, to be upstaged by a holocaust. If history, if current affairs were to reach a climax on November 5 during the full eclipse, then her own little drama, scheduled for the early minutes of the following day, would have no bite, no content – and absolutely no form. And no audience. No undivided attention. On the other hand, you wouldn't want to miss that either, the big event. I identify with the planet, thought Nicola, with a nod, as she started getting dressed. I know just how it feels. They say that everything wants to persist in its being. You know: even sand wants to go on being sand. I don't believe that. Some things want to live, and some things don't.

As she clothed them she consulted her breasts, which told her that the big event wouldn't happen, and that the little one would.

'It is thought by some', read Keith,

> that the secret of Stonehenge lies in darts. The circular stone ruins are shaped in a circle, like a dartboard. This may explain a mystery that has puzzled historians for literally ages. For Stonehenge goes back to 1500BC.

1500BC! thought Keith.

> What is a definite historical fact is that early English cavemen played a form of darts. This is definite from certain markings on the cave walls, thought to resemble a dartboard. Many top darters believe that darts skill goes back to cavemen times. The top caveman would be the guy who brought back the meat every time, employing his darts skills. So in a way, everything goes back to darts. If you think about it, the whole world is darts.

No matter how many times he pondered it, this passage never failed to bring a tear to Keith's eye. It entirely vindicated him. And Keith's plump teardrop might have contained tenderness as well as pride. The whole world was darts: well, maybe. But the whole world – on certain screens, in certain contingency plans – was definitely a dartboard. Keith bent open his notebook and slowly wrote:

> Remember you are a machine. Delivring the dart the same way every time.

While he was actually plagiarizing an earlier passage from *Darts: Master the Discipline*, Keith was also originalizing it in his inimitable way.

> Clear ideas from your head. You do'nt want nothing in your fukcing head.

396

Now he contemplated that last sentence with the stern eye of the true perfectionist. He crossed out *fukcing* and put in *fucking*. An observer might have wondered why Keith took the trouble to make these deletions and insertions. Why correct, O Keith, when the words are for your eyes only? But someone watches over us when we write. Mother. Teacher. Shakespeare. God.

Oy! Ooh. That itch again. That abdominal vacuum. Chronic, innit. And suddenly, in one fell swoop, all his women had disappeared: just like that. Petronella had gone to Southend with her husband, Clint, on their honeymoon. Analiese was back in Slough (and the M4 traffic you just wouldn't believe). Debbee was sixteen. Iqbala, following her misadventure in the Cavalier, wasn't talking to Keith, or indeed to anybody else. And Sutra (Sutra!) had levered herself back into the world from which she had so surprisingly emerged: hurry, hunger, seen through window and windscreen – other women, more women, women found and unfound, and Keith up above, multiform, like a murder of crows, saying *caw, caw, caw* . . . Which left Trish. And he wasn't going round *there* again, no danger, after this morning and the state she was in. About an hour ago, at noon, he had popped into Nick's for a video. But Nick's videos, Keith decided, were like Chinese meals. As for Nicola herself, on this side of the screen, Nicola in the flesh, the mysterious flesh, with dark-adapted eye and unaccustomed lips, and the way she filled her dresses, Keith was neither patient nor impatient: even sitting next to you with thighs touching she was both near and far, like TV.

The telephone rang. As Keith crossed the garage to answer it, he was firmly of the opinion that success had not changed him.

'Keith Talent? Hello there. Good afternoon there. Tony de Taunton, executive producer. *Dartworld.*'

Oh yeah: Marquis of Edenderry . . . *Dartworld*? *Dartworld*!

'Congratulations,' said Tony de Taunton. 'Sterling effort there the other night. Smashing effort. Tight thing.' With terrible candour he went on, 'You were all over the shop there for a while. And with Paul Go *well* out of form I thought, Hello. Dear oh dear. Blimey. It's going to be one of those nights. But you seemed to take heart there, with likkle Paulie throwing such crap. In the end, it was your character got you through.'

'Yeah cheers.'

'Now you watch the show don't you Keith.'

'Consistently,' said Keith fiercely.

'Right. Now with finals and celebrity challenges we do a short docu on the participants. You've seen them. Couple of minutes each. So we want to do you, Keith.'

Keith smiled cannily, unfoolably. '. . . But that's TV,' he said.

'Right. Like they say. You know: your lifestyle.'

'Kind of like a lifestyle feature.'

'You've seen them. Where you live, where you work, hobbies, family, interests: all this. Your lifestyle.'

Keith looked up: the stinking ruin of the garage. Tony de Taunton asked if they could start tomorrow and Keith said that they could.

'Address?'

Keith gave it helplessly. The wife, the dog, the joke flat.

'Smashing. See you there then. Goodbye there.'

Keith's face was all poll tax and means test as he dialled Nicola with shimmering fingers.

'Don't worry. Wait a while, and then try again,' said Nicola, and replaced the receiver. Then she put her hand back where it was before. 'My God. It's harder than the telephone. That was a wrong number. Another wrong number. It is. Even through this rather heavy tweed, it's harder than the telephone. It is. This isn't in nature, surely.'

Guy's face was trying to look pleasant; but its expression was unmistakably strained.

'Do other men become as hard as this?'

'Oh I expect so,' said Guy croakily. 'In the right circumstances.'

'Takes a bit of getting used to. I've been consulting my fiction shelves, without much luck. It seems to be the nature of the subject that the writer assumes a general stock of knowledge and procedure from which his characters subtly diverge. In code, usually. No help to me, I'm afraid.'

'Well this, after all,' said Guy (his head was tilted slightly), 'is definitely non-fiction.'

'Now what? . . . The idea is, I suppose, to move the outer skin very gently against the inner. This tweed doesn't chafe you, does it? I imagine you've got pants on too or something? . . . And of course there are all these arrangements further down. Do they play a part? I suppose stroked or squeezed they might – Guy. Guy! What a ghastly face you just made!'

He tried to speak, reassuringly.

'What? Is it painful or something?'

'A little,' he mouthed.

'I don't understand. I thought it was meant to be *nice*.'

Guy did some explaining.

'Oh, darling! Sweetheart. You should have *said*. Oh it's too pathetic of me. Well let's . . . I'll . . .' She reached for his belt buckle. Then her long fingers paused and she smiled up at him self-deprecatingly. 'I've just thought of something. It's – it's sort of a game. I think it'll do the trick. And I'll try something really daring. Guy?'

'Yes?'

'You couldn't just leave me alone for a little while first, could you? Half an hour or something.' Again the smile of childish challenge. 'To screw my courage to the sticking place?'

He said 'Of course' so sweetly that she had a mind to cup his narrow cheeks in her hands and tell him how many, many, many men had written their names in come all over her stomach and breasts and face and hair. What signing sessions. What autograph hounds . . . But all she said was, before she let him out, 'You know, you make me so happy sometimes that I think I must be going to die. As if just to go on living were really too much to ask . . .'

In the market street he kept seeing piles of shoes, piles of hats, vastly tumbled, piles of handbags, piles of belts. Woundedly he walked, with a thumping in the drool-damaged ear. Guess who'd been there, when Guy arrived at Nicola's? Keith. Keith was on his way out. Keith was just picking up his things: while he finished doing so, Guy had been obliged to wait on the porch, shielding his eyes as he searched for the Cavalier under the low sun. The two men passed at the front door; Keith was looking fantastically washed-out but otherwise seemed very pleased with himself, justifiably, some might say, after his recent efforts at the Marquis of Edenderry. It was as unlikely as anything could be, Guy thought: but if he was being deceived, well, then it was quite a deception; and if Nicola and Keith were lovers, then it was some love. Goats and monkeys! Now a San Marco of pigeons pattern-ed the street like iron filings drawn by the little boy's magnet. At the crossroads one pigeon in particular was eating pizza, and wanting more pizza, and risking pizzafication itself as a lorry loomed near.

Perverse and unchallengeable hunger attacked him. He entered the first food outlet he could find, a potato restaurant called the Tate or Tatties or was it Potato Love? The queue or flock was populous but swiftly flowing. At its head sat a Spanish girl in a steel pen. She took the laden paper plates from the hatch behind her and split each spud with a dab of marge or cheddar or hexachlorophene. Then she passed it through the Microsecond: and that's how long it took – half a pulse. Guy knew that the device used TiredLight, that adaptable technology. The food just goes on cooking, on your plate, in your mouth, in your guts. Even beneath the streets.

'Thank you,' he said, and paid the amount that was asked.

The girl was coarsely beautiful. But she probably wouldn't be that way for very long. There was the evidence of the mother, operating out of the hatch and framed in it like someone on a primitive TV set. But this was no cookery programme. It was about what kitchens tended to do to the female idea. And the daughter would get there quicker than the mother had, because the modern devices saved time but also used it up – sucked time out of the very air . . . Guy collected his plastic utensils and looked round for a stool. With difficulty he half-seated himself (that's better), and carefully parted the loose lips of his potato. Its core sizzled, smokelessly bubbling with TiredLight, but its surface was icy to the touch. He shuffled back to the penned girl.

'This potato', he said listlessly, 'is undernuked.'

Half a pulse later and it was dropped back on to his plate like a spent cartridge. Now it was overnuked. And suddenly ancient. Guy looked at the potato and then looked at the girl. With a pale smile he asked, 'Do you really expect me to eat this?' She just raised her eyebrows and inclined her head, as if to say that she had seen people eat worse. He left it there on the counter and walked back to Nicola. And on his way down the market street he kept seeing those heaps of gloves and hats and handbags, little shoes. And what was that supposed to remind you of? Guy thought he kept seeing heaps of glasses, heaps of hair.

'Now it's really a very simple game,' she began. 'And completely juvenile, of course. I learned it from some of the brassier girls at the children's home, years and years ago. It's called *dare*. It's also known as *nervous*. I believe it's played all over the world, as such things usually are. Playing *nervous*.'

'Don't know it. What happens?'

She laughed rosily. 'Not a great deal. You put your hand on my throat, say, and let it descend until I say *nervous*. Or on my knee. Or I put my hand on your tummy and move it slowly downwards.'

'Until I say *nervous*?'

'Or until *I* say *nervous*. Shall we play? I suppose,' she said, revealing the white strap of her brassière beneath her shirt and producing a blush, 'I suppose it would be fairer if I took this off. Turn away.'

400

Guy turned away. Nicola stood, unbuttoning her shirt. Leaning forward, she unhooked herself and slowly released the brocaded cups. She gave a special smile.

Next door, wearing Y-fronts, earphones, and a frogged smoking-jacket she had recently bought him, Keith lay slumped on Nicola's bed. He was watching the proceedings on the small screen. His peepers bulged. His kisser furled into a collusive sneer. Nicola rebuttoned briskly, to the top, to the brim of the brimming throat. Keith was shocked. He had always suspected that when Guy and Nicola were alone together they just talked about poetry. Keith shrugged limply.

'Jesus, some mothers,' he murmured to himself.

And so they played *nervous, nervous, nervous*. Nicola played *nervous*, though she wasn't nervous (she was playing), and Guy played *nervous*, though he wasn't playing (he was nervous). 'Undo the top button. And the next. Wait. . . *Nervous*. No, go on . . . Not *nervous*. You can kiss them.' And there they were, so close together, in fearful symmetry. Guy dipped his lips to them. What could you say about *this* breast. Only that it was just like *that* breast. Why compare them to anything but each other?

Hello, boys, thought Keith. Nice bouncers she got. Pity a bit on the small side. Still you lose respect after a while for the bigger tit. Good laugh at first. Now Analiese . . . He wiped his sniffer.

With blips and bleeps and scans and sweeps their hands moved up their thighs. His fingers reached the stocking tops and their explosion of female flesh. ('*Nervous!*' she sang.) Hers were warm and heavy as they moved in beneath his belt.

'*Nervous?*' she asked.

'. . . No,' he said, though he was. 'But *I* am,' she said, though she wasn't. 'But I'm not,' he said, though he was.

Working him up to a fever pitch innit, thought Keith. He made a liquid sound with his gnashers. Nervous? He'll be a fucking nutter in a minute. Here –

'Does it feel as it should feel?' she was asking.

'Yes very much so.'

Keith felt the soft arrival of sweat on the palms of his feelers. He looked away for a moment, as if in pain. Then he felt a lash of panic that almost flipped him on to the floor as Nicola said,

'Quick. Let's go to the bedroom.'

With a great jerk Keith struggled himself upright. He paused: it's okay. He lay back again, listening to his steadying ticker and Nicola saying,

'No – here – now. Stand up. All these buttons. It seems to . . . I'll have to . . .'

'Oof,' said Keith. He whistled hoarsely, and those blue gawpers filled with all their light. Blimey. No, you don't – you don't do that. Not. To a guy. You don't, he thought, as his flipper reached down for his chopper. You don't do that to a guy.

'Lie down. And close your eyes.'

So Keith saw it all and Guy saw nothing. But Guy felt it. Guy did all the feeling. He felt the hands, the odd trail of hair, the hot and recklessly expert sluicings of the mouth. And other strange matters. A suspicion (a fleeting treachery) that now, after this, he could be free and safe and home, the fever passed, and her forgotten, and the long life waiting with child and Hope. But then too there were consequences: immediate consequences (the male animal, never lost from thought). Soon, and with embarrassing copiousness . . . he might drown her. He might drown them both. Physical fear was never wholly absent in his intimate dealings here down the dead-end street, down the dead-end street with the mad beauty, when she was taken by sexual surprise. He held her head. The world was dying anyway. Towards the end, which never came, he said help-lessly,

'I'm . . . I'm . . .'

Then something happened – something tiny in the layered swell-ings. '*Enough*,' he said, and pulled her clear from the struggle, and at last was lost from thought.

She was kissing his eyes. He blinked out at her.

'You sort of fainted,' she said. 'Are you all right? You sort of fainted.'

He looked down. It was all right. He hadn't made a mess of things.

'You sort of fainted,' she said again. 'Oh, I see I've made another mess of things.'

'No no – it was heavenly.'

As she was showing him out, or, rather, helping him to the stairs (he had an eczema seminar to attend), she held him back and said,

'You know, you needn't have stopped. I was prepared – for your swoon to death,' she quoted prettily, though she thought she had timed it beautifully – that tiny reminder of her teeth. 'I mean the other swoon. In fact I was longing for you to fill my mouth. Because I'm prepared for everything now. I want you to make me,' she said, and gave him the Grand-A-Night Hooker. 'There's only one thing you'll have to do first.'

Guy wiped his dripping chin and said, 'What's that? Leave my wife?'

She started back. How could he be so wide of the mark? How could you! Guy had begun to apologize for his flippancy when she said,

'Oh no. I don't want you to leave her. What kind of person do you think I am?' And this was asked, not in reproach, but in a spirit of pure inquiry. 'I don't want you to leave her. I just want you to tell her.'

In the bedroom Keith was taking the liberty of savouring a well-earned cigarette. Technically, smoking was banned in the bedroom, although Nicola, a heavy smoker, smoked heavily in the bedroom all the time. Now she stood leaning on the door frame with her arms folded.

'Smoking-jacket innit.'

She gave him a slow appraisal, one of fascinated, inch-by-inch detestation, from the feet (red-soled and faintly quivering) to the face, which looked ruminative, grand, prime-ministerial.

'That smoking-jacket looks great on you, Keith. And you look great in *it*.'

'Yeah cheers.'

'I do hope you're not going to be spooked by this TV business,' she said, and watched his face instantly collapse. Keith's tongue now seemed to be trying to sort things out inside his mouth. 'Isn't this what you've worked for? What we've worked for? Well, Keith?'

'Invasion of privacy like.'

'Or darts stardom . . . TV isn't true, Keith, as you've just seen. Or not necessarily so. Darling, you must put all this out of your mind and leave everything to me. Let me translate you. I'll not fail you, Keith. You know that.'

'I appreciate it.'

'I've made a new video for you. But in a sense you've already seen one. And I can tell by the mischievous expression on your face that you – that you did it already.'

'Yeah,' said Keith perplexedly, averting his eyes. 'I did it already.'

Keith came down the passage and out through the front door whistling 'Welcome to My World'. As he passed he happened to glance at her name on the bell. 6: six. Six. 6! thought Keith. Double 3! . . . Nasty, that. Worst double on the board. Never go near it less you've fucked double 12 and then come inside on double 6. Murder.

3's the double all the darters dread. Right down the bottom like that, at six o'clock, you're sort of *dropping* it in. And if you come inside it's 1, double 1. Pressure darts. Old Nick. Double 3. 6. 6. 6. Nasty, that. Very nasty. Ooh wicked . . .

An old woman with hair like coconut fibre limped past whipping herself with a home-made switch. For a moment Keith stood there listening to or at any rate hearing the cries of the city, like the cries of dogs or babies, answering, pre-verbal, the inheritors of the millennium, awaiting their inheritance.

In tortoiseshell spectacles and grey silk dressing-gown Guy knelt poised over the Novac, his long back curved in a perfect semicircle, like a protractor, his curious nose inches from the board (this difficult position seemed to ease his nether pain, his tubed heart, which hurt a lot all the time): six moves in and he was only one pawn down, and half-expecting to survive into what used to be called the middle game. He wanted to survive as long as possible, because when he lost he would have to go to Hope with the truth.

Every few minutes without turning round Guy would take a wrapped toy from the straw tub and toss it back over his shoulder to Marmaduke. Thus, before he could wreck it, Marmaduke first had to unwrap it, and this took him a little while. Guy could hear his snarled breathing and the tear of paper; then the grunts of effort as the toy began to snap and give.

One of the troubles was that chess was over, chess was dead. The World Champion would now have no chance against Guy's Novac, which cost £145. As a human construct chess had challenged computers for a creditable period; but not any more. Once a useful sparring partner, chess now jumped off the stool, snorting and ducking in its trunks, and was explosively decked in the very first round. Games *between* the computers were unfollowably oblique and long-armed, a knight's jump away from human understanding, with all the pieces continually realigning on the first rank (as if there were an infinity of previous ranks, the minus one, the minus two, the minus nth rank), invariably drawing through elaborate move-repetition after many days, with hardly a piece being captured. When programmed for win-only the computers played like suicides . . . Guy's nose twitched as he saw that one of Novac's bishops was unprotected. This wasn't unusual: it was always lobbing minor pieces at him, and even the computer Queen was

404

regularly *en prise*. He could capture, but then what? He captured. Novac replied sharply.

'Yes. Brilliant,' Guy whispered.

Four moves later (how pitiless the silicon was) he stared blinking at his wedged king. At that moment Marmaduke, who must have held his breath as he approached, sank his teeth into the Achilles tendon of Guy's right heel. And by the time his wits returned the child had forced the busby end of a toy guardsman down his own throat and was turning an ominous colour as he fell backwards on to a bulky personnel-carrier. Luckily Petra was near by, as well as Hjordis, and together they were able (Marie-Claire was also at hand) to straighten things out with Paquita's help and the ever-calming presence of Melba and Phoenix.

Guy showered, and swabbed and dressed his heel. Later, in the kitchen, he inspected the guarantees on the lamb cutlets – the staggered dates, the fine print – and readied them for the grill. 'It must be true, all that,' he said to the room in general, 'you know, about food and love. Have you come across the idea?' He waited, with his back turned. 'When food gets too far from love . . . The preparation of food has to do with love. Mother's milk. And when food gets too far from love there's a breakdown, like a breakdown in communication. And we all get sick. When it gets too far from love.' He looked over his shoulder. The sisters were listening, Lizzyboo with full attention (she had even stopped eating), Hope with patient suspicion. As Guy addressed himself to the cooker he felt his wife's eyes busying themselves on the breadth of his back, on his hair, on the very prickles of his neck. How strong were their scrutiny and grip? What held them? With a few bags of pitta bread and an institutional tub of taramasalata, Lizzyboo repaired to her room. Now was the time: the time was now. Guy felt powers move in him but his face, with its rinsed blue eyes, looked especially weak – the weakness that was inevitable in him, the weakness he weakly cleaved to. How beautiful the truth is, he was thinking. Because it never goes away. Because it's always there, just the same, whatever you try to do to it. Hope was talking to him intermittently about various chores he hadn't done (domestic, social, fiscal); during her next breather he said intelligently, with his back aimed at her,

'I've got something to say.' And already he was on the other side. 'It'll sound more dramatic than it really is, I expect. I think you've got something to say too.' Here he turned. Here, of course, he was about to

405

introduce the gravamen that Nicola herself had recently stressed: the fact that Hope had, 'rather sordidly', taken a lover in Dink. But one look at the solar hatred in Hope's eyes and Guy thought: poor Dink! He's gone – he was never here. He's been unpersoned. He isn't even history. 'I mean, for quite a long time it seems to me there's been a need to . . . redefine our . . . All I'm proposing really is an adjustment. And I do think it's important, very important, vital, really, to be as honest as one can be. And I don't see why we can't just work this out like two reasonable human beings. With the minimum of disruptions all round. There's someone else.'

Guy experienced a certain amount of difficulty, as he checked into the hotel on the Bayswater Road. It was the fifth hotel he had tried. Although the injuries to his face would turn out to be mainly superficial, he must have cut an unreassuring (and unprosperous) figure at the reception desk, with his fat lip, swelling eye, and the dramatic lateral gash across his forehead. Then, too, the top five buttons of his steaming, rain-soaked shirt were missing; and all he had in the way of luggage was a plastic bag with a bit of wet Y-front hanging over the brim of it. But finally his osmium credit card prevailed.

In his room he cleaned himself up and called Nicola. There was no answer. He unpacked his belongings – two shirts and the few undergarments he had managed to pick up off the front lawn – and tried again. No answer: not even her disembodied voice, on the soft machine. He went out and plunged through the cabless streets, through the diagonal arrowshowers of reeking rain, through the desperate maelstroms of Queensway and Westbourne Grove: the inspired hordes of the poor. He splashed his way up the dead-end street and climbed her porch and rang her bell and then leaned on it. There was no answer. In the bright heat of the Black Cross he drank brandy, and talked to Dean and Fucker, who informed him that Keith was on the town up west with his sugarmummy, a dark bitch called Nick who gave him cash gifts and who, moreover to recommend her, could suck a lawnmower through thirty feet of garden hose. Guy heard them out with heavily rattled scepticism, and returned to her door, where he remained for the next two hours.

. . . On his way back to the hotel he went past Lansdowne Crescent. It seemed to him that the house, his house, was already unbearably lit, from within, like a house of death, a house where a child had chillingly died. On the other hand he found two drenched pairs of socks in the rosebed, and all his silk ties. He stopped in Queensway and purchased toiletries at the all-night chemist. Again he had some pleading to do at the reception desk before they delivered up his key. He called her, and went on calling, in between trips to the minibar. No answer. And there's nothing to be done when people can't be reached. When there is no answer, no answer.

Bright and early next morning (you got to be quick) Keith stood flapping his arms on the stone stairway to Windsor House.

Jesus, talk about a night out: dinner at the Pink Tuxedo, drinks in the Hilton, the special club with the models up on the ramp, and then back to her place for a couple of videos, to round the evening off. Keith spared a bitter thought for Guy, who had tarnished this last chapter with his incessant phoning. Still. Now Keith removed the souvenir menu from his inside pocket: he'd had *faisan à la mode de champagne* or some such nonsense. Refused the wine, mind, and stuck with lager. Can't go far wrong with lager. Lager's *kegged*. All the same, Keith wasn't fully convinced that rich food agreed with him; his suspicion rested on the five-hour visit he had made to the bathroom on his return. At such times you really felt the inconvenience of so compact an apartment. In that kind of spot, in that kind of groaning extremity, the last thing a man wants to hear is the wife and kid scuttling about and creating all night long.

A chauffeur-driven two-door saloon pulled up, followed by a van marked with the famed darts logo. Slightly dizzy from his first cigarette of the day enjoyed in an upright posture, Keith stepped forward to greet Tony de Taunton, executive producer, and Ned von Newton, the man with the mike himself. Shaking his head, Keith contemplated Ned von Newton, for a moment unable to believe his eyes. Ned von Newton. Mr Darts.

'A true honour,' said Keith. 'Listen, lads: slight change of plan.'

'We got the address right, didn't we Keith?' asked Tony de Taunton, lifting his rippled face to the tower block, which burned in the low sun as if at every moment all its glass were being hammered out of the clear sky.

'Moved, innit. Why don't I lead the way in the Cavalier?'

We can't stop. She can't stop.

Oh the dolorology of my face, with pains moving into positions like sentries, like soldiers who hate my life. This nuked feeling, the kind of ache you get from a vaccination – when the syringe is six feet long. And not in the arm or the ass. In the head, the head. The pain can't stop.

Christ, even that prick of a wasp prospecting for dust on the glass of the half-open window . . . It waddles up the pane, then drops and heavily hovers, then climbs again, and won't fly clear. Getting in and out of windows ought to be one of its main skills. What else is it any good at, apart from stinging people when it's scared? Just as the pigeon that Guy saw, that I saw, that we all see, faces a narrow repertoire of decisions: to go for pizza *now*, and risk becoming pizza itself, or flap uglily in the air for a second or two and go for the pizza *then*.

I find I have spent the last ten minutes looking out of the window, watching a twelve-year-old boy wearily stealing a car. While he accomplished this, a very old man limped by in running-shoes. It wasn't my car. It wasn't Mark's car. He phones me to say that he is coming over for a party on Guy Fawkes Night, or Bonfire Night as he calls it. He is full of praise for the Concorde. I'm not to worry – he'll find a warm bed elsewhere; but maybe we'll meet. After last night, I don't hate him any more. I can feel some new emotion waiting to form. What? Asprey asks if I enjoyed *Crossbone Waters*. I lied, and said I didn't. The book gave rise to some enjoyable scandal, he tells me: there's something about it among the magazines on his bathroom floor . . . This morning, Incarnacion came. Rather than sit around listening to her, rather than sit about listening to Incarnacion murdering the human experience, I went out. But I soon came back. Too many people denying themselves the pleasure, or sparing themselves the bother, of beating me up. When I see the fights I resolve to be incredibly polite to big young strong people. Incarnacion was in the study. She seemed to be looking at my notebook. Another thing. The toaster-like photocopier – I thought it didn't work, but there it was with its light on. It hummed warmly . . . Sometimes (I don't know) I take a knight's jump out of my head and I think I'm in a book written by somebody else.

The wasp is gone. But not out the window. I can hear it bumping into things. It'll be back. It will turn toward me. Insects and death always turn toward you. Gesture them away, and they turn toward you. All the awful things in the end turn toward you.

Now here's a revelation.

Dink doesn't do it. Lizzyboo told me. I wormed it out of her at Fatty's. I plied her with fudge sundaes and creme brulées until she finally came across. The food is sweet like chainstore romance, like happy-ever-after. The food is yuck. She hates what she's doing to herself but she can't stop, can't stop. (Nobody can. I can't.) Tears run down her cheek – sauce runs down her chin. We must have looked like the couple in the postcard joke. In the seaside café. Jack Sprat would eat no fat. Which is the cruel one?

Dink doesn't do it. Dink didn't do it to Lizzyboo and he hasn't done it to Hope either: so Hope's clean, more or less (though I won't use it. I don't need it). Dink'll roll around and everything, and neck and pet. You can see him in the nude if you really insist. But he doesn't do it. He fears for his tennis – his rollover backhands, his whorfing smashes. Dink hasn't come for thirteen years. And the hairy bastard is still only the world ninety-nine.

There's also the fatal-disease consideration. If Dink caught one of *them*, he'd stop being the world ninety-nine. And start being the world five-and-a-half billion. Dink's smart. Dink's hip. He knows that dead men don't play tennis. That's how come he has this rule.

The poor sisters, surrounded by these dud males with these dud rules. Even masturbation is too many for them. Guy, Dink; and now

I'm at it. Yes, I've quit too. Actually I have nothing against the activity. I always thought I'd babywalk into the bathroom with my pants around my ankles *maybe just one more time*. But recently, with these new lesions on my hands and everything, I've put all that behind me. I'm frightened of catching a venereal disease from myself. Is this a first? And why do *I* care?

Kath claims that Keith is cheerful around the house, when he's there. But not quite cheerful enough, evidently, to refrain from giving her a new bruise on her chin. All the women in the street suddenly seem black and blue and scarlet – violet eyes, crimson lips. Some of these cruelty instructions come from upstairs. Cruelty is being delegated.

$E=mc^2$ is a nice equation. But what is the theodicy of uranium? Ferocious physics. And the everyday medium-sized New-tonian stuff, the deckchair and map-folding and meter-feeding physics of ordinary life: all that has it in for you too. Babies are finding out about physics the whole time (how they slip and stagger) in their school of hard knocks.

A new bruise also on the little ass with its precocious nobility of curve, and three new cigarette burns, again in a triangle. The left buttock said *therefore*; the right buttock says *because*. I try, but I can't see Keith doing this. His eyes lit by the cigarette's coal.

It must be like an addiction, and addiction I can understand – as I surf on the crest of something irresistible and unholy. The heavy calm the ungratified addict feels, awaking to the sound of the voice that says today will be the day: the day of indulgence and an end to struggle – pleasureday. And the morning will pass so sweetly, with sin so secure.

'Nor her choo.'

I moaned with fright: the baby was awake, and staring, and naked. From the floor came Clive's growl, ticking over in warning.

'Nor her choo.'

'What?' I said (I was astonished). 'No. Not hurt you. Not hurt you. No, of course not, my darling.'

Is there someone else coming in here I don't know about? A social worker like Nicola in disguise? A smiling uncle, like me, myself. Is it me? I rub my face. Outside, the hell, the torment, the murder of the low sun, and its cruel hilarity. I say nothing. Kath says nothing. And Kim can't tell me. Kim can't tell. And somebody can't stop.

*

The life isn't over, not quite. But the love life is. I might as well get the love stuff wrapped up. 'Please. My darling,' I said, ninety-some days ago now, elsewhere. 'Do this one big last thing for me. Do it, Missy. Not here. Christ, no. We'll take an attractive little condo somewhere – say in Palm Springs, or Aspen. Do it, Missy. I'll be the dream patient. I promise. Do this one big last thing for me.'

Even nature was telling me I'd lost, that love had lost. She was hating everything, herself, me, contemporary circumstances. The second and final act of love had taken place that morning, and I had heard or felt (I believed) the fateful pop or pang of conception. She was hating everything, but most of all she was hating nature, the trees in their postures of injury and recoil, the spongy froth along the shore, that log on the path in the shape of a seal tragically or just pathetically overturned in death. She had loved it here.

I hid in plain sight. I took the boat out on the water. At first, the sky looked like one of Darwin's warm little pools, sugary blue, where life would ineluctably form; but the pond itself was tired. It didn't have too long to go now, with the ocean smashing at the dunes to the east and getting yards closer every week. The oars slid through the surface tracery of dead waterskaters. I gave a shout as I saw that the clan of snapping-turtles was still in occupation, huddled up among the reeds. In their heyday, when they had discipline and esprit, they looked like the ranked helmets of Korean riot police. Now these survivalists wallowed loose and exhausted: soiled bowls in the soup kitchen. And myself the old kitchen stiff with his sleeves rolled up. For an hour the sky was Cape Cod true blue, with solid clouds grandly gleaming like statuary. After that, just heat, with the sun and the sky slowly turning the same colour.

Nothing much was said. Nature continued to do most of the talking. The LimoRover came for her at dusk. It was driven by one of Sick's sidekicks, Mirv Lensor, another kind of Washington wretch. 'Mirv Lensor: Expeditor', said the card he flicked out of the window at me when I disobeyed orders and staggered out on to the drive – in preposterous defiance. Sheridan Sick has a ventilation system in his apartment which removes all nitrates from the air he and Missy breathe. The ageing process is thus measurably retarded. Time goes slower there, slower than it goes with me.

After she'd gone, night fell, and I worked on the fire. I spent the evening staring at the lamplit back window. It held me, it included me, it said everything: my reflected face, and then, a couple of millimetres beyond, the outer surface like a glass-bottomed boat, only deep-sea, heavy-water, with all kinds of terrible little creations out there, tendrilled, dumbbelled, gravity-warped; or like a preparation for the crazy scientist's microscope, disgraceful cultures in compound opposition, the ambitious maggot with its antennae rolling like radar sweeps, the gangly moth briefly clearing the decks with its continental wing-frenzy, the no-account midges, the haunchy ants and grimly ambling spiders, the occasional innocuous white butterfly fainting away from the glass, all of them seeking the atomic brightness, the nuclear sun of the lamp's bulb. And all the wrong things prosper.

It's happening.

At last, late at night, the cries of the city are coming together and turning into something, with the eclipse so close now – the city is finally finding its voice, like the thud of a sullen heart, saying, 'No . . . No . . . No . . .' It can't stop. And a mile from my window someone else is listening. And she can't stop saying, 'Yes . . . Yes . . . Yes . . .'

I'm helpless against these forces. You can't stop them – the century says you can't stop them. I must become the tubercular toreador, whom Hemingway knew. The bull weighs half a ton. You let him have the strength.

Manolito, was it? Dead in the sawdust of Madrid.

Chapter 21: At the Speed of Love

GUY GOT HIS night with Nicola. Guy Clinch reached the finals with Nicola Six. And got his night of love.

It happened, after a fashion, in its own way. The love force that swathes the planet, like weather, found a messenger or an agent, that night, in Guy, who had never felt so fully elemental. He didn't know that she was just a weatherwoman, with stick and chart. For him it was the real thing. He didn't know that it was just an ad.

First, though, she had to account for the asphyxiating vacuum of her absence: not just for that one night of rain, when Guy's house blew up in his face, but for the further thirty-six hours which she had selflessly devoted to Keith Talent and his needs. Helping her Keith. Oh, how she lived for others . . .

'I went', said Nicola, 'to visit my parents' graves. In Shropshire.'

Guy frowned. Nicola's men, and their vermicular frowns. 'I thought you said you knew nothing of your parents.'

'That', said Nicola, who had half-forgotten a lot of this early stuff by now, 'was a deliberate untruth. In fact long ago I bribed a nurse at the orphanage and she told me where they were buried.' She shrugged and looked away. 'It's not much, is it – just their graves?'

'. . . Poor mouse.'

'Goodness, the trains. Like Russia during the purges and the famines. I felt like Nadezhda Mandelstam. It's a pretty little cemetery, though. Tombstones. Yews.' If he had asked where she'd stayed, she might have hazarded, 'In a rude tavern.' But it didn't

413

come up. After all, he was dreadfully pleased to see her. 'I should have told you, I know. I was in a strange state. Strangely inspired.'

'Well. You're back safe and sound.'

They were having a candle-lit supper on the floor of her sitting-room, in front of the open fire. Firelight and candlelight paid their compliments to her full pink dress (in reply you could hear the whisper of petticoats, the faint gossip of gauze) and to the artless pink ribbons in her disorderly hair. How simple and sustaining: bread, cheese, tomatoes, a smooth but unpretentious *vin de pays* . . . Nicola had in fact peeled off the labels to disguise the thick claret she'd chosen, a Margaux of intensely fashionable vintage.

'This may sound fanciful,' she said wanly, 'but I felt I had to *square* it with them. You.'

Guy nodded and sipped, and sipped, and nodded. His palate, his tutored papillae, continued to savour the fruit, the flowers, the full body (stout, plummy, barrelly, tart) of the examined life, the life of thought and feeling so languidly combined. He was rich in understanding. He was also, by now, a rather poorly paramour: a sick man, in fact, and thoroughly distempered. The cold he had caught in the unwholesome rain soon developed into an arctic fever. Thrice he had called down to demand the complete replenishment of his minibar, on which he had depended for a diet of pretzels, cashew nuts, Swiss chocolate and every potable from brown ale to sweet sherry. Apart from bloodying his chewed fingertips on the telephone dial, he had been incapable of action, or of thought. In his dreams, when he wasn't escorting disfigured children through empty zoos, he was attracting many varieties of unwelcome attention, in moral nudity, and priapic disgrace . . . Now he was full of understanding, full of weakness – and what else? Such vigour as remained seemed to be packed into the logjam of his underpants. Visiting the bathroom soon after his arrival at Nicola's flat, he had been obliged to try a kind of handstand before eventually backing up to the toilet seat with his face almost brushing the carpet.

'I suppose I have some sort of obsession,' she said, now tasting the sensation of risk, 'with the sanctity of the parental role. Certainly for the great rites of passage. Like losing one's . . . like one's first act of love.'

So in a sense Guy got everything.

First, starting at around 10 45, on the rug, before the fire, the stroking of hair, and the gazing into one another's faces, and delicious avowals, and solemn kisses.

At midnight he was led by the hand to the bedroom. Left alone (she wouldn't be long), he unbuttoned his shirt with a battered smile, and tenderly winced as he sat to remove his shoes, and then with grateful fatalism entered naked the weird coolness of someone else's linen. At 12.20 he disobeyed her order to close his eyes as she ran through the doorway and jumped into bed in her flesh-coloured training bra and worsted tights, slipped on, perhaps, in a last whim of modesty . . .

It took her an absolute age to get warm! What playful stops and starts they had before she was fully enfolded in his robust caloricity. He never dreamed there would be so much laughter, so much childish gaiety. Adorable little sulks and grumps, too, and sudden failures of nerve and syrupy successes. At 1.15 the thick bra was unclipped. For the first time he felt the liquid coldness of her breasts on his sternum. At 2.05 the fizzy tights came crackling off. When he had got it really toasty he was allowed to run his hand down the shining power of her inner thighs.

Meanwhile and throughout, the hot compacts of kisses tasting of sleeplessness and fever and the intimate dismissal of tomorrow morning or any future. There was the sheer of light sweat every-where, and, for him, the jabs and volts of the uncovenanted caresses paid to his exterior heart. Her panties, innocently unfeminine in texture (their lateral elastic even suggesting some medical exigency), were last seen at 3.20.

The room had changed colour many times that night but it was full of the pallor of dawn, and of the unslept hours they had logged together, when at last he loomed above her, at 4.55. By now her flesh, too, had a sore transparency; the tracings of blue in her breasts appeared to rhyme with the queries of damp hair on her neck and throat.

'Yes. My darling.'

It seemed to push all the breath out of her.

'*How it hurts. Oh, how it burns . . .*'

He had entered on tiptoe; but by 5.40 he was fully and hugely established in the purple-lined palace of sweet sin. For an hour, her sharp inhalations, her arias of exalted distress, were the guides to his diminishing caution. By 7.15, with five toes on either shoulder, four fingertips in his buttock, a light palm weighing his scrotum, and most of his face in her mouth, Guy was swinging back and forth in the mystic give and take of a negro spiritual, hymned by all the choirgirls and choirboys of love.

'Now,' she said. 'Stop *now*.'

He stopped. She applied her little finger to his chest. And then she was gone, and Guy was falling down through thin air.

'I've just realized what is wrong. What's so terribly wrong.'

Guy blinked into the pillow.

'It would be awful. Quite inexpiable.'

Guy lay there, waiting.

'You have to tell your parents. And your wife's too, of course.'

Already, as if after a lucky escape, she was putting on her panties. They really did look like Elastoplast, there in the morning light. Guy laughed strangely and said, 'I've only got a father. And she's only got a mother. And tell them what?'

'Just square them.'

'I'll call them.'

'*Call* them?'

At 7.20, when they had finished discussing it, Nicola said, 'Then go to New York. Go to New England. Go to New London.'

Go to London Fields.

Keith was displeased.

'So there you was, basically,' he said to Kath as she served him a late breakfast, 'sticking your oar in again. With your questions. Eh? Eh?'

He stared out at her from the clogged seclusion of his hangover. Given a night off by Nick while she sorted it with Guy, Keith had ventured out to the Black Cross, and to the Golgotha, where, as the night progressed, he had so convinced himself with drink . . . Kath returned to the washing-up. She said,

'He volunteered the information.'

'I'll volunteer you in a minute. Tony de Taunton?'

'He just said they were making this little programme. About you.'

Wagging his head about, Keith said, 'And you goes "He's my husband" and all this.' He wagged his head about again. ' "We got little girl." All this.'

'I didn't say nothing.'

She offered this lightly. Keith seemed mollified – though it remained clear that he was thoroughly out of sorts. He dropped his knife and fork on to the plate as Kath asked,

416

'When's it on then?'

'What?'

'The TV programme.'

'Never you mind. Business, innit. Darts. It's not . . .' Keith paused. He was actually in great difficulty here. Himself on TV: he couldn't work out how the two worlds overlapped. Try as he might, bringing all his powers to bear, he just couldn't work it out. He straightened his darting finger at her. 'Like the news. You don't want to believe everything on TV. No way to carry on.'

'You can believe the darts, surely to God.'

'Yeah but . . . This thing. It's – it's not *on* TV,' he said. 'Obviously.'

'What isn't? The TV programme?'

'Jesus.'

Keith thought it prudent to change the subject. So he started talking about how ugly Kath was now and how depressed he became (he swore it broke his fucking heart) every time he looked at her.

'You know what I'm talking?' he concluded, much more moderately. 'Success. And I happen to be able to handle it. It's a lifestyle you couldn't conceive. It's out there, girl. It wants me. And I'm gone.'

The baby gave notice of waking: the labour of baby consciousness would soon resume. Soon, the baby would be rippling with grids and circuits. And Kath herself gave a jerk as she reflexively moved for the door. Keith's blue eyes filled with everything he could no longer endure: his lips tightened, then whitened, and then vanished inwards as he said, with unbounded venom,

'I intend to complete my preparation elsewhere.'

Sourly handsome Richard was present at the office to let Guy in, as arranged. For a while they stood there amid the Japanese furniture, conversationally revising their holding positions. The world they referred to now comprised about half a percentage point of Guy's reality; to Richard, it had always been everything.

'I see no alternative to riding it out,' Richard said. 'It's sheer cuckooland, of course.'

'Agreed.' Every time their eyes met Richard seemed to lean a further inch backwards, as if to put more distance between himself and Guy's impermissible disarray. I suppose (Guy thought), I suppose I must look . . . 'Agreed,' he said again.

'You know the new buzz word over there? *Cathartic war*.'

417

'Really.'

'Poor old deterrence is in bad shape, so you give it a little jolt. Two cities. It's good, isn't it. We'd all feel so much better after a cathartic war.'

Richard laughed, and Guy laughed too, with real amusement. Of course, it suited him, up to a point, if nothing whatever mattered. But then such generalized hilarity might be considered a necessary condition for nothing mattering. About a year ago he had at last finished Martin Gilbert's *The Holocaust*, and had sombrely decided that this thousand-page work could also be read as a treasury of German humour . . . Guy went to his desk and called his father on the direct line. He was connected quickly but he still had to get past all the staff: lessening densities of Hispanic bafflement giving way to the forensic interceptions of stewards, secretaries, lawyers, game-keepers. 'It's nothing to do with the office,' he kept telling a Mr Tulkinghorn. 'It's personal. And rather urgent.' Eventually his father lurched exhaustedly on to the line, as if the receiver itself were some new burden he was being asked to shoulder.

'What's it about?'

'I can't discuss it now. It's far too delicate.'

'But what's it about?'

Guy told him what it was about.

'Well, there's nothing much more to say, is there. You have my . . . my "okay". All the best, dear boy. I'm glad we talked.'

A few seconds later Richard knocked and entered.

'You're absolutely right,' said Guy. 'It's pure fantasy. It'll blow over.'

Guy hadn't come to the office to talk to Richard. He had come for his passport and travel cards – and for that spare cane which he elatedly glimpsed leaning against the wall by the door. As he moved across the room to get it, Richard, who was Guy's younger brother, said, 'Then why are you going to New York? Have you got a hernia or something? I was listening in. It sounds as though you've cocked things up nicely. You *tit*.'

Guy looked at the floor: Richard wouldn't understand, of course, but he had never felt happier in his life. Guy looked at the ceiling. 'You wouldn't understand,' he said, 'but I've never felt happier in my life.'

'You *tit*,' said Richard.

He took the tube to the Strand, where he bought a travel bag and lots of new stuff to put in it. In the golden silence of the department store he went from men's wear to women's, in search of a silk scarf for Hope's mother, and one for Nicola, while he was there. The vaults and galleries of female clothing, their catholicity of cut and colour, surprised and impressed him. Compared to all this, men went around in uniform. But then . . . But then, just now (and in a sense it had been this way for half a century): we are all in uniform. Not volunteers either, but pressed men and women, weeping conscripts. The children in anaconda file on the zebra-crossing are in uniform. The old lady over there dithering from hat to hat is in uniform. Our babies are born, not in their birthday suits, but in uniform – in little sailor suits. Hard for love. Hard for love, with everyone being in the army like this. Love got hard to do.

Now the revolving doors delivered him on to the street (the brass-topped cane really did make a difference). Above, the low sun painted the shape of an eagle on to the cirrus haze. Today an eagle, with eagle eye; tomorrow a vulture, perhaps, flexed over London carrion. Looking down, he saw a pretty cat behind the bars of a basement window; it yawned and stretched, outside history. An old man walked past; he was shyly stifling a smile as he remembered something fond or funny. Preserve this! Yes, certainly! Guy stopped a cab and reached quick agreement with the driver in his beefeater outfit. He climbed in. He was no longer afraid. On the way to Heathrow he looked at the books she had given him for his transatlantic reading and glanced again at the inscriptions. Towards the west, like madlady's hair, the thin clouds sucked him into the completion of his reality. He was no longer afraid; and he no longer feared for love. Partly it was her show of principle, so bravely self-sufficient, when you thought about it, with the eclipse only days away. Partly it was the recession of Keith's image in his mind: the only bane here was the recently revealed talent for literary criticism (what other charms and skills might Keith acquire?). But mainly, he admitted to himself, it was those panties. Guy smiled, and went on giving smiles of pain at every bump the cab took on its way. Quite a fright. Unpleasant to the touch, too (and his fingertips had explored their every atom). Exactly the sort of thing you'd expect a virgin to wear, at thirty-four.

Double 17, thought Keith. Bad one. Come inside, you're looking at 1, double 8. But she don't even look thirty. Not nice either. Better go 10, double 10. Moisturizers innit.

419

'Now where are my keys,' she said.

Keith stared moodily at her stocking-tops as she led him up the stairs. She paused and turned and said,

'When you had two darts for the 66 pick-off. I thought you'd go 16, bull. But no. You went bull, double 8. Magic. That's finishing, Keith.'

'Yeah cheers.'

'And the 125! Everyone was expecting triple 19, big 18, bull. But you go *outer* bull, triple 20, tops. Brilliant kill . . . Keith! What's the matter? Why are you looking at me like that?'

'It's *treble*. Not triple. Treble.'

Nicola climbed the last flight with her head at a penitent angle. In the sitting-room she said cautiously,

'Darling what do you think? We could go and eat quite soon, or do you want to relax here for a bit first?'

'Never do that,' said Keith with a wipe of his palm. 'Not when I just come through the door. I get my bearings, okay?'

'Forgive me. Would you like to take your coat off and try it out?' she said, referring to the new dartboard of which she had taken delivery that afternoon. 'Whilst I go and get you your lager?'

'All in good time.'

'Do you like it?'

'No it's smart.' Keith took off his jacket and reached masterfully for his purple pouch. 'Wood-grained wall cabinet. Of mature mahogany.'

Nicola hurried to the refrigerator, where the cans of lager were stacked like bombs in their bay. He hadn't actually *said* she could fetch him a drink, and she did hope she was doing the right thing. She hesitated, listening for the thunk of his darts.

Over the next few days she took him (Keith) to illustrious old-style restaurants in whose velvet and candlelight he fuzzily shone with class dissonance, with villainy, with anticharisma; he sat with the tasselled menus and heard Nicola translate. She translated him (Keith) to sanctums of terrible strictness, accusatory linen and taunting tureens, where he always had what she had. She bought him (Keith) the dinky black waistcoats and black trimmed trousers that he loved; as a result, when he returned from the toilet to their table, hands would go up all over the room, like in class, when the pretty teacher asked an easy question. He never talked (Keith). He never talked. At first she assumed that he was in the grip of an inscrutable rage. Was he still brooding on her solecism with the *triple*? Had someone spoken ill of the Marquis of Edenderry? Then she realized: he thought you didn't. He thought you didn't talk. Though others did. He sat there, chewing (Keith), with caution, without zest, deep in his dreams of darts. Or perhaps he was wondering why, in the fantasy, you felt at home in places like these, whereas of course you never did, and never would. With the waiters, Keith was as a fly to wanton boys; the lightest glance of the maître d' could harrow up his soul. Nicola supposed that this explained the proletarian predilection for Indian food — and Indian waiters. Who's afraid of those brown-faced elfs? He once tried a glass of Mouton Rothschild (Keith) and spat it out into his napkin. She paid, ostentatiously, always querying the bill, while Keith turned a pensive stare on the chandeliers. He knew the required demeanour of the man shedding humble origins: you act as if you feel it's all your due. But he was having a job feeling that, these days, and a job acting it. When the godlike greeter talked to her in what was presumably French, when he advised and beseeched, wringing his hands, Keith always thought they were asking her what she was doing, going out with someone like him. Like him. (Keith.)

At home, though, in her flat, Keith was *it*. He came in at around ten or eleven and looked at her through the shards, the swirling parquetry, of his shuffled hungers. She dressed wealthily for him, to win that admiring sneer. Before he started on his lagers or his Lucozades he was served croissants, and devilish espresso, and once or twice she coaxed him into humour with a Tequila Sunrise, where something sweet fought the heavy tug of the booze. Then he threw darts all day, pausing only to acknowledge receipt of an exquisite snack, for example, and a lager served in the engraved pewter tankard she had bought him, or to relish a new video; with Keith now needing four or five of these a day, Nicola was far from idle! To begin with he desisted from his darts when the telephone rang and it turned out to be Guy, shouting through the ambient clatter of some airport or gas station; but after a while, such was his local suzerainty, he practised right through the calls. On one occasion Guy rang from a deserted motel and remarked on the background noise: Nicola said that it was probably a monitor or money meter, thus covering for the slow triple thunks of Keith's tungstens. When she talked to Guy she sounded like Keats. For Keith, this was all low heaven. He loved her as he would his own manager, in the big time. You sensed it the instant you stepped in off the street: the whole house stank of pornography and darts.

On the eve of Bonfire Night, of Final Night, a couple of hours before the TV teaser – Keith's docu-drama – was about to be screened, Nicola decided to spare him the usual gauntlet of tuxed torturers and took Keith for a light supper at 192, the media restaurant in Kensington Park Road. He sat there with his orange juice, warily awaiting the sushi she had suggested he try.

'A penny for them, Keith?' said Nicola gently.

He said nothing.

192. The best thing with that is: smack in a maximum. Psychological body blow. Leaving 12. But if you come inside, leaves 6. 6. Double 3. Murder. Avoid it. Here's another way it can happen. You're on 57 and go for 17 to leave tops – and h't the treble. 51. Leaves 6. Or you're going for double 14 and hit double 11. Leaves 6. Wrong bed. Or you're on double 9, pull one, and hit 12. Leaves 6. Or God forbid you're on double 11 and you hit double 8! Wrong bed. Leaves 6. Wrong bed. Nasty, that. Fucking wicked. Murder.

A fourteen-hour wait in the VIP Lounge at Heathrow; the Mach II to Newark; the helicopter to Kennedy; the 727 to Middletown; the limousine to New London. America moved past him behind treated glass. The pain had now spread downwards as far as his calves and upwards as far as his nipples. Every tick of the second hand on his watch administered an exquisite squeeze to the trauma of his being. He looked out at the cordoned, the sweated fields of New England, and at the woodlands, also brutally worked, but still holding their twiggy, ribboned, Thanksgiving light. Impossible even to imagine that Mohawk and Mahican had once wandered here – yes, and Wampanoag, Narraganset, Pequot, Penobscot, Passamaquoddy, Abnaki, Malecite, Micmac. He had a sense, as you were bound to have in America now, of how a whole continent had been devoured, used up, chewed up.

The night before he had tarried in Middletown, at a recently opened airport hotel called the Founding Fathers. Again he had run into indefinable difficulties as he tried to persuade the managerial staff that he was neither poor nor mad nor ill. One of the troubles seemed to centre on his new habit of giggling silently to himself. Perhaps he looked like one of the first English sailors, panting with scurvy, his turn-ups swinging round his calves. In any case his

422

iridium and titanium credit-cards prevailed. After a shower he made a second successful call to the retirement home and confirmed the appointment with his mother-in-law. After a Virgin Mary in the Mayflower Room, he had an early dinner in the Puritan Lounge. By his plate lay the two books she had given him: one for the way out, one for the way home. It was over Stendhal's *Love* that he now frowned and chuckled and mused . . . In his room he made the last call of the day to Nicola, who despite the late hour and the bad line (the metronomic thunks of the money meter) gave him an extraordinary fifteen minutes on her plans for his return. This complicated his next action: a manoeuvre of long-delayed self-inspection, achieved naked, with one foot up on the writing-desk before the mirror. Mm, quite bad. Possibly rather serious. It really was the sort of sight that would have the nurses scampering from the Delivery Room. There were some tangy tints of green in there, and the surface was rippled as if in a sharp breeze; but overall his flesh was almost picturesquely blue. The blue, perhaps, of the blue lagoon. He fell asleep wondering what would happen if you transposed the heroines of *Macbeth* and *Othello*. With a Scottish Desdemona there would be no story, no plot, no slain kings. But with a Mediterranean Lady Macbeth you might have got a stranger tale, and a bloodier one, because such a woman would never have looked so kindly on Cassio's cares, and might have headed straight for Iago . . .

Now he rode on to New London. *Love* nestled on his lap, also the second book, as yet unopened, something called *The Light of Many Suns*. Guy wasn't reading: the migraine in his groin had somehow established connexions with the blinding ballsache in his eyes. He watched the news on the limousine's TV, as it were reluctantly and askance, in the same way that the chauffeur watched his unreassuring passenger, with stolen glances in the rearview mirror. The President had made his decision. They were going in. They had decided to operate on the President's wife.

The ninety-second biodoc on Keith Talent was watched by 27½ million people – in the UK, in Scandinavia, in the Netherlands, in the rockabilly states of America, in Canada, in the Far East and in Australia. It was watched by dartslovers everywhere, and then shot out into space at the speed of light.

It was watched by Nicola Six, perched on Keith's knee.

Go-getting Keith Talent is an upcoming merchandizer operating out of London's West Kensington.

To the hectic tumbles of a xylophone solo, Keith was seen nodding shrewdly into an intercom. Between his finger and thumb he rolled a biro shaped like a dart.

In the elegant West London flat where Keith lives and works, the calls come winging in from Munich and LA. In business as in darts, no way does Keith play to come in second best. Winning is what it's all about is Keith's byword. Never far from Keith's side is his trusty girl Friday Nicky with a helping hand.

Assistant Nicky, in T-shirt and jeans and dark glasses, appeared behind her boss with several sheets of paper, which Keith started nodding shrewdly at before they were in front of his face. One hand rested on his shoulder as she pointed with the other. Now an establishing shot of the Marquis of Edenderry, and then Keith's emotional face filling the screen.

'*I'm basically the sort of guy who likes to relax with a few drinks with the guys. Here. With the bestf – with the bestf – with the best support of any pub in London.*'

Nicky was sitting beside him. He seemed to have her in a kind of headlock. The xylophone solo had given way to Hawaiian guitar. Keith drew near-tearfully on his cigarette.

Dartwise, Keith is known for his clinical big finishes. The 170s, the 167s, the 164s, the 161s. 'The 160s.' (This was Keith, pitilessly offhand.) '*The 158s. The 157s. The 156s. That's correct. The 155s. Some question my power. But come Friday I intend to silence the critics.*'

Keith and Nicky strolled out into the carpark, hand in hand, their linked arms swinging.

A bachelor, Keith and Nicky have as yet no plans to wed. But one thing is certain.

There was a fish-eye rearview shot of the Cavalier, and the sound of heavy-metal, and then the car fired off into the distorted street.

Keith Talent is going a long, long way.

'. . . But Keith,' said Nicola in a stunned voice, during the commercial break. 'You were quite amazing. A true natural. The TV camera *loves* you, Keith.'

Keith nodded, rather sternly.

'I only wonder slightly what your wife will make of it.'

He looked at her with qualified hostility, as if unsure whether or not he was being trifled with. Nicola was aware that Keith was in a state of near-psychotic confusion on this point. And she didn't know the half of it. In fact he was still clinging to the notion that the biodoc would be screened only at those locations where it had been filmed: her flat, and, of course, the Marquis of Edenderry. But even Keith found the notion tenuous; growing doubts about it had tempted him to tamper with the TV at Windsor House, in the only way he knew how, by switching it off and putting his boot through it. In the end he shrank from such sacrilege, and just went on telling Kath that – although reason declared that there wasn't much point in the TV biodoc unless it was on TV – the TV biodoc wasn't *on* TV.

'Still,' she said, 'who stands behind you now? Who is it who really understands about your darts?'

'Shut it,' said Keith, who in a sense was feeling more and more at home down the dead-end street. A commercial break had just ended and before another one had the chance to begin a voice was saying,

. . . a little look at Keith's opponent for the big one, and Kim Twemlow will be saying why he thinks it's going to be a little bit special. After this.

Now although Keith never asked about an opponent, he'd naturally been keeping up with events (by means of half-hourly telephone calls). The second semi-final of the Duoshare Sparrow Masters was to have been disputed by Keith's old enemy, Chick Purchase, and the young unknown from Totteridge, Marlon Frift. But there'd been a problem, and a postponement. Following a night out, Marlon had had a heart attack; and there were still doubts about his fitness.

Nicola waited for the start of the organ solo and then said, 'Who is it, Keith?'

'Never ask about an opponent. Immaterial as such. You play the board not the – jammy bitch's bastard.'

. . . due to the very sad Marlon Frift tragedy. By a walkover.

On screen, big Chick patrolled his coin-op store, appeared at the races in morning-suit and topper, was seen on horseback himself, then fishing at some blighted canal. Chick down the gym, with the chest-flexer, in the plunge pool, all chest gloss in the solarium – Chick, big Chick, with his ponies, his birds, his pitbull . . . And then Kim Twemlow, the ex-world number one, with his white shoes, his white belt, his shot face, saying, 'Look at the averages and it's got to be big Chick, by a mile. All credit to Keith for progressing as he has.

Must have got his head beautiful for the big occasion and that. But on current form he's not fit to empty Chick's ashtrays . . .'

After a while Keith said hoarsely, 'So be it.'

'Who is this *Chick* person?'

He gave a taciturn version of the dispute with his old business associate. Of the rape of Chick's sister, and Keith's subsequent hospitalization, the smaller man had this to say: 'We came to blows over this bird, the big fella coming out second best. And now tomorrow night him and I have a rendezvous. To sort out who's number one once and for all.'

'Good, Keith. This could work for us. Now I expect you'd like to forget the pressures with a nice video. It's something a little bit special. On a Halloween theme. We're a few days late, but what of that, Keith.'

'Horror like?'

'In the old calendar it used to be the last night of the year. When all the witches and warlocks were abroad.'

As Keith trudged into the bedroom, Guy's limousine entered the grounds of the institution. The little TV screen within was now showing a colour-coded diagram of the uterus of the President's wife. The President's wife, so young, so blonde . . . Guy asked the driver if he wouldn't mind pulling over for a moment. The driver minded, but pulled over anyway. Guy bent his long body and out he climbed.

He made to straighten up – and nothing happened. The driver watched in settled distaste as Guy grunted, first with surprise, then with effort, and remained in a jagged crouch on the verge. After a second attempt, and a second failure, he backed himself on to a wooden bench. Here he rested with his fingers folded over the handle of the cane in soft support of his chin. Now he saw the L-shaped Tudor-type mansion, the slated roof and leaded windows, the pond like a silver coin pitched on to the front lawn; and he saw too the size and nature of the task ahead of him. Before, it was just something to be got out of the way as he sped towards something else – towards inevitability. But now of course it filled the sky. And the sky was falling.

The physics felt strange, the physics felt fierce. Gravity was pushing down on him, but if *Guy* pushed down, hard enough, on the cane, then, slowly, he went up, up.

As Guy straightened, Keith reclined, and made himself comfortable on Nicola's bed: a lengthy procedure. She plumped his pillows and pulled off his boots; Keith also suffered her to bring him a fresh can of lager from the fridge. Now he looked about with an inconvenienced expression for the box of paper tissues.

'Wait, darling,' she said. 'These might be more fun.' She opened a drawer and started browsing through it. 'All the good stuff seems to be in the wash. From the videos, Keith. Wait.' She turned, and bent forward, and reached up into her dress with both thumbs. 'Use these. We'll put them on your head until you need them. You can watch through the legholes. Might look rather comic on anyone but you, Keith.'

The black gusset puffed out for a moment as Keith said, 'Yeah cheers.'

She left him there, sprawled on the covers in his frilly gasmask. Then re-entered, in electronic form. On screen, she came into the bedroom slowly in black cape and thigh-high boots and witch's pointy hat. And as she turned and the black cape swirled you could see, within, the simple ways the simple shape (legs, hips, haunch, waist) can be made to shine on the reptile eye, and burn on the reptile brain. The glamour: charms, rhombs, wishbones, magic rings – gramarye, sortilege, demonifuge . . .

Keith was doing handsome.

Then she came into the bedroom slowly in black cape and thigh-high boots and witch's pointy hat.

Keith was doing handsome. Then the real thing – the necromancer – came into the bedroom.

It would go beautifully.

Guy muffled his delight when the matron or health-operative or death-concessionaire informed him that Mrs Broadener's condition was far advanced. She wouldn't understand what he said to her. And she wouldn't respond. With any luck. It would go beautifully. Hope disliked her mother, of course, and her mother disliked Hope; Guy had not seen Mrs Broadener for seven or eight years. The only thing he knew about this place, her last refuge, was a detail that Lizzyboo had let slip. Although no old lady would ever walk out of here, each old lady had to be able to walk in: company policy. Mrs Broadener had walked in; she wouldn't walk out. Now Guy moved through proliferating parlours: waiting-rooms, in various degrees of disguise. There appeared to be no other visitors.

'Priscilla?' he said, when they were alone.

He stared down. At what? Something caught up in the more or less disgraceful struggle at the end of existence: the process from which so little can be salvaged. He took this person's hand and sat beside her.

'You remember me, don't you,' he began. 'Guy? Hope's husband? You're looking well. Thank you for seeing me. Uh – I bring . . . I bring good news! Everyone is well. Hope's wonderfully well. Marmaduke, your little grandson, is in tremendous form. A handful, as always, but . . .'

She watched him as he spoke, or she seemed to. Her face minutely bobbled on its spindle; the eyes swam in their huge new pools, but never blinked. Priscilla's hands were tightly clasped or fastened.

'Lizzyboo is full of beans. She's put on some weight recently but that's not the end of the world, is it? No, everyone's well and they send their love. It's wonderful, isn't it, it's so absolutely marvellous, I do think, when a family is really close, and everyone loves one another,' he said, and hesitated as he realized how quickly his face had covered itself in tears, 'and they, no matter what, they protect each other. And it's for ever.'

Suddenly she spoke. She just said: 'It's all – '

Guy waited. Nothing followed. 'Well. I suppose I'd better be thinking about going. Goodbye. Thank you for seeing me.'

'Shit,' she said.

He waited. 'Goodbye, Priscilla.'

Nicola and Keith were sitting up in bed together, smoking. They drew huskily on their cigarettes. Nicola raised her chin as she exhaled. She said,

'You're not to reproach yourself, Keith. It happens to everyone.'

'. . . Oh yeah? Well it ain't never happened to me before. No way.'

'Really? Never?'

'No danger. Me – I'm in there. Boof. Ain't never happened to *me* before.'

In fact, of course, it *had* happened to Keith before. It happened to Keith, on average, about five times a week. But it also didn't happen to him pretty regularly too. And in this case he felt he was entitled to a certain amount of bafflement, and anger. What was it? Her skinny ankles, maybe. All the *talking*. Or the way that, despite her evident

428

litheness, she had felt so heavy – as heavy as an automobile, as heavy as the heavy Cavalier. It was like parking a pantechnicon, just trying to turn her over.

'I should imagine it even happens', she said, 'to Chick Purchase. Every now and then.'

'Way he treats minge he ought to be locked up,' said Keith soberly. He further reflected that Chick Purchase *was* locked up, pretty often, on bird-related matters, as well as in the normal course of business.

'You're a very sensitive man, Keith. As well as an incredible tyke and everything, with your rugged ways. You should give yourself credit for that.'

Keith flexed his eyebrows. Come to think of it, he was wondering why he didn't feel more angry. But anger didn't come. Self-pity came. Not the usual kind, which looked and sounded just like anger. A different kind: self-pity of a far nobler strain. 'Press₋res of darts,' he said.

'Yes. And a little difficulty switching from one medium to another. That's what this whole thing is really about.'

'Yeah. Well.'

She saw that Keith's eyes were starting to pick out articles of his own clothing, flattened on the floor: the grovelling trousers, for instance, trampled, twisted-out-of.

'Early night and that. Compose myself for the big one. See how Clive's doing.'

'Oh Keith. Before you go.'

She picked up her black dressing-gown and left the room, returning almost at once with a silver tray: an imposingly expensive-looking bottle and two glasses, and some sort of device like a foreign lantern with tubes.

'This is as old as the century. Try some. *This*', she said, 'is practically newborn, and just in from Teheran. I went to some trouble to get it.'

'Yeah I smoke a little keef,' said Keith. 'Now and again. Relax.'

'It may interest you to know, Keith, that the word "assassin" comes from *hashish*. Assassins – killers by treachery and violence. They used to give the men a good blast of this before they went out to do their stuff. And if they died in action, they were promised an immediate heaven. Of wine, women and song, Keith. And hash, no doubt.' A little later she said, 'But that's enough etymology for now.

I'm beginning to sound like a schoolteacher. Why don't you just lie back and let me find out what makes this cock tick?'

Guy linked up again with his courier or expeditor at the airport in New London. Here he was told that, if he wished, he could get an air-taxi straight to Newark. With luck he might catch an earlier Concorde and shave perhaps half a day off his journey. The courier smiled and twinkled potently; everything was possible; his was the maximum-morale specialism of deeply expensive travel. At this point he paid off the chauffeur, whose disaffection remained secure against Guy's reckless tip. Outside in the warm dusk the light was the colour of a grinning pumpkin, Halloween light, promising trick or treat.

Before he retired to the Celebrity Lounge (there would be a slight delay) Guy wandered the concourses, full of love's promiscuous interest, among pantssuit and stretchslack America. Even though there was said to be less of it now, the human variety on display, with its dramatic ratios of size and colouring, still impressed and affected him. It was true that you did see signs of uniformity (one nation), all the people wearing off-white smocks and pink, gymkhana-sized rosettes, like that family over there, four of them, in perfect-family formation, man and woman and boy and girl, each with the squeamish smile of the future . . . Guy threw away his painkillers – their tubes and sachets. Everywhere young women looked at him with kindness. But of course there was only one woman who could really kill his pain. The eyes of certain faces, children's faces, made him wonder whether this whole adventure of his, so agitated and inspired, and so climactic, wasn't just a way of evading the twentieth century or the planet or what the one had done to the other.

Because love . . . But wasn't nature constantly asking you what all the fuss was about? It was hard to shirk this question when you saw them trouped together like that, the old ladies, walking down passages at five yards an hour, or humped on chairs in parlours, their heads trembling in anger and negation, insisting, saying never, never, never. All of them had been adored and wept over, presumably, at one point, prayed to, genuflected in front of, stroked, kissed, licked; and now the bald unanimity of disappointment, of compound grief and grievance. It was written on their mouths, on their lips, marked in notches like the years of a sentence. In their heads only the thoughts that just wouldn't go away, cold and stewed, in their little

teapot heads, still brewing beneath frilled cozies of old-lady hair . . .
Whatever it was women wanted, few of them ended up getting it.

He advanced into the Celebrity Lounge, where there were complimentary coffee and free telephones, and where he hoped to finish
Love.

'Now,' she said. 'Stop *now*.' And she hadn't even heard the telephone
ring.

'Okay,' said Keith cheerfully (with that cheerful little throat-
clearance on the consonant).

He climbed up her body until she felt the scrawny sharpness of his
knees on her shoulders.

'Shut your eyes and open your mouth.'

But Enola Gay, being Nicola Six − Enola shut her mouth and
opened her eyes . . .

'. . . Hello? Darling? I was just thinking about you,' she said. 'And
having a rather blinding little weep.'

'Jesus,' said Keith.

'. . . Nothing. Do I? I can't imagine I'll be getting much sleep
tonight, so do call later if you like. I just can't sleep for thinking about
you. Yes, you know I sometimes suspect I'm never going to sleep
again.'

Settling on the pillows like, Keith ran a hand down her throat as
such, and reached for the brandy bottle innit.

'. . . Come to me, my darling. Come to me. At the speed of love.'

Dust storms grounded the midnight Concorde. Guy was driven from
Newark to New York, and spent a few pricy hours at the Gustave on
Central Park South. He couldn't sleep. TV said real estate and
wrestling and medical ads and fireside shopping and pulpit stuff and
last-best-hope stuff and dial 1–800. As he was driven through the
city, towards Kennedy and the rerouted morning flight, he thought
what he always thought when he was in New York now. He thought:
where have the poor gone? The places where the poor shop, the
places where the poor feed: where have they gone?

At the speed of love . . . He ran it through his head as he paced the
VIP Lounge at five miles per hour. She can turn a phrase, that girl.
Delightful. At the speed of . . . Yes, really quite lovely.

431

I guess it looks like a cheap shot, the revelation, at this stage, that Richard is Guy's brother. But I can only duplicate my own astonishment. It was news to me too. I could always go back and fix it. Now is not the time, though. It is not the time. It never is. It just never *is the time*.

You could have knocked me over with a feather. Of course, if knocking me down with a feather were what anyone was interested in, I'd never get off the deck. They wouldn't even need the feather. I reach for a fresh sheet of paper and there's this splitcrack in my arm, as if some spore-coven or fat maggot has just detonated in the crimson innards of a log fire. Dying reminds me of something, something I'd just got over and successfully put behind me when, all of a sudden, I started dying. Middle age: that's what. Yes, it's perfectly okay, so long as you don't try anything too butch or sporty, like walking down the street for a pint of milk, or pulling the flush handle, or kicking off your shoes, or yawning, or reaching too sharply for the vitamin E, or lowering yourself with any suddenness into the herb-green bath. All that stuff is out. Like middle age, like my dreams, death is packed with information. At last you really find out the direction time's taking. Time's arrow. Time works! And, more than this, you are monstrous . . .

When middle age comes, you think you're dying all the time. Dying is like that too. But here, finally, all resemblance ends. All resemblance ends.

*

432

Nine-thirty, on the morning of November 5.

Nicola has already been with me for over three hours. She's next door . . . I can hear her, pacing. Fortunately she is not demanding my undivided attention. She has had the decency, for example, to let me finish Chapter 21. I keep her fuelled with coffee. She had a shower. Later, she had a bath; and she asked for dental floss. When she isn't walking up and down she sits on the sofa in one of Asprey's dressing-gowns, not even smoking: she just stares at the window – at the low sun, which has now reached its apogee and will stay that low all day long until the moon intercedes, coming between the sun and our eyes. Every now and then she goes all trancelike and I can tiptoe off to the study, and write. But how she fills the flat, how her presence fills the flat, like a rich smell, or like anger. She's switched the TV on again, looking, no doubt, for news from Washington or Bonn or Tel Aviv, news of the storms, the tides, the moon, the sun (the sky is falling!), but looking through all this for a correlative, the thing out there that might say yes to the thing in here. Events, and possible events – the world has to *want* it. Whereas for me it's easier: the TV itself is my correlative, pandar, hack, mediator, foot-in-the-door, vile paparazzo.

It's in the nature of an obsession, I suppose, that one will get to the bottom of whatever's available. One will tend to get to the bottom of it.

Next to Mark Asprey's baronial can there's a hip-high stack of assorted magazines. All they have in common is a certain amount of editorial matter about Mark Asprey: a profile, an interview, what he's pulling down, his favourite colour, who he's fucking. The mags get older and Mark gets younger as I work my way down the pile (the effect is speeded up by the increasing frequency of my visits). Until, last night, I find myself staring through tears of strain at paired photographs of Mark Asprey and Cornelia Constantine under the heading, DID THEY OR DIDN'T THEY? She says they didn't. He says they did.

Of *course*. Marius Appleby is a pseudonym. It's Asprey. I knew it: I wasn't even surprised. It was almost bathetic. What else could explain the familiar taste, and the poundcake richness, of my love-hate for *Crossbone Waters*?

Digging deeper into the stack, I find additional earlier reports: scandal, accusation. She sued him; he settled out of court; doubts linger. 'The book is all lies,' say Cornelia and her lawyers. 'What happened happened,' Asprey insists.

Naturally I now root for Cornelia. But two puzzles remain. In all there are about a dozen photographs of her, including some swimwear poses, and physically she measures up, except in two particulars. First, it is clear that Cornelia is dramatically flat-chested. The second point has to do with her face, or her expression, which never changes, and which bespeaks (or so this reviewer feels) really helpless stupidity.

What actually happened? I guess the person to ask, if it's the truth you want, would be old Kwango.

Before I could even bring this up with Nicola she said abruptly, 'I hate it here.' 'Yes, it is a little rich for some tastes.' 'It's the acme of vulgarity. But it's not just that. The gowns, the baubles, the awards and everything. They're all fake.' 'No.' 'Look at that translation. It's gobbledegook. He has them printed up.' 'But he's, he's so —' 'He just writes schlock plays and cute journalism. Christ, why do you think you never heard of him?'

I said, 'Then why does he do it?'

'Why do you think? To impress the gullible.'

'Whoops,' I said. 'I do beg your pardon.'

Regrettably, disappointingly, altogether unacceptably, and like all the other dying people I've ever come across, I am suffering from eructation and its related embarrassments. If I extrapolate from the death of my father, the death of my brother, the death of Daniel Harter, and the death of Samson Young, then I may conclude that buying it is a pretty windy scene . . . I'm glad I no longer have to hang out in the Black Cross, where I've experienced many armpit-torching moments. Nobody recognizes me in there (every day is like the first day), and I have to stand around behaving 'characteristically'.

The baby cries, the baby cries and turns, in its awful struggle to be a baby. Its struggle is with all that is changeless and unworkable. She farts with the effort. Whoops. Maybe farts are frowned on for no other reason than their connexion with mortal weakness, with being a baby, with dying. To her, to Kim, evidently, or so I've read, the breasts, the penis – these mean life. And the stool, the piece of ordure, this means death. But she shows no natural aversion, and babies find nothing disgusting, and don't we all have to be trained quite hard to hate our shit?

*

434

I am the father of Missy's baby. Or Sheridan Sick is. ('I suppose it's Sick's.' 'Don't *call* him that.' 'It's his *name*, isn't it?') She flies over to England. To be by my side. Or for an abortion. I hear a ring on the bell and I go and answer and she's there . . . I'd have no time for her, one way or the other. Only time to write it down.

Missy had to go. For reasons of balance. Reasons of space. She belongs to some other version. She preferred to run her own life. She didn't want artistic shape. She wanted to be safe. Safe, in America, at the end of the millennium.

I still believe love has the power to bring in the loved one, to reel her in. You can send the line out half way across the planet and it will bring the loved one in. But I don't even try and call her any more. Love failed, in me. It was sapped by something else.

She has her slot in my dreamlife, as if the dreams were vestiges of the love power. These dreams of Missy are like Missy's dreams, very logical and realistic – not like the nuclear sizzlings of my nightmares. We keep having this conversation. On the Cape. I say, 'Nurse me.' She says, 'What about your book?' I say, 'I'll give it up. I want to give it up. It's a wicked book. It's a wicked thing I'm doing, Missy.'

Then she says, 'Watch the girl. Be careful. There's going to be a surprise ending. It isn't Keith. It's the other guy.'

When I let her in this morning around six-thirty she looked so transparently ruined and beat – and so transparent: ghostly, ghosted, as if the deed were already done and she had joined me on the other side. After a few showers, and several cups of laced coffee, she started telling me about it: the night of hate. At one point, quite early on, I looked up from my notes and said, 'That's outrageous. Oh, my poor readers. Shame on you, Nicola. Shame on you.' I asked why in Christ's name she hadn't kicked Keith out after the initial fiasco. So much better thematically. And a nice contrast with Guy. 'It would have meant that nobody really had you.' 'Only you.' 'This doesn't have anything to do with me . . .'

'You're worried about Guy, aren't you. You think he's the one. You think it's going to be him, don't you. It won't be. I swear. You love him, don't you.'

'I guess I do. In a way. He must have called me twenty times from the States. He says I'm his best friend. *Me*. Where *are* everyone's friends? Where's everyone's family? Where's Kath's family? Why isn't she smothered in sisters and mothers? You can rest up but I'm going to be tearing around all day. I can't handle this physically. The airport! How'll I get a cab? I can't bear these novels that end in mad activity. "Jane? Call June and tell Jean about Joan. Jeff – get Jim before Jack finds John." All this goddamned fetching and carrying. How're you supposed to do any *writing*? My leg hurts. Heathrow!'

'*Easy*. Calm down. It'll all work out. Here's what you do.'

It didn't sound too bad, after she mapped out my schedule for me. And I was more relieved than intrigued, for instance, when she said I'd get a three-hour writing break between nine and midnight . . . I looked up at her. She had just brought me another cup of coffee and was standing beside me, carelessly stroking the back of my neck with the knuckles of her left hand.

'Mark Asprey might show up,' I said. 'I really hope there's no unfinished business between you two.'

'He won't be here until tomorrow,' she said. 'When I'll be gone.'

Nicola was looking out, at the window, at the world. Her slender throat tautened, and her eyes filled with indignation or simple self-belief. She had about her then the thing of hers that touched me most: as if she were surrounded, on every side, by tiny multitudes of clever enemies.

Just come in again. And must now go out again.

I write these words to keep my hand steady. And because nothing means anything unless I write it down. I can't go out there, not just this very second. But of course I'll go. I'll go. There is some kind of absolute obligation here.

The phone rang and the instant I picked it up I felt a breeze of awfulness whistling liplessly down the line. How could I get it so wrong? How could I not see? Everywhere there are things that I'm not seeing.

'Kath,' I said, 'what happened? Where are you?'

'Somewhere else. The baby – go and get the baby. I'm a wicked woman, Sam.'

'You . . . No you're not.'

'Then what is it? Tell me what it is.'

'It's just the situation.'

As I hung up, Nicola came out of the bathroom and I said,

'You're wearing *that*? Oh my God, look at us. And you know what the worst thing about everything is? About you. About the whole story. About the world. About death. This: it's *really happening*.'

436

Chapter 22: Horrorday

THE FIRST THREE events – light, sound and impact – were all but instantaneous. First, the eye opened to the scalding bulb of the foundered standard lamp; next, the rushing report of some lofted cherrybomb or megabanger; and then the brisk descent of the crammed glass ashtray. This ashtray had been teetering for hours on the shelf above the bed: now it was dislodged – by the frenzied physics of everyday life. It fell at the usual rate of acceleration: thirty-two feet per second per second: thirty-two feet per second squared. And it flipped in mid-air. So Keith copped the lot. Impact, crushed butts, a shovelful of ash – right in the kisser. Right in the mush. This was the fifth of November. This was horrorday.

Keith spat and struggled and thrashed himself to his feet. She was gone. Where? With his eyes bobbing and rolling in their sockets, he focused on the horrorclock. *No.* He swore through a dry cloud of horrordust. In the spent tempest of the bedroom he sought out his clothes. When he pitched himself towards the toilet he barked a horrortoe on the bed's brass stanchion. Tearfully he mollified his incensed bladder. In the mirror Keith's reflection started getting dressed. A split horrornail kept snagging in the blur of fabrics, all of them synthetic: made by horrorman. On the wall Keith's shadow straightened and dived headlong from the room. He paused in the passage and roughly freed a segment of his scrotum, nastily snared in the seized teeth of his horrorzip.

Out on to the street he stumbled. He made for the car – for the

437

heavy Cavalier. Builders' dust and builders' orange sand formed an orange mist at the level of his eyes, his agent-orange vision, which was itself engrained with motionless impurities, like a windscreen splattered with dead insects. In a ditch, in a bunker full of pipes and cables, a workman was giving his drill a horrid kneetrembler, louder than an act of God. Like me, myself, last night, with her. Underfoot the pavement crackled with horrorgrit. It went crackling right into the roots of Keith's horrorteeth.

The car *looked* funny. Keith scrunched up the parking tickets. Then he froze. The front window on the passenger side had been stove in! Keith's body throbbed from the sudden wound. He went round and unlocked and opened the door – and felt the horrorslide and horrortrickle of the crushed glass. The welded stereo had been scrabbled at, its dials torn off, but . . . Keith's library of darts tapes! It was okay: intact, entire. They hadn't stooped that low. For a while he stared at the faulty burglar alarm he had recently stolen. Without thinking he reached down and with his right hand brushed from the seat the jewelled horrorglass.

Fresh catastrophe: the stained tip of his middle finger had been sweetly pierced by the horrorshard. No pain: only mental anguish. A fat dome or bulb of horrorblood now pulsed above the yellow rind. It started dripping. On the car floor he found a crumpled pin-up with which he rudely dressed his damaged darting digit. And the digital on the dash – what was the horrortime? – remained garbled, made nonsense of, by the rays of the low sun, which had surely never been lower (he was on his way now), bouncing at bus height over the spines of traffic. Through the open window the sound of passing cars came like the zip and sniff of a boxer's feints and punches. Ten-twenty. His appointment with Mrs Ovens had been scheduled for 9.15. But there were always queues. As he drove, motes of the shattered glass, quarks of glassdust, seemed to tickle his scalp like particles of horrorlight.

He arrived at the tricky junction on the Great Western Road: familiar horrorspot, with zebra-crossing, bus station, and hump-backed bridge over the canal, all complicating access. Fifteen minutes later, he was still there. Timing their runs to split-second perfection, the launched horrorcars, the bowling horrorlorries successively denied the heavy Cavalier. Whenever a gap appeared, so would some contrary vehicle, seeming to pounce or spring into position. Either that, or, as Keith inched forward, the underground station would emit a resolute trainload on to the crossing before him. Keith pounded his fists on the steering-wheel's artificial leopard skin. At his rear he sensed the climbing volume of thwarted hurry: how it groaned and squirmed . . . In his face he felt the low sun like a lamp bent for interrogation. Now the road cleared but as Keith revved and shuddered, and yearned forwards, another watch of horrorsouls bobbed on to the zebra – the passing faces of the horrorsouls.

Finally he churned his way through with his bloodied hand on the horn. And into what? Driving was like a test film or a dramatization of the Highway Code, whatever *that* used to be, with every turn and furlong offering multiple choice, backing learner, swearing cyclist, peeking perambulator. Richly sectioned with doubleparkers and skip-collectors and clamp-removers, the roads became a kiddy-book of excavators, macadam-layers, streetlamp-changers, white-line painters, mobile libraries, armed-personnel-carriers, steamrollers, bulldozers, tanks, ditch-diggers, drain cleaners. For an extended period he was wedged behind a leaf-disposal truck. From its rear a vacuum tube slurped up the sear broomed roadside pyramids. He watched the suck, the feathery flip; sex re-entered his head and found no room there. Everything he had ever done to womankind he had done again ten times last night, with her. The whipped dance of the moistened leaves. Defoliated, deflowered, stripped of leaves and flowers, with trees sharp-lined like old human faces, and wringing their bare hands, London could still drown in all its horrorleaves.

At the civic building, at 10.55, a stroke of good fortune – or motoring knowhow. The back street was double, tripleparked, parked out, with cars parked beside, athwart, on top of. But as usual nobody had dared block the old dairy exit (which Keith knew to be disused) – or so it seemed, when he peered into the dusty fire of his rear window. Keith backed in smartly. This was horrorday, however. Therefore, a horrorbike was waiting there, leaning on its stick, and Keith heard the eager horrorcrunch. Worse, when Keith crept out to disensnare his bumper, the horrorbike's own horror-biker formidably appeared – one of that breed of men, giant miracles of facial hair and weight problem, who love the wind of the open road, and love the horrorbikes they straddle there. He hoisted Keith on to the boot of the Cavalier, and banged his head on it for a while, and then direly raised a gauntleted horrorfist. Keith whimpered his way out of that one, offering up a stolen credit card in earnest of his false address. He went and parked about three miles away and tearfully sprinted back through the fuming jams and the incredible crowds of the horrormany.

Guy Clinch was heading towards London at twice the speed of sound, one of half a dozen passengers on the hurled dart of the Concorde. He had missed the earlier flight by ten minutes and had spent three hours trying to sleep, in a kind of capsule hotel at Kennedy, before taking off, smoothly but dramatically, in the still centre of Hurricane Lulu. Now he was in another capsule, his eyes rinsed by the coldly beautiful blue of the troposphere. Through his porthole Guy could also see both sun and moon, the former discreetly filtered by the treated plastic. Because of the elevation and velocity of this particular observer, the two bodies seemed to be moving towards each other with uncelestial haste. Below, the turning planet fell through its curve of spacetime, innocent (though much traduced) in its blond fur coat. Beyond, inanely vast, the inanity of space.

Two glamorous, multilingual stewardesses exhaustively pampered him; he had recently relished a plateful of scrambled eggs and smoked salmon; and he was reading *Love*. Even so, Guy happened to be in dramatic discomfort. Bending to refill his cup with the excellent coffee (a mixed roast, he would guess), one of his stewardesses had noticed the odd tilt of the meal tray: she had given it a careful nudge and then, suddenly, leaned on it quite hard with the full weight of her shoulder. When Guy reopened his eyes, probably about ninety seconds later, he was confronted by the frown of the cabin steward, solicitously crouched in the aisle. The stewardess was hanging back with the knuckle of her forefinger pressed against her teeth. Guy apologized to them and eventually they went away. But the pain went nowhere.

The last chapter of *Love* was called 'Concerning Fiascos': ' "The whole realm of love is full of tragic stories," said Madame de Sévigné, relating her son's misfortunes with the celebrated Champmeslé. Montaigne handles so scabrous a subject with great aplomb.' Guy finished the chapter, wonderingly, and then flipped through the copious appendices. It would be a relief to be done with *Love*: this famished sampling of erotic thought would never ease his hunger pains. *Concerning Courts of Love*. Guy smiled modestly as he thought of that last telephone call and the delightful carnality he seemed to have awakened in her. 'The plea of marriage is not a legitimate defence against love.' No doubt she would meet him halfway up the stairs, with all that colour in her face. 'A lover shall, on the death of the other lover, remain unattached for two years.' As they kissed, he would place both palms on the back of her thighs, beneath what might well be that black cashmere dress with the buttons, and almost lift her whole body on to him. 'Success too easily won soon strips love of its charm; obstacles enhance its value. Every lover grows pale at the sight of the beloved.' As they moved through the sitting-room her breath would be sweet and hot (and *hers*: everything would be *hers*); teardrops, too, perhaps, rather deliciously. 'Suspicion and the jealousy which derives from it aggravate the condition called love.' It didn't matter what happened in the bedroom and in a way one feared for the loss of individuality (in the blinding rapture and so on); yet how strange her face would look from that angle, when, as she had laughingly promised, she knelt to remove his trousers and undershorts. 'A person in love is unremittingly and uninterruptedly occupied with the image of the beloved.' So brown, so close together. 'Nothing forbids a woman to be loved by two men . . .'

Guy put *Love* aside and took up the second book, *The Light of Many Suns*. For a moment he vaguely wondered what Keith was up to; but then his eyes fell on Nicola's inscription, over which he had already done some puzzling:

> Thou art the grave where buried love doth live,
> Hung with the trophies of my lovers gone,
> Who all their parts of me to thee did give,
> That due of many now is thine alone:
>   Their images I loved I view in thee,
>   And thou – all they – hast all the all of me.

One of the Sonnets, of course (and Guy knew the Sonnets tolerably well); a complete sestet. How did it . . .? Ah yes: Thy bosom . . . Thy bosom is endeared with all the hearts . . . Rather a knotty one, this. Addressed by the man to the woman. The past lovers aren't just 'gone': they're dead. But people died earlier in those days. Wish I had a copy. And there reigns Love, and all Love's loving parts. Absolutely fascinating.

'That leaves four hundred', said Mrs Ovens, 'for the nose.'
'Nose? What nose? There weren't no *nose*.'

'Same incident, Keith.'

'That was an earhole.'

'You can't *fracture* an ear, Keith. And we're coming to that. The torn ear.'

'Bitten,' said Keith firmly. 'Bitten.'

'Which reminds me: the tooth'll be twelve-fifty.'

'Twelve-fifty! Blimey . . . Gone up again, has it?'

'The seven-fifty's for a molar. This is an incisor. Canines are seventeen-twenty-five.'

'Jesus. I mean, I'm just a working *man*.'

'It's what the law considers fair, Keith.'

'Capitalism innit,' said Keith. 'Just bloodsuckers as such.' He sighed longsufferingly.

'And then there's the split tongue.'

Keith now raised a dissenting forefinger. 'When there was all this,' he said carefully, 'I, *I* was hospitalized on thirteen occasions. Sustaining permanent injury to me chest. We don't hear nothing about that. No danger.'

'Yes, but what were you *doing* at the time, Keith?'

'Trying, in my own way, to establish a small business. Escape the poverty trap. That's it. Go on. Laugh.'

'The split tongue, Keith.'

'Jesus.'

In the end Keith agreed to up his weekly payment from £5 to £6.50. On top of that, to show good will, he committed himself to forty-eight hours of community service. Consisting as it did of stealing odds and ends from very old people, community service was nowhere near as bad as it sounded. Community service, in Keith's judgment, had been much maligned. But on a day such as this a man's thoughts should surely be with his darts. Not haggling here with some old hippie about the price of horrornose, of horrortooth, of horrortongue.

Keith drove to the garage in Rifle Lane. Fortunately Fucker was on shift.

'Who did *this* fucker?' asked Fucker. 'It'll be a rough job. But you'll have security.'

Gratefully Keith relaxed on a winded carseat in the back room. He read the ripped mags: nude skirt. Peace at last. Beside him in a large cardboard box an even larger cat lay dying. Cruelly cramped, it struggled and sneezed and sighed. It began weeping rhythmically.

442

Keith was used to noise, incessant and unwelcome noise. Most of his life was played out to a soundtrack of sadistic decibelage. Noise, noise — noise on the brink of bearability. He was used to unwelcome nearnesses, also, to stinging proximities; but did the bald cat's sneezes really have to bubble and dampen the very thigh of his trouserleg? It wept in rhythm. Sounds almost like . . . The nude birds in the book. Nothing on Nick. She'd show them. He closed his eyes and saw himself naked and twanging back and forth with incomprehensible violence and speed, as if in controlled preparation for spaceflight. There she was, just a G-spot in a G-string. And there was Keith in his G-suit, ready to take on gravity . . . A new noise, a new nearness, a new order of alarm: Keith was staring at the horrorcat.

'Gone, has she? It's a rough job,' said Fucker.

They stood there inspecting the Cavalier's warped windowframe, the mauled glass, smothered in fingerprints.

'But you've got security.'

'Appreciate it.'

And Keith bent into his pocket and parted with the money: endlessly, horrornote after horrornote.

With the low sun like a prickly sweater gently pressed into his unshaven face, Keith drove to the Black Cross, for his breakfast. The backslaps and the fagsmoke, the lagers and the Scotch eggs, did not combine well. A pork pie, Keith decided, was what he really fancied. Then you feel twice the price. Shakespeare staggered over and fiercely tousled Keith's hair for at least a minute. When he had stopped doing that, Keith looked down at the bar: a new soft-fallen mask of dandruff now salted his food, and melted into the lager's horrorhead. At that moment his teeth lanced a spectacular impurity among the knotted gristle inside his mouth. Keith, who took his chances and ate a great many pork pies, was no stranger to impurity; but he had never encountered anything so throatfloodingly gangrenous as this. Without interrupting the conversation he was having with somebody else, Pongo handed him the bottle of green mouthwash kept under the bar, and Keith loped off to the Gents. Half an hour later, when the tortured gagging had subsided, to the relief of everyone in the building, Keith returned and drank the complimentary Scotches and dabbed at his eyes with a piece of newspaper tenderly torn by Pongo from his own tabloid. Keith nodded as he studied the pork-pie wrapping: the eat-by-date was placed well into the next millennium. He had a few more Scotches and was cheering up enough to make a start on telling the lads about his night with Nick. His stomach still bubbled and spat, still noisily rueing that horrorpie.

When everything began to go dark.

'Look!'

Through the stained glass they stared, or some of them did, as in perfect parallax the two white balls conjoined like something unanswerable under the microscope, and the moon began to burn like a little sun.

'It's eclipse . . . Eclipse! . . . What fucking clips? . . . Fucking power-cut . . . It's the fucking eclipse . . . Put the fucking lights on . . . Eclipse, innit . . . It's the fucking eclipse . . .'

Keith turned away, in horror. To his left a dartsman waited at the dimmed oché with his arrows, head dropped in a martyrdom of impatience. Someone pitched a coin on to the counter. It clattered on its rim, noisily, like a cold car just before it fires. And the coin went on wobbling, clattering, faster, tighter. That was him last night, himself, twirling to the very end of his band . . . Shivering Shakespeare stood ten feet away with his face between the double doors of the Black Cross. Today was the day when, in Shakespeare's scheme of things, he was due to lead his chosen people to the mountains of Eritrea: the promised land. As he looked round the Black Cross that morning, though, it didn't look terribly likely . . . Outside, he had sensed the cold, the eclipse wind, the silenced pigeons. Four hundred miles across, the point of a dark cone of shadow a quarter of a million miles long was heading towards him at two thousand miles per hour. Next came the presentiment of change, like the arrival of weather-front or thunderhead, with the light glimmering – but getting fierier. Then a shade being drawn across the sky. Totality. Shakespeare was crying. He knew that something awful had to happen, when horrorday was horrornight, when horrorsun was horrormoon.

Up above also (if anybody had been able to find her), and looking her very best in the sudden twilight, proudly shone Venus, daughter of Jupiter, wife of Vulcan, lover of Mars, and never brighter than when the darkness of totality played across the earth.

Where was Nicola Six?

Nobody knew.

The Light of Many Suns turned out to be a war memoir: rather remarkable in its way. Guy finished his *faisan à la mode de champagne* and shamefacedly went on drinking the claret, which he suspected would have a restaurant price of about three times the minimum weekly wage. Group Captain Leonard Cheshire, VC, OM, DSO, DFC, the author, a Catholic and obviously a good egg, was one of the two British observers of the atom-bombing of Hiroshima.

Guy looked out of the porthole. The 'second contact', or the first moment of full eclipse, had occurred twenty minutes earlier. The pilot of the Concorde, an eclipse-enthusiast and member of the Thousand Second Club, had announced his intention of staying within the eastward-moving umbra until he began his descent over Ireland. Thus totality was lasting far longer than its terrestrial three minutes. When it came, Guy had tensed, as if for an impact. Or he had tried to. But he realized then that he couldn't get any tenser than he was already. Just as his phallus couldn't get any harder. At the moment that the moon's shape fully covered the sun, then with fantastic simultaneity the solar corona bathed the circumference with unforgettable fire. Guy was amazed, harrowed, by the tightness of the fit. Surely only the divinely privileged observer would be blessed with this full-true billiards shot, straight, dead straight, for ninety million miles. Perhaps that was the necessary condition of planetary life: your sun must fit your moon. The umbra began to overtake the plane; the pilot came on again and with emotion commanded his few passengers to admire the 'diamond-ring' effect of the 'third contact', when the leading slice of the sun re-emerged. Yes, yes, yes: just like a sparkler on its band. Like a ring for her, perhaps. Heavenly engagement.

The descent began. Guy picked up *The Light of Many Suns*. On page forty-six he dropped the book to the floor. He reached for his paper bag and opened it in front of his mouth. He waited. Perhaps there was an explanation. Perhaps, after all, it was something quite innocent . . .

'Enola Gay' was the plane that flew the mission to Hiroshima. The pilot named the aircraft after his mother. He was once her little boy.

But Little Boy was the name of the atom bomb. It killed 50,000 people in 120 seconds.

Keith stood on her stoop, fumbling weepily with his great ring of keys – Keith's keys, his gaoler's keys, keys for Debbee, Trish and Analiese, keys for flat, for car, for go-down and lock-up. But keys for

Nicola? He rang the bell again; he tried all the keys again. Now Keith was close to panic, to cursing, rattling panic. He wanted to see her very badly, not for the act of love and hate, which, to his surprise, and so far as he could tell, he wanted never to perform again with anybody. No: he wanted her for her belief in him, because she was the other world, and if she said that Keith was real then the other world would say it too. But hang on. Suppose she's under a bus somewhere? His darts boots, his darts strides, his darts shirt, his very – ! Keith clapped a hand to his horrorchest. Then his knees gave with relief. All is not lost. His darts pouch remained in its rightful place, in the pocket closest to his heart. He buzzed the buzzer again; he tried all the keys again. Throughout he was aware of eyes on his back. Today, even the dead-end street was crowded, and sharply charged in voice and gesture: a sense of population shift. Keith turned. A lone policeman was watching him from the pavement, motionless against the plunging figures beyond. Just a kid. In a uniform. Fucking tithead. Keith was fairly confident that the policeman wouldn't try nothing here, or he'd get lynched. But now he was coming forward, his shoulders interestedly inclined, and – okay – maybe it didn't look too good, unkempt Keith crooked over his keys. So he did a great mime of casually patting his pockets, then swivelled, shaking his head. He sauntered down the path and, with a bit of the old insouciance (the Scotches and supplementary *pornos* were about their work), hopped into the heavy Cavalier. Keith started off with an unintended bound, just missing an unattended pram, and monitoring in his rearview mirror the shape of the tapering horrorfilth.

With the low sun playfully tickling the hairs in his nostrils, Keith drove to Windsor House. Nick'd show up later: call her from there. And, besides, he wanted to see how Clive was doing. The radio worked all right. As he drove home he listened irritatedly to the news, the dissolution of the Crisis, the improving condition of the President's wife, the delegations leaving simultaneously for Paris and Prague (not a summit: more like twin peaks), and wondered if this explained the pronounced congestion he encountered in Ladbroke Grove. He doubleparked outside Maharajah Wines. On the way to the lift his gait changed from its accustomed boxy shuffle to the sudden dance of a paddler entering a cold sea. His right foot, deep in horrorturd. Luckily, on the other hand, the lift was working, more or less. It came all the way down in answer to his punched summons.

But it didn't get very far up. Sitting on the floor, waiting the twenty minutes for the next power surge, Keith took a matchstick to the slender grids of his tarnished sole. One mercy: the dog responsible for such a dropping was by now almost certainly dead. His thoughts were all with horrordog and horrorcat as, after a sickening drop, he shuddered his way tormentedly upwards, wedged in the pungent horrorlift.

On the narrow walkstrip Keith attacked the lock, which was often recalcitrant. But today was horrorday. He stared down at the single gnarled key. On the outer mat were four horrorletters: two horrorbills, a horrorsummons, and a horrororder of distraint. Keith had had enough with all this locks and keys: he took a step back and detonated himself against the door. Normally it would have given like a dunked biscuit. But the devices Keith himself had sometimes deployed were evidently in place: the bars and braces used by him to keep out bailiffs, bad-debt buyers, repo men, cheated horror*cheats*.

'Kath,' he said in a low voice.

He flinched at the misted glass. A warning shape moved away, then reappeared, like a figure glimpsed in church.

'I saw you,' it whispered.

'Fuck off,' coaxed Keith. 'What? When? Come on, darling.'

'On the telly.'

'. . . That weren't nothing. Just for the telly like. Load of nonsense. *For* the telly.'

'You told the world,' she said. 'On the telly.'

And Keith had no answer.

Even the old Metrocab coming in from Heathrow had its own slant about forms of torture. For one thing, the vibration, the cauldron-bubble beneath the seat, appeared to whet the pain in Guy's groin, assuming that any kind of increase was possible down there. But it was stranger than that. The driver treated his cab as a peasant might treat his horse or ass, with numb and proprietorial cruelty. The bursts of acceleration were like long-toothed, lip-flapping exhalations; then came the looping whinny of the brakes. It was diversion of a kind to listen to the grades of neigh and whinny, of anger and submission, that the driver thrashed out of his livelihood, the black machine.

As he paid, a passing child tossed a jumping-jack in through the window, and paused to watch it raise hell in the back of a cab – its headbanging ecstasy of entrapment.

'Bombfire night,' said the driver, listlessly.

Guy walked on down the dead-end street; he had called her from the airport, without success; he didn't expect her to be home. Nor was she. He let himself in at the front door and climbed the stairs. The second key opened up an olfactory world that Guy remembered from his schooldays: duckboards and lockers, the lavatory where the smokers went. He saw the dartboard, the pewter tankard engraved to him, to Keith. Next door, through the thin passage, he saw the ruin of the bed, the upended ashtray on the pillow and its droppings on the sheets. Scattered about the floor were shiny puddles of exotic underwear. He saw the three empty brandy bottles, the hookah pipe. On the chair, as if laid out ready for school, brocaded trousers and the red shirt saying, KEITH TALENT – THE FINISHER.

Next door again he found an envelope marked *Guy*, unprominently displayed among the fashion and darts magazines on her crowded bureau. The note said: 'Gone to the darts.' There was a pass or ticket attached. The telephone rang. He waited before picking it up.

'Where the fuck a you been?' said a voice Guy knew well.

'. . . Guy here.'

'. . . Oh, hello, mate. I uh, I had some stuff I was picking up. She there is she?'

'No, she's not here.'

'Know when she be back?'

'No, I don't know.'

'Minge,' said Keith indulgently. 'Never around when you want them. Always there when you don't. I couldn't, I couldn't pop – Nah. Yeah well cheers.'

Guy waited.

'Okay. See you later then, pal.' He added monotonously, 'Yeah well she said you'd want to be there. As my virtual sponsor. Helping with the funding like.'

'No doubt.'

'Onna darts.'

No joy there then, thought Keith. He can't be feeling too brill neither. Either. But this is it, *it*, success in this life always going to the guy who . . . The dartboard in Keith's garage looked on as he finished his *porno*, removed his clothes, and, jogging lightly on the cold floor, washed himself, horribly, in the horrorsink. Keith's lifestyle. Sceptically he connected the electric kettle he had recently stolen. It hummed faultily for several seconds, and Keith's hopes soared. But then the machine gave a scorching fizz and pooped the blackened plug from its horrorrear. He shaved in lukewarm water before the mirror's acne. Next, with the jellied shampoo, colder still, his horrorhair. He donned his number-three darting shirt, so damp and creased. It said: KEITH TALENT – THE PICKOFF KING. He dried his hair with some old horrorrag.

A sudden orange cockroach rushed past and Keith stamped on it, urbanely, out of grooved urban habit. But the glazed and tendrilled body of the cockroach, even as it collapsed inwards, sent Keith a reminder that his foot was unshod, unsocked. Just a horrorfoot. Keith yanked his whole leg up with a senile yodel of disgust. So he was still capable of disgust; and he didn't go all the way through with that skilful stomp of his. The look he gave the half-crushed roach might even have been mistaken for appalled concern. The vermin lay there, half-turned; its various appendages were all moving at different speeds – but none of them were human speeds. Me, myself, only hours ago, thought Keith, with intense lassitude . . . He put on his left shoe. After many unsatisfactory minutes with a scrubbing-brush, he put on his right shoe. Reckon I get there early, in good time. Soak up the atmosphere. He got to his feet. Blimey. You just decide you're going to enjoy every minute of it. Wouldn't miss it for the world. Never ask about . . . He zipped up his windcheater. Relax, few drinks. Take the opportunity of using the celebrity practice boards. And generally compose myself, Tony. It's fortunate, Ned, that I seem to respond to the big occasion. On his way out he took a last look at the hate-filled face of the flickering horrorroach.

Guy had gone home.

Or he had gone to Lansdowne Crescent. His housekeys were still in his pocket, but manners – and caution – demanded that he ring the bell. Through the half-glass door and its steel curlicues a redoubtable figure loomed. Guy thought it might be Doris – the one who couldn't climb stairs. Because of her knees. The one who feared and hated all stairs.

The door opened. It was Lizzyboo. He couldn't help staring. And he couldn't help thinking of the helium blimp he had seen that day, effortfully hovering over Terminal Four.

'Isn't it wonderful? Isn't it *wonderful*.'

She said this joyfully. And as Guy listened he clearly saw the other Lizzyboo, the one he had loved for a month, the one he had kissed and touched among the trembling porcelain. The other Lizzyboo was still there all right, hiding within; and now it was safe to come out.

'Everything's okay again.'

Of course this was neither here nor there to Guy, because she only meant the planet. 'How's Hope? How's the boy?'

'You'd better go on up.'

He went on up. As he turned the corner of the stairs he was disquieted by the sight of a silhouette in the passage, near the bedroom door. Something about the waiting shape was admonitory, ritualized, ecclesiastical. As he approached he saw that it was a little boy, in full armour.

'Who is it?' came a voice. 'Darling?'

Guy was about to frame a grateful reply. But the little boy answered sooner. 'A man,' he said.

'What man?'

'. . . Daddy.'

Marmaduke stepped aside, with some formality, and Guy entered the room. The little boy followed, and then moved quietly past his father to the side of the bed, where Hope lay, on her barge of pillows.

'Where is everyone?' said Guy, for the house was eerily staffless.

'All gone. There's no need. He's different now.'

'What happened?'

'It was quite sudden. The day after.'

As they spoke, Marmaduke was undressing, or unbuckling himself. He laid down sword, dagger, pike and shield, neatly, on the chair. He freed his breastplate. Finger by finger he loosened his gauntlets.

'And you?' said Guy.

Her face expressed, in terms of time and distance, the kind of journey he would have to undertake if he were ever to return. It was a long journey. Perhaps even the earth wasn't big enough to contain it . . . One by one Marmaduke removed his shin-guards, then the little chainmail slippers. Next, his authentic-looking tights were meticulously unpeeled.

'No nappy!' said Guy.

Marmaduke stood there in his underpants. These too he stepped out of. He climbed into bed. 'Mummy?'

450

'Yes, darling?'

'Mummy? Don't love Daddy.'

'I won't. I certainly won't.'

'Good.'

'. . . Byebye, Daddy.'

Guy came out into the fading afternoon. He looked at the pass or ticket she had left for him and wondered how he would ever kill all that time. Bent with his bag, he stood by the garden gate. He looked up. Already the sky was dotted with firebursts, rocket-trails: its proxy war. Soon, all over London, a thousand, a million guys would be burning, burning.

It's weird: you pull the sunguard down and it don't – the sun's still there, like Hawaii. Keith motored to the studio, which was very convenient, being amongst the refurbished warehouses down by the old canal. Once there, he availed himself, as instructed, of the private carpark. A janitor came hurdling out from behind the dustbins and told Keith, in no uncertain terms, to park elsewhere. On Keith producing ID, the janitor huddled over his faulty walkie-talkie. Keith listened to denial, to horrorfizz and horrorsquawk, and endless denial. When the clearance eventually came through Keith sniffed and realigned his jacket, and decisively shoved the car door shut with the flat of his hand. The window on the passenger side exploded outwards. Firmly the janitor brought him dustpan and horrorbrush.

Celebrity practice boards? *What* fucking celebrity practice boards? He was taken through the canteen and into a stockroom that happened to have a dartboard in it. Incredibly the sun sought him out even here. What was the sun made of? Coal? Oxyacetylene? Glologs? What was the matter with it? Why didn't it go away? Why didn't it go *out*? No: it went on funnelling its heat into his exhaustedly hooded eyes. He blinked into the numbered orb of the board, itself like a low sun, the vortex of all his hopes and dreams. His head bowed in its horrorglare. With the purple pouch in his hand (how very worn and soiled it looked) Keith paced out the distance, turned, sniffed, coughed and straightened himself. The sun vanished. The first dart was flying through the horrornight.

I return from my latest mission to find a note from Mark Asprey on the mat. Hand-delivered. Out of the Connaught. Now wait a minute . . .

Dear Sam: *So* glad you toiled your way to the crux of the Cornelia Constantine business. She was telling the truth when she said that *Crossbone Waters* was 'all lies'. There was no cerise lagoon, no rabid dog, no tears by the campfire beneath the throbbing stars. There was, above all, no marathon seduction. In fact, in truth, I had the idiot in hysterics on the very first day, after lunch, at the hotel – a location from which, during the entire fortnight, we seldom strayed.

No doubt you're wondering about those 'magnificent breasts' of hers. Those also I created with two deft dabs of my facile fancy: they had no more reality, alas, than the courtly Kwango. You know the type – great fat arse but racing tits. And *so* stupid. With a peculiar habit of –

There follow three or four hundred words of the grossest pornography. The letter concludes:

You don't understand, do you, my talentless friend? Even as you die and rot with envy. It doesn't matter what anyone writes any more. The time for it mattering has passed. The truth doesn't matter any more and *is not wanted*.

452

'Wait a minute,' I said. Nicola was coming out of the bathroom. I looked up at her. 'My God, you won't get fifty yards. It's grotesque.'

She had noticed the letter, with her intelligent eyes. She said, 'Are you ready to hear the bad thing I did to him? It might perk you up. Come in here. I want to keep doing my hair. Actually it has certain affinities with your own case. He wrote this novel,' she said, as I followed her into the bedroom. 'He'd been trying to write it for years. He showed it to me. It was in longhand, in a big exercise book. And it had something. It wasn't the usual trex he writes. It was from the heart.'

'And?'

'I destroyed it. I locked him in the bedroom and fed it to the fire. Page by page. Taunting him a lot and everything.'

'Hey, not bad.'

She was watching the way my eyes moved. 'Don't worry. I haven't destroyed yours.'

'Thanks. Why not? What came over you?'

'No need.'

'I don't understand you, Nicola.'

'That's right. You look terrible. Aren't there any *pills* you can take?' She sighed and said, 'Tell me about the child.'

Pain travels through diffuse interconnexions, through prolix networks of fibres, past trigger zones, along branches, through thickets . . . You want it to be over. Over! But *fear* is *all* about wanting it to be over. This might be its defining characteristic. The immediate physical symptoms are mild, and not distracting, as pain is.

I felt the baby's fear when I entered. A sudden pall of mid-afternoon, and silence, and no Keith and no Kath: just Kim, the squirming bagel at my feet on the kitchen floor. She seemed unhurt, only soaked and crying – and afraid. And that was enough, too much, should never happen. Oh I know when the babies come how we patter and creep like mice through the dark tunnels, to tend them, anticipate them, to pick them up and give them comfort. But it must be like that. It must always be like that. Because when we're not there, their worlds begin to fall away. On every side the horizon climbs until it pushes out the sky. The walls come in. Pain they can take, maybe. Pain is close and they know where it comes from. Not fear, though. Keep them from fear. Jesus, if they only knew what was *out* there. And that's why they must never be left alone like this.

453

Or not quite alone. When I knelt down to take her I heard a warning growl – from Clive, sitting erect in the Clive-sized square between the four joke rooms. 'It's all right,' I said. 'I'm good. I love her. I'm not bad. Good dog.' You can apparently tell this to a dog: a dog will believe it. He came forward; with sigh and half-leap he had his front paws up on the sink, watching for Kath or Keith; from the rear he looked like a trained gunman, ready, knees bent, weapon up. When the child was calmer I noticed on the table a box of matches, and a single cigarette. This was Kath's note to me.

Because I'd gotten everything wrong. And life is always forcing you into yet stranger positions. *Got to stop hurting K*, Keith had written. *Just takeing it out on the Baby.* But *K* wasn't Kim. *K* was Kath. But Keith couldn't stop. And Kath couldn't stop.

I had only one idea. I dressed her. When I changed the diaper I saw without surprise that there were no new marks. Kath had resisted the force of her own powerlessness, this time. I left a note, and a number, and I might have written there and then that some people get others to perform their greatest cruelties. They get others to do it for them.

And then this.

With her bobbing, rolling face on my shoulder I carried the child through the streets – and through a sudden carnival: an outbreak of human vigour and relief, with balloons and steel bands, loudspeakers propped on window-sills, pubs turned inside out. We were caught up in the beat of it and jounced along through the swiftly gathering crowds. One of those moments when everybody wants to be black, lithe, hellraising; and against their dark brilliance, the white faces, shyly smiling, ashamed to go out in the light, to be seen at all. The streets were infantile and drunken. There the donnish indulgent stroll of the policemen. There a black lady dancing in a bobby's hat. There a child's rapt uplifted face.

Life! Like the warm life in my arms. But then there can suddenly be too much of it, too much life, and different breathlessness, different danger . . . A tight intersection on the Portobello Road, and life pressing in from all four directions, more headcounts everywhere, like stacks of cannonballs, and the mysterious arrival of panic, with arms now windmilling as they fought their way to the edge. And there *was* no edge, only life, more life. I held Kim above my head, right up there among the screams. And the crowd, the large creature of which we formed a cell, started to topple centipedically, and (I thought) only one outcome, as you must fall or trample or do both.

Then it was over and we were on the other side. I used the basement door at Lansdowne Crescent. Lizzyboo could do it. She was all healed and clear. I said that Kath would call. I said I knew she would do what was right. I said she had all my trust.

'It's all right for you. You just had a whole chapter off. I've been dicing with death out there.' 'Yes, so you claim.' 'I swear I was *that close*.' 'I too have been far from idle.' 'Putting your warpaint on.' 'Yes. And reading.'

I waited, and watched her brow.

'You made me ridiculous. How did you *dare*? I thought I was meant to be tragic. At least a bit. And all this stuff as if I wasn't in control. *Every second*.'

'I'm sorry,' I said. 'I don't see you that way.'

Then she said something I didn't quite catch. And didn't want her to repeat. I started getting ready to leave.

'Do you think this dress is sufficiently disgusting?' she called out. 'I'd better tell you something I'm going to do on the way there.'

She told me. 'Nico*la*.'

'You'd be surprised how eloquent a bit of dirt can be. Carefully applied.'

'I've just thought. I'll see you at the studio and everything – but this is *goodbye*.'

'Take my flat key. Get there early and you'll have a good view.'

I looked for challenge in her coldness. I said coldly, 'You're going to be gone from nine to twelve, right? I can't imagine how you're going to work it.'

'The story of your life. Off you go. Kiss.'

'Let's stop it. Let's abort . . . Oh, wear a coat, Nicola. It's not working. It's not working out. I'm losing it, Nicola. There are things I'm not seeing.'

I'm going.

I'm back.

It seems for the time being that Nicola has confounded us all.

Chapter 23: You're Going
Back With Me

THE BLACK CAB will move away, unrecallably and for ever, its driver paid, and handsomely tipped, by the murderee. Disgustingly attired (how *could* she?), she'll click on her heels down the dead-end street. The heavy car will be waiting; its lights will come on as it lumbers towards her. It will stop, and idle, as the passenger door swings open.

His face will be barred in darkness, but she will see cracked glass on the passenger window-frame and the car-tool ready on his lap.

'Get in.'

She will lean forward. '*You*,' she will say, with intense recognition. 'Always you.'

'Get *in*.'

And in she'll climb . . .

Disgustingly attired: how *could* she? In white thinstrapped tanktop picodress, cauterized at the waist, promoting all the volume of the secondary sexual characteristics, and so tight below that the outlined panties give a nappy-puff to the rounded rear; and bare-legged, with scarlet satin shoes, the heels unforgivably long, heels that would look longer still (the suggestion was) when their shadows played on the backs of berks! Her hair was sprayed with glitter, and savagely tousled. As she made her way to the studio she selected a good brick wall, steeped in London smoke and moisture, and went and pressed her rump against it. The dress was man-made, drulon, trexcett, man-made in every sense, made by men with men in mind. She wanted to walk the whole way there, to test her nerve and tauten her breasts.

She shimmied her rump against the moist brick wall. Of course, there was no mirror, and she couldn't really check; but the contact felt just right.

Keith said, 'Where's the pub then?'

'Pub? What pub?' Tony de Taunton looked at Keith curiously.

'The venue. The —' Keith snapped his darting finger — 'the Chuckling Sparrow.'

'There's no *pub*. Don't you think we have enough grief already, Keith. Without wheeling a couple of hundred pissers in and out of here four nights a week.' As he spoke, Tony de Taunton gave Keith a glass of low-alc and led him by the arm to the window. 'No no, friend. All those jolly butchers and smiling grannies — that's library stuff. We use cutaways and dub the pub later.'

'Common sense,' said Keith. They were standing in a cavernous lot, full of hidden noise. Shifters and fixers moved stoically about with planks under their arms. All were expert noisemakers. Sheets of silver cardboard imparted the spectral light of watery dreams. On the wall was a sign bearing the saddest words Keith had ever read: NO SMOKING. Also a mirror, in which he made out a funny-looking bloke in a wrinkled red shirt: TV's Keith. There *was* a bar, though, with four or five stools you could perch on. But none of that fog and gurgling clamour that he had come to think of as his darting lifeblood. Where the pub parrot, effing and blinding on its soiled hook? Where the pub dogs, whinnying in nightmare beneath the round tables?

'Look. Here comes Chick,' said Tony de Taunton. 'You got to like his style.'

A cream Rolls-Royce had pulled up in the carpark below. Two men climbed out slowly.

'Where are *your* guests, Keith?'

'Be along. Who's that with him?'

'Julian Neat.'

Julian Neat: agent to the darting stars. Agent to Steve Notice, to Dustin Jones.

'Yes. They say Chick's all signed up.'

*

457

Nick and Chick had come in through different doors but they made their entrances together, which was frankly ideal for television's Keith Talent, who, by this stage, felt he could do with a little support – felt, indeed, that he might die or go mad at any second. She pushed past the greeters and moved with hesitant hurry towards him. He had never seen her looking quite so beautiful.

'Oh my Keith.'

'Where you *been*, girl?'

'What happened? Did you lose your keys? I saw your darts clothes were still on the chair.'

'Where you *been*, girl?'

Imploringly she flattened herself up against him. 'I'll tell you about it later. Making arrangements. For us, Keith. We're going on a wonderful journey.'

'Break it up, you two,' cajoled Ned von Newton: Mr Darts. 'Come and be friendly.'

They went to join the others at the semicircular bar. Keith strolled over with some insouciance (he saw the way that Chick clocked Nick). She was holding his hand – gazing, with the demurely gratified eyes of love, at TV Keith.

Guy stood with his back to the building, facing the flatlands of demolition. Squares of concrete, isolated by chicken wire, in each of which a bonfire burned, baking the potatoes of the poor. Apparently cleansed by its experiences of the afternoon, the moon outshone these fires; even the flames cast shadows.

As he turned he saw a hooded figure by the doorway. He halted.

'They're in there,' it said.

Guy thought: it's a girl. He moved closer. One of Keith's women. The ruined blonde who –

'Keith,' said Trish Shirt. 'And . . . Nicky.' She sighed nauseously. 'Now they getting married like.'

'I hardly think so.'

'They are. It was on the telly.' She leaned forward and placed a hand on his arm. 'Say I'm waiting. Tell Keith. Forever in a day like. I'll always be waiting.'

When Guy got up to the lot he hung back by the door, able to linger, it seemed, in a frenzy of unobtrusiveness. At first all he felt was simple disappointment. He had hoped Nicola would be there, and she wasn't. Nicola wasn't there. He could see a girl in the group

458

round the bar, under a bulb of light: she looked a lot like Nicola. She *was* Nicola, almost certainly. But she was somebody Guy didn't know.

He'd thought Trish seemed disembodied, in her hood, neutered, an *it* not a she – or just non-human. But the girl at the bar, unhooded, turned to the light, indeed fully opened out towards the world, was less human than the thing in the hood.

Nicola was laughing with her mouth as long and wide as it would go. The energy equation here could be represented as something like $x=yz^2$, y being a certain magnitude of solitary female beauty, z being the number of men present, and x the Platonic gang-rape which, in certain possible futures, might harden into action. It had to be said that the men around her only frowned and smiled, as if chastened by her colour, her volume, her spin of ravenous risk. Where does the guest look when the host's little girl is doing her somersaults for him: it's so transparent? But this was no little girl. As she worked herself backwards on to her stool she gave a vivid flinch and turned to Keith like one confidently seeking forgiveness; and there was no way out of joining Nicola in her amusing struggles with the hem of her dress. Their indivisible attention: that's what she had.

Keith watched her proudly. And Chick watched her – Chick, Chick Purchase, large, delicate, deliberate, thick-haired, deep-voiced, and dangerous, with hardman or just criminal glow, like an actor, like a star, who accepts the role that the ordinary imagination assigns him. In his face you could see the associated pleasures of making love to women and of causing harm to men, or beyond that even, to the links between disseminating life and ending it. There was also something ridiculous, sinisterly ridiculous, in the way he looked: he dressed like a girl, he dressed like a chick. He filled the flow of his trousers with some of the lilt that a girl would, and his shirt had a flounce to it, the kind of flounce chicks like. But this was no little girl. There was no mistaking his sex. Chick? In the tight waist-to-thigh panels of his orange trousers, it was visible, and sinisterly ridiculous. A slobberer for skirt: that was how come he hadn't yet gone all the way, in crime or darts. Tonight, no roadshow hopeful or wet T-shirt at his side: only, in the cream Roller, Julian Neat, who looked like what he was, a successful middleman, in an exhausted culture.

'The past is past,' Keith was saying. 'Let's forget any unpleasantness and shake on it. Fair enough, mate?'

'Okay,' said Chick deeply. 'Tell me something, Keith. What's a girl like this doing with a little coon like you?'

'Chick,' said Julian Neat.

'See?' said Keith.

'I think that's very unfair, Chick,' said Nicola earnestly. 'Keith's very good at darts.'

'Okay, break it up, you lot,' said Miles Fitzwilliam as he approached, pulling his headphones away from his ears. 'Pre-match interview.'

The two contestants slid ponderously from their stools.

Guy saw his chance. But his chance of what? For one thing, he seemed to have forgotten how to walk.

Nicola saw him: she smiled and waved with puppet animation. As he crossed the vault the hope gathered in him that she would become the woman he knew; but she just went on getting stranger. Stranger smile, and stranger eyes. When he was near enough he said experimentally,

'Hello.'

'*Silence. Oi!*'

She pouted a kiss at him and prettily crossed her lips with a cautioning forefinger.

'Obviously,' Keith was saying to the camera, which was jack-knifed in fascination a foot from his face, 'hopefully'll the best man win. When we go out there.' He realized that more was expected of him. 'So let's hope the bloke, the guy with the, the superior technique will, will run out winner against, against the man with the . . . least good equipment. Dartwise. At the death.'

Nicola applauded silently; then her palms came to rest, as if in prayer.

'I'm confident, Miles,' Chick was chipping in. 'Got to be, with those averages. And – see, Keith and I go back a bit. And I know he's got this funny habit. Of bottling it. At the death. Frankly, I just hope it's not too one-sided. For darts' sake.'

'Thanks, lads. Five minutes, yeah?'

Nicola wiggled a finger and Guy moved closer. 'Darling,' said her hot breath, 'don't worry! – this is only a dream.'

Keith's heart leapt or jolted when he saw the new arrival: Kim Twemlow, the ex-world number one, with his smile, his jewelled shirt, his white shoes. The guy was like a god to Keith, no matter about his orange-peel face. Let others dwell on that funny lump in his side, that walking-frame. He had a good head of hair, for thirty-eight. Just that some of us live so full, our flames burn so bright, that the years go past not singly but six or seven at a time, like the years of dogs.

As for Guy, Keith saw him and closed his eyes and reopened them elsewhere.

Julian Neat was telling another one.

Nicola was laughing with her mouth as long and wide as it would go, when Guy stepped forward.

'*You're going back with me.*'

They all turned.

'*You're going back with me.*'

They all stared. They all stared at this bit of unnecessary unpleasantness. The pale loiterer with his boiled eyes. Nicola's expression showed that although she always tried to see the amusing side of things, well, on this occasion she really *was* rather shocked.

Guy seized her wrist and she gave a practised shriek as her stool slewed. Round about now Keith was always going to be stepping in.

'It's over. Don't be a prick.'

'You're going back', said Guy, with immaculate enunciation, as if perhaps she hadn't heard or understood, 'with *me*.'

She looked at him. Her upper lip hovered over her teeth. 'No I'm not. What for? To talk about love, and Enola Gay? No I'm not. I'm not going back with *you*.'

'Right,' said Keith to the nape of Guy's neck. 'She's going back with me. For more of what she got last night. She's going back with me.'

'No I'm not. No way. Innit. I'm not going back with *you*.'

They all waited.

'I'm going back with *him*,' she said, leaning forward and placing her hand on the penis of Chick Purchase.

Guy left, but Keith was going nowhere.

They said they'd put the sound on later, that inimitable pub bustle, the whoops, the laughter, the crack of glass, even the computerized thunks of dart meeting board. So the buzzers buzzed, and shifters fixed, and fixers shifted: each noisemaker made his noise. Also the steady belching of the cigarette-smoke simulator, sending its grey

461

clouds out over the occluded oché. Laughter remained, but it wasn't pub laughter. It was the laughter of Julian Neat, Kim Twemlow, and Nicola Six.

'Keith . . ? Shame it didn't go your way, Keith,' said Malcolm McClandricade. 'But it's not the end of the world. Sorry, Dom?'

'They're saying they can't use it.'

'There you go, Keith! Spare your blushes down the Marquis. Well. That's a relief all round.'

'They're saying they're using it. Thought they had a ladies' semi but they ain't.'

'Sugar. How'll they fill it? All we got's ten minutes.'

'They going to bung in a pub song or something. A knees-up. And a raffle or something.'

'Jesus. Still, Keith. Not surprising you didn't do yourself justice. With that handful. Talk about trouble. Keith? Keith? Dry your eyes, old son.'

'He's okay?'

'What do you think?'

'Get a car round?'

'Keith?'

But Keith snapped out of it, out of his ruined dream, his trance of darts. He stood up and said with boyish directness, 'I could point to the finger injury I was nursing. But tonight's been a valuable experience for me. For my future preparation. Because how's your darts going to mature, Malcolm, if you don't learn?'

'That's the right attitude, Keith.'

'Because she's dead. Believe it. You know what she is, Malcolm? She's a fuckin organ-donor. Do that and live? No danger. She's history, mate. You hearing me?'

'Anything you say, Keith.'

Will be taken down and used . . . He spun round the shaking cage of the spiral staircase. Every impact of his boot was louder, harsher, his force and mass growing with all that was neg and anti. Then he hit the cold night air, and saw the moon – redder, to his eyes, than the midday sun.

Keith ran low towards the heavy Cavalier.

I must go back to London Fields – but of course I'll never do it now. So far away. The time, the time, it never *was* the time. It is a far, far . . . If I shut my eyes I can see the innocuous sky, afloat above the park of milky green. The traintrack, the slope, the trees, the stream: I played there with my brother as a child. So long ago.

The people in here, they're like London, they're like the streets of London, a long way from any shape I've tried to equip them with, strictly non-symmetrical, exactly lopsided – far from many things, and far from art.

There's this terrible suspicion. It isn't worth saving anyway. Things just won't work out.

Be gone now, for the last act.

Chapter 24: The Deadline

DOWN THE DEAD-END street the car was waiting. And so was I . . .

I'm here. I'm in it. And how *strange* it is in here, fish-grey, monkey-brown, all the surfaces moist and sticky, and the air no good to breathe. Already destroyed. And not worth saving.

The car was there on the other side of the dead-end street. When midnight struck or tolled I crossed the road and bent my body and looked in through the broken window, broken by my own hand, so long ago. The murderer turned toward me.

'Get out of the car, Guy. Get out of the *car*, Guy.'

He was crying. But so what? We're all crying now, from here on in.

It was Guy. Of course it was. After a thousand years of war and revolution, of thought and effort, and history, and the permanent millennium, and the promised end of mine and thine, Guy still had all the money, and all the strength. When Keith came running low across the carpark, Guy was waiting, with all that strength. They squared up to one another. And Keith lost. For the second time that night, Keith tasted defeat: obliterating defeat. He got driven into the ground like a tentpeg. Where was he now? Somewhere: cradled, perhaps, in the loving arms of Trish Shirt.

'Look what she's done to me.'

'Get out of the car, Guy.'

'Look what she's *done* to me.'

We closed our deal. As he walked away he hesitated, and turned with a wide wag of the head.

'Jesus, Sam, don't do this for me.'

'Isn't it always someone else? Who does it.'

'Don't do this for me.'

But he kept on going.

The black cab has pulled away, unrecallably. Here she comes now on her heels, crying, shivering, through the smell of cordite. There are still fireworks in the sky, subsiding shockwaves, the memory of detonations, cheap gunfire, whistling decrescendo and the smoke of burnt guys. I can see marks on her face. Another hour with Chick and he might have saved us all the trouble. He might have saved us all the goddamned grief. I flicked on the lights and the car lumbered forward. It stopped and idled. I opened the passenger door. I said,

'Get in.'

My face was barred in darkness. But she could see the car-tool on my lap.

'Get *in*.'

She leaned forward. 'You,' she said, with intense recognition. 'Always you . . .'

'Get in.'

And in she climbed.

There are one or two things left to write.

That pill went down easily enough. I have about an hour. All told. For now I feel great luxury. I was seven when I learned the facts of life. I learned the facts of death even earlier. Not since then, I realize, not once, have I felt such certainty that the world will keep on going for another sixty minutes.

She outwrote me. Her story worked. And mine didn't. There's really nothing more to say. Always me: from the first moment in the Black Cross she looked my way with eyes of recognition. She knew that she had found him: her murderer. I wonder if she knew there'd be a queue . . . 'I've found him. On the Portobello Road, in a place called the Black Cross, I found him.' Imagination failed me. And all else. I should have understood that a cross has four points. Not three.

I've just taken a casual glance at the beginning – who knows, with a little work, it might somehow accommodate a new ending. And what do I see? Chapter 1: The Murderer. 'Keith Talent was a bad guy . . . You might even say that he was the worst guy.' No. I was the worst guy. I was the worst and last beast. Nicola destroyed my book. She must have felt a vandal's pleasure. Of course, I could have let Guy go ahead and settled for the 'surprise' ending. But she knew I wouldn't. Flatteringly, she knew I wasn't quite unregenerate. She

466

knew I wouldn't find it worth saving, this wicked thing, this wicked book I tried to write, plagiarized from real life.

Originally I'd planned to do a final chapter, in the old style: Where Are They Now? It hardly seems appropriate. But still, in life's book a little I can read. Pale Guy will go home, on his hands and knees. We made a deal. Keith's fate is of course more uncertain – Keith, with his cultured skills, his educated release. But he will be linked to Guy, through the child. I made Guy swear. To do *what's right*. In the end, he delegated cruelty. I, kindness, or paternalism, or money. It was the best I could do.

And Nicola. Necropolitan Nicola, in her crimson shoes. Poor Nicola – she was so *cold*. It made it easier: even that she planned. 'I'm so cold,' she kept saying. 'I'm so cold.' And: 'Please. It's all right to do it . . . It's all right.' And after the first blow she gave a moan of visceral assent, as if at last she was beginning to get warm.

Yesterday, in the hour before dawn and her arrival, I had a prophetic dream. I know it was prophetic because it's now come true. Yesterday I dreamt I ate my teeth. *That's* what murder feels like. I failed, in art and love. I wonder if there's time to wash all this blood off my hands.

Endpapers

Letter to Mark Asprey

You return, I fear, to a scene of some confusion. I will be lying on your bed, quite neatly, I hope, eyes open to the mirrored ceiling, but with a stoical smile on my face. In the car on the ledge, under a sheet, lies another body, rather less peacefully composed.

On your desk in the study you will find a full confession. That's all it is now. Perhaps it is also an elegy to the memory of an unfortunate lady, whom you knew. But I can't justify any of it and am indifferent to its destiny. I die intestate, and without close family. Be my literary executor: throw everything out. If an American publisher called Missy Harter makes inquiries, do me the courtesy of delivering a final message. Send her my love.

Even the dream tenant should always sign off by apologizing for the mess – the confusions, the violations, the unwanted fingerprints. This I do. You will encounter the usual pitiful vestiges of an existence. The usual mess. I'm sorry I'm not around to help you put everything into shape.

PS: If you have an hour or two, you might care to look at a little something I left on the drawing-room table: a brief critique of the Drama.

PPS: You didn't set me up. Did you?

I find I am thinking of the words of the exemplary War Poet: 'It seemed that out of battle I escaped . . .' The poem is a vision or a premonition of death (accurate, alas: his death was days away), in which the war poet – himself a forced collision, himself a strange meeting – joins his counterpart, his semblance, from the other side: 'I am the enemy you killed, my friend:

> I knew you in this dark: for so you frowned
> Yesterday through me as you jabbed and killed.
> I parried; but my hands were loath and cold.
> Let us sleep now . . .'

There is a third sense in which the poet was himself a strange collision. He was young; and the young aren't meant – the young aren't scheduled – to understand death. But he understood.

Also I am haunted by the speech of surrender of the Indian Chief Joseph, leader of the Nez Percé: subjugated, and then defeated in battle (and then routinely dispossessed):

> I am tired of fighting . . . I want to have time to look for my children and see how many I can find. Maybe I shall find them among the dead . . . From where the sun now stands, I will fight no more forever.

Even when we don't have any, we all want time to do this, time to look for our children and see how many we can find. With fingers all oily from being rubbed together, in ingratiation, vigil, glee, fear, nerves, I cling to certain hopes: hopes of you. I hope that you are with your mother and that you two are provided for. I hope your father is around somewhere – controllably. Your beginning has been hard. Your continuation, not so hard. I hope.

Two years ago I saw something that nobody should ever see: I saw my little brother dead. I know from the look on his face that nothing can survive the death of the body. Nothing can survive a devastation so thorough. Children survive their parents. Works of art survive their makers. I failed, in art and love. Nevertheless, I ask you to survive me.

Apparently it was all hopeless right from the start. I don't understand how it happened. There was a sense in which I used everybody, even you. And I still lost. . . Blissful, watery and vapid, the state of painlessness is upon me. I feel seamless and insubstantial, like a creation. As if someone made me up, for money. And I don't care.

Dawn is coming. Today, I think, the sun will start to climb a little higher in the sky. After its incensed stare at the planet. Its fiery stare, which asked a fiery question. The clouds have their old colour back, their old English colour: the colour of a soft-boiled egg, shelled by city fingers.

Of course you were far too young to remember. But who says? If love travels at the speed of light then it could have other powers just on the edge of the possible. And things create impressions on babies. It really is the case. Everything created impressions on you. The exact crenellations of a carpet on your thigh; the afterglow of my fingerprints on your shoulders; the faithful representation of the grip of your clothes. A bit of sock elastic could turn sections of your calves into Roman pillars. Not to mention hurts, like the bevel of some piece of furniture, clearly gauged on your responsive brow.

In a way, too, you were a terrible little creature. If we were out together, on a blanket in the park – whenever you caught my eye you would give a brief quack of impending distress, just to keep me on alert. You were a terrible little creature. But we are all terrible little creatures, I'm afraid. We are all terrible little creatures. No more of that. Or of this.

So if you ever felt something behind you, when you weren't even one, like welcome heat, like a bulb, like a sun, trying to shine right across the universe – it was me. Always me. It was me. It was me.